THE SUMPTUOUS, SEDUCTIVE NEW NOVEL BY THE NATIONAL BESTSELLING AUTHOR
JACQUELINE CAREY
KUSHIEL'S SCION

The candles had burned halfway down, and the room was filled with the scent of lovemaking. I heard Claudia get up and move about, and then the bed dipped under her weight as she returned. She knelt behind me, pressed against my lower back, the tips of her breasts brushing my shoulder blades. I felt the fingers of her left hand twining in the locks of my hair.

And at my throat, the keen edge of a dagger.

ACCLAIM FOR THE NOVELS OF
JACQUELINE CAREY

KUSHIEL'S SCION

more . . .

"A truly remarkable series." —Bookloons.com

KUSHIEL'S AVATAR

"Stunning, clever, sultry, and mysterious."
—**Associated Press**

"Lush, sensuous . . . a savory feast for mind and heart."
—*Booklist* **(starred review)**

KUSHIEL'S CHOSEN

"Elegant, intricate, sensual, and captivating. Once you pick it up you won't want to put it down." —ROBERT JORDAN

"There is seemingly something for everyone here: a great love story, intense spirituality, high eroticism, and lots of adventure, intrigue, and swordplay."
—*Booklist* **(starred review)**

KUSHIEL'S DART

"Brilliant and daring . . . magnificent . . . catapults Carey immediately into the top rank of fantasy novelists."
—*Publishers Weekly* **(starred review)**

"Superbly detailed, fascinatingly textured, and sometimes unbearably intense; a resonant, deeply satisfying, and altogether remarkable debut."
—*Kirkus Reviews* **(starred review)**

BOOKS BY

JACQUELINE CAREY

Kushiel's Legacy

Kushiel's Scion

Kushiel's Avatar

Kushiel's Chosen

Kushiel's Dart

JACQUELINE CAREY

KUSHIEL'S SCION

WARNER BOOKS

NEW YORK   BOSTON

Copyright © 2006 by Jacqueline Carey
Excerpt from *Kushiel's Justice* copyright © 2007 by Jacqueline Carey
All rights reserved. Except as permitted under the U.S. Copyright Act of 1976, no part of this publication may be reproduced, distributed, or transmitted in any form or by any means, or stored in a database or retrieval system, without the prior written permission of the publisher.

Warner Books and the "W" logo are trademarks of Time Warner Inc. or an affiliated company. Used under license by Hachette Book Group USA, which is not affiliated with Time Warner Inc.

Cover design by Don Puckey
Cover illustration by John Jude Palencar

Warner Books
Hachette Book Group USA
237 Park Avenue
New York, NY 10169
Visit our Web site at www.HachetteBookGroupUSA.com

Printed in the United States of America

Originally published in hardcover by Warner Books
First Paperback Printing: May 2007

10   9   8   7   6   5   4   3   2

ALBA

THREE SISTERS

AZZALLE

KUSHETH

NAMARRE

TERRE D'ANGE

THE

CAMLACH

L'AGNACE

SIOVALS

City of
Elua

EUSKERRIA

Montrève

Milazza

Gisande

Marsilikos

CAERDICCA

ARAGONIA

Lucca

Tiberium

MENEKHET

NORTH

Dramatis Personae

Sidonie de la Courcel—elder daughter of Ysandre; heir
   to Terre d'Ange
Alais de la Courcel—younger daughter of Ysandre
Imriel nó Montrève de la Courcel—cousin; son of
   Benedicte de la Courcel (*deceased*) and Melisande
   Shahrizai
Barquiel L'Envers—uncle of Ysandre; Royal
   Commander; Duc L'Envers (Namarre)

HOUSE SHAHRIZAI

Melisande Shahrizai—mother of Imriel; wed to
   Benedicte de la Courcel (*deceased*)
Faragon Shahrizai—Duc de Shahrizai
Mavros, Roshana, Baptiste Shahrizai—cousins of
   Imriel

MEMBERS OF THE ROYAL COURT

Ghislain nó Trevalion—noble, son of Percy de
   Somerville (*deceased*)
Bernadette de Trevalion—noble, wed to Ghislain, sister
   of Baudoin (*deceased*)
Bertran de Trevalion—son of Ghislain and Bernadette
Amaury Trente—noble, former Commander of the
   Queen's Guard
Julien and Colette Trente—children of Amaury
Marguerite Grosmaine—daughter of the Secretary of
   the Presence
Nicola L'Envers y Aragon—cousin of Queen Ysandre;
   wed to Ramiro Zornín de Aragon
Raul L'Envers y Aragon—son of Nicola and Ramiro

THE NIGHT COURT

Nathalie nó Balm—Dowayne of Balm House
Emmeline nó Balm—adept of Balm House
Didier Vascon—Dowayne of Valerian House
Sephira—adept of Valerian House

ALBA

Drustan mab Necthana—Cruarch of Alba, wed to
    Ysandre de la Courcel
Necthana—mother of Drustan
Breidaia—sister of Drustan, daughter of Necthana
Talorcan—son of Breidaia
Dorelei—daughter of Breidaia
Sibeal—sister of Drustan, daughter of Necthana, wed to
    Hyacinthe
Hyacinthe—Master of the Straits, wed to Sibeal
Grainne mac Conor—Lady of the Dalriada
Eamonn mac Grainne—son of Grainne and Quintilius
    Rousse

TIBERIUM

Master Piero di Bonci—teacher of philosophy
Lucius Tadius, Aulus, Brigitta, Akil, Vernus—students
    of Master Piero
Deccus Fulvius—senator
Claudia Fulvia—wife of Deccus; sister of Lucius
Anna Marzoni—widow
Belinda Marzoni—daughter of Anna
Canis—beggar
Master Strozzi—teacher of rhetoric

Master Ambrosius—incense-maker

Erytheia of Thrasos—painter

Silvio—assistant to Erytheia of Thrasos

Denise Fleurais—D'Angeline ambassadress in
    Tiberium

Ruggero Caccini—ruffian commander

Priest of Asclepius

Titus Maximius—princeps of Tiberium

Oppius da Lippi—captain of the *Aeolia*

LUCCA

Publius Tadius—father of Lucius

Beatrice Tadia—mother of Lucius

Gallus Tadius (*deceased*)—great-grandfather of Lucius

Gaetano Correggio—Prince of Lucca

Dacia Correggio—wife of Gaetano

Helena Correggio—daughter of Gaetano and Dacia

Bartolomeo Ponzi—enamored of Helena

Domenico Martelli—Duke of Valpetra

Silvanus the Younger—commander of Valpetra's
    mercenary company

Arturo—captain of the Luccan guard

Orfeo, Pollio, Calvino, Matius, Adolpho, Baldessare,
    Constantin—soldiers in the Red Scourge

Quentin LeClerc—captain of the D'Angeline embassy
    guard

Romuald—soldier in the D'Angeline embassy guard

Marcus Cornelius—commander of the Tiberian
    contingent

OTHERS

Maslin of Lombelon—unacknowledged son of Isidore
   d'Aiglemort (*deceased*)
Lelahiah Valais—Queen Ysandre's chirurgeon
Emile—proprietor of the Cockerel
Quintilius Rousse—Royal Admiral
Favrielle nó Eglantine—couturiere
Bérèngere of Namarre—head of Naamah's Order
Amarante of Namarre—daughter of Bérèngere
Brother Selbert—chief priest in the Sanctuary of Elua
   (Siovale)
Gilles Lamiz—Queen's Poet
Roxanne de Mereliot—Lady of Marsilikos (Eisande)
Gerard and Jeanne de Mereliot—children of Roxanne
   (Eisande)

HISTORICAL FIGURES

Baudoin de Trevalion (*deceased*)—cousin of Queen
   Ysandre; executed for treason
Isidore d'Aiglemort (*deceased*)—noble; traitor turned
   hero (Camlach)
Thelesis de Mornay (*deceased*)—Queen's Poet
Waldemar Selig (*deceased*)—Skaldi warlord; invaded
   Terre d'Ange
Fadil Chouma (*deceased*)—Menekhetan slaver
The Mahrkagir (*deceased*)—mad ruler of Drujan; lord
   of Daršanga
Drucilla (*deceased*)—Tiberian prisoner in Daršanga;
   chirurgeon
Kaneka—Jebean prisoner in Daršanga
Jagun (*deceased*)—chief of the Kereyit Tatars
Ras Lijasu—Prince of Meroë in Jebe-Barkal

PROLOGUE

WHAT DOES IT MEAN to be good?

When I was a child, I thought I knew. It was easy then. I knew nothing of my birth or my heritage. My childhood was spent in the Sanctuary of Elua, where I was a ward. My days were spent in work like play: scrambling the mountainsides and tending goats with the other children of the Sanctuary, climbing trees and swimming in the swift stream while our charges grazed.

I was steeped in the precept of Blessed Elua: *Love as thou wilt.* And I did. I loved without reserve, freely and easily—my playmates, the priests and priestesses of the Sanctuary, the goats I tended, the earth beneath my feet and the sky above my head. I am a D'Angeline; I loved Terre d'Ange, the country of my birth. With all my heart, I loved our gods, Elua and his Companions, and I knew myself loved in return. I was happy. I never thought to be anything else.

When I was ten years old, everything changed.

I was stolen by Carthaginian slave-traders and sent on a journey into hell. And I thought I'd die there, but I didn't. I was rescued. I was brought out of damnation into safety.

And everything changed again.

In a distant fortress on the far verges of Khebbel-im-Akkad, the D'Angeline Queen's delegate bowed his head and greeted me as Imriel de la Courcel, Prince of the Blood.

All that I knew of myself was a lie.

I learned my father was Benedicte de la Courcel, the great-uncle of Queen Ysandre. For many years, he was her closest living relative in House Courcel. But by the time I heard the news, he was long dead. He was a traitor to the throne, and if he'd lived to be tried, he would have been convicted of it. He didn't, though.

My mother was another matter.

When I was eight years old, before I knew who she was, Brother Selbert took me to La Serenissima to see my mother. He had told me that my parents had been D'Angeline nobles who had died of an ague during a ship crossing, bequeathing me with their dying breaths to the priest as a ward of the Sanctuary. He told me that this woman had been a friend of my parents and would stand as my patron when I came of age. And he told me that she had dangerous enemies and that I must never speak of her, for it would put her in grave danger. That last bit, at least, was true.

I believed him. Why shouldn't I? I'd spent my life trusting him. But everything else was a lie. And he didn't tell me that she had earned each and every enemy she made. My father's treachery pales in comparison to her deeds. In all its history, Terre d'Ange has never known a deadlier traitor than Melisande Shahrizai de la Courcel.

My mother, whom I learned to despise.

In hindsight, it seems strange that I didn't recognize her at the time. And yet how was I to know? There were no mirrors in the Sanctuary of Elua. Betimes we children used to lean over the goat-bridge and peer at our wavering reflections in the stream's surface, but that was all. I was as ignorant of my features as I was of my identity.

Of course, that was before the slave-traders took me. Then I had ample opportunity to hear myself described. In the country of Drujan, they were looking for perfect, unblemished sacrifices. I was sold to one of the bone-priests who served the Mahrkagir, the ruler of all Drujan. The Mahrkagir was cruel, ruthless, and utterly mad. And I was bought for his foul harem, the zenana in the palace of Daršanga. Beauty is scant comfort on a descent into hell.

I resemble my mother

I know it now. I see it in mirrors—there are always mirrors, in my foster-mother Phèdre's household—and I hate it. I wear my mother's face. My eyes are her eyes, a deep twilight blue. My skin is her skin, a shadowed alabaster, the color of old ivory. I see the generous curve of her mouth reflected in my lips. My hair, like hers, grows in gleaming, blue-black waves.

The resemblance cannot be denied.

There are those—even now, after all she has done—who marvel that I don't welcome it. Although she was the greatest traitor our nation has known, Melisande Shahrizai was one of its greatest beauties, too. A deadly beauty, bright as the sun, keen as a blade. In certain circles, she is still admired for it. If there is a nation on the face of the earth with a people more vain than Terre d'Ange, I've yet to find it. And in my twelve years, I've seen more of the world than most D'Angelines will ever glimpse.

But I have seen beauty, and it does not wear my mother's face.

When I gaze in the mirror and see her features reflected in mine, I am filled with uncertainty. What does it mean to be good? When I look inside myself, I see only darkness and confusion. I do not know why what happened to me, happened. I do not know what I did to deserve it, or if I am bearing the price of my mother's sins. I fear the resemblance between us. I fear that one day I may prove to be like her. But when I look outside myself, it is easy to point to *goodness.* I was stolen out of paradise and sent into the depths of a depravity the likes of which decent folk couldn't begin to comprehend, but I was rescued. The ones who rescued me . . . when I think about what it means to be good, I think about them.

Phèdre.

Joscelin.

Phèdre.

I don't know—I will never know—where they found the courage to do what was needed to save me. Phèdre says that although it is my mother who charged her with the task, it was the will of Blessed Elua himself that sent her forth across that terrible threshold. I cannot reckon the cost. I know what the Mahrkagir did to her. All of us who were slaves in the Mahrkagir's zenana knew what he did to his favorites. I don't know how she endured it. And I don't know how Joscelin, Phèdre's consort and protector, survived knowing the abuse she suffered at the Mahrkagir's hands without succumbing to madness.

I love them so much that it hurts inside.

I am theirs, now; their foster-son. Queen Ysandre allowed it, although she has little liking for the arrangement. My mother consented willingly to it; indeed, she made a concession that it might come to pass. As far as I know, it is one of the only concessions my mother has ever made in her life. Although they have been opponents in her intrigues, there is a bond of long standing between her and Phèdre. I don't understand it, and I don't want to; I think, somehow, that I will rue the day I ever do. My mother remains in sanctuary in the Temple of Asherat-of-the-Sea in La Serenissima. Unlike my father, she was tried and convicted of high treason long before I was born. Her life is forfeit if ever she sets a foot beyond the temple walls.

She writes me letters, which I don't read. I tried to burn the first letter she sent, but Phèdre snatched it from the brazier. After that, she began keeping them for me. She says that I will want them one day, and mayhap it is true. In my short life, I've seen many things no one would have believed possible. But I cannot ever imagine wanting to read my mother's words.

It doesn't happen often, but sometimes Phèdre is wrong.

It is strange, now, to think how I despised her at first. In the zenana of Daršanga, Phèdre nó Delaunay, the Comtesse de Montrève, did not look like a heroine bent on my rescue. She looked like a D'Angeline courtesan, delicate and lovely, and willing to wallow in the foulest depravity the Mahrkagir offered. It was true, too. For that, I hated her. I hated her so much I could barely stand to look at her. And Joscelin . . . Joscelin, too. I thought he had betrayed all that was noble and good about Terre d'Ange, sinking as low as a warrior can go.

I was wrong.

They were more, so much more. They were my salvation, and the salvation of many others. Not all, but many. A deadly evil was removed from the world the night that we— all of us together in the zenana—overthrew the Mahrkagir's forces. It was Blessed Elua's will, Phèdre says. Perhaps that, too, is true. I wish to believe it. In the daylight, enfolded in their affection, it is easy. We are a family. We emerged from the terrible stronghold of Daršanga, the three of us, damaged and broken, and healed ourselves into a new whole.

I pray that what befell us will never come again, not so long as I live. Whatever becomes of me, I will live my life in the shadow of greatness, but I will never begrudge it. When all is said and done, I do not think I have greatness in me. I would like to, but I don't. Not like Phèdre; not like Joscelin, whose role was even harder in some ways, who ever stood at her side, whose scars bear testament to his courage and valor. All I want to do is come to manhood in a manner that does not disgrace those I love.

This, I pray, is not too much to ask.

In the daylight, I can be happy and filled with hope. Sometimes the emotions well within me so strongly—love, joy—that it feels as though my skin is too tight, as though my heart will burst out of my chest. And I am happy, and glad to be alive.

But the nights are different. At night, I remember. I remember the Mahrkagir and his fathomless black eyes; the things he did to me, and the things he made me do. I remember his voice, whispering joyous promises of agonies to come. I remember the others, the warlords who made a plaything of me. I remember the lash against my skin and the agonizing sizzle of a branding iron, the stink of my own seared flesh. At times I dream and wake myself screaming.

It is hard, then, to believe in *goodness*.

Still, I try. I try not to think too hard about the tangled threads of destiny that led me into hell as a child, and out the other side as something at once more and less. I lost my childhood in Daršanga, but I have reclaimed bits of it, here and there. Most of all in Montrève, Phèdre's estate. She inherited it from her lord Anafiel Delaunay de Montrève, who bought her marque when she was but a child, who adopted her as she had adopted me. But that is a long story and not mine to tell.

Montrève lies in the foothills of the D'Angeline province of Siovale. It reminds me of my childhood at the Sanctuary of Elua. There, I am at home. I am Imriel nó Montrève, not Imriel de la Courcel. I have the mountains, the mews and the kennels, and even friends—the seneschals of the estate have a clan of good-natured youngsters. I would be content to stay there always. So too, I think, would Joscelin, for he has little love for Court intrigue. But the Queen demands her due and betimes we must return to the City of Elua and attend her. Joscelin is her acclaimed Champion, and Phèdre is one of her most valued confidantes.

And I am a Prince of the Blood, third in line for the throne.

It is the blood of Blessed Elua that runs in my veins, at least on my father's side. I have never boasted of it. Elua and his Companions spread their seed widely; there is no one in Terre d'Ange who cannot claim descent from one or another. But the Great Houses have kept their lines pure, or so they claim. It is a source of pride and vanity, and at times, intolerable prejudice.

I should know. I was conceived because Benedicte de la Courcel wished to provide Terre d'Ange with a purebred D'Angeline heir. He thought the goal worthy of treason.

To her credit, Queen Ysandre does not subscribe to this vision. Her marriage was a love-match to Drustan mab Necthana, the Cruarch of Alba. Together, they rule over two countries. I like Drustan very well, and wish that I liked the Queen better. It is hard for me. I travelled with Phèdre and Joscelin for a long time after I was rescued. Ysandre was angry, so angry, that it took them so long to restore me to Terre d'Ange. She didn't understand that I needed to be with them. And I didn't understand her anger.

It was a cold anger. Phèdre, who forgave her for it long

ago, says it was the Queen's right to be concerned about the safety of her kin. Still, I am uneasy with Queen Ysandre. It is unfair, I suppose, when she had championed me against the united mistrust of the peers of the realm. There are those who would gladly see me dead, despising the fact that Melisande Shahrizai's son is three heartbeats away from the throne.

Such is the dubious gift of my mother's legacy. The mistrust of these nobles is deserved. If my mother had triumphed, if her intrigues had born fruit, even now I might be sitting upon the throne of Terre d'Ange, a boy-king with a treacherous regent.

And yet I have no such desire. I would be content to be left in peace, to be Imriel nó Montrève, would the world allow it. To spend my days hawking and hunting and fishing, learning from Joscelin the fighting skills of the warrior priests of the Cassiline Brotherhood, listening to such tutors as Phèdre lures to the estate, bickering and coming of age among the children of her seneschals. This, I know, is not to be. Yet I will cling to it for as long as I may.

Until I can't, anyway.

I fear my mother's legacy will make it difficult. It is only on my father's side that I am descended from Blessed Elua. My mother's lineage is different. The Shahrizai are among the Great Houses of Terre d'Ange; but they are not descended from Blessed Elua, but from one of his Companions. Their blood is very old and very pure, and it is that lineage that frightens me. They are Kushiel's scions.

Kushiel's name means "the rigid one of God," and he was once charged with administering punishment to the damned, but abandoned his post to accompany Blessed Elua in his wanderings. It is said that he had an excess of compassion for his charges. It is said that they, in turn, loved him so well that they wept with gratitude beneath his lash. This I find difficult to believe. And yet, in Terre d'Ange, his temples endure.

Sometimes Phèdre visits the temples of Kushiel. What absolution she finds there under the lash, I cannot comprehend. I know that when she returns, she is tranquil and at peace. Joscelin says it is a mystery in the truest sense of the word. Although he will never be easy with it, there are things he grasps that are beyond my ken.

Me, I cannot fathom it. I know that she is an *anguissette*, Kushiel's Chosen. She was marked by it for all the world to see: Kushiel's Dart, a mote of scarlet in her eye. I understand that she is condemned to find pleasure in pain, and that somehow this redresses an imbalance in the world. I know, too, the source of this imbalance: my mother, Kushiel's greatest scion, born without benefit of a conscience.

It is whispered that Kushiel's lineage carries its own dark gift, the ability to perceive the flaws and fault-lines in another's mortal soul. To discern those forms of cruelty that are kindnesses unto themselves, to administer an untender mercy. And like all gifts, it can be used for unworthy ends.

I hope it is not true.

But at night, I sense its presence like a shadow on my soul, waiting. And I lie awake in my bed, clinging to the brightness I have known, fighting back the tide of darkness, the memories of blood and branding and horror, and the legacy of cruelty that runs in my own veins, shaping my own secret vow and wielding it like a brand against the darkness, whispering it to myself, over and over.

I will try to be good.

ONE

WE WERE ATTENDING a country fair when the news came.

For a while, a long while, after our final return to Terre d'Ange, life was blissfully uneventful. Having had enough adventures to last me a lifetime, I was grateful for it. Whether in the City or at Montrève, I tended to my studies, immersed in the daily business of living and content to let the affairs of the world pass me by untouched. Phèdre and Joscelin did all they could to allow this respite to endure, sensing there was healing in it for me.

There was, too. As the slow months passed and turned into years, I felt things knotted tight inside me ease. My nightmares grew less and less frequent, and the times of happiness longer.

Still, even Phèdre and Joscelin couldn't protect me forever.

It was my third summer in Montrève. I had turned fourteen in the spring, though I looked younger, being slow to get my full growth. The Queen's chirurgeon claimed it was due to the shock of enslavement and what had befallen me in Daršanga, and mayhap it was so. I only know that I chafed at it. My parents were both tall; or so I am told. I cannot say, having never known my father. If it's true, it is the only gift of theirs I'd ever wished for.

The fair was held in an open field on the outskirts of the village, alongside the river. It was a small gathering. Montrève was not a large estate, and the village it bordered—which was also called Montrève—was modest in size. But it was a fair, and I was young enough to be excited at the prospect of it.

We made for a merry entourage as we rode forth from the estate: Phèdre, Joscelin, and I, accompanied by her chevalier Ti-Philippe, his companion Hugues, and a few other men-at-arms, all of them clad in the forest-green livery of House Montrève. The Friote clan was already there, tending to our wool-trading interests. The bulk of our wool would be shipped elsewhere for sale, but there were always small landowners looking to buy.

There were other goods available for purchase or trade, too: fabrics and yarns, livestock, produce, spices, and other uninteresting items. Of greater interest, at least to me, were the crafters' booths, which displayed a fascinating array—leather goods, arms and bits of armor, jewelry, mirrors, mysterious vials of unguents, musical instruments, and intricately carved toys. Not all of them were meant for children, either.

Best of all, there were Tsingani, with horses for sale. Not many—the pick of the lot sold at the great horse fairs in the spring—but a few. We spotted their brightly painted wagons from the road, and I saw Phèdre smile at the sight. There was a time when the Tsingani wouldn't have been welcome at a small country fair, but a lot has changed since those days. In Montrève, they were always welcome.

There were a few good-natured cheers and shouts of greeting as we arrived, which Phèdre acknowledged with a laughing salute. She was always gracious that way, and well-loved because of it. We tethered our mounts at the picket line and Joscelin gave a few coins to the village lads who hung about to attend them.

Ti-Philippe and the others remained mounted. "I'll take Hugues and Colin and ride a quick circuit," he said to Joscelin, who gave a brief nod in reply. "Marcel and the others will cast an eye over the fair proper."

I hated hearing that sort of thing. It cast a pall over the day's brightness, knowing it was because of me. Queen Ysandre was insistent that my security was paramount, and a fair brought strangers into the area. They were only being cautious; but still, I hated it.

Joscelin eyed me, noting my expression. "Take heart," he said wryly. "When you come of age, you'll be free to take all the risks you like."

"Four years!" I protested. "It's forever."

A corner of his mouth twitched. "You think so?" He tousled my hair lightly. I hated when almost anyone else did it—I didn't like people touching me—but my heart always gave a secret leap of happiness when Phèdre or Joscelin did. "It won't seem it, I promise." He glanced at Phèdre then, and something passed between them; a shared and private understanding.

There are those who laugh at their union, although not many. Not now, after all they have endured together. It's true, though. 'Tis an unlikely pairing, Kushiel's Chosen and a Servant of Naamah in love with a Cassiline warrior-priest.

Phèdre was a courtesan, sworn to the service of Blessed Elua's Companion Naamah, who gave herself to the King of Persis to win Elua's freedom, and who lay down in the stews of Bhodistan with strangers that he might eat. It is a sacred calling in Terre d'Ange, though it is not one practiced by many peers of the realm. But Phèdre was a Servant of Naamah long before she inherited Delaunay's title and estate, and although she has not practiced it since Daršanga, she has never renounced Naamah's Service.

And Joscelin—Joscelin was a Cassiline Brother when they met, although he left the Brotherhood for her sake. From the age of ten, he was trained to be a warrior-priest, sworn to celibacy. Alone among the Companions, Cassiel claimed no territory in Terre d'Ange and begot no offspring, but remained ever at Blessed Elua's side. That is the vow of the Cassiline Brotherhood: To protect and serve.

The Cassilines are very good at what they do; but Joscelin, I think, is better.

"What will you, love?" he asked Phèdre, indicating the fair with the sweep of an arm. His steel vambraces glinted in the sun. "Pleasure or the duties of the manor? The Tsingani or the Friotes?"

"Ah, well." She cocked her head. "We *could* glance at the fabric stalls on the way to either one. If there's aught of interest, it won't last long."

I groaned inside. I hated looking at fabric.

Although I made no audible sound, Phèdre's gaze settled on me, dark and unnerving. Her eyes were beautiful, deep and lustrous as forest pools, with a mote of scarlet floating on the left iris, vivid as a rose petal. And she was capable of a look that saw right through one. There were reasons for it.

"All right." She smiled and beckoned to another of the men-at-arms. "Gilot, will you accompany Imriel to—to the Tsingani horse-fields, is it?"

"Yes, please!" I couldn't help the grin that stretched my face.

Gilot swept an extravagant bow. "Lady, with a will!"

He was my favorite retainer, after Ti-Philippe and

Hugues, who were almost family. He was the youngest—only eighteen, the age of majority I coveted. But he was good with a sword and quick-thinking, which were qualities Joscelin looked for in hiring retainers. I liked him because he treated me as an equal, not a responsibility.

Together we plunged into the fair and began forging a path toward the horse-fields. "They've got one of those spotted horses from Aragonia, did you see?" Gilot asked. "I spied it from the road. I wouldn't mind having one."

I made a noise of agreement.

"Whip-smart and smooth-gaited, they say." He shrugged. "Next year, mayhap, if I save my coin!" A stand of leather goods caught his eye. "Ah, hold a moment, will you, Imri? My sword-belt's worn near enough to snap near the buckle. It was my brother's anyway. I ought to buy new."

I loitered at Gilot's side while he perused the goods available, and the leather-merchant made a great show of exclaiming over my own belt. It was a man's belt, though it held only a boy's dagger. "What have you there, little man?" he asked in a jovial, condescending tone. "Boar-hide?"

"No." I smiled coolly at him. "Rhinoceros."

He blinked, perplexed. Gilot gave a sidelong glance, nudging me with his elbow. The belt had been a gift from Ras Lijasu, a Prince of Jebe-Barkal. Gilot knew the story behind it. The merchant blinked a few more times. "A rhinoceros, is it? Good for you, little man!"

"Imriel!"

I turned, recognizing the voice. At an adjacent stall, Katherine Friote beckoned imperiously, shoving up the sleeve of her gown.

"Come here and smell this," she said.

I went, obedient. Katherine was in the middle of the Friote clan, a year and some months my elder. In the past year, she had begun to . . . change . . . in a fascinating manner. The skinny, bossy girl I had met two summers ago had become a young woman, a head taller than me. She thrust her wrist beneath my nose.

"What do you think?" she asked.

I swallowed hard. She had rubbed a dab of perfumed ointment on her skin, and the scent was strong and cloying, like overblown lilies. Beneath it, faint and elusive, I could smell her own scent, like a sun-warmed meadow.

"I think you smell better without it," I said honestly.

The perfume-seller made a disgusted sound. I thought Katherine would be annoyed with me, but instead she wore a look of amusement. She bobbed a teasing curtsy in my direction. "Why, thank you, Prince Imriel."

"You're welcome." My face felt unaccountably warm.

"Prince, is it?" The perfume-seller turned his head and spat on the ground. Obviously, he was a stranger to Montrève. "Prince of sheep-dung, I'll warrant!"

At that moment, Gilot appeared at my side, wearing a sword-belt so new that it creaked over his Montrèvan livery. "Well met, Demoiselle Friote," he said cheerfully. "Would you care to accompany us to the Tsingani camp? His highness has a fancy to see the spotted horse, and the Comtesse has given us her blessing."

Now it was Katherine who blushed at Gilot's chivalrous attention, while the perfume-seller opened and closed his mouth several times, fishlike, then squinted hard at me. I muttered somewhat under my breath about spotted horses, which all of them ignored.

"Shall we?" Gilot asked Katherine, extending his arm and smiling at her. He had a lively, handsome face and brown eyes quick to sparkle with mirth. Still, it irked me to see Katherine dote on him.

We made our way through the stalls, pausing for Gilot to purchase a sweet of candied violets for Katherine. Through the crowd, I caught a glimpse of Phèdre at a cloth-seller's stall, examining bolts of fabric. The merchant was fawning over her. At her side, Joscelin observed the process with an expression of long tolerance. He stood in the Cassiline at-ease position, arms crossed, hands resting lightly on the hilts of his twin daggers.

I mulled over my irritation as we continued walking, kicking at clumps of foot-churned grass. "I wish you wouldn't say such things," I said at length. "Not here."

"What things?" Gilot gave me a perplexed look.

"Prince," I said. "Highness."

"Well, but you are." He scratched his head. "Look, Imri, I know—I mean, I understand, a bit. But you are who you are, and there's no changing it. Anyway, there's no call to let some tawdry peddler insult you. I'm not one to let it pass unnoted."

I shrugged. "I've heard worse."

"You didn't mind so much when *I* said it." Katherine glanced at me under her lashes. The sun brought out golden streaks in her glossy brown hair, and sparkled on tiny crumbs of sugar clinging to her lips.

I looked away. "Please, forget I spoke of it."

These new feelings Katherine evoked shouldn't have dis-turbed me. In Terre d'Ange, the arts of love came to us eas-ily and young; or so it should be. I was different. It wasn't that I was immune to the promptings of desire—in the past several months, I had grown uncomfortably aware of desire stirring in my flesh. But in the zenana of Daršanga, death and desire were inextricably linked. I couldn't think about one without the shadow of the other hanging over it. So at a time when boys my age were conducting fumbling experiments with one another and begging kisses from girls, I kept myself aloof, afraid and untouchable.

Gilot sighed. "Come on, let's go."

I forgot my grievances in the Tsingani camp. There were two *kumpanias* present with three wagons between them. The wagons were drawn in a circle, with their horses tethered at the rear. At the front of the wagons, women tended cooking fires where kettles of stew and pottage simmered. The unwed women wore their hair uncovered and loose and made long eyes at the Tsingani men, and all of them wore *galb* displaying their wealth, necklaces and earrings strung with gold coins. A few of the men were engaged in haggling with potential buyers, but most of them idled in the center of the circle. Bursts of music issued forth as one or another began to play—fiddle or timbales, accompanied by rhythmic clapping and snatches of song.

It would be a good life, I think, to be one of the Travellers; or at least it would be for a man. It was harder for Tsingani women, who must abide by a stringent code of behavior lest they lose their virtue; their *laxta*, they called it. If that happened, they were declared anathema.

It is better now than it once was. Much of that is due to Hyacinthe, who is the Master of the Straits and wields a power beyond the mortal ken. I know, for I have seen it; seen wind and wave answer to his command. He was one of them, once—a half-breed Tsingano, born to a woman who lost her virtue through no fault of her own. In the end, they would have had him as their king, but he refused it. Still, he has urged change upon them and many of the Tsingani have eased the strictures they impose on their women. Hyacinthe has reason to be concerned with the lot of women, since it is to Phèdre that he owes his freedom.

I shivered in the warm sunlight, remembering the day she

spoke the Name of God and broke the curse that bound him to an immortality of dwindling age on that lonely island. There are some memories so profound they cannot be conveyed in words.

Some of them, for a mercy, are good ones.

Gilot let out a low whistle, breaking my reverie. "Look at him, will you! What a beauty."

There was an admiring crowd around the spotted horse staked on the outskirts of the circle. I had to own, the horse *was* a beauty—a powerfully arched neck, strong, straight legs, a smooth back. His coat was a deep red-bay, speckled with white as though, in the middle of summer, he stood amidst a snowstorm. He basked in the adulation of the crowd, tossing his head and stamping his forefeet, almost as though to beat time with the nearby timbales.

"Imriel, Katherine!" Charles Friote detached himself from the throng of admirers and waved us over. He was my age, though to my chagrin, he too had grown in the past year, overtaking me by a head. "Hello, Gilot," Charles added belatedly, then dropped his voice to a whisper. "He's not for sale, the Tsingani say. But maybe for Lady Phèdre . . . ?"

I was opening my mouth to reply when the Tsingano holding the spotted horse's head beckoned to me, calling out. "Hey, *rinkeni chavo*! Come meet the Salmon!"

It was the spotted horse's name, I guessed. While Charles squirmed with envy behind me, I moved forward. The Tsingano who had beckoned me grinned, his teeth very white against his brown skin.

"Here, *chavo*," he said, pressing something into my palm. "Give him a treat."

It was a bit of dried apple; the end of last autumn's stores. I held my hand out flat. The Salmon eyed me, lordly and considering, then bent his head to accept the tidbit, his lips velvety against my palm. I began to think about what a glory it would be to ride him—to own him—and wondered if perhaps the Tsingani might sell him to Phèdre after all. I could repay her for him. There were monies that were mine to spend, held in trust for me; the proceeds of estates I had never seen, nor cared to.

"A *gadjo* pearl, with black hair and eyes like the deep sea," the Tsingano horse-trader murmured.

I jerked back, startling the horse.

"Peace, *chavo*." The Tsingano raised one hand, palm outward. His dark eyes were calm and amused. "We remember, that is all. Does it trouble you?"

It was the second question of the day I had no chance to answer. On the far side of the field, familiar shouts arose— the battle-call of House Montrève, giving an alarm. I turned to see a single rider departing from the road to race hell-for-leather toward the fair. Whatever his intentions, the sight didn't bode well. I was abruptly aware that I had only Gilot for protection.

Ti-Philippe and his men were on a course to intercept the rider, but they were too far away. The rider would reach us first. Gilot swore and drew his sword. In three swift steps, he reached me, grabbing my arm and yanking me behind him. Katherine and Charles were round-eyed with fearful awe. The spotted stallion reared against his tether, trumpeting, while his Tsingano owner sought to soothe him.

In the midst of the fair, pandemonium broke loose. A handful of villagers sought to rally to our aid, seizing weapons from the arms-sellers' stalls. Protesting merchants blocked their way, grabbing at their purloined goods. Here and there was a struggling knot where one of Montrève's retainers sought to shove a path through the throng.

I watched the rider loom nearer and drew my dagger, flip-

ping it to hold it by its point. At fifteen paces or less, my aim
was good. In front of me, Gilot maintained a defensive
stance, legs planted, sword tight in his fist. A muscle in his
jaw trembled. Katherine's fingers dug into my left forearm.
I pried them loose, shoving her toward Charles.

"Take care of her," I said, the words coming harshly. He
nodded, his face pale, brown hair flopping over his brow.

A single voice, raised, called my name. "Imriel!"

I raised mine in reply, and though it cracked, it carried.
"Joscelin, *here*!"

There; bursting free of the crowd. He came at a dead run,
crossing the horse-fields to the Tsingani camp, passing
Gilot. The rider thundered toward us, Ti-Philippe and the
others following hard behind, a few seconds too late.

Not Joscelin.

His sword sang as he reached over his shoulder and drew
it; a high, keening note. Tradition holds that Cassiline Brothers draw their swords only to kill. When it came to my defense, Joscelin observed no such niceties.

"Stand down or die!" he called to the rider, angling his
sword across his body in a two-handed grip.

The rider drew rein, hard, turning his lathered, hard-
ridden mount. Froth flew from its bit. A hafted pennant, now
visible, fluttered from a hilt mounted on the pommel of his
saddle—a square of rich blue with a diagonal bar of silver.

"Queen's Courier!" he shouted. "In the name of Queen
Ysandre, hold your hand!"

Joscelin did not shift, his voice remaining taut. "Stand
down, man!"

In that moment, it seemed everyone else converged. Ti-
Philippe, Hugues, and Colin arrived in a thunderous flurry of
hoofbeats, blocking the rider's retreat. Tsingani armed with
light hunting bows emerged from the circle of wagons. Vil-

lagers armed with sticks, cudgels, and appropriated swords ran into the field.

And Phèdre.

She stepped lightly past me, touching my shoulder briefly in passing. At her appearance, everyone grew quiet. She wore a gown of vibrant blue, the color of the summer sky; the color of Joscelin's eyes. It was trimmed with gold embroidery, a handspan deep, and a caul of gold mesh bound her dark, shining hair.

"Queen's Courier?" she asked, frowning slightly. Joscelin adjusted his stance, angling his sword to protect her. "What news is so urgent?"

The rider dropped his reins. His mount lowered its head, blowing hard, its nostrils flaring. "My lady Phèdre nó Delaunay de Montrève?"

"Yes." She regarded him calmly.

He raised his hands, showing them to be empty. "I bear an urgent dispatch from the Queen," he said. Reaching slowly into a pouch slung over the crupper of his saddle, he drew forth a sealed missive. "Here."

Joscelin took it from his grasp, examined it, then handed it to Phèdre. It was a slim envelope, sealed with the swan insignia of House Courcel. She cracked the wax seal and read the single sheet of parchment within. I watched the frown lines reemerge between her graceful brows. "The Queen requires our presence in the City of Elua," she said. "There is a situation."

"What is it?" Joscelin asked brusquely.

Phèdre handed him the missive, but it was on me that her gaze settled, pitying and grave. "It is Melisande," she said gently. "It seems she has vanished."

TWO

WE MADE THE RETURN ride to the estate in silent haste, all thoughts of the fair forgotten. One new thought preyed on my mind, over and over. I gnawed on it like a dog with a bone until I could stand it no longer. I brought my mount alongside Phèdre's.

"Her letters," I said. "The ones she wrote to me."

Phèdre nodded. "Do you think there may be somewhat in them?"

"I don't know," I said miserably. "Do you?"

She was quiet for a moment, gazing at the road ahead. "I don't know," she said finally. "I think not. But one may never be certain, with Melisande." She turned her head to look at me. "Do you want to read them?"

I shuddered. "No." I waited, hoping she would offer, until it was clear she wouldn't. "Will you?" I asked. "Please?"

For a long moment, Phèdre studied me. "If you're sure it's what you want, love."

I sighed with relief. "Yes. I'm sure."

"All right, then." She shifted in the saddle, squaring her shoulders. "I will."

I felt guilty then, thinking on it. I didn't like to be a burden to anyone, and least of all to Phèdre, who had borne so many. I'd asked out of selfishness, little thinking how it might be painful to Phèdre to read words my blood-mother had written to me. When all was said and done, Melisande could claim what Phèdre could not—she was my mother, whether I liked it or no. And yet I could not bear to read them myself. My stomach churned at the thought. "You don't need to," I said. "We could give them to Queen Ysandre."

"*No.*" Phèdre's reply was swift and certain. "Not unless we must."

I looked away. "Why do you always protect her?"

"Imriel." She waited until I looked back at her. "I made a promise," she said. "I am keeping it in the only way I know."

It was that simple for her. I wished sometimes that she had never made a promise to my mother, never extracted one in return. She had, though. My mother had promised not to raise her hand against Queen Ysandre and her daughters. In turn, Phèdre had promised to adopt me into her household, to deliver such letters as Melisande might send, and never to seek to turn me against my mother. To allow me to make my own choices. How she could bear it, I do not know. I didn't know, for a long time, the whole of what my mother had done to her—how she had betrayed her, twice. It was a long time before I grasped the whole of my mother's infamy.

And yet they understood one another.

My mother had been one of Phèdre's patrons, once. The very marque inked on Phèdre's back, the vast and intricate briar rose that signified she had paid her bond-debt as a Servant of Naamah, was completed thanks to Melisande's patronage.

What *that* entailed, I never wished to know.

Upon our return to Montrève, Phèdre retreated into her study to read my mother's letters. Elsewhere, the household was a flurry of activity as our staff and retainers began to prepare for the unexpected journey, packing trunks and loading provisions. I prowled the manor in a state of nervous anxiety, until I was shooed out of every room I entered.

It was Joscelin who took me in hand, finding me making a nuisance of myself in the pantry where Katherine was helping her mother. "Come with me." He beckoned with one hand, holding a pair of wooden swords in the other. "Let's have a bout."

"Now?" I protested. "I'm in no fit mood for it."

"You're wound up like a top," he said pragmatically. "It will do you good."

I followed him out to the courtyard, beyond Richeline's herb gardens. Joscelin practiced there every morning, flowing through the forms of the Cassiline discipline. Although he had been teaching me for over two years, I didn't know them all, nor ever would. For ten years, until the age of twenty, Joscelin had studied little else—and he practiced every day.

He is not as good as he was, once. I saw him at his finest, on that terrible night in Daršanga, when he built a wall of corpses in the Mahrkagir's hall. That was before his left arm was shattered by a blow from a morning-star mace. I don't think anyone will ever match what he did there, and I pray no one ever need to. Still, it wasn't Joscelin who struck the blow that mattered the most that night.

That was Phèdre, who killed the Mahrkagir with a hairpin.

"Come." Joscelin tossed me one of the practice-blades and took a stance. "Have at me."

I struck a halfhearted blow which he parried with ease, unbalancing me.

"Watch your feet." He pointed toward them with the blade's tip. "Your weight was on the rear."

Scowling, I shifted my weight to my lead foot, raised my sword, and drove a straightforward strike toward his unprotected face; or as near to it as I could reach, given the disparity in our heights. Our blades clattered as he reacted, startled, and brought his up in an awkward horizontal parry. "I told you I was in no fit mood!" I shouted.

Joscelin grinned at me. "Better," he said. "Now again."

We practiced in earnest, then. The Cassiline fighting style was a circular one; spheres within spheres. There was the inner sphere of one's own space, and the outer sphere encompassing one's opponent's. If there were multiple opponents, there were multiple spheres. Each sphere was defined by its own quadrants, marked and measured like hours on a sundial. It was a hard thing to keep in mind, and only long practice made it possible.

There was also the sphere of one's ward, which was integral to the philosophy of the Cassiline Brotherhood, and in many ways the most important of all. It was the essence of their training—to protect and serve. Indeed, the final strike the Cassiline Brothers were taught—the ultimate blow, the last resort—was called the *terminus*. It was one of those performed with the twin daggers, not the sword. In it, the Cassiline throws his right-hand dagger to slay his ward, slitting his own throat with the left-hand dagger.

Joscelin came within a hairsbreadth of performing it on Phèdre once. So Gilot told me, not realizing I had never heard the tale of what happened on the battlefield outside Troyes-le-Mont, where the Skaldi warlord Waldemar Selig attempted to skin her alive.

I'd never told them I knew.

My mother was Selig's ally.

The sphere of the ward was one that Joscelin never tried to teach me, reckoning I would be best served by learning to protect myself, which was true enough. But he taught me the others. So we circled one another in the courtyard, testing one another's spheres, probing at each angle of every quadrant with quick, flickering two-handed blows.

I watched his face and his body, too.

This, Phèdre taught me. She was trained by her lord Anafiel Delaunay in the arts of covertcy—how to watch and remember, how to listen to what is said and unsaid. How to discern the tell-tales of a lie. How to move in silence, how to pay heed to those senses beyond sight, and how to find the deeper patterns linking one thing to another.

I saw, as we sparred, that Joscelin was careful on offense, taking only the obvious openings I afforded him, pressing them hard enough to make me aware of my errors, but gently enough that he did not injure me unwitting. Wooden or no, our practice-swords carried a considerable sting at best; at worst, they could crack heads.

And I saw, too, what Joscelin did not realize. Mindful as he was, waiting for my attack, he was slower to parry on his left. Although his broken arm had long since knitted, his speed lagged.

Sweat dripped from my brow into my eyes; impatiently, I shook my head. I had forgotten Phèdre in her study, reading my mother's letters. I had forgotten that I didn't want to spar. I circled, paying heed to my footwork on the slate tiles of the courtyard, waiting for a chance.

When it came, I feigned an error, leaving myself open. Joscelin moved to press me. I took a quick step backward, feinted left, and spun. He parried and missed, and I came around hard, completing the circuit of my inner sphere and leveling a hard blow with the edge of my wooden blade against his upper left arm. He winced, left hand going numb, losing its grip on the hilt. His sword, wielded in his right hand, swept up and past my guard, the wooden tip coming to rest beneath my chin.

Feeling the point dent my skin, I laughed. It was the first time I'd ever breached his guard to provoke an unintended attack.

"Very clever." Joscelin smiled, lowering his blade. "You'd have had my arm off."

"Well, you'd have had my head," I replied. "Did I hurt you?"

"Gave me a bruise to remember," he said, flexing his hand and shaking off the stinging residue of pain. "That will teach me to be soft on you."

"I'm sorry."

"Don't be." Joscelin shook his head. "It means you're learning and improving. Anything that might save your life one day is worth a thousand bruises." He grinned. "Which is likely what my future holds. You've got a lot of promise. You're quick, and you *think*."

I felt my face flush with pride at the praise. "Thank you."

Joscelin regarded me with affection. "Feeling better?"

To my surprise, I realized I was. I was hot and tired and sweaty, but the lump of tension that had sat heavy in my belly since the Queen's Courier had delivered her missive had grown smaller. "Yes," I admitted. "A bit."

"Good." He nodded toward the manor. "Let's go wash up."

Inside, I scrubbed down at the washbasin in my room, stripping off my shirt and plunging my whole head in the cool water. It felt good. Most of my clothing had already been packed for travel, but I rummaged in the clothespress and found a clean, loose shirt of unbleached cotton, well worn and much mended. It was one I wore for mucking about in the kennels with Charles. I'd not worn it yet this summer, and I was pleased to find that the sleeves were inches too short.

Thus fortified, clean and dripping, I went to find Phèdre.

The door to her study was open, but I paused before speaking. She was seated at her desk, gazing at nothing, her chin propped in her hand. A pile of unsealed letters sat beside an open coffer on the desk before her, neatly refolded.

"Phèdre?" I asked hesitantly.

She lifted her head. "Come in, love."

I entered and pulled a chair over to sit across from her. "Was there . . . anything?"

"No." Her voice was gentle. "Nothing to hint at her plans. Nothing to suggest you might have known, or might know now."

"Oh," I said. "Good."

Phèdre gazed steadily at me. "Do you want them?"

I shrank under her gaze. It was hard to hold, sometimes. *Lypiphera*, one of the Hellenes in the zenana called her: pain-bearer. She looked weary, her eyelids shadowed and bruised. I wondered whose pain she bore today and suspected, with an uncomfortable certitude, that it was my mother's. "No," I said. "I don't . . . no." Ducking my head, I fidgeted with a loose thread on my too-short sleeve. "What does she say?"

"A lot." A wry note crept into her voice, coaxing a reluctant smile from me. "Imri, it's not for me to say. Her words were written for you, and if you ever wish to understand your mother better, you'll read them." She was silent for a moment, then added, "If you're wondering if she attempts to justify her deeds, no, she doesn't. She does say that there is much she would have done differently, had she known what would happen to you."

I looked up at her. "But that wasn't her fault."

It was true, though I was surprised to hear the words come from my mouth. My mother had me hidden away in the Sanctuary of Elua, yes, while all of Terre d'Ange searched for me. That was her doing, and there was a deep plan behind it that would have taken years to come to fruition. Still, it was no fault of hers that I was kidnapped by Carthaginian slave-traders and sold into hell. I was taken at random. That, not even my mother Melisande could have foreseen.

"No." Phèdre smiled. "It wasn't." With deft motions, she straightened the stack of letters and returned them to the coffer. "They'll be here for you."

"Thank you," I said, meaning for reading them. Meaning for many things.

"You're welcome." She closed the lid, locking the coffer with a tiny key. With my mother's presence banished, the air within the study seemed to grow easier to breathe. Phèdre pushed her chair back, tucking an errant lock of hair behind her ear with the sort of absentminded grace that was as deeply ingrained in her as Joscelin's Cassiline reflexes were in him. "We should go," she said. "Richeline has everything in readiness, and I'd like to put a few hours of road behind us before sunset."

Obliging, I stood. "I'm ready."

"Good." Phèdre glanced at me, then glanced again, her brows rising. "Imriel nó Montrève, what in the name of Blessed Elua are you wearing?"

I grinned at her, plucking at my shirt-front. "What, this? It's only for travel."

Phèdre shook her head, but the shadow had gone from

her eyes, and I was happy to see it. "Sometimes," she mused, "I think Joscelin Verreuil is a bad influence on you."

"I'll change," I promised.

Coming around the desk, Phèdre gave me one of her mercurial smiles: the rare ones, the ones that came from the deep and mysterious reserves of her being, where her own peculiar sense of humor made the unbearable bearable. "Not too much, I hope," she said lightly, dropping a kiss on my cheek. "I'm rather fond of you as you are, love."

"No," I whispered. "Not too much."

THREE

WE WERE ON THE road in short order. I daresay few households in the D'Angeline peerage were capable of mobilizing as quickly as Montrève's. For all that she enjoyed her luxuries—and she did—Phèdre was able to forgo them on a moment's notice.

As for the rest of us, we thrived on it.

No one entered the service of Phèdre nó Delaunay de Montrève out of a craving for security and a staid lifestyle. Ti-Philippe, who had been with her the longest, pledged his loyalty after the battle of Troyes-le-Mont. There were three of them, then—Phèdre's Boys, they called themselves. I never knew the others, Remy and Fortun. They died in La Serenissima, where I was born, killed on my father's orders.

But the others I knew. Like Gilot, they were a high-spirited lot, men who sought service with the Comtesse de Montrève because they had heard the stories and the poems. Some of them, I think, were hoping to bask in the glory of further adventure. And if they were disappointed that it was not forthcoming, still, life in our household was never dull.

It would have been a pleasant journey, were it not for the purpose. The weather was hot and dry, but the breeze of our passage rendered it comfortable. I would have been content to have it last forever. The City of Elua was a buzzing bee-hive of gossip, and I had little desire to confront the results of my infamous mother's latest piece of infamy.

"You could always run away and join the Tsingani," Gilot offered helpfully, sensing my mood. "Think of the horses!"

"I wouldn't mind," I said, remembering the Salmon. "Want to come with me?"

"Why not? I've a fancy to see the world." He laughed, then glanced uncertainly at me. "You *are* jesting, I hope. Joscelin would skin me alive."

"Yes." I shuddered. "And no jests about skinning, please."

"Oh." He fell silent, chastened. "Right."

It wasn't Gilot's fault. He was only four years older than me. It was only a story to him; something that had happened when he was still clinging to his mother's skirts. But I, who had not yet been born at the time, had seen too much horror not to feel it deeply. I was glad, actually, that Gilot forgot at times—that he told me the stories others feared I couldn't bear to hear. I would rather know, always. Still, there were times when I felt myself the older of the two of us.

Travelling light, we made good time and came within sight of the white walls of the City of Elua within several days, arriving in the late morning. Despite the circumstances, I could see Phèdre's mood lighten. Unlike the rest of us, she was City-bred to the bone, and it was where she was most at home.

To be sure, the City of Elua returned the sentiment.

The City Guard at the Southern Gate hailed her with a clamorous salute, shouting and whistling. One of them importuned a flower-seller within the walls, and lavender sprigs came showering down from the guard towers as we passed through the gate. The news of my mother's disappearance, I thought, must not yet have been released. They wouldn't greet us so if it had been. I watched Phèdre's eyes sparkle as she caught a sprig of lavender and tossed it back with a blown kiss; watched the guardsmen scramble for it, and Joscelin's amused, long-suffering patience.

I thought of the shadow descending over that happiness, and I hated it.

We made our way to the townhouse, where Eugènie, Phèdre's Mistress of the Household in the City of Elua, was expecting us. After greeting Phèdre and Joscelin, she turned her prodigious affections on me.

"Sweet boy!" she cried, enfolding me in her considerable embrace. "Name of Elua, I swear you've grown a handspan since you left!"

I smiled, hugging her unreservedly in return. I still remembered my first encounter with her. To this day, she is the only person I have ever seen who dared take Joscelin by the shoulders and shake him. But she dealt gently with me for a long time, until I grew fond enough to suffer her affection gladly. "It's only been a couple of months, Eugènie."

"Ah, well." She patted my cheek. " 'Tis ever too long."

Although we had ridden hard and fast to arrive within mere days of receiving the courier's message, the Queen's summons awaited us. Phèdre dispatched a messenger to the Palace with word of our arrival, and by the time we had changed from our road-dusty attire and partaken of a light refreshment, a reply was waiting. Phèdre read it and sighed.

"Now?" Joscelin asked.

She nodded. "Now."

For this last, shortest leg of the journey, we took the carriage, with the arms of Montrève etched and painted on the doors. There were protocols to be observed. Ti-Philippe,

Hugues, Gilot, and another of our men-at-arms served as outriders, guarding our passage.

Upon our arrival at the Palace, we were ushered directly into the Queen's presence.

It was a formal reception, which I had not reckoned on. Although I was seldom able to forget my parentage, I forgot, betimes, that it meant I was a Prince of the Blood, and entitled to due courtesies. Drustan was present, which was not always the case. But during the summer months, the Cruarch of Alba crossed the Straits to abide with his wife, the D'Angeline Queen.

When it came my turn to greet them, I bowed; the courtier's bow that protocol dictates when acknowledging those whose rank is higher than one's own, yet within the same echelon. "Your majesties."

"Prince Imriel." The Queen inclined her head. "Thank you for coming."

Drustan mab Necthana smiled. "Well met once more, Prince Imriel."

They were an unlikely couple, as unlikely as Phèdre and Joscelin—more so, in appearance. Ysandre was tall and fair, a quintessentially D'Angeline beauty, with pale gold hair and violet eyes. She resembled her mother's side of her family, House L'Envers.

Drustan was one of the Cruithne, the Pictish folk of Alba—dark-haired and dark-eyed, his skin tattooed in whorls of blue woad. Even his face was decorated thus. Although it was strange and barbaric to the D'Angeline eye, I thought there was an odd beauty in it.

There were three others present, one of whom made me grit my teeth. I didn't like Duc Barquiel L'Envers, who was the Queen's maternal uncle. He had proved himself a hero twice over, which I knew. It was Barquiel L'Envers who

launched a daring rescue from behind fortress walls onto
the field of Troyes-le-Mont, where Waldemar Selig wielded
his skinning knife and Joscelin had begun the *terminus*.
And it was Barquiel L'Envers who held the City of Elua
some two years later against the forces of Percy de
Somerville, another pawn my mother duped into treachery.

For that, Duc Barquiel was made Royal Commander, but
I still didn't like him. When he looked at me, he saw a threat
to Ysandre's throne, nothing more. Also, I was certain it
was his daughter who tried to have me killed in Khebbel-
im-Akkad, far from D'Angeline justice.

Whether he suggested it to her, I didn't know, but I had
no doubt he would gladly see me dead. I didn't think he
would be so foolish as to try anything here in Terre d'Ange.
Ysandre made it clear that a crime against me is a crime
against House Courcel. But I still remembered the words
with which Barquiel L'Envers greeted her proclamation.

So don't assassinate the little bugger.

I bared my teeth in a smile, inclining my head. "My lord
Duc."

By rights, he should have responded with the same
courtier's bow with which I had greeted the Queen and Cruarch; instead, he lifted one hand in a lazy, languid gesture.
"Hail, Prince Imriel."

If the gesture was meant to offend, it was somewhat un-
dermined by what followed, for the other two present were
Drustan and Ysandre's daughters, my young cousins.

"Imriel!" Heedless of the protocol of adults, Alais, the
younger, launched herself at me with a shout of delight.
"Welcome back! I missed you!"

I caught her, staggering a bit under her weight, and tried
to fend off her kisses. Slight though she was, at ten years of
age, her exuberance carried an impact. "Hello, Alais."

"Did you bring me a puppy?" she demanded. "You promised you would, from the spring's litter in Montrève."

"I forgot," I said honestly. "But I wasn't expecting to be here so soon."

"Oh." Her violet eyes, like unto the Queen's, darkened. It was her only resemblance to Ysandre. For the rest, she looked purely Cruithne, like her father. "Of course. I'm sorry, that was thoughtless."

"That's all right," I said. "I'll remember, next time."

"Well met, cousin." Sidonie, the elder, greeted me, extending her hand with a coolness that belied her twelve years of age. I bowed over it.

"Well met, Dauphine," I said politely to her. If there was any other way to deal with the Dauphine Sidonie, the Queen's Heir, I hadn't found it.

"Have we done here, Ysandre?" Duc Barquiel asked pointedly. "May we dispense with the *children* and proceed? There is a matter of state at hand."

The Queen leveled a look at him that would have quelled a less insolent soul. "And it is a matter of importance that House Courcel stands united in this time," she said. "You know my feelings on this, Uncle."

He grimaced. "All too well."

I didn't give Ysandre enough credit. There was treachery and betrayal and blood feud in her history, too. She had always stood above it and sought to break the cycle that continued it. That was why she wanted me found—to bring me into the fold of House Courcel, to acknowledge to the world that the innocent should not be persecuted for the sins of their parents. I should have respected that, and I did; still, it was hard to be grateful for a gift I would rather not need.

Ysandre beckoned to an attendant. "Please escort the princesses forth and seal the room."

"Oh, please!" Barquiel L'Envers gestured at me in disgust. "You don't mean to—"

"Barquiel." It was Drustan who spoke; one word, uttered in his soft Cruithne accent, but there was the full weight of the Cruarch's authority in it. The Duc subsided. The attendant escorted Alais and Sidonie from the room, closing the doors firmly behind them. Drustan took a deep breath. "Please, my friends, be seated."

We all sat.

Without preamble, Ysandre related the news. In truth, there wasn't much to tell. A little less than a week ago, she had received a letter from Lorenzo Pescaro, the Doge of La Serenissima. He had sent one of his swiftest couriers; there, it seemed, his sense of urgency ended. In the letter, the Doge wrote that he regretted to inform her majesty that he had received notice from the Priestess of the Crown that Melisande Shahrizai de la Courcel was no longer present in the Temple of Asherat.

I felt sick.

Joscelin uttered a violent oath. "That's *all*?"

"Nearly." Ysandre sighed. "He claims to have had the Priestesses of the Temple questioned. They disavowed all knowledge of Melisande's disappearance, and he was satisfied with their answers."

"A priestess may lie as well as a priest," I said, remembering Brother Selbert.

"I know." There was kindness in Ysandre's regard. I looked away, finding it hard to bear. "But Lorenzo Pescaro reckons it is a D'Angeline matter, and little concern of his. He will not challenge the Temple of Asherat over it."

"Well, someone aided her," Phèdre mused aloud. "It's her way. She wouldn't leave without a plan in place, not after fourteen years of biding her time." She glanced at Joscelin. "Do you remember Allegra Stregazza's warning?"

He muttered under his breath.

"What?" Barquiel L'Envers' voice cracked.

"There were rumors." Phèdre glanced at me. "She took the Veil of Asherat, claimed sanctuary, and made herself into a mystery. A legendary beauty, bereft of her child, condemned by her country—"

He stared incredulously at her. "A cult of *worship*?"

I felt sicker.

"Well, a very small one," Phèdre said. "She wouldn't cultivate it, that would skirt too close to blasphemy."

"No." The Duc shook his head. "Oh, no! Not even Melisande—"

"Oh, she would. It's a means to an end." Phèdre rose without thinking, pacing the room. She wore a familiar look, vivid and distracted. "Have you sent for Duc Faragon?"

"Yes. He's coming from Kusheth. He should arrive in a few days." Ysandre watched her. "Do you think the Shahrizai are involved?"

"No." Phèdre frowned. "On the balance, no. Melisande hasn't trusted them fully since Persia's betrayal. She didn't trust them with the knowledge of Imriel's whereabouts, and I doubt she would with this."

"Mayhap," Ysandre said. "I'd like you to be there when I discuss the matter with him."

"As you wish, my lady." Phèdre tilted her head, thinking. "I'll write to Allegra today; and Severio, too. Among the Stregazza, they're two I trust. If we leave immediately after speaking to Duc Faragon—"

"No."

Joscelin's voice cut through hers like a blade, flat and

implacable. Among the six of us in the room, only Phèdre, lost in thought, failed to startle at it. She blinked at him, un-comprehending. Barquiel L'Envers opened his mouth to speak, then closed it as Drustan shook his head in warning.

"No," Joscelin repeated, sounding weary this time. "No. We are not going to La Serenissima. We are not embarking on another search for Melisande Shahrizai. No."

"But I can find her," she said simply.

"I don't care." He held her gaze. "Isn't this why you ex-tracted a promise from her? You claim to understand her. You thought it worthwhile. Do you have so little faith in your own claim? Will you once more risk everything we have?"

Everyone was silent.

Phèdre closed her eyes briefly, then opened them and looked at me. I clenched my hands into fists, afraid of what she would say. I didn't want her to go to La Serenissima. I didn't want her to chase after the damned spectre of my damned mother. But my heart was in my throat, choking me speechless.

"No," she whispered at last. "You're right."

I unclenched my hands and breathed a sigh.

"Well, and that was hardly my intention!" Ysandre's voice was acerbic in the aftermath of tension. "What I want is your counsel and your wits, Phèdre. Here, beside me, in Terre d'Ange, serving the interest of the nation. Do you understand?"

She inclined her head. "Your majesty."

"Oh, *stop* that!" Ysandre said irritably. Gathering her-self, she turned to me. "Imriel, heed me. I have kept the news silent for some days, but I cannot for long. The mem-bers of Parliament must be notified. There may be . . . re-newed suspicion."

Barquiel L'Envers raised his eyebrows.

"I understand," I said to the Queen, ignoring him.

"Good." Ysandre nodded. "I wish you to know, also, that we do not share this suspicion. The throne of Terre d'Ange stands behind you, privately and publicly."

To my annoyance, I felt tears sting my eyes. For the first time, I caught a glimpse of the courage and nobility in Ysandre that inspired such loyalty in those I loved. Once again, I had to look away. "Thank you, my lady."

"No thanks are needed," she said. "But there may be duties in the bargain. You are a Prince of the Blood and a member of House Courcel. There are those who should be reminded of this." The Queen of Terre d'Ange stood, and we all stood with her. "We will speak more of this anon," she said to me, and to Phèdre and Joscelin, "You will abide in the City of Elua?"

Joscelin gave his sweeping Cassiline bow, arms crossed.

"We will, my lady," Phèdre said.

With that, the Queen dismissed us. It was a quiet ride back to the townhouse. What Phèdre was thinking, I could not guess. Joscelin looked stoic. I reached over and squeezed his hand in silent thanks. He gave me a brief nod and the hint of a smile, and I felt better.

In the small courtyard at the front of the house, our outriders dismounted and the stable-keeper Benoit came to unhitch the carriage horses. It was crowded with all of us present and so much horseflesh milling around. Benoit squeezed past one of his charges as Phèdre made her way toward the door.

"My lady," he called. "A man came while you were gone and gave me somewhat for you."

Phèdre turned. "What man?"

Benoit shrugged. "He wouldn't say, so I didn't open the

gate to him. He handed me this through the portal and said it was for you. Then he left." Reaching into his pocket, he withdrew a small parcel wrapped in oilskin and tied with twine. "Here."

"Ah, Blessed Elua," Joscelin muttered. "Not again."

"Should I not have taken it?" Benoit asked anxiously. "I didn't let him in."

"No, that's fine, you did right." Phèdre took the parcel and caught Ti-Philippe's eye. He nodded and beckoned to Gilot and the others. "Benoit, tell Philippe exactly what the man looked like. How tall, how old, the color of his hair, what he was wearing—everything you can remember. Did you see which way he went?"

"No." He sounded miserable. "Sorry, my lady."

"That's all right. Just tell Philippe everything you can remember." She glanced at Joscelin with a trace of defiance. "We *do* have to look."

He crossed his arms. "You'll notify the Captain of the City Guard," he said to Ti-Philippe. "Not that I expect it will do much good."

"Yes." Ti-Philippe looked a trifle bemused. "Notify him of what, exactly?"

Joscelin eyed the parcel in Phèdre's hand as though it were a live adder. "I've no idea, but we're about to find out."

With careful fingers, Phèdre untied the knots that bound the parcel and unwrapped it. Inside the oilskin wrapping was a velvet pouch with a drawstring. She opened it and spilled the contents into the palm of her hand.

Gilot gave a low whistle.

It was a large diamond, strung on a length of black velvet cord, old and worn, fraying at the ends. Phèdre stared at it without speaking, her eyes wide and dark. There was a slip of parchment caught in the mouth of the pouch.

She withdrew it, smoothed it flat, and read what was written on it.

"Is it signed?" Gilot asked.

"No," she murmured. "It didn't need to be."

"Well, what does it say?"

She looked up. " '*I keep my promises.*' "

FOUR

THEY FOUND THE MESSENGER in a wineshop that day, deep in his cups, and learned that a stranger had paid him a gold ducat to deliver the parcel. All he could say was that the man wasn't D'Angeline. From there, although they searched the City, the trail went cold.

I learned the story from Gilot, who had it from Ti-Philippe. The diamond had been a patron-gift from my mother, long ago. Phèdre had worn it until the day she gave the testimony that condemned my mother to execution.

"In front of the Queen and the peers of the realm," Gilot related with relish. "She dropped it at your mother's feet and said, 'That is yours, my lady. I am not.' After so long, can you believe she kept it?"

"Yes," I said shortly. "I can."

I could, because Phèdre kept things for remembrance, too—painful things. There is a small carved dog of jade that was the Mahrkagir's gift to her. I was the one who brought it out of Daršanga, but she kept it, along with an ivory hairpin.

It is important to remember.

Phèdre told me as much the night of the slaughter there,

in the small hours, before the Tiberian chirurgeon Drucilla died. *Remember this*, she said. *Remember them all.*

I thought about that in the days after the diamond was delivered, and wondered what it was that my mother remembered, and if she had learned anything by it.

The news of her disappearance was released quietly. There was no great outcry of shock and condemnation, for which I was grateful. She had been gone for a long time, and most people's memories are short-lived. Still, wherever I went in the City, there were whispers of renewed speculation.

On the fourth day, the Shahrizai arrived, and we were summoned back to court.

It was the first time I had encountered my mother's kin.

The meeting was held in the Queen's formal chambers. Duc Faragon had brought an impressive retinue, and there must have been a score of the Shahrizai among them. The stamp of my mother's House was unmistakable.

Duc Faragon was venerable, his skin wrinkled like parchment, his hair a rippling silver. Still, he was solid and doughty, and his eyes were undimmed. The kindred who ranged behind him were younger. The women wore their black hair loose, while the men wore theirs in a myriad of small braids, falling like linked chains to frame their faces. All of them were clad in black velvet adorned with gold brocade, the colors of the House.

They looked beautiful, proud, and dangerous.

One of the young men glanced over at me and smiled as we entered the chambers. It was a friendly smile, and a clever one, too. He winked at me. His eyes were a deep, starry blue.

I took a step closer to Phèdre.

If she was perturbed by the Shahrizai, she gave no indi-

cation of it. We made our greetings to the Queen and Cruarch, and took our places standing beside their thrones.
Joscelin, as the Queen's Champion, provided a note of quiet
menace, vambraces glinting, his daggers at his belt and the
hilt of his broadsword over his shoulder.

"My lord Duc." The Queen inclined her head. "I trust you
know why I have summoned you here?"

"Your majesty, I do." Duc Faragon's voice was melodious
and resonant. With a grace that belied his years, he dropped
to one knee and bowed his head before Ysandre. As one, the
other members of his kindred followed suit, the men kneeling, the women sinking into deep curtsies. "In the name of
Blessed Elua and merciful Kushiel, House Shahrizai pro-
claims its absolute loyalty to the throne."

On the far side of the Queen, Barquiel L'Envers stirred.
Several of the other peers assembled murmured. Ysandre
glanced once at Drustan, then rested her chin in her hand
and contemplated Duc Faragon and his entourage.

None of the Shahrizai moved

"Very well," Ysandre said at length. The Duc rose, the
others following. He met the Queen's gaze without fear.
"Have you had any communication from your kinswoman,
Melisande Shahrizai de la Courcel?"

"Yes," he said calmly. "Several times, over the years." He
beckoned, and a woman came forward with a small packet
of letters. "That is everything," Duc Faragon said. "There is
no sedition in them."

"And the rest of you?" Ysandre raised her brows. "Are
there any among you who possess any knowledge of your
kinswoman's latest deeds?"

There was a faint rustling sound as they shook their heads
in denial.

"We are at your service, majesty," Duc Faragon said. "We

place ourselves before you, trusting to the wisdom of your justice."

Ysandre sighed. "What does the Cruarch say?" she asked Drustan.

"Alba's justice is more direct than that of Terre d'Ange." He smiled slightly. There was nothing reassuring about the expression. "Did I believe them, I would accept their oath of loyalty. Did I not"—he touched the hilt of the ceremonial sword at his belt—"they would not leave these chambers alive."

Someone drew in a sharp breath. Several of the Shahrizai raised their heads, eyes blazing. Not scared, I thought; angry. They had come in good faith. Still, members of the Queen's Guard posted around the room took a watchful stance, and Joscelin's hands, resting on his dagger-hilts, twitched.

"Phèdre?" Ysandre glanced at her. "What does Kushiel's Chosen say of Kushiel's scions?"

Phèdre considered the Shahrizai. Some of them, the younger ones, the angry ones, returned her gaze with a hint of mocking challenge. Duc Faragon did not. He inclined his head to her, grave and respectful.

I thought about the diamond lying in her palm, the note. *I keep my promises.*

"I would accept their oath, my lady," Phèdre said thoughtfully. "One at a time."

So it was that the members of House Shahrizai came forward, one by one, and swore oaths of loyalty to the throne. I watched them all, searching for the tell-tales of a lie, and knew Phèdre did the same.

There were none, and I was glad.

Afterward, Duc Faragon approached us, with several of the younger Shahrizai behind him. "Comtesse," he said courteously to Phèdre, and to Joscelin, "Messire Verreuil." To me, he gave the courtier's bow. "Prince Imriel."

I inclined my head. "Your grace."

"I have a favor to ask." He drew a breath, addressing Phèdre. "It is in the letters I gave to the Queen, but I do not ask for my kinswoman's sake alone. I ask for all our sakes, and the boy's."

Phèdre frowned. "Yes?"

"Let him know us," Duc Faragon said simply. "We are kin. Let him come to Kusheth for a summer to be fostered among the Shahrizai."

I felt a lurch of alarm in the pit of my stomach, mixed with a dark excitement that was unexpected. Behind the Duc, the young man who had winked at me nudged the young woman beside him and grinned.

"No." Phèdre's response was gentle, firm, and immediate. "Forgive me, your grace, but I cannot consent to that; nor, I think, would her majesty allow it."

"Then consider this." With a sweep of his arm, Faragon indicated the young Shahrizai nobles behind him. "Mavros, Baptiste, and Roshana are yet of an age to be fostered. It is why I brought them here. Will you consider extending the hospitality of Montrève to them for a summer?" He paused. "I do not request an offer of threefold honor. Only a chance for the boy to know his kin."

Phèdre looked at me.

I wished I knew what to say. A part of me wished to decline; another, to accede. I was afraid of the dark tide that stirred in me. I did not want any part of my mother's blood. And yet it called to me.

"I will consider it, your grace," Phèdre said formally. "Will that suffice?"

He smiled. "It will."

"Prince Imriel."

The Queen's voice, cool and commanding, summoned us. Taking our leave of the Shahrizai, we approached the throne.

"When last we met," she said, "we spoke of duties. Now that this matter is settled, it is time to speak further."

I bowed. "Your majesty."

"You hold estates in title," she said, her violet gaze resting on me. "Estates which belonged to my great-uncle, Benedicte de la Courcel."

"So I understand, your majesty." I remembered the Salmon, and thinking about how the proceeds from those estates might purchase the spotted horse. In two years, that was as much consideration as I had given them. "I do not need them, if you wish to bequeath them elsewhere," I added honestly.

"No." Ysandre smiled. "I do not. But I think it would behoove you to make a tour of your holdings. It is important that they know you. And it is important that they understand the support of the Crown is behind you. To that end, I have asked the Royal Commander to prepare an escort. With, of course, the consultation of House Montrève."

I looked at Barquiel L'Envers with dismay.

He gave a short, wry bow.

It was in my heart to protest. In truth, I needed no estates. I was Imriel nó Montrève; Phèdre's heir, her adopted son. That was all I sought to be, all I wanted to be.

But it was not the hand I was dealt.

And there were such things as duty and honor.

I bowed to the Queen. "As her majesty bids," I murmured.

FIVE

So IT WAS that we spent the balance of the summer of my fourteenth year touring my holdings in Terre d'Ange, rather than spending it as I would have chosen, hunting and fishing and hawking in Montrève. It was not ill done, I suppose. To my profound relief, while Barquiel L'Envers delegated a squadron to escort us, he didn't deign to accompany them. They were good men—Montrève's retainers ensured it, for Ti-Philippe maintained ties to the Royal Army—and seemed to welcome the light duty.

There were three estates, all told: two in L'Agnace, and one in Namarre. We visited Heuzé in L'Agnace first, where I admired the grain-fields and prizewinning cheeses, and from thence rode to Namarre.

Namarre was Naamah's territory. There was a shrine there, where the River Naamah rises from beneath the ground. Phèdre visited it upon our travels. It was sacred to the Servants of Naamah, and Joscelin and I were not allowed to enter.

She went.

What transpired there, I do not know; only that there was a brightness about her when she came back. Hugues sighed a great deal afterward, and wrote more of the abysmal poetry he dedicates to Phèdre, which we had ample time to hear him recite on the road.

We made our visit to the duchy of Barthelme, the largest of my holdings, where I discovered I was responsible for producing, among other things, a very fine red wine. All of the estates, truth be told, ran themselves. They had done so for many years, for my father had dwelled in La Serenissima until he died. The Queen had appointed wise seneschals. They made their accounts to her factors, and those monies were held in trust. It was all very exacting. I shook the hands of the seneschals and they bowed, putting a face to the name, taking heed of the squadron of the Royal Army that stood behind me. At each estate, we spent a day or two touring the holdings and an evening exchanging social courtesies, and then rode onward.

The third estate we visited was different.

Lombelon, it was called. It was in L'Agnace, no more than a half-day's ride from the City of Elua, which was why we saved it for last. There was little more to it than a manor house and a handful of outlying orchards, but it bore a strange history. It had once belonged to my mother, who had inherited it upon the death of her first husband as part of his holdings. Some years later, she deeded it in turn to Isidore d'Aiglemort, the Camaeline traitor, doubtless as a gift to seal their alliance.

When d'Aiglemort betrayed the realm, his holdings were declared the property of the Crown. Ysandre bestowed Aiglemort itself on the Unforgiven, those Camaeline warriors who have dedicated themselves in perpetual penitence to defending the border of Terre d'Ange against the Skaldi. But the tiny holding of Lombelon she deeded to my father, Benedicte, as a gift upon his second marriage. Thus it came to me.

It was a pleasant place, dedicated to growing pears. We toured the pressing-yard, where they made perry cider, and then the distillery shed. That was where I first saw Maslin, though I did not know his name.

He was tending to the gleaming copper alembic that distilled Lombelon's perry cider into brandy. It was the rapt concentration with which he did it that I noticed; that, and the way a shaft of sunlight from the doorway caught his hair, a blond so pale it was silvery. But he averted his head and slipped away when we entered, and I thought nothing of it.

All of us endured a lengthy discourse on harvesting, pressing, and distillation techniques, for which we were rewarded with a sample of Lombelon's pear brandy. It was heady stuff. I sipped mine with care, while L'Envers' soldiers quaffed theirs with a good will. Afterward, the seneschal took us on a stroll through the closest orchard, boasting of the healthy crop. The air was warm and sweet with the scent of pears, alive with the drone of bees.

That was the second time I saw Maslin.

He was working in the orchard, wielding a wicked-looking pruning hook on a long shaft. It was one of the older trees, one the seneschal informed us they were trying to prompt to bear further fruit in the years to come. The silver-haired youth circled it, shirtless and barefoot, working the pruning hook with savage grace. Although the rapt look was gone from his face, as in the distillery shed, his focus was absolute. He assailed the highest branches, the muscles in his arms bunching and gliding with the effort. With each stroke, a flurry of twigs and green leaves descended, and his strokes were so fast and unerring, it was as though the tree shook itself, shedding a hail of detritus.

I envied him.

I envied his assurance of his place in the world, his height and broad-shouldered strength. I envied the simplicity of the task, and his utter concentration on it. I gauged him to be some two years older than me, and I envied that, too. I found myself lagging as the seneschal moved on without me, more than happy to have Phèdre's ear to bend. Our escort was scattered, Montrève's retainers and soldiers of the Royal Army wandering amid the orchard.

Within a few moments, the silver-haired youth sensed my presence. He lowered the pruning hook and fixed me with a dark-eyed stare. "What do you want?"

"Nothing." The surliness of his tone took me by surprise, but human nature is a peculiar thing. Because I had admired him, I wanted him to like me. I came forward, extending my hand. "I'm Imriel."

He didn't move. "I know who you are . . . Prince."

I felt a touch of unease, like a cold finger on my spine. "Then you have the advantage of me," I replied in a calm tone. "Will you give me your name and render us at quits?"

"Maslin." He spat the name. "Does it mean anything to you?"

"No." I shook my head, genuinely perplexed. "Should it?"

"It *should*." He smiled grimly and took a step forward. The pruning hook in his right hand cast a long shadow on the grass. "I had it from my father. It was *his* father's name."

In my mind, the pieces fell into place like a puzzle—the strange history of Lombelon, the genealogies of the peerage, the youth's pale hair. I had heard the stories of Isidore d'Aiglemort, the traitor-hero. *Kilberhaar*, the Skaldi called him: Silver-hair. Though my mother led him into treachery, he redeemed himself at the very end. It was he who slew Waldemar Selig on the battlefield of Troyes-le-Mont, though he got his death-wound doing it.

"You're Duc Isidore's son," I said.

"His *bastard*!"

"There is no shame—" I began, bewildered.

"He would have acknowledged me!" Maslin shouted, cutting me off. The pruning hook lowered like a spear, aimed at my heart. "This was to have been mine, Lombelon, *mine*! But there was no time!"

"I'm sorry, Maslin." I took a step backward. "But it's nothing to do with me."

"Puling princeling." He spat on the ground. "My father died a hero. By what right do you, the son of a bitch-whore-traitor, lay claim to Lombelon?"

"By right of the Queen's will," I said coldly. I had no intention of defending my mother, but Maslin had succeeded in making me angry. My hand strayed to the hilt of my dagger. The pruning hook made a vicious weapon, but I reckoned I could throw faster than he could lunge. "Will you challenge it?"

There was shouting, somewhere, and the muffled sounds of footsteps racing through the long grass toward us. We both ignored it, staring at one another. Maslin was breathing hard, his bare chest heaving. He wiped the back of his free hand over his brow, leaving a dark smudge.

"Will you?" I repeated.

"No." Gritting his teeth, he put up his impromptu weapon. "Not here, princeling, not now. But one day, when we are men, there will be a reckoning. I mean to make something of myself. And you will rue the day I do."

I nodded. "So be it, if it must. But I do not seek your enmity."

"No?" His mouth twisted. "Nonetheless, it is yours."

My escort arrived in belated, thunderous array, swords drawn, clad in the livery of Courcel and Montrève. The seneschal of Lombelon lumbered in their wake, puffing. There was nothing to be seen by then. Only two youths, conversing beneath a pear tree. I made light of the exchange, and we moved onward.

Phèdre knew, of course.

There was little that escaped her attention. Still, she was angry at herself for being careless, and I found myself reluctant to discuss it. I begged her not to speak to the Royal Army Captain of it, reckoning it not worth his trouble. In that, she acceded, saying only a quiet word to Joscelin and Ti-Philippe. We did not speak of it that day, not until the next day, as we rode toward the City and she drew the details of the encounter from me.

"Isidore's son," she murmured. "I wonder who his mother is."

"I don't know." I shook my head. "It didn't seem prudent to ask."

"D'Aiglemort was reckoned a hero until he turned," Ti-Philippe commented. "There's any number of L'Agnacite lasses might have lit candles to Eisheth on his behalf."

Gilot laughed. "You ought to know, chevalier!"

At that, Phèdre smiled. There are a good many children in the area surrounding Montrève who bear a certain resemblance to the last of Phèdre's Boys, although not so many in the years since Ti-Philippe took up with Hugues. "Well, Isidore d'Aiglemort didn't strike me as a man given to casual dalliance. There must have been somewhat in it if he was willing to acknowledge Maslin as his heir, at least to Lombelon."

"There's always somewhat in it, my lady!" Ti-Philippe sounded aggrieved. "You of all people should know."

Joscelin cleared his throat.

"Well, yes." Phèdre glanced at her Cassiline consort with amusement. "But betimes more than others."

Despite all the years they have been together, Phèdre and Joscelin have never wed; nor, I think, will they. He was her consort, declared and acknowledged, but he did not share her title. It had to do with the vows he swore as a Cassiline Brother. Although he had broken all of them save one—the one that mattered most—he would not exchange them for the vows of marriage. There was somewhat in it that his sense of honor could not abide. This, Phèdre understood in him.

"Well, that's true enough," Ti-Philippe said, mollified. "Still, whoever the lad's mother was, why blame Imriel? No one forced d'Aiglemort's hand to treason. He was offered a gambit to seize the throne from a young, untried Queen, and he took it."

I was silent, listening to them argue the matter with half an ear. I understood full well why Maslin of Lombelon hated me. We were both the sons of treasonous parents. The difference was that he was landless and poor, laboring in the orchards that would have been his inheritance, while I strolled through them and claimed ownership; a Prince of the Blood, clad in silk and velvet, with the Queen's Champion and a squadron of the Royal Army at my side.

"He's bitter," I said aloud. "Do you blame him?"

Phèdre gave me one of her deep looks. "For being bitter, no. For drawing a weapon on you, yes."

I shrugged. "A pruning hook."

"You can do a lot of damage with a pruning hook," Hugues offered cheerfully. "*I* could."

"But he didn't," I pointed out.

I thought about it for the remainder of the journey. Once we were within the walls of the City, we dismissed our

Royal Army escort. I thanked the men by name, having memorized them as Phèdre had taught me to do, and gave a purse to the Captain to share among them. They saluted me with a good will, and I was glad of that, at least. Any tales they carried to Barquiel L'Envers would be benign. I'd always gotten on well with soldiers, given half a chance.

Therein lay the challenge.

I thought more about Maslin.

He might be a friend, if he knew me. If he gave me half a chance. Why it mattered, I could not say, except that we shared the heritage of a tainted lineage. And because I had envied him; admired him. He could not know that in some ways, I would gladly trade places with him; that I would happily surrender my claim to Lombelon and the other estates in exchange for the childhood I had lost in Daršanga.

For two days, I mooned around the townhouse, fretting and neglecting my studies, until I came to a decision. When I did, I went to find Phèdre.

She was in her bathing-room, which was the one altar to sheer luxury that she maintains in her household. I paused and would have gone away without knocking, but Eugènie's niece Clory opened the door, her hands glistening with oil.

"Imri." Phèdre's voice, coming from beyond the door, was mild. "Will you out with it now, or later? 'Tis yours to choose, love."

The mingled scent of lavender and mint made me wrinkle my nose. "Now?"

"Come in, then."

I entered and took a seat on the low stool there, hooking my heels over the last rung and propping my chin on my fists. The bathing-room was warm and humid. Candles flickered, burning low in waxen pools. Phèdre lay on the cushioned massage-table, draped only in a short length of finespun linen. Her head was pillowed on her arms. She looked heavy-lidded, languid and indolent, which would have deceived anyone who did not know her.

"Is it Maslin?" she asked.

I nodded. "Do you promise you won't laugh at me?"

"Yes," Phèdre said. "Do you want Clory to leave?"

"No, that's all right." I shook my head. Among those who served in Phèdre's household, discretion was paramount. Women know how to keep secrets. I learned that in the zenana. "I don't mind."

Clory, resuming her duties as masseuse, clicked her tongue against her teeth, doubtless responding to some slight tension in Phèdre's body. She had trained at Balm House, and she took a great deal of pride in her skills. It was soothing to watch. In the warm candlelight, Phèdre's skin glowed like new cream, the black lines and crimson accents of her marque in stark contrast. I perched on my stool in silence, watching Clory's strong, clever hands at work, while Phèdre watched me, patient and waiting.

At last I met her eyes. "I want to give him Lombelon."

Phèdre folded her hands beneath her chin. She didn't look surprised. "You know his claim will have to be substantiated."

"Yes." I took a deep breath. "I know. Do you doubt it?"

"No." She smiled wryly. "Not really. He looks like d'Aiglemort."

I watched a candle gutter and die. "Could you see to it, then? That part?"

"Yes." She shifted one shoulder. Clory halted and, without a word, went to wash her hands in the basin. Wiping them dry, she picked up Phèdre's silk robe, spreading it open and obscuring my view. With the ease of long practice,

Phèdre stood and slid into it, knotting the sash. "Thank you, Clory."

"Always, my lady." Clory's smile was warm. As she left, she touched my shoulder lightly with one fragrant, oil-scented hand. "Young highness."

When she had gone, Phèdre sat cross-legged on the thick cushions of the table. She arranged the graceful folds of her robe, studying me. "Why, love?"

"Because I don't need it." I picked at some pooled wax with my thumbnail. "I don't even *want* it. And if it was meant to be his—it's not fair, that's all." I lifted my chin. "That's a good thing, isn't it? To set right something that's wrong?"

"In theory, yes," she said. "It doesn't always work as simply as it ought. For one thing, the Queen may not approve."

I frowned. "But it's my decision, isn't it?"

"Yes." Phèdre twisted her damp hair into a coil, smiling with a trace of rue. "And mine, since you've not reached your majority."

"She'll be angry at *you*." I hadn't thought of that.

"No more than usual." A flicker of genuine amusement crossed her features. "I was thinking of you, love. Ysandre does not like to have her generosity rebuked. And then there is Maslin."

I found her jeweled hairpins and handed them to her. "What of him?"

"He may not be grateful," she said. "He may even be angry."

It made no sense, and I felt my frown deepen. "Why would he? He loves Lombelon, I could see it. And it's nothing to me."

"You answer your own question," Phèdre said softly, affixing her hairpins.

I sat and thought about it until I came to understand how Maslin of Lombelon might hate me for giving him his heart's desire. For caring so little that I could afford to toss it to him as a sop, the least of my undeserved holdings. How my careless charity might be a hateful reminder of the disparity in our status. How he might hate me for being forever in my debt, and how his pride would gall him at the sight of me.

"Do you see, Imri?" Phèdre asked after a while.

I nodded.

"Do you still want him to have it?"

"Yes." I rubbed my eyes with the heel of one hand. "It's still the right thing to do, isn't it?" I blinked at her, clearing my stinging eyes. "Isn't it?"

Phèdre shook her head and slid from the table. "Come here," she said, opening her arms. I walked into her embrace, resting my chin on her silk-clad shoulder. I had grown tall enough to do that now. She hugged me hard, kissing my temple. "Yes."

After a moment, I freed myself. "Phèdre? What would you have done?"

"Me?" One corner of her mouth curved upward. "Ah, well, love . . . remind me sometime to tell you the story behind Favrielle nó Eglantine and her notorious ill-temper."

I smiled at her. "Joscelin told me that one."

She ruffled my hair. "Then you know."

Six

IN THE MONTHS that followed, the matter was slowly concluded. Phèdre sent Ti-Philippe to make discreet inquiries in the area of Lombelon, where he learned that Maslin's mother was one Anne Livet. Her father, who had died some years ago, had been the master gardener in d'Aiglemort's day. The dalliance had been an earnest one, well-known by the L'Agnacite folk in the area, and d'Aiglemort had claimed the child in the womb. No one doubted that he would have acknowledged Maslin had he lived to see his birth.

Autumn came, and Drustan the Cruarch sailed back to Alba. Phèdre sought a private audience with the Queen to discuss the matter. What she said, I do not know, but if Ysandre was angry or hurt, she held her tongue.

I had to sign the deed before the Chancellor of the Exchequer, sealing it with the stamp of the signet ring Ysandre had given unto my possession after we returned from Jebe-Barkal, with the swan insignia of House Courcel. It felt very strange. Phèdre signed it, too, pressing the seal of Montrève with its crescent moon and mountain crag below mine. When it was done, the Chancellor wrote out a fair copy, signing and stamping it with his own seal. This he gave to me. One way or another, it was mine to deliver.

I agonized over the decision. How to do it? A courier would be impersonal; and yet, if there was hatred in Maslin's eyes, I wouldn't have to see it. And yet, if he were pleased—if he were willing to accept the gesture in the spirit of goodwill and kinship I intended it—I would miss that, too. I would miss that half a chance to befriend the only person I had met who labored under a burden of unwanted heritage similar to mine.

It was Alais who forced the matter, although not, in the end, who decided it.

"You're not paying attention," she said, rapping the back of my hand with the fan of cards she held. "I played trumps, Imriel! You're not paying attention at all." She paused. "Will you tell me why?"

I raked one hand through my hair. In truth, I didn't mind these days, when the Queen bade me to Court and decreed the scions of House Courcel must further their acquaintance. I was fond of Alais, and Sidonie—well, Sidonie left us well enough alone, content to read a book while Alais and I played cards under the watchful eyes of the Queen's Guard.

"I'm sorry," I said to Alais. "I was thinking of somewhat else."

"Yes," she said impatiently, "I know. *What*?"

I told her, then; a shortened version, one fit for a child. Alais listened gravely. She could be serious, when she wished; sometimes she had dreams that came true. That came from Drustan's side and his mother's blood.

"I think you should tell him yourself," she said. "It's nice, what you're doing. What are you afraid of?"

I explained, as best I could. Alais knew a good deal of what I had endured—Ysandre did not want her daughters sheltered from knowledge of the world's ills, and Alais had heard it long ago. But she was born of a love-match, and young, and it was hard for her to understand.

"Well, I think he *should* be happy," she said.

"Yes," I said. "But we do not always do what we should."

Sidonie's voice intervened, cool as water over rocks. "I have heard many things of you, Cousin Imriel, but never that you were a coward."

I stared at her, furious.

She raised her brows; gold, a deeper hue than her mother's. Unlike Alais, the Dauphine looked almost wholly D'Angeline. Only her eyes were pure Cruithne, dark and unreadable.

"That," I said coldly, "I am not."

"Well, then." Sidonie returned to her book, dismissing me.

By what right a twelve-year-old girl who had never known a day's fear or hunger or want of any kind thought to insult the courage of a fourteen-year-old boy who had endured a hell that would break many a grown man, I cannot say. It was, however, singularly effective. I was still chafing at the condescension in her tone when I made my decision to go to Lombelon.

There was a good deal of discussion. I wanted to go alone, with only a pair of men-at-arms, which Phèdre adamantly refused to allow. In turn, I argued against the entire household appearing in a show of force. Sidonie had pricked my pride, and I did not want Maslin to think I was afraid.

In the end, I was allowed to go with a handful of men-at-arms under Ti-Philippe's command, although Phèdre did not like it. Neither did Joscelin, but he understood.

The day was blustery, with a chill edge to the wind hinting at the winter to come. We departed in the early morning under dull grey skies. It was strange to see the City quiet and empty; the shop doors bolted, the streets almost deserted. Only a few scattered members of the City Guard were about, and a few weary revelers weaving their way home from a late night's debauch. One of them greeted Ti-Philippe, calling out a slurred salute.

He grinned in reply. "To the flowers of Orchis!"

I felt myself redden. Orchis was one of the Thirteen Houses of the Night Court, where Naamah's finest Servants plied their trade. Phèdre was raised in one such—Cereus House, First among Thirteen.

"Philippe?" I cleared my throat. "What's it like there?"

He glanced at me. "Orchis House?"

"The Night Court."

"Well, it depends on the House." He shrugged. "I like Orchis. They're lighthearted; merry. It suits me."

"What about the others?" I asked.

"They're all different." Ti-Philippe smiled. "Heliotrope's nice. The adepts there will make you feel like the only man ever to touch their hearts. And Eglantine—it's worth visiting for the poets and players alone. Jasmine . . . ah, there's adepts at Jasmine will leave you limp as a dishrag, half-drowned in the sweat of desire."

Phèdre's mother was an adept of Jasmine House, but she left. And when she sold her daughter into indentured servitude, it was to the First among Thirteen; to Cereus House. "What about Cereus?"

"Ah." His gaze sharpened. "Well, all beauty's transient, so they say; but I'm not one to ache at its passing—or at least not to relish the ache."

"No," I said slowly. "I suppose not."

Ti-Philippe chuckled. "Ah, don't worry, Imriel, you've got plenty of years to choose."

The men in earshot laughed, and I blushed deeper. "That's not why I asked."

"I know." He grinned, but nicely. "Well, if you choose to visit Cereus House one day, you'll see where her ladyship got her manners, but that's about it. Anyway, it's not the House I'd pick for you."

"Which one, then?" I was curious despite myself. The Night Court wouldn't accept me as a patron until I'd gained sixteen years, but the mere thought of choosing among the Thirteen Houses made my stomach feel unsettled with a sick excitement.

Ti-Philippe opened his mouth to reply, then paused and shook his head. "I'm not sure." His eyes had gone grave and thoughtful. "For you, I'm not sure."

"Well, what do think you might fancy?" Gilot asked cheerfully. "I'll tell you, I hear Bryony's more fun than you might reckon. If you like to wager, you're a lad will have the coin to spare. Or maybe Alyssum, eh? A little modesty, a little hesitation?" Leaning over in the saddle, he nudged my leg. "That might suit you, Imri."

Unaccountably, I shuddered. Something in his words summoned a memory of the zenana, so powerful that I could almost smell the stagnant water in the abandoned pool. I remembered the Bhodistani women fasting there, hollow-eyed and serene. Somehow they had maintained dignity and modesty alike in that terrible place. It had carried a cost. One of them had died at the point of a knife rather than consume a morsel of food in the Mahrkagir's hall.

"No." My voice was thick. "Not that."

"Ah, well." Gilot was oblivious. "There's Dahlia if you

like 'em haughty instead; or Camellia, they're a proud lot. Or, of course—"

"Enough, Gilot." It was Hugues who intervened. His voice was mild, but there was somewhat implacable in his pleasant blue eyes; and too, the set of his broad shoulders. "As Philippe said, Prince Imriel has years to choose."

I smiled my thanks at him.

"Sorry, Imri." Gilot shrugged. "I meant no offense."

"None taken." I shook my head. "It's no matter."

It was, though. I did not want to hear him name the other Houses—not Balm or Gentian; healers and dreamers I did not mind—but the other two. Mandrake and Valerian, those given over to the sharper pleasures; the one giving, the other receiving. Their clientele was smaller, but it was select.

They played with dangerous toys there.

I knew too much about those.

We passed through the Northern Gate and turned up the collars of our cloaks against the cold wind. I felt it whip against my cheeks, scouring away the City's clinging touch, and I was glad. Although a part of me yearned for it, I was not ready yet to be a man among men, speaking casually of desire and the pleasures of the flesh. Not yet, not really.

Besides, there was Maslin.

What was the truer test of manhood? To know another, to plumb the depths of desire? Or to face one's fears and accept the burden that responsibility entails? Anyone could do the former. It was in the latter that the challenge lay.

We reached Lombelon before midday. The seneschal, Jerome Bargot, greeted us with startled good manners, calling for mugs of hot perry cider and ushering us into the great room, where we might warm ourselves before the fire.

"Welcome, Prince Imriel," he said when we were settled. "Forgive us for not being prepared to better receive you."

"No matter." I smiled to put him at ease. "The fault is mine for coming without notice. But have no fear, we will not trouble you long."

"As you will, highness; it is no trouble." He paused. "How may I serve you?"

I cupped my mug, feeling its warmth seep into my cold hands, and took a sip of perry cider. It was sweet and spicy, blazing a trail of heat into my belly, and I felt stronger for it. "I wish to see Maslin," I said. "Anne Livet's son."

Jerome Bargot, who was a florid man, turned pale. "Has he . . . has he given offense, highness?"

"No." I shook my head. It was strange to have so many people worried about offending me; although I suppose the seneschal had cause for concern. I reached into the pouch at my belt, withdrawing the sealed deed. "I have come to set right a certain matter. Will you summon him?"

The seneschal's eyes bulged. "Highness!" he croaked. "He is . . . he is in the orchards, tending to the fall mulching. Perhaps you would prefer to wait until—"

"Bring him," I said simply.

Jerome Bargot bowed. "As you will."

We lounged in the great room and waited while Maslin was summoned. The fire crackled. We grew warm and threw off our cloaks. Hugues brought out his wooden flute and played a simple, merry tune. A serving maid brought a plate of bread and meat and strong mustard, and Gilot caught her eye, grasping her hands and convincing her to dance a measure with him until she drew away, laughing and protesting.

It reminded me of Montrève, and I was smiling when Maslin arrived.

He brought with him a strong whiff of dung. I rose when he entered the great room. We took each other's measure at a glance. Hugues' flute fell silent. Firelight laid a ruddy crown on Maslin's pale hair. He clenched his fists, with half-moons of dirt under the crescents of his nails, and inclined his head. His voice, when he acknowledged me, was grating. "Your highness."

I saw him, and for the first time, it was as though I stood outside myself. I saw the fierce pride and the anguished betrayal. I saw the fault-lines in his soul and where they lay, and how they could be exploited. There was a game to be played. He hated me, yes, but we were victims in common. I could play to that, speak cunning words, turn his hatred to a shared target. One whose justice was too harsh for his angry soul, whose mercy galled my unrestful one.

Ysandre, the Queen.

Or I could wound him with disdain, and earn his undying enmity, sealed and immaculate. There was power in that, too. Those whose hatreds are simple are easy to manipulate. He could become my creature, all unwitting.

I trembled at this knowledge. It was my mother's legacy, Kushiel's gift, and I did not want any part of it.

What I wanted was to make a friend of him.

It was not to be. That, too, I saw; and I was grateful to Phèdre for her warning.

"Here," I said, thrusting the deed forward. "I cannot undo what is done. I know only that this is right. Lombelon is yours."

Maslin grabbed the parchment and broke the seal. For a long moment, he read, lips moving silently. At last, his dark eyes met mine.

"Why?" he asked.

I shrugged. "Because I could."

It was not answer enough; it would never be answer enough. But it was all the answer I could afford him. Maslin shuddered, his dung-stained nails tightening on the deed. "Shall I bow and scrape in thanks, princeling?" he asked harshly. "Is that what you wish to see? Groveling gratitude, a sop for your miserable soul?"

Someone's breath hissed between their teeth, and I motioned my retainers to be still. I gazed at Maslin. "You do not know me," I said to him. "Do not presume that you do."

He looked away. "Nor you me," he muttered.

"Fair enough," I said evenly.

"What is it?" He looked back at me, scowling. "What do you *want*?"

I considered the question. "I want to be good."

This was an answer he understood. I saw the flicker of recognition in his eyes. His scowl eased and he nodded, half to himself, as though I had spoken his thoughts, thoughts no one else in the room save we two could know. "People make it hard to do," he said.

I thought about my mother who had borne me, the priest who had lied to me. I thought about the Carthaginian slavers, the Mahrkagir, the mocking, distrustful face of Barquiel L'Envers. And I thought, too, about Phèdre and Joscelin—and strangely, Sidonie, with her cool, disdainful words. "Some do," I said. "Not all."

"Most," said Maslin.

"Too many," I agreed.

What the others in the room made of our conversation, I cannot guess. But we understood one another, we traitors' sons. It was not friendship, but it would do. I put out my hand, and this time, Maslin clasped it. His grip was callused and strong.

"My thanks," he said. "I didn't mean . . ." He shrugged, wordless.

I nodded. "I know."

So it was done, and I was glad. We took our leave in short order, leaving behind a manor abuzz with the news. The folk of Lombelon seemed well enough pleased with my decision, and I was glad of that, too. I had not made a friend, but I had not made an enemy, either.

I thought a great deal about Maslin on the homeward ride, wondering about those people in his life who made it hard to be good. His life seemed so much simpler than mine—it was one of the things I had envied him. And yet I had complicated it.

Was it right? I believed it was. Was it *good*?

I thought so, yes; but I was not certain. I had acted out of self-interest. In the end, I could not say. And I thought, too, about my own perceptions—about the fault-lines and flaws I had discerned in Maslin, and how they might best be exploited. It was not so different from the arts of covertcy which Phèdre had taught me; and yet it was.

I had seen how Maslin could be *used*.

I was my mother's son.

But I had seen, and I had walked away from it. It gladdened my heart to know this. That was the secret of Kushiel's gift to his scions—power, to be used for good or ill. Even so, it could be rejected. It need not be used.

Therein, I thought, lay true strength.

Dusk was falling by the time we returned to the City of Elua, the long shadows tinting the white walls of the City with blue. We were all of us cold and hungry, blowing on our chilled fingers as we rode into the narrow courtyard. All the windows of the townhouse were ablaze with lights, awaiting our return. For the first time, I felt a strong sense of homecoming; here, in this place. We poured through the open door into the welcoming parlor, set about with warming braziers and the bust of Anafiel Delaunay on its marble plinth, smiling his subtle smile.

"Well?" Phèdre set her hands on her hips, eyes sparkling. I could see so many things in them—relief, concern, curiosity. And love; always love. So much it made me dizzy, so much it made my heart ache. "How was it?"

"Good." I smiled at her; at Joscelin, who stood beside her, his Cassiline stoicism not hiding his own vast relief at my safe return. It had cost him, letting me go without his protection. "It was good. I'm glad I did it."

We celebrated that night with a long meal around a crowded table. What exactly it was that we celebrated, I could not say. I only knew I was glad to have gone and glad to be back, and I felt lighter in my heart than I had since setting foot in Lombelon.

I held on to the moment, and wished nothing would ever change.

SEVEN

THAT WINTER, in the City of Elua, I grew.

It was as though I had crossed some invisible thresh-old in giving Lombelon to Maslin, crossing out of boyhood and toward manhood, and my body sought to keep pace. My bones seemed to lengthen daily, and betimes they ached. My voice, which had been breaking for the better part of a year, settled into a deeper register.

I felt strange to myself. Though I had longed for it, when it came, I felt uneasy in my own body. My limbs seemed too long, my hands and feet outsized. Never in my life had I been clumsy; now I found myself bumping into objects, ca-reening off balance.

Joscelin laughed at me.

We kept up our practice in the Cassiline drills, training in the chilly inner courtyard. Although he still had the advan-tage of me in height and reach, it had lessened; yet now I found myself overreaching, flailing and floundering, my feet slipping on the frosty flagstones.

In contrast, Joscelin never made a misstep. Every move was controlled and precise. Time and again, I measured my-self against his fluid grace and found myself sorely lacking.

"This never happened to *you*," I complained.

"Oh, it did." He grinned, his summer-blue eyes crinkling. "Colts' Years, we called them in the Brotherhood. Everyone goes through it. Don't worry, you'll grow out of them."

It was a good term. It was how I felt; half-grown and gangly with it. It gave me a shock the first time I looked at Phèdre and realized I was taller than her. I saw the knowledge reflected in her face, along with a bittersweet sorrow.

"Ah, love," she whispered, touching my cheek. "Don't grow up too fast."

It is an awkward thing to be caught between one state and another. When I went to Court, I felt newly self-conscious. I was no longer a child, and people looked differently at me, speculative and assessing.

In the self-absorbed way of the young, I had supposed the news that I had given Lombelon to Isidore d'Aiglemort's son would be on everyone's lips; but that had passed without remark. No one, it seemed, was particularly interested in the fate of a minor untitled holding, and a nobleman's bastard get was hardly news in Terre d'Ange. If d'Aiglemort had lived to acknowledge and adopt him, it might have been different, but he hadn't.

After all, it wasn't as though Maslin were a Prince of the Blood.

Not like me.

There was no news of my mother, which was a mercy. Wherever it was she had gone to earth, she showed no signs of resurfacing. There were no further letters from her, no correspondence. Phèdre exchanged a regular correspondence with her acquaintances in La Serenissima and elsewhere, and no news was forthcoming on any front.

Still, her memory lived, and where I went, whispers followed. At Court, I treated everyone I met with unfailing politeness; but I was wary, and I got a name for being aloof.

Midwinter came upon us, and with it an invitation to the Masque at the Palace. It was one of those rare things that showed up the divide between Phèdre and Joscelin. I hated to see them argue; but over this, they did.

"Will you not accompany me?" she asked. "Surely, Blessed Elua can spare you."

He shook his head. "It is the Longest Night, Phèdre. I ask for little. If nothing else, let me keep his vigil."

"Even now?" she said. "What of Imriel?"

It was the first year I had been invited to attend; a courtesy of Ysandre's, recognizing that I was no longer a child. There was a part of me that yearned to do so. Long ago, before Daršanga, the idea of a grand fête with fancy dress would have delighted me. Even afterward, I'd held a fondness for it. I still remembered plotting with Favrielle nó Eglantine to make Joscelin splendid, wearing the lion's mane that had been a Jebean queen's gift. But, too, there was a part of me that abhorred the idea, yearning for something simpler, clean and pure.

"What *of* Imriel?" Joscelin retorted. "Have you asked him?"

Both of them looked at me then. I squirmed under their scrutiny.

"What will you, love?" Phèdre asked gently.

I opened my mouth and blurted, "I want to go with Joscelin."

Phèdre raised her brows. "Are you certain?"

I wasn't, not at all. And yet Joscelin looked surprised and pleased; and proud, too. I imagined the two of us, kneeling side by side in the Temple of Elua, stern and disciplined. It was a picture I very much relished.

"Yes," I said. "I'm certain."

That got me one of Phèdre's deep, searching looks; one

of those that owed nothing to the arts of covertcy, and everything to the fact that she had held the Name of God in her mind, and there was little or nothing in the human soul that could be concealed from her.

"As you will, love," she said simply.

"What of you?" Joscelin asked her, and there was an edge to his voice. "You know there is . . . speculation."

Somehow, word had gotten out that Phèdre had made the pilgrimage to Naamah's shrine. Ysandre's Court, which was not overly concerned with the disposition of my holdings, was keenly interested in whether or not the most famous courtesan in Terre d'Ange would return to Naamah's Service.

"I know." Phèdre smiled, touching the bare hollow of her throat. "Let them wonder. You keep your vigil in your way, and I in mine."

What it meant, I could not say; but Joscelin seemed satisfied with it.

And so it was that on the Longest Night, when all of Terre d'Ange celebrated the sun's return and the lengthening days to come with a riot of love and libation, that I found myself in the Temple of Elua, shivering and miserable.

We rode there alone, Joscelin and I, while the setting sun threw long streaks of red fire in the western skies. Elsewhere in the City, the revelry had already begun. Twilight settled over the streets, challenged by music, shouting, and torches. Above the river, the Palace was ablaze with light; farther inland, Mont Nuit echoed its brilliance. There would be a fête there, too, hosted by Cereus House, welcoming all the adepts of the Night Court.

The streets were crowded with early revelers; most onfoot, making way for the carriages that forged a path through them. Overhead, the sky grew dark, stars emerging. I marveled at Joscelin's composure. He sat at ease in the saddle, starlight glinting on his steel vambraces, the hilt of his sword jutting over one shoulder. Everyone who passed gave us a wide berth.

I wanted to be like that.

It was cold. Our horses snorted, their breath frosting in the cold air. Near the Temple of Elua, the streets grew quiet. We dismounted, giving our mounts to the ostler, then passed through the gate into the vestibule. There we were met by blue-robed priests and priestesses. They welcomed us, smiling, giving us the kiss of greeting.

"Cassiel's child," said one, old and venerable, laying his hands on Joscelin's shoulders. "You have ever chosen truly. Be welcome on this Longest Night."

Joscelin smiled. "Thank you, my lord priest."

An acolyte knelt before me, drawing one foot into her blue-robed lap, unlacing my boot. I balanced awkwardly on the other foot, meeting the old priest's gaze. It was amused and kind, deep with unspoken wisdom.

"Kushiel's scion," he said to me. "What seek you here on this Longest Night?"

"I don't know," I said honestly. My foot freed, I stood, half unshod. The marble floor felt like ice. "What will I find, my lord priest?"

The wrinkles around his eyes grew deeper as he smiled. "Love, child! What else? You will find it and lose it, again and again. And with each finding and each loss, you will become more than before. What you make of it is yours to choose." He laid a hand on my cheek, and a shadow of sorrow darkened his expression. "Ah, lad. I would that your path was easier. But rejoice that you have loving guides to set you on your way."

I nodded, not knowing what was expected of me. "I do."

"Yes." He patted my cheek. "I pray that you do."

It was not entirely reassuring; but with that, he left us. The kneeling acolyte removed my other boot and rose, pointing the way with a smile. Unshod, Joscelin and I ventured into the Temple proper.

There was no roof over the inner sanctum; Blessed Elua's temples were always open to the heavens. In the Sanctuary of Elua in Landras, where I spent my childhood, his altar was in a field of poppies. Here it was contained within a vast walled garden with pillars marking the four corners and ancient oaks flanking the altar.

In other seasons, it was a lush and verdant place. Now the oak trees lifted crowns of stark bare branches against the night sky. Nothing remained of the weeds and flowers that had once flourished here save bent stalks, brown and brittle. Only cypress and holly lent a semblance of life.

Before us was the effigy of Blessed Elua on his altar, carved from a massive piece of marble. It is one of the oldest ones in existence. The workmanship is crude by today's standards, and yet there is a raw power in it. Elua stands, smiling, gazing downward, both his hands open in offering. The left bears the mark of Cassiel's dagger, the wound with which Blessed Elua answered the summons of the One God.

My grandfather's Heaven is bloodless, and I am not.

We approached, soundless on bare feet. The ground was frozen hard beneath our soles, so cold it burned. There were already two others maintaining vigils, kneeling on the cold earth; Cassiline Brothers, both of them. They wore the ash-grey garb of their order, the vambraces and twin daggers, hair bound into a club at the nape of their necks. No swords, though. Cassiline Brothers are no longer allowed to carry swords in the City. Both of them lifted their heads at our approach and favored Joscelin with long, silent stares.

He ignored them. For a long moment, he stood before the altar, gazing on Blessed Elua's face. I stood behind him, shivering in the still, frosty air, and wondered what he thought. Although Cassiel's order declared him anathema, Joscelin has always honored the one vow that mattered, his loyalty as unswerving as Cassiel's devotion to Elua himself. Drawing a swift breath, he stooped to kiss the effigy's feet, then stepped away. Finding an open space to one side, he knelt and composed himself, arms crossed over his breast.

I followed suit. The marble was icy beneath my lips, worn smooth by thousands upon thousands of supplicants' kisses. I made my way toward Joscelin and knelt beside him. The frozen ground was rock-hard, uneven and lumpy. Already I could feel the cold seeping into my bones, and my bare feet were chilled through. I sat back on my heels to warm them, rubbing my palms on my thighs.

The Longest Night was going to be long indeed.

No one spoke. In the distance, we could hear the City rejoicing, but within the Temple walls, all was quiet and still. I glanced sidelong at Joscelin. He knelt, head slightly bowed, motionless as the effigy. His expression was calm and grave in the starlight.

I tried my best to emulate him.

I willed my mind to silence, seeking to find a small, still place within myself to contemplate Blessed Elua's gift to his children; love, in all its myriad glories. Once upon a time, I had it. But that was before the slave-traders, before Daršanga. It was harder to believe, now; harder to *worship*. And yet, by the same token, who had greater cause than I? If Elua allowed me to be cast into a living hell, he had not suffered me to be abandoned.

I gazed at Elua's enigmatic visage, wondering, for the thousandth time in my life, *why*. Wondering if what had befallen me had been necessary. Wondering if it were true, after all, that we had defeated a terrible darkness in Daršanga. Ill thoughts, ill words, ill deeds; such were the tenets of the Mahrkagir and the priests of Angra Mainyu, who sought to conquer the world. And there was power in them—I had seen it. I had witnessed the bone-priests there wield death and madness as weapons, killing with a thought. A mighty army of Akkadian warriors had been destroyed by the dark sorcery begotten there.

And against this legion of horror, where other gods sent forth armies, Blessed Elua had sent an unarmed courtesan and a single swordsman.

Love.

It had been the Mahrkagir's undoing. He had loved Phèdre in the end. So much that she would have been his perfect sacrifice, the offering that would have sealed his power. So much that he allowed her within the circle of his trust. And there, she had killed him.

My knees were beginning to ache. I shifted, trying to find a more comfortable patch of ground. I wondered how Joscelin could bear it. Surely his old wounds must ache in the cold. He has earned enough of them in his lifetime—the shattered bones of his arm, the long scar that curves around his rib cage, the myriad lesser gashes he has sustained. But if they did, he gave no sign of it. No sign that his joints were stiffening. No sign that the cold was leaching all the warmth from his body, leaving him shivering to the core.

The others did. Out of the corner of my eye, I could see them move from time to time. I could hear them rustle, and the occasional cough. Only Joscelin had gone so deep inside himself that he scarce seemed to breathe.

Once, Phèdre told me, he sat cross-legged in the snow all night long. That was in Skaldia, where my mother betrayed them into slavery. And yet Joscelin says it is Phèdre whose will sustained them there; who goaded him into hope when he despaired.

Rejoice that you have loving guides to set you on your way.

Did Elua's priest think me unaware? Ungrateful? I knew it all too well. I was not worthy of the sacrifices they made. No one mortal could be. I didn't forget it, ever.

I didn't rejoice in it, either. Not often. Joy came hard for me.

Perhaps, I thought, that was the priest's meaning. Not a reminder, but an injunction. All darkness, even that of the Longest Night, gives way to dawn. I had passed through darkness, but I had emerged. Not unscathed, but alive.

I bore the scars of Daršanga, though only a few were visible; a handful of faint lines crosshatching my back where the deeper welts healed, and the Kereyit rune branded on the flank of my left buttock. That one wasn't the Mahrkagir's doing. It was Jagun, a warlord of the Kereyit Tatars, who marked me for his own.

He died for it, one of many Joscelin slew there. We made our way out of darkness together and found brightness on the far side of hell.

Rejoice.

It was hardest at night. There was no daylight in the zenana, never. Not until the day Phèdre found a way to pry open the boards sealing the walled garden there. I remembered how it had felt to see the sky, cold and grey, and found my eyes filling with tears.

Somewhere in the distance, a horologist was crying the hour. It was later than I had thought. I tilted my head to gaze at the night sky, remembering. The stars were cold and bright. They had seemed closer in Saba, where we had fol-

lowed the constellations across the Lake of Tears in search
of the Name of God. That night, too, had been terrible in its
way. And yet we had succeeded in the end.

I thought about what the priest had said of love.

You will find it and lose it, again and again.

It seemed a harsh fate, and yet, strangely, there was comfort in it. The priest had not offered me false kindness. I preferred a hard truth to a well-meant lie. There would be love,
and while it was mine, I could cling to it. I could rejoice—
in life, in the existence of love. In the existence of people
like Phèdre and Joscelin. Although the standards they set
were impossibly high, still, I could rejoice that such courage
and compassion existed in the world.

I could hope and aspire.

Blessed Elua, I thought, forgive me. I am unlike them,
and my faith is imperfect. There is a part of me that cannot
forget. There is anger in my heart, and a darkness within me
which I fear. And yet I have come here tonight. Lend me
strength, and I will try, wherever my path leads me.

There was no answer, but as I gazed at Elua's gentle
smile, a sort of peace settled upon me. My anger, my fear,
my pride—Blessed Elua was above these things. It felt good
to confess to them in my thoughts, to lay them before him
and ask his mercy.

I resolved then to offer up this night's suffering as a sacrifice; a penance for my doubt, for my anger. Three hours of
shivering and freezing had dispelled any romantic illusions
of my own fortitude. I had come in pride and vanity, and
whatever foolish whim had prompted my words. I could not
hope to match Joscelin's discipline.

But I could suffer and endure. That, I could do.

Much of what followed that night fades in memory. Hour
by slow hour, the faint cries of the horologists tracked time's

passage. I grew colder, so cold I began to tremble violently. Since I didn't want to shame Joscelin with my weakness, I wrapped my arms around my body and bent over double, my brow touching my knees. I felt the presence of Blessed Elua looming over me, filled with compassion and regret. A sense of mystery touched me, like the brush of a vast wing. Perhaps, I thought, even gods must make difficult choices. Without words, I told him that I forgave him what had befallen me, that I understood it had been needful.

Then the mystery went away, and there was only endless misery. I huddled and held myself, rocking and shaking on the frozen ground. My bones ached to the marrow. All my joints became locked and rigid save my jaws, which I could not stop from chattering. Using my chin, I worked a fold of my woolen cloak between my teeth to silence the noise.

At some point, the cold went away.

There was a mighty clamor in the City when dawn's first rays pierced the eastern horizon. In the Palace, in the Night Court, everywhere across the City, people cheered and drank *joie*. In the Temple of Elua, there were only stifled groans of relief from the two Cassiline Brothers, and the slow lift of Joscelin Verreuil's bowed head.

This, I sensed without seeing. With my own head pillowed on my enfolding arms, I smiled drowsily at a clod of soil. The sparkle of frost was beautiful in the grey light of dawn.

"Imriel!" Joscelin's voice was hoarse and alarmed. He was on his feet in a heartbeat, stooping over me. "Name of Elua, what was I thinking?"

"I'm fine," I said; or tried to say. My lips were too stiff to move and my mouth was clogged with wool. With an effort, I worked it free and spat it out. "Let me sleep."

"You're freezing to death," he muttered. "Why didn't you say something?"

I felt his arms slide under me then, preparing to lift me, and I struggled, waking. "No!" I croaked. "I can do it."

"Messire Verreuil." It was one of the Cassilines who spoke in a flat tone. "Permit us to assist you with the Prince."

"No," I whispered, raising my head. I met Joscelin's eyes. "Please."

After a moment, he nodded. Rising, he took a step backward. "The Prince," he said, "does not require your aid."

It hurt to awaken. The cold returned, and with it came pain. I unfolded my arms, placed my palms on the cold hard earth, and pushed. My spine crackled as I levered myself to kneel upright, and I gasped aloud. I tried to get to my feet and found my legs would not obey me.

Silently, Joscelin extended his hand. I hesitated, then clasped it. His hand felt warm to my frozen touch, firm and calloused. With a single, seamless effort, he hauled me to my feet.

There I stood, wavering, on numb feet and nerveless legs, only his careful grasp keeping me upright. Every muscle in my body was protesting. I drew a deep breath, feeling it sear my lungs with cold. My sluggish blood began to move in my veins, bringing pain like fire. But the Longest Night had ended, and I had survived it. I grinned at Joscelin, as nearly as my frozen lips would allow. "I did it, didn't I?"

"You did." Joscelin regarded me. A corner of his mouth twitched. "Phèdre is going to kill me for this."

"I know." I glanced at the hovering Cassiline Brothers, and gave them a regal nod of dismissal; the sort of thing I had seen Sidonie do. It worked, for they went without a word. I looked then at the effigy of Blessed Elua, and remembered the edge of mystery that had touched me, vowing silently to keep my resolve. At last, I looked at Joscelin, patient and waiting. "Let's go home."

It was a slow process. I limped over the frozen ground, supported by Joscelin's strong arm. Once we reached the vestibule, warmed with braziers, the agony of my thawing flesh grew unbearable; I was only glad the Cassilines were no longer there to see it.

In the end, Joscelin hired a hackney to bring us home, for my hands trembled too hard to hold the reins. He wrapped me in a carriage blanket, folding his arms around me and sharing the warmth of his body. For the moment, with no one watching, I was content to feel myself a child under his protection once more. In Daršanga, Joscelin's presence at my side meant no one could touch me; no one could hurt me. Here, it made the pain diminish. I lolled against him, feeling loose-limbed and warm, thinking about how calmly he had endured this travail, thinking about the stern beauty of his bowed profile against the night sky. "Joscelin?" I asked sleepily. "Do you think I'll ever be like you?"

He looked down at me. "Who said you should be?"

"No one," I said. "I just want to, that's all."

I felt his lips, then, touching my brow, and his arms tightened around me, a promise of safety and security. "Ah, love!" he said roughly. "Don't wish for that. You're too much like me for your own good."

"Never enough," I murmured. "Never be that."

"Mayhap," Joscelin said, stroking my hair. He gave me a wry smile. "Never fear, love. It seems being *you* is dangerous enough."

EIGHT

AFTERWARD, I WAS ILL, with bouts of chills and a
fever that refused to abate.

Joscelin's prediction proved true; Phèdre was angry. At
him for his thoughtlessness, and at me for my folly. The
chirurgeon who examined me ordered a period of extended
bed rest, extra braziers, and vats of weak tea sweetened with
honey, but I heard them quarreling while I lay in bed, their
voices fading in and out of my fevered dreams.

"It's not his fault," I said to Phèdre in one of my lucid
moments. "I wanted to do it."

She perched on the edge of my bed, wringing out a cloth
in a basin of cool water. "I'm aware of that," she said, laying the damp cloth on my brow. "But you took it too far,
Imri."

"Like you do," I whispered. "In Kushiel's temple."

Phèdre opened her mouth to reply, then shook her head.
"Somewhere," she murmured, "Anafiel Delaunay is laughing at me."

Once word of my illness reached the Queen, my plight
worsened. It wasn't that my condition grew worse; it remained unchanged, merely fluctuating on an hourly basis. If
anything, I thought, it was improving. But Ysandre was

angry, too; angry and worried, enough so to order me brought to the Palace to convalesce under the care of her personal chirurgeon.

I protested to no avail. It was a royal command and not to be disobeyed. The Queen's carriage was sent round, and I was bundled in blankets and carted off to the Palace, where I was installed for the duration. If it was a punishment, it was an effective one. Lelahiah Valais, the Queen's Eisandine chirurgeon, examined me with humiliating thoroughness, poking and prodding, peering into my ears and eyes and open mouth, even a sample of my urine and stool.

In the process of examining me, she discovered the brand on my left flank. Lying helpless on sweat-soaked sheets, I felt her cool fingers brush over the scar tissue and shuddered with shame and revulsion.

"What caused this?" Lelahiah asked, frowning.

With fever-heightened perceptions, I could see the thoughts flickering across her mind. I had come from the household of an *anguissette*, to whom such pain was pleasure. I bared my teeth at her. "His name was Jagun," I said. "And he is dead."

After that, she withdrew, but she left orders for administering a series of foul-tasting brews. Whether they proved effective or the illness merely ran its course, I cannot say, but within three days, the fever broke for good.

It left me weak and irritable. There are worse things than being confined to a sickbed, but from the perspective of a fourteen-year-old boy, not many. Gilot and Hugues had been allowed to accompany me, which was a mercy, but it was dull duty for them, and I dismissed them as often as they would go.

I had visitors, of course. The Queen herself came to see how I was progressing, and Phèdre was there every day. She brought me books to read, and we played many of the study-games that she had either invented or learned from Anafiel Delaunay. We shared the same favorite, which was one of her own—the game of tongues, which involved reciting famous works of poetry to one another, back and forth, line by line, translating each line into a different language. It was fun, for there was a dual challenge in it. One could hope to stump the other in choice of poem, or outwit the other in strength of language. When pressed, both of us would resort on occasion to zenyan, the pidgin argot spoken in the zenana. It was not a proper language, but it was a private one, and it made us laugh in the way survivors do. Otherwise we played in polyglot tongues: D'Angeline, Caerdicci, Hellene, Cruithne, Skaldic, Jeb'ez, Habiru, Akkadian, and Aragonian.

. Mostly, I lost; Phèdre was very good at languages. But every now and then I won. My Jeb'ez was as good as hers, and she spoke little Aragonian, which I had been studying.

There were other memory games, and those I knew were Delaunay's, having to do with the arts of covertcy. We played it on the Cassiline Brothers who had been present in the Temple on the Longest Night, and Phèdre made me speculate on their history.

"Their garments were worn and mended," I said. "They were older, in their forties, and unhappy to see Joscelin there." I shrugged. "At a guess, I would say they are two who found service with the Palace in their youth, and still resent its loss. Since they remain in the City, probably they found service with one of the lesser Houses of nobility, or one of the Great Houses fallen upon ill times. Still, they resent him for their dismissal."

She nodded. "Any danger?"

I thought about it. Once, the Cassiline Brotherhood had

enjoyed considerable prestige. Old King Ganelon, Ysandre's grandfather, had been attended by two Brothers at all times. So had Ysandre, until one of them tried to assassinate her. It was Joscelin who prevented the assassination; but that was after the Brotherhood had declared him anathema.

"I don't think so," I said honestly. "Just a trace of ill will."

"Good," Phèdre said, knitting her brow. "You'd tell me if there was more?"

"Yes." I wrapped my arms around my knees. "Are you still mad at him?"

"Joscelin?"

"Yes." I rested my chin on my folded arms. "Are you?"

She sighed. "A little."

"It was my choice," I repeated, still stubborn. "He let me make it. Is that so wrong?"

"No." Phèdre's gaze deepened to that uncomfortable level of acuity. "I know, Imri, you need to make your peace with Elua. Believe me, I know. But until you reach your majority, your choices are not wholly your own. And Joscelin knows that as well as you do."

At that I squirmed, knowing it was all too true. "Where did *he* learn it?" I asked, casting out a question to distract her. "Delaunay, I mean. Where did he learn the arts of covertcy?"

It worked. She frowned, thinking. "I don't know," she said at last. "I've wondered at it, too. What he taught us, Alcuin and me . . ." Phèdre shook her head. "It's not taught in any academy nor army, not in Terre d'Ange. I cannot think he learned it here. That leaves—"

"Tiberium," I whispered.

"Tiberium," she agreed, favoring me with an absent-minded smile. "He attended the University there. But who, and why? It's no part of the official curriculum." She gazed into the distance, remembering. "I asked Maestro Gonzago about it, once."

"What did he say?" I had never met the Maestro Gonzago de Escabares, but I knew his name. He was an Aragonian historian who had been one of Delaunay's teachers at the University of Tiberium. He had also been chosen by my mother as an unwitting messenger, many years later.

"Nothing," she said. "He disavowed any knowledge."

"Did you believe him?" I asked.

Phèdre smiled at me again. "No," she said. "Not for a minute."

I had other visitors, too. Alais came almost as often as Phèdre, and I was glad of her company. We played cards together and she chattered freely of Palace gossip. For a young girl, she overheard a great deal.

Most of it was inconsequential. Ysandre was a strong ruler; even I, who found it hard to love her, was willing to admit it. For as much as her early reign was fraught with challenge and upheaval, she had since presided over great peace and prosperity. Her marriage to the Cruarch of Alba lends strength to both realms.

And yet it was also the greatest abiding source of contention, for in Alba, the lines of succession were matrilineal.

So it had been from time out of mind among the Cruithne. There had been efforts to change it—indeed, Drustan's throne was usurped in one such. He reclaimed it at the battle of Bryn Gorrydum, triumphing over Maelcon the Usurper as the true and rightful heir of the old Cruarch, his uncle.

It was a sticking point, and a hard one. In accordance with Cruithne tradition, Drustan's heir should be his sister's son; and it was in his heart that it would be a betrayal of his people to do aught else. There was reason for it—Maelcon the Usurper was the old Cruarch's son. To violate tradition now would undermine the legitimacy of his own claim. Although Drustan had made no formal declaration, in Alba, his nephew Talorcan, the eldest son of his sister Breidaia, was widely regarded as his heir.

D'Angelines held a different view.

It sat ill with them to give the succession of Alba over to a complete and utter stranger, a Cruithne with no blood ties to Terre d'Ange. And it sat doubly ill because my cousin Sidonie, Drustan and Ysandre's daughter, had been, from the moment of her birth, the acknowledged Dauphine of Terre d'Ange. It was a double standard, and one that did not favor Terre d'Ange.

If the peers of the realm were willing to accept Sidonie as Ysandre's heir, half-Cruithne though she was, they wanted somewhat in return. They wanted Drustan to name an heir with D'Angeline blood, preferably Alais. They feared that if he didn't, Alba's influence in Terre d'Ange would grow, while our influence in Alba would dwindle.

"What is it your mother wants?" I asked Alais one day, curious.

She sat cross-legged at the foot of my bed, her small face serious. "Truly? She agrees, although she's not willing to say it publicly, not yet. She wants Father to name me his heir."

"Do you think he will?" I asked.

Alais shook her head. "No," she said somberly. "I don't think he can." She paused, furrowing her dark brows. "They're not like us, are they, Imri? Their women don't light candles to Eisheth."

"No," I agreed. "They don't."

We were silent a moment, both of us pondering the mysteries of procreation, of which we had no firsthand knowledge. It was one of Eisheth's gifts to the women of Terre d'Ange—they did not conceive ere they chose, lighting a candle in her name and praying that she open the gates of their wombs. But there were no guarantees, even so; a prayer might be years in the granting.

And a prayer, once made, could not be rescinded.

There were D'Angeline women who had gotten unwanted children. Not many, for rape was a crime of heresy and punishable by death. Still, it happened; as did errors in judgment.

"What do *you* want?" I asked Alais.

She rested her chin on her propped hands. "I wouldn't mind," she said. "Alba, I mean. But it won't happen, so I don't know . . . do you know what I would like?"

I shook my head. "No," I said. "Tell me."

"I'd like to learn to use a sword." Alais' face brightened. "Would you teach me, Imri? No one else will."

I opened my mouth to demur, and the royal guards in attendance snickered. I watched the eager light fade from Alais' face. I thought about the stories I had heard; about Grainne of the Dalriada, who had ridden to war alongside her brother in her wicker chariot, fighting as fiercely as a man. I remembered Daršanga and the women there. I saw Kaneka's hand covering Gashtaham's mouth from behind, her dagger flashing. Blood spurting from the Âka-Magus' throat, and Phèdre dragging me out of its spray.

"I would be honored," I said, drawing my bedclothes around me and bowing. "Princess."

Alais beamed.

The following day, I sent Gilot to fetch a pair of wooden practice-swords from the townhouse, but it was Joscelin who brought them. I was so happy to see him, I clambered out of bed and flung my arms around him.

"Gently, love!" He laughed. "You're meant to be a-bed still."

I made a face. "I'm weary of bed rest. Are you in disgrace? I've missed you."

"Only a bit." Joscelin lifted one shoulder in a half-shrug.

"I'm sorry," I said.

He grinned at me. "I know. Well, now we've both been punished for our folly. What's this about teaching Princess Alais to use a sword?"

"She asked," I said simply. "And I said I would."

Joscelin nodded as though it were the most reasonable thing in the world. "I brought the daggers, too," he said. "Better to start with those; the swords are a bit heavy."

So it was that I regained my strength by teaching my young cousin to wield a blade. I started with the simplest rudiments, reckoning her interest would flag. If nothing else, I could teach her how to hold a weapon, and those areas on an opponent which are least guarded and easiest to strike.

To my surprise, I found it was fun. Alais was a quick study, and neat-handed. Once I had taught her a few basic thrusts and parries, we made a game of it, playing out roles of villains and heroes, chasing one another around the bedchamber under the amused gazes of her guards. At first I found them galling, but it brought Alais such joy, I was hard put to resist. In time, I learned to forget their presence.

And she was clever; skipping around charcoal braziers, ducking behind hanging drapes, vaulting atop the bed. I stumbled after her in pursuit, dizzy and easily winded. On a few early occasions, I was forced to surrender, laughing and gasping for air. It took several days before I was steady enough on my feet to catch her without a considerable effort.

It was in the midst of such a game that the Princess Sidonie paid a visit.

The guard announced her at the precise moment that a cornered Alais let out an earsplitting shriek and launched an attack at me. I was laughing too hard to hear aught else. I took the brunt of her onslaught, staggering and catching her dagger-hand. We both fell backward onto the bed and I twisted, falling uppermost and pinning her.

"Surrender, villain!" I cried, raising my wooden dagger.

Alais giggled breathlessly, hiccoughing.

"Let her go!"

The words rang with the unmistakable tenor of command, brittle and furious. I turned my head and saw Sidonie standing in the doorway. Her slight frame was rigid, and her face was pale and taut. Her black Cruithne eyes were stretched wide, blurred with terror and fury.

I knelt on the bed, opening my hands and dropping the dagger. The guards moved forward uncertainly.

"Hold," I said to them, and to Sidonie, carefully, "Greetings, cousin."

She drew a short, sharp breath and looked past me. "Alais?"

"I *had* him!" Alais complained. "Or I would have, anyway." Scrambling to her knees, she smacked me hard on the shoulder with the wooden blade of her dagger. "You ruined it, Sidonie!"

"Ah, you weren't even close." I ruffled her hair and gave her a nudge. "Go on to your sister, villain." I watched her flounce her way off the bed. "It's a game," I said to Sidonie. "One we've been playing for days." I rapped my knuckles against the wooden dagger. "See?"

She nodded, slow and wary. "I see. Forgive me, cousin."

"Highness?" one of the guards interjected, sounding

nervous. "We've been watching all along. There's been no cause—"

Sidonie held up one hand. "I see," she repeated. "Cousin Imriel, I'm pleased that you are convalescing. Perhaps it would be best if I came another time."

I felt at once tired and sad. "Why would you think it was anything else, Sidonie? Who told you to be afraid of me?"

Alais glanced between us and kept wisely silent.

"Too many," Sidonie murmured. "I'm sorry, Imriel." For a moment, her slender shoulders slumped; with an effort, she squared them and reached out a hand to her sister. "Come, Alais."

I watched them go, two small figures, fair and dark. I wanted to be angry, yet I was not. At that moment, anger seemed too heavy a burden to lift. Their guards trailed after them, casting dubious glances behind at me.

Once they had gone, I packed my things. There was not much—a few items of clothing, including a luxurious robe of deep blue silk that had been the Queen's gift, two books Phèdre had left, and the wooden daggers, the blades chipped and splintered, the hafts polished and smooth. I stroked the worn grain, hearing Alais' giggles echoing in my memory, seeing the look of shock and terror on Sidonie's face.

When I had done, I left my chamber. There was a guard lounging in the hallway outside my door, clad in the blue livery of House Courcel. On the smallest finger of his left hand, he bore a ring of solid silver, a subtle indicator that he was one of the Queen's personal guard. As I emerged, he came to attention with a start. "Your highness! You're not supposed—"

"Yes," I said wearily, cutting him off. "I know. Where are my retainers?"

"The . . . the Hall of Games," he stammered. "B-but . . ."

I gave him a long, hard stare. "Take me there."

He obeyed without arguing, escorting me down the long hall with its fretted balustrade and down a broad marble stair to the main floor of the Palace.

The Hall of Games was a vast, bustling space, surrounded by a colonnade for strolling. There were tables reserved for all manner of game-playing and wagering, and other areas for conversing, made intimate with chairs and low couches. Other than the theatre, it was the single largest space within the Palace proper, larger even than the Hall of Audience. It was said that half the business of Terre d'Ange is conducted within its confines.

"Prince Imriel!" The head guardsman saluted me, exchanging a wary look with the guard who accompanied me. "Shouldn't you—"

"Montrève's retainers?" I asked coolly.

He shut his mouth and pointed. Following his finger, I made my way through a host of royal peers toward the Dicers' Corner, Ysandre's guardsman trailing in my wake.

It was a familiar sound: the rattle of shaken dice, the tumble of the cast. All around the world, men dice for pleasure and wager on it. But I used to hear it in the zenana, where the women would consult Kaneka's oracle, to determine when the Mahrkagir would summon them. She used to draw circles in a tray of sand: a day, a week, a month.

Only Phèdre threw all ones, ever.

The sound and the memories it evoked made me unsteady. I'd overtaxed myself, and it had taken its toll. I wobbled, brushing against a tall nobleman clad in a maroon velvet, with golden silk showing in his slashed sleeves. He cast an irritable glance at me, then checked himself, features turning smooth with diplomacy. I knew too well what he saw; me, gaunt and pale, knobby-limbed, my eyes sunken into dark-hollowed sockets. A traitor's ill-gotten son to whom he was forced to pay respect.

"Your highness," he said, inclining his head a scant inch. "Forgive me."

"My fault," I said hoarsely. "Sorry."

One immaculate brow arched. "As you say."

It made me angry at last. Ysandre's guard hovered ineffectually behind me. The unknown nobleman looked down his nose. I wanted to spit at his feet, on his glossy, shining boots, and wished I were a commoner who could do so.

"*Cousin!*" A voice cleaved the crowd, light and friendly. I looked up to see one of the Shahrizai approaching. It was one I had seen before, a few years older than me. He reached out to clasp my forearm. He was smiling, filled with assurance, midnight braids framing his face with its high cheekbones. "Remember me?" he asked, winking.

"Yes," I said, remembering. "You're Mavros."

"So I am." He turned his smile on the nobleman, at once pleasant and dangerous. A kind of heat seemed to emanate from him, playful and predatory. "I suggest you be gone, Messire Bauldry." He paused. "Or . . . forgive me . . . did you wish to offend?"

"He jostled me!" Bauldry spat.

"Oh?" Mavros raised his brows, still smiling pleasantly. "As you say."

Somehow he had turned it all around, and I was grateful to him for it. I returned his arm-clasp; glad, for the first time, to see a face that echoed my own. Both of us laughed as Messire Bauldry stomped away. "Who is he?" I asked.

"No one," Mavros said, amused. "A minor lordling with aspirations. Look, highness—"

"*Imriel!*" At the dicing table, Gilot broke away, hurrying

toward us. "What are you doing here?" he asked. "You're supposed to be resting."

"I've rested," I said irritably. "I want to go home."

Gilot ran a hand through his disheveled brown hair. "Queen Ysandre—"

"Surely the Queen would not deny her kinsman the comfort of his own home," Mavros remarked, sounding eminently sensible. "Not after he has been given insult under her very roof!" He laid a hand on my shoulder, still smiling. "The Shahrizai do not countenance such treatment of their kin."

Gilot eyed me dubiously. "Given insult? Is that so?"

"Yes," I said. It was, though not for the reasons Mavros thought. Still, it felt good to have an ally at my side, one who understood how to negotiate the treacherous shoals of Court intrigue with effortless ease. I sighed. "Gilot, let it be. I'm fine. The Queen's chirurgeon will attest to it. I don't want any fuss. I just want to go home, that's all."

"All right, Imri." His expression softened. "Let me find Hugues, and we'll fetch your things. Stay put and I'll come for you." Patting his pockets, Gilot grinned. "Time enough, any road! I've precious little left to wager."

As Gilot plunged into the crowd, Mavros steered me toward the colonnade, sensing my discomfort. "Here," he said. "Walk with me." We strolled together. Away from the sound of rattling dice, I felt my head clear.

"Thank you," I said to him.

He shrugged. "'Tis nothing." He gave me a sidelong glance. "Your retainer is familiar with you. Is he a lover?"

Heat rose, scorching my cheeks. *"Gilot?"*

"No, then." Mavros laughed softly. "Ah, well . . . Imri, is that what you are called?"

"Sometimes." I drew away from him.

"Forgive me." Mavros halted, turning his hands outward. Everything changed; his tone, his demeanor, all of it turning somber. "Cousin Imriel, you are the last person on earth I wish to offend. I forget that you were not raised as I was. What you have suffered, I cannot begin to guess. I spoke out of turn. Can you forgive me for it?"

I studied his face. He let me measure his expression. I did, and found no trace of a lie in it. Whatever his reasons, he was sincere. I nodded, slowly.

"Good." Mavros blew out his breath in a sigh of relief, shaking his braided head and grinning at me. "So it's girls for you, then, is it?"

I thought about the Thirteen Houses of the Night Court, and I thought about Katherine Friote, and the scent of her flesh, like a sun-warmed meadow. The memory was overlaid with the odor of the zenana, the fecund stench of its stagnant pool. And still, all of it stirred desire. Something in my throat grew tight.

"Yes," I said thickly. "Someday."

"You have desires you fear?" Mavros asked.

All I could do was nod.

He smiled, nodding in return. "Don't be afraid," he said. "There are reasons, and Kushiel is merciful." Once again, he laid his hand on my shoulder, squeezing it gently. "Think on our offer, cousin. It yet stands. It would be good for you to know your kin."

With that, he left me.

I watched him go, swaggering with insouciant grace, his thumbs hooked onto his belt. Left alone with my thoughts, I walked slowly along the colonnade, accompanied only by Ysandre's worried guardsman.

In time, Gilot and Hugues came for me, and I dispatched my escort with a terse message of gratitude to the Queen. If

Ysandre learned what had transpired earlier, she would know why I left; if not, well, it was true. I was on the mend, and there was no reason to stay at the Palace throughout my convalescence. If not for Alais, I might have left sooner.

There was some commotion upon our arrival at the townhouse, though not as much as I feared. Phèdre took one look at me and ordered me back to bed. I obeyed without arguing, feeling bone-weary.

She got the story out of me that evening, after I had slept for a few hours and eaten a light dinner. There are some things it was easier to tell Phèdre than anyone else, and this was one of them. It seemed almost silly now, and I felt foolish telling it, even to her. Still, when I closed my eyes, I could still see the look on Sidonie's face, stricken with the utter, terrified certainty that I was murdering her sister. Phèdre understood. I didn't have to tell her that it had hurt, or why.

"I'm sorry, love," she said when I had finished. "I'm so sorry."

I shrugged, sitting propped against pillows. "I shouldn't blame her, not really. She saw what she saw." Resting my chin on my knees, I smiled a little. "She was brave, actually, shouting like that. Like you did in the zenana that time, remember?"

"I remember," Phèdre said quietly. "But I had cause."

We were both silent, then, remembering. It had been one of the times I had been sent to attend Jagun; afterward, when a few of the Chowati women were tormenting me. There was no reason for it, save that cruelty begets cruelty. Phèdre does not raise her voice often, but it had cracked like a whip that day. It was the moment, I think, when the women of the zenana began to believe that perhaps the gods of Terre d'Ange were not as soft as they had reckoned.

Thinking about the zenana, I remembered the rattle and cast of dice in the Hall of Games, and Mavros Shahrizai coming to my aid. "Phèdre?" I asked. "Has Duc Faragon pursued his request to send some of the Shahrizai to summer in Montrève?"

"How did you know?" She cocked her head, regarding me. "He sent a letter the other week. I was waiting until you felt better to discuss it. We can speak of it later, Imri. You need to sleep now. There's time enough to think on it."

"I know," I said. "But I don't need to think. If you're willing, I'd like them to come."

Phèdre looked surprised. I hadn't told her about the Hall of Games. "Are you sure?"

I nodded. "I'm sure."

"All right," she said, bending to kiss my cheek. "We'll talk about it." As she straightened, a glimmer of deep amusement lit her eyes. For some reason, it made me think about my vigil on the Longest Night, reminding me that darkness fades, and there is reason in life for rejoicing. "This," she said, "ought to be interesting."

NINE

WINTER GAVE WAY to spring, and I turned fifteen. My favorite gift on the occasion came from Joscelin, who commissioned a pair of daggers for me modeled after the Cassiline style. With Phèdre's aid, he even contrived to have scabbards made to fit my rhinoceros-hide belt, which was one of my most prized possessions.

The Queen hosted a small private dinner in my honor, which might have been pleasant, if not for the awkwardness. Sidonie and I were polite to one another. The incident was never discussed. I felt worst for Alais, who didn't wholly understand why her favorite cousin had begun avoiding her. Perceptive though she was, there were some things she was simply too young to grasp.

"I wish you would visit more," she complained. "You're better now, aren't you?"

"Much better," I said. The lingering aftereffects of my sickness had vanished at last, leaving me thin but hale. "I'm sorry, Alais. I've been busy, that's all."

She wrinkled her nose. "Doing *what*?"

"Practicing," I said. "Fighting villains."

That earned me a look of disgust. Alais had a child's keen

sense of when she was being humored. "You will, you know."

"Will what?" I asked.

"Fight villains." She nodded. "I dreamed it. You were helping a man with two faces."

I almost laughed, but I didn't. Alais had dreamed true things before, though never anything so fanciful. Small things, usually, that came to pass. "Two faces? Did he have a face on the back of his head?"

"No." Alais shook her head. "He didn't wear them both at once."

"Ah," I said. "He wore a mask, then?"

"No," she said patiently. "He had two *faces*. And you were older."

"Why was I helping him?" I asked. "Was he a friend?"

She considered the question. "One of him was."

Though I questioned her further, I got no more from her on the subject of the man with two faces; instead, she extracted in turn a promise from me to visit before we left for Montrève. I gave it gladly enough, though I could not help glancing at Sidonie as I did. There was a pink flush on her cheeks as she met my eyes, but she held them as coolly as ever.

It was galling, but at least it was a familiar annoyance.

Once the ordeal of my natality was behind me, I set my sights on Montrève. Summer could not arrive soon enough for me that year. I was tired of the City and yearned for the freedom of the countryside. I longed for open air, to scramble over the mountains and swim in the brisk streams. I wanted to see the puppies from last year's litter, grown into young dogs, long-limbed and gawky. I wanted to see Charles Friote and measure my growth against his; I wanted to boast to Katherine how I had endured Elua's vigil on the

Longest Night. I wanted to be surrounded by people whose loyalty was as solid and dependable as the earth itself: villagers, country folk, the manor household.

And of course, there were the Shahrizai, who were none of those things.

They were coming. The matter had been discussed at length. Joscelin, predictably, misliked the idea. Although he would never say it, betimes I think he would not mind if the province of Kusheth fell into the sea, taking every last member of House Shahrizai with it.

"I made a promise," Phèdre said to him. "Would you have me renege on it?"

He gritted his teeth, and I knew he was thinking about a diamond strung on a frayed velvet cord and a note reading, *I keep my promises.* "Unless her kin have lied, this has nothing to do with Melisande."

"It does," she said. "I promised to let Imriel make his own choices."

"Unto the point of folly?" Joscelin asked. Phèdre raised her brows at him, and he had the grace to look abashed. "All right," he grumbled. "But they're not bringing their own guards to be lodged at Montrève."

"They're not asking to," she said dryly. "It seems they have confidence in the ability of the Queen's Champion to ensure their safety."

It wasn't a real argument, though. They had made up their quarrel over the Longest Night, for which I was glad, having been the cause of it. When Joscelin looked mortified at the thought of defending the Shahrizai, Phèdre laughed and kissed him until he forgot his concerns, and all was well between them.

Afterward, she consulted Ysandre, that the arrangement might be made openly with no hint of intrigue. I daresay the

Queen shared Joscelin's misgivings, but she had accepted the Shahrizais' oaths of loyalty, and there was little she could do without giving insult. So it was decided, and letters flew back and forth from the City of Elua to Kusheth, until all was agreed.

They would not come until midsummer, and I was just as glad. I wanted Montrève to myself for a while. I chafed my way through the long spring, awaiting word of Drustan's arrival. After the Cruarch of Alba had returned, we would be free to take our leave of the City. It seemed later than usual this year; although perhaps that was due to my own impatience.

At last, the red sails of his flagship were sighted, and the City made ready to receive him. Since their marriage, it has always been a joyous occasion. While that had not changed, there was a measure of reserve. Not among the D'Angeline commonfolk, who adored Drustan mab Necthana. They never forgot that he and his Cruithne, with the aid of the Dalriada, saved our nation in its direst hour, falling upon the forces of Waldemar Selig.

Among the peers of the realm it was different. They muttered about the line of succession in Alba, and the imbalance of power that might ensue. And they muttered about how to redress the inequity, and the line of succession here in Terre d'Ange. Although my thoughts were fixed on Montrève, I kept my ears open as we attended the procession, and I heard the muttering. Not a lot, but here and there it was evident.

Cruithne half-breeds.

That was the term that made me break into a cold sweat, for it was the one they used for Sidonie and Alais; especially Sidonie, for she was the Dauphine. I shouted and clapped and threw petals with the others as Drustan entered the gates, and wondered if she knew. I guessed that she did, and felt sorry for her. In some ways, perhaps, her lot was no easier than mine.

If Sidonie felt the disapproval, she never showed it. It was a piece of irony. When impetuous Alais flung herself on her father and Drustan caught her up with a smile, setting her on the pommel of his saddle, everyone cheered. How not? Though her features were pure Cruithne, she was a lovable child—and she was not the Queen's Heir. Sidonie, though . . . she was so much the mirror of her mother, from her upright carriage to her clean-cut profile, her chin raised in cool defiance. And yet it earned her few cheers. The commonfolk liked her well enough, after a fashion. They remembered Ysandre's ride toward the walls of the City of Elua, when Percy de Somerville had sought to make it his own. They remembered how she faced down an entire army through sheer courage.

So did the peers, who muttered. Because Ysandre was pure-blooded D'Angeline, and Sidonie was not, and there were powerful people in several of the Great Houses of Terre d'Ange who mistrusted her for it, who despised the fact that the sacred bloodlines of Elua and his Companions had been rendered impure. Because some of them supported Percy de Somerville's goals, although they would never say it aloud in earshot of anyone loyal to the Queen.

I saw them glance my way, sometimes.

Not often, and not for long. The shadow of my mother's infamy hung over me. But I saw the speculation in their eyes, and I knew they were asking themselves, which is less tolerable? Melisande's son or a Pictish half-breed?

Thus far, the answer yet favored Sidonie. After all, my mother's machinations nearly gave Terre d'Ange into the hands of Waldemar Selig. An alliance through marriage with

Alba, even one that favored the Cruithne over time, was preferrable to conquest by Skaldia. Still, I hated knowing anyone thought it.

It would help if Ysandre would promise Sidonie's hand in marriage to some pure-blooded young D'Angeline nobleman who could trace his lineage back in an unbroken line to Elua or one of his Companions. She wouldn't, though. It was politics, in part. It might silence the muttering, but those who disapproved were too few to pose any meaningful threat. There were too many favorable alliances to be made while the possibility yet dangled, and Sidonie was only thirteen. And too, it was idealism: Blessed Elua's precept, *Love as thou wilt*. Ysandre did not, I think, cling fast to the conviction that her daughters would make love-matches to equal her own. But she had every intention of allowing them the opportunity to do so, insofar as the pragmatic constraints of politics permitted.

I wished them luck; especially Alais, since it was hard to imagine that Sidonie would grow into the sort of woman apt to inspire true ardor. But perhaps that was true of her mother at that age.

For my part, I was glad to be well out of it.

We attended the welcoming festivities for the Cruarch at the Palace, the last of our courtly obligations. I didn't mind overmuch, as I was pleased to see Drustan. Since it was not a formal audience, he gave Phèdre the kiss of greeting and hailed Joscelin as a brother. Me, he greeted as an equal, gripping my arm in a strong clasp. I was startled to realize we were of a height.

Drustan noted it, too. His teeth flashed in a grin, unexpectedly white in the mask of blue woad. "You've grown, young Prince."

"So I'm told," I said, feeling awkward. Somehow, it

didn't seem right that I should be as tall as the Cruarch of Alba. But Drustan's presence was greater than his stature. One forgot it, as one forgot that his clubfoot makes him half a cripple.

"Don't know what to do with it yet, do you?" He laughed, patting my shoulder. "Never fear, you'll make sense of it."

"I hope so," I said, meaning it.

"You will, lad." There was an unexpected gentleness in his eyes; dark eyes, warm and compassionate, so like and unlike Sidonie's. "Never doubt it." Drustan turned to Phèdre. "Phèdre nó Delaunay, I bear greetings to you from Grainne mac Conor, and somewhat more."

"Oh?" Phèdre smiled, one of her small, inward-looking smiles. "How fares the Lady of the Dalriada?"

"Grainne is well, as ever." Drustan smiled back at her. For reasons unknown to me, Joscelin rolled his eyes. "She sends her affections. Also, she is minded to send her second son to be fostered in Terre d'Ange for a time. Ysandre has agreed to welcome him to the Palace. Still, it is in Grainne's thoughts that you might open your home to him. I have spoken to her of your household, and she is much intrigued."

"Her second son," Phèdre murmured. "Is he—"

"Quintilius Rousse's son," Drustan said, pronouncing the words with care. "So Grainne says, yes."

"Why us?" Joscelin asked bluntly. "Why not the Admiral's folk?"

Drustan turned his dark, masked gaze on him. They were not equals, not in a physical sense. Joscelin stood head and shoulders above the Cruarch of Alba. But Drustan shifted his weight onto his good leg and tilted his head, not in the least intimidated. He was accustomed to carrying the burden of rulership and all its attendant responsibilities. "Because you are two of the best people she has ever met, my brother," he said calmly. "That is Grainne's reasoning."

At that, Joscelin flushed.

"Also." Drustan's smile returned, crinkling his eyes. "Admiral Rousse has no family, only a fleet to command. It is impractical."

Phèdre gave me an inquiring look. I shrugged, feeling at once curious and dismayed. "As long as it's not *this* summer."

"No," Drustan agreed. "Not this summer, but perhaps next. Will you consider it?"

"Grainne's second son," Phèdre mused aloud. "How is he called?"

"Eamonn," Drustan said.

I felt the word drop like a stone into the pool of conversation. All of them looked at one another. I knew the stories. Eamonn mac Conor had been Grainne's twin brother; together, they were Lord and Lady of the Dalriada. He had died on the field of Troyes-le-Mont.

"Yes," Phèdre said. "Of course."

Although I chafed at it, I raised no word of protest. I knew that Phèdre carried a burden of guilt for his death. She was the Queen's ambassador in a desperate time, and it was she who convinced the Lord and Lady of the Dalriada to go to war. If fostering this second Eamonn would help alleviate it, I would suffer his presence.

"Well," Joscelin said philosophically, "at least he's likely to be less trouble than the Shahrizai."

Drustan chuckled. "Do not be certain of it."

Afterward, he and Phèdre spoke at greater length; mostly, I think, about Hyacinthe. The Master of the Straits was wed to Sibeal, Drustan's younger sister. They had a child—a girl, born over a year ago—and Sibeal carried another in her womb. It was a matter that could further complicate the issue of succession in Alba, although it had not done so yet. They had remained silent on the matter, and no one, Alban or D'Angeline, was likely to intrude on the Master of the Straits' private affairs. If Hyacinthe were to put his and Sibeal's daughter forward as the Alban heir . . . well. That was another matter. It would be hard to negotiate with a man who possesses arcane powers and single-handedly wards the safety of both our nations' shores.

But Phèdre did not think he would do so, ever, and she knew him better than anyone. And in truth, the greater question was whether or not he would train a successor.

Hyacinthe spent ten long years in bleak isolation learning his trade. The Straits had another Master, once; for eight hundred years, in fact. It was a curse that bound him to it— the curse of Rahab, Lord of the Deep, one of the One God's angels. The curse passed to Hyacinthe, but it was broken now. Phèdre broke it with the Name of God, compelling Rahab to release him. Hyacinthe was no longer condemned to his lonely isle, shackled to an immortality of decrepitude.

Still, such power was a fearsome burden, more fearsome than rulership. I didn't know the Master of the Straits well, but I'd seen the awful strain of it in his eyes. No one knew, not even Phèdre, if Hyacinthe would see fit to pass it on to another, or let the knowledge die with him. I suspect even Hyacinthe does not yet know.

Sometimes I thought it would be best if it passed from the world forever. Power is a dangerous tool to wield. In the wrong hands, it is deadly. What I saw in Drujan, I can never forget.

Then I thought about Phèdre, and the day she spoke the Name of God.

It is a thing I will never forget. No one who saw it will;

how Hyacinthe made the waters bear her weight, and she stood upon them before the terrible, bright presence and spoke the Sacred Word. Her, I would trust with almost any power on earth, but there are few people born capable of making the choices Phèdre has made.

There were no easy answers, and I was glad the matter is not mine to decide.

Indeed, as the days lengthened and we made ready to depart for Montrève, I felt the simpler burdens I carried lighten. I visited Alais, and promised to bring her a puppy, as I had forgotten to do last year. I said my good-byes to Eugènie and the rest of the household staff.

"Ah, lad!" Eugènie embraced me, then took me by the shoulders and shook me. "You needn't be so happy to leave."

"I'm sorry," I said, feeling a moment's flicker of guilt. "It's just—"

"I know what it is." She patted my cheek. "Go on, it will do you a world of good to get away from those nattering nobles and breathe fresh country air. Put a few pounds on that skinny frame of yours, and come back!"

I laughed. "I will, Eugènie."

It was a lighthearted trip, unlike the one that had brought us to the City. We travelled at our leisure, staying at inns along the way. Phèdre liked to sit in the common room and listen, taking the tenor of ordinary D'Angeline folk from all walks of life. Invariably, someone would recognize her. The scarlet mote of Kushiel's Dart made it hard to hide her identity, and Joscelin was not exactly inconspicuous with his Cassiline arms. Then there were songs and poems, and the wine would flow freely into the small hours of the night.

I wondered, sometimes, what it must be like to be thus beloved.

Make no mistake, I did not begrudge either of them, not for a single heartbeat. I knew, better than anyone, the price of their heroism. Daršanga nearly destroyed them both; nearly destroyed all of us. In the City, some envied them and accused them of false modesty. It was no such thing. If Phèdre accepted praise with a quiet smile, or Joscelin shook his head and demurred at telling the story of his duel against the Cassiline traitor-assassin, it was because they were mindful of the true story that lies beneath the poems; the blood and toil and sacrifice. Still, I wondered.

They were my stories, too; some of them. But there was scant heroism in my role. I was abducted and sold into slavery; I was rescued, and stowed away on my rescuers' ship. For the most part, I was baggage.

Not everyone is meant to be a hero.

I did stab a man once, on Phèdre's behalf. It was in Saba, on the isle of Kapporeth, on the very doorstep of the Temple of the Holiest of Holies. I spilled blood on sacred ground. The Sabaeans would have killed me for it. It was Phèdre who intervened. She offered herself in my stead, and they accepted it. I remember sunlight gleaming on the bronze blade, and turning my head to see the door of the temple opening, and the tongueless priest framed in the dark doorway, clad in a robe of white linen.

I cried out, and the Sabaean captain stayed his hand. And Phèdre walked into the temple, and when she emerged, she held the Name of God, and the glory of it shone in her face.

I wondered, sometimes, what would have happened if the door had not opened. If I would have let it happen. If I would have had the courage and the swiftness to throw myself in front of the blade.

I wondered about a lot of things.

Well, that was what passed for lighthearted, at least for

me. When we reached the borders of Montrève, I put such thoughts from my head. Remembering the lesson of the Longest Night, I gave myself over to rejoicing.

The estate of Montrève was beautiful. It lay upriver from the village and the manor was nestled in a green valley, surrounded by low mountains. The valley held gardens and a small olive grove. The lower slopes were terraced, and given over to chestnut orchards; the province of Siovale was famous for its chestnuts. A bit farther up, there was pasturage for the sheep that were Montrève's primary source of wealth, and a cluster of stone cots perched on a plateau for the shepherds who tended them.

Beyond that, the mountains were wild. Forests of spruce and oak grew there, and there were unexpected meadows filled with flowers. There was a spring-fed lake, round and perfect, that Joscelin and I found my first summer, and there were caves, too. Although Montrève was a small holding by some standards, it was large enough to contain secrets.

There was an escort to meet us. We had been spotted on the road, which was as it ought to be. Denis Friote, the oldest of Purnell and Richeline's clan, was leading them. And among them, to my surprise, was Charles, his younger brother.

"Charles!" I shouted his name.

"Imriel, hey!" He rode over to me, grinning. Leaning over in the saddle, he thumped my shoulder with his fist. "Well met, your highness. What have you been up to? You're skin and bone."

I thumped him back. "Nothing *you'd* understand, I reckon."

"Oh, aye, the secret doings of nobility." He nodded, brown curls bouncing on his brow, and ran his thumb over the hilt of his sword in a casual gesture. "I'm perishing with envy." He paused, eyeing the daggers at my belt. "Those are nice, though."

"These?" I asked carelessly, and saw Joscelin's head turn slightly, one corner of his mouth lifting in amusement. "They are, aren't they?" I added with haste. "So, you're riding with the guard now?"

"Sometimes." Charles shrugged, then burst out laughing. "Ah, Denis let me come, he knew I was pining after it. Otherwise, they say I've got to wait until next year. But it's good to see you, Imri."

"And you." I thumped him a second time, his shoulder solid and meaty under my fist. Charles, too, had grown in the past year. "How are you? How is the clan?" I paused. "Katherine, and the others?"

He grinned. "Come and find out."

TEN

WE FOUND MONTRÈVE in fine fettle, as always. The chestnuts were thriving, the high pastures were lush and green, the sheep grazed in placid good health, lambs gamboling at their side. Every surface and every item within the manor house had been dusted and polished and waxed to a fine gleam. The stables and the kennels and the mews were immaculate. All the accounts, as always, were in order.

And Katherine Friote was infuriating.

For a start, it was the way she hugged me. She ran into the front courtyard and flung both arms around me as I dismounted, crying, "Imriel!" I held her in return, breathing in the scent of her hair, like new-mown hay. "I'm so glad you're here," she whispered, her breath warm against my ear. "I've missed you."

"And you." My words came huskily.

Then she let me go, and looked me up and down. "Name of Elua!" she exclaimed. "You're thin as a lathe. What do you get up to in that City?"

I drew myself up. "Actually—"

With a friendly smile, Katherine thumped me on the shoulder. "It's good to see you, Imri," she said, then turned to give a nice curtsy to Phèdre and Joscelin. "Welcome, my lady, my lord," she said, and gazing past them, simpered. "Hello, Messire Gilot."

Gilot coughed and avoided my eye. "Demoiselle Friote."

And that was that.

During the days that followed, Phèdre gave me leave to run wild, sensing my need for freedom after the constraints of the City and Court. As long as I remained within the generous boundaries of the area patrolled by Denis Friote and the guard, I was free to wander.

I spent most of my time with Charles. He and Katherine and I had become fast friends during my first summer at Montrève, being the closest in age. At thirteen, Katherine had been willing to spend hours in the mews, listening to Ronald Agout, the old falconer, or tussling with the puppies in the kennels. She still had a little white scar on one hand where a hound-bitch snapped at her.

But now she was sixteen, and a young woman. It was beneath her dignity to play children's games. This, Katherine made abundantly clear.

She regarded Charles with the amused condescension of an older sister. By virtue of my status, I warranted a measure of respect, but only a small one. It was not that I minded, exactly—one of the things I cherished about Montrève was that my status as a Prince of the Blood was held in light regard—but I wanted her to see me as more than an old playmate yet to grow up.

I wanted her to see me as . . . what?

Not a man, exactly; but not a boy, either. I wanted Katherine to look at me as someone worthy of regard in my own right. It didn't have to be the way she looked at Gilot, which was downright foolish, but . . . well, perhaps a little bit.

I told her the story of Joscelin's and my vigil on the

Longest Night and my dramatic illness that followed it, but women have a pragmatic streak when it comes to such things. Katherine merely cast an acerbic eye over me and said, "Boys and their folly! I hope Lady Phèdre had his hide for it."

Charles, at least, was properly impressed.

We had measured ourselves against one another, standing back-to-back in the stables. I was the taller by a good two inches, though I daresay he outweighed me. I envied his solid frame, the breadth of his shoulders. Colts' Years, Joscelin had said, but Charles was as sturdy as a plowhorse.

"Ah, well." He shrugged when I complained of it. "It's hard work that does it. But you wouldn't know about that, would you, *highness*?"

I thought about the hours I spent drilling with Joscelin. "Oh, indeed? Would you care to spar a few rounds with the Queen's Champion, *farm boy*?"

"Swordplay and scholarship," Charles scoffed. "You want to speak of hard work, try clearing a pasture or chopping wood."

It made me think of Maslin in the orchard, attacking a pear tree with a warrior's skill. "All right," I said. "I will."

Charles eyed me as though I'd gone mad. "Why? You don't have to, Imri."

"So?" I said stubbornly. "I want to. Set me a chore, and I'll do it."

He eyed me for a minute longer, then grinned. "Swear it?"

I nodded. "I swear."

I had cause to regret it within a day. Charles' father, the seneschal, had set about a plan to expand the pasturage of Montrève in order to increase its flocks. By my oath, I was bound to help with the task.

It was backbreaking work. Most of it was done by small-holders; crofters willing to do the labor and pay a tithe from their proceeds to the lord or lady of the estate. But in Siovale, there is a long-standing tradition of the manor-folk and crofters working side by side to the betterment of all, carving out fresh portions of pasturage or arable land. Not all the peers, obviously; few of them deign to dirty their hands.

I did.

The first day, we cleared rocks. Not small ones, either, but great chunks of stone that must be dug out from the earth and carried to the verges of the new pasture, where they were used to build meandering stone fences to mark its boundaries. I sweated and swore and dug. I worried rocks loose from their deep beds, tugging at them until my nails bled, hearing my sinews crack as I wrenched them free. I carried them, staggering under the weight, to drop them on the mason's piles.

By the end of the first day, every fiber of my body was in agony.

Phèdre very nearly forbade me to continue. It was Joscelin who eyed me at the dinner table, hunched in misery, and dissuaded her.

"It's his will," he said to her, raising his brows. "You did promise to let him make his own choices, did you not? Besides, he'll take no harm from honest work."

So I continued, laboring under the hot summer sun. Like the crofters, I threw off my shirt and labored bare-chested. Charles worked beside me, laughing and jesting. Together, all of us cleared the pasture of nearly all the stones small enough to carry. It took many days, but I grew hardened to the work. There was a certain satisfaction in seeing the land open to new growth and watching the fence lengthen, stone by stone, foot by foot. When it was done, I thought surely we were finished, but Charles shook his head.

"Those have got to come out," he said judiciously, pointing at a pair of monstrously tall pine trees that jutted at an angle from the sloped ground. "That one and that one."

"Those?" I looked incredulously at him. "They're trees, Charles. Other pastures have trees. Can't the sheep graze around them?"

"Look." He led me uphill to the far side of one. "See how the ground is bulging and the roots are pulling loose? They grow shallow, you know. A hard rainfall or a strong wind, and they're ready to topple. Besides," he added, "where do you think the firewood that cooks your supper and warms your bathwater comes from?"

I sighed. "So they come out?"

Charles grinned. "They come out. And then we chop."

Felling the trees was a spectacle unto itself. The work was undertaken by an expert woodsman, and Charles and I were ordered to stand well clear of the site. Joscelin came, too. We all watched as the woodsman wielded his axe, swift and deliberate. It cut through the air, thunking deep into the wood, over and over. Chips flew fast and furious, and yet the woodsman moved with calm efficiency, not a single motion wasted.

"Could you do that?" I asked Joscelin.

"Me?" He shook his head, amused. "A sword's not an axe, Imri. Strange, though. I was just minded of Waldemar Selig."

"Selig?" I asked. "Why?"

Joscelin nodded at the woodsman. "Selig wielded a sword the way he does an axe. As though he were born to do it."

"Was he the best swordsman you ever saw, Joscelin?" Charles asked eagerly. "Other than you, I mean?"

"On the field of battle, yes, he was one of them." Joscelin was quiet a moment, and I knew he must be thinking about his duel against a fellow Cassiline. "Not the best, though, in the end."

"Isidore d'Aiglemort," I murmured.

"D'Aiglemort," Joscelin agreed. "He was like that, too. Born to it."

"He wasn't better than *you*, though," Charles said in stubborn defense. "No one is."

"Selig was." Joscelin smiled gently at him. "He beat me the first time we crossed blades. And Isidore d'Aiglemort defeated him. Who can say?"

"I can," I said. "You're the one left alive."

Joscelin glanced at me, thoughtful. "True," he said. "There is that."

The woodsman stepped away from the tree and pointed downhill, then stepped back to the mighty trunk. Once, twice more his axe bit into the wood. With a groaning creak, the tree toppled. It fell exactly where he had pointed, with a massive and resounding thud that shook the earth. Charles and I shouted, jumping about with unrestrained glee. Even Joscelin grinned like a boy at the sight. The woodsman allowed himself a small nod of satisfaction, then shouldered his axe and trudged toward the second tree.

It came down as handily as the first, though there was little cause for glee afterward as we set about the hard labor of removing the felled trees. Charles and I were given hatchets and charged with the task of trimming large branches to be used as rollers. I chopped away at the springy branches, thinking about the woodsman, Selig and d'Aiglemort, and Maslin, too. That was part of what I had envied in him—the effortless ease, the sense that he had been born to the blade, even if it was a pruning hook.

And I thought about Joscelin, too. His skill was harder-won. He had a gift for it—it was impossible to believe otherwise—but it was years of training and discipline that had made him what he was, instilling it in every muscle and sinew.

When the field was clear, I resolved, I would practice harder. For now, I would apply myself to this task as though it were a sword-bout. With the sun beating down on my bare back, I bent to the work, grasping branches, chopping and hacking with as much precision as I could muster, until I lost myself in the rhythm of it.

"Hey," Charles said, surprised, glancing at the pile of smooth shafts I had accumulated. "Nice work, your highness!"

I grinned at him. "A fair match for you, farm boy."

The task didn't end there. We moved one of the huge trunks that day, lashing it with a dozen ropes and hauling it in fits and starts over the rollers, pausing every few yards to move the shafts. It was grueling work, but we managed to get it into the manor's wood-yard before the day's end. There it lay, hulking.

"We chop?" I asked Charles dubiously.

He clapped my shoulder. "Tomorrow. Let's go sluice off."

Montrève's well was in the courtyard. It was a deep well and gave good water, clean and icy cold. Both of us were filthy; sweat-drenched and stuck all over with bits of pine bark and needles, our skin scraped and bruised, our hands stinging from the rope's burn. As the lowering sun cast a warm honey-colored glow over the courtyard, Charles drew the first bucket.

"Ready?" he asked, and without waiting, hurled the contents at me.

"Charles!"

I heard Katherine's voice at the same moment the water struck, and gritted my teeth against a gasp of shock. When I opened my eyes, she was staring at me.

"It's all right," I said. "We were working." I felt foolish, half-clad, runnels of cold water streaming over my bare skin and soaking my breeches.

"So I see," Katherine murmured. She raised the kettle she held. "May I?"

"I'll get it for you." Glad to have something to do, I took the bucket from Charles and lowered it. The crank seemed to turn more easily these days. My sodden hair dripped into my eyes, and I tossed it back as I straightened, lifting the refilled bucket from its hook. "Here," I said, pouring it carefully into her kettle.

A little smile played over Katherine's lips. "Thank you, Imriel."

"You're welcome." I watched her go.

"Elua's Balls!" Charles exhaled explosively. "Did you see the way she looked at you?" He punched my shoulder. "Watch out, or she'll be lying in ambush for you, highness."

I glanced at him. "You're not serious."

"Oh, aye." He grinned at me, pine bark stuck in his curly hair. "I told you hard labor would put meat on your bones." His grin faded, eyes turning serious. "Whatever you do, just don't hurt her, Imri. She's my sister, and I'd have to kill you for it."

"I wouldn't," I said automatically. "I would never."

"You'd better not." Charles refilled the bucket and handed it to me. "Here, my turn."

In the morning, nothing had changed. Using a double-handled saw, Charles and I set about the task of cutting the monster log into manageable sections. These we split into firewood with axes and wedges. It was more grueling work, resulting in new blisters and a fresh set of aching muscles, and once it was done, the second log awaited.

And yet, things *were* different.

It took several more days to complete the work of clearing the field. To my vast disbelief, we even pulled the stumps, which made hauling the logs look easy. The Siovalese prided themselves on their ingenuity and despised waste. The tough, gnarled wood of the roots was slow-burning, ideal for smoking chestnuts.

When it was done, I felt different. It was true, the long hours of solid labor—and the ravenous appetite it had given me—had given me a measure of strength. For the first time in almost a year, I felt at ease in my own body. I even grew to relish the lassitude and deep muscle-ache of fatigue.

It was more than that, though. It was a sense of pride and accomplishment, and a truer grasp of the workings of the estate, the division of labor and profit that made it all function to sustain its folk. I found myself inexplicably interested in knowing.

And then, too, there was Katherine.

Once the field was cleared, Phèdre suggested mildly that I might resume my studies, at least for a portion of each day. For as long as I had summered at Montrève, Phèdre had always welcomed the Friotes—and indeed, any of the crofters' children as might be interested—to attend lessons at the manor.

It was always different, depending on the day. There was a Siovalese scholar in the village who was well-versed in the basic elements of grammar, rhetoric, logic, arithmetic, and geometry, and she often came. Other times, it was a master musician, or an astronomer, or an engineer. Those times were more interesting, although I did enjoy the study of logic.

The best times were when Phèdre played tutor.

She taught us what Delaunay had taught her—the art of covertcy. One day, when Charles and Katherine and I were all in attendance, she blindfolded all of us and bid us wander the manor estate for an hour's time. We were to report back on all we had observed while deprived of sight, including each other's doings.

I will own, I had an advantage. I had long since memorized the layout of the manor house and the surrounding area—it was the sort of memory game that Phèdre and I played often. And I had more practice than the others with moving in stealth. There is a certain trick to it, walking on the balls of one's feet.

Also, I knew them.

I knew Charles would make a beeline to spy on the maidservants in the laundry. Katherine . . . Katherine, I thought, would make for the gardens.

I made an audible exit toward the front of the manor, then changed course soundlessly, heading for the kitchen. There I hovered in the doorway, listening and sniffing the air. I marked the rattle and clamor of luncheon dishes being scrubbed in a pan. It was too early for the aromas of dinner cooking, but I could smell sage and onion. I could hear the damp thud, slap, and roll of dough being kneaded, and the steady sound of a knife chopping. Root vegetables, I thought: carrots or turnips.

"One of her ladyship's games, is it?" Although I couldn't see her, Richeline's voice held a smile. "Are my youngest at it as well?"

"It is and they are," I said, edging my way through the

kitchen, trying not to bump into anyone. On the far side, there was a door onto the herb garden. "You won't tell them you saw me, will you?"

Richeline laughed. "Go on, and stay out of my kitchen! And mind you don't trample my herbs."

Outside, I stood for a moment, basking, turning my blindfolded face toward the hot sun. The rear courtyard of Montrève was a delightful place, even unseen. I knew its configuration by heart. Richeline's herb gardens nestled comfortably against the manor walls. Beyond was the well, and the laid-slate square where Joscelin and I often sparred. Flower gardens surrounded the area, bringing forth a profusion of blooms in every season. There were footpaths through them, set with simple stones.

I picked my way to the square, mindful of Richeline's herbs. Once I felt smooth slate beneath the soles of my boots, I stood and listened. It was easy to detect Katherine. Her skirts rustled. I heard her exhale softly as they caught on a flowering shrub, and the rasp of fabric as she tugged them loose.

Smiling to myself, I set out on a course to intercept her.

Silent and stealthy, I removed my boots. It was easier to move quietly in bare feet, and I could feel my way unerringly. I crossed the slate courtyard and plunged into the gardens, feeling the way along the footpath with my toes and listening to her passage. Katherine was making for the stone bench in the rose arbor. I placed myself in her way, and listened to her approach.

With outstretched hands, she blundered into me and gasped.

"Katherine." I grinned beneath my blindfold. "It's me."

"Imriel!" She pounded my chest with one soft fist, then laid it flat against me. "How did you get here?"

"Through the kitchen." The pressure of her touch was unbearably sweet. All around us, the heady mingled scents of a dozen species of flowers perfumed the air. I inhaled, my chest rising under her hand. "I guessed you'd come here."

"I can feel your heart beating." Like her mother's—and yet not like, not at all—Katherine's voice held a smile. "It beats fast."

"It does for you." The words seemed impossibly daring, but there they were, emerging from my mouth, sounding far more confident than I felt. Somehow, with both of us locked into our own private darknesses, it was easier.

Katherine's outspread fingers curved, the tips digging into my linen shirt, bunching the fabric. "You're a sweet boy," she whispered, and I would have taken offense at the words, except her tone said somewhat altogether different. I sensed her rise onto her toes. There, blindfolded and shrouded in darkness in the sun-shot beauty of the garden, I felt her soft lips touch mine in a brief, fleeting kiss.

I drew a sharp breath.

A world of *wanting* opened like an abyss beneath my feet.

Katherine laughed, dancing away from me. And in that moment, I understood better how swiftly games may change, how quickly power shifts from one to another in the games that men and women play with one another.

"So," she said, her voice lilting. "We are here, you and I. Where is Charles?"

I breathed deeply, willing my pulse to subside. "The laundry," I said, sounding harsh to my own ears. "That's where he will have gone."

"Then let's follow him," Katherine said.

We did, and found him there, crouching in a hallway, listening to the maidservants stirring the vats with their paddles, laughing and jesting, the air moist and warm, fragrant with the scent of soap. What he imagined in his private darkness, I can only guess.

Afterward, there seemed no point in continuing, so we peeled off our blindfolds and trouped back to Phèdre's study to make our reports. She listened to them with a bemused look; especially to Charles, who was red-faced and stammering. I made a better job of it—I was at least able to hazard a guess regarding our dinner menu—but I still felt the unexpected thrill of Katherine's lips touching mine, and Phèdre was not easily misled.

"Well," she said when we had finished. "Next time, perhaps, I'll seek a less . . . distracting . . . game."

I felt myself flush to the roots of my hair.

Phèdre glanced at me. "After all," she said, "the Shahrizai will be here in a week's time, Imriel. And if you think *this* a distraction . . ." She shook her head, and the expression on her lovely face hovered between mirth and rue. "Blessed Elua have mercy on us."

Eleven

IT WAS RAINING the day the Shahrizai arrived.

Not a hard rain, but a gentle one; scarce more than a dense mist. The Montrèvan border patrol spotted them on the road and gave them an escort, sending a single rider to the manor to report. We turned out to meet them in the courtyard.

Three were coming: Mavros, who was two years my elder; Roshana, a year older than me; and Baptiste, who was a year younger. I was not yet entirely clear on the exact nature of their kinship to me, save that they were cousins. House Shahrizai was clannish, and the ties that bound it were intricate and complex.

As if to fulfill Joscelin's anxieties, they came with an entourage—armed retainers clad in the black-and-gold livery of the House, surrounded by Denis Friote and the Montrèvan guard, who looked uneasy at it.

My young cousins showed no evidence of discomfort. They rode bareheaded astride their richly caparisoned horses, comfortable in the saddle, chatting with one another as they approached. Raindrops clung like diamonds to their blue-black hair. Mavros and Baptiste wore theirs in a myriad of braids; Roshana's hung free, loose and rippling.

Joscelin grimaced as they entered the courtyard.

"Comtesse de Montrève!" Mavros saluted Phèdre from the saddle, then dismounted gracefully and accorded her a deep bow. The others followed suit. "Lady Phèdre," he said, rising, "we are grateful for your hospitality."

"Montrève welcomes the Shahrizai," Phèdre said, smiling.

"Lord Joscelin." Mavros turned to him, inclining his head in a gesture of respect. "To you, too, we give our thanks. And rest assured, our men-at-arms do but guarantee our safety in the passage. They will depart anon, and return for us in a month's time."

I think Joscelin very nearly rolled his eyes; and yet it was courteously done. He gave his Cassiline bow in return, fluid and precise. "Your men are welcome to pass the evening here, Lord Shahrizai. There is ample room in the guardhouse."

"My thanks, Messire Cassiline, but we will not strain your hospitality." Mavros turned toward me. "And you, cousin!" He strode forward, then paused to deliver an elaborate courtier's bow. "Your highness, I should say."

"Imriel," I said. "Just Imriel, here."

"Imriel, then." Mavros grinned as he straightened, his teeth flashing white in the muted daylight. Our eyes met on a level. I had grown since we had met in the Hall of Games. He reached out to clasp my forearm in a strong grip. "Mayhap I might aspire to *Imri*, one day?"

I returned his grip with more strength than he expected, enough to make him wince. "Mayhap, cousin."

Mavros laughed with unabashed delight. "Ah, well, I'm pleased to see you in excellent health! You remember Roshana and Baptiste?"

"Cousin Imriel." Roshana's voice was melodious.

Though I seek to avoid memories of my mother, that is one thing I have never forgotten—her voice, as sweet as strong honey. When I was a child of eight, before I knew aught of who or what I was, I had loved her for it. Before I could flinch, Roshana stepped forward. "Well met, once more," she said, giving me the kiss of greeting as though we were both adults. Her lips, brushing mine, were soft and full.

Two kisses in as many weeks. I glanced toward Katherine, who was near the entrance to the manor. She was staring, wide-eyed. I sensed, without fully knowing *why*, that the nature of the game had shifted once more. Charles, standing beside her, glowered.

"Well met, indeed!" I laughed, extending my hand to the third member of the party. "Baptiste, is it?"

"Aye, cousin!" The youngest Shahrizai nodded exuberantly, braids flying. He clasped my hand with boyish goodwill, his face alight with eagerness. "So," he said cheerfully, "what do you do for *fun* here?"

Over the course of the days to follow, Baptiste's question was answered. For the most part, we roamed and hunted, spending hours afield. I had feared the Shahrizai would disdain the pleasures of the countryside. I had been wrong. Kusheth is a harsh land, and they understand vigorous pleasures. There was nothing soft about my Shahrizai kin.

They were skilled.

They were skilled, and they charmed the folk of Montrève with their skills. Not Phèdre, no, who beheld them with an amused tolerance—and of a surety, not Joscelin. But the others, yes. They charmed the manor-folk with unfailing courtesy, and Richeline conceived a particular fondness for high-spirited young Baptiste. Within days, they charmed most of the men-at-arms; even Ti-Philippe, who had been almost as dubious as Joscelin about their arrival. They

charmed Katherine and Charles, who regarded them with reluctant fascination.

They charmed the old falconer Ronald Agout, and Artus
Labbé, the kennel-master. The hounds of Montrève were a
distinct breed; wolfhounds, they were called in Siovale, although they will hunt almost any game. Our dogs hail from
Verreuil. Joscelin's brother Luc sent one to us my first summer here, a pregnant hound-bitch ready to whelp. Since
then, her offspring have stood us in good stead, interbreed-
ing with other Siovalese wolfhounds.

They were loyal dogs, majestic and fearless. Betimes,
when we rode out with them, we would pass one of the
shepherds in the hills. They kept a different breed of dog:
tawny-haired herders, small and tireless, with quizzical
faces. It made me smile to see the shepherds' little dogs stare
after the lordly, pacing wolfhounds, wondering if they posed
a threat and what in the world could be done about it if they
did.

Seeing the Shahrizai in Montrève was similar.

They seemed a breed unto themselves. It was something
beyond the strong familial resemblance; I, who looked much
the same, didn't have it. It was in the way that they moved
through the world at their own pace. It was in the way they
seemed to share a deep private jest among them, one that
made life's pleasures sweeter. It was in the aura of danger
that clung to them—not menace, no, but somewhat different.

It wasn't something I could readily identify. In the end, I
asked Mavros about it.

We were hunting in the high meadows, coursing hares
and other small game. He smiled at the question and did not
answer, watching Baptiste struggle with a goshawk's tangled jesses.

"Should we help him?" I asked at length.

He shook his head. "Roshana will do it," he said. "She's neat-handed." He turned his intent gaze on me. "Do you remember what I asked you in the Hall of Games?"

In the bright sunlight, I felt my throat tighten. "You asked if I had desires I fear."

Mavros nodded. "Everyone does, Imriel. You, I suspect, more than most. You're one of us, Kushiel's scion. But after what befell you, well . . ." He paused. "The difference is, among the Shahrizai, we're taught to gaze upon them without fear."

"Why?" My voice was blunt.

"Because Blessed Elua bid us to," he said simply. "Love as thou wilt. We do. And betimes it makes others . . . uneasy . . . because in so doing, we hold up a dark mirror that reflects their own desires."

"To *hurt* people?" I shuddered, thinking of the zenana. "But I don't, Mavros. Not anyone, not ever."

"No?" He smiled, leaning over in the saddle. "Take my hand."

I did, and felt his clasp tighten. Mavros bore down hard, exerting a painful pressure on the web of flesh betwixt my thumb and forefinger. His mocking gaze dared me to retaliate. I bared my teeth in an involuntary grin, squeezing back. My stint of hard labor stood me in good stead. I burrowed into his flesh with the ball of my thumb and squeezed his knuckles until I could almost hear the small bones grinding.

We swayed in our saddles together, locked in foolish combat.

"See?" Mavros gasped. He laughed, disengaging, and shook out his hand, eyeing it ruefully. "Ah, Imriel! It's a part of you. And there's pleasure in it, isn't there?"

Across the meadow, Baptiste crowed in triumph as Roshana succeeded in untangling the goshawk's jesses. At

the same moment, one of the wolfhounds flushed a ptarmi-
gan, nosing the air in vague, dignified perplexity as the bird
took flight. The goshawk burst from Baptiste's fist in a feathered blur, striking hard and fast, landing in a tumble.

"It's not the same," I said eventually.

"No?" he asked. "How does it differ?"

How indeed? It was a game, a moment's challenge, one
we entered willingly. How, truly, did that differ from love-
play that tested the boundaries between pleasure and pain?
Since I could not say, I asked a question instead. "You
told me there were reasons for it," I said. "That Kushiel was
merciful."

"There are." Mavros grimaced, massaging his hand. "And
he is."

I watched Baptiste swing the lure, calling the goshawk
off her quarry. He managed it nicely. The disinterested
hounds ranged farther afield, seeking prey of their own.
"Tell me more," I said. "I want to understand."

"Imriel." Mavros sighed. "Ah, Imri! How can I explain it
to you? It is purging, Kushiel's gift. In the loss of self, there
is expiation, and grace. Like a bright fire, it purges all, and
makes everything new. It is a gift, and it is ours to give. And
to receive, betimes. All of us will know it at least once, that
we might better understand Kushiel's gift."

I ignored him for a moment, whistling for the hounds.
They came, loping and obedient, jaws parted and tongues
lolling. My horse snorted through its nostrils as they
crowded around. I dug into my game-bag, quartering one of
the hares they had caught earlier, tossing bits to them.

"It's not enough," I said tersely.

"No?" Mavros smiled. "What does *Phèdre* say?"

I glared at him, my heart filled with sudden fury. "You
know nothing of her!"

"No." He swallowed then, hard. "Forgive me, I do not. Once again, I have overstepped my bounds, Imriel." He was silent for a moment, thinking. "I only want you to understand. What you are . . . there is beauty and majesty in it. But perhaps . . ." He glanced across the meadow. "Perhaps it is better if I let Roshana explain."

We spoke no more of it that day, and for several days afterward. They were sensitive to such things, the Shahrizai, and capable of great delicacy. I knew why. It was what I had experienced with Maslin in Lombelon when it seemed I stood outside myself and saw into him—they saw the faultlines in my soul, my flaws and weaknesses, and trod gently near them.

For a time, at least.

And that, I thought, was what truly made them dangerous. It was a comfort to know that my kin were capable of kindness, and not necessarily wont to exploit Kushiel's gift for personal gain or vaunting ambition. But they saw too much, and they were drawn to what they saw. In time, Mavros—or perhaps Roshana—would prick me once more where I was sore.

In the meanwhile, we spoke of less consequential matters.

I learned a great deal of my heritage. House Shahrizai was the oldest family in Kusheth; one of the oldest, indeed, in Terre d'Ange. Their holdings were extensive, lying on both coasts of the province. For all that, theirs is not the sovereign duchy in Kusheth—that falls to Quincel de Morhban, who holds the Pointe d'Oest. To hear Mavros speak, it was by choice; although I didn't wholly believe him. I suspect it has long served the Crown's interest to keep House Shahrizai in check. They were powerful and numerous enough to be a threat, if they chose.

But it *was* true that they were a strange and insular clan in their own way. Cousins often wed within the family, and they held their own traditions. Other than the ruling Duc de Shahrizai, they did not use land-titles among themselves—only the Shahrizai name, as though it superseded any holdings. And they were fearsomely loyal to one another.

Mavros claimed that my mother acted without her House's blessing or knowledge. Whether or not it is true, I cannot say, but he believed it to be so. He thought she did so in order to protect the Shahrizai, should matters go awry. Perhaps he was even right. They held her in a strange mix of awe and . . . I did not even know a word for it. Regret, perhaps?

"*I* wish I had known her," Baptiste announced when we spoke of her late one evening, sitting in the manor's great room. "I do, truly."

Roshana, who was unbraiding his hair, smiled quietly. "She was dangerous to know, my heart. Even for family."

It was a cardinal sin among them, to endanger the well-being of the family; and yet their greatest disdain was reserved for Marmion Shahrizai, who accidentally caused the death of his sister Persia. It was she who aided my mother in escaping from Troyes-le-Mont, loyal to the end.

Roshana spoke truly; my mother was dangerous to know.

"Why did she do it?" I asked my cousins that night. "Why did she do what she did?"

They exchanged glances and shrugs. There was a moment of silence, broken only by the soft sound of Roshana running a boar-bristle brush through Baptiste's unbound hair.

"Did she never tell you?" Mavros asked me.

"No," I said, and thought of Phèdre seated behind a pile of unsealed letters, looking pain-bruised and weary. I was abashed. "I don't know. She sent . . . she used to send letters, before she vanished. But I never read them."

"*I* would!" Baptiste raised his head, an eager light in his eyes.

"Hush, my heart." Roshana stroked his cheek until he subsided under her touch. "Imriel must make his own choices." She set about the work of rebraiding his hair. They were half-siblings, both of them born to my mother's first cousin, Fanchone. That much I had learned. Mavros was the youngest son of Sacriphant, who was my mother's uncle. "Do you still have the letters?" she asked me.

I glanced involuntarily toward Phèdre's study. It was there, somewhere, the coffer containing every letter my mother had written to me. Phèdre hadn't spoken of it since my mother vanished, but she always travelled with it. She still believed I would want them one day. "Yes," I said. "I have them."

"Well, then." Roshana smiled. "Mayhap they hold the answer."

"Mayhap," I muttered. "*Her* answer." I watched her deft fingers fly, the miniature braids taking shape beneath them. Baptiste had his eyes half-closed, luxuriating under her touch. If he was a cat, he would have purred. "Why do you do that?" I asked. "Why only to the men?"

"This?" Her smile deepened. "It teaches patience, cousin. It is a lesson all men need to learn." Roshana ran one finger along Baptiste's nape, making him shiver. "And for us, it improves dexterity," she added, a note of mischief in her tone.

"He's your brother!" I exclaimed, half-horrified.

Mavros chuckled.

"Oh, aye." Roshana laughed softly. "We're not meant for one another. Still, we may learn from the game. And who knows who will reap the benefit of it? Such is the purpose of such games." She glanced sidelong, sensing a presence, and somewhat in her voice shifted toward composed politeness. "Is it not so, my lady?"

Standing in the doorway, Phèdre regarded her mildly. "Indeed, so they say in the Night Court. I did not know they said it in Kusheth."

"Ah, we Shahrizai are adepts after our own fashion, my lady." Mavros, sprawling on a sheepskin rug, propped himself on his elbows and flashed a lazy white grin. "Surely, no one would deny we pay Naamah her due and honor her to the fullest."

Phèdre smiled despite herself. "Surely not," she said. "Imriel, 'tis late, and I've dismissed the household. Will you be sure to snuff the lamps?"

"Yes, of course." I found myself on my feet. It was still disconcerting to look *down* at her. I laid my hands on Phèdre's shoulders. "Thank you," I said. "Don't worry, all is well here. These are things I need to understand, no more."

"I know, love." There was a shadow of sorrow in her gaze. She touched my cheek gently. "Good night to you. I'll see you anon."

When she had gone, Mavros flopped back down on the rug, blowing out his breath. "Name of Elua!" he sighed, folding his arms under his head. "Kushiel's Chosen, alive and in the flesh. Surely, Imri, you must have wondered—"

Roshana made a warning sound.

"No," I said. "And don't. Just . . . don't."

Mavros blinked at me, his eyelashes long and sooty. "Ah, but surely . . ."

There was a high-pitched ringing sound in my head. I hunched my shoulders against it, tensing. Memories haunted me: the pervasive stench of stagnant water in the zenana, the searing odor of my own flesh. Phèdre's voice, aboard a ship bound for La Serenissima, where she granted my deepest wish, warning me that it carried a danger.

You've Kushiel's blood in your own veins. One day, you will know it.

"No," I said firmly. *"Never."*

"No?" Mavros sounded disappointed. He closed his eyes. "I do," he murmured. "I cannot help it. I wonder and wonder."

I glanced toward Roshana for aid, but she averted her head, concentrating on Baptiste's braids. The youngest of my Shahrizai kin was oblivious, lost in the pleasure of her grooming. "I wish you wouldn't, cousin," I said to Mavros, hearing a note of despair in my voice. "Please. I truly wish you wouldn't."

"I know." His eyes opened, slitted. He regarded me through his lashes. "But it is who I am. I cannot help it. And it is who *you* are, cousin."

Another voice swam to the surface of my memory, accompanied by a gust of frosty air and the image of stars, cold and distant, glittering above the Temple of Elua, where the old priest had spoken of my fate.

What you make of it is yours to choose.

"You don't know me," I said, my voice trembling. "What I am. *Who* I am."

"Do you?" he asked.

"Mavros." Roshana spoke his name like a command. He turned his head and stared at her. "Let him be."

"I'm only—"

She shook her head at him.

"Oh, all right." With a single motion, he unfolded himself from the floor and stood upright. "I'll take myself off to bed, then, since it seems I'm not fit for pleasant company this evening."

"You would be if you'd stop baiting me," I said.

"Don't be angry at me, cousin." Mavros gave me the disarming smile he used to charm kitchen-maids and stablelads. "I'm only trying to help." When I made no reply, his smile faded, replaced by something deep and wondering. "What did they *do* to you in that place, Imriel?" he asked, genuinely curious. "What did they do to make you so afraid of what you are?"

I had never told him any of it; I have never told anyone all of it, except for Phèdre.

"You don't want to know," I said.

"I do, though." He touched my arm. "We understand these things."

Ill thoughts, ill words, ill deeds.

"No," I said gently, no longer mad at him. "You think that you do, but believe me, Mavros, you don't. Not these."

After a moment, he nodded. "If you ever want to speak of it, I've a willing ear."

When he had gone, I sat down and watched Roshana's deft hands at work. There was something soothing in the rhythmic motion of it. Baptiste had fallen into a peaceful doze, his half-braided head drooping, lips parted. The sight made me smile.

"Patience, is it?" I asked Roshana.

"Well." She smiled back at me. "Patience, like love, takes many forms."

TWELVE

ALTHOUGH I HAD MADE peace with Mavros, his words made me restless.

In truth, the Shahrizai themselves made me restless. To their credit, they had been perfectly well-behaved during their time at Montrève. What I had expected, I cannot say—perhaps, in the recesses of my mind, I half feared there would be some rampant manifestation of orgiastic behavior, or at the least, that I would find Mavros doing somewhat unspeakable to a chambermaid in a dark stairwell.

But no; although they flirted and charmed, they kept their behavior within the bounds of propriety. And yet it was there. It was present in the careless sensuality with which they interacted with one another, in the sense of desire simmering beneath the skin, predatory and . . . well, patient. Even in young Baptiste, it was there.

To gain a respite from it, I went to visit Phèdre in her study, where I found her reading through a pile of correspondence. A courier had come from the City, bearing a packet of missives which had arrived for her there. I stood in the open doorway, watching her read, her face alight with pleasure.

"Imri." She noticed me and beckoned. "Come in, love."

"I won't trouble you?" I asked. I had not seen her much; I had been busy with my cousins, and I thought she was merely being generous in giving me leave to spend time with them. After Mavros' words . . . I was not so certain.

Phèdre smiled. "Never. Where are our guests?"

"Ti-Philippe and Hugues are escorting them to the village. Roshana had a fancy to see it." Entering the study, I seated myself on the floor beside her chair. "Who's the letter from?"

"Nicola L'Envers," she said. "She's coming to the City to spend the winter at Court this year, with her younger son Raul."

I made a noncommittal sound. I knew the name well enough; she was a kinswoman of the Queen on her mother's side. She was wed to an Aragonian nobleman, and her influence there had been instrumental in aiding Phèdre and Joscelin in tracking down the Carthaginian slavers who had kidnapped me. I also knew she had been one of Phèdre's favorite patrons.

"What is it?" Phèdre stroked my hair with cool fingers. "Trouble with the Shahrizai?"

"No." I leaned against her chair and closed my eyes. For a moment, I could pretend I was a child again. After Daršanga, I used to wish Phèdre was my mother, but I always knew it was impossible. She wasn't. She had saved my life, and I would lay my own down for hers in a heartbeat, but she was not my mother.

"What, then?"

Reluctantly, I raised my head and met her gaze. Her eyes were dark and lustrous, the scarlet mote vivid against the iris. A slight line of concern was etched between her winged brows; otherwise, her skin was creamy and flawless. In Terre d'Ange, one would say Phèdre was in the full summer of her beauty—past spring's fresh charms, not yet touched by the sere frost of autumn.

"Nothing," I said. "I've missed you, that's all." I hesitated. "Have you been avoiding the lot of us?"

"A little bit." Her face held a look of candor. "I thought it would be easier for you."

Mavros' words haunted me. *I wonder and wonder.* I looked away. "Why? Do you . . . think about them?"

"Your *cousins*?" Phèdre sounded surprised. "Not at their age!" She laughed. "I do have some measure of self-control, you know."

"Mavros is seventeen," I said.

"Yes, with a head full of a seventeen-year-old's thoughts and a belly full of a seventeen-year-old's desires." She touched my cheek. "I know. He cannot help it, and the others are not far behind him. That's why I thought it would be easier this way."

"It scares me," I murmured. "I don't want . . . I don't want things to change."

"Ah, love. Life is full of change. Not all of it is bad." Phèdre tugged a lock of my hair, making me look at her once more. "Imriel nó Montrève, you have a heart as true as an arrow's flight, and courage enough for ten. Whatever manner of man you will become, it will be a worthy and good one. Believe me, love, there is nothing in *you* that you need fear."

"There is, though," I whispered.

"No." She shook her head. "Only shadows."

"How can you be so sure?" I said.

Phèdre raised her brows. "You question the word of one who knows the Name of God?"

It made me laugh, as she intended. We did not jest about such matters; indeed, we seldom spoke of them, for they ran too deep for speech. But today, somehow, it was needful and right, reminding me of what we had shared together.

Rising, I stooped to kiss her cheek. "Thank you."

Nothing had changed; and yet I felt better. I went to the kennels and spent time talking with Artus Labbé. He had helped me choose the pick of the spring's litter for Alais, a bitch-pup with lively brown eyes and a curious disposition. We discussed the finer points of training dogs. It pleased me to think of the wolfhound pup at Court, where lapdogs were the order of the day. When this one was full-grown, she would stand nearly shoulder-height to Alais. I had brought an old chemise of Alais' with me, that the pup might get to know her scent.

Afterward, I sought out Joscelin and asked him to spar with me, which he did willingly.

I didn't bother to ask if he had been avoiding us; I knew full well that he had. If danger threatened, he would honor his vow. He was Phèdre's consort and the Queen's Champion; he would protect and serve. But so long as it did not, he would absent himself insofar as courtesy allowed. Out of consideration to me, he didn't flaunt his antipathy to the Shahrizai; yet he couldn't altogether hide it, either.

We had a good bout, one that left me dripping with sweat. First with the wooden daggers, then with the swords. I was handier with the latter. Something about the singularity of the weapon appealed to me. It cleared my mind, and I could perceive more acutely the spheres of defense and opposition in which we moved, back and forth, to and fro.

Somewhere in the middle of the bout, I heard the sound of the Shahrizai party returning. They were in high spirits. There was laughter and chatter, and I could hear Charles' and Katherine's voices among them. It gave me an unexpected pang of envy. I pushed it aside, focusing on my swordplay.

It worked, until Roshana and Katherine came into the garden to watch us.

I saw Joscelin's gaze flicker sideways, and missed a chance to attack him. I began to lower my wooden blade to greet the girls, and he pressed me harder, forcing me into a retreating defense. Anger stirred in me, and I fought back, circling around to get at his left side.

"You're right," Roshana whispered behind me. "He *is* quite good!"

That did it.

I put a foot wrong and missed a parry. Joscelin's blade battered it aside, sweeping inside my guard to score a gouge over my right eyebrow.

"Imri!" Katherine said in alarm.

Joscelin winced. "Are you all right?"

"Yes." I clapped one hand over the gouge and glared at him. "I'm *fine*."

"Let me see." He pried my hand away. "Ah, you will be, just wash it well." There was a hint of amusement in the curve of his mouth. "Sorry, love." He turned, then, and gave his Cassiline bow. "Ladies."

I sat down on one of the stone benches. Katherine hurried to the well and drew a bucket, soaking a handkerchief, then set about dabbing my bleeding graze. Roshana watched Joscelin stride toward the manor house.

"He doesn't like us, does he?" she murmured.

"It's not your fault." I cleared my throat. Katherine was bending over me, the tops of her breasts swelling against the bodice of her gown. I snatched the handkerchief from her, clamping it to my brow. "Here, I'll do it."

"I don't mind." She smiled at me.

My face grew hot. "Did you have a nice excursion?"

"We did." Roshana came alongside Katherine, laying a hand on her shoulder. "We were thinking, Imriel. Mayhap tomorrow we should take an excursion of our own, the three of us. The boys may not be tired of hunting, but *I* am. Katherine says there's a lake up in the mountains you promised to show her."

"We could take a picnic luncheon," Katherine added.

I stared at them, wondering if I looked as stupidly befuddled as I felt. "The three of us?"

Roshana smiled lazily. "Why not?"

My mouth worked, but no sound emerged. I swallowed hard. "All right."

"Good!" Katherine clapped her hands. Her grey-blue eyes sparkled, and her color was high. I wondered what in Elua's name they had discussed during their trip to the village, and decided I'd rather not know. "I'll take care of luncheon."

"All right," I repeated, pressing her kerchief to my bleeding head.

Definitely befuddled.

I slept poorly that night, lying awake, tossing on my sheets. It seemed to me a strange and remarkable thing that I could have survived what I have undergone, that I could have seen horrors and marvels, and still have my composure thoroughly undone by a pair of sixteen-year-old girls who had suggested nothing more daring than a picnic on the surface of the matter. It was the promise, the hint of somewhat more that undid me.

I wanted . . . ah, Elua! I *wanted*.

But with desire came the shadow. And mayhap Phèdre was right, there was nothing to fear from shadows. I believed it when I was with her. But she had gone into

Daršanga of her own volition, a grown woman, already knowing what darkness she carried inside her, the terrible urgings of Kushiel's Dart. I had been a child. What had it done to me?

Mavros was right; I didn't know myself.

I wasn't sure I wanted to.

In time I slept. The day dawned fine and bright. I still felt muddle-headed. Katherine had undertaken all the arrangements with cheerful efficiency; the luncheon was packed, and our mounts were saddled and ready. Amid promises not to stray beyond Montrève's guarded border, we took our leave.

I led them along the prettiest route I knew, up the terraced slopes of the chestnut orchards, winding past the high pastures, where grazing sheep dotted the hillsides. I pointed out the new pasturage which Charles and I had helped clear.

"It's hard to believe you're the same age, Imri," Katherine observed, turning to Roshana. "Charles seems so much younger, doesn't he?"

"All younger brothers seem thus to their sisters," Roshana said pleasantly.

I eyed her. "Does Baptiste?"

"Well." Her smile brought out a dimple. "Yes, in his way."

My cousin was looking lovely that day. In truth, both of them were. Roshana wore a deep blue gown that brought out the hue of her eyes, her hair loose over her shoulders. It fell the way mine did, in blue-black waves. Katherine wore a pretty linen gown of golden yellow, that made one think of flowers blooming. She had a little coronet of braids, and in the sunlight her brown hair gleamed with honey-colored streaks.

A distant shepherd raised one hand in salute, and I waved back.

It was a long trek into the mountains. There were places where we had to ride in single file, our mounts picking their way with care amid the scattered boulders. I led the way, trying to recall in which direction the spring-fed lake lay, listening to the girls' easy conversation. I had not known, until yesterday, that they had bothered to befriend one another.

Women are a mystery.

At the summit, I paused to rest our mounts. While our horses stood along the mountain's crest with lowered heads and heaving barrels, blowing through their nostrils, we gazed into the valley below. The manor house and its sprawl of outlying buildings looked small and snug in the distance, held fast in the cupped green hand of the valley, while the river meandered through it like a silver ribbon.

"Oh, Imri! I'd forgotten how pretty it is in the mountains." Katherine drew a deep breath of fresh air and looked at me, eyes shining. "It's beautiful, isn't it?"

In an instant, I felt ashamed of the thoughts I had harbored, and of how little consideration I had showed her this summer. Katherine was the seneschal's daughter. Since she had left childhood behind, it was duty that had bound her to the manor house, not disdain of my company. "Yes." I smiled at her. "It is."

Roshana gave me a curious glance. "You love this place, don't you?"

"Very much so." I thought about Montrève and all its inhabitants, then gave myself a little shake. "Let's go. 'Tis this way, I think."

Although it took the better part of an hour, I found the lake without too much difficulty. It lay in one of the high, hidden meadows, where the grass and wildflowers grew in unchecked profusion. The lake was as I remembered it, perfect and round, surrounded by a stony ledge of sun-warmed granite, a blue eye giving a secret wink unto the heavens.

After letting the horses drink their fill, we tethered them. I unloaded the saddlebags and spread our blankets in the meadow, pressing the grass flat. It was truly an idyllic spot. All around us, flowers nodded on tall stalks, and insects flitted on translucent wings. Katherine removed her leather shoes and peeled off her stockings. Her bare feet were fine and white. Hoisting her skirts, she crossed the rocky ledge, dipping a toe into the lake.

"It's *cold*!" she cried in dismay.

I laughed. "I told you. It's spring-fed."

Her chin lifted, and she nodded toward the lake. "I dare you!"

Somewhat in her tone reminded me of the children's dares we had once undertaken together, that first summer in Montrève; and somewhat, to be fair, did not. But I was weary of my own caution and cowardice.

"All right," I said recklessly, standing and stripping off my shirt. "I will."

"Imriel." Roshana, reclining on the spread blankets, roused herself. "Are you sure—?"

I ignored her, shedding my boots and untying my breeches and linen undergarments, kicking them loose until I stood naked beneath the vast blue sky. In the bright daylight, the faded weal-marks on my back and the pale brand on my flank must surely be visible. Pretending they were not, I ran the few paces to the lake's verge and launched myself in a shallow dive.

The water was cold.

It was very cold.

I came up sputtering, my teeth already chattering. "Satisfied?" I gasped.

They stood on the edge, peering at me while I trod water. "Well, you've proved you can swim," Roshana said. "Was there some other point to this?"

I splashed a bright spray of water at them until they retreated to the blankets, laughing. I hauled myself out of the water onto the stone ledge. There I stood, dripping in the warm sunlight, my skin prickling with gooseflesh from the lake's chill. Though I stood on solid ground, I still felt strangely buoyant, suspended between the carefree child of the Sanctuary I had once been and the confident adult I wished to become.

"I don't know," I said to them. "Was there?"

Roshana chuckled, and Katherine ducked her head, a curtain of her honey-brown hair swinging forward to conceal her smile. She groped for my clothing and tossed my shirt at me. "Go on, dry off! You don't want to take ill again."

At that I made a face, but I did as she said. My clothes clung to my damp skin. I wrung out my soaked hair, leaving it to hang in a sodden mass down my back. "So," I said, joining them to sit cross-legged on the blankets. "What now?"

"Lunch," Katherine said, eyeing me sidelong.

We ate well, our appetites honed by the long ride and the clean air. The food was shepherd's fare, simple but good—Richeline's crusty bread, sharp cheese and sausage, seasoned ham and oil-cured olives sprinkled with rosemary. We ate everything we had brought, sharing a skin of crisp white wine to wash it down.

When we had finished, I felt replete and lazy. The sun had dried my clothing, and I was warm and content. I lay on my back, closing my eyes, listening to the hum of the meadow, the long grass rustling. It didn't matter why we were here, what scheme the girls had concocted. The world was good, which was reason enough to rejoice. I let go of desire, content to relish the moment and my own sense of well-being.

"Mavros says there are things you wish to understand," Roshana said softly.

I opened my eyes, squinting.

Her deft fingers were at work, plucking stalks of tall grass and weaving them into a neat plait. "We were talking," Roshana continued. "Katherine and I, on the ride back from the village. About the games that we learn to play in Kusheth and Siovale, and the differences between them."

I sat upright. "What games?"

"*You* know!" Katherine blushed. "Games, Imri!"

I shook my head. I had an idea of what she was trying to get at, but I had no experience in such matters. "You'll have to teach me."

Katherine sighed. Leaning over, she grasped a handful of trailing bindweed, tugging the blue-flowering vines loose and gathering them into a loop. "'I cast a net to catch true love,'" she chanted, tossing the impromptu noose aloft. It fell onto the blanket, half draped over my foot. "You never learned that one?"

"No." I frowned at the length of vine. "What am I supposed to do?"

"Nothing!" Katherine's voice held a trace of acerbity. "I didn't catch you. If it had landed over your head, you would have owed me a kiss."

"So—" I began.

"This is a game we play in Kusheth," Roshana intervened. "It has a sharper edge than those you play in Siovale." She gave her grass-plaited quirt an experimental snap, and smiled when both Katherine and I jumped involuntarily. "There's no harm in it, Imriel."

"For whom?" I asked uneasily. "And why?"

"For anyone." Her smile deepened. "'Tis a light game." She touched the trailing end of her grass quirt to my cheek. "You're afraid, aren't you?"

I brushed away the plaited grass in an irritable gesture. "Of you? No."

"Of your own desires," Roshana said calmly. "Of those things you crave and fear to give voice to. This is only the merest taste of them, and one you should enjoy." She turned to Katherine. "You understand, do you not?"

I opened my mouth to answer for her, to say *No*. But Katherine raised her chin as she had when she dared me; this time, daring my cousin. "I'm not afraid," she announced.

"So we play." Roshana trailed the ticklish end of the grass quirt along Katherine's cheekbone, circling her ear. "This is the nature of the game. If you squirm or make a sound," she whispered, "you earn a lash. If you don't . . . you win a kiss."

Katherine whimpered.

The grass-plaited quirt cracked.

I winced at it. Katherine's eyes flew wide open, and she gasped, startled and half-laughing. It was a teasing blow, landing harmlessly on her upper arm, but even so, it was sharp enough to raise a faint pink welt. The sight of it stirred dark unease in me. I knew, altogether too well, how deep a welt a *real* whip left. I still bore the scars. It had taken a measure of bravado to bare them today; a bravado I no longer felt.

"Let's not do this," I said, finding my voice. "Roshana, please don't."

"It's only a game." She let the grass quirt trace a path

down Katherine's throat, tickling the hollow at its base where her pulse beat visibly. "But it is a game of resistance and surrender." She traced a delicate pattern on Katherine's skin, watching her pulse quicken. "You ask *why*, Imriel. Because in a game of wills, the stakes are raised and pleasure is heightened. And in the playing of it, we come to know ourselves—and each other—more deeply." The quirt trailed lower. "Already, I'll wager Katherine has learned something new of herself since first we met," she said, meeting her eyes. "Is it not so?"

Katherine returned her gaze with mute, sparkling defiance.

"You see?" Roshana smiled. "She has won a kiss." Rising on her knees, she leaned forward, laying down the quirt. With my mouth agape, I watched her deliver on her promise. It was a real kiss, deep and lingering, and Katherine returned it ardently. I felt a rush of desire so intense I ached. It left me feverish, lightheaded and sick. When they parted, strands of their hair remained caught together, blue-black and honey-brown, shimmering in the sunlight like spider's silk.

"Your turn, cousin." Roshana picked up the grass quirt and placed it in my hand. "You may choose either one of us."

I clutched it hard, feeling the neat plaits press against my sweating palm. I envisioned myself swinging it, the smart snap and the ensuing welt. Both the girls regarded me with amusement. It was true, it was only a game; a silly game. And I, who had reveled in the sense of being suspended between childhood and adulthood only an hour ago, now felt at once too young and too old to play. I couldn't do it. As much as I wanted them—both of them, either of them—I couldn't. Not like this. My mouth went dry, desire shriveling.

"I can't." I tossed the quirt onto the blanket. "I'm sorry, but I can't."

Katherine colored and looked away, and I knew I had embarrassed her. Whatever, exactly, had been offered here today, I had spurned it. She would not be quick to repeat the offer in any form. I wished we'd played the Siovalese game instead. I put my head in my hands and sighed.

"It's all right, Imriel." Roshana's voice was surprisingly gentle. I lifted my head and saw concern in her face. "You know we mean well, don't you?"

I nodded. "I *do* want to understand. It's just . . ." I tried to find words that would encompass the enormity of it, that would explain how and why, here in the open air of a flowering meadow, I was haunted by the fetid stench of stagnant water. How plaits of fragrant grass evoked the shadow of knotted leather crusted dark with old blood. "Daršanga," I said.

It was the first time I had said the word aloud to anyone but Phèdre. They exchanged a glance.

"That was the name of the place?" Roshana asked.

"Yes," I murmured.

"I'm sorry, Imri," Katherine said impulsively. "I forget sometimes. You seem so . . ." She shrugged, giving me a sweet smile. "Well, like a brother, only not."

I smiled back at her. "I try to forget, too."

"Try harder," she said, teasing.

So at least a day that bid fair to end in disaster ended in goodwill. We gathered our things and made the long trek down the mountain, arriving at the manor house in ample time for supper. Afterward, Katherine bustled about her duties, while I sat and spoke with my cousins in the great room, as we had done every evening since they arrived.

Nothing had changed.

Save that once again I lay sleepless. And this time it was not the fevered conjecture of my imagination that made me wakeful, but memory, and the piercing desire that accompanied it. When I closed my eyes, I saw Roshana and Katherine kissing. I sweated and tossed, tangled in my sheets, and cursed myself for an idiot.

Try harder.

Would that it were so simple.

THIRTEEN

IN THE FINAL DAYS of their visit, I quarreled with Mavros.

I own it freely; the fault was mine, although Mavros played his part. In truth, after the day at the lake, I was wound tighter than a child's top. Montrève, my respite and haven, had become fraught with tension and desire.

It was not the fault of the Shahrizai. They were what they were; they sought to deal fairly with me. The shadow on my soul was no fault of theirs. I was the one who was unfair. I beseeched them for understanding, and fled when it was offered.

After the lake, Roshana understood. She had caught a glimpse of what I had undergone in that single word: Daršanga. She did not press me, for which I was grateful. And Baptiste . . . Baptiste was a joy. I saw much in him of what I might have been, had it not been for Daršanga, by turns merry and indolent, partaking in life to its fullest. No priest of Elua would ever need remind Baptiste to rejoice; it was part and parcel of his nature.

But there was Mavros.

In some ways, we were the most alike. He was older and understood the burden of obligation imparted by his birth, even as I was forced to contend with my status as a Prince of the Blood. Over the course of their visit, he had given a good deal of helpful counsel on dealing with Court intrigue and nobles who looked sideways at me and muttered under their breath. But Phèdre had spoken truly; he was seventeen, with a head full of seventeen-year-old thoughts, and a belly full of desire.

And he was living under her roof.

We were outside the mews when it happened, watching Ronald Agout transfer the hawks to their blocks, where they crouched and sidled, hooding their eyes and preening in the warm sun. I was telling him about keeping Elua's vigil with Joscelin on the Longest Night.

"It sounds perishing dull if you ask me." Mavros laughed. "And to think, your mother once—" He broke off his words, glancing toward the manor house.

"Once what?" I asked when it became evident that he wasn't continuing.

"Nothing." Mavros stroked the peregrine's speckled feathers with one careful finger, avoiding my gaze. "If Phèdre never saw fit to tell you, it's not my business to do so."

"Saw fit to tell me what?" I bristled. The peregrine shifted restlessly, ruffling. Across the yard, Ronald made a disapproving sound.

Mavros shrugged, taking a step backward. "It doesn't matter. It was a long time ago, Imriel, before either of us were born."

"But *you* know," I said, growing increasingly irritated with him.

"Well." There was an edge to his smile. "It's family lore, you know. I daresay half of Kusheth knows."

"So tell me," I said. "There's no point in being coy."

"You wish to know?" Mavros gave me a long look. "All

right, I will, then. Better you should hear it from me than some backwater Kusheline lordling. Your mother contracted Phèdre for the Longest Night and brought her to the Duc de Morhban's fête on a velvet leash."

"No," I said automatically. "It's not true. You're lying."

"I'm not lying!" he said impatiently. "Name of Elua, Imri! Phèdre's an *anguissette*, and she was sworn to Naamah's Service. What do you think that meant? It's what she *does* to earn a livelihood—or did, at any rate, before Queen Ysandre made her a peer. And yes, it's true. On the Longest Night, your mother paraded her before the Duc de Morhban, in order that he might be consumed with envy and understand that in certain matters, the Shahrizai will always be his betters. Melisande put a collar around her neck, a velvet collar with a diamond the size of—"

He got no further, for I lowered my head and charged him.

Mavros grunted under the impact, and I bore him down hard. The two of us flailed in the dust while Ronald shouted ineffectually and the birds, alarmed, bated and strained at their tethers. We rolled over and over, and I came up on top. Hugues, kindhearted as he was, had taught me well. In Siovale, wrestling is reckoned a science. I clamped both of Mavros' legs with mine and braced one forearm across his throat.

"Take it back!" I hissed, leaning my weight on him.

He glared at me, eyes slitted. "I won't lie for you, cousin!"

"Imriel!"

It was Joscelin's voice—his battle-voice, clear and carrying. I had scarcely time to process the fact before his hand descended, grabbing the back of my shirt and lifting me by main force off Mavros.

I dangled briefly in midair, meeting Joscelin's furious summer-blue gaze. "I didn't—"

He slammed me down onto my feet. "Intend to disgrace the hospitality of Montrève?" he asked, hard and intent.

"No," I said in a small voice.

Mavros sat up, coughing. Joscelin turned to him. "Are you all right?"

"Yes, thank you." He sounded subdued. "It was a misunderstanding, that's all."

"He said—" I began.

Joscelin cut me off. "It doesn't matter, Imri. He's your guest, and you're responsible for honoring the rules of hospitality. They don't extend to throttling visitors." He let go of my shirt and wiped his hands, eyeing me with disgust. "Phèdre will not be pleased."

"Do we have to tell her?" I asked in dismay.

Folding his arms, Joscelin glanced around the yard. Mavros was on his feet, beating dust from his clothing, trying to appear unobtrusive. The hawks were still in an uproar, and poor old Ronald Agout bustled from block to block, trying to calm them. Two young goshawks were near-frantic, and I knew such an incident could set their training back by weeks or months.

"Oh, I think we do," Joscelin said coldly.

It was a rare thing to see Joscelin truly angry. It was not that he lacked the temper for it—indeed, I have gathered from things I have heard that he was fairly ill-tempered during his younger days as a Cassiline Brother. Perhaps it was the celibacy that caused it; of a surety, it had done little for my mood. But I believed that the trials he has undergone since those days were so severe that they established a threshold for anger, true anger, that was much higher than it is for ordinary mortals.

In some ways, Daršanga was harder on Joscelin than anyone.

So it was rare, and frightening; but it was doubly rare to see Phèdre angry. Joscelin marched us to the manor house, and there, in her study, he made me relate the incident. She listened to my account without expression, then turned to Mavros.

"My lord Shahrizai, please accept my deepest apologies on behalf of House Montrève," she said, her voice grave and sincere.

"Yes, of course," he said awkwardly. "It was just a misunderstanding."

"He said you let my mother parade you on a leash!" The words burst from me in anguish. "It's not true, is it?" At the back of the room, Joscelin made a small, unintelligible sound. Phèdre turned her head to regard me.

I wanted so badly for Mavros' words to be a lie. Under the weight of her dark, luminous gaze, I knew they were not. She had done what he said. And yet, somehow, she bore no shame for it. She was Kushiel's Chosen; an *anguissette*. Shame could not touch her. She rose above it, beyond it. It rolled off her and clung to me, and I could not even say why.

In the zenana, they called her Death's Whore. Every depravity the Mahrkagir visited upon her, she bore willingly. I knew that. In the zenana, everyone did.

The first time I met Phèdre, I spat in her face.

Across the study, Mavros began to smirk.

"Oh yes, it's true," Phèdre said quietly. "I made my marque that Longest Night." She turned her gaze back to Mavros, and his smile ebbed. "But I do not think," she said, "that House Shahrizai has had cause to boast of it since."

He looked at her for a long moment, his face naked beneath her steady regard. I knew what he saw. The whole entangled history of their Houses—of Phèdre, my mother, Anafiel Delaunay—lay between them; and yet, it was somewhat more. Phèdre nó Delaunay walked into hell willingly and walked out alive. And somehow—Blessed Elua alone knows—she retained the ability to *love*. She carried the Name of God in her thoughts, and there was nothing in the human soul that could be concealed from her.

There were times when all she needed to do was lay it bare.

"Forgive me, my lady." Mavros' voice was hoarse. "I was cruel."

"Youth is cruel." Phèdre caught Joscelin's eye. Something passed between them and she sighed, shaking her head. "Go on, get out, the both of you. And mind, no more fighting."

We went with alacrity.

For a time, by common accord, neither of us spoke. We walked together, wordless and aimless. I stole a glance at Mavros and found him looking uncommonly pensive. As we departed from the manor grounds, our unplanned course took us to the river. We walked alongside, following it toward the northern end of the valley. I found a sturdy stick and slashed at the reeds that grew along the river's edge, watching them bend without breaking, springing upright as we passed.

"I'm sorry," Mavros said abruptly, breaking our long silence.

I halted, watching the water tumble over gleaming rocks. "The fault was mine."

"Not entirely." He stood beside me. "I begin to think mayhap the Shahrizai have an imperfect grasp of what it means to be Kushiel's Chosen."

I prodded the ground with my stick. "It's true, though. What you said."

"You wish it were not?" he asked. "Why?"

I nodded. "I can't help it. Mavros . . ." I sighed and tossed the stick away. "It's hard. I cannot explain it."

He sat down on a dry tussock of grass. "I told you that Kushiel is merciful," he said slowly. "It is a hard and demanding mercy. If we are the dark mirror of the world's desire, then I think mayhap Phèdre is the bright mirror of ours, showing us those things we cloak in pride and vanity. I beheld my own pettiness in her gaze, and I did not like what I saw."

"I'm familiar with the feeling," I murmured.

"And yet you are ashamed of her?" he asked, curious.

"*No.*" I pressed the heels of my hands against my eyes. "I don't know! Why did it have to be my *mother*?"

"Oh." Mavros' tone changed. "Yes, well . . . yes. That must be awkward."

I lowered my hands and glared at him. "Awkward?"

He shrugged. "What do you wish me to say, Imri? The situation is what it is; I cannot change the past, any more than you can. You're carrying around a world of fear. I cannot help you if you refuse to confront it. No one can," he added, "not family, not Phèdre. You have to face the mirror yourself."

"Which one?" I asked dryly. "Bright or dark?"

"Both of them." He laughed. "Listen to me! Deigning to speak to you of fear."

I smiled a little. "Ah, well, you're not wrong."

"No." Mavros rose, dusting his hands. "But you're not ready. And as Roshana reminds me, I am supposed to practice *patience*." He held out his hand. "Are we friends?"

"Friends," I said slowly, clasping his hand. "All right, yes."

"Good." He grinned. "I don't fancy going another round with you! You're a nasty fighter, cousin."

So it was that our final days passed in amity. In the end, I was both saddened and relieved to see the Shahrizai depart. I had grown fond of them, fonder than I had reckoned. Mavros had spoken truly; they were a dark mirror, and there was much of myself I saw in them that I did not disdain. But too, there were other things.

Their escort came for them on the appointed day, and we gathered in the front courtyard to bid them farewell. They looked as splendid as they had when they arrived, and I could not help but feel a certain pride at their beauty. Baptiste whooped and shouted, standing in his stirrups and turning his mount in a tight circle; Roshana smiled and blew me a kiss. Mavros raised his hand in farewell, winking.

"I'll see you at Court, cousin!" he called.

Once again, nothing had changed, yet everything was different. I had a sense of myself that was different and new. I was a member, albeit at a distance, of a strange and exotic family. And if I was not prepared to embrace this bond wholeheartedly, neither did I regard it in abject horror.

Other things had changed, some to my sorrow.

In the month of my Shahrizai cousins' visit, I had grown apart from Charles. Although our friendship endured, he seemed to me younger than he had before, and simple and rustic in his desires. At the same time, Katherine had grown more mature. Whatever else had transpired in the meadow, Roshana had spoken truly; Katherine had learned somewhat of herself during their visit that she had not known before. She moved with a new surety, aware of her own blossoming sensuality and confident in the knowledge. It made me wonder at the cause.

After the Shahrizai had gone, I watched her set her sights once more on Gilot.

This time, there was no simpering. She stood, easy and sure, and crooked her finger at him; and he trailed after her, blindsided and besotted.

It would have made me laugh, had it not hurt. I'd had my chance, there in the meadow, and I let it slip through my fingers. There beside the lake, Katherine had offered herself, had dared to make herself vulnerable, and I had spurned her. And yet she accepted it without blaming me and moved on with ease. It was no more and no less than the old priest of Elua had foretold when he spoke to me of love on the Longest Night.

You will find it and lose it, again and again.

With a heart full of youthful rue, I watched it go.

We finished the summer at Montrève. After a month's indulgence with the Shahrizai, I flung myself into labor. I helped Charles with chores around the estate, and if our camaraderie was less than it had been, still, he was glad to have my aid. I sparred with Joscelin, who spoke well of my progress. And I resumed my studies with Phèdre.

There were no more tutors, and we did not practice the art of covertcy. Instead, sensing my need to lose myself undisturbed, she gave me a series of texts to read—histories and philosophies, for the most part. I liked reading the arguments of old Hellene philosophers.

After her anger, I was careful with Phèdre. It was not that she held a grudge, not by any means. There was no one in the world quicker to forgive. But it was because she understood human failing all too well; and in the bright mirror of her regard, I was reluctant to gaze upon my own shortcomings.

I spoke to Joscelin about it one day after we had sparred.

"Well," he said judiciously, "you *did* act the fool."

"Yes, I know." I flushed. "It's just—"

"I know." Joscelin's gaze softened. "Your mother." He sighed and ran a hand through his wheat-blond hair, darkened with streaks of sweat. It was hot and we had fought hard. "Imriel, I don't relish the knowledge any more than you do."

I traced a pattern on the slate with the toe of one boot. "How do you bear it?"

"I tried doing without Phèdre once." His voice was light and wry, but I lifted my head to meet his gaze, and his expression was not. "I discovered anything else was preferable."

"Even Daršanga?" I asked.

"Yes." Joscelin was quiet for a moment. "Even Daršanga," he said at length, and gave his half-smile, reaching out to tousle my hair. "Even her inexplicable affinity for your cursed mother. And if you ask me which of the two is worse, love, I would be hard put to answer. But we got *you* out of it, didn't we?"

It was one of those moments that made my heart soar. I grinned foolishly. "You reckon it was worthwhile?"

"Of course," Joscelin said simply. "Don't you?"

I thought a good deal about his words. It was not only that they warmed my heart, but they held a double meaning. Like Drustan mab Necthana, when he speaks, it is to good effect; like the Cruarch, Joscelin is more subtle than he appears. When all was said and done, I did reckon it worthwhile. They had found me, and redeemed me out of hell.

It was enough; it was more than enough.

Still, I did not know how to make my peace with Phèdre.

The strain persisted between us until the day she caught me browsing in her study. She has an extensive library, both at Montrève and in the City, but it was a common text that had caught my eye—an edition of the *Trois Milles Joies*, which is a famous D'Angeline compendium.

It was Enediel Vintesoir, the founder of the Night Court, who compiled it; or so legend claims. It contains every form of lovemaking in which men and women may partake, in every possible form and combination. All of them were illustrated by finely cut woodblock prints.

I scanned its pages in appalled fascination, dry-mouthed and taut with desire.

"Do you wish to borrow it?"

Phèdre's voice broke my reverie. I dropped the volume, wincing at the sound of parchment crackling, and stooped and caught it up quickly, holding it before me to hide the swelling in my breeches.

"No!" I said, quick and high-pitched. "I'm sorry. I was only looking."

"You may, you know." She turned away in a graceful gesture, scanning the shelves. "You probably should. Here." Phèdre handed me a leather-bound copy of *The Journey of Naamah*. "This one, too."

I felt the blood rise in my face, which was an improvement. "It's not necessary."

"They're only texts, Imri." Phèdre leaned against the bookshelves, a delicate frown knitting her brows. "You're curious. It's good to learn."

"Did you?" I asked, clutching both volumes.

"I did," she said gravely. "For a long time. You need not put it into practice. I didn't, not for years. But all knowledge is worth having."

"My thanks," I whispered, and fled.

I read the books she had lent me, and I learned. Strangely, it broke the long tension between us. The *Trois Milles Joies* dealt wholly with erotic instruction, but *The Journey of Naamah* examined the divine aspects of carnal love. When I read about how Naamah gave herself to the King of Persis to win Blessed Elua's freedom, and how she lay down with strangers in the stews of Bhodistan to earn coin that Elua might eat, I began to grasp an inkling of the link between desire and divine compassion—and in so doing, I gained a deeper understanding of Phèdre. What she had done was not so different. Both of them gave of themselves and somehow gained in the process. And there was no shame in it, only love.

As for the rest of it, I felt easier knowing that such desires as plagued me were simply part and parcel of the human condition. I spent many hours poring over those tomes, yet when I returned them to her, although they'd made me restless with yearning, I felt a bit easier in my skin.

"So," Phèdre murmured. "Do you have questions?"

I shook my head. "No," I said honestly. "Not yet." I thought of Mavros' words and laughed. "I'm not ready."

"All right." She smiled at me. "You know you may always ask."

"I know," I said. "And I'm grateful, but to be truthful, I'm not sure you're the best person to give me answers."

A flicker of pain crossed her face. She drew a deep breath and released it. "That may be true. But I would always try."

I nodded. "I'll think on it."

When summer began to give way to autumn, we made ready to return to the City. It was the first time that I did not do so with a heavy heart. Montrève had grown smaller, and I had changed. When I thought about showing myself

FOURTEEN

T HERE WAS THE USUAL fanfare upon our return to
    the City of Elua—a merry welcome at the gates, a joy-
ous reception at the townhouse and an official one at Court.
For once, I didn't dread the latter. Part of it, of course, was
my newfound confidence, a good deal of which I own I
owed to my Shahrizai kin. But there was a large part of it
that was due to a different reason, one that had nothing to do
with anything save Alais.

I was bringing the pup I had promised her, and I was
eager to see her response.

At five months, she—the wolfhound bitch—was almost
half-grown. I called her Celeste. She was a tall, lean shadow,
grey and hairy, with intelligent brown eyes and long-toed
paws that promised further growth.

"You're sure you want to do this?" Joscelin asked dubiously. "At Court?"

"She'll be good," I assured him. "And Alais will love it."

In the parlor of Phèdre's townhouse, Celeste sat with her
narrow jaws parted, red tongue lolling. Her hairy, whiplike
tail swept the marble floor in a steady beat, while the bust of
Anafiel Delaunay sat on its plinth, regarding her with an

austere smile. She had been well-behaved on the journey, and I was proud of her.

Phèdre laughed aloud. It was a musical sound, scintillating and filled with pure delight. "Why not?" she said to Joscelin, eyes dancing with whimsy. "He's right, you know."

So it was that we arrived at the Palace.

With Phèdre's help, I had ordered a collar commissioned before we departed for Montrève: a wide band of gilded leather set with seed pearls, such as ladies of the Court use to adorn their lapdogs, only much larger. It looked very fine on Celeste. I held tight to her leash of soft, braided leather, admiring her regal pace as we proceeded down the hallways of the Palace, ignoring the perambulating nobles.

Ysandre's herald announced us at the threshold of her drawing room.

I heard Alais squeal.

I let go of the leash, already grinning. Celeste bounded forward, her leash trailing.

In a heartbeat, half a dozen guards were there, swords drawn. Alais had sunk to her knees, and she had her arms wrapped around Celeste's neck, half adoring and half protecting. The wolfhound, familiar with her scent, sat on her haunches and lapped her cheek with a long red tongue. The guards exchanged perplexed glances.

"You remembered!" Alais exclaimed.

"I remembered," I said gravely. "Her name is Celeste."

"Celeste." Alais repeated the word, sinking her face into the wolfhound's ruff. "Oh, Imri! I already love her."

I grinned like an idiot. "I knew you would, villain."

At my words, the Dauphine Sidonie's chin rose. She turned slightly to her mother.

"Prince Imriel," said the Queen, her voice restrained. "Be welcome."

I swept her a low bow. "Your majesty," I said.

Ysandre turned to her left. I had paid scant heed to those who stood beside her; now I did. "Cousin," Ysandre said, her voice warming, "I pray you greet Imriel de la Courcel. The Comtesse de Montrève and her consort Joscelin Verreuil, I trust you know full well."

I shuddered, bone-deep.

"Well met, your highness."

Nicola L'Envers y Aragon smiled at me. Even before Ysandre made the introduction, I knew who she was. She had a look of the L'Envers side of the family, with deep violet eyes and shining bronze hair. I made myself reply politely and greet her son Raul. He must have favored his Aragonian father, for he was dark-haired; a blade-thin youth with a somber gaze.

"Nicola!" Phèdre's voice held a lilt. "I didn't know you'd be at Court already."

She laughed. "I thought I'd surprise you, my dear. Greetings, Messire Cassiline."

"A pleasure, my lady." Joscelin bowed. He sounded surprisingly good-natured. I could not imagine why. It was the first time, to my knowledge, that I had ever met one of Phèdre's patrons in the flesh—save for my mother, whom I already despised.

I hated it. I hated every moment of it.

If not for the pup Celeste, it would have been unbearable. Excited by the new surroundings and exchange of greetings, she bounded around the drawing room, creating havoc. Amid Alais' shrieks of glee, I managed to calm the wolfhound and get her to sit, obedient.

Joscelin rolled his eyes. "Forgive us, your majesty."

"I usually do," Ysandre said wryly.

"I think she's lovely." Nicola stooped gracefully beside

us, scratching the pup behind her ears. A garnet seal dangled from the gold bracelet on her slender wrist. "You trained her yourself?"

"Yes," I said shortly.

"She's mine!" Alais announced with pride. "I'm going to have a pillow at the foot of my bed for her to sleep on, and she'll have a special silver platter so she can eat with me."

I caught sight of a bemused, long-suffering expression on the Queen's face, and the quick flash of a grin on the young Aragonian, Raul's. He ducked his head to hide it.

"What fun that will be." Giving the now-adoring pup a final pat, Nicola straightened. "But remember, Alais, Celeste is used to having room to run and play with other dogs. Betimes she might be happier in the royal kennels."

"Mayhap." Alais sounded unconvinced.

"You *are* a diplomat's wife," Phèdre murmured. Nicola glanced over her shoulder and smiled at her.

"Well, yes." She turned to me. "And I am reminded, Prince Imriel, that I have a gift for you. A small token from the House of Aragon."

"It's not necessary," I muttered.

"It is." Nicola's violet gaze was disconcertingly frank. "I would that we had done more to prevent what happened in Amílcar."

I looked away. It was not something I cared to remember. "It wasn't your fault."

"Ah, well." She touched my arm lightly. "I have a gift for you nonetheless."

It was agreed that Nicola would call upon us within a few days. I paid scant heed to the conversation, making an escape with Alais on the pretext that Celeste must needs be walked in the gardens. A quartet of guards accompanied us.

There, I breathed easier in the fresh, cool air. The royal

gardens were filled with a riot of autumn blooms. We strolled along its paths, and I taught Alais the commands with which Celeste had been trained. She learned them quickly, her small, dark face intense with concentration.

"I do love her, Imri," Alais said to me as we sat side by side on a garden bench, Celeste sitting obediently at her feet. The guards waited at a respectful distance. "I truly, truly do. I wish Father were here to see her."

"He's gone back to Alba?" I asked.

She nodded. "They argued a lot this summer. About the succession there."

"Has anything"—I hesitated—"been determined?"

"No." Alais shook her head, bending to pet Celeste. "Why don't you like the Lady Nicola?"

I pulled a face. "Was it that obvious?"

"Yes," she said, reflecting. "She's nice, I think. *I* like her."

I shrugged. "Mayhap."

"Well, I do." Alais scratched behind Celeste's ears the same way Nicola had. The wolfhound laid her lean jaw on my young cousin's knee, rolling her brown eyes at her new mistress. "Is it because of what happened in Amílcar?"

"No," I said, and sighed. "Oh, Alais! It doesn't matter."

"That's where they sold you, isn't it?" Her voice was low. "The Carthaginians?"

Alais knew the story. She had been there, although I had not known her for my cousin and a Princess of the Blood, when we told it to Thelesis de Mornay, who was the Queen's Poet. Thelesis is gone now. She died of a long wasting illness, not so very long after Phèdre broke Rahab's curse. I was sorry I had not known her better.

"Yes," I said to Alais. "That's where they sold me."

"Celeste would have protected you," Alais said to the pup. "Wouldn't you?"

Celeste beat the hairy whip of her tail in agreement, stirring the dried leaves that littered the paving-stones.

"She would have tried," I said fondly. "Alais, why is the Lady Nicola here?"

"I don't know, not for sure." She stuck out her legs and frowned at her shoes. "I heard Mother say there is a chance her son Serafin might inherit. A long chance, though."

"Inherit?" I felt stupid.

"The throne of Aragon." Alais glanced at me. "The King doesn't have an heir of his own get. But it's a long chance. So I don't know." She knocked the heels of her shoes together, contemplating them. "Mayhap they are courting Sidonie for Serafin. Or mayhap they want *me* to wed Raul. I don't know."

I felt strange and sick. "Oh, Alais! What do *you* want?"

She shrugged. "I don't know, Imri. Do you?"

"No." I regarded her bent head, the spring of her black curls. The sight filled me with tenderness. "We'll figure it out together, shall we?"

"All right." Alais frowned in thought. "What about Sidonie?"

"What about her?" I asked.

"Will you help her, too?"

I laughed. "Alais, I don't think Sidonie needs my help, or anyone's, in that regard."

Alais looked at me out of the corner of one eye. "You don't know her very well, do you?"

"No," I said. "I suppose not."

I felt a bit guilty at this; it was true, although I spared a sympathetic thought for the young Dauphine's plight, I had not gotten to know my cousin Sidonie well. Perhaps if I had, she would not have reacted as she did that day last winter, with distrust and horror. But then we returned to the Queen's drawing room, where the adults were laughing and chatting like old friends, and the young people were making quiet conversation. When Alais and I entered with Celeste, Sidonie raked me over once with her cool, measuring gaze, and any feelings of guilt vanished.

Thus I returned to the City and found myself once more treading warily amidst the coils of intrigue. I had learned more than I reckoned from my Shahrizai kin. They had returned to Kusheth for a time, but the summer's lessons stayed with me. At Court, I bethought myself of Mavros' counsel. I was pleasant and polite to everyone I encountered, but I remained mindful of my own status. Let them think me aloof; it did not matter. As a Prince of the Blood, I held an edge of power over almost every peer of the realm.

To use it would be unwise; but it did not hurt to know it. *All knowledge is worth having.*

At home, it was another matter.

The Lady Nicola called upon us within days of our Court reception, and I found out what gift she had brought me. Like my long-promised gift to Alais, hers took living form.

It was one of the spotted horses of Aragon; like the Salmon, whom I had admired at the fair the day I learned of my mother's disappearance, over a year ago. Phèdre, it seemed, had seen fit to mention it in a letter. But I had known nothing of it.

I walked into the front courtyard, and my mouth went dry.

He was two years old, broken to the saddle, but still a little green with it. Unlike the Salmon, he was mostly white, generously speckled with reddish spots, the color of old blood. Secured on a lead-line in the narrow courtyard of the townhouse, he glared, rolling eyes that showed the whites, stamping striped hooves, making the courtyard ring. His strong neck arched, particolored mane breaking like a wave over his spotted hide. As I drew near, he wrinkled his lips, showing teeth like ivory plates.

"Do you like him?" Nicola L'Envers y Aragon leaned out of the open carriage door, laughing. "Phèdre said you would."

I loved him.

I hated her.

"Name of Elua!" Gilot breathed fervently. He had been moping ever since we had left Montrève; now he grabbed my shoulders and shook them in an excess of excitement. "Ah, Imri, look at him, will you!"

"His name is Hierax," Nicola said, descending lightly from the carriage. "Though Ramiro says the Tsingani who bred him called him the Bastard."

I knew Phèdre and Joscelin were watching. I walked forward. I wished someone else had given me this horse; I wished I had found him by myself. I grabbed his coarse mane in both fists, bowing my head and leaning against him, feeling the hard, bony plate of his forehead against mine.

"Hello, Bastard," I whispered.

He whuffed hard through dilated nostrils, our breath mingling.

Mindful of courtesy's demands, I made myself release him and turned, bowing deeply to Nicola. "My thanks, my lady, to you and the House of Aragon. He is a splendid gift."

She smiled. "You're quite welcome."

After that, of course, nothing would do but that Nicola was invited inside. Phèdre called for cordial, and I served it myself. We sat on couches in the salon and made polite conversation. It was a double agony, for all I wanted to do was acquaint myself with my magnificent new horse, and what I least wanted to do was be pleasant to the Lady Nicola.

It was unfair, I know. She had done nothing to merit my dislike, and I had cause to be grateful to her. But I hated knowing what I knew, and I hated the way Phèdre's eyes sparkled in her presence. They bantered, light and teasing and fond, but there was an undercurrent of tension between them. I could feel it on my skin, the way one feels lightning's charge in the air before the flash.

How Joscelin could bear it, I do not know; and yet he seemed untroubled. Perhaps, I thought glumly, it was my own heritage that made me sensitive to it. Although they are mostly Naamah's line, there is old Kusheline blood in House L'Envers. But no; although Joscelin harbored no dark desires—indeed, in the eyes of the realm, he harbored unnaturally *few* desires—he was no fool, and he knew Phèdre too well. For whatever reason, he willingly tolerated Nicola L'Envers y Aragon.

I knew what she had done. It was not just the aid she had given in Amílcar. Long before, she had entrusted Phèdre with the password of House L'Envers, the phrase that its members are compelled to honor. And Phèdre used it, too— twice. She used it to compel Barquiel L'Envers to hold the City against Percy de Somerville's army, and she used it to compel his daughter in Khebbel-im-Akkad. Valère L'Envers, who is wed to the Khalif's son, petitioned her husband for aid in retrieving me from Drujan because of it.

He didn't grant it, though. Even the Khalif's son feared the bone-priests of Drujan, having lost two armies to them. All he did was give Phèdre and Joscelin a guide to Daršanga. And when they brought me out of that living hell, Valère L'Envers tried to have me killed.

It was small wonder, I suppose, that I had trouble with the Queen's kin.

All except Alais.

She would love the Bastard, I thought. Perhaps we could go on a hunting excursion together. I could teach Celeste to course hares, as we did in Montrève. At eleven, Alais was old enough to begin learning such pastimes.

"Imriel."

The sound of Phèdre's voice made me startle. Curled into the corner of her couch, she regarded me with bright amusement, then nodded toward the door.

"Go," she said. "Off to the stables with you. You're not fit for conversation."

Not needing to be told twice, I went.

In the stables, I found the Bastard stamping and tossing in his new stall, churning the sweet-smelling straw. Gilot hung on the half-door of the stall, watching and admiring, while the stable-keeper Benoit cursed and wrapped a bandage around his left hand.

"Careful, highness," he said. "He's a hellion."

I approached the door. The Bastard ceased his stamping and stood, eyeing me. Gilot nudged me with his elbow. "Want to go for a ride?"

"Just the two of us?" I knew Phèdre and Joscelin would disapprove.

Gilot shrugged. "A quick one, eh? Just to try his paces."

I took one look at the Bastard, who pricked his ears at me. "All right. Let's do it."

He was docile enough while being saddled, but when I swung astride him and took up the reins, I could feel him quivering with tension. Gilot rode a tall, rangy bay gelding that he favored. We jogged into the courtyard. With a dubious look on his face, Benoit opened the gates.

"Go!" Gilot shouted.

I gave the Bastard his head. He sprang forward, bursting off his haunches, hooves clattering on the paving-stones. I laughed like an idiot, exhilarated. It was a foolish thing to do; I knew it, and knew it at the time. And yet it was thrilling. Together, Gilot and I raced like madmen through the City of Elua, reckless and swift. For all his unruly temperament, the Bastard had a gait as smooth as silk. Gilot's bay mount caught a taste of the Bastard's fervor, and together they were like swallows on the wing. We crossed the arched bridge over the Aviline River, heading for Night's Doorstep. Pedestrians scattered before us and carriage-horses reared in their traces, alarmed.

Here and there, people shouted, waving to us.

I heard my name. *"Im-ri-el! Prince Imriel!"*

It felt good, bringing a fierce grin to my lips.

In Night's Doorstep, we halted. Gilot's mount was lathered and blown. The Bastard arched his neck and pranced, huffing. He was not even tired. The spotted horses of Aragon were known for their endurance.

"Come on." Gilot raked a hand through wind-tangled brown curls, then patted the money-pouch that hung from his belt. "We need to breathe them a spell; or at least I do. I'll stand you a round at the Cockerel, Imri."

"You said a short ride," I reminded him.

"I know." He grinned at me. "But you looked like you needed a bit of an escape, and I've heard the Lady Phèdre herself say none of her household would ever come to harm at the Cockerel. If you're scared, we can head back."

It stung my pride. "I'm not *scared*!"

"Come on, then."

Inside the Cockerel, there was a great deal of shouting. I whispered a word to Gilot, promising restitution, and he stood a round for the inn. Here they remember Hyacinthe, the Prince of Travellers, who became the Master of the Straits.

"Ah, my prince!" A barrel-shaped man came toward me, weeping openly, arms outstretched. "You came! You remember!"

"Emile," I said, exhaling his name as he embraced me hard. "Yes, of course."

"A *gadjo* pearl," he said, taking my chin in his thick fingers. "A *gadjo* pearl!"

A foaming tankard of ale was placed before me. I drank it down and wiped my lips. Afterward, more came. I was not sure who purchased it; Emile, mayhap. It was strong ale, and more than I was wont to drink. We toasted Hyacinthe, and Emile coaxed me to tell the story of the breaking of his curse to a rapt audience. After that, the story of the fête that Phèdre threw in Night's Doorstep to celebrate his return was rehashed with great relish by the patrons there.

By the time Gilot and I left, I was unsteady on my feet. I tried three times to put my foot in the stirrup, missing twice. The Bastard rolled his white-rimmed eyes at me. "Hup!" someone said, giving my buttocks a boost, and there I was, astride.

"Home," I said firmly, peering at Gilot. "Do you want to race?"

"Name of Elua!" Gilot looked pale. "I'm an idiot. Her ladyship will have my hide."

"All right, then." I was weaving in the saddle. "We'll race."

I put my heels to the Bastard's flanks, and he sprang forward like an arrow shot from a bow. I crouched low over his neck, laughing. His mane stung my cheeks. In the gloaming twilight, we raced through the streets. I could hear Gilot thundering behind me, trying in vain to catch us, his voice raised in a fading shout.

"Imri! Imri, *stop*!"

I didn't, not until I came within a hairsbreadth of running down a party of young nobles on the outskirts of Night's Doorstep. One of the women cried out in fear. The Bastard shied hard, flinging me onto his neck, then reared, hooves flailing the air. I managed to keep my seat and fought to regain his head.

"Fool boy!" A young lord in russet velvet scowled and drew his sword. "I've half a mind to lesson you with the flat of my blade!"

I felt chilled and very sober. "My lord, forgive me. I was careless."

He pointed at the paving-stones with the tip of his sword. "Apologize on your knees, whelp."

I heard an echo of the Mahrkagir's commands in his voice, and felt the shadow of Daršanga fall over me. I sat very still in the saddle, and the Bastard stood motionless beneath me, ears pricked and attentive. "No," I said softly. "I apologize, my lord, most sincerely. But I will not kneel."

"Oh, you will—" he began.

"Imriel!" Gilot burst upon us in a rattling clamor. Without an instant's hesitation, he drew his sword, pointing it at the angry lord. "Messire, drop your sword! *Now*!"

After a pause, the lord obeyed. His blade fell with a clatter. "Your highness," he said stiffly, "I pray your pardon. I did not know you in this light."

"It's all right," I said, embarrassed. "The fault was mine, truly."

"It certainly was," Gilot muttered.

Even so, they bowed to me as protocol dictated. We took our leave, riding at a sedate pace. I felt a thorough idiot. I stole a chastened glance at Gilot.

"I'm sorry," I said. "That *was* foolish."

"No," he said. "*I* was foolish. It was an ill-advised excursion, and I hold myself to blame." In the dim light, the corner of his mouth twitched. "Though I will say, you've got a wild streak in you, my prince. You and your spotted horse both."

"He's something, isn't he?" I patted the Bastard's neck. "Gilot . . . I'll keep this quiet if you will. If I go back through the garrison door, they don't have to know how long we were gone."

He looked sidelong at me. "Are you trying to save me trouble?"

"Yes," I said honestly.

"You shouldn't." Gilot's jaw set in a hard line. "I deserve it. I deserve to be dismissed."

"I'd rather you weren't," I said. "And I don't want to have to explain it to Katherine."

At that, he sighed. "Katherine!"

I put out my hand. "It's agreed, then?"

Gilot looked at my hand for a long moment. "All right," he said, clasping it. "Agreed."

At the townhouse, we found Benoit in a state of guilt-ridden agitation. It took no coaxing to enlist his aid in keeping quiet about our absence. Once the horses were stabled, we slipped into the garrison quarters where Gilot and Ti-Philippe and the others were lodged. I often spent time there visiting with them, and no one would think anything strange in it.

Still, I entered the townhouse warily, moving in silence.

I needn't have worried. Although the Lady Nicola had left, Phèdre and Joscelin were still in the salon, enjoying a rare moment of privacy. I heard their voices, low and murmuring, and stole toward the doorway.

"Do you think you will see her?" Joscelin asked. He was

reclining on one of the couches, unusually relaxed, idly stroking Phèdre's hair as she leaned against him.

I stood in the shadows and watched.

"I don't know." Phèdre's voice was low. "After Daršanga . . ." She shook her head. "Ah, love! I've forfeited the right to ask you to endure aught else."

"Oh, will you make *me* the villain, then?" Joscelin asked dryly, winding a lock of her hair in his fingers. "Don't, Phèdre. I made my peace with it long ago. I survived Daršanga, though it nearly destroyed me. And for three years you have trod on eggshells because of it, attempting to protect me from what I know full well. I am telling you, Nicola is far easier to bear."

"Joscelin." She breathed his name, lowering her head to kiss him. I drew back into the shadows. "You're sure?"

I could not see him when he replied, but his voice was breathless and half-laughing. "Sure? I stand at the crossroads and choose, again and again. How can you ask?"

She answered him without words. I would have left then, save that I heard my name when Phèdre did speak.

"It's not only you," she murmured. "It's Imri."

"Yes," Joscelin said. "I know." I peered around the doorway. He had both hands sunk deep into her hair and was gazing up at her. "Would you live a lie for his sake, love, and pretend to be somewhat you are not? Because I do not believe, in the end, he would thank you for it."

I did leave then. I stole away and returned, making a noisy, cheerful entrance. I caught them out, flushed and laughing. D'Angelines are not shy in matters of love. If I had not eavesdropped on them, it would have been nothing more than one of those silly, joyous moments such as may occur in a small household.

And insofar as they knew, it wasn't.

"Imriel, my love." Phèdre smiled at me, running her fingers through her disheveled hair. "Did you have a pleasant time gloating over your new gift?"

"Yes, thank you." I smiled back at her and lied. "Very pleasant."

Any other time, I suspect she would have known it; but I had caught her in a moment of distraction. And it was Phèdre herself who taught me the nine tell-tales of a lie. As well as she knows them, she was not terribly good at dissembling.

I learned that evening that I was.

FIFTEEN

T HERE WAS SOME GOSSIP at Court, though not as much as I expected. Once again, it seemed I was the last to learn what every other living soul in Terre d'Ange had known. The Lady Nicola had been more than a favorite patron. Phèdre had given her a lover's token long ago. It was something Naamah's Servants did on occasion, exalting a favorite from the status of patron to lover. It was the only time Phèdre had ever done so. No one expected her to do aught else but resume the liaison. They were more interested in whether or not she would return to Naamah's Service, a matter on which Phèdre had remained silent.

Still, letters bearing offers came every week.

There was nothing strange in it. In Terre d'Ange, such liaisons were commonplace. Blessed Elua was free from jealousy, and we strive to emulate his example. Betimes we fail, being mortal and weak, but we strive.

I knew this. It was part of my earliest teaching in the Sanctuary: Elua's precept, *Love as thou wilt*. And yet, I struggled with it. All that I had learned in childhood, I had unlearned under the Mahrkagir's tutelage. I had been so proud of the understanding I had gained during my reading of *The Journey of Naamah*. And though I could cling to it in my thoughts, in my heart it slipped away from me the first time Phèdre returned home from a liaison with the Lady Nicola.

It was the way she looked.

I used to see it in the zenana, when the Mahrkagir sent her back, at once pain-stiff and languid. A part of her went away at those times to a place where almost no one could follow. I hated it then, and I hated it now. I could not even wholly say *why*.

"Are you all right?" Joscelin took her cloak. He had remained at the townhouse while Ti-Philippe escorted her, but he made himself greet her upon her return.

"Yes." Phèdre smiled up at him. Her dark, wide-set eyes were soft and unfocused with the aftermath of desire, the scarlet mote floating in the left. When she shrugged out of her cloak, one sleeve of her gown fell back, revealing a rope-burn on one slender wrist. "Fine."

He exhaled hard. "Good."

"Are you?" she asked him.

"Nearly." Joscelin traced a line on her cheek beneath her dart-stricken eye. "Very nearly." He nodded toward the stairs. "Go on, Clory's drawn you a bath."

I got out of the way fast, and stayed out of her way. I could not help it. Something in me shrank from seeing her thus. A bright mirror, Mavros had called her; but Phèdre was a dark mirror, too, as surely as the Shahrazai. And although I scarce admitted it to myself, I was afraid of what I might see in it. It was easier to hate it.

It was a piece of irony that she warned me of it herself. It was a day etched on my heart, one of the happiest I had ever known. We were aboard a ship sailing from Iskandria to La Serenissima when Phèdre granted my heart's desire and told me that she and Joscelin meant to adopt me into their household. I remembered the warning she gave, taking my hand, revealing the underside of my wrist where the blue veins throbbed, pulsing with the blood of Kushiel's lineage.

Betimes you will despise me, like you did in Daršanga.

I had denied it with all the fervor of my eleven-year-old soul. Now, four years later, it was true, and I had to learn to live with it. In some ways, it was a matter of honor.

One day I took my courage in both hands and marched into her study.

"I have a question," I announced.

"Imriel." Phèdre looked up from the strange alphabet she was studying—somewhat that Hyacinthe had sent her some time ago. She wore her faraway look and focused slowly on me. "Yes? What is it?"

"Are you going to return to Naamah's Service?" The question came out abruptly. "It's just . . ." I sighed. "I'm tired of being the last to know."

"I see," Phèdre said. "Are you angry because of Nicola?"

"No." I looked away. "Yes, a little."

"She is a friend of long standing," Phèdre said gravely. "And I am very fond of her."

"I know that *now*!" I heard my own voice rise, petulant.

"Come here." Phèdre beckoned. I went with reluctance, then gave myself over with a certain relief, sinking to my knees and laying my head in her lap, letting her stroke the hair from my brow. "Imri, I'm sorry. I should have told you."

"You know why," I whispered.

"I know," Phèdre murmured. "But, love, I promise you, this is nothing like Daršanga. Do you know about the *signale*?"

I did, only because I had read the *Trois Milles Joies*. It

was the password established when violent pleasure was in play, overriding all false protestations. It meant, on pain of heresy, *stop*. "Yes," I said. "I know it."

"It exists here," she said. "There, it didn't."

"Ill thoughts," I said, remembering. "Ill words, ill deeds."

"Yes." Phèdre's hands went still. "I would have spoken it were there ears to hear."

I raised my head from her lap, peering at her. "So?"

"So." She smiled, one of those irresistible smiles, filled with all the impossible, enduring love and unlikely merriment that was part and parcel of her nature. Once again, it made my heart overbrim with feeling. How could anyone endure what we had known and still be capable of so much *goodness*? "There weren't. And now I am home, in Terre d'Ange, where matters differ. And now I am given to choose, as I have done, but the answer, love, is no; most probably, no."

"What answer?" I asked.

"To your question." Phèdre stroked my hair. "Do you remember how I made the pilgrimage to Naamah's river shrine in Namarre last fall?"

I nodded.

"I may be called," she said gently. "Such a possibility ever exists. But if I am not . . ." Phèdre shrugged. "I will not answer. I have received Naamah's blessing and her gratitude for my service. Nothing more is needful."

I was glad, fiercely glad. "And Nicola?"

"That is different." Her touch lingered on my brow. "It was a different choice, and one I do not regret. It is Elua's business. But the others . . ." Phèdre shook her head. "No. Not unless I am impelled. And if I am," she added, "I will tell you. All right?"

"Yes," I said. "Why don't you let it be known at Court, then? It would put an end to the guessing and wondering."

"Ah." Phèdre raised her eyebrows. "But I am Naamah's Servant still, and guessing and wondering is part of our stock-in-trade. If I am ever called, I will draw upon years of speculation for my asking price. Does it trouble you so much?"

"Not as much as the Lady Nicola," I said truthfully.

She laughed. "You would like her, you know, if you gave her half a chance."

"I'll try," I muttered.

"Ah, love." Phèdre cupped my face in her hands. "I don't mean to make your life harder. I'm sorry if I have handled this poorly. I should have spoken to you before."

"I wouldn't have listened." I turned my head, resting my cheek against one cool palm. Something in my heart ached, sensing that one day, this, too, would be lost to me. "And I *will* try harder, I promise."

After that, I did.

In a rare moment of whimsy—one that was prompted by the Lady Nicola—Queen Ysandre decreed a Celebration of the Harvest in the royal apple orchard that year. It is a small orchard of no more than twenty trees, contained within the Palace walls, but the trees were lovingly tended and bore an abundance of fruit.

I will own, it was a pleasant affair. After a cold spell threatened to blight the last apples of the season with frost, the weather relented, and autumn flung out one last, glorious gasp of warmth. Everyone was clad in rustic attire; rustic, by Court standards. I wore a simple white shirt and laced breeches; but the shirt was sewn of the finest white cambric and the breeches were fawnskin, soft as a glove.

They had been made to measure by Favrielle nó Eglantine's chief apprentice.

Phèdre fussed over me before we went, making sure my collar lay just so.

"Oh, Imriel!" She laid one hand over the soft deerhide laces that crisscrossed my breast. There were unexpected tears in her eyes. "Wearing that, you remind me of—" She caught herself, shaking her head. "Do you have to grow up so *fast*?"

I smiled down at her. "I'm going as slowly as I can."

We arrived in the early afternoon to find the fête in full resplendence. Tables set with sumptuous linens were set here and there, laden with savories. Rich carpets had been spread beneath the trees that the D'Angeline nobles might picnic upon them. Musicians strolled along the tree-lined aisles, pausing to serenade various parties. At the center of the orchard stood a great cider press, gleaming with gold inlay. It must have taken eight men to carry it there. It made me laugh aloud to see it, and I found myself wondering what Maslin of Lombelon would make of this courtly idea of a working orchard.

"Imri!" Alais' high voice greeted us. She ran into me hard, wrapping both arms around my waist. "You came," she said, muffled.

"Of course." I hugged her back, bemused. The wolfhound pup Celeste circled us, frisking. "Why wouldn't I?"

"I don't know," Alais said. "I'm always afraid one day you won't."

"Are you afraid I'm going to run away with the man with two faces?" I teased her. "The one from your dream?"

"You might," she said gravely.

I ruffled her hair. "Not likely, villain!"

As befitted our status, we were seated on the Queen's

carpet along with the other royal kindred. Fortunately for me, Duc Barquiel L'Envers was not in attendance. I kept my word and greeted the Lady Nicola and her son Raul with unforced courtesy. If no one else found the situation awkward, I had no intention of rendering it so.

Shortly after our arrival, Ysandre proclaimed a contest. She was in fine fettle that day, smiling and at ease, clad in a simple velvet gown the color of ripe chestnuts with a wreath of chrysanthemums and anemones adorning her fair hair. It made me realize how seldom I had seen my cousin the Queen *happy*.

"My lords and ladies!" she called. "I summon you to the harvest! In a quarter hour's time, let each of you gather as many apples as you may, and the victor may claim a forfeit of any of the losers!"

There were cheers and mock groans; the latter, mostly from the women, who were disadvantaged by their skirts. The lower limbs of the apple trees had been picked bare, and only the upper limbs remained full, dangling with tantalizing fruit. Servants began to circulate with wooden baskets and the Court horologer stepped forward officiously, consulting the small sundial he wore on a chain about his neck.

I noticed various lords and ladies flirting and striking bargains to work in tandem. Raul gave a courtly little bow to Sidonie. "With your permission, it would be my honor to assist you, your highness," he said to her in D'Angeline with a trace of a soft Aragonian accent.

"Thank you." She colored slightly. "And please, call me Sidonie."

"Sidonie." He smiled at her. "All right, Sidonie."

"Heartless child of mine!" Nicola laughed. "Will you leave me to fend for myself?"

"Are you willing to accept the aid of a humble chevalier, my lady?" Ti-Philippe asked promptly.

"A hero of the realm?" She laid a hand on his sleeve. "With pleasure."

Phèdre looked at Joscelin, who rolled his eyes. "You have to ask?" he said.

No one had spoken to Alais. She bowed her head, fidgeting with Celeste's collar. It was not easy on her, always being the youngest in Court gatherings. Although she was near to becoming a young woman in her own right and carried the burden of her birthright, she was treated like a child. I knew what it was like to be caught between both worlds.

I got to my feet and made her an absurd, sweeping bow. "Your highness," I said, "shall we demonstrate the proper picking of apples to these fine people?"

Her face brightened as she looked up at me. "Yes, thank you."

"It is," I said solemnly, "my deepest pleasure."

At a nod from the horologist, Ysandre called the start. The strolling musicians came together in a neat band and struck up a lively tune. Everyone scattered, the men racing for trees, the women gathering their skirts and hurrying after them, trailed by servants bearing baskets.

With the speed of youth on our side, Alais and I got a good tree, still heavily laden on top. I clambered easily onto the lower limbs, then made the mistake of looking outward.

It was something to see, a handful of D'Angeline noblemen attempting to scale apple trees without soiling their rustic finery. They were spectacularly inept. I laughed so hard I nearly lost my perch.

"Imri!" Below, Alais danced from foot to foot. "Hurry, please!"

"I'm going." I climbed higher and began plucking apples. I tossed them down lightly. "Catch, cousin!"

It was an absurd scene, with most of the participants manifestly unsuited. Some acquitted themselves well; one, at least, was handicapped by his skill. I wrapped my legs around a sturdy limb and picked everything within reach, dropping apples one by one. Alais gathered them and put them into a wooden basket, aided surreptitiously by the servant bearing it, while Celeste looked on in bewilderment at the inexplicable activities of humankind.

Elsewhere, I could hear the thud and squelch of ripe apples being hurled with unerring accuracy, and Phèdre's aggrieved voice rising. "Joscelin, stop throwing them so hard!"

"Sorry!" he called in an unrepentant tone.

There was no contest, in the end. Ti-Philippe had been a sailor under the command of the Royal Admiral Quintilius Rousse. He scaled the upper limbs of his tree as easily as a ship's rigging, and shook the limbs hard. Apples rained down like hailstones. When he had stripped it barren, he clambered back down and assisted the Lady Nicola in filling their baskets.

When a quarter hour had passed, the musicians' instruments fell quiet and a laughing Ysandre called an end to the contest. I descended, twigs catching at my hair.

"We didn't do too badly, did we?" Alais said complacently, eyeing our half-full basket.

"No," I said. "Quite well, I think."

The formal count was pointless; Ti-Philippe and Nicola had filled two baskets to brimming: No one else had filled even one.

"Will you claim your forfeit, chevalier?" Ysandre asked.

Ti-Philippe bowed to the Lady Nicola. "I cede it to you, my lady."

"Oh, do you, now?" Her face was alight with mirth. If I had not disliked her so, I would have owned, she was a lovely woman. "Well, then, I claim a kiss." She surveyed the orchard, taking in the assembled nobility. I saw her gaze linger on Phèdre.

I gritted my teeth.

Nicola turned to Ti-Philippe. "And since you were gallant enough to cede it," she said mischievously, "I shall do you the courtesy of returning it." It was prettily done, and she kissed him to cheers of approval.

For the remainder of the day, we ate and drank and played such games as the Queen decreed. Servants filled the cider press with apples, and everyone took a hand at turning the crank. A set of quoits inlaid with silver filigree was brought forth, and there was a roar of protest when Joscelin stepped up to take his turn. With good grace, he submitted to being blindfolded with a silk sash; even so, he acquitted himself well, pausing and listening for the sound of the discus hitting the pin. I daresay with enough practice he might have won. Although I am no Cassiline, I have good aim, and I came near to winning at quoits; but a few lucky tosses by a young lord named Hubert Arundel put me out of contention.

And somewhere in the course of the day, I realized I was enjoying myself.

As twilight settled over the orchard, servants moved around with tapers, hanging oil lamps of clear glass until it looked as though a shower of stars had fallen to adorn the stripped apple trees. The day's lively entertainment had given way to the tranquil pleasures of song and conversation. When it grew time to leave, I found to my surprise that I was sorry to see it end.

"Thank you, your majesty," I said to Ysandre. "It has been a rare pleasure."

"Too rare." Ysandre smiled. She put out a hand as though to touch me, then halted. A shadow of distant sorrow surfaced in her gaze. "You know it has ever been my wish that you feel a welcome and beloved member of House Courcel, Imriel."

I wondered if it had wounded her that I had to be compelled to Court, yet had freely invited my mother's kin to Montrève. I had not given it a thought; now I saw the discourtesy in it. Once again, absorbed by my own private agonies, I had been thoughtless.

"I know, my lady," I said softly. "And for that, too, I am grateful."

Ysandre shook her head, her wreath of chrysanthemums rustling. "I seek no gratitude," she said. "But I am pleased that you enjoyed this day."

"I did." Because it was true, I smiled at her. "Very much so."

I turned away to see the Dauphine Sidonie regarding me with a considering look. In the charmed illumination of the faery-lights strung from the apple trees, she looked very pretty. At thirteen years of age, the woman she would become was beginning to emerge from the girl she was. Tonight it held an unwonted softness instead of her customary hauteur.

Filled with goodwill, I accorded her the sweeping bow I had given Alais earlier. "Cousin, I bid you good eve!"

"Thank you." Sidonie's lips twitched. She cocked her head in a manner that reminded me of Phèdre, continuing to consider me. What thoughts passed behind her dark

Cruithne eyes, I could not begin to fathom. "You know," she said at length, "you're not so bad when you smile, Imriel."

"My thanks, your highness," I said wryly.

If she had been older, I would have sworn her expression was one of suppressed laughter; then it passed, and Sidonie inclined her head to me, raising it with an imperious tilt of her chin. "You're very welcome, I'm sure."

No matter what their age, women are a mystery.

SIXTEEN

AFTER THE FÊTE in the apple orchard, I found it easier to be pleasant at Court, relinquishing some of my aloofness. Sidonie's observation, irritating as it was, held a measure of truth. Once I allowed myself to relax and smile, I found a number of people were willing to smile back at me. I even made some friends among them.

There were always young gentry at Court. While their elders vied for influence or status, the younger folk played at love. For most D'Angelines, courtship prior to marriage was a long, drawn-out affair. It began at an early age and continued for years. Save for the scions of ruling sovereigns—and betimes sovereign ducs in their own provinces—childhood betrothals were rare. And since Queen Ysandre had thus far refused to see her daughters betrothed young for political gain, it set the fashion for the realm. Families of the Great Houses brought their children to the City to begin the Game of Courtship.

It was not a game in which I took part. It began in earnest around the age of sixteen; before that, youthful flirting—the sort of games Katherine and Roshana taught me in the meadow—was accorded little or no weight. At fifteen, I was exempt.

Still, because I was often at Court, I was around it. And because I was a Prince of the Blood, I was not *wholly* exempt. Even Sidonie, at thirteen, had her would-be suitors. They trod carefully, fearful of the Queen's ire, but one could see them seeking to curry favor that she might be kindly disposed to them in the future.

It didn't work very well.

Those nobles, I avoided. To my surprise, I had to own that Raul L'Envers y Aragon was not one of them. He was pleasant and attentive to her, but in a respectful fashion. Once I got past, to some degree, my dislike of his mother, I found him quite tolerable. He was quiet and thoughtful, with a shrewd sense of humor that surfaced on occasion. If he was laying the groundwork to court Sidonie on his brother's behalf, it was with surpassing discretion; and if his interest was in Alais, it was nowhere evident.

"Why did your mother bring you to Court?" I asked him bluntly one day.

Raul looked at me with surprise in his brown eyes. "To learn my heritage," he said in his softly accented D'Angeline. "Why else?"

"To effect a betrothal," I said.

"Oh." Surprise turned to amusement. "You speak of rumors." He shook his head. "D'Angelines are a funny people. If my brother Serafin wishes to make a bid for the throne of Aragonia, he will marry an Aragonian girl of high standing, not another D'Angeline."

"What about you?" I asked.

We were in the Salon of Eisheth's Harp. Raul glanced around. "I like it here," he said. "I would consider it."

"Alais?" I pressed.

"She's a little girl!" He laughed, spreading his hands. "I have no designs on the throne, any throne. I am like my mother. I like beautiful things. Some things are that simple, your highness."

"Not in my experience," I said.

It could be, though. Raul spoke truly; most of the young nobles flirting and courting did so with exuberance, playing the game for pleasure's sake, reveling in their own youth and beauty, and the multitude of choices available to them. It would not end once they wed, but it would change. To marry or take a formal consort was to establish a household. One might take lovers, afterward, or dally with Naamah's Servants—indeed, most did—but marriage would fix the domestic framework of one's life.

I found it hard to imagine.

When I did try, it was Montrève I thought of. I could envision myself wed to someone like Katherine Friote, a country girl of good family, presiding over the manor; and yet I could not envision Katherine at Court, where I was beginning to feel a certain sense of belonging.

For one thing, Mavros Shahrizai had returned to winter there. At seventeen, he was beginning to play the Game of Courtship to the hilt, and he cut a dangerous swathe. Still, I was glad to see him, and we resumed our uneasy friendship.

But there were others, too, I began to think of as friends; those whom I found to be good-hearted and decent. Bertran de Trevalion, who was another cousin; his grandmother, Lyonette, had been my father's sister. They used to call her the Lioness of Azzalle. He was a tall young lord with an earnest, open gaze, only a half a year older than I. He was also the heir to the duchy of Trevalion, and knew somewhat about contending with treason in his family lineage. And there were Colette and Julien Trente, whose father, Lord Amaury, had served as Commander of the Queen's Guard and led the

expedition to rescue me; and Marguerite Grosmaine, whose
mother was the Secretary of the Presence.

They were not boon companions, but they were easy
ones. In the countryside, autumn was a time of hard labor,
spent putting up the summer's harvest, salting and smoking
and preparing for winter. At Montrève, I would have worked
alongside Charles and the others, lending a hand in the Siovalese tradition. Here in the City, the peers merely played at
such things. Hunting in particular was a popular autumn
sport, and it was over the course of several hunting parties
that I found myself falling in with the same young people.

Owing to their backgrounds, they knew a bit of my history; unlike my Shahrizai kin, they did not press me on the
dark and painful aspects of it.

They were more interested in the adventures.

I hadn't given thought to the fact that it made me exotic
in their eyes. Colette and Julien had grown up with the story:
How I had deceived Lord Amaury Trente in the harbor at
Tyre, bribing a street lad to take my place while I stowed
away on Phèdre and Joscelin's ship. I winced to hear of his
fury at the deception, but they found it amusing; a parent's
foible.

"You did it out of love!" Colette exclaimed. "He
shouldn't have been *that* mad, should he? Tell us about
Meroë and the oliphaunts."

So I did. I told them about our voyage down the mighty
Nahar River, and the crocodile temple of the god Sebek. I
told them about the terrible desert crossing, and the splendor
of Meroë, where Queen Zanadakhete granted us passage
across Jebe-Barkal. I told them about the strangeness of
Saba, a realm forgotten by time, where the soldiers wore
armor of worn bronze older than Terre d'Ange itself.

Some parts, I kept to myself. I did not think they would

marvel at Kaneka's village of Debeho, which was a collection of mud huts. It was special to me, a haven of happiness and kindness, but I did not think these fine young D'Angeline lords and ladies would understand. And I did not tell them about the day Joscelin and I caught the giant fish, which was special to me for other reasons.

But I told them other stories, and the women gazed at me with wide-eyed awe while the men looked envious. They knew the stories, of course; nearly everyone does. Thelesis de Mornay set a portion of them to verse before she died, and her onetime apprentice Gilles Lamiz, who was named the Queen's Poet after her, has crafted many others. Still, Jebe-Barkal was little more than a distant rumor to most D'Angelines, and it was different to hear such things from someone who could say, *Oh yes, I was there.*

They wanted to hear tales of Phèdre and Joscelin, too. Owing to their exploits, it had become somewhat of a fashion among the young gentry to be enamored of one or both of them. At first it set me on edge to hear it, but I grew accustomed to it. In truth, it probably did me some good. It was romantic fancy, nothing more, and I came to accept this.

So I told them those stories, too; not Daršanga, but the others. How Phèdre coerced the Pharaoh of Menekhet into aiding us, how we rowed an entire night across the Lake of Tears, how Joscelin fought single-handedly against the army of Saba.

That one set Colette Trente to sighing. "Is it true he's never taken a lover other than her?" she asked, gazing wistfully at Joscelin. "Man or woman? *Never?*"

I shrugged. "Insofar as I know."

"He's a Cassiline Brother," Marguerite reminded her. "He broke all his vows for Lady Phèdre, and now he's bound not to love anyone else, so long as he lives."

They sighed in unison at the terrible, wonderful romance of it.

"Lucky him," Bertran said.

"Lucky *her*," Julien added.

It made me laugh. I told Joscelin about it later for the sheer amusement of seeing his blank stare in response.

"Name of Elua!" he said. "Why *me*?"

We were sparring in the inner courtyard, and I paused to look at him. Phèdre once said that Joscelin was as careless of his beauty as a spendthrift of his coin, and it was true. It was more than true. Whatever else a childhood spent in the Cassiline Brotherhood did to him, it rendered him almost wholly insensible of his own appearance.

"Because," I said gravely, "you are a figure of great and terrible romance."

Joscelin rolled his eyes. "And you are spending over-much time in the company of foolish young women."

I grinned at him. "Even foolish young women are right sometimes."

Thus passed a pleasant autumn, sliding into winter; and I found myself a different person than I had been a year ago. It is passing strange, what a fluid thing is one's own identity. I did not think mine could change more than it had, from a goatherding ward of the Sanctuary to a barbarian's slave to a Prince of the Blood.

And yet it did.

It was only a year ago that I had been an undersized stripling, shrinking under the news of my mother's disappearance, brooding over Maslin of Lombelon, despising the Queen's Court. Now I was becoming someone new; someone tall for his age and strong with it, able to engage in light banter with friends, envied for his fine spotted horse, his rhinoceros-hide belt, and the stories that accompanied it.

I liked it.

I liked it enough that I forgot, sometimes, it was only a portion of the truth. And then Mavros would catch my eye in the Hall of Games and smile his knowing smile, and I would remember. Or I would see Phèdre with Lady Nicola . . . That happened, once.

It was at a small salon gathering in the L'Envers quarters at the Palace. I knew Joscelin would not be in attendance. And I shouldn't have gone; I didn't intend to go, but I was with Bertran de Trevalion, and he had a mind to coax Raul to join us in the Hall of Games. Because we were who we were, the footman manning the door of the L'Envers quarters admitted us without question.

In truth, it was nothing. A handful of guests lounged on couches in the salon, conversing. And Phèdre was there, kneeling gracefully beside a couch; *abeyante*, they call the pose in the Night Court, except that her head was leant against the Lady Nicola's knee, and I could see Nicola's hand entwined in Phèdre's hair in a caress that was not quite a caress.

"Imri?"

I was already backing away as Phèdre rose, leaving Bertran to make our apologies. Gilot, who was attending me that evening, caught up to me in the hallway outside, putting his hand on my shoulder.

"Are you all right?" he asked.

"I'm fine!" I shook him off. "Elua's Balls, stop being such a nursemaid!"

"Fine," he said dryly. "Stop being such a child." I rounded on him with a glare, clenching my fists. Unimpressed, Gilot crossed his arms. "Well?"

I sighed, unclenching my fists. "It's just . . . never mind."

"You know, Imri, it's no concern of yours," he said.

"They *are* all adults, and they have the right to enjoy one an-other's company without you having tantrums over it." He shrugged at my expression. "What? I'm not stupid, you know. Why does it bother you so?"

"I don't know," I murmured.

"Well, Raul's escorting the Dauphine and the young princess to the theatre," Bertran said cheerfully, emerging into the hallway. "So we're on our own. Why the sudden dash, Imriel? Do you need the privy?"

"He needs to get bedded, is what he needs," Gilot said. "Right and properly bedded."

"Gilot!" I flushed.

"What?" He eyed me. "It would do you a world of good, if you ask me."

"There's a thought!" Bertran fingered the purse at his belt with a rueful expression. "My father's allowance doesn't stretch far enough to cover the Night Court, not unless I have a lucky night in the Hall. But mayhap if we pooled our monies on Imriel's behalf . . . You've not turned sixteen yet, have you? Well, we could go to Night's Doorstep—"

"No!" I cut him off, feeling my face grow warmer. "No Night's Doorstep, no bedding."

There wasn't; not that night, nor any other. We returned to the Hall of Games, where Bertran lost a portion of his fa-ther's allowance at dice, and I mulled over Gilot's words.

It wasn't that I lacked desire.

If anything, I had a surfeit of it. I thought about it all the time. I remember how Phèdre laughed when I asked her if she thought about my Shahrizai kin, about Mavros. *A belly full of a seventeen-year-old's desires.* What were those? She made them sound simple and urgent. And yet I was fifteen, and mine weren't. They were deep and awful. At fifteen, I felt there should be a yearning sweetness, and there wasn't.

I remembered the way Katherine had kissed me in the courtyard, tender and fleeting. It had opened up a pit of *wanting* in me. And in the meadow . . . ah, Elua! I was sick with it.

Betimes the desire was so intense, it seemed to swell my whole body to bursting. Such a vastness seemed out of place in the pleasant, bantering courtship that went on at the Palace; and what I *wanted* was neither tender or sweet, but dark and intense, tinged with the odor of violence and the stagnant-water stench of the zenana. And so I shied from it as a horse will shy at a high fence; and like a spooked horse, I built it higher in my mind.

"I'm not ready," I said to Gilot as we rode home that night. "Not yet."

He looked at me out of the corner of his eye. "Any readier and you'll burst, Imri."

"I'll take that chance," I said.

Gilot shrugged. "As you will."

It was that, as much as anything, that led to my decision regarding the Longest Night. Once again, I was invited to the Queen's fête. It was taken for granted that I would attend this year, not only because I had fallen ill after maintaining Elua's vigil last year. I had grown easier at Court; I had made friends, all of whom would be in attendance. Everyone expected me to go, even Joscelin.

It was at the dinner table that I announced otherwise. "I want to go with you to the Temple of Elua."

Joscelin dropped his fork with a clatter and stared at me. "After last year? No. Oh, no."

Somewhat to my surprise, Phèdre did not refuse me out of hand. Instead, she turned her searching look on me until I squirmed in my chair. Silence stretched and grew around the table. Out of nowhere, unbidden, a vision of her lodged in my head, accompanied by Mavros' voice. *Melisande put a collar around her neck, a velvet collar with a diamond . . .*

"All right," Phèdre said mildly. "But dress warmly."

"Are you out of your mind?" Joscelin asked her.

"No," she said in an absent tone, still looking at me. I had the horrible feeling that she could see the vision in my head. Her brows creased, a little furrow forming between them. "This is what you want, love? How you want to deal with it?"

I nodded fervently.

"Well, then, let him," she said to Joscelin. Her gaze sharpened. "Only this time, don't be a fool about it."

"I'll do my best," he said, fixing me with a wry look. "You *will* say something if you're on the verge of perishing of cold this time?"

"I will," I said. "I promise."

SEVENTEEN

T HIS YEAR'S VIGIL at the Temple of Elua proved less
traumatic. It was long, it was bitterly cold, and at
times, deadly dull. Wearing an extra layer of thick woolen
attire and a heavy, fur-lined cloak, I knelt and shivered beside Joscelin while the City reveled, and this time I gained
no epiphany for my efforts, nor words of prophetic warning. But I survived it with no ill effects, and I left feeling
clear in my thoughts and pleased by my own hard-won self-
discipline.

It had an unexpected effect at Court.

Of course, I had to hear about the marvelous gala I had
missed—the costumes, the dancing, the varying liaisons that
resulted from the Longest Night. It is ever a time of license
in a City not known for its restraint, and in the eyes of my
male friends I was a fool for forsaking the opportunities it
afforded. But in the eyes of the women, what I had done was
a gesture of great and terrible romance.

"I can't imagine!" Marguerite Grosmaine shivered at
the thought of it. "Why do they do it? Why did *you* do it,
Imriel?"

"Cassiel's servants do it to affirm his choice and the sacrifice it entails," I said solemnly. "I do it because I owe my life to Joscelin and to Blessed Elua, whom he serves."

"That's so lovely," murmured Colette Trente. "So noble!"

"So foolish," muttered her brother Julien. "If you ask me."

I shrugged. "I owe a debt."

It was true; and yet I was conscious of using it for my own ends. I saw the way Marguerite looked at me. She had long, red-gold hair. I imagined seeing it fanned across a white pillow, and hearing her ragged breath gasping lewd words in my ear.

"*I* think it's noble, too." She smiled at me, touching my arm.

I gritted my teeth and withdrew from her. "No," I said in a thick voice. "It's not. It's just . . . what is needful."

During the long, dark months of winter, that Longest Night's vigil served as my touchstone. I clung to it; to the discipline of it. When desire surged in me, I put myself there, remembering the frozen ground beneath my knees, and the sight of Joscelin's profile against the stars, his head bowed, serene and meditative.

It got me through the winter.

Then came spring, and the thawing of the earth.

Blessed Elua himself was nurtured in Earth's Womb. He was engendered by the blood of the Yeshuite *mashiach*, Yeshua ben Yosef, and the tears of his lover, Mary of Magdala; the Magdalene. He is the One God's ill-gotten son; but it is Earth herself who brought him to term.

In the spring, the Earth quickened; and I quickened, too.

And I turned sixteen years of age.

I knew somewhat was afoot. There are no secrets in a small household; and when all was said and done, House Montrève was that. I heard the talk and laughter among the men-at-arms as they debated, and Gilot arguing strongly among them. But I did not know what they had decided, and I was afraid to ask.

In the end, it was Phèdre who told me. She summoned me to her study on the eve of my natality. "Do you know what they're planning?" she asked without preamble.

My lips had gone dry, and I licked them. "Something to do with the Night Court."

"It's a rite of passage among young D'Angeline noblemen." Her tone was neutral. "Staging a mock abduction with all a young lord's friends, and hauling him off to taste the pleasures of the Court of Night-Blooming Flowers."

"Oh," I said.

"Somehow, the women seem to manage with less fanfare." Phèdre smiled slightly. "Imri, if the notion pleases you, I won't speak against it. I'm sure your friends would think it a grand lark. They're young and heedless enough to give little thought to what memories it might evoke. But if you are uneasy at it, I will see it goes no further."

"What . . ." I cleared my throat. "Which House?"

"Which House would you choose?" she asked, curious. "They're like to make the choice for you if you can't say."

"I don't know." I looked away. "I don't think . . . I don't think I want this." I did and I didn't, and it made a sickening knot of desire and revulsion in my belly. When I imagined my friends and the Montrèvan men-at-arms around me, laughing and jesting as they accompanied me to Mont Nuit, the revulsion grew stronger. I didn't know which would be worse: the mock abduction, the agonizing indecision, or the terribly public nature of it all. "Not like this."

"How, then?" Phèdre asked gently.

"I don't know!" The words burst from me. "I want . . . oh, Blessed Elua, I *want*, but I don't *know* how! It's all mixed up, and it keeps getting bigger, and I don't know how to sort it out!" I was on my feet, pacing the length of her study in a fit of agitated misery. "And I don't even know how to talk about it, or who to talk to! Mavros thinks he understands, but he doesn't, not this, not"—I swallowed—"Daršanga. And you . . . you . . ." I shook my head, unable to explain. "You, I can't—"

"Imriel." Reaching into the purse at her belt, Phèdre withdrew a small ivory disk. "Here," she said, tossing it to me.

I caught it by reflex and stared foolishly at it. It bore the image of a flowering plant in raised relief, and nothing more. The plant looked vaguely familiar; I thought I might have seen it growing in Richeline Friote's herb garden.

"What is it?" I asked at length.

"It's a token for Balm House," she said.

"Balm House?" I echoed.

Phèdre nodded. "If it's your will to use it, then speak to Hugues before the end of the Queen's fête tomorrow. He will escort you, and Joscelin will ensure that the others plan no mischief."

"All right." I closed my hand around the token. It felt cool and smooth. I knew little of Balm House, save that it was a house of healing and Eugènie's niece Clory had studied the art of massage there. "Why . . . why Balm House?"

She smiled, and for a moment I thought she would remind me again that she carried the Name of God in her thoughts. But instead, she said, "I do have some experience in these matters, love."

"I know." The coiled anxiety in my belly had eased. "Thank you, I think."

The day of my natality dawned cool and bright. I felt strange unto myself. I had crossed an invisible threshold on this day, and it might be that I would cross another ere it ended; a visible, very tangible threshold. I felt at the ivory token in my purse, wondering if I dared use it, thinking about Phèdre's choice. Was I so broken that I was in need of healing?

Yes, I thought; mayhap I am.

What they would do there, I couldn't imagine. I had watched Clory at work many times. Not lately, because . . . well. But Clory was not Naamah's Servant, she had only studied to learn massage. What I wanted was far more than any mere massage. I thought about the *Trois Milles Joies*, much of which I had endeavored to commit to memory. It spoke much of pleasure, but little of healing.

As she had done last year, the Queen held a fête in my honor. It was a little larger with my new friends in attendance, and there was music and dancing afterward. I danced with Alais, feeling guilty for having neglected her.

"Are they going to do the abduction, Imri?" she asked me.

"What?" I held her at arm's length. "You know about that?"

"Of course. It's only boys who aren't told." She looked up at me. "Well, are they?"

"No," I said. "No abduction."

"Oh." She sounded disappointed. "I was looking forward to seeing you fight them."

I laughed. "It's not that kind of abduction, villain."

"I know," she said, considering. "But you might have made it so."

I started to laugh again, then stopped and thought about it. I had been abducted once in earnest. What my own reaction to this nobleman's game would have been if I'd truly been caught unwitting, I could not say. Phèdre was right, my friends were heedless in their youthful folly; and my little cousin was nearly as clever as Phèdre. "You're awfully smart, Alais."

"I know," she said complacently.

After our dance, I sought out Hugues. He was talking with Ti-Philippe, but he turned away the moment he saw me. I fished the Balm House token out of my purse and showed it to him, and he merely nodded. Phèdre had chosen him wisely. I remembered how he had silenced the others on the way to Lombelon when their talk of the Night Court began to make me uncomfortable. Out of all Montrève's household, he had the kindest heart.

The remainder of the affair passed in a blur. I endured sly looks from Bertran and Julien, and Gilot and the others; and I watched them fade in resigned disappointment as Joscelin circulated, speaking quietly to them. Somewhat to my surprise, Mavros did not appear to be among my would-be abductors. He shook his head when Joscelin spoke to him, his expression unchanged. Then again, he knew me better than the others. I was easier in their company than I was in his, but I had never opened my heart to them, and they had no skill to see inside it.

I wonder, sometimes, what it would be like to have a true friend—one I could speak to openly and without fear, or strange undercurrents of tension. I was friendly with Gilot, but it wasn't quite the same. In truth, Alais was probably the nearest thing I had . . . but there are certain things one cannot speak of to an eleven-year-old girl.

Like tonight.

The fête ended at a reasonable hour. I made my thanks and farewells, and in the flurry of activity as the footmen hurried about fetching cloaks and summoning coaches, Hugues tapped me on the shoulder, Ti-Philippe beside him.

"Our horses are saddled and waiting," he murmured.

"You, too?" I said to Ti-Philippe.

"Joscelin's orders. A two-guard minimum." He smiled. "He'll come himself, if you'd rather."

"No," I said slowly. "He's not overly fond of the Night Court, I think."

"True," said Hugues. "Let's go."

Under cover of darkness, we slipped away from the Palace and rode through the City toward Night's Doorstep. The Bastard huffed and snorted beneath me, arching his neck and picking up his hooves in an odd prancing gait. Anxiety had returned to settle in my belly, and I wondered if he felt it. As though to alleviate it, Hugues sang aloud as we rode, an old Siovalese ballad about a shepherd lad who loved Blessed Elua for a brief time, until Elua left him, wandering across Terre d'Ange.

You will find it and lose it, again and again . . .

It was cold and clear that night; almost wintry, except for the moist odor of spring in the air, rising in a mist from the damp, quickening soil. The inns and wineshops of Night's Doorstep were doing a rollicking business, but it took place behind closed doors and sealed windows, leaving the streets relatively quiet.

"Mont Nuit." At the base of the hill, Hugues breathed the name. "Ready, Imri?"

I nodded. "I'm ready."

We passed other parties leaving as we arrived; riders and coaches, some of them unmarked. Ti-Philippe exchanged good-natured greetings with several of them, and I found myself glad he was there. He was Phèdre nó Delaunay's chevalier, and no one thought it strange to find him on Mont Nuit. For my part, I kept my head low, gazing at my hands on the reins.

All of the Thirteen Houses had their estates on Mont

Nuit, and all of them were splendid in different ways. Each estate was gated and fenced, with the insignia of the House rendered on the gates. Cereus House, first and oldest, sat atop the hill's crest. The others lay lower. We reached Balm House before I had a chance to see the place where Phèdre spent her childhood. The insignia on the gates matched the relief on my ivory token.

"Here we are," Ti-Philippe said softly.

There was a gatekeeper. Behind bars of wrought iron, he bowed to us. "What seek you, my lords?"

I showed him the token. "Healing."

He bowed again, deeply. "Then find it," he said, opening the gates.

We rode up to the courtyard of Balm House. It was a pleasant place, low and sprawling. The air smelled green and good, like Richeline's herb garden. Ostlers descended on us, solicitous and friendly, taking our horses to be stabled and directing us to the main door. I found my feet faltering.

Hugues nudged me. "Go on, Imriel."

The door of Balm House opened, spilling a square of lamplight. There was a figure silhouetted in it; a woman's figure, broad-hipped and solid.

"Young highness," she said in a grave voice. "I am Nathalie nó Balm, the Dowayne of this House. Be welcome here, you and your men."

I took a deep breath and entered. "Thank you."

She looked like a mother; or someone's mother. Not mine, surely. There was somewhat in her presence and her manner that eased me. "So," she said, smiling at me, ushering us into the foyer, where servants in the livery of Balm House bowed and took our cloaks. "You seek healing here."

I held out my hand with the token on it. "Phèdre sent me."

The Dowayne Nathalie took it from me, her eyes crinkling. "Yes, I know. We have spoken. Phèdre nó Delaunay de Montrève is wise in Naamah's ways, and you are wise to trust to her wisdom. Will you trust to mine?"

I hesitated. "How so, my lady?"

"Ah." She steepled her fingers and touched her lips. "Come and see."

She led us into the reception salon. It was a vast space, but it was arranged on an intimate scale, divided by carved screens which formed a number of smaller spaces. There were clusters of couches, with hanging oil lamps casting a warm glow above them. Everywhere, potted plants grew, lending an herbal fragrance to the air and mingling with the scent of beeswax candles. In the center of the room, a small fountain trickled gently, and somewhere a flautist was playing, low and sweet. A handful of patrons were arrayed on the couches, conversing with graceful adepts. Apprentices circulated with wine jugs and trays of cordial, quiet and unobtrusive.

"A peaceful place," Ti-Philippe observed. "Very pleasant, my lady."

"My thanks, chevalier." The Dowayne inclined her head to him, then turned to me. "Balm House is not like other houses. If it is your wish, I will arrange a showing of those adepts available and willing to serve you. But if you permit, I will use my own judgment, and choose." Her smile deepened. "And thus do I judge, young highness. A woman, not a man; although there might be healing there, too, it is too soon and not what you seek. A woman, a young woman, close to your own age, but far enough from it to impart a wisdom of her own."

"All right," I said. "Yes." My mouth had gone dry again, but I steeled myself against it, reading her face. "You've already chosen, haven't you?"

"You see much." She touched my cheek with surprising tenderness, and her gaze was gentle. "Is it through your mother's blood, or your foster-mother's training?"

"Both," I whispered.

"Poor lad," murmured the Dowayne Nathalie. "It's a hard burden to bear."

Caught between empathy and desire, I merely nodded.

The Dowayne rang a small silver bell that hung from her belt. Its tinkling chime was scarce audible above the murmur of conversation and the sound of fountain and flute, but an apprentice was there in an instant. "Please summon Emmeline," the Dowayne said. The apprentice bowed, and the Dowayne indicated a nearby cluster of couches. "I pray you, sit and refresh yourselves."

I was too nervous to remain seated. Within a few moments, the adept Emmeline arrived. She was some twenty years of age, tall and slender, with solemn grey eyes and lovely features. Her hair was the color of Katherine Friote's, a honeyed brown, spilling like silk over her shoulders.

"Welcome, Prince Imriel," she said gravely, curtsying. "I am Emmeline."

"Have I gauged you well, young highness?" Nathalie nó Balm asked shrewdly, appearing at her side.

I stared at Emmeline and nodded. "Well met," I said to her, feeling awkward. "I'm . . . well, yes. Imriel. Which you already knew."

"Indeed, it is my honor, your highness." She smiled at me. It was one of those smiles wholly without guile, that make one feel as though the sun had broken through the clouds, and I found myself smiling in return.

"The Comtesse has taken care of all arrangements," the Dowayne said. "If you are well pleased, then go and find the healing you seek. Your men will be well attended and there are quarters where they may seek repose, should the hour grow late."

I glanced at Hugues and Ti-Philippe.

"Well?" Ti-Philippe smiled, not unkindly. "Go on, then."

I glanced at Emmeline.

"Come," she said simply, holding out her hand. I took it and let her lead me through the salon. A few patrons looked up as we passed, and I found myself ducking my head to hide my features. My heart was beating as hard as though I'd run a race. After the salon, we passed through a series of halls, where we encountered no one, to Emmeline's room itself. There she closed the door behind us.

Like everywhere else in Balm House, it was pleasant: large and spacious, with fretted lamps casting intricate shadows on the walls. A charcoal brazier warmed the air. The bed was vast, piled high with white pillows and hung about with sheer curtains. I tried not to stare at it.

"Imriel." Emmeline still held my hand. Now she turned it over, bowing her head and tracing a line over my palm and the inside of my wrist with one fingertip. Surely she could feel my pulse racing. I swallowed hard. We were standing so close, I could smell the faint scent she wore, a light perfume with notes of citrus.

"Yes?" I said hoarsely.

"Imriel nó Montrève de la Courcel." Raising her head, Emmeline looked into my eyes. We were almost of a height. "Understand, there are desires in your blood that will not find fulfillment here tonight."

It was at once a disappointment and a relief to hear it said. I nodded, preparing to clamp down on my ardor with an iron will. "I understand," I said grimly.

"No." She gave me that brief sunburst of a smile. "You

don't, not yet. It is a gift I wish to give you; Naamah's gift.
But there is a gift I ask in return."

"A patron-gift?" I said stupidly.

Emmeline shook her head. "Your trust," she said softly.
"Already, you have given it twice this evening; to Phèdre nó
Delaunay and to the Dowayne. I ask you to give it a third
time; to trust yourself, and to trust me to guide you in this.
It is only for a little while, for this charmed space of time.
And I swear to you, I will hold it in Naamah's keeping. No
harm will come to you, only good."

Unexpected tears stung my eyes. "'Tis hard to do, my
lady!"

"I know," she said gently.

I drew a harsh, ragged breath. This was neither the scene
of tender romance nor torturous passion I had envisioned.
"What must I do?"

"Be still," Emmeline murmured, "and *trust*." She laid
one hand on my breast, splaying her fingers over my hard-
beating heart and gazing into my eyes. The air in the room
seemed to thicken, and I felt the presence of something—
Naamah, or Blessed Elua himself—hover over us. "Can
you do that?"

"I think so," I whispered. "I will try."

"Good," she whispered in reply. "It is all any of us can
ask."

And there, in that room of fretted shadows, Emmeline of
Balm House stripped me bare. She did it slowly, with an
adept's grace. Her delicate fingers undid the buttons on my
velvet doublet, and she removed it with care. She teased my
silk shirt loose from my breeches, sliding her hands beneath
it. I hissed as she eased it over my head, her hands sliding
along my ribs, over my shoulders. Her touch was gentle and

warm, not yet meant to arouse. It might have been soothing were I not strung tighter than a harp-string.

"This is sacred, Imriel." Her fingers, dipped in scented oil, anointed my chest, tracing a line toward my navel. "You; all of you. Do you understand?"

I stood, shuddering like a fly-stung horse while she moved around me. "Yes," I said helplessly. "Yes."

Emmeline's fingers found the weal-marks on my lower back, the faded scars of Daršanga. "Oh," I heard her murmur, and then I felt the touch of her soft lips, and the tip of her tongue tracing them, learning them. "And this, too."

Something knotted deep within me began to ease, almost painfully. My body began to respond to her touch. I unclenched my fists and gazed at the flickering lamps.

"There is no part of you that is not sacred." Emmeline rose before me, her hands sliding over my oil-slick breast. "And there is no shame here, only love. This is a benediction. Do you understand?"

"I am beginning to," I said, breathless.

She laughed. "Ah, Elua!" Her pupils were dilated. "You *are* a beautiful boy!"

I swallowed. "There is more."

I didn't want to have to explain; and I didn't need to. Emmeline nodded. She sank to kneel on her heels, removing my boots and undoing my breeches. My phallus, freed, sprang erect, straining. She anointed me with oil, murmuring a blessing. At the touch of her lips, I gritted my teeth and stared at the ceiling.

"This."

Emmeline's fingers found the brand on my left buttock; Jagun's brand. I looked down at her, seeing tears in her wide grey eyes.

"Oh, my love," she whispered. "Oh yes, this, too."

I started crying when she kissed it; and once I started, I could not stop. I wept as she led me to the bed, that big vast bed with all its white pillows. And there I lay and watched, tears trickling from the corners of my eyes, as she stripped off her silken gown, bare skin gleaming in the lamplight, and came to straddle me.

"Here," she murmured, grasping my phallus, guiding the tip to her hidden aperture. I could feel it parting her inner lips, dewy-moist, emanating heat. "Here, there is healing and Naamah's grace."

She lowered herself, and I gasped. Inside, her flesh was as slick and hot as blood, and as soft as silk. It was more intimate than anything I could have imagined.

Inch by slow inch, she sank down onto me.

Ah, Elua! I was sheathed in her to the hilt, and it was heaven.

"Is it not so?" Emmeline asked softly.

"Yes," I whispered through my tears. "I understand."

And suddenly, there was tenderness and ardor, too. Emmeline leaned forward, her hair falling to curtain our faces. She kissed me; kissed away my tears, kissed my tear-swollen lids, kissed my lips. Her hips moved, only a little. If it had been more, I couldn't have stood it. I took her face in my hands and kissed her back, sinking my fingers deep into her shining hair. Her lips were soft, so soft. They parted beneath mine, and I felt the tip of her tongue touch my own. It was so lovely and sweet, I could have wept anew.

Is it possible to fall upward? It seemed it to me. Lying on my back, I fell upward into Emmeline; into her mouth, into her. Every part of me she had touched and made sacred blazed with a desire that was Naamah's gift, clean and pure, untouched by any shadow. I offered it back as tribute, and she accepted it with gladness.

Toward the end, everything gathered. Emmeline let out a gasp, lifting her head. I held her hips hard as she rode me, seeing for the first time the way a woman's face changes with pleasure, going soft and abandoned. It was impossibly beautiful.

With a sense of awe, I felt her inner walls ripple and flutter. Ah, Elua! It was too much to bear. I wanted the moment to last, I wanted to gaze at her face and fix it in my memory, but everything gathered. I was falling, falling so fast. Her face, the lamplight; everything blurred. I gave up and closed my eyes, letting myself fall.

"This, too," I heard her whisper. "This, too, is sacred."

Groaning aloud, I spent myself like a shooting star.

It seemed to go on forever. All the vast desire in my body was concentrated in my aching loins; my throbbing phallus and testes. A year's worth of awful, complicated longing was released in a surge of seed, and Emmeline rode the crest of my desire as a ship rides a tall wave.

But at last, it ebbed. I returned to myself enough to hear the harsh sound of my own breathing, its frantic pace slowing. I felt the tickle of her hair against my face and opened my eyes to see her face, her grey eyes shining with tears.

"You have given me a gift," she said. "Thank you."

"No." I touched her eyelashes. "You have." I paused. "Am I still crying?"

Emmeline smiled. "A little bit." She brushed away a tear with the ball of her thumb. "I don't mind."

She moved off of me, then. There was a fleeting sense of loss as my limp phallus slipped from her warm recesses. I turned my head on the pillow to gaze at Emmeline as she reclined beside me, propped on one arm. I felt strangely at peace, languid and good.

"My beautiful boy," she whispered, sliding one thigh over

mine and tracing my lower lip with one fingertip. "It must have been bad."

"It was," I said simply. "How did you know?"

Her smile deepened. "It's my calling."

The night did not end there. After having lanced the poisonous wound of my desire, Emmeline showed me such things as I wished to learn; things I had read about in the *Trois Milles Joies*. I learned. As the Dowayne had said, Emmeline was near my age, but old enough to impart a wisdom of her own. I learned how to kiss properly, with all the niceties and subtleties. I held her breasts in my hands, marveling at the wonderful heft of them, and felt her nipples harden beneath my touch. I learned how to adore them with lips and tongue, teasing and suckling, until I exerted the pressure that pleased her most.

And I learned her innermost parts.

Emmeline showed me without shame, leaning against the pillows and opening her thighs. She spread her outer lips with her fingers, and then the inner, revealing Naamah's Pearl.

"There," she said, sighing as I made reverence to it. "Oh, yes!"

She taught me myself, too. It was true, there was no part that was not sacred. I caught my breath when she performed the *languisement*, one hand grasping my shaft, the other easing back my foreskin to expose the sensitive glans. I cried aloud as her mouth descended on me, one hand sliding beneath me to cup the sac of my testes.

"It is *all* sacred, Imriel," she murmured before proceeding.

It was. All of it was. And these things I had known in my head and heart, I learned in my flesh that night. When I fell asleep at last, my head pillowed on Emmeline's breast, it was the sleep of true exhaustion. Emotionally and physically, I was replete.

I slept soundly and without dreams, waking at dawn. Balm House was quiet. I stooped over the bed, watching Emmeline's eyelids crease as the sun's first rays slanted through her room's garden window, laying a ruddy coverlet on the bed.

"Thank you," I whispered. "I thank you so much."

"Beautiful boy." She stirred and touched my face. "Will you remember this?"

"Always," I said. "Always, and with joy."

Emmeline smiled. She was as beautiful in the morning as she had been the night before. Before I left, she rang for a servant, who came to fill the washbasin with steaming water. She bathed me herself, sponging away the oil with which she had anointed me and the dried traces of our lovemaking that lingered on my skin. The soap had the same light fragrance as her perfume.

On her nightstand was a sculpture carved of gleaming wood, depicting a pair of cupped hands; Naamah's Hands. I placed a purse of coin in it, my patron-gift. I wished I had something more personal to give her, a keepsake of some sort.

"I'll come back to see you again," I promised.

"You may," she said, stroking my cheek. "I will always welcome you gladly, Imriel. But I think you have found what you sought here."

It was true. If I had felt strange to myself yesterday, it was nothing to what I felt this morning. Emmeline escorted me to the reception salon where Ti-Philippe and Hugues had already been summoned. They were waiting, yawning and sleepy-eyed. I wondered if I looked different to them. Surely, I felt different.

"Good-bye, my beautiful boy," Emmeline said, giving me a farewell kiss.

"Good-bye," I whispered.

Outside, the sky was growing brighter. I stood in the courtyard, listening to birdsong, while the ostlers brought our mounts. The Bastard's spotted hide was vivid in the dawn light. He snorted as I mounted, but was otherwise docile. I swung astride him and settled myself in the saddle, feeling a heightened awareness of my body. I have known a woman since last I did this, I thought.

The world seemed very beautiful today.

We were halfway down Mont Nuit before either Ti-Philippe or Hugues spoke of it. It was Ti-Philippe who gave me a sidelong glance. "So," he said. "Riding with our head held high today, are we?"

I laughed. "Am I?"

"You are." Hugues smiled at me. "Well done, Imri."

"Yes," I said. "It was."

EIGHTEEN

AFTER MY VISIT to Balm House, I was at peace with myself for the first time in many months. Word had gotten out, of course, and there were knowing looks to be endured, but I found they did not trouble me.

"Thank you," I said to Phèdre. "You chose rightly."

"Good," she said simply. "I thought so."

I grinned at her. "You weren't *sure*?"

Phèdre raised her brows. "In matters of love, nothing is certain."

I thanked Joscelin, too, for his role in quelling my would-be abductors. He merely nodded, then asked cautiously, "So you were pleased with your evening?"

"Yes." I hesitated, then asked him. "Joscelin, have you never wondered?"

"About the Night Court?" he said.

I shrugged. "About the Night Court, or anything. Anyone. Others."

"Of course." Joscelin laughed at my startled expression. "Imri, I *am* human. It's just . . ." He shook his head, searching for words. "I was a middle son, and my family keeps the old traditions. I grew up knowing I was meant for Cassiel's service. In my father's household, one's word of honor was a sacred bond. When I swore my oath to the Cassiline Brotherhood, I meant it, every part."

"But you broke it," I murmured.

"I fell in love," he said quietly. "Yes. And I will not dishonor my vows for aught less."

"How did you know?" I asked. "When?"

Joscelin frowned. We were cleaning our gear together, oiling the leather straps and polishing metal bits. "It was in Skaldia," he said. "I'm not sure exactly when. Mayhap when Phèdre crawled into the rafters to spy on Selig's plans. Or mayhap it was when she cursed me for giving up hope." Remembering, he smiled slightly. "She threatened to write to the Prefect of the Brotherhood and tell him Blessed Elua was better served by an adept of the Night Court than a Cassiline priest."

"She did?" I asked, half-enthralled and half-horrified.

"Oh, yes." He laughed. "And somewhere in there, I realized that I would willingly lay down my life and die in the service of such glorious, foolish, improbable courage, although it took a good deal longer for me to realize what it meant. Why?" Joscelin asked belatedly, frowning. "Do you fancy yourself in love?"

"No," I said honestly. "I just wondered."

Laying down the tangled straps of his baldric, Joscelin touched the back of my hand. "I'm a poor model for you, I know. I'm sorry, Imri. I can only be what I am. But I am pleased for you, truly."

I hugged him then, hard and fierce. "Thank you," I whispered. "And it's not true. You are the best model there ever was, ever."

"You're welcome," Joscelin said, bemused.

I thought a great deal about love in those days; and a great deal about lovemaking. Over and over again, I relived my night with Emmeline, poring over every detail of it. The awful desire that plagued me was not gone, but it had changed. I knew myself to be capable of giving and receiving pleasure; Naamah's gift in its purest form. The hurdle I'd built in my mind was nowhere near as high or vast as I'd imagined it, and the terrible uncertainty of sheer inexperience was gone. I still had desires I was unready to confront, but I wasn't scared of the act of love itself anymore.

This, too, is sacred.

If nothing else had changed, I might have flung myself into the Game of Courtship. At sixteen, I had reached the age where it began in earnest, and although I could not envision marriage, I could well envision the rituals of courtship and the pairings that accompanied it. But that spring brought another change, borne across the Straits on the Cruarch's flagship.

It brought Eamonn mac Grainne.

I had nearly forgotten Drustan's request, made almost a year ago. When Phèdre made mention of it, I found myself torn between curiosity and annoyance. I wondered what he would be like, this Prince of the Dalriada whose mother had fought like a tigress on the battlefield, all the while carrying him in her womb. At the same time, I dreaded the thought of bringing a stranger into our midst when I was at ease with myself and the world.

Still, it was a matter of honor, and I meant to welcome him with all due courtesy. There would be time to take this Eamonn's measure before he became a part of our household. Our departure for Montrève would be delayed until Admiral Rousse returned from a posting to Illyria some weeks hence, and until that time, Eamonn would be Ysandre's guest at Court.

The Cruarch's reception at the gates of the City was lavish this year. Ysandre meant to demonstrate that Terre d'Ange had not forgotten its debt of gratitude to the Dalriada. Unfortunately, the weather was foul, spitting down a cold rain. Hordes of D'Angelines milled about shivering, festive spring attire plastered to their skin. A squadron of the Royal Army stood at attention, rain dripping from their parade armor. Barquiel L'Envers, commanding them, bore a look of profound distaste, which I found heartening.

Usually, the Alban contingent looked splendid, riding bare-chested beneath their cloaks, displaying their intricate woad tattoos, silver torcs flashing at their throats. Today they were huddled under their cloaks, hoods drawn tight, looking sodden and miserable.

All except two.

One was Drustan mab Necthana, who knew the importance of making a kingly impression. He sat upright in the saddle, hood thrown back, already searching to meet his wife's gaze. And the other . . .

"That must be Eamonn," Phèdre murmured.

I would have known him at a guess. Among the dark Cruithne, he shone like a torch, half a head taller than the rest of the company. Rain beaded on his bright coppery hair and cascaded from his broad shoulders. He didn't seem to notice, gazing around him with frank delight. When the herald bawled his name after Drustan's, he flashed a wide grin.

They made their way through the gates and the formal greetings were exchanged. Ysandre made a pretty speech welcoming Eamonn mac Grainne, and then introduced the members of her household.

"Well met, Prince Eamonn," I said to him when it came my turn, leaning over in the saddle and extending my hand.

"Ah, yes!" He clasped my forearm hard; a warrior's grip.

His grin broadened, and I found myself returning it. "Well met to you, Prince Imriel!"

I found myself liking him.

I could not help it; there was something infectious about his joy. If I suffered from a lack of it, this Eamonn appeared to have a surfeit of it. And he was utterly heedless of its effect. I watched him greet Duc Barquiel with the same cheerful enthusiasm. It took Barquiel L'Envers aback, and that, too, cheered my heart. His D'Angeline was faulty, uttered with a peculiar lilt; Eamonn could not have cared less. Sidonie regarded him with mild shock, and Alais with alert interest.

When he met Phèdre, he insisted on dismounting, going to one knee and kissing her hand. "Dagda Mor!" he exclaimed. "Now I see why the Dalriada went to war."

Phèdre laughed. "It was a long time ago, your highness."

"Ah, no." Climbing to his feet, Eamonn grinned at her. At close range, one could see his resemblance to Quintilius Rousse—the broad, rugged features that were at once homely and handsome. "Surely that must be a bard's lie, lady!"

We rode in procession to the Palace, while the chilled folk lining the streets cheered and attempted to throw rain-soaked flower petals that clung damply to their hands or fell limp on the cobblestones. Eamonn stared around him in openmouthed wonder. I found myself riding beside him, and he turned to me. "This city . . . It's so big! All the houses!"

"You don't have cities in Alba and Eire?" I asked.

He shook his head. "Not like this."

Somewhere behind me, I heard the word *barbarian* muttered. I turned around to meet Barquiel L'Envers' bland expression.

"It was the Tiberians who began it," I said to Eamonn.

"You put up a better fight than we did. They were building cities and roads in Terre d'Ange while the Cruithne were driving them back across the Straits."

It was true. It was also true that after the fall of Tiberium and the advent of Blessed Elua, the Master of the Straits had rendered Alba and Eire isolated for eight centuries, while D'Angeline civilization had flourished.

"Oh, we're great fighters, we are!" Eamonn agreed cheerfully. He patted the sword-hilt at his side and gave me a sidelong glance. His eyes were grey-green, and there was a trace of shrewdness in their mirth. "You don't wear a blade. Do you not fancy a good fight?"

I smiled. "It's not customary to carry a sword until one comes of age. But I know how to use one."

"He's the warrior, is he not?" He nodded toward Joscelin, who was riding nearby, ignoring the rain with his usual impervious Cassiline disdain. "The one they speak of."

"He is," I said. Whoever *they* were, it seemed a fair likelihood.

Eamonn scratched his chin. "Hard to reckon, pretty folk like you," he said in a dubious tone. "Do you think he might give me a bout?"

"He might," I said, adding, "and if he won't, I will."

Eamonn laughed aloud, though there was no malice in it. "Ah, boy! No offense to you, but I'd break you in two."

I sized him up. He had the advantage of height and reach on me—indeed, strapping as he was, he had the advantage of Joscelin—but I was willing to bet he didn't have the speed. "Care to wager?"

"Oh, aye." He grinned lazily. "That's a fine horse you ride."

"Not the horse," I said in alarm.

He laughed. "The crow's bigger than the cock, is it?"

I gritted my teeth, suddenly aware of Barquiel L'Envers' mocking gaze at my back. Eamonn's voice carried; surely he had heard the exchange. "All right, then," I said slowly. "The Bastard . . . my horse . . . against your torc."

"This?" Eamonn's eyes narrowed. He fingered the necklace that circled his throat, an intricate gold cable. "It is a sign of who I am. My lady mother set it around my neck with her own hands."

I raised my brows. "You spoke of cocks and crows?"

He paused, then loosed another full-throated laugh. "Dagda Mor! You have ballocks, Prince Imriel." Leaning over, he slapped me on the shoulder with enough force to make me regret my offer. "It is a wager."

So it was settled.

We made our way to the Palace, where Eamonn mac Grainne was installed as a guest to the appalled delight of the Court. It wasn't until afterward that I confessed to Phèdre and Joscelin what I had done.

"You *what*?" Phèdre was dismayed. "Imri, that's no way to treat a royal guest."

"He wanted to!" I said, defending myself.

"Phèdre." Joscelin was trying not to laugh. "He's a young man. That's what they do."

"Yes, and it's foolish and unnecessary!" she said, adding to me, "And it's a discourtesy, too, wagering that horse in a bet. It was a gift of state from the House of Aragon."

I already felt remorse over letting myself be goaded into risking the Bastard, and her words pricked me. "You're only saying that because of Nicola," I retorted.

Phèdre drew a sharp breath, then let it out in a sigh, throwing up her hands in surrender. "I leave this to your auspices," she said to Joscelin. "Since it is *men's* business."

He gave her his Cassiline bow, nearly sober-faced. "And

I shall handle it accordingly, love." When she had gone, he turned back to me.

"Well?" I asked, still defensive.

"Oh, you're in trouble," Joscelin said, grinning openly. "He's a big lad, and I've seen the Dalriada fight. They're fierce, all right, and handy with a blade. You've come a long way in your training, Imri, but even I've lost on occasion. Remember what I told you about Waldemar Selig?"

"Am I going to lose the Bastard?" The thought made me feel awful.

"Mayhap." His expression softened. "There's nothing wrong with being proud of hard-won skills, Imriel; but it is a mistake to be ruled by pride. It's a hard lesson to learn. Believe me, I know."

"How did you learn it?" I asked in a small voice.

"I had a cursed *anguissette* inform me that Blessed Elua was better served by a courtesan than a Cassiline Brother," Joscelin said dryly. "And it was true." He tousled my hair. "Come on, let's spar. You're going to need the practice."

It was my hope that our wager would remain a private thing; one, perhaps, that could be played out at Montrève. It was a vain hope. Eamonn had spoken openly of it at Court; and why not? He had no way of knowing it would be received as a novelty. Outside of martial Camlach and the training-fields of the Cassiline Brotherhood, noble-born D'Angelines seldom dueled with one another for sport.

Certainly not at Court, where grudges were played out by seducing one another's lovers or circulating cutting poems.

So the story got about, and nothing would do but that it be made into the centerpiece of a fête. I daresay Ysandre was no more pleased about it than Phèdre, but she acquiesced to the Court's eagerness for spectacle. And, too, there was a symbolic component to it. I was a Prince of the Blood, the only pure-blooded D'Angeline scion of House Courcel. Like her own daughters, Eamonn mac Grainne was of mixed heritage.

Betimes I wondered who the Queen wished to see victorious.

A date for our bout was fixed. It was to take place on the Palace grounds, followed by a picnic on the greensward. I found myself hoping for rain, but no; the day dawned fair and bright, promising a hint of warmth. There would be no delay.

For the first time since Balm House, dread made a lump in my belly. I curried the Bastard myself that morning. He was in high spirits, eager and restless. On the ride to the Palace, the lump in my belly made its way to my throat. "I'm sorry," I whispered, leaning forward in the saddle. His spotted ears flicked backward in response. "I'm so sorry."

Phèdre glanced at me and shook her head.

There was a considerable crowd assembled on the greensward: almost all the young gentry, and the Queen and Cruarch themselves. The grounds had been made festive, with a dais and chairs for select guests. Cheers greeted us as I rode the Bastard onto the field, where he would be held as my stake in the wager. He pricked his ears and pranced as though on parade.

"Cousin!" Mavros Shahrizai hailed me. He crossed over to us with his easy feline grace and put one hand on the Bastard's bridle, a glint of amusement in his dark blue gaze. "As a kinsman, I'd be honored to hold him for you."

"My thanks," I said glumly, dismounting.

"Not at all." He looked curiously at me. "Any chance you'll win?"

"A very slight one." I eyed him. "Did you place a wager on me?"

He pursed his lips. "Not exactly."

"Thanks," I said. "I appreciate the nod of confidence."

Mavros shrugged. "Look, Imri, I've seen you spar with Joscelin and I'd back you against Bertran or Julien or any of that lot. But you're not a real Cassiline, and the Dalriada learn to fight as soon as they're weaned." He glanced over at Eamonn, who was conversing animatedly with Marguerite Grosmaine. "He's already killed two men, did you know? Some tribal spat or other."

"I killed a man once," I said.

"You did?" Mavros shot me a startled look. "When?"

"When I was ten." It was true, too; or almost. I stabbed Fadil Chouma, the Menekhetan slaver who bought me from the Carthaginians, in the thigh with a carving knife. Phèdre told me in the zenana that the wound took septic later, and he died of it. "Anyway, it doesn't matter. We're using wooden blades, not real ones."

"Yes," Mavros said thoughtfully. "Prince Eamonn was most disappointed."

Indeed, he greeted me with it.

"Prince Imriel!" Eamonn called in his Eiran lilt. "I thought we were to have a bout!" He glanced at the wooden sword in his hand, coppery brows knitting in perplexity. "These are children's toys. How are we to have a proper fight?"

"I'm already risking my horse!" I said in exasperation. "Do you want to take my head as well?"

"Ah, no!" His eyes widened. "Not on *purpose*."

In the end, Drustan intervened, explaining to Eamonn in the Eiran tongue—which I nearly understood, it being a dialect of Cruithne—that Queen Ysandre did not take kindly to the notion of either her kinsman's or her guest's blood being shed for sport.

Resigned, Eamonn shrugged. "Well, then," he said, removing his gold torc and giving it unto Drustan's keeping. "I will honor my wager with children's toys."

It was, I thought, an unfair assessment. A fine pair of practice-blades had been commissioned for the occasion, carved of solid walnut with gilt inlay on the carved hilts. A pair of wooden bucklers had been provided, too. Eamonn's was painted green and bore the device of a white horse; mine was blue, with the silver swan of House Courcel. He slid his left forearm through his shield's straps, testing the heft of it. I ignored mine.

"No shield?" His brows arched pointedly.

I shook my head, checking the buckles of my vambraces. They weren't real ones, but were made of boiled leather, thick and sturdy. I wore them when Joscelin and I sparred, and the leather was scuffed and scarred.

"Ah." Eamonn glanced over at Joscelin, comprehension dawning. "He has trained you, your foster-father? Perhaps this will be fun after all!"

It took some time before everyone was settled to their satisfaction: members of the royal family, their kin and valued friends seated; others grouped around in a loose circle, jostling for the best view. Mavros stood off to one side, holding the Bastard's reins. He jingled his purse and pointed at me with a meaningful look. I could see my other friends laughing and conferring, caring only for the spectacle.

I did not dare look at Phèdre, knowing she thought this was a foolish endeavor; nor at Joscelin, for fear I would let him down. On the dais, Ysandre looked calm and resigned. Drustan, having taken custody of Eamonn's torc, appeared to take a lively interest in the proceedings. Sidonie, seated at her mother's side, seemed bored. Only Alais, knotting her hands under the wolfhound Celeste's collar, watched me with a worried, anxious look.

I smiled to reassure her, blowing her a kiss.

"The little princess." Beside me, Eamonn chuckled. "She's . . . what is the word? Clever. I like her very much."

I bristled. "Let her be! She's only a child."

"Dagda Mor!" He blinked at me. "Of course. She's like one of my little sisters. What did you think I meant?"

"Nothing," I muttered. "Never mind."

"You D'Angelines are strange," Eamonn commented. "I'll tell you, though, her older sister's a right bitch."

I bit my lip to keep from laughing.

"What is it?" Eamonn asked. "Is that not the word?"

"Oh, no," I said. "It is, most assuredly."

We had already agreed on the proceedings. Drustan nodded at an attendant, who struck the bronze gong he held. Eamonn and I stepped back and faced one another.

The world shrank, dwindling to hold just the two of us. I watched him settle on the balls of his feet, moving lightly, and thought I may have underestimated his speed. He brought his buckler up, guarding his vital parts. He held his wooden sword in a deceptively gentle grip. I was clutching mine with both hands, too tight, my palms already sweating. We gazed into one another's eyes, each trying to read the other.

The gong sounded again.

Eamonn burst forward at me with a wild shout, shield high and sword low. Only my Cassiline-trained reflexes saved me; and just barely, at that. I chopped down hard and away, deflecting his blade, but the upper edge of his buckler caught me on the chin. It knocked me off balance and it was all I could do to absorb the blow, letting myself fall and somersault backward, coming to a crouch and launching a sweeping strike at his shins.

He dodged away from it, laughing. I got to my feet, sword angled before me.

"Are we fighting or dancing?" Eamonn asked.

"You tell me," I said, going on the offensive.

Within moments, I realized I should have spent my practice sparring with an opponent other than Joscelin. In truth, Cassiline swordplay *was* like dancing. The steps of the forms were intricate, one flowing into the other. "Telling the hours," they called it, each motion designed to defend or attack a segment of a sphere, even as the gnomon's shadow sweeps around the face of a sundial. I knew the twelve basic forms well enough, and the strokes that accompanied them.

Eamonn didn't.

And I couldn't predict his reactions; I had gotten too accustomed to the Cassiline style. In earlier days, I had spent time sparring with Ti-Philippe and Hugues that I might learn to handle myself against conventional opponents, but in the past year I had spent most of my time with Joscelin. And this was very different.

The buckler was the worst of it. Given his reach, I couldn't figure out how to get past it. After his initial onslaught, Eamonn settled into a surprisingly patient defense. I circled around him to the left, flickering quick blows at him. He turned in a slow circle, deflecting them with the shield, letting me tire myself and grinning at me all the while. Every now and then he would surprise me with a parry, and there was so much force behind it, it nearly tore the wooden blade from my hands. There was no question I was outmatched in sheer strength.

At first, the watchers cheered and shouted at each exchange, but as our bout wore on and on, their interest waned. The sun stood high overhead and the day was growing warmer. I began to grow hot and tired and careless, recovering slowly and leaving myself open.

And Eamonn began to press me.

There was no finesse to it. He merely hacked at me. But he had the advantage of height and reach and strength, and as I parried blow after blow, my arms became leaden.

"Had enough?" he asked cheerfully.

I shook my head. Sweat dripped into my eyes. I swiped one forearm over my brow, and barely parried in time as Eamonn lunged forward. I disengaged, spinning away from him.

"No," I said, panting. "You?"

He beat the flat of his wooden blade on his shield, then spread his arms wide. "Come and get me, D'Angeline!"

I glanced over at the Bastard, his spotted hide vivid against the greensward. And then I looked at the dais, and for the first time, at Phèdre. She was watching intently, chin in her hand, her expression unreadable. I thought about how many times she had defied her adversaries' expectations: refusing to acquiesce, refusing to surrender to despair.

That which yields is not always weak.

For the first time in our bout, I began to think.

I launched a blistering attack on Eamonn, forcing him to block me high and low. He grunted as he caught the strokes on his buckler. It had to have taken a toll on him, that long, patient defense. And then I let myself sag, lowering my guard. When he gathered himself to hack at me, I began a slow, careful retreat.

It went on for a long time. I feigned stumbles and offered false openings, recovering in the nick of time. I parried with the merest flick of the wrists I could manage, hoarding my strength. Step by step, I led Eamonn mac Grainne on a dull, wearying dance back and forth across the greensward, and I watched his grin fade, replaced by exhausted frustration. He grew slow to raise his buckler, and I began to attack him once more.

How long it lasted, I could not say. It felt like hours.

Our audience jeered and made catcalls and eventually lost interest altogether, except perhaps for a few. Locked together in a private world, Eamonn and I continued to trade blows, sweat-drenched, moving as slowly as one does in a dream.

In the end, I got inside his guard, beating his sword aside; but once I had gotten there, I lacked the strength to regroup. Keeping his sword-arm pinned low and outside, I leaned against his shield, breathing hard. Both of us were swaying on our feet, nearly holding each other upright.

"Truce?" Eamonn said hoarsely.

"Truce," I agreed.

With a groan, he dropped onto the grass and sprawled on his back. I dropped beside him, staring at the blue sky, my chest heaving. I could not remember being more exhausted, not even after helping clear the new pasture in Montrève.

"Imri?" Alais' face appeared in my field of vision, disconcertingly inverted. "Is it a draw, then?"

Too weary to speak, I nodded.

"Oh, good!" Her upside-down face vanished, and I heard Drustan proclaim the match a draw to a fresh round of jeers. I was too tired to even consider rising.

Beside me, Eamonn began to chuckle. "Good bout," he said.

I turned my head toward him. "Not bad."

Lying on the grass, too weary to move, both of us laughed like idiots. Phèdre was right, it was a foolish and unnecessary thing we had done; but it was a glorious one, too. And somehow in the process, we had become friends.

NINETEEN

WHAT FOLLOWED was one of the happiest times of my life.

True friendship must be akin to romance, I think; only without all the anguish and anxiety. After our bout, Eamonn and I became inseparable.

At Court, we made an odd pair. The rumor went about that we were lovers, of course, though there was no truth to it, or at least not in the physical sense. Although it was common practice in Terre d'Ange, after Daršanga, I had seen too much of men's cruelty for the notion to appeal for me. As the Dowayne of Balm House had noted, I was unready to address that wound.

Eamonn thought it was funny. "You people do like your buggery!" he said, laughing.

"Oh, and the Dalriada don't?" I asked him. "Tell me truly."

"Only on long hunting trips." He grinned, unperturbed. "I'm game if you are! Dagda Mor, you're pretty enough for it, Imriel."

"True," I said. "But you're not." It only made him laugh harder.

My Court friends thought it strange. Eamonn was well-liked—it was hard to dislike him, good-natured as he was—but he had no head for the subtleties of the Court, and no great command of the tongue. He was simple, direct, and honest.

It made it easy to be in his company. But it was a mistake to underestimate his intelligence, as most of the gentry did. Most D'Angelines, I fear, are terrible snobs. I loved my country as much as anyone and perhaps more than most. I had cause, having been snatched from it, having witnessed the impossible heroism of which our people are capable at their finest. But I had witnessed acts of heartbreaking valor by people of other nations, too, and I was under no illusion that D'Angeline blood confers any superiority.

We are a pretty folk, as Eamonn said. It is a legacy of Elua and his Companions, whose blood runs in our veins. I had seen one of the One God's angels, and the beauty of Rahab in his true form was almost unbearable. But physical beauty was meaningless in and of itself. I should know, being my mother's son. It was Blessed Elua's precept, not his bloodline, that offered us a chance to make ourselves truly *better*. It meant somewhat more than license to conduct endless affairs, a fact my fellow countrymen often forget.

Eamonn and I spoke of such matters.

He was endlessly curious about Terre d'Ange and eager to meet his father, although he attached less weight to it than I would have reckoned. I suppose it shouldn't have surprised me, since I had little interest in my own. I learned Eamonn was one of five children born to Grainne mac Conor, the Lady of the Dalriada. All of them had different fathers, save his two younger sisters. He was the restless one among them, not content to stay bound by Alba's shores.

"It is my father's blood, my mother says," he told me. "He is a wanderer, too."

"It must run in the family," I said. "They say his grand-father was Tiberian."

"Ah, yes!" Eamonn beamed. "I plan to go there, to Tiberium. It is something no other Dalriada has ever done. Is it not a center of learning?"

"The University is," I said. "Eamonn, do you speak Caerdicci?"

"No," he said cheerfully. "I was hoping you would teach me."

Word came that Admiral Rousse's flagship had made port at Marsilikos. Messengers were sent to meet the Admiral, who blazed a path up Eisheth's Way to the City of Elua, rid-ing hard to meet his half-Eiran son.

That, too, was a spectacle.

"Elua's Balls!" Quintilius Rousse roared, grabbing Ea-monn by both shoulders. "You've a look of your mother, lad! You're one to make a man proud, you are. By the seven hells, that was a magnificent woman, eh?"

"Oh, she still is, Father!" Eamonn grinned.

"No doubt." Quintilius Rousse swatted Eamonn on the back, staggering him. "No doubt, lad!" He winked at Phè-dre. "Right, my lady?"

Phèdre smiled. "The Lord and Lady of the Dalriada were magnificent alike."

"Ah, Eamonn." Rousse grew pensive. "A fine man, your uncle. I mourned his loss. I hope you're honored to be his namesake, lad."

"Oh, yes," he said earnestly. "I am."

There was a lengthy fête that night to celebrate their re-union, and one unlike most Court affairs. There were more of Drustan's Cruithne present than usual, and Ysandre had invited a number of men from Rousse's old crew; sailors who had risen to appointments of their own.

Phèdre's Boys.

It was a raucous night. Sidonie and Alais, who attended the supper, were dismissed early. I felt sorry for Alais, who dragged her feet, departing reluctantly. Sidonie's expression was cool and unfathomable, and I supposed she was glad to go. For my part, I was glad to stay.

They were all survivors, and some things only survivors may share. They did, that night, reliving the experience and retelling the stories—the battle of Bryn Gorrydum, the crossing of the Straits, the battle of Troyes-le-Mont. Eamonn and I both listened in fascination, catching one another's eye, nodding in understanding. In different ways, this was our common heritage.

Toward the end of the evening, Drustan ordered a keg of *uisghe* breached. It was a strong, fiery drink, and even though I sipped it with care, it made my head spin. I heard laughter as it circulated, and then impassioned toasts drunk to the fallen dead—to Eamonn mac Conor, to Drustan's sister Moiread, to Remy and Fortun, two of Phèdre's Boys who lost their lives in La Serenissima, thanks to my mother's treachery. And after those and many others, too many to count, I heard the D'Angeline voices of Phèdre's Boys raised in a marching-chant.

"Man or woman, we don't care; give us twins, we'll take the pair!"

In the grip of a sudden, unwelcome understanding, I squinted at Phèdre. Her face, lovely and alight with memory, swam in my vision. "Did you bed his . . ." I gestured vaguely at Eamonn. "What, *both* of them?"

Phèdre glanced at Joscelin, who shrugged. "It's a peculiar form of diplomacy," he said. "But oddly effective in its own way."

"I'm sorry, love," Phèdre apologized to me. "I thought you knew."

"No." I seized the pitcher of *uisghe* as it passed, pouring a cup and draining it. "Is there a list I should consult? Mayhap in the Royal Archives?"

"There's a thought." Joscelin's dry voice was the last thing I heard before my head struck the table. Much later, I awoke in my own bed to a vague memory of being led, stumbling, from the Queen's banquet hall, my arms slung over the shoulders of Joscelin and Ti-Philippe. It was a good thing we had come by carriage, as I'm sure I couldn't have ridden that night.

I avoided Eamonn as best I could for several days, pleading illness. Of a surety, it was true the first day. But then the time came for Quintilius Rousse to depart and for us to make ready to travel to Montrève, and once that occurred, I could no longer avoid Eamonn's company.

On the road, it was he who broached the subject. "Why are you angry at me, Imriel?"

I stared straight ahead through the Bastard's pricked ears. "I'm not."

"You are," he said simply.

I stole a sidelong glance at him. His face was so open and earnest, it made my heart ache. "It's not you," I said, sighing. "It's just . . . ah, Elua! Does everything always have to be so entangled?"

"No," Eamonn said slowly. "But I think it is what happens when people are at the center of great events. Maybe we are lucky to live in the aftertimes." He rubbed his chin in thought. "Do you know what my mother said about Phèdre?"

"Do I want to?" I asked in a sour tone.

He ignored my comment. "She said she was probably the

bravest person she had ever met." He smiled a little, remembering. "She said it was something most people would not recognize, especially men, who think courage only matters in fighting. But that it is true."

"Oh." Whatever I had expected, it wasn't that. I looked over at Phèdre, riding some distance away, and felt ashamed. Eamonn's mother didn't know the half of it. Even Joscelin wouldn't have gone into Daršanga if not for his vow. "Eamonn, I'm sorry. I'm an idiot sometimes."

"True," he agreed. "Are you finished?"

"For now." I smiled. "It may happen again."

"That's all right," he said cheerfully. "If I had a foster-mother so beautiful, I would be jealous, too."

"It's not *that*!" I said.

He merely looked at me.

"All right." I flushed. "A little, mayhap."

"*I* would be," Eamonn said.

There was no talk of dark mirrors and frightening desires. I was sixteen years old, and my foster-mother was the most famous courtesan in the realm. Eamonn made it seem so simple and normal.

It wasn't, of course; not really.

I still had dreams that woke me in a cold sweat, at once nauseated and aching with desire. I knew the shadow lay in me, waiting. But Eamonn's sunny company drove it into hiding, as surely as that of my Shahrizai kin brought it to the fore. And for that, I was grateful.

For his part, Eamonn regarded Phèdre with frank awe; and Joscelin, too, for different reasons. And as they came to know him better on the ride to Montrève, I could see that they began to return his regard with amused affection. It made me feel good, almost as though I had a brother, albeit an unexpectedly large and ebullient one.

We had fun at Montrève.

In the countryside, Eamonn fit in more than he had in the City, and there was no snide talk from the Siovalese commonfolk as there was among the gentry. The Dalriada were heroes of legend, and they were delighted to have one in their midst.

Especially the young women.

It took me by surprise, although it shouldn't have. Eamonn loved women with the same unabashed passion with which he did everything else. At Court, his lack of sophistication at the Game of Courtship was regarded with a certain amused tolerance; in the country, his candid ardor met with approval. And he was a strapping figure. If he lacked a pretty face, it was an interesting one, revealing an odd, rough-hewn beauty at times.

"I think he's quite handsome," Katherine declared. "In a funny sort of way."

"You're mad," Gilot observed. Their romance had resumed upon our arrival, stronger than ever, and I wondered if Gilot would accompany us when we returned to the City this fall, or request to remain at Montrève.

"*You* don't understand women," Katherine teased him.

"I understand *you*," he retorted. "Don't I, now?"

At that, Charles and I rolled our eyes at one another in a rare moment of accord. I saw less of him this summer; in part because at sixteen, he was old enough to ride regularly with the Montrèvan border patrol headed by his older brother Denis, and in part because of Eamonn. Mostly, it was because our lives had gone in differing directions, furthering the process that had begun when the Shahrizai visited. But we could still agree on the fact that Katherine and Gilot were deadly cloying together.

Even so, Katherine had the right of it. The young women

of Montrève and its surroundings liked Eamonn mac
Grainne, and he cut a glad swathe through them—house-
maids, crofter's daughters, villagers. They seemed to regard
bedding him a grand lark.

I learned why.

It was on a day when we rode into the village. Eamonn
had a fancy to visit Shemhazai's temple there. It was a small
one, but they are all marvels of engineering. Gilot, Hugues,
and Ti-Philippe accompanied us, but they let us enter alone.
The priestess tending it was clad in simple grey robes. She
bowed, offering us bowls of incense in exchange for a tribute of coin.

Taking them, we approached the altar.

The figure of Shemhazai was scarce taller than a man,
cunningly wrought of gilded metal. An empty bowl lay at its
feet. It stood in a niche, head bowed, studying a tablet it held
in its left hand. As we approached, it began to move.

"Dagda Mor!" Eamonn gasped.

I chuckled.

Shemhazai's right hand, grasping a stylus, rose. It moved
over the tablet. His head lifted, facing us with his austere,
unseeing gaze. The tablet spun slowly in his gilded palm, ro-
tating outward so we could read the words written on it.

All Knowledge Is Worth Having.

Somewhere below us there was a whispering sound, and
a flame erupted in the empty bowl at the figure's feet. Re-
pressing a brief shudder at the memory of the firepits of Drujan, I knelt in homage, then rose to pour my incense in a
stream. Sweet-smelling smoke trickled upward. Eamonn
followed suit, eyeing the figure warily.

As we retreated, the tablet rotated once more. Shemhazai
lowered his right hand and bowed his head, settling once
more into a pose of contemplation.

"May you find wisdom in knowledge," the priestess said, offering the formal blessing.

Remembering my own upbringing in the Sanctuary of Elua, I bowed to her. "Our thanks to you, sister."

Outside, in the bright light of day, Eamonn shook himself. "You people!" he exclaimed. "What are you to make such a thing? It seems almost you mock your own gods!"

"It is the gods themselves who taught us," Ti-Philippe murmured.

Eamonn squinted at him. "There is another thing I do not understand. You call them gods. And yet I have heard that others claim they were merely the One God's servants; the One God of the Yeshuites. Is it not so?"

"Not Elua." Hugues' face was set in unwontedly stubborn lines. "Never Blessed Elua! And the others, who became somewhat more, did but follow him."

"Out of love," Gilot added. "That is the promise of Elua's precept. Through love, we become greater. We become more."

I said nothing.

Eamonn looked at me and sighed. "Is there not a tavern in this town?"

There was. It was a tavern and inn, called the Golden Fleece. It was one of those names beloved of D'Angelines, referencing alike the wealth of Montrève and an ancient Hellene tale. It was there that we went to quaff a cup of wine, and there that I beheld Eamonn in action.

Let me be clear; it was the innkeeper's daughter who chose him. She perched on his knee, flirting, wrapping her arms around his neck. Eamonn embraced her, seeking refuge in that which was solid and knowable. He jiggled his knee and lowered his head, burrowing his face between her breasts, inhaling deeply of her scent.

"What else?" he asked me, raising his h
What else matters?"

"All knowledge is worth having," I said; echo
echoing Anafiel Delaunay, echoing Elua's Co...   ...ion
Shemhazai.

"Mayhap," Eamonn said. He smiled at his companion,
the innkeeper's daughter. "Pretty Jeannette, I am a stranger
in this land. I see that you are as fresh and fair as a lily kissed
by dew, and there is laughter in your eyes to gladden a man's
heart. And yet there are mysteries here I do not understand.
Pray, tell me what knowledge I lack. What does it mean
when D'Angelines speak of *love*?"

She giggled and whispered in his ear.

His smile broadened. "Ah, well! *That*, I understand."

He called for more wine then. After several cups, my
head was spinning. I watched the innkeeper's daughter Jeannette lead Eamonn away. They disappeared to the upstairs of
the Golden Fleece, returning some time later with grins on
their faces.

"Why him?" I asked Jeannette as we took our leave. Unsteady on my feet, I gestured vaguely in Eamonn's direction.
"I mean . . . I just wonder, that's all."

"Because he is happy." She smiled up at Eamonn, touching his cheek. "It's nice."

He beamed down at her.

"Is that enough?" I asked, genuinely curious.

"For a moment's pleasure, aye." Her gaze rested on me,
filled with womanly shrewdness. "Ah, highness! I could
dash my heart to pieces against your brooding beauty; and
make no mistake, I have thought upon it. I daresay a great
many young women do, and there will be many more. Each
one will think mayhap *she* will be the one to pierce your
mystery to the core, the one to open your proud, secret

heart." She shook her head. "I am a simple woman, and I will not delude myself. This I can remember, and smile."

"Oh," I said.

"I will always smile at the thought of you," Eamonn promised her cheerfully.

The innkeeper's daughter winked at him. "I daresay you will!"

Eamonn whistled all the way back to the manor, periodically breaking into snatches of Eiran song in a resonant, tuneful voice. Whatever unease he had felt at beholding the simulacrum at the Temple of Shemhazai, it had wholly departed.

Blessed Elua, I thought, would have approved.

"Brooding beauty!" Eamonn broke off his singing to laugh aloud. "It is true, is it not?" He eyed me affectionately. "One day you will have to tell me *why*."

"I will," I said. "One day."

And I did.

I had spoken to Eamonn of my mother. Somehow, it was easier with him. He knew little of Melisande's treachery; it was not a story that had stirred the Dalriada, having naught to do with them. It made him blessedly objective, and easier for me to accept his sincere, untainted sympathy.

I had not spoken of Daršanga.

He knew, of course. It was common Court gossip that I had been abducted and sold into slavery. What that meant— truly meant—no one knew. None of us had spoken openly of those horrors.

It was in the high lake meadow that I told him, the one I had visited with Roshana and Katherine last summer. It seemed a long time ago. We rode there together, Eamonn and I, scaling the mountains' heights. As I had guessed, he loved it. We tethered our mounts, and he greeted the lake with an exuberant shout, stripping off his clothing and plunging into its translucent depths.

I followed suit.

It was cold, so cold! We trod water and splashed one another; laughing as our teeth chattered and our lips turned blue. And when we could stand it no more, we hauled ourselves onto the slate lip and sprawled there, basking in the warmth of the sun-drenched stone.

"What is *that*?" Eamonn asked, pointing at the pale scar on my left buttock. "Dagda Mor! It looks like a cattle-mark."

In the warm sun, I shivered. "It is. Or something like it."

"This is the thing you do not speak of, is it not?" Eamonn grew quiet, watching me with his grey-green eyes, damp hair plastered over his brow. "We are like brothers, you and I. I will never betray your trust. If you can bear to say it, I can bear to hear it, Imriel."

And so I did.

Taking my courage in both hands, I told him about Daršanga. Not all of it; not the worst, in some ways. Only Phèdre knows *that*, and it is her secret to keep. But I told him about Jagun of the Kereyit Tatars, who set his brand on me. I told him of the Âka-Magi, who kept death on a leash like a hound. And I told him about their anointed ruler the Mahrkagir in all his awful madness, and what it was like before Phèdre came.

I told her, long ago. I had never told anyone else.

"He wanted to break me," I said to Eamonn. "Not all at once." I gave him a bitter smile. "I was lucky, if you can believe it, at least compared to the others. He was saving me for something special, or at least he was until Phèdre came. I wouldn't have lasted as long as I did if he hadn't. But he did . . . things."

"The Mahrkagir?" he asked softly.

I nodded. We were sitting face-to-face now, both of us cross-legged on the sun-warmed slate. It had been hours in the telling. The lake-dampened attire we had donned had long since dried. In that bucolic setting, it seemed impossible to envision. I hugged my knees, hunching over them. "Yes," I whispered. "He did things."

Eamonn gazed steadily at me. "Do you want to tell me?"

"No. I don't know." I stared over his shoulder at the lowering sun. "One time . . ." I began, and then halted, shuddering. "Oh, Eamonn! It's vile."

"No." He touched my arm. "It may be. *You* are not, Imriel."

I nodded, shoving away unbidden tears with the heel of one hand. "One time," I said roughly, "there were two of us. Before Phèdre came. There was a woman, one of the Chowati, named Lilka, who was kind to me." I heard a ragged laugh escape me. "Ah, Elua!"

"What happened?" Eamonn leaned forward.

I gritted my teeth. *"Duzhmata, duzhûshta, duzhvarshta,"* I intoned. "Ill thoughts, ill words, ill deeds. That was his Three-Fold Path. He marked her for death in his chambers, and offered me a bargain to spare her life, if I was willing."

"Were you?" Eamonn asked.

"Of course!" My pride stung, I flared at the words. "I tried." I scrubbed at the sockets of my eyes. "I tried," I said softly. "I did. He bade me to kneel and open my mouth. And then he pissed into it." Eamonn made a sound; I smiled dourly. "That was the Mahrkagir's price," I said. "If I could swallow his piss without gagging, he would spare Lilka."

He flinched. "Did you?"

"No," I murmured. "I tried. I truly tried. But it was hot and it stank and oh, Elua! There was so much of it, and I was so scared. I swallowed what I could, and choked on the rest."

"I'm sorry," Eamonn whispered, looking sick. "So sorry. Dagda Mor, Imri! Did he . . . ?"

"He took her from behind," I said. "While I knelt there in a puddle of piss and bile and watched it. That was my penalty for failure." I turned my head to gaze at the lake, watching a breeze ruffle the water's surface. "He didn't use his iron rod, since it was already an act that would end in death. I didn't tell you about that. It was part of it, you know; sowing death in place of life. But he held a dagger to Lilka's throat the whole time—a filthy, old, rusty dagger. She kept her eyes closed," I added. "To spare me from seeing the look in them, I think; or mayhap from seeing the look in mine. I was grateful for that. Especially at the end."

Remembering, I fell silent. Eamonn said nothing, waiting.

"He spent himself in her," I said without looking at him, "and he pulled her head back by the hair and slit her throat. Her blood . . ." I paused, swallowing hard. "It was like a fountain, Eamonn. I was drenched in it."

With an effort, I made myself meet his eyes, fearful of the shock and disgust I might see in them. Instead, there was only shared grief and steadfast compassion.

"Ah, Imriel!" Eamonn grasped my right hand, clutching it hard. "I almost wish he were not dead, this Mahrkagir," he said fiercely. "So I could swear a blood-oath to avenge you!" He paused. "He is dead, is he not?"

I nodded. "Phèdre killed him."

"Phèdre?" His eyes widened. "*Our* Phèdre?"

It made me smile, a little. "She did. With a hairpin."

"Mother Mebh have mercy!" Eamonn's mouth hung open; he shut it with a click. "By all the cows in Connacht, Imriel, I cannot believe you lived through this." He shook his head. "All of you. But *you* . . . how old were you?"

"Ten," I said. "I was ten years old when they took me."

Tears shone in his grey-green eyes. "Ah, you poor lad!" He squeezed my hand. "People don't know, do they? Those poncey Court friends of yours?"

"What I told you?" I said. "No. No one. Only Phèdre."

Eamonn released my hand and made a fist, pressing it to his breast. "What you have told me, I will keep close to my heart," he said soberly. "Your secrets are mine, Imriel. Only know that I honor them, as I honor your courage."

"My thanks." I knuckled away a fresh onslaught of tears, sniffled, and laughed. "I did precious little to deserve it, other than survive. Ah, Elua! Well, if I am betimes brooding, now you know the reason why."

"I do," he said simply. "And it is enough that you survived. It is more than enough."

"There are other stories, other times," I cautioned him. "Some of them . . . are worse."

Eamonn squared his shoulders and nodded. "Do you wish to speak of them?"

"No. One was enough." It was true. And yet, strangely, I felt lighter and happier. Having shared the burden of my memories, it had grown easier to bear. The adepts of Balm House were right; there was healing to be found in trusting others. I got to my feet. "Come on," I said. "Richeline will be waiting supper on us."

That night, my sleep was dreamless and peaceful.

I wished it might always be so.

TWENTY

SUMMER IN MONTRÈVE passed quickly.

It was a time of high-spirited adventure and youthful daring. My confession to Eamonn had released a streak of wildness in me, and together we rode roughshod over the countryside. There was no harm in it, only an excess of exuberance. Together, we dared one another to find higher trees to scale, higher crags from which to leap, larger prey to hunt. Within the confines of Montrève, we sought ways to outwit the border guard; outside it, we sought ways to give the slip to our own men-at-arms.

We found girls, too.

Many of them were eager and willing in the Siovalese countryside. I learned to carry the baggage of my past more lightly and, like Eamonn, engage them with a smile. I put the lessons Emmeline of Balm House had taught me to good use, and I learned a few more in the bargain. Although it was never quite the same.

As much as I hungered for it, I never felt the same hovering presence of blessing. This was carnal pleasure, pure and simple; young human animals coupling for the sheer joy of it. Betimes I lost myself in it, and yet it never seemed I went far enough. Not as far as I wanted, so far that I escaped from my very self.

Afterward, it left me melancholy.

I never showed it to the girls I bedded, although some of them sensed it. With them, I was ever courteous and respectful. If they wanted for naught, I made them pretty gifts. If they had need of aught—for some of the crofters' families were impoverished—I made discreet inquiries and tried to see to what was needed. Still, it did naught to assuage the black mood that sometimes befell me after lovemaking.

Eamonn always knew.

We spoke seldom of it, but I could tell. Betimes, he would seek to lift my spirits through his own ebullience; at others, he merely left me to brood in peace. And at other times, he would goad me into sparring with him. Being evenly matched, we honed our skills against one another.

It was good to have a friend.

He still yearned for a bout with Joscelin; a real bout, steel on steel. Throughout the summer, Eamonn begged and wheedled until at last Joscelin assented. They fought in the inner courtyard, with all of Montrève turned out to watch. When Joscelin appeared wearing only his daggers, Eamonn was sore disappointed.

"You promised me a *real* bout!" he said, aggrieved. "Where is your sword?"

Joscelin caught my eye and gave his half-smile. "I was trained as a Cassiline Brother, Prince Eamonn. We draw our swords only to kill. I will not draw mine against you, even in sport." He set himself, drawing both daggers and bowing, vambraces crossed. "Try me."

It went fast; impossibly fast.

Eamonn charged with a shout. It was the same attack he had used against me in our first bout, buckler high and sword low; but Joscelin was prepared for it. However ill-suited the Cassiline style might be to a formal battlefield, Joscelin had learned to adapt it to a thousand situations. There were few warriors in any discipline who have fought so many battles as he, for such deadly stakes. He caught the tip of Eamonn's blade on the quillons of his right-hand dagger and turned it aside with a twist of his wrist. In one deft step, he slid inside Eamonn's guard, his left arm forcing away the thrusting shield. He hooked his right foot behind Eamonn's heel and shoved hard.

Clattering to the ground, Eamonn fell onto his back.

I grimaced at the impact and tried to memorize the sequence Joscelin had used to get inside his guard so effortlessly.

Joscelin lowered one knee on Eamonn's chest, both daggers at his throat. He looked mildly down at his conquest. "Are you satisfied, Prince of the Dalriada?"

"Dagda Mor!" Eamonn gasped, laughing. "Oh, aye! Let me up!"

Altogether, we gave Phèdre a fearful headache.

There were other times, though. Eamonn was sincere in his desire to study at the University of Tiberium. And in truth, he had a keen intellect, albeit limited in its tutoring. So it was that Phèdre found ways to teach us both. Of her own accord, she taught Eamonn the rudiments of the Caerdicci language. And once it was done, she discerned those elements of scholarship that most interested Eamonn—the dissertations of the philosophers—and set us both to studying them, working to translate their theses from Caerdicci into D'Angeline, and thence to discussing them.

For Eamonn, it came hard. He stewed over his translations, mumbling to himself in a mix of D'Angeline and Eiran, struggling with the Caerdicci. I grew envious, watching the way Phèdre hovered over him, murmuring advice, guiding and aiding him. Yet once he grasped the ideas at stake, his mind ran apace of mine, overtaking it. And for some perverse reason, it galled me to see him grapple so eagerly with the questions that haunted me in my darkest hours.

"What *does* it mean to be good, Imri?" Eamonn's grey-green eyes glowed. "You and I, we have cause to wonder! What is the pursuit of goodness? Is it pleasure? Is it honor? Is it justice? Where does the true essense of *goodness* lie?"

"I don't know," I muttered, wishing I did.

"Well, then!" Eamonn clapped his hands. "That's what we must determine, isn't it?"

"I suppose," I muttered.

"These are fine questions to ask," Phèdre said gently to me. "Philosophers have debated them for many centuries."

I glared at her. "Is that what your beloved Anafiel Delaunay learned at the University?" I asked in retort. "For it seems to me he learned somewhat more. Yet not even you can say where he learned the arts of covertcy."

"No." Her dark eyes were clear, save for the floating mote of Kushiel's Dart. "He kept his secrets. And he died too young." Her mouth quirked. "How could he have guessed? To me, he ever seemed a man grown, and wise with it. And yet, I realize now, he was scarce older than I am now when he bought my marque. He must have believed he would live forever."

"He used you grievously," I commented. "Was that *goodness* at work?"

Phèdre's gaze deepened. "Anafiel Delaunay didn't shape my nature, he merely turned it to a purpose. Even so, I think he did not do it lightly. He had a sense of what would be needful," she mused. "The question is, who taught it to him?"

"Someone in Tiberium," Eamonn observed helpfully. "I will ask when I go there in the spring."

Phèdre laughed. "I hope you find an answer!"

I didn't like to think about Eamonn leaving next spring. Already, I knew I would miss him. And I envied his freedom. Although he would not gain his majority until this winter, the Dalriada reckoned him a man grown. He had no obligations or responsibilities. His mother was content to send him off with a fistful of gold, free to wander the world, trusting him to make his way back home, older and wiser.

By contrast, I chafed at my own restraints.

Outside of Montrève, I wasn't allowed to go anywhere without an armed escort. In the early days, with assassination attempts in Khebbel-im-Akkad fresh in my mind, it had seemed a sensible precaution. Now it seemed unnecessary. After all, no one in Terre d'Ange had tried to kill me. My mother had vanished without a trace, and the peers of the realm were beginning to forget her existence. Barquiel L'Envers wouldn't mind if I fell into a hole and broke my neck, but he didn't appear willing to do the job himself.

Summer ended too soon.

I was in two minds regarding our return to the City. A part of me looked forward to it; and a part of me mourned the further loss of freedom. At least in Montrève, I was free to roam within the borders of the estate. In the City, I would be kept on a shorter leash.

Still, there was nothing to be done about it. Summer gave way to autumn, and we returned to the City of Elua.

To no one's surprise, Gilot decided to stay in Montrève. The rest of us went back.

One always supposes that life elsewhere stands still in one's absence, but it doesn't.

Things had changed.

For one thing, Alais had grown. It took me by surprise. Over the course of the summer, my irrepressible little cousin had become a gawky girl of twelve, with dark scowling brows and a nose that seemed too large for her face. Although she was still slight, she seemed all sharp elbows and knees, limbs akimbo.

Colts' Years, I thought.

For the first time, she greeted me with shy reserve. The only familiar element was the wolfhound Celeste, beating her tail on the marble floor.

"It's good to see you, villain," I said, hugging Alais despite her reluctance.

She drew away. "Don't call me that! It's silly."

I hunkered down on my heels, scratching Celeste's ears. "What's wrong with silliness? It's only because I like you, Alais. I thought we were friends, you and I."

"She's not a child, you know," said a familiar voice. "Don't treat her like one."

I looked up at Sidonie. She stood behind her sister, her hands resting on Alais' shoulders. For all the coolness in her voice, her face held an expression of fierce defiance. Her liquid dark eyes smoldered in her delicate face. Sidonie, too, had grown. Unlike Alais, she had done so with effortless grace. It seemed unfair.

I stood and bowed. "My greetings, Dauphine. I meant no offense."

"Then give none," she retorted.

I caught Eamonn's eye and grimaced. He grinned and

came over to us, uttering a few florid phrases in Eiran, then translating them for their benefit. It made Alais laugh, almost like her usual self, and even Sidonie smiled.

And so the moment passed.

But there were other moments.

The Game of Courtship had carried on without me. Reuniting with my friends, I was hard put to keep pace with the gossip. Some players had left the field, like Raul L'Envers y Aragon. It was rumored he would return in the spring, but he was wintering in Amílcar this year. I will own, I was not sorry for it. Though I had come to like him well enough, I would not miss the Lady Nicola. But there were other players, too; new players. Many, I did not know. Others, I did. One was my cousin Roshana Shahrizai, who had come to winter in the City.

Another, I would never have expected.

"The new lieutenant in the Queen's Guard?" Julien Trente fanned himself in jest. "Name of Elua! He's got the look of a chained leopard. A few more like him, and *I'll* enlist in her majesty's service."

"It *is* your birthright," his sister Colette reminded him. "Mayhap you ought to."

"It's a stepping-stone," he said peaceably. "Ysandre rewarded Father generously for his service, and rightfully so. Our family has risen high in the Queen's regard. For you and me, he wants somewhat more. But you've got to own, Maslin de Lombelon has a . . . certain appeal."

I gaped at the name, dumbstruck.

"Wasn't Lombelon one of your holdings?" Colette asked me curiously. "I seem to remember hearing Father say somewhat about it years ago."

"Yes." With an effort, I collected myself. "I gave it to him."

"To Maslin?" Her brows arched. "Why on earth?"

"I thought he wanted it," I murmured.

Already there were stories about him. Upon attaining his majority, he had entrusted Lombelon to its old seneschal's care and left to take service in the Queen's Guard. He had arrived, ill-mannered and untaught in the ways of swordsmanship, and demanded an appointment with Diderot Duval, the Captain of the Queen's Guard. Upon ascertaining his background, Captain Duval put Maslin to the test, setting him against one of his best swordsmen. They all laughed at Maslin's untutored stance, and Captain Duval promised him a lieutenancy if he won.

He did.

Remembering his skill with a pruning hook, I wasn't surprised. After all, he was Isidore d'Aiglemort's son. Captain Duval kept his word. And all summer, Maslin had set himself to mastering the sword and the arts of diplomacy and command with dedicated ferocity. If he was not exactly well-liked, he was admired. And out of some whim, Barquiel L'Envers had taken a liking to him, and was rumored to be highly supportive of Maslin's career.

I met him in the Hall of Games.

It was an awkward moment. There was a quarrel over a game of piquet, with accusations of cheating hurled on both sides. I was no part of it, but I was near. Indeed, I was backing away when I literally bumped into Maslin. As the lieutenant on Palace duty, he was sending his men to escort the quarreling Azzallese lordlings from the Hall.

I turned around with an apology on my lips. Seeing him, I lost the words.

"Maslin!" I said stupidly.

"Prince Imriel." He bowed, crisp and correct. Only a

flicker of his lids betrayed any emotion. "I beg your pardon."

"No, it was my fault." Why was I always jostling people in the damned Hall of Games? Discomfited, I stared at him. With his pale blond hair and his fine-honed features, he looked splendid in the deep blue uniform of the Queen's Guard, his doublet adorned with the swan badge of House Courcel and the silver braid of his office. But there was a restless glitter in his dark eyes that belied his courtly appearance. I understood what Julien had meant about the leopard. "Why?" I asked Maslin, not bothering to frame the question.

He understood. "It wasn't enough," he said, then paused. His voice roughened. Only slightly, but I, who had been taught by Phèdre to notice such things, heard it. "You made it small."

"I'm sorry," I whispered. "Maslin—"

His shoulders squared, and he looked past me toward the yet unsettled quarrel. "Forgive me, your highness. I have a job to do."

"Who was *that*?" Eamonn asked cheerfully, forging a path toward me.

"Someone I knew once, a little bit." I slapped his shoulder. "Come on, let's go."

I told him about it that night, though. Since we had returned to the City, Eamonn and I shared my room in the townhouse. The oil lamp on the stand burned low while I sought to explain myself. Lying in the adjacent bed, Eamonn listened without comment, his arms folded behind his head. In the guttering light, his face looked strange and shadowed. He did not speak until I had finished.

"You were trying to do a good thing," he said softly. "How can that be wrong?"

I sighed. "But for what reason, Eamonn? For whose benefit? His, or mine?"

"Does it matter?" he asked.

"I think it does." I plucked at my bedsheets. "Phèdre tried to warn me that he might hate me for it. And I thought I understood. But what did I do? I took a thing he cherished, and I disposed of it as carelessly as though it held no worth. I made it small in his eyes."

"No," Eamonn said simply. "*He* did."

"I don't understand," I said.

"Imriel." He propped himself on one arm. "You D'Angelines, you are so quick to speak of love. Do you even know what it means?" He shook his head. "If he had truly loved this place . . . what is it called? Lomblon? Nothing could have made it small in his eyes. No," he continued thoughtfully. "I know. I hear what your friends say about me, about the Dalriada. I'm a barbarian, aye? Rough and uncouth." He laughed deep in his chest, sounding like his father. "Do you think it makes me love my home the less? My mother, my family, my people?"

"No," I admitted.

Eamonn flopped onto his back, staring at the rafters. "Ah, it's a beautiful place!" he said. "I hope to show it to you one day. I mean to go back, you know, when I've grown a bit in the world. The thing is, when you come to it, it's not that Innisclan is too small for me." He glanced over at me, and his shrewd eyes glinted. "*I'm* too small for me."

I grinned at him. "Not according to the innkeeper's daughter!"

"Lewd bugger!" He laughed and threw a pillow at me. "Ah now, you know what I mean. But this Maslin of yours, he doesn't. He reckons the world's cheated him, and it's left a hole in his heart. He's trying to fill it somehow, but nothing ever fits. It's not your fault."

"Whose, then?" I asked.

"No one's." Eamonn shrugged. "Life isn't fair, Imri. You of all people ought to understand. Still, we can but try to do good. And you did. What he's done with it is up to him."

I tossed his pillow back to him. "You make it sound so simple."

"It is." He tucked the pillow under his head, stretching and sighing. "Oh, Imri! You should come to Tiberium with me in the spring. Think of what a time we'd have."

"I can't," I said. "Not until I turn eighteen."

"Ah well, you *could*," he said slyly. "If we were clever about it."

We had talked about what a grand adventure it would be. I'd even given it thought. It was hard always being surrounded by intrigue, encumbered by a net of safeguards. I'd give a lot to be like Eamonn, feckless and unfettered. Even if the Queen sent a company of guardsmen to haul me back to Terre d'Ange, it would be a glorious escape.

I couldn't do it.

It came back to the same thing: Phèdre and Joscelin. I couldn't betray their trust. It wasn't just a matter of all we had been through together. I remembered that day in the throne room when I was formally adopted into their fosterage. I remembered Queen Ysandre's outrage and genuine disbelief at the request, and how Phèdre had held forth the Companion's Star in silence, claiming a boon the Queen herself had promised long ago. I'd had no idea the stakes would be so high. What had I known of Court? Until then, I'd never been aught but a goatherd or a slave.

"I can't, truly," I said to Eamonn. "It's a matter of honor."

"Oh, honor!" he said. "All right, then. Next year, mayhap, you'll join me."

"Mayhap."

The lamp on the nightstand between us gave a final sputter and died. Near me, I heard Eamonn settle into sleep, his breathing growing heavy and slow. I lay awake with my eyes open onto darkness, envying him.

Afterward, I made it a point to avoid Maslin. Most of the time it was easy. To be sure, he wasn't eager to seek out my company, either. Still, there were times when it was unavoidable. And despite Eamonn's words, which I knew to be sensible and true, I often felt obscurely guilty in his presence.

Other times, I was angry at him.

Those were the times that frightened me. I found myself studying him, gauging his fault-lines, imagining the perfect way in which to drive a wedge into them that would crack his pride asunder. It wouldn't be hard to do. With a few well-chosen, well-timed words—a careless mention of my own generosity, say, and how I had granted Lombelon to him while he stood before me with dung under his nails—I could humiliate him before the Court. He would hate me for it, but no one would ever forget it.

I didn't, of course. But I thought about it.

The only good thing about Maslin's presence was that it restored a piece of common ground between Alais and me. She didn't like him.

We discussed it during a hunting party in late autumn. It was one of those invigorating days when the air was crisp and bright, cold enough to see one's breath. We rode to hawk and hound, and everyone turned out in fine new warm attire: velvet gowns and padded doublets, sweeping cloaks trimmed with ermine and marten.

I rode with Alais, who had had little chance to go a-hunting with Celeste. It was a scene of merry pageantry as the party spread out across the meadow. Patient cadgers carried the birds of prey for the gentry, transferring them to gauntleted arms. The beaters and bird-dogs plunged into the brush, seeking to flush quarry. Wineskins and flasks were passed back and forth, laughter and wagers were traded. Alais and I set ourselves apart. Celeste was the only coursing hound present, but I reckoned sooner or later the beaters would flush a hare.

Sure enough, one burst from the sere grass, its powerful hind legs propelling it in mighty leaps. Alais gave the command I had taught her, and Celeste bounded to the chase.

It sowed chaos on the hunting field.

The hare doubled in a panic, zigging and zagging between riders and attendants. Celeste followed in hot pursuit, a tall lean shadow. At the same moment, a covey of partridge flushed from the underbrush. Horses shied in alarm, jolting their riders. Hawks bated, battening the air with their wings and straining at their jesses. Everyone was shouting: gentry, cadgers, guardsmen. I could hear Eamonn's loud whoop amid the clamor.

Alais and I laughed harder than we had since the Queen's harvest celebration in the apple orchard, laughing until our sides ached.

When it was over, Celeste had caught the hare. Alais gave the command for her return and she loped over to us, the hare's limp body drooping from her mighty jaws, blood beaded on its grey-brown fur. I dismounted and praised her as I took it from her.

"Poor thing," Alais murmured, regarding the hare.

"'Tis a harsh sport," I agreed. An attendant came forward with a game-bag. With a deft move, he slit the hare's belly, tossing the entrails to Celeste. In Montrève, I'd have done it myself. "We needn't continue, if you'd rather not."

"No." Alais' chin rose. "I don't need to be coddled."

I sighed, putting one hand on her stirrup. The Bastard nudged me from behind, whuffling at my hair. "No, you don't. And I'm not. I'm just trying to be your friend, Alais."

"I know." Her violet eyes darkened. "You're not like *him*."

Following her gaze, I saw Maslin, who was in charge of the company of the Queen's Guard escorting this outing. Until now, I had managed to ignore that fact. Clad in his lieutenant's finery, he had dismounted to aid Sidonie; calming her mount, helping gentle the goshawk on her arm. Her head was bent toward him, her hair hiding her face in a golden curtain. The sight made my stomach give an unexpected lurch.

"Maslin of Lombelon?" I asked.

"I don't like him!" Alais said fiercely. "I know what you did for him, Imri. And he's not even grateful. He doesn't even care."

"He does," I said. The old guilt plucked at me. We were both born to treasonous parents, but he had suffered more than I for it, at least in those ways under mortal jurisdiction. At Court, that was all that mattered. "It's just . . . what I did wasn't enough."

Alais fixed me with a hard look. "Oh, please!"

"I know, I know." I watched him with Sidonie. "Name of Elua! Tell me he's not thinking of courting her."

"No, not exactly." She shrugged. "But she likes him."

"Sidonie?" I asked, incredulous. "Why?"

Alais shrugged again. "I don't know. Because he's not like the others. He doesn't mince words or tell pretty lies. But I don't like him. He looks through me, and there's something cold in his eyes." Her mouth twisted. "I know what he sees. I'm too young. I'm not pretty, not like Sidonie. It's not my fault."

"That's not true." I gazed up at Alais. Her violet eyes were wide and vulnerable, fringed with sooty lashes, set in her awkward young face like twin jewels. "I think you're beautiful."

Color rose to her cheeks, and she scowled at me. "Don't lie to me!"

"I'm not." I smiled, seeing at once the whole of Alais—the clever, impulsive, and open-hearted girl she had been, and the proud and prickly adolescent she was becoming. I could see the fault-lines in her, and it filled me with nothing but tenderness. Alais was young and insecure, and she struggled so hard not to let the whispers of Court bother her, not to be resentful of her older sister to whom so much seemed to come so easily. And yet she was fierce and loyal, too. No one would ever find it easy to exploit her faults, and I would gladly kill anyone who tried. "You *are* beautiful, Alais. Never believe otherwise."

"Thank you," she whispered.

Sitting on her haunches at my feet, Celeste beat her tail like a whip, grinning with bloodstained jaws. I laughed. "See, even Celeste agrees. And everyone knows dogs can't lie." I reached up and squeezed Alais' hand. "Come on, love. Let's see if we can catch another hare."

I made a show of mounting, giving her time to wipe away the tears I'd pretended not to see. The Bastard obliged by turning in an abrupt circle, forcing me to hop on one foot until I gained enough leverage to swing myself astride. By the time I did, Alais was smiling. Across the field, I could see a few people laughing, too, but it was worth it.

"Do you know, I had a dream once that we were brother and sister," Alais said. "Really and truly, I mean. When I woke up, I wished it were so." She paused. "I do love you, Imri."

I grinned at her. "Me too, villain."

Her brows drew into a scowl. "Stop calling me that! It's silly."

"All right, villain."

TWENTY-ONE

FOR THE FIRST TIME, I attended the Midwinter Masque.

I told myself it was for Eamonn's sake, though it wasn't entirely true. I wanted to go. I'd heard too many stories of the splendor and gaiety of the Longest Night. And this would be my only chance to attend it with a friend, one true friend, in tow.

If Joscelin was hurt, he didn't show it; I daresay he understood. He would keep Elua's vigil as always, while Ti-Philippe stood in as Phèdre's escort. For her part, Phèdre was pleased. Once the matter was determined, nothing would do but that we all accompany her to the salon of her couturiere, Favrielle nó Eglantine, to be fitted for costumes.

It was customary for the members of a household to be costumed around a single theme. Favrielle took one look at the four of us—Phèdre, Ti-Philippe, Eamonn, and me—and put her hands on her hips.

"What do you expect me to do with *this*, Comtesse?" she asked in an acerbic tone.

"I thought you might have some ideas," Phèdre said mildly.

Favrielle shook her head and muttered, pacing around the

comfortable antechamber of her salon and studying us. She was a pretty woman, with disheveled curls of coppery gold and a delicate face poorly suited to its customary expression of ill-temper; but then, I suppose irascible genius doesn't choose its vessel.

"Stand up," she said abruptly to Eamonn. He did, towering over her. "Name of Elua! How am I supposed to handle a giant in your midst?"

Phèdre shrugged. "Are there no popular themes this year that would suit us?"

"Popular?" Favrielle shot her a scathing look. "I *set* trends, Comtesse. I do not follow them."

"Of course." Phèdre inclined her head, hiding a smile. "Forgive me, Favrielle."

Ignoring her, the couturiere walked around Eamonn, studying him as though he were prize livestock. He stood, patient and bewildered. The rest of us sat waiting while Favrielle nó Eglantine's sharp gaze flickered from him to us and back again. Finally she dismissed Eamonn with a wave of her hand, then resumed pacing, biting her thumbnail, deep in thought.

"I have an idea," she announced at length. There was a rare note of uncertainty in her voice. "You may not like it." She rang a bell, and an apprentice appeared. "Bring me Dorian's folio."

In short order, the apprentice returned with a handsome leather-bound folio. Favrielle handed it to Phèdre, who paged through it, gazing at the woodblock prints. Her hands went still, and she looked up at Favrielle. "These are Skaldic myths," she said.

Favrielle nodded. "I told you you might not like it." Stooping beside Phèdre, she pointed at a print of a handsome, hulking deity, a mighty hammer in one hand. "Donar, the thunder-god. That's who I thought of for the Dalriadan prince."

Eamonn peered over her shoulder. "I like the look of him!"

"Your country wasn't invaded by the Skaldi," Ti-Philippe muttered.

"It wasn't their gods who ordered it." Phèdre rose and walked a little distance away. "Believe me, I know." She looked at Favrielle. "What else?"

"Loki." The couturiere pointed at Ti-Philippe, then me. "And Baldur the Beautiful. For you, Comtesse, the goddess Freyya." She took a deep breath, expelling it through pursed lips. "Color. Everyone will be doing strong color, bright color this year. I'd keep you all in white: frost, ice, snow. Silver accents, nothing more."

Phèdre nodded at the folio. "Where did you get that?"

"The artist is Dorian nó Eglantine. He's a friend." Favrielle watched her. "He spent a year travelling through the southern reaches of Skaldia, gathering their myths and making the sketches on which these are based. But he's been afraid of going public with the prints."

"I don't blame him," Ti-Philippe said sourly. "He wasn't on the battlefield at Troyes-le-Mont."

Favrielle shrugged. "It's art, chevalier." She turned back to Phèdre. "I would not suggest this for just anyone. But you . . . you have earned a certain right. It would be respected as a gesture of peace and accord. As you say, it was not Skaldia's gods who made war upon us."

Returning to the folio, Phèdre traced the lines of one print with her forefinger. "This is strong work," she murmured. She met my eyes. There was a shadow in the depths of hers that only I understood. "What do you think?"

I answered in one word. "Erich."

There had been a young man of the Skaldi in the zenana of Daršanga. How he came to be there, I never knew. We never learned his story. No one spoke his tongue, and after the Mahrkagir had him gelded, he spoke to no one until Phèdre arrived. He recognized her, though he did not say it for a long time. In Skaldia, they tell stories about her. I still remembered the words he spoke when he finally broke his silence, uttered in crude zenyan.

The defeated always remember.

Erich fought bravely for our freedom, though he did not live to see it. He kept his head when others lost theirs, and he spent his life protecting theirs. He took a dozen wounds before he died, and I had wept at his death.

"I made him a promise," Phèdre said quietly, remembering. "I swore I wouldn't blame the Skaldi for Waldemar Selig's war." She touched Ti-Philippe's arm. "Philippe, can you live with this? I will not do it if it pains you."

He sighed, studying the ceiling. "My lady, I would walk through fire for you, and well you know it. If it is your wish that I be attired as an Ephesian dancing girl, I will do it. If it is a Skaldic deity, I will do that, too. Whatever it be, I trust you have your reasons."

Phèdre kissed his cheek. "My thanks, Philippe."

I was watching Favrielle during the exchange and saw her expression soften for a moment. It hardened the instant she noticed, and I smiled to myself.

"You people!" she exclaimed. "Name of Elua, it's just a Masque. Must everything always be a matter of life or death with you?"

So it was decided.

The costumes were gorgeous. How not? Favrielle was a genius, after all. She had a knack for making fabric sing like poetry, and whatever she might claim, she took a good deal of pride in dressing Phèdre nó Delaunay de Montrève and her household. On the afternoon of the Longest Night, she even sent one of her apprentices to assist with the preparations.

It was a lengthy process.

When it was done, I gazed at myself in the mirror and beheld a stranger.

As Favrielle had promised, I was clad all in hues of white. Mine was one of the simplest costumes. A shirt of ivory silk, open at the throat and fastened below with silver buttons shaped like mistletoe berries; a pair of white velvet breeches with a silver sash about the waist. Even my leather boots were white. So simple; and yet. Favrielle's apprentice had spent ages twining silver ribbons throughout my hair. It framed my face in an unlikely starburst, the silver bright against my blue-black locks.

Baldur the Beautiful, the Skaldi god of light, slain by a sprig of mistletoe.

But it was the mask that made all the difference. It was a half-mask of ivory silk, modeled on my own features, but motionless and still. The upper half of my face looked smooth and serene, distant as a god. I leaned forward, peering into the mirror. Yes, those were my dark blue eyes; those were my lips, looking unwontedly ripe. It was a strange interplay, the tension between the living flesh and the remote whiteness of the mask.

"Well, aren't *you* pretty!"

I jumped at Eamonn's voice. He leaned in the doorway, grinning at me, his mask shoved onto his forehead. He wore white boots, a cloak of ivory wool, and a long white jerkin trimmed with ermine, belted around the waist with a chain of silver links, leaving his brawny arms and lower legs bare. He lowered his mask to show me. Unlike mine, it was sculpted into an expression of thunderous intent. He hoisted a crudely shaped hammer covered in silver leaf.

"You look . . . imposing," I said.

"I feel a right dolt." He raised his mask. "Are we ready?"

"Nearly, I think."

Downstairs, Ti-Philippe joined us. He wore a doublet and breeches of ivory velvet, glittering with a tracery of silver embroidery. Like us, he had a silken half-mask, but his bore an expression of clever malice. Whether or not any of us looked like the Skaldic ideal of their deities, I doubt; I daresay we didn't. But we didn't look like ourselves, either.

And then Phèdre descended.

"Dagda Mor!" Eamonn whispered fervently.

She scintillated from every angle. Her gown was made of ivory satin, and it clung to her waist and torso as though it had grown there, leaving her shoulders and arms bare. It was adorned with ornate beadwork, refracting light. Below the waist, it flared and frothed, breaking like the crest of a wave upon the stairs. Her dark hair was loose, but a hundred small brilliants were fastened in it, looking like a net of stars. An intricate necklace of silver links and pale gems circled her throat. Unlike the three of us, she wore a small mask; a simple white domino that lent mystery to her eyes and hid none of her beauty.

"Well?" Phèdre smiled.

Eamonn knelt, offering up his silver hammer. "Lady, I lay myself at your feet!"

"You look like a goddess," I said honestly.

Ti-Philippe merely gave a low whistle, glancing at Joscelin, who was following his consort down the stairs, clad in plain woolen attire. "Sure you don't want to change your mind, Cassiline?"

He laughed. "I don't think your costume would fit me,

chevalier." Joscelin turned to Phèdre, touching her hair. His steel vambraces glinted dully. "I'll see you after sunrise."

"Joie," she whispered to him.

"And to you, love." He kissed her, then. "Joie to all of you on the Longest Night!"

I thought about him on the journey to the Palace. Already, the City was ablaze with mirth. We made slow progress through the revelers. At every intersection, someone darted up to the carriage, proffering a flask or wineskin. We declined, laughing, and tossed them silver centimes for luck. Somewhere, I thought, amid all this gaiety, Joscelin was making his steady way toward the Temple of Elua. While we would pass the night in revelry, he would spend it kneeling on the frozen ground, immersed in silent prayer.

"This, too, is sacred."

The words startled me. I stared at Phèdre, the blood warming my cheeks, remembering how Emmeline of Balm House had spoken them. "What?"

"This celebration." She gestured at the revelers outside the carriage window. "We celebrate the passing of darkness and the return of the light. It's a sacred ritual, as old as Earth herself."

"I know," I said. "I was just thinking about Joscelin."

She smiled below her mask. "In his heart, he will always be Cassiel's servant. The Longest Night means a great deal to him. Only know, this path is no less worthy."

"And a lot more fun!" Ti-Philippe added.

I nodded. "I will be mindful of it."

By the time we arrived, I had already ceased to fret. The stories I had heard failed to do justice to the pageantry of the Midwinter Masque. Every inch of the Palace was ablaze with light. Although we were not late, the ballroom was already filled with a throng of masked celebrants. Favrielle had guessed rightly; it was a riot of color, jewel tones, deep and rich. We made a stark white splash as we entered, the herald bawling our names. Eamonn stared about him, his eyes wide behind his mask's thunderous scowl, his mouth agape.

I nudged him. "Act like a god."

He raised his hammer and roared aloud.

It was a bit more than I had intended, but what could one do? I thought about Erich the Skaldi and laughed. I daresay they are not so different, the Daldriada and the Skaldi. With sublime disregard for the whispers and stares, Phèdre took Ti-Philippe's arm and plunged into the throng; trusting us to follow, trusting the others to make way for her.

We did; and so did they.

"Phèdre!" It was Queen Ysandre herself who hailed us. She came toward us, Sidonie and Alais in tow, flanked by members of her Guard. The Queen was dressed as the personification of Summer, while her daughters were Spring. She gave Phèdre the kiss of greeting. "My dear, what *are* you tonight?"

"Freyya," Phèdre said calmly. "A Skaldic deity."

There was a little pause. The Queen's brows rose. "All of you?"

"I am Donar!" Eamonn said helpfully, brandishing his hammer. "God of thunder!"

Ysandre blinked. Her gaze passed over Eamonn and Ti-Philippe, coming to rest on me. "And you, Prince Imriel?"

I bowed low, my head heavy with silver ribbon. "Baldur, your majesty, god of light."

The moment made me tense, but in the end, Ysandre merely sighed. "You do like to make matters interesting, my dear," she said. "So be it. Let this be a measure of the peace we have established. Be welcome. May the Longest Night pass swiftly, and light return."

We toasted one another with *joie*. It is a rare liqueur distilled from flowers that blossom in the snowdrifts of the Camaeline Mountains and its taste is indescribable, at once cool on the palate and burning in the belly. Alais' eyes widened as she sipped hers.

"Your first taste?" I asked her.

She shook her head vigorously. "No, Mother let me try it last year, but I'd forgotten." She laughed breathlessly. "It's my first Masque, though! I've leave to stay until the Sun Prince arrives."

"You look lovely, young highness," Eamonn said gallantly. "Will you save a dance for me?"

"Oh, yes!" Alais blushed. "Thank you."

"I am honored." He bowed to her, giving me a wink.

It was true. She did look lovely, clad all in lavender with a matching mask, and a golden wreath on her black curls set with amethysts fashioned to look like violets. Sidonie, clad in pale green the color of new leaves, complemented her. She stood upright as a little spear-maiden beside her younger sister, inscrutable behind her mask. In the background, the Queen's Guardsmen hovered, chosen to attend as a special honor. They wore domino masks with their usual uniforms, but I knew Maslin by his silver-gilt hair. An imp of perversity goaded me.

"Since Eamonn has claimed your sister, mayhap you will honor me with a dance later," I said to Sidonie.

Her lips curved in a faint smile. "Mayhap. I've never danced with a god of light." Sidonie studied me. "You look the part, cousin. Were you thinking to be asked to play the Sun Prince?"

I opened my mouth to reply, then frowned, remembering.

Long ago, another Prince of the Blood had done so in the Night Court's pageant: Baudoin de Trevalion, who had been at the center of a plot to replace Ysandre as heir to the throne of Terre d'Ange.

In the end, he had been executed for it.

"Not I," I said lightly. "Trust me, highness, I've no such ambition."

She nodded slowly. "We will see."

Mercifully, Julien and Colette Trente appeared, tugging me away into the festivities. I spent a few minutes brooding over the exchange, then forgot it, losing myself in merriment. Wine and *joie* were flowing freely, and there was so much to see. Everywhere one turned, there was an array of fantastical figures: gods and goddesses, sprites, nymphs and demons, creatures out of story and legend, animals of all ilk. The masks lent a sense of abandon to the proceedings. One knew who one's companions were; and yet they were strange and unfamiliar, no longer themselves. It made one sense anything was possible.

"Wait until midnight," Julien whispered in my ear.

"What happens then?" I asked.

He brushed one finger along my jaw. "Almost anything you like, highness." I shook my head at him, and he made a face. "Oh, come! It's the Longest Night, Imri. You needn't be so untouchable."

"Do you need rescuing, cousin?"

I turned at the sound of Roshana's voice, rich and amused. She was clad and masked in black velvet, a miniature huntsman's horn around her neck and a braided quirt of black leather about one wrist. "From this one?" I said, slinging my arm around Julien's shoulders. "I might."

"Come dance with me, then." She held out her hand.

We danced well together. Roshana moved with supple

grace, her lower body melded against mine, following my lead effortlessly. Growing aroused, I drew back a few inches, holding her away from me. The quirt that dangled from her wrist hovered between us.

She laughed low in her throat. "You *are* afraid of me!"

"No," I said. "It's just—"

"Then dance with me." Behind the black velvet of her mask, Roshana's eyes were a dusky, phosphorus blue, aglow with challenge. I wondered if mine looked the same.

"All right." Reckless, I drew her close.

When it was done, we were both of us breathing hard. Roshana regarded me with new respect. "Your friend's right, you know," she said. "Anything can happen on the Longest Night." Tilting her head, she kissed me, swift and unexpected. I felt her tongue dart between my lips, tasting of *joie*. "Don't forget your family." She laughed, leaving me.

I stood for a moment, swaying, gritting my teeth against the sharp stab of desire.

"Imriel!" Eamonn's hand descended on my shoulder. He looked happy and a little drunk, his mask shoved up onto his disheveled hair. Somewhere, he had lost Donar's silver-leafed hammer. "I've been dancing with one of the married ladies. I think she fancies me. Come on, let's get some wine, and you can tell me about her."

I took a deep breath. "I need to sit down."

He glanced down at me. "Dagda Mor! I think maybe you do."

We found chairs at the Queen's table, which was piled high with food. There was no formal dining hour on the Longest Night, only a constant supply of abundance. Revelers paused to eat or drink, plunging back into the fray. It was a relief to have a respite from it. Once the ache of desire passed, I filled a plate, listening with half an ear to Eamonn's story.

"Will her husband challenge me, do you think?" he asked.

"What?" I glanced at him. "Who?"

"Lady Osmont's husband," Eamonn said patiently. "Like Fionn mac Cumhaill, when Diarmuid stole Grainne from him; my mother was named for her, you know. He hunted them without mercy. I wouldn't mind if he did; challenge me, that is. But I don't want to marry her, that's all."

I looked blankly at him. "I wouldn't worry, Eamonn. The lady knows her mind. And this is Terre d'Ange, not Alba."

"Eire." He sighed. "It's an Eiran tale, Imriel." Across the ballroom, a horologist called the hour. It was later than I had guessed. Eamonn heaved himself to his feet. "Ah, now! I owe the little princess a dance. I'd best claim it, hadn't I?"

"I'll go with you," I said. "I asked as much of Sidonie."

He chuckled. "Mind you don't get chilblains."

It was somewhat to behold, Eamonn and Alais. He was twice her height, and her small hand was lost in his brawny grip. To his credit, he was gentle and kind. Knowing full well he danced poorly, he deferred to her, letting her lead him in subtle ways. I smiled to see it, then turned to Sidonie and bowed.

"Shall we dance, Dauphine?" I asked her politely, conscious of Maslin's watching gaze.

She raised her chin. "All right. Why not?"

Although she was skilled, it could not have been less like dancing with Roshana. Sidonie's hand was cool in mine, almost impersonal. She held herself at a distance and I touched her lightly, scarce letting my right hand rest on the small of her back, formal and proper. I wanted to think of her as a sister, as I thought of Alais; and yet I couldn't. We were kin, but we were strangers to one another.

"You dance well," she said grudgingly.

"Phèdre taught me." I smiled, whirling her into a complicated turn. She followed it with ease, her dark eyes watchful. "You know, you can trust me, Sidonie. I'm not your enemy."

Her throat moved as she swallowed. "I'd like to believe it."

"Who says otherwise?" I asked.

As I watched, her glance slid sideways. Who did it seek? Ysandre, her mother? Maslin? Duc Barquiel L'Envers, clad in Akkadian finery? "It doesn't matter," she murmured.

I tightened my grip on her hand, feeling the small bones shift. "It does to me."

"Imriel." Something flared behind her mask; stubbornly, she held her ground, continuing to follow my lead with effortless grace. "You're hurting me."

I was, and I knew it, and ah! Elua help me, it felt good to draw a reaction from her. Even as the musicians ended their tune, I loosed my grip, turning her free. "Forgive me," I murmured, bowing. "It wasn't my intent, Dauphine."

Sidonie shook out her hand and eyed me with infuriating composure. "You're not exactly your own best advocate, are you, cousin?"

First it stung me, and then it made me laugh. "No," I admitted. "Not exactly."

She smiled a little. "I do want to like you, Imriel. You've been good to Alais, and I'm grateful for it. It's just . . ." She shrugged, looking very young and lonely. "I can't afford to make any mistakes."

I nodded. "I know."

"How could you?" she asked simply.

"I hear the whispers," I said. "I know what some of the peers say."

"Cruithne half-breed." Sidonie gave a bitter laugh. "And then they look at you and your pure D'Angeline blood, and they wonder."

"Sidonie." I steered her off the dancing floor. "I swear to you, I have no designs on the throne." On impulse, I dropped to one knee, taking her hand. "Sidonie de la Courcel, Dauphine of Terre d'Ange, in the name of Blessed Elua, I give you my oath of loyalty. For so long as I live, I will uphold your honor as my own and lay down my life in your defense."

She stared at me, lips parted in shock. "Are you mad?"

I grinned at her. "Mayhap. Do you accept my oath?"

"I . . . yes. All right." She steeled her spine. "I do."

"Good." I rose, then bowed and kissed her hand. "Now I'm going to go get drunk and usher in the Longest Night."

I succeeded in both goals.

At midnight, Night's Crier entered the ballroom, sounding his bronze tocsin. We all fell silent and watched as the vast hall was plunged into near-total darkness. Phèdre had spoken truly; it was an ancient ritual, unchanged since before the coming of Elua. It was all done by players' tricks, but in ancient Hellas the theatre was sacred. We do not forget. I gasped with the others when the false mountain crag in the musicians' grotto split to reveal the Winter Queen hobbling on her blackthorn staff. I cheered with the others when the ballroom doors were flung open to admit the Sun Prince in his chariot. He pointed his gilded spear at the Winter Queen and her rags fell away, revealing a beautiful maiden.

In a rush of oil-soaked wicks, the light returned.

"Oh, Imriel!" Eamonn sounded dazzled. "It's so beautiful!"

"Yes," I said softly. "It is."

I found Phèdre then, and asked her for the first dance of the reborn year. Like light after darkness, she was impossibly beautiful, luminous as a pearl. I held her as close as I dared, and mayhap it was the *joie*, but it seemed we floated together over the polished parquet, both of us clad in ivory white. People stopped their revelry to watch us, and my heart swelled with pride and love.

"Thank you," I whispered. "Always, for everything."

Phèdre shook her head, the brilliants in her hair scattering myriad points of light. "When darkness shattered our lives, you made them whole, Imri. There is no need for thanks, now or ever." She touched my silken mask with tenderness. "Only be happy. It is all I want for you."

"I am," I said honestly. "Tonight, I am."

And I was. I drank cup after cup of *joie*, until my mouth felt numb and I was untethered from my being. I danced with a great many women that night, their masked faces swimming in my sight. I do not even remember the last one, only that Mavros and Roshana introduced us, laughing. She must have been from Kusheth. She was an undine, a waternymph. I remember her drawing me into the shadows of the colonnade. By that time, some of the lamps had been extinguished and the shadows were alive with the half-glimpsed couplings, the heady whispers and gasps of love. I remember her mouth, hot and devouring on mine. I remember struggling with her attire, my hands seeking her smooth flesh beneath layers of frothing silk.

I remember her freeing my erect phallus from the confines of Baldur's tight breeches, and her face above me, gone soft with pleasure behind its mask.

I remember the feel of her buttocks, taut and yielding beneath my urging fingertips.

"Joy!" she gasped. "Oh, yes!"

Holding her braced against a column, I closed my eyes. Behind my lids, I saw too much. It was better open, staring into the face of masked anonymity. "Joy," I echoed, feeling the leap of desire in my loins, as urgent and mindless as a salmon surging upstream. With a vast sense of relief, I spent myself and shuddered. "Joy."

"Ah, Elua!" With a breathless laugh, my masked companion slipped away from me. I stayed there for a moment, gazing at the lights and revelry, feeling the familiar aftermath of melancholy threaten. I thought about Joscelin, kneeling beneath the frozen stars, and the careless oath I had sworn to Sidonie. And then I pushed away such thoughts and left the shadows.

So passed the Longest Night.

TWENTY-TWO

THE DAYS FOLLOWING the Midwinter Masque were
filled with gossip and hearsay. To be honest, there was
little else to do in the City during the dead of winter. I found
myself growing weary of it, feeling cooped and cloistered.

The Game of Courtship recovered from whatever blows
were dealt it on the Longest Night and continued apace, but
I held myself back from it. There were young women I liked
well enough among my friends, but it was a tame emotion,
fond and easy. I listened to my friends' protestations of
heartbreaking passion, and measured them against what I
knew of love, which was all at once terrible and wondrous
and cruel. I could not imagine any of them surviving what
Phèdre and Joscelin had endured.

I could play at pleasure, but not love.

Since it seemed unfair to play the game while my heart
wasn't engaged, I didn't. There was pleasure to be found
elsewhere. When Eamonn and I weren't continuing our respective studies, we went often to Night's Doorstep, accompanied by Montrève's none-too-reluctant retainers. It was
still the fashion for daring young gentry to do so, but we
were more welcome than most. There were more Tsingani

than ever in Night's Doorstep, and they had not forgotten what Phèdre had done.

I liked it there, as did Eamonn. There was an honesty and a spontaneity present that was lacking in mannered Court life. We sat for hours, talking and arguing over jugs of wine or tankards of ale, joined by folk from all walks of life. And too, Naamah's Servants plied their trade in Night's Doorstep. They were of a less rarefied ilk than the adepts of the Night Court, but they took their calling no less seriously.

The Night Court, alas, was beyond our everyday means. I received an allowance from the proceeds of my estates, but most of that was held in trust until I reached my majority. I daresay Phèdre would have had it increased if I had asked, but I felt awkward. Her father had been a merchant's son, and it was owing to his feckless ways that she came to be sold into indentured servitude in the Night Court. I would sooner cut off my right hand than ask her.

As for Eamonn, he had little concept of money's value. Isolated from the rest of the world for long centuries, Alba's trade remained a fledgling industry; and the Dalriada were not at its forefront. Eamonn had arrived in Terre d'Ange with a purse of newly minted gold coin, and left to his own devices, he would have spent it until it was gone. It was Phèdre who hauled him to meet with her factor, who taught him about banking houses and shrewd investments. Eamonn had sufficient funds to live on, but it was not enough for the luxury of the Night Court.

So we made do.

For as much as I fretted at winter's confines, I dreaded spring's arrival. But as surely as dawn follows dusk, it came. Snow melted in the passes of the Camaeline Mountains. In the south, the earth thawed. Dormant plants burst forth with green growth. I celebrated my natality and turned seventeen, one year closer to my majority. Along the western coast of Terre d'Ange, watchers vied for a sight of the Cruarch's flagship.

And Eamonn mac Grainne scented the air and looked toward Tiberium.

I held my tongue for days, then blurted the words. "I wish you wouldn't go."

We were drinking in the Cockerel when I said it. Eamonn was hunched over the table, a foaming tankard dwarfed in his hands. He always seemed too big for his surroundings. His coppery brows knit into a perplexed frown. "Why, Imri? You know it's what I want."

I stared at the table, tracing lines in the scarred wood. "I'll miss you, that's all. What does Tiberium offer that Terre d'Ange doesn't?"

"I don't know," he said peaceably. "That's the point." He blew foam from his tankard and sipped. "I'll miss you, too."

"Not enough," I said darkly.

Eamonn laughed. "Are we friends or lovers?"

I shrugged, picking at the scarred wood with my thumbnail. "You know the answer. You're like a brother to me, Eamonn." I paused. "What I told you in Montrève . . . I've never told another living soul, except for Phèdre."

"Daršanga," he murmured.

I nodded. "I trust you."

"Imriel." Eamonn covered my hand with his, stilling it. "I will take that trust to my grave, and you know it." His grey-green eyes were wide and earnest. "But you must find your own way in the world, as I must find mine." He shook his head in frustration, words failing him. "This . . . your friendship is a gift unlooked for. I will treasure it, always. But this thing, I must do it for me."

I clasped his hand hard. "You won't forget me?"

"Never," he said simply.

This year, Quintilius Rousse timed his return to the City of Elua to coincide with Drustan's arrival. Ten days later, he departed with Eamonn in tow. With the Queen's blessing, the Royal Admiral would escort his unlooked-for Dalriadan son to Tiberium.

We turned out to bid them farewell. Ti-Philippe knew a couple of the City Guard on duty at the Southern Gate, and they let me mount the guard tower. From that vantage point, I watched as the Admiral's party rode toward Marsilikos. Eamonn turned in the saddle, waving. I waved back, watching until they were small in the distance and I could only pick out Eamonn by the gleam of sunlight on his coppery hair.

And then they were gone.

It began a moody time for me. Although I had known it, even I failed to fully reckon how much Eamonn's unwavering cheer balanced my own brooding tendencies. My Court friends irritated me with their endless prattle. Night's Doorstep seemed a hollow pleasure without Eamonn's company. By the time we departed the City for Montrève, I was glad to leave.

In Montrève, it was a little better. As I had done before, I sought refuge in physical labor, assisting in the day-to-day business of running the estate. I worked as hard as I had played the previous summer, often laboring from dawn until dusk. It raised a few brows, but the Friote clan welcomed my assistance with good-natured tolerance.

Phèdre worried, I know.

Some weeks into the summer, she called me into her study, regarding me with concerned affection. "I didn't exactly get my Longest Night's wish for you, did I?"

"Happiness?" I asked.

She nodded. "It is just that you miss Eamonn?"

"No." I shrugged. "It's a part of it. But there's more, too." I propped my chin on my hand, thinking. "I don't know. I don't know what to *do* with myself. Everyone else seems to be content with their lot or sure of their goals, and I'm not either. Not because of you," I added hastily. "The discontent, I mean. Ah, Elua! I ought to wake up every day grateful to be alive. And I do, I am, but—"

"Imri." Phèdre cut me off gently. "It's all right, love. You can't force happiness."

"Were you happy at this age?" I asked.

"I was." She smiled. "Happy, shallow, and vain."

It made me smile, too. "How did you know what you wanted?"

"They were simple wants," she said wryly. "I wanted to make my lord Delaunay proud of me, and mayhap to love me. I wanted to make my marque and be hailed by the City as the Queen of Courtesans." Phèdre shook her head. "The other things, those came later."

"Saving the realm, you mean?" I teased her.

She flushed. "I never meant to. Well, I didn't set out to. I was only trying to do what was right. And somehow, there always seemed to be one more thing to be done. It added up to more than I reckoned." A delicate furrow formed between her brows. "They were terrible times, Imriel, a lot of them."

"I know." I sighed. "But now it seems like there's nothing left to be done."

"No room left for heroes, you mean?"

Even in Phèdre's gentle tone, it sounded foolish said aloud; and yet she had cut to the quick of it. I looked away. "I just feel . . . trivial, sometimes."

"So it's not enough to be good?" she asked.

The question caught me out, and I glanced sharply at her. "It should be, shouldn't it?"

Her eyes were dark and sympathetic. "It is, love; but the truth is, it doesn't always feel that way. Don't worry, your time will come."

I took a deep breath. "I feel like I ought to do . . . I don't know, *somewhat*. I could find my mother," I said slowly. "Find her and bring her to justice. That would be a worthy gesture." I imagined Sidonie's expression. "It would silence a lot of doubt."

"Mayhap," Phèdre said. "You'd have to start by reading her letters."

"Why?" I asked.

"Because the first step in dealing with Melisande is understanding her," she said. "It's true for anyone and doubly true for your mother."

I shook my head. "I don't want to understand her."

"Then you're not ready. Someday, mayhap, but not today." Rising, Phèdre stooped to kiss my brow. "Imri, it's all right to yearn for things you can't even name."

"Other people don't," I said.

"Oh, they do." She smiled at me. "They just don't know it."

In some oblique way, it made me feel better. I couldn't even say why. It was true, Phèdre had a gift for understanding people. It reminded me of what Mavros had said two summers ago. Whatever the mirror of otherness reflected, bright or dark, she was willing to look into it without fear. Even in Daršanga, it had been true; and what she had seen reflected of herself in the Mahrkagir's mad gaze, I shuddered to think. Death's Whore, we called her.

Yet she had given hope to us all, she and Joscelin.

And saved us.

That summer, I renewed my resolve to be worthy of them. I stopped brooding and sought to be somber and conscientious, grateful for what I had and mindful that, in Phèdre's words, it was all right to yearn for things I could not name.

When sorrow struck Montrève, it stood me in good stead.

It happened to Katherine. Although she and Gilot had yet to wed, they had settled contentedly into a life together. She had lit a candle to Eisheth in his name and gotten with child. By the time we arrived, her belly was already beginning to swell. She sported her little bulge with pride, carrying on with her chores, stroking it smugly. For his part, Gilot went about beaming.

She lost the child.

It happens, I am told. Still, it was a terrible thing. I remember servants hurrying from the bedchamber, their arms laden with bloody linens, and Gilot's pallid face, his fearful eyes stretched wide to show the whites. The Eisandine chirurgeon Phèdre had summoned could do nothing. She emerged, shaking her head in regret.

"Your lady will recover," she said softly. "But I fear this babe is lost."

Gilot shook and wept.

I went with him into the bedchamber, where Katherine reclined, pale and drawn. Phèdre had drawn up a chair beside her; without comment, she laved her seneschal's daughter's temples with a cool, damp cloth. Our eyes met, filled with mutual sympathy.

"Oh, my love!" Choking, Gilot knelt at the bedside. "I'm so sorry!"

"It's not your fault," Katherine murmured, turning her face away.

Such is the nature of love, wondrous and terrible. It cannot always withstand life's cruel vicissitudes. So I beheld that summer, although it wasn't evident that night. After a decent amount of time, I drew Gilot away, murmuring well-meaning sentiments. With Joscelin's tacit nod of approval, I ordered a keg of brandy breached, and got Gilot well and truly drunk.

Afterward, I went to see Katherine on my own.

"I'm sorry for your loss," I said humbly. "Truly, I am."

"Thank you, Imri. You've always been a good friend to me." Her fingers curled into mine. She smiled wanly. "What is it, do you think, that Blessed Elua sought to impart to me with this lesson?"

I shook my head. "It's not my place to say, Katherine. Sometimes bad things happen."

"They happened to you." Her head rolled on the pillows, her hollow gaze seeking mine. "Oh, Imriel! How did you endure it?"

"One day at a time," I said. "One hour at a time, minute by minute." I stroked her hand. "Then, and for a long time afterward. But it does get better, I promise."

Katherine mended, at least in body. Her heart was another matter. After the miscarriage, nothing was the same between her and Gilot. Why, I could not say; I'm not even sure she knew herself. But although she was apologetic for it, she withdrew from him and remained distant, saying only that perhaps they had committed to one another too young.

For his part, Gilot was hurt and bewildered.

I grieved for him, but there was nothing anyone could do to help. He tried to ply her with tenderness, to no avail. Whatever it was that had broken between them, it could not be fixed by love alone; not now, and mayhap never.

That autumn, when we departed for the City, Gilot came with us.

I watched them say their good-byes in the courtyard. It was a strained moment and a sad one. When we struck out on the journey, I made it a point to ride beside Gilot, offering my silent commiseration. From time to time, I glanced at his clean-cut profile. He was quiet and sober, every inch the professional man-at-arms, his brown hair bound unwontedly in a tight braid. All the lively merriment gone from his eyes. We rode for several leagues before he spoke, and when he did, his voice was harsh with pain and impotent anger.

"Don't fall in love, Imri," he said. "It will only break your heart."

"No fear," I murmured. "I haven't yet."

Gilot shuddered. "Don't."

TWENTY-THREE

I N THE CITY, my restlessness returned.
I couldn't help it. I was seventeen and I wanted ...
something. Love, despite Gilot's warning; adventure, despite what I knew of its rigors. It didn't matter. I wanted, with passionate intensity, to feel. I wanted *more*.

Most of the time, I kept it in check. At others, it would break free. I lashed out at friends and earned a name for having a sharp tongue.

And once, I lashed out at Nicola L'Envers y Aragon.

She had returned for the winter, along with her son Raul, who was contentedly courting several of the young women of the Court, including Colette Trente. Betimes, Phèdre saw Lady Nicola. Although she was quiet about it, I knew. I always knew. I saw what I had seen in Daršanga; the languor, the remote echo of violent pleasure. And despite my attempts at resolve and maturity, I still hated it.

It was an awkward encounter, taking place in the Salon of Eisheth's Harp; a small fête in honor of a minor dignitary from one of the Caerdicci city-states. At the Queen's behest, the musicians struck up a tune and everyone took part in a Caerdicci pavane in which one changed partners according to intricate rules.

At the end, I found myself partnered with the Lady Nicola.

I forced a pleasant smile as we danced, and we spoke lightly of inconsequential matters. She was a diplomat's wife; she was good at it. But there was another line of thought running behind her eyes, and when the dance ended, she gave voice to it with unexpected honesty. "You don't like me overmuch, do you?"

In the middle of a polite bow, I stiffened. "No," I admitted, straightening. "Not overmuch, I'm afraid."

Nicola studied me. There was no offense in her expression, only curiosity. "Why?"

I glanced over at Phèdre. She was conversing with the Caerdicci dignitary, her face alight with lively intelligence. A rush of love and anger overcame me. "Tell me, what manner of toys do you prefer, my lady?" I asked. "Whips? Brands? Blades?" With satisfaction, I watched Nicola blanch. "If you knew . . ." For a moment, words failed me. With an effort, I gathered myself. "If you knew," I said coldly, "if you had *any* idea, the slightest idea, what Phèdre has endured, you would never lay a hand upon her. You would never conduct such cruel outrage and call it *love*." I shook my head. "You have no idea."

I was trembling, filled with righteous fury. I expected . . . I don't know. I expected the Lady Nicola to apologize, to retreat in humility. Instead, she looked at me with profound compassion and spoke three words in a low tone.

"Duzhmata, duzhûshta, duzhvarshta."

It struck me like a fist to the gut, hearing them spoken here. I doubled over, gasping, hearing her voice at a distance. Vaguely aware, I suffered myself to be led to a low couch. There I collapsed, pale and sweating.

"I'm sorry." Nicola's face swam in my gaze, concerned. "Imriel, forgive me."

"You know," I whispered.

Her warm hands chafed my cold ones. "Yes."

"How?" I asked helplessly.

There was a world of sorrow in her gaze; an ocean of sorrow. "Because I could bear to hear it. Oh, Imriel! In a thousand years, I could never come between Phèdre and Joscelin, nor would I try to. What they are to one another . . ." Kneeling before me, Nicola shrugged. "The gods alone have decreed. And yet this thing, this one thing, I can hear and understand, in a way that he cannot. Altogether, they are stronger for it." She paused. "Have you never felt the need to tell anyone what befell you in that terrible place? Someone you trusted without reservation?"

Thinking of Eamonn, I nodded.

"Then you know," she said softly.

"But you hurt her," I whispered. "You *hurt* her!"

The Lady Nicola L'Envers y Aragon smiled. "No," she said. "There is a point where pleasure and pain commingle. Believe me, I would violate neither Elua's precept or Phèdre's trust." She touched my cheek, the garnet seal bearing the mark of Kushiel's Dart dangling from her wrist, brushing my skin. "And there are points, too, where being a friend and a lover intermesh. Is it hurtful to explore these?"

"Don't!" I shrank from her touch. "Please, don't."

She sat back on her heels, violet eyes grave, her gold-embroidered skirts pooling around her. "As you wish," Nicola said. "Only know . . ." She opened her hand, regarding her empty palm, contemplating the lines etched upon it. "Only know."

"Know *what*?" I cried.

"Know yourself." Nicola touched the center of my brow

with the tip of her forefinger. "It's a good place to start, Prince Imriel."

I tried.

I tried so hard to be *good* that winter. All the while, all I yearned for was freedom: freedom from my past, freedom from my present, hedged all around with safeguards. I let go my antipathy toward the Lady Nicola, gaining a new sympathy and understanding. At Court, I tried hard to be pleasant and lighthearted. Making an effort, I tried, very hard, to be a good brother to Alais and Sidonie.

Half the time, I even felt like it.

At thirteen, Alais was as prickly as a thornbush. With her, I pretended nothing had changed. Betimes she would relent and speak openly to me; about her fears regarding the unsettled succession in Alba, about the long-standing quarrel between her parents. At other times, she was bristly and removed.

Sidonie was another matter.

Elua help me! I came to respect her in that year. No, that is a lie. I came to admire her. I watched and I saw. Attending an increasing number of Court events, she shouldered her burden as the Dauphine of Terre d'Ange squarely, aware of all it entailed. There was a constant undercurrent of intrigue and speculation, which she ignored with remarkable thoroughness. If it made her seem a touch cool and removed, so be it. It was a heavy burden.

I thought about my oath.

Impossible as it seemed, it remained a secret between us. No one except Sidonie had heard me swear it on that Longest Night. I had told no one; not even Phèdre. Nor, it seemed, had Sidonie.

We had a secret.

It felt strange, though not in a bad way. We never spoke

of it. But betimes, in a crowded room, I would catch her eye and see a faint smile hover at the corner of her mouth. I knew, then, she thought of it, too.

And that year, for the first time, my loyalty was assailed.

It happened in Night's Doorstep, a few weeks after Mid-winter. A party of us had ventured forth, defying the bitter cold. It was my usual group of friends—Bertran de Trevalion, the Trentes, Raul L'Envers y Aragon, Marguerite Grosmaine. Gilot was there, and a handful of men-at-arms attending the others. All in all, we made a considerable crowd.

I had scarce been to the Cockerel since Eamonn had left, and I reveled in the reception I received. There were always Tsingani there, and as Phèdre's foster-son, I was always welcome among them. Whether or not I knew them, they knew me. They knew the story. And in some ways, I felt more at home among them than I ever did at Court.

"The *gadjo* pearl!" a Tsingano man cried, grinning. He flung his arm around my shoulders. "We Tsingani saved your life, didn't we, *chavo*?"

"You did," I agreed, ignoring the shocked stares of my Court companions. I beckoned to the barkeep. "I'll stand a round for the Tsingani!"

They cheered and I laughed.

"Are you mad, Imriel?" Bertran asked quietly.

"Not at all," I said cheerfully. "It's true, they did. If not for the Tsingani, I'd still be a slave in Drujan. A *dead* slave."

He gave me a troubled look. "You shouldn't speak of such things in public."

"Why not?" I asked. "It's true."

"Oh, yes!" My Tsingano comrade gave my shoulders a friendly shake. "And if not for your *gadjo* foster-mother,

Anasztaisia's son would be a prisoner!" He let me go and extended his hand, dark and sinewy. "I am Viktor."

I clasped it firmly. "Imriel."

For a moment, I thought it would go badly with my Court friends; then Julien Trente let out a whoop of enthusiasm. "All right, then! *I'll* stand a round for the Tsingani!"

After that, all was well. A pair of fiddlers began to play, and everyone mingled and drank together. As if summoned by magic—or more likely, a well-organized system of messengers—others came, including several of Naamah's Servants. There was one I knew, a pretty girl named Hélène. I whispered in her ear, pointing her toward Gilot. He had a dazed look on his face as she led him away toward a back room. I hid my smile in a tankard of ale, reckoning it well worth the patron-fee.

By the time we left, it was late and the moon was high overhead, small and distant. We milled around in the crisp air, laughing and talking over the night's adventure, waiting for the stable-lads to fetch our mounts from the livery. The Trentes had come by carriage, and there was some fuss over a fraying harness strap. I paid it scant heed. Viktor and two of the other Tsingani were admiring the Bastard, discussing his lineage in Tsingani dialect. I was listening to them, trying to make out their comments, when a figure stepped from the shadows.

"Prince Imriel."

"Yes?" I frowned. It was a man, and no one I knew. His lower face was swathed in a heavy scarf, muffling his voice, and he wore a rustic woolen cap pulled low over his brow.

"You have friends in Parliament." His eyes glinted in his shadowed face. "True of heart and pure of blood."

Every ounce of camaraderie and warmth left me. "Who are you?"

"No one." He began backing away. "No one."

"Wait, stop." I moved to detain him. "Stop!" Bertran's mount swung around abruptly, blocking me. Bertran stared down at me, incredulous.

"What did that fellow just say to you?" he asked.

The mysterious messenger was disappearing around the corner of the Cockerel into a dark alley. "Stop!" I shouted, shoving at solid horseflesh. "Damn it, Bertran, help me catch him or get out of the way!"

He tried to do both at once. I slipped past him and was nearly run down. Bowled over by his charge, I ducked my head, trying to scramble out of the way of his mount's churning hooves. I heard Bertran swearing, Gilot shouting at him, and the ring of a sword being drawn.

"Gilot!" I pointed toward the alley. "That way!"

Montrève's men-at-arms don't need to be told twice. Gilot took off at a dead run, boots skidding on the icy cobblestones, and plunged into the alley. I got to my feet and felt Bertran's hand descend on my shoulder.

"What did he say to you?" he repeated.

"Later." I shook him off, racing after Gilot.

Once I passed beyond the faint illumination from the street, it was pitch-black in the alley. Within twenty paces, I slowed to a walk, then halted. Closing my eyes, I listened. I could hear footsteps and someone's breathing. "Gilot?"

"Aye." He sounded disgruntled. "He's gone, Imri."

Bertran appeared at the mouth of the alley with a lit torch. "Any luck?"

"No," I said. "Bring that here, will you?"

By torchlight, it was obvious the alley grew too narrow to admit him on horseback. Bertran dismounted and came on foot. With the torch casting wavering shadows on the crowded buildings of Night's Doorstep, we searched to no avail. The back alleys branched and branched again. There were too many paths my unwelcome messenger could have taken, and all of them were silent and empty.

"Come on." Gilot clapped a hand on my shoulder. "Let's go back; the others must be freezing."

A dozen yards from the mouth of the alley, Bertran pointed. "What's that?"

I stooped and picked up the object. "His cap. He was wearing this."

"Let me see." Bertran held out his free hand. I gave it to him. He examined it, frowning, then peered inside it. I saw his mouth tighten.

"What is it?" I asked.

"Hold this." He thrust the torch at Gilot, who took it without comment. I watched as Bertran worked at a scrap of parchment sewn into the interior of the cap. There was a message written on it. He read it silently to himself, and I felt my blood run cold.

"Bertran," I said. "Please."

He met my eyes and his were dark with distrust. "Read it."

I took it from him, squinting at the blurred ink. "'Dolphin fountain, sunset, two days hence,'" I read aloud. "Bertran, I have no idea what that means. I swear to you, I have no idea who that man was or what he was talking about."

"Friends," he said softly. "'True of heart and *pure of blood.*' Don't play me for a fool, Imriel. *Prince* Imriel."

It was like a nightmare. I shook my head. "No," I said. "You know me. Name of Elua, Bertran! I don't want the throne. I don't want the holdings I have! Have I ever given you any reason to doubt me?" I asked fiercely. "*Any* reason?"

"No." The torchlight made a mask of his face, strange and

unfamiliar. "But your mother played a long game, didn't she? So my own mother always said, and she's cause to know." A muscle in his jaw twitched. "Melisande Shahrizai destroyed my grandfather, too, and he was a hero, once. Percy de Somerville. My father gave up his *name* to be free of the taint of her treachery." He laughed bitterly. "Imagine that! Baudoin de Trevalion was executed for treason, and the stench of the Trevalion name still reeked less than Somerville's after your mother was done with it."

"I know," I said quietly. "And I am sorry for it. But I am *not* my mother's son."

"Pray you're not." Bertran looked hard at me. "Pray you're not, Imri! Because I will see you dead before I let you follow in her footsteps."

"My lord de Trevalion!" Gilot interceded, cool and crisp. "Do you question the honor of House Montrève?" He shifted the torch into his left hand, placing the right on the hilt of his sword. "If you do, I will be pleased to answer for it."

"Enough!" I moved between them. "Gilot, stand down. This is absurd. Bertran . . ." I spread my hands. "Whatever is going on, I have no part in it. The first thing in the morning, I'll take the matter to the Queen."

Nothing in his expression changed. "Give me the note. I'll do it myself."

"Fine." I shoved it at him. "Take it."

He took it without comment and we returned to the Cock-erel. Our companions were waiting, shivering with cold and excitement, stamping and hugging their cloaks around them as they speculated on what had transpired.

"Was it a cutpurse?" Julien called. "Did you catch him?"

Bertran eyed me.

"No, and no." I took a deep breath. "It's nothing. I've no

idea who he was. He tried to imply that I'm involved in some manner of intrigue, that's all."

"Oh, good!" Julien said happily. "Are you?"

"No!" The word burst from me. I sighed, taking the Bastard's reins from a wide-eyed stable-lad. "Come on," I said. "It's late. You'll hear all about it on the morrow."

We made our respective ways home. Gilot and I rode the last few blocks alone. I kept silent for as long as I could stand it, and then finally spoke.

"I am telling the truth, you know," I said.

"Of course!" He looked surprised. "Imri, I've known you since you were thirteen years old. I never doubted it."

A wave of gratitude overtook me. "My thanks."

Gilot shook his head. "No thanks needed." He grinned at me. "Well, except mayhap mine to you, young highness. Hélène is a peach."

I smiled. "I'd forgotten. It seems like days ago, doesn't it?"

"Aye." His face turned sober as we entered the townhouse courtyard. "Whatever this business is, it's no good. I think you'd best wake her ladyship and tell her."

"I mean to," I said.

We woke the household and held a conference in the salon. Everyone sat or stood around, blinking and stifling yawns. Phèdre listened without interrupting, the vague softness of sleep giving way to a fierce clarity.

"What of the man?" she asked when I had finished.

I shrugged, feeling stupid and helpless. "I couldn't *see* well enough! I know, you trained me better than that, but it's just like the assassin in Nineveh. I wasn't expecting it, I didn't think."

"That's all right," she said gently. "Go slowly, and tell me what you remember."

I closed my eyes, hearing his muffled voice in my memory. "He was youngish," I said. "Older than me, but still young. And he knew Night's Doorstep, but he's not City-born. He had a provincial accent; Namarrese, mayhap." I thought about it. "Yes, Namarrese. He sounded a little like the master cheese-maker at Heuzé."

"Good," Phèdre said. "How tall was he?"

Opening my eyes, I held my hand out a few inches above chin level. "Not tall. He stood about so high to me. Slight, and quick."

"He knew what he was about," Gilot agreed. "He vanished like a rabbit."

"Lucky for him," Joscelin said darkly. He looked absolutely thunderous. For the first time in years, I shivered a little at the sight of him.

"Not lucky," Phèdre said. "This was carefully planned. But why?" She paced the salon, frowning in thought. "Imri, is there anything you might have said or done to give someone reason to believe you might welcome such an overture? Anything?"

Her words were an unexpected blow. "How can you ask?" I said bitterly. "I wouldn't, not in a thousand years! How can you think it? How can you possibly?"

"Imriel." She touched my hand. "I don't. But people hear what they wish to hear, and a careless jest may be taken in earnest."

It calmed me enough to think. "No," I said. "It's not somewhat I'd jest about. Only . . ." I paused. "Last year, at the Midwinter Masque, when I came as Baldur . . . because he was a god of light, Sidonie asked if I thought I might be asked to play the Sun Prince."

"Like Baudoin de Trevalion," Phèdre said softly.

I nodded. "Someone might have taken it for a sign."

She looked a little sick. "I never thought of that."

"Nor did I." I squared my shoulders. "But that's all. There's nothing else."

"So why this?" Phèdre mused. "Why *now*?"

"Because Imriel turns eighteen and gains his majority in the spring," Joscelin said in a blunt tone. "And there are members of Parliament unhappy about a half-Cruithne heir to the D'Angeline throne while Drustan's damned nephew appears to be laying claim to the succession in Alba without a D'Angeline in sight."

They exchanged a glance.

"Mayhap," Phèdre said slowly. "Or it may be somewhat else altogether."

Joscelin raised his brows. "What are you thinking?"

She shook her head. "Nothing, yet." Her dark eyes focused on me, clear and impossibly deep, save for the scarlet mote. "Go to bed, love. There's naught to be done about it tonight. We'll speak with the Queen in the morning."

TWENTY-FOUR

M Y STATUS AT COURT was altered overnight.
It wasn't Ysandre's doing. To her credit, the
Queen heard me out with aplomb. By all appearances, she
was unwavering in her support. But Bertran was there, a
shadow of suspicion in his eyes, the damning note in his
hand.

He told her it was he, and not I, who found the cap.

He told her I fouled his pursuit of the messenger.

"Oh, please!" I said in disgust. "You're the one who
blocked my path. And for all I know, *you're* the one planted
that note. You were awfully quick to assume the worst of me,
Bertran."

He bristled. "I would never stoop—"

Ysandre raised her hand for silence and we both com-
plied, chastened. She looked somberly at Phèdre. "What do
you think?"

"I don't know yet," she said. "But I think it's time to start
asking some serious questions about what members of Parliament may have been overheard using the phrase 'true of
heart and pure of blood.'"

The Queen raised her brows. "An open inquiry? Surely
we have more to gain by concealing our hand."

Phèdre glanced at Bertran. "How many people have you told of last night's encounter, my lord?"

His face turned brick red. "Only those who were there!"

"So," Phèdre said mildly, "I imagine it will be all over Court by this evening."

"Name of Elua!" I clenched my fists. "I'm an idiot. I should have sewn my mouth shut." I pointed at Bertran. "I should have sewn *your* mouth shut!" ·

"Oh, you'd like that!" He glared at me. "Look, I saw what I saw."

Ysandre sighed. "Did you tell your companions about the note's contents?"

Abashed, Bertran nodded. "On the way home," he muttered.

"My thanks," I said sardonically. "You're a loyal friend, Bertran."

His flush deepened. "I'm loyal to the Crown, is what I am! You know damned well what it's like, Imriel. I'll do whatever it takes to keep the Trevalion name above suspicion."

"Your ambition is to be commended, young lord de Trevalion." The Queen's tone was cool. "But a measure of forethought would not go amiss with it." She beckoned to Diderot Duval, her Captain of the Guard. "Lord Duval, see if your men can locate these companions before their tongues can wag and bid them to silence. I would proceed quietly for a day and place a covert watch over the dolphin fountain in Elua's Square on the morrow." She looked at me. "Are you willing to keep this purported appointment, cousin?"

"Yes," I said. "Of course, your majesty."

"Good." For a moment, Ysandre looked unspeakably

weary. "If naught transpires," she said to Phèdre, "I will stage an open inquiry."

Phèdre inclined her head. "My lady."

On the following day, I went to Elua's Square a little before sunset. It had all been arranged with Captain Duval. In the warm months, it was a bustling place. There was a great oak tree in the center of the square, rumored to have been planted by Blessed Elua himself. Four fountains played beneath it, and it is a popular meeting place for friends and lovers. But in the winter the fountains were dry, and only a few hearty souls strolled the square.

For the sake of appearances, Gilot accompanied me, then wandered some distance away, ostensibly immersing himself in a game of dice with a pair of idlers—members of the Queen's Guard in disguise.

I sat myself on a bench beneath the oak's barren branches, contemplating the dolphin fountain. There were four of them, dancing on their tails amid the marble waves, bodies arching. In the summer, water spewed from their smiling snouts, but they were dry now.

There had been dolphins in the harbor at Amílcar. I remember how they raced alongside the ship, breaching to blow plumes of water into the air. Fadil Chouma, the Menekhetan slaver, had pointed them out to me as I stood beside him aboard the ship, scared and sick, dizzy with the lingering effects of opium.

I was scared now, too.

No one came. We waited until darkness fell. I sat for a long time without moving on that bench. By the time Captain Duval and his men came to fetch me, the cold had sunk deep into my bones.

"Go home, young highness," the Captain said almost

kindly. Almost, but not quite. "The Queen thanks you for your service."

I gazed up at him. "I didn't ask for this," I whispered.

He hesitated. "Of course not."

"Move aside." Joscelin's voice was as clear and cutting as a blade. "I'll take him."

The Captain paused, then moved, gesturing to his men to do the same. I could have wept at the sight of Joscelin, his face at once furious and tender, a thick woolen blanket over his arm and the worn hilt of his sword jutting over his shoulder, silhouetted against the stars. He placed the blanket around me.

"Come, love," he said. "Let's go home."

Rumor kills.

I learned it that winter. The Queen's inquiry came to naught. If there was a conspiracy seeking to recruit me, it was well and truly hidden. There were a few nobles embarrassed, forced to admit to seditious comments. All of them fervently denied acting upon them.

No one remembered hearing the phrase "true of heart and pure of blood."

Nonetheless, I had been tarred with the brush of suspicion—and it stuck. Old friends eyed me askance and were cool in my company. My relationship with Bertran turned bitter, bordering on outright enmity. Only the Queen's continued show of support kept me from becoming a pariah at Court. Even Phèdre and Joscelin's support was reckoned suspect. Beloved as they were, it was whispered that they were naïve, too good-hearted to recognize that they had taken a serpent to their bosom.

It hurt.

It hurt a lot; more than I had reckoned. When my mother

vanished, I had been braced for it. But this . . . this was unlooked for. It was unfair. I hadn't done anything wrong.

To my surprise, the Shahrizai stood by me.

"You *are* family, Imriel," Mavros said dryly. "After all, we've withstood worse."

Alais stood by me, too. If there was anything in the world she disliked, it was being told what to think. The mill of rumors only made her more staunch in her friendship, and I was more grateful for it than I could say.

"What does Phèdre think about it?" she asked me one day. "*Really* think?"

"I don't know," I admitted. "She's been quiet about it."

"She suspects somewhat," Alais said with certainty.

"Mayhap." I shrugged. "But I don't know what." I changed the subject. "What passes in Alba these days?"

Alais looked away. "Prince Talorcan is coming this summer."

"Drustan's heir?" I asked in surprise.

She smiled with a wryness that belied her thirteen years. "He hasn't named him formally." We were sitting together in her quarters, talking in low tones to avoid the ears of her attendants. "I imagine Father will ask me after I've had a chance to meet him."

"Ask you?" I repeated.

"If I'm willing to consent to a betrothal." She hugged her knees. "He thinks it's the only way. The Cullach Gorrym have threatened to revolt if he changes the tradition."

"Well, we always knew it might come to this," I said. "What will you do?"

Alais shrugged. "I'll meet him. It would only be a betrothal; we wouldn't wed for a few years, at least." She smiled again, this time wistfully. "Mayhap he'll be nice, like Eamonn. Wouldn't it be nice if he were like Eamonn?"

"Eamonn!" I laughed. "So he's what you'd look for in a bridegroom?"

"Oh, yes!" Her eyes glowed. "He's kind and funny, and . . ."

"Tall?" I suggested.

She scowled at me. "Don't be silly. Who would you have me wed, Imri? Some pretty-faced D'Angeline lordling with a smooth tongue? True of heart and pure of blood?" she said, an edge to her voice.

I winced. "No, of course not."

"I *liked* Eamonn."

"I liked him, too, villain," I said softly. "I miss him a lot." I reached out to stroke a lock of her hair. "In fact, you're right. I can't think of anyone else I'd sooner see you wed when it comes time. But I'm afraid the kingdom of the Dalriada is but a tiny portion of Alba, and Eamonn's a younger son with little stake in it. You might make a love-match out of it, but don't look for the Queen or your father to arrange it."

"I know." Alais sighed, exhaling so hard it lifted the black curls from her brow. "And it's not exactly a love-match, is it? I'm nothing more than a child to him. He went off to Tiberium without a backward glance." She frowned. "I wish I were older."

"Me, too, villain," I said with sympathy.

"You've no cause to complain. You've almost reached your majority," Alais said tartly. "And stop calling me that."

Thus, Alais.

And then there was Sidonie.

In her own way, she stood by me, too. Over a year had passed since I made my impulsive oath of fealty to her, and still, throughout this ordeal, neither of us spoke of it. Instead, we treated one another with increasing degrees of courtesy and respect. It was a strange thing, this framework; so distant and formal, built around a shared secret.

Why did neither of us invoke it?

I could not say, save that for my part, it proved nothing. Oaths may be broken. Even Joscelin, whom I idolized, had broken most of his Cassiline vows. Surely my detractors would point to that example. What did I have in response? My mother's word, a diamond strung on a fraying velvet rope. A note reading *I keep my promises.*

Mayhap it was even true; still, I did not think it would play well at Court. And mayhap Sidonie knew it, too.

She turned sixteen that spring, becoming eligible for the Game of Courtship. Her natality fell a few weeks before mine. The Queen staged a gala for the occasion. I hovered on the outskirts of it, watching suitors declare themselves in relentless pursuit. Bertran de Trevalion was numbered among them, which was another reason I kept my distance.

"Have you ever seen men fishing for sharks?" Mavros murmured in my ear.

I shook my head.

His hand tightened on my shoulder. "They go into a frenzy at the scent of blood in the water," he said. "I'm almost tempted to pity the lass."

"I wouldn't," Roshana said. "Look at her! She's capable of holding her own."

Sidonie was, too. She was coolly polite to all her suitors, encouraging to none. The frenzy was held at bay. There were other factors, of course. There was Amarante of Namarre, appointed as one of her ladies-in-waiting. Her mother Bérèngere was the head of Naamah's Order, and I suspected she had been recruited to instruct Sidonie in Naamah's arts.

And there was Maslin de Lombelon.

I came to hate him that spring. It is a piece of irony, since

I had wanted so much for him to like me, once. But a schism had emerged at Court, and we found ourselves on opposite sides of it. Like Bertran, he had reason to abhor the scent of treachery, and he made no secret of his mistrust. Like Bertran, he had an interest in Sidonie. Although he didn't declare it openly, it was obvious. Maslin's, I think, ran deeper than mere political ambition.

It all came out in the hunt.

I wouldn't have gone if Alais hadn't begged me. Drustan had brought her a Pictish bow on his last visit—Cruithne women are skilled with the bow—and she had been practicing with it, but this would be her first time trying her hand at bringing down live game.

It fell on one of those rare spring days when all seems right with the world. Gilot and Hugues and Ti-Philippe all accompanied me. With their company, riding at Alais' side, I felt buffered from the unpleasantness. Most of my former friends were in the cluster surrounding Sidonie. There were so many of them, I couldn't even see Maslin, taking his usual place as Sidonie's self-appointed personal Captain of the Guard.

Hugues sang aloud as we rode to the Queen's Wood, his voice ringing in the bright air. At Ti-Philippe's urging, he declaimed a few of his own verses. I winked at Alais, who ducked her head to hide a smile. Hugues sang beautifully, but he was a wretched poet.

All in all, I was in good spirits by the time we reached the wood.

The Queen's Wood was a small forest, but an old and stately one, preserved for the royal family's hunting pleasure. Mostly it is fallow deer they hunt there; we had been cautioned against bringing down aught but bucks, since the does were likely to be carrying or new mothers. I bade Alais to keep a sharp eye on Celeste, pacing at her side. She nodded, her jaw set.

We ventured into the forest, stringing out in a long, ungainly line. At this time of year, it was open, almost airy. The trees had yet to attain their full foliage, and broad shafts of sunlight pierced the canopy. All the young gentry in their spring finery made a pretty picture, moving in and out of the columns of light. They laughed and chattered, calling to one another. The Master of the Hunt and his men went about their business quietly, scouting in advance.

Despite the clamor, they found game.

We all heard the huntsmen's horns sound in the distance. Heels were clapped to horses' flanks and a mad, scrambling dash ensued.

There were two of them; a pair of young bucks engaged in contest. By the time the royal party arrived, they had bolted in opposite directions.

"That way!" I shouted, pointing toward the nearest.

"Celeste, *hunt*!" Alais cried.

What followed was pandemonium. Half the party went left, half right. The Queen's huntsmen moved to circle round and drive the quarry back to us. A laughing Sidonie and half of her lot had a few paces on us, but we were ranging close behind. Before us, the fleeing buck gained ground, light-dappled as it passed through shafts of sun; but Celeste was hot in pursuit, a low, grey shadow. For a time, we lost sight of them, but we heard the huntsmen's horns, merry and gallant, urging us onward.

And then the sound changed to an alarm.

I saw the glade.

I saw the Master of the Hunt waving his arms, his face pale and terrified.

I didn't see a deer.

It was a boar. It was a damned *monstrous* boar, the kind the veterans of the battle of Bryn Gorrydum talk about. It was massive and irritable, and it snorted as we straggled to a halt, lowering its head and presenting its tusks, its small eyes glinting.

"Alais, get behind me," I said quietly.

"Celeste," she whispered, strained.

The wolfhound was braced and snarling, her hackles standing on end. By some fluke of fate, she had positioned herself in front of Sidonie. The Dauphine sat motionless atop her fractious young mare, her face drawn and white. Her mount trembled beneath her, hooves shifting in the soft loam.

"Your highness, *don't move*," said the Master of the Hunt. She nodded stiffly.

Out of the corner of my eye, I saw Gilot and Ti-Philippe dismount, drawing their swords. Half a dozen other men did the same, Maslin included. None of them had boar-spears.

The boar scraped the earth with one trotter, whuffled, and charged. It was like a small mountain in motion.

"Celeste!" Alais screamed.

The wolfhound leapt aside, snapping at the boar as it passed. The Dauphine's mare let out a terrified squeal and bolted. Branches broke and crackled as it fled, and the boar rounded for another turn, eyeing us all.

"Guard Alais," I said briefly to Hugues.

He gave a grim nod. "Go!"

I turned the Bastard in Sidonie's direction and heeled him hard. "Yah!"

He answered; ah, Elua! I gave him his head and crouched low over his neck. The trees were a blur; everything was a blur. I clamped down hard with my thighs and silently thanked the Tsingani for breeding such a magnificent mount—and yes, Nicola L'Envers y Aragon for gifting him to me.

"Sidonie!" I cried, catching sight of her.

She was upright in the saddle, sawing at her runaway mare's reins. There was a massive deadfall in their path. Coming upon them from behind, I saw her mare check hard, planting her forelegs and refusing the jump; I saw Sidonie soar over her head, falling hard on the far side of the deadfall. I hauled on the reins, veering to the right. "Please," I whispered. "Oh, please!"

The Bastard gathered his haunches and leapt.

He tucked his striped hooves as neatly as a dancer. We cleared the fallen tree; we cleared Sidonie's recumbent form. I dismounted, scrambling on foot. I could hear somewhat stirring in the underbrush, coming toward us.

"Stay down!" I flung myself atop her.

Was it the boar? I couldn't be sure. I angled my body to best protect her, so that its gouging tusks would find my flesh first. And then I heard Sidonie de la Courcel's laugh, her true laugh, deep-throated and unexpectedly buoyant.

I stared at her, gaping.

"Oh, Imriel!" She pointed beyond where I had her pinned. "Look!"

It was a deer; only a deer. A young buck. Like as not, it was the one we had first pursued. It peered at us from the underbrush, ears pricked, its eyes moist and lambent, then beat a prudent retreat.

I sighed. "A deer."

"Oh, your face!" Sidonie gasped. "You should have seen it! It's not funny, I know, but . . ." Her laughter trailed off. Something in her expression turned soft and quizzical. "You really meant it, didn't you? Your oath."

I swallowed hard. Of a sudden, I was acutely aware of her

body beneath mine, all firm curves and tender limbs. Of her honey-gold hair, spilled across the damp loam. Of her face, inches from mine, lips parted. My own hair fell forward, curtaining her face. We were so close our breath mingled.

I saw her realize it, too, the blood rising beneath her fair skin. In the hollow of her throat, I could see her pulse quicken.

I felt . . . what? Dizzy and disoriented, as though I'd seen the sun rise in the west. I was a stranger in my own skin. Something deep in my chest felt wrong, as though a piece of me had gone missing.

Neither of us moved.

"Yes," I whispered. "I meant it."

The Bastard chose that moment to amble over and investigate. He leaned his spotted head down, snuffling at my hair. I startled and cursed, then got hold of myself and clambered to my feet. I extended my hand to Sidonie.

"Are you hurt?" I asked, helping her rise.

"No. Bruised a little, that's all." Averting her head, she brushed dirt and leaf-mold from her skirt. "Thank you, Imriel."

"For protecting you from a deer?" I asked wryly.

"For protecting me." Sidonie looked at me, her dark Cruithne eyes direct and honest. I saw, for the first time, our shared heritage in her face. Our brows were the same shape, straight and firm, tapering at the ends. Hers were burnished gold where mine were black. Otherwise, they were the same.

It made me feel strange all over again.

"I'll see if I can't catch your mare," I said.

As it happened, I couldn't. I spent some time at it, stamping and swearing. The fractious beast skittered away, showing the whites of her eyes, her reins trailing. The Bastard watched the proceedings with mild interest. Sidonie laughed. Not the same laugh, but a laugh.

"Never mind," she said. "Someone will fetch her. We'd best find out what's happened." She sobered, shivering. "Elua! I hope no one was hurt."

So I boosted her astride the Bastard and led him on foot. We hadn't gone farther than a few hundred paces before we heard the searchers calling. I gave a shout in reply. And my cursed luck held true; Maslin de Lombelon was the first to find us, bursting from the forest on horseback, his face a mask of streaked blood, none of it appearing to be his own. He rode us down furiously, drawing his sword and pointing its tip at my heart. It, too, was bloody.

"Unhand her!" he said tautly.

I stood stock-still, holding the Bastard's reins with one hand. "Maslin," I said cautiously, raising my free hand and showing it empty. "The Dauphine is unharmed."

His blade trembled. *"Unhand her!"*

"Maslin!" Sidonie's voice was sharp. "I'm fine. Leave him be."

He breathed hard, staring at her. And I knew in that moment with utter surety that he loved her; or thought he did. There was somewhat between them. I knew it. He bowed his head and sheathed his sword. "As you command, Dauphine."

In the glade, we found the others; or most of them. The boar was dead, lying in a vast unseemly mound. Alais was sitting on the ground, weeping, cradling Celeste in her lap. I winced, seeing the wolfhound's side gored, a long slash that laid her rib cage open nearly to the bone. Celeste beat her tail feebly at my approach, unable to raise her head, brown eyes apologetic.

"Oh, Imri!" Alais raised her tearstained face. "Help her, please!"

I got the whole story from her later. How the boar had charged and charged again; how Celeste had snarled and fought. How she had been gored, and how Maslin de Lombelon had stepped into the breach, shoving his blade home in the boar's mighty breast, sinking it to the hilt, holding it while it raged, until others came forward and struck a succession of death-blows, until it sank and subsided.

None of that mattered, then.

"Needle and thread," I snapped, gazing around at the ring of silent faces. "Name of Elua! Does no one carry it?"

"Here." A calm voice; Sidonie's lady-in-waiting, Amarante. From somewhere in her purse, she procurred an embroidery kit. Kneeling at my side, she handed me a threaded needle. "Do you know what you're about, highness?"

"Not really," I said grimly. "Anyone?"

No one answered. So I set about the unpleasant process while all the fine gentry of Terre d'Ange busied themselves trying to catch Sidonie's mare. I thought about the Tiberian chirurgeon, Drucilla, whom I had known in Daršanga. I remembered the advice she had given, dying; the lives she had saved. I thought about Phèdre and Joscelin. She had done as much for him, once, when they were lost in a Skaldic blizzard. He bore the scar to prove it.

I sewed up Alais' dog.

It was a messy business, but I did it. Amarante of Namarre knelt at my side, blotting away the welling blood with a wadded piece of what looked to have been fine embroidered cloth. Alais wept, holding Celeste's head. For a mercy, the wolfhound was too weak to struggle.

"Will she be all right?" Alais pleaded when I finished. "Will she?"

I wiped my brow with the back of my hand, unwittingly smearing it with blood. "I don't know, Alais," I said honestly. "Let's get her to a proper chirurgeon and see."

Maslin had not been idle while I worked. He had sent for a wagon and ordered his men to build a makeshift stretcher out of a pair of saplings and his own cloak. I stood aside, watching them ease Celeste into it.

"Hold out your hands, highness." It was Amarante who spoke, her apple-green eyes grave. I obeyed and she tipped a waterskin over them, sluicing away the blood. When she had finished, she drew a silk kerchief from her bodice, wetting it. "Here, bend down."

"My thanks, lady." I let her mop my brow. "You were a great help."

She smiled slightly. "The young princess loves her dog very much."

It was an oblique comment; but then, she was a priestess' daughter. I merely bowed in response and said, "Yes, she does."

It was a somber party that returned from the Queen's Wood. Maslin's men did their job, carrying the injured wolfhound out of the forest with care, slung between them on his cloak. Once we were out of the forest, I rode with Alais in the wagon while Gilot led the Bastard for me. Together we cradled Celeste, cushioning her as the wagon jounced along a rutted path. Alais wept steadily, tears forging two shining paths down her cheeks.

"She saved us," she said. "She did, Imri!"

"I know, love," I said softly. "I know."

On one side of the wagon, Maslin rode, glancing at me with stony hatred in his eyes, dried blood flaking on his face. On the other side was Sidonie. I didn't dare look at her; for fear of remembering the feel of her body beneath mine, for fear of the strange flutter in my chest.

Ah, Elua!

What had happened between us?

I was not sure.

And I was afraid.

TWENTY-FIVE

ALAIS' DOG CELESTE lived, and I turned eighteen.
The credit for the former went to the Queen's
Eisandine chirurgeon, Lelahiah Valais, who tended her with
the same deft professionalism she accorded her human pa-
tients. She clucked her tongue over the shoddy workmanship of my stitches, crude as they were. When the
wolfhound's wound festered, she induced maggots to clean
it, then packed it with an odd allotment of bread-mold and
spiderwebs. It looked ghastly, but it worked.

The dog survived.

And I gained my majority.

I had thought, a great deal, about Tiberium. Since Eamonn had departed, I had thought about little else. The
thought of leaving Phèdre and Joscelin filled me with anxious misgivings; and yet there was exhilaration, too. I
yearned to escape from the web of rumor that surrounded
me; the suspicion, the sly mockery. I yearned for the freedom to reinvent myself; the freedom to learn and explore the
world. But on the day of my natality, the Queen herself
begged a boon.

"Stay," she said simply. "Please stay, Imriel; at least until
Drustan returns."

I glanced at Phèdre, who was frowning. She had that look about her, like a soldier who hears horns in the distance, but cannot yet discern their call. Meeting my eyes, she shrugged.

"All right," I said to Ysandre. "I'll stay."

Drustan came, along with a panoply of Cruithne. His sister's son Talorcan, Prince Talorcan, was among them. I watched them enter the City, my arms folded, thinking of Alais.

I found little with which to quarrel on first glance. He was a well-made young man, not tall, handsome in the manner of the Cruithne. Intricate woad tattoos covered his arms and the upper half of his face, indicating he was a skilled and tested warrior. He bowed respectfully to Alais when they met, showing no sign of presumption. When we were introduced, he clasped my forearm firmly and gave me a pleasant smile.

"Well met, Prince Imriel."

His D'Angeline was flawless. Drustan, I thought, had been grooming him for this for a long time. I stole a glance at the Cruarch out of the corner of my eye. His face, behind its tattoos, was unreadable.

Talorcan bowed in the Queen's direction, then turned and beckoned. "And may I present my sister, Dorelei."

The ranks of Cruithne guards parted, and she trotted forward astride a bay mare, her face at once shy and vivid with excitement. There was a murmur of surprise and a few good-natured cheers from the assembled crowd. Beneath it, I heard Phèdre's soft indrawn breath, and a cold finger of foreboding brushed my spine.

When my time came, I bowed over her hand. "Well met, Princess Dorelei."

She laughed; almost a giggle, catching in her throat. "Thank you!" Like her brother, she was pure Cruithne, slight and dark, with twin lines of blue dots etched high on her cheekbones. Something in her manner made me think of a woodland animal, curious, yet poised to startle. "Well met to you, too."

There was a formal reception following their arrival.

I attended it, going through the empty motions of courtesy. I wanted, urgently, to speak to Phèdre; but there was no time. She merely shook her head at me, cautioning patience. So I watched her instead, reminding myself how the game of intrigue was played. In her own way, no one played it better.

"Comtesse de Montrève!" Amarante, Sidonie's lady-in-waiting, greeted her with a deep curtsy. "It is an honor to meet you."

Phèdre smiled and raised her up, giving her the kiss of greeting. "Amarante of Namarre. You have a look of your mother. How is she?"

"Very well." Amarante smiled in reply. She had a ripe mouth, her lips as plump as cushions. I hadn't noticed that while we were busy sewing up poor Celeste. "She sends her greetings," she added, sliding a sealed letter from her bodice and passing it to Phèdre. "And says that Naamah does not forget her Servants."

"No," Phèdre murmured. "She doesn't."

The letter vanished. I swallowed my impatience and forced myself to circulate, making polite conversation. If I found no chance to speak to Phèdre in private, I did catch a quiet word with Alais. If Talorcan was here to court her, he was in no hurry to do it; but then, Drustan would have advised him to be subtle.

"So?" I asked her. "What do you think thus far?"

She shrugged. "He's nice enough," she said noncommittally. Her face brightened. "I like Dorelei, though. I like her laugh. Do you remember, Imri, I dreamed it, once; that you and I were truly brother and sister. That would be nice, wouldn't it?"

I opened my mouth to reply and caught sight of Sidonie across the room. As though I had called her name, she met my gaze. Her brows, the exact same shape as mine, creased into a helpless frown. I felt anew the strange flutter in my chest; the ache of something missing.

"I don't know, villain," I said slowly. "You dreamed I'd meet a man with two faces, too. And that hasn't happened yet."

"Stop calling me that!" Alais followed my gaze; her voice rose, incredulous. *"Sidonie?"*

"No." I shook myself. "Look, Alais . . . this sister, Dorelei. Did you know about this?"

"Of course not!" She scowled at me. "I'd have told you if I did. Do you trust me so little as that?"

"No." I touched her hair. "I'm sorry, love. This is just . . . unexpected."

"I *do* dream true dreams." Her jaw set. "And you haven't even asked after Celeste."

I knelt humbly before her. "Forgive me. How is she?"

"Well enough." Her face softened. "You saved her, Imri."

"That's me." I stood lightly. "Savior of dogs, defender against deer. A right and proper hero of the realm."

"Yes." Alais regarded me. "That's you."

Though it seemed endless, in time, the Queen and Cruarch dismissed us. The carriage-ride to the townhouse was fraught with silence. Joscelin and I exchanged glances, both of us silent and wondering.

"Well?" he said at length. "Do you mean to divulge, love?"

Phèdre's gaze rested gently on me. "You can guess as

well as I. If this is some machination of Ysandre's, she's not taken me into her confidence."

"What about the letter?" I asked bluntly. "What's *that* about?"

"Bérèngere's letter." She smiled, absentminded and distant. "Do you know, she was an acolyte when I was first dedicated to Naamah's Service. I remember. I knew her later, when she rose to head Naamah's Temple here in the City. We worked together, she and I. And now she's the head of the order." Phèdre touched her bodice, where the letter was concealed. "I've no idea what it contains," she said. "I've not read it yet."

Joscelin eyed her, wry and knowing. "Oh, you've plenty of ideas."

She leaned forward to kiss him. "A few."

We returned to the townhouse, where Phèdre cracked the seal on Bérèngere's letter and read it. She tossed it silently onto the low table. Joscelin read it, and I read it after him.

Both of us swore.

"What do you mean to do?" Joscelin asked her.

Phèdre shook her head. "It's not my decision," she said. "Imriel's of age. It's his choice to make."

I was angry, angry enough that it was hard to think. I paced the room in a fury. "I'll challenge him," I spat. "On his honor, what little he's got of it!"

"Or," Phèdre said mildly, "you could speak to Ysandre."

"Ysandre!" I laughed. "For all we know, this is *her* doing!"

"No." Something adamant surfaced in her gaze. "The other, mayhap. Not this."

I took a deep breath, forcing myself to dispel the image of Barquiel L'Envers pleading for mercy at the point of my blade. "All right." I pressed the heels of my hands against my lids. "All right. I'll speak to the Queen."

"Wise choice," Joscelin murmured.

"Will you come with me?" I lowered my hands. "I'd rather not do this without counsel."

Phèdre nodded. "Of course."

On the morrow, Ysandre met with us in her private chambers, rearranging her schedule with alacrity to accommodate our request. I daresay she thought she knew what it was regarding. Drustan was there, too; no one else, not even a guard. Two days ago, that indicator of her trust would have cheered me. Today, I was still too furious to care.

She saw the anger in my face and confronted it in a straightforward manner. "Imriel, hear me out. No doubt you've guessed that we wished for you to meet Talorcan's sister, Dorelei mab Breidaia. Before you leap to conclusions in this matter, Drustan and I would like you to hear our thoughts—"

I handed her the letter that implicated Duc Barquiel L'Envers in a plot to bring suspicion of treason against me. "Read this."

Ysandre stared blankly at me, too astonished by my tone to take offense at it.

"My lady." Phèdre sounded apologetic. "I think you should."

She did. I watched her face turn pale as she read. When she finished, she set the letter aside and sighed. "Barquiel."

"What has he done?" Drustan asked.

"He tried to make me out a traitor," I said grimly. "Did a good job of it, too."

The Cruarch looked unwontedly perplexed. "I don't understand."

"The letter is from Bérèngere of Namarre, my lord," Phèdre said. "The head of Naamah's Order. I asked her aid. Five days ago, a courtesan in the city of Valtrice reported an assignation with a young man who boasted of a dangerous task he performed for his lord. He is a member of Duc Barquiel's household."

"Are you sure?" Drustan frowned. "A dangerous task could be many things."

"The lad had a loose tongue. There are details." Ysandre picked up the letter with distaste and passed it to him. "How did you know?" she asked Phèdre.

"I didn't," she said. "But I knew he was Namarrese, and young. And I know where young men are apt to spend coin they've come into suddenly. It was worth a try."

Ysandre rubbed her temples. "Name of Elua! *Why*? What possessed my uncle?"

"Sport, mayhap," I said sourly. "No doubt he's had a good laugh watching my friends turn against me."

"Oh, he's more cunning than that." Phèdre turned to Ysandre. "My lady, tell us honestly. What lies behind the presence of the Cruarch's niece here at Court?"

"I will answer." Drustan glanced at his wife, then set his shoulders and looked straight at me. "The idea was mine. You are aware of the difficult matter of succession in Alba?" he asked. I nodded. Drustan rested his hands on his knees, his eyes somber in his blue-masked face. "Imriel, I will be truthful. If I were to follow my own heart and Ysandre's wishes, I would name Alais my heir. But it is not worth the cost. We have gone to war once over this issue. *I* have gone to war over it. Since I became a father, my heart has changed. Even so, I cannot, in good conscience, change my stance and put my country through it again. Can you understand this?"

"Yes, my lord," I said. "Alais and I have spoken of it."

He smiled a little. "Ah, she's a clever lass! And she'd be a fine Cruarch. But . . ." He shook his head. "My people want Talorcan. And he's a good lad, my sister-son, with a level head on his shoulders. If Alais consents to wed him, she will rule at his side one day."

I nodded again. "But their children wouldn't stand to inherit. That's it, isn't it?"

"Yes." His gaze softened. "Talorcan would name his own sister-son his heir."

"Imriel." Ysandre leaned forward. "After all you have endured, I will place no demands upon you. I do not ask this thing, only that you consider it. We have fought"—she glanced around at Drustan, Phèdre, and Joscelin—"we have *all* fought so very hard for this bond between our nations. It has brought peace and prosperity to all of us, and it galls my heart to think of losing it."

"You want me to wed Dorelei," I said.

She spread her hands. "It would keep the peace. It would placate those who insist Terre d'Ange must maintain an equitable foothold in Alba."

"You mean those who murmur against *your* heir," I whispered. "Your Cruithne half-breed heir."

Ysandre didn't flinch. "Yes."

"Your children would inherit Alba," Drustan said quietly.

I felt like crying, but I was a man grown; instead, I laughed, wild and uncontrolled. It was what I had guessed, what I had suspected from the first moment I beheld Drustan's niece. Still, it was somewhat else to have it stated and confirmed, spoken aloud. "Ah, Elua!" I gasped. "That would amuse my absent mother, wouldn't it? What a fine twist she would think it!"

"Ysandre." Phèdre's cool, thoughtful voice intervened. "Did Barquiel L'Envers know of this plan?"

The Queen looked away. "He knew."

"Then I suspect you have your answer." Phèdre folded her hands before her. Her eyes were clear and grave. Joscelin stood at her side, silent. He didn't need to speak. His scars, his battered vambraces, the grip-worn hilt of his longsword over his shoulder, were testimony enough. "Your uncle the Duc thought to give Imriel a bit of added incentive to accept your proposal and leave the shores of Terre d'Ange behind him. Barquiel cares naught for Alba, but he would very much like to see the last of Imriel." She smiled sadly. "My lady, why didn't you tell me?"

"I thought you would oppose it." Ysandre met her gaze. "Would you?"

"No," Phèdre said. "I would have let Imri choose. It's what I promised."

I thought about the diamond lying in her palm, its facets sparkling in the sunlight. The note that accompanied it. *I keep my promises.* For the first time, I felt less than ashamed at being my mother's son. At least there was a measure of honesty in it.

"What *do* you choose, Imriel?" Ysandre asked me.

"I don't know." I faced her squarely. "I need to think."

She nodded. "That's fair. I ask nothing, only that you think on it."

"What about Duc Barquiel?" I asked, my voice hard. "You know now what he has done. What penalty for him?"

Ysandre looked weary. "If you wish, you may bring a case against him in Parliament. I can tell you what he will say. He will claim it an ill-conceived jest at your expense, and nothing more. I tell you truthfully, it is best dealt with in private." She sighed. "Let me keep the letter. I will ask him to step down from command of the Royal Army. Will that suffice?"

"Oh, he'd hate that." Joscelin grinned.

I thought about the suspicion in Bertran's eyes, the way former friends avoided me at Court. "It's not enough," I said. "Barquiel L'Envers smeared my name with treason. I want a public apology from him."

"You won't get it." The Queen's voice was candid. "I know my uncle, and he doesn't bend easily. This"—she waved the letter—"this is insufficiently damning. It's third-hand innuendo from a source admittedly biased toward Phèdre nó Delaunay."

"Then we'll find Barquiel's man," I said. "And make him testify."

"You might," Ysandre said. "Or Barquiel might put him out of reach, or worse. Do you think he doesn't keep a watch posted over his estates? One move from House Montrève in that direction, and I wouldn't give a fig for the man's chances."

My blood ran cold. "So you'd just condone this? Let him get away with it?"

"That's not what I said." Her eyes flashed. "Name of Elua! Imriel, he slandered you. It's unpleasant and under-handed, but it's not a crime against the realm. If you pit yourself against him openly, you will earn his outright enmity. I do not want House Courcel torn apart over this. Use your head," she said grimly. "Barquiel will acquiesce if I reckon with him privately. He won't want to force my hand. And I will make a public proclamation that our investigation has proved you to be the butt of an unfriendly jest by unknown persons. Such is my offer."

I glanced at Phèdre, who looked troubled. "What do you think?"

She addressed Ysandre instead of answering me. "My lady, are you scared of him?"

"Of Barquiel?" The Queen's lids flickered slightly. "Of course not."

It was one of the tell-tales of a lie. Because of what Phèdre had taught me, I knew it. With an effort, I stepped away from my anger and stood outside myself, regarding Queen Ysandre. I beheld a woman who had been thrust into the role of greatness unprepared, who had faced tremendous challenges, who had fought long and hard with all the courage of her convictions to do what was best for her realm.

But the Ysandre de la Courcel who had ridden fearlessly between the ranks of a rebellious army was not the woman who sat the throne today. The burden of the Crown had taken a long, exhausting toll. She *was* afraid—afraid for her daughters, afraid for the future of relations between Terre d'Ange and Alba, afraid of what her ruthless uncle Barquiel L'Envers would do if openly provoked.

Afraid for me.

I sighed and wished I had seen less. And I thought about my oath to Sidonie, and what it would do to her if I forced House Courcel into schism—and to Alais, the one member of my kin who had always trusted me unreservedly.

"Your majesty, it will suffice." Though my heart was heavy and the words left a bitter taste in my mouth, I said them. "As to the other . . . I'll think about it."

Ysandre inclined her head. "Thank you."

"Imriel." Drustan hesitated, then spoke. "I think you would like Dorelei. I would never have proposed this if I thought you were ill-suited."

I had always liked and admired the Cruarch of Alba. Today, I didn't. "Do you know what, my lord?" I said to him. "Right now, I don't care."

With that, I turned on my heel and made my exit.

TWENTY-SIX

ALL WAS DONE as the Queen promised. Within a day, her proclamation of my innocence was released. Several days later, it was quietly put about that Duc Barquiel L'Envers was stepping down from command of the Royal Army, citing a desire for respite after years of long service. Ghislain nó Trevalion, Bertran's father, was named in his place.

No one at Court thought it overly strange. After all, L'Envers was rising sixty and had held the command for most of my lifetime. And Ghislain nó Trevalion had proven himself an able commander during the Skaldic War and a loyal Queen's man during his father's insurrection. I daresay some of L'Envers' enlisted men wondered at it, but they kept their mouths shut. As a leader, he was admired, but not greatly loved.

My lot improved . . . somewhat. The Queen's proclamation was accepted by some, and regarded with mild skepticism by others. In turn, I was not inclined to forgive my former friends their betrayal, and my relationship with Bertran remained awkward. An open admission from Barquiel L'Envers would have been infinitely more satisfying, and I wondered every day if I had made the right choice.

I asked Phèdre about it.

"I don't know, love," she said gently. "Some things are never given us to know, and some choices are not between right and wrong, merely different paths. You chose with a great deal of maturity, and that will have to suffice."

It was true, I know, but not terribly reassuring.

We tarried in the City that summer, delaying our departure for Montrève. My plans for Tiberium lay idle. Simmering with inward resentment, I kept my word to Ysandre, attending affairs at Court. I made an effort to be pleasant to Prince Talorcan's sister, Dorelei mab Breidaia.

It wasn't hard.

Somewhat to my annoyance, Drustan was right—I did like her. Although D'Angelines made her shy, she had a lively, curious mind, and I suspected in Alba she was far more forthcoming. When she laughed, there was somewhat infectious about the way her laughter broke to end in a whimsical giggle. I found it hard to brood around Dorelei. I found it hard to envision her as a bride, too. Although she was seventeen, she seemed younger. Somewhat about her put me in mind of Alais as she'd been as a child, fond and impulsive.

And then there was Sidonie.

On the surface, nothing had changed between us. After all, what had happened? Nothing. And yet everything was different. I found myself looking for her without thinking when I entered a room. When she looked for me, I felt her gaze like a touch.

I felt Maslin's, too; only it was more like a blow. He was there, too often, escorting her. They made a pretty pair, the Dauphine and her handsome lieutenant. Already there were murmurs beginning—that they were lovers, that she had promised to make him her Captain of the Guard and keep him on as her consort no matter who she wed. Such things had been done before in Terre d'Ange.

At a fête in honor of Roxanne de Mereliot, the Lady of Marsilikos, I was watching them together and thinking about those very rumors when a voice interrupted.

"It's not true, you know."

I glanced at Amarante of Namarre. "What's not?"

She smiled, the kind of smile one would expect from someone whose mother was a Priestess of Naamah. "What you're thinking."

I folded my arms. "And how would you know what I'm thinking?"

Her smile deepened. "Go ask her to dance, your highness."

I felt unaccountably nervous at it. For some idiotic reason, the words Eamonn had spoken the last time I asked Sidonie to dance rang in my head. *Mind you don't get chilblains*, he had said with a chuckle. At the time, I had laughed, too. Now I found myself constructing an argument with him in my thoughts, and it got in the way of my tongue.

"Do you . . . ?" I pointed at the dance floor, words failing me.

Sidonie looked bemused. "Are you all right, Imriel?"

I nodded. "Will you dance with me?"

She smiled. "Yes, all right."

It was so strange; like and unlike. Sidonie was scarce less formal than before, and yet her fingers quivered slightly in mine. The space between us was charged. I was acutely aware of my hand on the small of her back. My palm felt hot and I yearned to press her to me, feeling her young body firm against mine. My cousin, my near-sister. I didn't, but I wanted to. Instead, as I swept her across the floor, I broke the silence between us.

"Are we going to speak of this, Sidonie?" I asked.

For a moment, she didn't answer, and I thought mayhap she would pretend igorance. Then her chin rose, and I saw her dark eyes were filled with pain and regret. "I don't know," she said. "Mayhap it's better if we don't."

"Is that Naamah's counsel?" I asked. "Or your own?"

She glanced involuntarily toward Amarante. "No. I don't know." She changed the subject. "Will you wed Dorelei? I know what my parents are plotting."

I bared my teeth in a smile. "I don't know. What's Maslin de Lombelon to you?"

"One of the only people at Court who never lies to me," she said honestly. "A safeguard, often. A friend, betimes. Nothing more yet, and mayhap ever. I cannot say for sure. Why do you care? Why do you hate one another so?"

"I didn't want to." I tightened my grip on her hand; too tight. This time, though her eyes widened, she didn't protest. "Ah, Elua! Sidonie, I only ever wanted him to *like* me. And you . . ." The music ended and I let her go. "And you," I repeated softly, bowing to her.

"Imriel . . ." she began.

I waited.

Sidonie shook her head, impatient and despairing. "It's not that simple!"

"No," I said. "It's not. Mayhap if we obeyed naught but Blessed Elua's precept, it would be. Elua cared naught for thrones or mortal politics." I paused, remembering where I had heard those words before. "You know," I said, wondering, "Phèdre once told me that when she asked Melisande what Elua would make of her treason, my mother said that very thing in reply. The older I get, the closer I come to understanding her." I saw Sidonie's look of alarm and laughed softly. "Don't worry, your highness. I will keep my oath to you. On pain of death, I will keep it. You see," I said to her, "I always keep my promises."

On that ironic and self-righteous note, I strode away, ignoring the wrench of pain in my heart, the subtle tug that urged me to stay.

I thought about going home, and didn't. If Eamonn was there, I would have confided in him, but he wasn't. For a good hour, I wandered the City with only a worried Gilot to attend me. And then I made up my mind and turned to the only people I knew would understand my bitter, complicated mood.

The Shahrizai maintain a multitude of domiciles in and near the City. I went to Lord Sacriphant's townhouse, where I knew Mavros abided. Gilot was uneasy at accompanying me, though once we arrived, he relented, awed by the effortless grace of the household. Everything moved so smoothly there, the polite servants with their eyes downcast, in stark contrast to the free and informal nature of Montrève's household.

"Cousin!" Mavros greeted me effusively, kissing me on both cheeks. His blue eyes glinted, ambiguous as twilight. "Have you sewn up any good dogs lately?"

"Mavros." I returned his embrace. "You have always offered me the solace of family. May we speak?"

His expression sobered and sharpened at once. "Of course," he said, guiding me inward with a sweep of his arm. "Enter, and speak. What you say shall not pass these thresholds." He glared at a passing servant. "Shall it?"

The servant shook his head. "No, my lord," he murmured. "Never."

"So!" Mavros slung his arm around my neck, escorting me into the inner salon. It was gorgeously appointed with tapestries on the walls depicting scenes from the history of

Kusheth and muted lamplight gleaming on gilded statuary. Mavros gestured to a couch and sent the servant to bring a cordial. "Speak, Cousin Imriel."

I told him everything, or almost.

I told him about the hunt and what had transpired between Sidonie and me, and the tension between us that followed it. I told him about Dorelei and the Queen's request. And I told him about what Barquiel L'Envers had done.

Mavros listened silently, moving only to refill my glass. Only when I told him about L'Envers did he seem surprised, hissing through his teeth.

"Sodding bastard!" he spat. "He should know better than to cross the Shahrizai!"

His lamplit face was suffused with demonic cunning. "Mavros, no," I pleaded. "Don't do anything rash. I made my choice to keep the peace and I'll abide by it."

"Very noble." He eyed me wryly. "For Sidonie's sake?"

I shrugged. I hadn't told him about my oath. "For the sake of House Courcel."

"House Courcel!" he scoffed. "They don't do a very good job of protecting their own, do they? If it were us . . ." He shook his head, a myriad of braids shifting.

"Well, it's not." I cradled my half-empty glass in my hands.

"More's the pity." Mavros poured cordial into the glass. "Fine, I'll behave. So do you fancy yourself in love with the young Dauphine?"

"Love? No," I said. "I don't know. Betimes, I don't even *like* her. But I think about her. A lot. Too much. And I . . ." I raised my glass and took a gulp of cordial, shuddering. "I want her."

"She's a cold one," Mavros observed.

I remembered the way the blood had risen beneath her

skin as I lay atop her in the Queen's Wood, her pulse quickening in the hollow of her throat. "Oh, I don't believe it. But, Mavros! Name of Elua, she's only sixteen, and nearly my sister."

He looked amused. "Oh, please! She's playing the Game of Courtship, isn't she? And she's—what? Your father's great-niece. By Shahrizai standards, that's barely related."

"We have the same eyebrows," I informed him.

"So?" he said. "All the better to recognize one another. What about the little Pictish princess?"

I drained my cordial in a second gulp. "Lorelei?" I frowned, realizing I was a little drunk. "Dorelei. She's a sweet girl. A child."

"You don't want to marry her, then."

"No." I set down my empty glass. "I don't want to marry anyone. I want . . . I don't know what I want."

"Oh, you do." Tilting his head, Mavros regarded me through his lashes. "Barquiel L'Envers' head on a stake, and Sidonie de la Courcel whimpering in your bed."

I opened my mouth to deny it, but a rush of heat flooded me at his words, and I closed my eyes instead. Anger and desire were all bound up together in a knot inside me, urgent and pulsing, making my tongue thick and my limbs heavy. I bit my lip, willing it to subside.

"Come on." Mavros got to his feet. "It's early yet. We're going out."

I opened my eyes, gazing at his extended hand. "Where?"

He smiled. "Out."

TWENTY-SEVEN

I N SOME PART of me, I knew.

But I would sooner lie to myself and claim ignorance; and Mavros gave me the pretext to do so, refusing to tell me where we were bound and making a mysterious game of it. We travelled by carriage to another of the Shahrizai domiciles, where Roshana's mother Fanchone kept a household. There were several of the young Shahrizai gentry in residence, Roshana among them.

"Imri!" She greeted me with a lingering kiss, sinking both hands into my hair. "You have such beautiful hair," she whispered. "Will you let me braid it tonight?"

"All right," I agreed. "Why not?"

Mavros waved a magnanimous hand. "There's time."

So while other members of the household primped and made ready, I sat cross-legged in the Lady Fanchone's salon while Roshana hummed, brushing my hair and dividing it into an infinity of small locks, braiding each one deftly and tying off the ends with waxed thread. It took nearly an hour. Gilot, who had followed on horseback, looked on with marked disapproval.

"Are you sure you want to do this, Imri?" he asked me.

I shrugged, careful not to disturb Roshana's work. "Do

what? Allow my hair to be braided? Gilot, do me a favor. Go back to the townhouse and let Phèdre know I'm here. I don't want her to worry."

He raised his brows. "Young Lord Shahrizai has already sent a messenger," he said, nodding toward Mavros. "I'm staying with you."

"As you like." I shrugged again.

Roshana moved around to my front, blocking my view of Gilot. I kept my gaze on her face and my head still, breathing slowly, admiring her concentration and the speed of her dexterous fingers. She gave me a quick smile.

"You've good discipline," she said. "Have you done this before?"

I smiled back at her, thinking of the vigils I had endured in the Temple of Elua, kneeling on the frozen ground. "Something like it. This is easier."

"And more fun, I'll warrant." She planted a kiss on my brow. "There, you're done."

I shook my head experimentally, feeling the braids fly. My head felt strange and heavy, the way it had on the Longest Night when I had worn the costume of Baldur. And yet there were no masks here. I was only me, but different.

"Thank you," I said to Roshana.

A mischievous smile flirted across her lips. "You look beautiful."

Mavros clapped his hands. "Come!" he said decisively. "Let's go."

We went, piling into two carriages. Mavros and Roshana I knew; there were others, Aprilios and Thiela and Sonoril, all young Shahrizai gentry, none of them much over twenty. Their own outriders accompanied them, and Gilot came, too, following slowly and leading the Bastard by the reins.

It was not hard to guess where we were bound.

They laughed and gossiped and kept themselves from telling me, and I kept myself from knowing it. And yet, as our carriages ascended the slope of Mont Nuit, in my heart, I knew. When the drivers drew rein before the gates of Valerian House, I was not surprised. I wanted to be, but I wasn't. Anything else would be a lie.

"Mavros." I stirred against the padded seats of the carriage. "I don't want to go here."

"Yes, you do, Imri." In the shadows, his face was unexpectedly sympathetic. "You needn't do anything you don't want. But you need to *see*. It's time." He paused. "Or are you afraid?"

"Yes," I said honestly.

He clapped his hand on my shoulder. "All the more reason."

So I went to Valerian House.

The entrance is a long one, warded by trees on either side. In the courtyard, we were met by a pair of adepts, male and female. They ushered us into the receiving room with downcast eyes, and there the Dowayne met us. He wore tight-fitting leather breeches and a loose shirt of sheer linen, and he bowed low before the Shahrizai.

"My lords and ladies," he murmured. "Your quarters await you as always. Shall I send a selection of adepts?"

Mavros drew him aside, whispering.

"Very good, my lord." The Dowayne bowed again, then beckoned to Gilot. "Come, messire. We will make you comfortable while their lords and ladyships take their pleasure."

Gilot hesitated, glancing at me. "Imri? Are you sure?"

"I'm sure," I said, though I wasn't. "Go."

He departed, led by a pair of adepts.

Didier Vascon, the Dowayne of Valerian House, bowed low. "This way."

We followed him down a hallway, then a narrow, winding stair. The Shahrizai chattered among themselves, clearly at ease. It was only at the bottom of the stair that they fell silent, kneeling one by one.

I saw why.

There was an altar to Kushiel there; a niche with a raised dais and a bronze sculpture contained within, an offering bowl on the dais at his feet. Once the others had departed, I stood alone, gazing at Kushiel. His face was stern and calm, filled with implacable mercy. His hands were crossed on his breast, one holding a rod, the other a flail.

Mighty Kushiel, of rod and weal . . .

I knelt, shivering.

"Come." A sympathetic voice sounded in my ear. Kind hands encircled my upper arms, lifting me. I turned to face Didier Vascon. "You have known his touch, have you not?" asked the Dowayne of Valerian House. "In all its cruelty?"

"Yes," I said softly. "I have."

"Go." He gave me a gentle nudge. "Know his mercy."

I went, stumbling a little, following my Shahrizai kin. In the dimly lit hallway, Mavros paused, waiting for me. "Come on, Imriel!" he said. "This will be fun."

I hadn't reckoned on it; any of it. I should have. But it was more than I had imagined. Here at Valerian House, the Shahrizai maintained their own quarters—a private dungeon appointed for their usage. There was a fireplace with a roaring fire on the hearth, rendering the room stiflingly warm. Lush carpets covered the stone floors, woven in the black-and-gold interlocking key device of the Shahrizai.

On the barren walls, there were . . . other devices. Manacles and chains, a whipping cross. A wooden wheel with clamps.

"Behold!" Roshana said happily, opening the doors of a tall cabinet. "The toy chest."

It was a well-stocked flagellary, filled with whips and tawses and paddles, all manner of bonds and blinds and gags, collars and pincers, rings and pleasure-beads and aides d'amour. They were all beautifully crafted and maintained, the leather oiled, the metal gleaming.

The Mahrkagir had such toys in Daršanga, rusted and dark with old blood.

I stared at them, my shivering intensifying. I could smell the fetid water of the zenana's stagnant pool and there was a foul taste in my mouth.

"Mavros." I clutched the front of his doublet. "I can't do this."

"Here." He steered me to a couch near the fire. "Sit." Glancing around, he snapped his fingers. An adept appeared almost instantly, a shy lad as graceful as a fawn, proffering cordial on a tray. "Drink this," Mavros ordered.

I obeyed, downing the glass. It was perry brandy, sweet and spicy. I wondered if it had been distilled at Lombelon. I could hear my cousins laughing and chatting pleasantly among themselves. A tightness in my chest loosened and the memories of Daršanga receded. This was Terre d'Ange, and there was no Three-Fold Path here.

"Better?" Mavros asked, crouching before me.

I nodded.

"Good." He frowned. "Imriel, listen to me. These are Naamah's Servants, bound to her worship in their own way. And yes, they serve Kushiel, too, and find pleasure in it. No one is here against their will. All here have chosen this. You need not take part in it. But it is time you understood your heritage. Are you willing?"

I drew a breath, feeling better. "I'm willing, Mavros. It's just . . ."

"I know," he said softly. "A little of it, anyway. But I swear to you, we honor Blessed Elua's precept here. Any one of us would sooner die than dishonor it."

"I understand," I said faintly. "Believe me, I do."

Mavros nodded. "We have a standing agreement with Valerian House. By coming here with us, you agree to abide by it." Rising to his feet, he ticked off the points on his fingers. "No maiming, ever. No branding and no flechettes; no wounds that will scar unless it has been agreed upon in separate contract beforehand. You will ascertain the *signale* of any adept with whom you engage, and honor it on pain of death. Is that clear?"

I looked away. Valerian adepts moved gracefully throughout the dungeon, lighting sconces, stoking the fire, proffering wine and cordial. Others lit lumps of opium, letting them smolder in fretted incensors. Thin threads of blue smoke rose, rendering the air heady.

That, too, reminded me of Daršanga. I pushed the thought away.

"Yes, I understand," I said to Mavros. "It won't be necessary."

"As you say." His twilight gaze rested on me. "I only ask that you abide."

"I will," I said stubbornly.

Mavros bowed to me. "So be it."

What ensued was an orgy. If there be any other name to give it, I do not know it. I sat there, glued to my couch, and watched all manner of love given license. And ah, Elua! I yearned at what I saw; yearned until it hurt.

This is what I saw.

Valerian's adepts, filing into the Shahrizai dungeon and

presenting themselves to the Shahrizai, their eyes downcast. And yet, oh Blessed Elua! There was pride there in a manner I failed to expect. I saw it in the set of their shoulders, in their covert sidelong glances. They *wanted* to be chosen.

They wanted to be challenged.

And they were. Oh, gods above and beyond, they were! I watched my Shahrizai kin smile, their fingers beckoning. They played dangerous games, shameless before one another. Chains jangled and leather snapped, the wooden wheel spun. Flesh, nubile flesh, was laid bare. I groaned at the sight of emerging weals. Ah, Elua! There was a terrible beauty in it. For the first time, I saw it. A part of me yearned to claim it for myself; another part yearned to reject it. Torn by my own conflicting desires, I watched in helpless fascination.

"My lord!" A naked adept knelt on the floor alongside me, her golden hair spilling over her bare shoulders. She gazed up at me in entreaty. "Why do you hold yourself apart? Is there nothing here that pleases you? No one?"

I stared past her, gritting my teeth. Aprilios Shahrizai had another adept on the wooden wheel, laughing as it spun, slinging his arm sidelong with a cat-o'-nine-tails, his aim unerring. Each knot raised a welt.

"It's not that," I said shortly.

The adept lowered her eyes. "Do you find me displeasing, my lord?"

"No." I drained my glass and set it down. "No, of course not." I touched her cheek, raising her chin. "What's your name?"

"Sephira, my lord." Her eyes were hazel, her tawny brows a shade darker than her golden hair. Sidonie's coloring, except for the eyes.

"Mine's Imriel," I told her.

She blushed, the blood rising visibly beneath her fair skin. There was somewhat appallingly erotic about her kneeling there, naked and vulnerable, while I sat fully clothed. "Yes, my lord, of course."

"You may use it, you know," I said. "My name."

Sephira shook her head. Averting her gaze, she leaned away and picked up a decanter of perry brandy, neatly refilling my glass. Her hair trailed over my clad legs, making my skin prickle all over. "Oh no, my lord. I couldn't."

"Why not?" I asked.

She replaced the decanter and folded her hands in her lap. "It's not done, my lord."

"So?" A wave of recklessness overcame me. I drank off the brandy, slamming down the glass. "Elua's Balls! Does it always matter what's *done*? Must we always be bound with restrictions? Look at this, this"—I waved my hand at the participants—"utter carnal madness. How can it matter what's *done* in the midst of this?"

"It matters to me, my lord." A note of stubborn pride crept into Sephira's voice.

"Why?" I asked, then sighed. "Never mind. I don't care." I tangled my fingers in her hair, gripping it hard, forcing her head up. It felt horribly good. "Why are you here?" I asked. "What do you want of me?"

"To please you, my lord," she breathed.

I tightened my grip. "That's not good enough."

"All right." A flare of defiance crossed her face. "I want to see what Melisande Shahrizai's son is capable of."

I swore aloud and nearly slapped her. Sephira never flinched. Her breathing quickened, her breasts rising and falling visibly, pink nipples erect. I felt a thread of tension binding us together. It grew tighter as I gazed at her.

"This is a game of wills, isn't it?" I said slowly. "One I am losing."

"My lord." Sephira turned her head, kissing my palm that had nearly struck her. She took my hand in hers, stroking and kissing it. "It is within your power to give me what I crave," she whispered. "And it is within your power to withhold it. That is the only game that matters here." Her voice dropped lower. "Do you want me to beg you? I shall. Please, my lord. Allow me to please you."

"I can't." I looked at the scene beyond her. "Not like this."

"There are private chambers, my lord," she murmured.

Across the dungeon, Mavros met my gaze. He stood, legs braced, one hand twined in the hair of a kneeling adept who performed the *languisement* on him. Male or female; I couldn't tell from the bare slender back and glossy brown hair. Mavros' eyes were at once fever-bright and strangely grave. Roshana whispered in his ear, a crop held loosely in her hand.

I looked into the dark mirror of my desire and beheld my reflection.

"All right," I said. I got to my feet, swaying, dazed and a little drunk, dizzy from the opium fumes. "All right, then. Why not?" At my feet, Sephira knelt, looking hopefully up at me. I held out my hand to her. "Show me."

She led me first to the flagellary, opening its doors wide. "Will you choose, my lord?"

"I don't . . ." I swallowed hard. Almost of their own accord, my hands rose, touching the objects within. I selected a few items. My skin was hot and they felt cool to the touch. "Go on," I said, my voice thick.

Sephira led and I followed. Firelight danced over her naked skin. She had already begun to make her marque, a

•

scrolling base of Valerian leaves etched on the small of her back, beginning to climb her spine. I watched the way her buttocks moved beneath it, round and enticing. With each step, it felt as though I were falling into an abyss, as though the floor was opening beneath me. And yet I kept going, following her to a private chamber, lit by flickering torches and warmed by a charcoal brazier. The floor was strewn with thick cushions, and there was a whipping cross on one wall. When she closed the door behind us, it was blessedly quiet, save for the sound of my own harsh breathing resounding in my ears.

"Here, my lord." She turned to me, smiling.

"What . . ." I cleared my throat. "What is your *signale*?"

"Sunshine," she said.

"Sunshine." I echoed the word, thinking inadvertently of Daršanga, remembering the day Phèdre had convinced Erich the Skaldi to help pry away the boards walling off the garden; the day I had seen the sun for the first time in months, cold and grey and unspeakably marvelous. I shuddered.

"My lord?" Sephira took a step closer. "Are you well?"

"Yes." I thrust one of the items I had chosen at her, a black silk blindfold. "Put this on."

She obeyed, tying it in place. When it was done, a thick swathe of silk obscured her features. She might have been any woman. She might have been Katherine, playing at one of Phèdre's covertcy games back at Montrève. With her golden hair loose and unbound, she might have been Sidonie. I took a harsh breath.

"How old are you, Sephira?" I asked.

Her blind face tracked my voice. "Eighteen last autumn, my lord."

"The age of majority." I laughed humorlessly. "Do you know what you want?"

"You, my lord," she said simply.

"Why should I believe you?" I asked.

She took another step closer and reached for my hand, placing it between her thighs. I fingered her, finding her slick and wet. Her nether-lips were plump. Naamah's Pearl throbbed as I rubbed it, and Sephira gasped.

"Believe me, my lord," she said raggedly.

I did believe, then. Grasping her head with both hands, I kissed her hard, feeling her lips part beneath mine, her body swaying against me, desperate and yearning.

It was nothing like Balm House; it was nothing like anything I had ever known. All the pent longing I had endured, all the shadowy desires I had feared to express found voice that night. I devoured her mouth, plundering it with my tongue. I ran my hands down her sides, grasping her buttocks, pulling her against me, grinding her naked loins against my rigid phallus, trapped beneath my breeches. All was permitted, all was encouraged.

"Do you like that?" I asked harshly.

"Yes, my lord!" she gasped. "Oh yes!"

Groping on the cushions, I found items I had dropped: a pair of ring-shaped pincers. They were made of silver, weighted and heavy. I cupped her breasts, thumbing her erect nipples, dropping a kiss upon each one.

"Here," I murmured. "And here."

Sephira moaned as I attached the pincers, her breasts swaying, nipples stiffening further as the weights dragged at them. The sight of her was enough to drive me mad.

"Turn around," I grated.

She obeyed my unspoken command, making her way blindly to the whipping cross and standing spread-eagled before it. I fastened the leather cuffs to her wrists and ankles and found myself weeping without realizing it, soundlessly. Sephira turned her blindfolded head toward me.

"Yes, my lord," she said softly. "Like this, please."

I dashed away tears. "Why?"

She strained against her bonds, rubbing her pubis against the rough wood of the cross, heedless of splinters. "We want it alike, my lord. Does it matter?"

"Yes," I said. "It matters to me."

"I don't know!" Sephira's voice broke. She ground herself helplessly against the wood. "*Please*, my lord! I beg you, grant me ease!"

I could have withstood her desire, or mine; I could not withstand the weight of their combined urgency. The thread that bound us had grown taut. I made my way behind her, fumbling on the cushions for the deerskin flogger I had dropped. I grasped it hard, feeling its braided grip imprinting my sweating palm, and swung it.

A dozen soft thongs smacked Sephira's buttocks.

She jerked in her bonds, sighing.

Oh, Elua! It felt good, so good. Over and over, I swung the flogger, watching the sweet pink welts rise on her skin, kissing her buttocks, curving around her rib cage. There, yes; there and there. The surge of her pleasure drove us both; the sting and smack of the thongs, the profound release in submitting to it. I rode atop it like a ship on a wave's crest. My arm grew tired as I swung it, losing myself in the rhythm, yearning to drive her higher and further, to make her squirm and moan; to force her to utter her *signale*. The flogger was a gentle weapon as such toys go, and I had chosen it as such, knowing myself a novice. But it made its point, giving rise to other possibilities; those glimpsed in the Shahrizai dungeon, in the dank shadows of Daršanga.

I dared not think of those.

"Have you had enough?" I whispered at length, my voice husky.

Sephira writhed. "Yes, my lord!"

I undid the leather cuffs that bound her to the whipping cross, tumbling her onto the soft cushions and pinning her there. I was hard and erect, my phallus aching, my testes drawn up so tight and full I thought they might burst. Propped above her on one arm, I freed myself with fumbling fingers, grasping my shaft and parting her swollen nether-lips with its crown.

"Is this what you want?" I whispered.

She threw her blindfolded head back. "Oh yes, my lord! *Hard!*"

It pushed me over the edge. I thrust into her, driving hard, over and over. My turn, my pleasure. There was no rational thought in my mind, only a blind, urgent need to conquer the pliant, willing flesh beneath me. I could feel her loins rising to meet mine, thighs spreading wider to take me deeper inside. I felt her climax, hidden muscles milking my shaft. There was no voice here saying, *This, too, is sacred*; only her breath panting at my ear, "Yes, yes, oh yes, my lord!"

I hated myself.

With a surge of self-loathing and the most excruciating pleasure I had ever known, I groaned and spent myself in her.

It was over.

I rolled off Sephira and lay on my back, breathing hard and staring at the rafters. After a moment, she sat up, one hand reaching blindly. "My lord?" Her voice was tentative. Beneath the black swathe of the blindfold, her lips were bruised and swollen. I could see the marks of my nails on her bare, creamy shoulders. "Did I displease you, my lord?"

"No," I said wearily. "Please, take off the blindfold."

Sephira obeyed. She blinked at me, her golden hair tangled and disheveled. There was no shame in her face, only confusion mingled with the vague aftermath of pleasure. Gathering herself, she knelt beside me, straightening my clothing with an adept's deft touch. When she had finished, she sat back on her heels and folded her hands in her lap.

"You're not like the others," she said softly. "Are you, my lord?"

"No," I said. "I'm not." The room was spinning. I closed my eyes to blot out the sight of the rafters moving overhead. Drunk, spent, or soul-sick, I couldn't tell. I only knew the abyss was opening beneath me. "Tell Mavros . . ."

She waited a moment. "Yes, my lord?"

I smiled faintly. "Sunshine."

And with that, I let darkness claim me.

TWENTY-EIGHT

I AWOKE to a splitting headache.

"And a fine morning to *you*, sunshine!" Mavros announced cheerfully. I winced, pushing myself upright, and found myself in a strange bed, luxuriant and canopied. He lounged in a chair nearby, legs outstretched, the heel of one boot propped on the toe of the other.

I squinted at him. "Where am I?"

"Valerian House," he said. "Patrons' quarters." Getting to his feet, he clapped his hands. "Come along, cousin! Let's get you dressed and out of here. Your man Gilot's been looking daggers at me all morning."

"Where are my clothes?" I glanced around. My aching head felt stiff and heavy, and I felt at it with numb fingers. "What's wrong with my head?"

"Too much perry brandy," Mavros said, tossing me my clothing. "Here."

"Braids," I mumbled. "I forgot."

"Oh, right." He sat on the edge of the bed, gazing at me. "That didn't exactly go as we might have hoped, did it?"

I went to shake my head and winced again. "No. I'm sorry."

"No, I am." His voice turned sober. "It was too much. I

shouldn't have pushed you." He gave me a curious look. "What did you mean, telling the girl to give me her *signale*?"

I shrugged and began dragging on my clothes. "I didn't have one of my own."

He raised his brows. "You're not supposed to need one."

"I know." I took a deep breath. "Mavros . . . it's not your fault. This, what happened here. You were right, it's a part of me, and I needed to confront it. There had to be a first time, and mayhap it won't be the last. The craving's in my blood. But I'm not like you. I can't play such games and call them *fun*. I can't escape the shadow of the past."

"That place," he said. "Daršanga."

"Daršanga." I pulled on one boot, then paused to rest. "Do you know, Phèdre once said that she would have given her *signale* there, were there ears to hear it."

"I'm sure she would have," he murmured.

I thought about the zenana, the women and boys who died there, their flesh rent and suppurating. I thought about kneeling in a puddle of the Mahrkagir's piss and my own bile, the foul taste of it in my mouth, the gouts of blood and Lilka's slit throat gaping. I put on my other boot and got to my feet, grabbing his arm for balance.

"You have no idea," I said.

"So you keep telling me." He steadied me. "We've taken care of the accounts and the patron-gifts. Are you ready to go home?"

I nodded my aching, braid-heavy head. "Please."

Outside, I felt a bit better. The bright sunlight and the City's clamor were jarring, but the fresh air cleared my head. I was glad to be astride the Bastard and riding, not cooped up in a carriage, and I thanked Gilot for waiting for me.

"Don't thank me," he said bluntly. "I did it for her lady-ship. She worries."

Unease stirred in the pit of my belly. "I *am* of age, Gilot."

"Aye," he said. "That's what worries her."

Mavros rode with us, elegant and cheerful atop a tall black gelding. The others, I learned, had departed in the small hours of the morning, long after the Dowayne's guard had carted my unconscious self to the patrons' quarters. He had gone with his kindred and come back for me on his own.

"My thanks, Mavros," I said to him outside the gates of the townhouse. "You're a good friend in your own right."

He grinned at me. "She was quite taken with you, you know."

I flushed. "Who?"

"The adept, Sephira." His grin broadened. "Even at Valerian House they do gossip, especially when they think we can't hear. An odd lad, with a streak of disarming sweetness. That's what she said."

Gilot chuckled despite himself.

I thought about what I'd done to her and nearly choked. *"Sweetness?"*

"In your own way." Mavros touched my arm. "Take care, cousin. If you've a need to speak, I've always an ear to hear."

I watched him ride away, a part of me envying him. The same blood flowed in our veins, the same dark desires plagued us. Would it be so bad to be able to carry it so lightly? After what I had seen, I was unsure. The adepts and patrons of Valerian House found unalloyed pleasure in what they were, honoring Blessed Elua's precept and basking in their own natures, free to enjoy the subtle exchanges of power.

I was the one who did not fit.

"Imri." Gilot jerked his head toward the townhouse. "Let's go."

The stable-keeper Benoit unlocked the gates to admit us, taking our mounts. I patted the Bastard on the neck as Benoit led him away, promising him a lively ride on the morrow when the cobwebs were gone from my head. Gilot and I entered the townhouse together.

"Your highness!" Eugènie scolded me. "We were growing worried."

"I'm fine, Eugènie." Her tone worsened my headache, irritating me. "Didn't Mavros send a message?"

"Yes, but . . ." She bit her tongue. "I'll tell her ladyship you're here."

Phèdre appeared in the doorway behind her. "Thank you, Eugènie. There's no need." She moved past her Mistress of the Household, tilting her head and regarding me, a concerned crease between her brows. "Are you all right, love? You left Roxanne's fête with scarce a word."

It seemed like so long ago, I'd nearly forgotten. "I'm fine," I repeated shortly. "Tired, that's all. I'll talk to you later."

"You look fevered." Her frown deepened. "Let me see."

I grabbed her wrist as she reached for my brow. "I'm *fine*!"

In that instant, one instant, everything changed forever.

I felt Phèdre's pulse give a startled leap under pressing thumb and I beheld her, for the first time, through my birthright as one of Kushiel's scions. Her eyes gazed at me, wide and dark, the scarlet mote floating on the left iris; the mark of Kushiel's Dart, a blood-pricked challenge. My blood surged in answer, roaring in my ears. I felt the abyss around me and knew I had never left it. I understood, in that instant, that the game I had played in Valerian House was nothing more than that, mortal and harmless. And I knew that to play them with Phèdre nó Delaunay was to play with a god's chosen, capable of yielding in ways I could scarce imagine.

And I saw Phèdre knew it.

For a moment, neither of us moved, frozen by the knowledge. Then I thrust her away, hard, in the same instant she wrenched her wrist free. I took two steps and doubled over, vomiting onto the floor. Bile and stale brandy splattered my boots.

"Imriel . . ." Her footsteps sounded behind me.

"Stay away!" I braced one hand on my knees, holding up the other. Small braids hung over my eyes and curtained my face, obscuring my vision. "Leave me. Just . . . leave me alone."

"All right, love."

There was a world of sorrow in her voice. Phèdre had known; had always known. I waited until I heard her withdraw, then straightened and wiped my mouth, heading for the stairs and the sanctuary of my room.

The washbasin was full. I plunged my head into the cool water, then raised it, dripping. I stared into the mirror above the stand at a stranger's face. Phèdre was right, I looked fevered. My skin was pale, drawn tight over my cheekbones. My eyes were over-bright, blue and incandescent. Dripping braids framed my face like hundreds of linked chains.

I snarled and began to undo them.

It went too slow. The waxed thread Roshana had used was tightly knotted, and the heat of Valerian's dungeon had softened it, letting it cool and fuse. I worked at one, then another, without success, growing impatient. Giving up, I plucked one of my daggers from the sheath at my belt, sawing through the braid itself. I severed one after another, dropping them on the floor. There was a certain grim satisfaction in it.

"Your highness!" A gasp, and the sound of a dish rattling.

I turned, dagger in hand, to see Eugènie's niece Clory. She held a tray with a bowl of steaming broth. A bit had slopped over the sides. "Go away, Clory."

She looked terrified. "Eugènie said . . ."

I raised my voice. "Go *away*, Clory!"

She set down the tray on a nightstand and fled. I finished cutting off every last damned Shahrizai braid on my head, then sank down on the edge of my bed and put my face in my hands. I wanted to cry. I wanted to curse and rail against the gods.

I wanted the last day of my life back.

I wanted to be someone else.

Since none of it would do any good, I didn't. I picked up the bowl of broth Clory had brought and drank it down, then hurled the empty bowl onto the floor. It shattered in a spray of crockery shards. Dashing the back of my hand over my lips, I got up and went to do the only sensible thing I could think of.

"Imri!" Gilot leapt to his feet as I strode through the salon. "Where are you going?"

"Out," I said briefly.

"I'm going with you." Although his eyes were red-rimmed with weariness, his face was set and stubborn. He had good instincts, Gilot, waiting here for me.

I shrugged. "Suit yourself."

At the stable, Benoit looked at us with surprise, but he made no comment, saddling the Bastard and Gilot's mount and opening the gates for us. We rode out into the City of Elua. Gilot glanced at me. "Where are we bound, highness?"

"How many wineshops and inns does the City hold?" I asked him.

"Dozens," he said. "Why?"

"Because," I said grimly. "I mean to get blind, stinking drunk."

I met my goal that day.

I don't know how many places we visited. Some of them, like the Cockerel, I knew. But I found no respite there or anywhere. We downed tankards of ale, jars of wine, and moved on to the next place, from Night's Doorstep to the heart of the City proper. Or at least I did; Gilot accompanied me, keeping a sober head. At some point he managed to get some food in me, though it didn't help. Yet as much as I drank, it wasn't enough to fill the abyss.

I couldn't escape from myself.

"That's the trick," I said drunkenly to Gilot. By that time, the sun had long since set. "To make of the self a vessel where the self is not. That's how she did it, you know." I hiccoughed. "Phèdre, I mean."

He moved my winecup out of reach. "Did what?"

I wagged my finger at him, then lurched over the table to retrieve it. "Got the Name of God." I refilled my cup, wine spilling over the rim. "She holds it in her head, you know."

"Yes, I know." Gilot sighed. "Are you ready to go home yet?"

"*No!*" I hunched over my winecup and glared at him. "You don't . . . you don't understand. We were there, at the temple. Kapporeth. I stabbed one of Hanoch's men, right there on the threshold. She was ready to give her *life* for me, Gilot! And I repay it like this?"

"If you want to repay it, go home and face her," he said patiently.

I drained my cup and inverted the jar over it. A single

drop of wine clung to the lip. I shook my ill-shorn head. "No," I said. "Not yet."

We ended at a disreputable tavern along the Aviline River. It was a rough place; truly rough, not one such as the City's gentry frequent for a thrill of the forbidden. They served only ale, no wine. Broad-shouldered boatmen hunched over their tankards. I liked it because no one knew who I was, or cared.

I picked a fight with one of the boatmen.

I don't remember what it was about. Nothing, like as not; I didn't even know the man. But I managed to insult him to the point where he hauled me off my stool, grasping the front of my doublet and threatening me with a ham-sized fist. There was a surge in the tavern as Gilot sought to come to my defense and went down under a pile of the boatman's comrades, thrashing and cursing.

"Apologize, lordling," the boatman rumbled.

I hung in his grip, laughing. "For what?" I asked. "Tell me, have you a sister? I wouldn't mind giving her a tumble if she'd let me close my eyes."

The front door opened and the whole tavern went inexplicably silent.

My assailant turned his head. Lolling in his grip, I followed his gaze.

Joscelin leaned in the doorway, the hilt of his longsword protruding over his shoulder.

"See that?" I gave a bleary grin, secure in his sudden presence. "*I* want to be able to do that. Just show up, and have everyone go dead quiet. Why can't *I* do that?"

Joscelin nodded at the boatman. "Go ahead. I reckon you owe him one."

"Jos—"

I only got out the first syllable of his name before the

boatman's fist smashed into my face. Drunk as I was, I felt it, a starburst opening behind my eyes. It hurt. It hurt a lot, more than anything had hurt me since Daršanga. I gaped, bloody-mouthed, hanging in the boatman's grip and seeing his fist cocked for a second blow, the sinews in his arm taut and swelling.

"I said *one*."

Joscelin's gauntleted right hand caught the boatman's fist. His other hovered over the hilt of his left-hand dagger. The boatman nodded, ceding to good sense, thrusting me toward him.

"Take him," he said in disgust.

I staggered into Joscelin's arms. "Thank you," I slurred.

He held me up effortlessly, gesturing toward the back of the tavern. "Gilot."

The horde parted, letting him rise. Gilot bounded to his feet, hand on his sword-hilt, fury in his face, abating as he took in the scene. Joscelin jerked his head toward the door.

"Go on," he said quietly. "You've earned your rest."

With a profound sigh, Gilot departed.

Holding me up with one arm, Joscelin fumbled in his purse, tossing a few silver ducats on the bar. "Apologies," he said.

The innkeeper nodded. "No trouble, my lord."

Outside, Joscelin let go of me. I squinted at him, seeing three wavering figures, and concentrated hard on standing upright. The ground seemed to be moving under my feet and my knees felt watery. Mercifully, after the first burst of pain, it had faded. My face felt hot and numb, a wet warmth trickling over my chin. Joscelin regarded me with folded arms.

"Lose any teeth?" he asked.

I spat out a mouthful of blood and probed with my

tongue. "Don't think so," I said thickly. "Loosened a couple."

He nodded. "Don't fuss with them." There was a street lad standing by, holding the Bastard and Joscelin's horse. He paid him and took the reins. "Come on." He started walking, leading both horses. They followed docilely. After a moment, I stumbled after them.

We walked for a long time. It was late and the City was quiet. After a while, I began to feel more sick than drunk. I had to pause a few times to vomit, heaving the contents of my stomach on the cobbled streets until I felt empty as a scraped gourd.

At Elua's Square, Joscelin tied up the horses and let me rest. I dunked my head into the cool waters of the dolphin fountain, scrubbing my battered face and swilling my mouth, then cupped my hands and drank deeply. It was the best water I ever tasted.

"Feel better?" he asked.

"Yes." My face was beginning to ache and stiffen and my swollen lips made talking difficult, but I was beginning to sober. "A little." I sat down on the stone bench where I had waited for my nonexistent conspirator to contact me.

Joscelin sat down beside me.

"Did Phèdre tell you?" I asked him.

He didn't answer at once, gazing at the stars. They were dense tonight, bright against the black sky. "I can't look at the stars without thinking of that night," he mused. "Searching for Kapporeth." He looked at me. "She said she suspected you'd come face-to-face with your heritage."

"I went to Valerian House," I said. "And I—" I looked away.

"And then you went home," he finished.

He knew.

I felt sick in a way that had naught to do with rotgut ale. Sick at heart, sick with guilt and shame. I said nothing, swallowing tears, trying to act like a man.

"Imri, love." The gentleness in Joscelin's voice nearly undid me. "You are what you are. We cannot choose the gifts the gods bequeath to us, only what we do with them. Believe me, no one knows it better than Phèdre." He smiled a little, stroking my shorn locks. "Though I may run a close second."

I did cry, then; hot tears, bitter and silent. They leaked beneath my lids and dampened my cheeks, salt-stinging on my split lips. Joscelin let me, offering no words of false comfort, only wordless solace. At last they ran their course, and there, on a bench in Elua's Square, I gathered my resolve and made a choice.

"I'm leaving," I said. "I'm going to Tiberium."

"Are you sure?" He searched my face with shadowed eyes. "We can find a way through this, Imri. We've faced worse together."

"I'm sure." I thought about what else awaited me in the City of Elua. The Queen and Cruarch urging me toward Dorelei, with her sweet child's laugh and Alban innocence. My young royal cousin Sidonie and the banked heat between us. Knowledge of Valerian House, where a beautiful adept proclaimed herself taken with me. All of those things added up to a disaster. I rubbed away tears with the heel of my hand. "I can't stay."

"I wish you would," Joscelin said simply.

"I know." I smiled at him though it made my face ache. "It's not that the City is too small, or Montrève, or even Terre d'Ange. It's me. I need to grow. I need to find out who I am. And I can't do it here. Not without hurting the people I love."

He nodded. "So be it, then. We'll begin making arrangements on the morrow."

We both rose. On impulse, I embraced him, flinging both arms around his neck and hugging him hard. Joscelin returned my embrace, his vambraced arms firm around me. For the last time, I stood in the charmed circle of his protection, knowing nothing bad could happen to me while he was there.

For the space of a few heartbeats, it was true.

But I wasn't a child anymore, and he couldn't protect me from myself. He was wise enough not to try, and I knew it.

"I'll miss you," I whispered. "So much!"

"So will I," he murmured. "So will I, love."

His arms tightened, and then he released me. In the shadowy starlight, I saw, for the first time I remembered, the gleam of tears in Joscelin's eyes.

He shook his head, dispelling them.

"Come," he said. "Let's go home."

TWENTY-NINE

O N THE MORROW, I had to face Phèdre.

I put it off as long as I could. Joscelin and I had arrived in the wee hours of the morning, with most of the household sleeping, only a bleary-eyed Hugues to greet us. I took to my bed and slept, too; the sleep of the dead, or nearly so.

But eventually, I had to rise.

Hunger drove me from my chamber. My belly, purged of all it had contained for the past day, rumbled ominously. When I heard Eugènie ring the bell for luncheon, I stumbled downstairs on wobbly legs.

"Good day," I mumbled, taking my seat at the table. Phèdre stared at me in mild shock. The surge of remembered desire, the way her pulse had leapt beneath my thumb, struck me anew. My empty stomach roiled. "What?" I asked, defensive. "What is it?"

"Your hair," she said. "And your *mouth*!"

Joscelin coughed.

I licked my split lips and winced. "I deserved it. And the hair . . ." I felt at the multitude of ragged, severed stumps of braids that dotted my scalp, half-unraveled. "I was angry," I said lamely.

"I know." Her voice softened. "Will you at least let me trim it?"

It would be a test of sorts. The thing lay between us, acknowledged but unspoken. I nodded and began to fill my plate.

Afterward, I bathed, soaking in a tub of heated water and fragrant oils. I felt better for it. And when I had done, Phèdre attended to my hair.

I sat on a footstool, wrapped in a dressing gown, hunkering low. Every muscle in my body was strung taut. Phèdre undid the tangled remnants of my Shahrizai braids, teasing them out with an ivory comb. She had a deft touch. How not? She had been trained as an adept of the Night Court. And yet this time there was somewhat impersonal in it, somewhat that quelled desire. I had heard rumors that adepts of all the Thirteen Houses were so trained. It was one of the Night Court's untold secrets. Mayhap it was true. I only know I was grateful for it.

"Hold still, love," Phèdre murmured.

I felt the cold kiss of steel shears against my cheek. "I trust you," I said, closing my eyes. "I always will. Always."

The shears moved in a steady flurry, snipping and slicing. I hugged myself and sat unmoving, bits of hair flying. It took a while. When the flurry had ended, Phèdre laughed, soft and low, a sound filled with quiet regret.

"Look," she said, directing me to the mirror. "A proper Tiberian gentleman."

I looked. My hair lay in a loose, shining cap, cut high enough to bare my ears, breaking over my brow in waves. I met her eyes in the mirror. It was easier that way.

"I'm sorry!" I said. "Ah, Elua! I'm so sorry."

"Don't be." Phèdre's hands rested on my shoulders, her touch cool and light. Looking into the mirror, she matched my gaze. "We are what we are, Imriel. Blessed Elua has his reasons."

"I pray he does," I whispered.

"He does." She turned me loose. "Go and make your plans."

I met with her factor first; my factor, now. As I had reached the age of majority, I had the right to draw upon the proceeds of my estates. Jacques Brenin arranged for a transfer of funds, giving me a note that would allow me to make a claim on one of Tiberium's foremost banks. And then I faced the Queen and gave her my decision. It was the first time I had met with her alone, with only the two of us present.

Ysandre was wroth.

I watched her pace the length of her private receiving-chamber, a scarlet flush on the lines of her cheekbones. Ysandre de la Courcel, the Queen of Terre d'Ange, did not like being thwarted in her plans.

She fetched up before me. "Why, Imriel?" she asked, frustrated. *"Why?"*

"Because," I said softly. "Dorelei mab Breidaia seems like a nice girl, your majesty; sweet and kind. And I'm not nice." I shook my head, weightless and shorn. "I'm not nice at all. She deserves better."

"Imriel." The Queen drew herself up. "A kingdom rides on this."

"What is a kingdom?" I asked philosophically. "Blessed Elua himself cared naught for thrones or the concerns of mortal politics." Beholding her expression, I laughed. "Have you heard those words before? Yes, your majesty. It seems, in the end, I am my mother's son after all. Will you not bid me good riddance?"

"No." Ysandre paused. Something surfaced in her gaze,

courageous and indomitable. "No," she repeated. "That I will not do. Whatever your choices, you are a member of House Courcel, now and always."

I bowed to her. "Nonetheless, I am going."

I said my farewells to those who mattered. Foremost among them was Alais. She tried very hard to ignore me, kneeling on the marble floors of her chambers and hugging Celeste, who bore it with worried patience.

"Don't go," she pleaded. "Don't leave me, please!"

"I'm sorry, villain." I crouched before her, trying to get her to look at me. "I have to."

She averted her head stubbornly. "You were supposed to be my brother!"

"And so I am, in my heart." I touched her hot tearstained cheek. "Have you decided to consent to the betrothal?"

Alais nodded. "I couldn't think of a reason not to," she said in a small voice. "But I thought you'd be coming too, Imri."

"Oh, Alais! I *am* sorry." Shifting to my knees, I gathered her in my arms. She relented and flung herself against me, dampening my neck with tears, her narrow shoulders shaking. I held her, swallowing against the lump in my throat. With Alais, I was my better self; my best self. I would miss her. "I'll come back," I whispered into her tangled hair. "I promise I will."

She drew away, sniffling. "*Swear* it!"

I raised my hand. "In Blessed Elua's name, I swear it."

Although I did not bother to speak with any of my former friends from among the young courtiers, I did pay a visit to Mavros, calling upon him at his father's domicile. Mavros merely nodded when I told him, calm and unsurprised. After the scene with Alais, I was grateful for it.

"When will you leave?" he asked.

"In three days' time," I said. "There's a merchant ship sailing out of Marsilikos. I mean to book passage."

"Alone?" he asked.

"I'd like to." I smiled crookedly, trying not to tear my healing mouth. "And I'd be within my rights, too. There's naught anyone could do about it since I've gained my majority. But no. Gilot is coming to Tiberium with me. He's not been good for aught else since he got his heart broken, so he reckoned he might as well. And I didn't have the heart to argue."

"Good." Mavros raised his brows at me. "Like it or no, you do have enemies, Imriel. An entourage would be better, but at least two are stronger than one." He paused. "Will you see Sidonie before you leave?"

I shrugged. "Why? There's no merit in it."

He merely regarded me.

"All right!" I scowled at him. "No. I couldn't think of a way. A discreet way."

Mavros chuckled, beckoning to a servant. "Paper and pen," he said, and then to me, "You're not very good at this, are you? We'll send a note to her attendant. Naamah's folk live for this sort of thing. You know the one. What's her name? The priestess' daughter, the one with the luscious lips that make you think about how they'd look wrapped around your shaft."

I flushed. "Amarante of Namarre."

He snapped his fingers. "Amarante! That's the one."

I argued; he coaxed. In the end, I conceded. Whatever else one might say of the Shahrizai, they are persuasive. We drafted a note to be sent under his aegis to Amarante for Sidonie, inviting her to a private meeting on the afternoon before my departure.

"So, we have the when," Mavros said, his pen poised. "Where?"

I thought about it. "The place where I first smiled at her."

He looked skeptical. "It's a bit vague. You think she'll remember?"

I shrugged again. "If she doesn't, then I'm right, aren't I? There's no merit in it."

Mavros shook his head, dipping his pen in the inkwell. "As you will," he said, finishing the letter and signing it with a flourish. "You don't make it easy for people to care for you, cousin."

"No," I said. "I suppose not."

We said our farewells, and he embraced me for the first time, hard and firm. I was glad, I realized, to call him kin.

"Thank you," I said. "For everything. For this"—I gestured at the sealed letter—"for everything you've tried to do. I appreciate it, truly. And tell . . . tell Roshana good-bye for me."

"You're family," Mavros said simply. He ruffled my short-cropped hair and grinned. "No matter what you look like."

So it was done and the worst of it over, save for the last. It would not be so hard, I thought, to bid farewell to Sidonie as it had been to Alais, whom I loved dearly, without complication or reservation. No harder, perhaps, than confronting the Queen. Of a surety, it would not be as hard as it would be to leave Phèdre and Joscelin, who were the stars by which I set the compass of my soul, uneasy though it was.

That part was true.

Still, it was hard; harder than I anticipated, and for reasons I hadn't.

I spent the day prior to our meeting immersed in the final

arrangements. There was so much to be done! Ti-Philippe had taken the travel arrangements in hand, having long experience with such matters, and I was glad for it. I pored over letters Eamonn had sent me, written in his painstaking scrawl. The earlier missives were filled with complaints about the tedium of mastering the Caerdicci tongue; the latest held a glowing account of being accepted to study with a philosopher he admired. I filed away letters of reference Phèdre had given me, written by her and by other tutors with whom I had studied. I wrote letters to the seneschals of my estates, instructing them to heed Phèdre's authority in my absence should need arise. I packed and unpacked my things half a dozen times. We would be travelling light, Gilot and I, with only whatever a pair of pack-horses could carry and no attendants.

It had sparked considerable dissent.

Mavros was right; it was dangerous. Joscelin had argued against it at considerable length, reckoning he had a better chance of convincing me. I refused, putting my foot down for the first time since I had gained my majority.

"How many times did you and Phèdre make such journeys alone?" I asked him.

"That was different!" he said, frustrated.

"Why?" I asked. "Because *you* were there?"

"You're a Prince of the Blood," he reminded me. "You have enemies and a responsibility to the Crown."

"I know," I said. "That's part of what I'm trying to escape."

In the end, seeing I wouldn't be swayed, he capitulated. We went to the armorers' district together, yet another final chore to be done. With Joscelin's counsel, I had commissioned a sword upon turning eighteen, and I was anxious that it be finished. I had spoken to the master smith two days prior, and he had assured me it would be ready.

It was a handsome blade. After much debate, I had opted for a nobleman's sword such as any member of the gentry might carry. It was shorter and slimmer than the warrior's longsword Joscelin wore, designed to be worn on the belt and not slung over the shoulder in a baldric. When all was said and done, I was not a Cassiline Brother or the Queen's Champion, and to outfit myself as such would only invite ridicule or outright challenge.

A nobleman's sword was another matter.

Joscelin examined it, drawing it in one fluid motion. It chimed faintly as it cleared the scabbard. The workmanship was plain, the hilt wrapped in leather, the pommel unadorned. The edges were honed to a blue glint. He studied the glimmering patterns in the blade, indicating the metal had been folded many times.

"Well crafted," he said.

The master smith was a laconic Camaeline with dense black eyebrows, and he knew an expert when he heard one. He nodded at a thick post, sturdy and notched. "Try it."

Joscelin handed me the sword. The hilt was longer than the average nobleman's blade, the tang wider and heavier. It could be wielded with a one- or a two-handed grip. Facing the post, I gripped the hilt in both hands and moved through the first of the Cassiline forms, telling the hours, getting a feel for the blade's balance. I told the hour of noon, shifting to attack and defend each of the sphere's four quadrants. The blade cut cleanly through the air.

It felt good.

I saw Joscelin's lips curve. The master smith's brows twitched.

Stepping forward, I finished with an attack on the midpoint, sweeping the blade in a high, arching parry to my right and swinging it in a level blow, hard and straight. It bit deep into the heavy wood. I felt the shock of it clean up both arms to my shoulders. The blade belled, clear and true.

In the depths of the smithy, an apprentice let out a whistle.

"Nicely done," said the smith.

"My thanks," I grunted, struggling to wrench the blade out of the post.

The scabbard fit nicely on my rhinoceros-hide belt, which was shiny with wear, but still as sturdy as the day Ras Lijasu gave it to me. It was on its last notch, but it fit. The Ras had been right, there was room to grow in it. Joscelin eyed it as we left the armorers' district. "We can get you a new belt."

I shook my head. "I don't want a new one."

We purchased one item in the leather district, though; a leg sheath to hold a second dagger, for with the addition of a sword, only the right-hand dagger fit on the belt. Joscelin knelt in the marketplace, strapping it to my left calf. When he was done, between the scabbard at my side and the dagger alongside my leg, I felt strange and a little stiff.

"It's an awkward draw," Joscelin commented.

I tried it. The first time, the pommel of my new sword drove into my ribs. The second time, I adjusted, coming out of a quick crouch with both daggers in my hands. Out of habit, I tossed my head, forgetting my hair was too short to obscure my vision. "Smooth enough, with practice."

Joscelin sighed. "Speed's not everything."

"No," I said. "But be honest, Joscelin. I'm better with the sword than the daggers, I always have been. If I need to go for them, I'm already in trouble. Besides," I added, "I haven't sworn an oath to draw my sword only to kill."

"Good," he said grimly. "Because I want you to draw it at need."

"I will," I promised.

"Better yet," he said, "stay out of trouble."

I grinned at him. "I'll try."

Under other circumstances, I daresay I would have swaggered a bit. Most young men do, upon getting their first sword. But I didn't have the heart for it. This was no courtly accessory; it was a weapon. And Tiberium was an eminently civilized city, but there was a long journey before I reached it.

And one farewell to make before the last one.

I rode out the following day to keep my appointment with Sidonie, unsure whether or not she would show. It was the second time I exercised my independence, for I went alone. No one knew but Mavros and Amarante, and I trusted him to keep my secrets. I trusted her, too. Priestesses' daughters have closed mouths. I knew, having grown up in a sanctuary.

The Queen's Guard admitted me onto the Palace grounds without a fuss, and I made for the royal apple orchard. The Bastard was in fine fettle, arching his speckled neck and snorting, picking up his forelegs in his odd, prancing gait.

I wondered if he sensed the journey to come.

We entered an aisle of trees, their gnarled limbs dense and leafy, bearing a myriad of tiny green apples. I glanced around as I rode, spotting Amarante at the end of another aisle. She stood, her hands folded, sunlight gleaming on her apricot-colored hair. As I rode closer, I could see her smiling. Her eyes were the color of green apples.

"Prince Imriel," she said. "You look quite the hero."

I laid one hand on the hilt of my new sword. "Defender against deer, savior of dogs."

Amarante laughed.

"So Sidonie knew the place," I said softly. "Did she come?"

"I came." She stepped out from behind a tree. Her sun-dappled face was somber and unreadable. "I don't have long. I told my guardsmen we wanted a private stroll. They'll come looking for us if we don't return soon."

I dismounted and looped the Bastard's reins over a tree branch. "Thank you."

She smiled ruefully. "I thought I owed you as much. Although you've well-nigh broken Alais' heart, and Mother's not pleased." Sidonie turned to Amarante, touching her sleeve. "Will you give us a moment?"

"Of course." The priestess' daughter inclined her head.

We both watched her withdraw, then Sidonie sighed. "Why?" she asked me.

"Many reasons," I said. "The foremost of which is me."

She looked at me sidelong. "Yes, I heard. You told Mother you weren't *nice*."

"I'm not," I said. "I try to be, but I'm not."

"Nice can be dull." Sidonie laughed at my expression. "Does that shock you? I'm a Queen's heir, Imriel. I've never been able to afford the luxury of niceness. And I have found, all too often, that a pleasant mask hides the face of ugliness."

I shook my head. "That's not what I mean."

"What, then?" she asked. "You've a good heart. For a long time, I didn't believe it. But I saw it the day you tried to protect me. And I've seen it in the way you treat Alais."

"Alais is different," I said.

"From what?" Her brows rose. "Me?"

I looked steadily at her, remembering the feel of her body beneath mine; remembering the adept in the private chambers of Valerian's dungeon. It was too easy to picture Sidonie the same way. Even now, I could envision taking her here in the orchard, destroying her cool composure. Pinning her wrists, feeling her writhe, golden hair splaying over the grass. Her fair skin bruised by the marks of my teeth and nails. "Yes," I said. "You."

Her chin rose. "I'm not afraid of you."

"You should be," I said. "You used to."

"Yes, and things have changed between us, haven't they?" Sidonie regarded me. "You swore an oath. Do you recant it?"

I let out my breath in a hiss. "No!"

"Then I have no cause for fear," she said.

I grabbed her upper arms, hard enough to bruise. "You don't know me," I said hoarsely. "You don't know what I'm capable of."

"Don't be so sure." She stood unmoving in my grip, chin tilted. Deep below the surface of her gaze, a nameless emotion flared. Dark eyes, Cruithne eyes, rendered strange and unfamiliar in her D'Angeline face. "I'm not a child, Imriel. I know you're Kushiel's scion. I know your House. And I know my own heritage, too. Do you forget that Kusheline blood flows in the veins of House L'Envers?"

I had forgotten.

For a moment, we stood motionless, both of us. I could feel my heart thudding in my chest, the blood throbbing in my veins. I could sense her breathing quicken. And I reminded myself that she was only sixteen and nearly a sister to me.

I pushed her away. "Name of Elua, no!"

She stumbled on the grass, then caught herself and laughed wildly. "No? Then go ahead, cousin. Run! Invoke Blessed Elua's name. Why not? You didn't hesitate to do it before when I drew away. Run, run away from desire. Run away from responsibility. Run!"

I strode to the Bastard's side and unhitched his reins, swinging astride. "Stay," I said coldly, gazing down at her from the saddle. "Wed some pedigreed D'Angeline nobleman, take Maslin de Lombelon as a lover, do as you will. Stay. I wish you the joy of it."

Sidonie sobered. "I don't have a choice," she whispered. "Oh, Imriel! I never have."

I swallowed, feeling an ache in my heart. "I don't want to part like this."

"Nor do I." Bowing her head, she laid a hand on my stirrup, fingertips brushing the glossy leather of my boot. "Go," she murmured. "And may Blessed Elua hold you in his hand and keep you."

I nodded. "And you, my lady."

She looked up at me. "You made a promise to Alais. Keep it."

I'll come back.

I laid my clenched fist on my heart. "On my oath, I will."

I went, then, setting my heels hard into the Bastard's flanks. He blew out his breath, snorting through his nostrils. We cantered between the apple trees and I dared not look behind me, knowing she watched us go.

In my haste to depart, I nearly ran down a handful of the Queen's Guard.

They were idling on the outskirts of the orchard. I checked the Bastard hard. I saw Maslin de Lombelon a few paces away, conversing with a familiar figure. Their heads turned as we plunged to a halt. A stab of fury went through me, and I tasted bile.

"You're back," I said to Duc Barquiel L'Envers.

"And you're still here. I'd hoped to find the rumors true and you in Tiberium." He looked me over archly. "I like the hair."

Maslin had gone rigid. "What are you doing here?" he demanded. L'Envers glanced at him. "The Dauphine," Maslin said to the Duc, "is in the orchard without a guardsman in sight. I find myself mistrustful of the Prince's intentions. 'Tis not the first time he's sought a means to be alone with her."

"I see," Barquiel L'Envers said quietly. He took two steps toward me. I put my right hand on the hilt of my new sword. Beneath his close-cropped blond hair, his face was cold, as cold as anything I'd ever seen. There was no malice in it, merely a deadly calm, implacable and calculating. "You don't want to play that game, princeling. Trust me, you do not."

I leaned over in the saddle and spat at his feet.

L'Envers never moved. "Go away, young Imriel," he said. "Far, far away."

"Guards!" Maslin said crisply, drawing his sword. They unsheathed their weapons, approaching warily. My blade rang as it cleared the scabbard. I kneed the Bastard in a tight circle, extending my blade and keeping them at bay.

What would have happened if Sidonie had not emerged from the orchard at that moment, strolling arm-in-arm with Amarante, I cannot say. I daresay they wouldn't have attacked me in broad daylight, without provocation, there on the Queen's grounds.

But I am not certain.

Sidonie's voice carried, cool and imperious. "Lieutenant Maslin, what on *earth* are you doing?"

He hesitated, then bowed and put up his sword, gesturing to his men to follow suit. "Your pardon, your highness. A misunderstanding, nothing more."

"I should hope so," she said evenly. Barquiel L'Envers narrowed his eyes, studying her. She returned his gaze without flinching. "Well met, Uncle. I trust your respite agreed with you?"

"Oh, indeed." He gave a pointed nod toward the orchard. "As, I trust, did yours."

"Very much so." Tender years or no, Sidonie didn't so much as flush. I ducked my head to hide a grin. From my vantage point on horseback, I could see the slightest hint of a smile hovering in the corner of her lips. She shifted her gaze to me, inclining her head. "Cousin."

I returned her nod. "Dauphine."

No one else spoke. I sheathed my sword and took up the Bastard's reins in both hands. He was edgy, body quivering between my thighs, hooves shifting. Sidonie and I exchanged a long silent glance.

"I'm going," I said to Barquiel L'Envers. "But I'll be back one day."

He said nothing, his eyes narrow and calculating.

I repeated my salute, pressing a clenched fist to my heart. And then I turned the Bastard and gave him his head. We fled, startling the guards at the Palace gate, bursting into the cobbled streets of the City, leaving behind a knot of intrigue and desire I'd no wish to unravel. Passersby stared, and I didn't care. Let them think what they might.

I felt the wind of our passage on my face, and it felt like freedom.

Run, I thought.

Run.

THIRTY

I SAID NOTHING of the encounter. There was nothing new in Barquiel L'Envers' enmity. Maslin was another matter, but I wasn't sure whether his animosity was born of his dislike of me, his feelings for Sidonie, or L'Envers' seditious lies. Either way, I found myself reluctant to speak of it. There was no merit in worrying Phèdre and Joscelin. I didn't want to talk to them about Sidonie, either. Although I couldn't say why, what lay between us seemed best left unspoken.

Anyway, it didn't matter.

On the following day, we left.

The rumor of my departure was already circulating, but we kept the timing of it quiet. I hadn't told anyone but Mavros, and no one else had spoken of it. We rode out from the City in a large party, attended by almost all of Montrève's retainers; even Eugènie and her niece. To all appearances, we might have been going on a household pleasure-jaunt, amply stocked with provisions. A league outside the City, we would part ways. Gilot and I would continue on toward Eisheth's Way and Marsilikos, and the others would return slowly to the City.

It wouldn't fool anyone, not for long. But it would buy us a little time.

As merry as our party looked, it felt like a funeral procession. I had put off thinking about this moment. I had known it would be hard. I hadn't reckoned on feeling like something inside me was breaking.

On one of the smaller country roads that connects to Eisheth's Way, we halted and said our farewells. Everyone there seemed impossibly dear to me. Eugènie was the first to weep, embracing me and turning away. I bid farewell to her, to Clory, to all our men-at-arms, to Hugues and Ti-Philippe.

Gilot said his own farewells, and when he was done, he led our mounts and pack-horses a way down the road. On Ti-Philippe's nod, the household withdrew in the opposite direction, leaving Phèdre and Joscelin and me alone.

I could scarce bear to look at them.

The sun stood high overhead. Our shadows pooled at our feet, mingling on the dusty road. The scent of lavender hung in the air. After all we had endured, it seemed impossible that we would part. There should have been words for it; torrents of words. But it was hard to breathe past the lump in my throat, and all words failed me.

"Imriel," Phèdre whispered.

I nodded and looked at her, seeing past her undimmed beauty and the mark of Kushiel's Dart; even past the sorrow brimming in her eyes. I saw the profound compassion and courage. Love. I saw love in its truest, purest form.

You will find it and lose it, again and again.

"Be well," she said. "Be happy. Come back safely to us one day."

Unable to speak, I nodded again, stepping into her embrace. I bowed my head against her shoulder. In that moment, I remembered only how many times she had held me when I awoke from nightmares, sweating and trembling, my throat raw from screaming. How many times I had taken comfort from her mere presence. In a part of me, I wished nothing had ever changed. But it had, and I could not undo it. The silent leap of desire lay between us, deep as a chasm. After a moment, Phèdre planted a kiss on my brow and let me go, turning away.

I looked at Joscelin and knew there was nothing left to say. In a way, we had already said our farewells. He reached out his hand and we clasped forearms like men. It gave me strength to draw a shuddering breath and speak.

"I love you," I said to them. "I love you both so much."

If I stayed, I feared I would lose my resolve. And so I went. Behind me, I heard a small sound escape Phèdre; I heard the sound of Joscelin's vambraces creaking as he put his arm about her. It was she who had taught me to listen for such things. And he was doing what he had always done, being strong for us both when we needed him the most.

My steps dragged on the dusty road. Ahead of me was Gilot, sweating under the hot sun as he sat astride, holding two lead-lines and the Bastard's reins. I kept going though my heart felt like a stone in my breast.

"You're sure about this?" Gilot asked when I reached him.

I leaned my head against the Bastard's muscular neck, breathing in the odor of hot horseflesh. I could feel Phèdre's kiss on my brow like a blessing. "I'm sure," I mumbled through the Bastard's coarse mane.

"Let's go, then." His voice was firm.

I forced myself to mount, though my limbs felt heavy and reluctant. Gilot secured the lead-lines of the pack-horses and we set on our way, treading our shadows beneath us.

I looked behind me only once. They were still standing

there, Phèdre and Joscelin, growing small in the distance. She looked small beneath his arm. He raised one hand in salute, vambrace glinting. I raised my hand in reply and turned my gaze forward.

Ah, Elua! It hurt to leave them.

I wiped my eyes, scrubbing my tearstained cheeks. And then I drew a deep breath, tasting the air as a free man. "Gilot?"

"Aye, highness?" he asked.

"I'm done with weeping," I said. "I'm sick unto death of my own tears. No more, do you hear me?"

"I do." He smiled wryly. "Tell the truth, I've had enough of my own."

"Good." I straightened in the saddle. "And no more *your highness* or *my prince*, either. Call me what you will in front of others, but not that. I'm not going to Tiberium as a Prince of the Blood or a member of House Courcel."

Gilot eyed me sidelong. "No? How do you want to be called?"

"Imriel," I said. "Imriel nó Montrève."

He nodded. "As you wish."

We made good time to Marsilikos, arriving a day and a half before the Tiberian merchant ship was due to depart. Gilot and I made our way to the quais, booking our passage with the ship's captain. He was an affable Tiberian fellow, glad to have our company and our gold, happy to recommend an inn where we might abide for a night.

Gilot was disgruntled.

"Surely the Lady of Marsilikos would receive you!" he complained, fussing at the threadbare blankets that covered his pallet. "My Lady Phèdre counts her as a friend. Do you mean to live as a peasant, Imri?"

I reclined on my own pallet, thin and lumpy, folding my

arms beneath my head. Our rented room had one small window. Through it, I could glimpse the Dome of the Lady high atop its hill, overlooking the harbor, gilded and glorious, impervious to the knowledge of our presence. I smiled to myself.

"Mayhap," I said to Gilot. "Or near enough as makes no difference."

He scowled at me. "Why?"

I closed my eyes. "Because that's how I was raised, Gilot. As a peasant. As an orphan taken in by Brother Selbert of the Sanctuary of Elua in Landras, taught to herd goats for a living. And I wonder, betimes, who *that* boy might have grown up to be." I opened my eyes. "Does that trouble you?"

"No." His scowl deepened. "I'm the fourth son of a poor manor. It's why I sought service in her ladyship's household; that, and her reputation. But why hold yourself cheap? You don't *need* to compromise, Imri."

I sighed. "Let me do this in my own way, Gilot. If you don't like it, you needn't come."

He snorted. "Oh, I'm coming! Make no mistake. If you want to be the only peasant in Tiberium with a bodyguard, so be it."

I grinned at him. "Well, mayhap not a *peasant*, exactly."

Our ship sailed on the morrow. We presented ourselves at the quai. Our mounts and pack-horses were ushered belowdecks, our belongings stowed. I made my way to the prow of the ship, cheering alongside the sailors as we hoisted anchor. The rowers bent to their oars and stroked. The ship turned slowly in the harbor of Marsilikos, green-blue waves breaking along her prow. Its sails began to fill and belly, and we picked up speed as we went.

Gilot shivered. "I've never left Terre d'Ange."

We passed Eisheth's Isle, narrow and barren. A few fishermen watched us go. I touched Gilot's arm. "I know," I said. "It's all right. Believe me, I have gone farther than this. I promise you, all is well."

It was a good journey, though a strange one. Gilot retired to our tiny cabin, where he spent most of his time. It wasn't that he was seasick—not like Joscelin—but the sight of all that open water made him uneasy. For the most part, I stayed abovedecks. It all came back to me: how to stand, how to walk. I helped where I was able, and tried not to make a nuisance of myself otherwise. I leaned in the prow and watched the dolphins that toyed in our wake, leaping and smiling their enigmatic smiles.

I remembered Fadil Chouma pointing them out to me.

I remembered the fountain in Elua's Square.

But mostly, blessedly, I forgot. Aboard the ship, I was only Imriel, a paying passenger who was less trouble than not. I gazed out at the four quarters of the world, bounded only by water and more water, and felt giddy with freedom. In the wind's salt spray, I felt scoured clean of my own dark desires. I diced with sailors and scrambled in the rigging when they dared me. I perched, swaying, in the crow's nest athwart the mainmast, hollering at the sight of land.

It came too soon.

"Ostia!" one of my shipmates shouted, crowding into the narrow space beside me. He flung his arm out like a spear, pointing straight and true. "Ostia!"

I clambered down from the rigging, sobering. As we neared the lighthouse, Gilot emerged from belowdecks, staring at the shore. "So," he said. "That's where we're bound."

I clapped my hand on his shoulder. "It's a start," I said. "'Tis the gateway to Tiberium."

It was a massive, bustling port. Once we disembarked, we had to wait for the horses and our gear to be unloaded. Gilot stared around at a loss, having never been away from native soil. The quais were crowded with folk from different nations—Caerdicci of every ilk, Illyrians, Carthaginians, Aragonians, Menekhetans, Jebeans, and Umaiyyati. Here and there, one saw a D'Angeline face, but not many. A babble of languages and dialects filled the air.

I caught Gilot gaping at a crew of dark-skinned sailors aboard a Jebean ship, busily unloading cargo. "Don't stare," I said, nudging him. "You look provincial."

He shut his mouth with an audible click. "I *am* provincial, Imri!"

One of the sailors pointed at us, grinning. I daresay we looked like a fine pair of idiots, standing around open-mouthed in the midst of all that activity. I laughed and waved to him, calling out, "Selam!" He mimed surprise at my greeting him in Jeb'ez, then gave a cheerful wave in reply and went about his business.

At length our horses and baggage were unloaded. The Bastard was nearly as unnerved as Gilot, spooking in all directions, threatening to wreak havoc on the quai. After I got him calmed, I hired a porter to lead us to the river wharf.

The wharf was as crowded as the quai. Barges docked beneath the shadow of a guard tower, their captains shouting for business. Throngs of merchants and porters clogged the wharf, dotted with vendors selling food cooked over open-air braziers. Realizing our bellies were rumbling, we paused at one to purchase meat pies wrapped in pastry.

"Name of Elua!" Gilot swallowed with difficulty. "What's *in* this thing?"

I chewed reflectively. The taste was strange, peppery and pungent, with an underlying saltiness. "I don't know," I said. "I'll ask."

The vendor beamed when I asked him in Caerdicci. "You

like it? Only good things, young D'Angeline lord! Minced meat and peppercorns, pine kernels and garum." He chuckled. "The garum is a family recipe, a secret. That's what makes my pies the best."

"Garum?" I asked. Without divulging his family's secret, he told me the essence of what it contained. I nodded my thanks. "Fish paste and herbs," I said to Gilot. "Fermented in the sun for several weeks."

He gagged.

I grinned and took another bite. "Better get used to it. It seems the Tiberians are very proud of their garum."

Once we had eaten, we set about booking passage up the Tiber River. On our porter's advice, I spoke to several barge-captains. I remembered how Kaneka had haggled with the caravan drivers at Majibara, and took her example to heart. When all was said and done, I struck a decent bargain. Along with a few other passengers, we loaded our mounts, our baggage, and ourselves aboard a shallow-bottomed barge. At the tiller, the captain gave the command, and the oarsmen struck out.

We began to glide up the wide, flat expanse of the Tiber River.

The other passengers were a family of Menekhetan merchants, slight and dark, ferrying a cargo of linens. I listened to them speak amongst themselves, catching a word here and there. I wondered if the Tiber disappointed them after the great river of the Nahar.

"You seem different here," Gilot observed.

"Do I?" I smiled. "I feel different. I feel . . . free." We glided beneath the arch of a massive bridge. I pointed out a carving on one of its supporting columns. Although it was worn, one could still discern the doubled features of a deity, looking at once north and south. "Do you see that, Gilot?

Janus, god of bridges and doorways, of crossroads. I'll warrant it was already old when Blessed Elua first trod the earth."

Gilot shuddered. "I'll take my gods with one face, thank you!"

A tickle of foreboding brushed my spine as I remembered Alais' dream. Our barge passed beneath the bridge's shadow, emerging into sunlight. "I'm just saying, look about you, Gilot," I said lightly, gesturing toward the banks. "There is a world beyond Terre d'Ange, and much of it is worthy of admiration."

He looked sourly at me. "What's Tiberium done lately?"

The barge-captain muttered somewhat in Caerdicci about D'Angeline snobbery and spat into the river. I watched his sputum swirl in the oars' wake.

"Plenty," I said to Gilot. "It reinvented itself as a center for learning, for one. Even Terre d'Ange acknowledges the preeminence of the University of Tiberium. That's why Eamonn came, and that's why I'm here. If you don't like it, bear in mind, *I* didn't ask you to come here with me."

Gilot hunched his shoulders and looked miserable. "I'm not a scholar," he muttered.

"I know." I touched his arm. "You don't have to stay, you know."

He looked at me with obdurate stubbornness. "Oh, I'm staying!"

"Fine," I said. "Then stop being an ass."

Once we glimpsed Tiberium proper, even Gilot had to own himself impressed. It is an old city, and if it no longer possesses the power it once held, it was still vast; bigger by far than the City of Elua. We both fell silent, gazing at the sprawl of buildings and monuments that covered its seven hills.

"It's . . . big," Gilot said faintly.

"That it is," I agreed.

As in Ostia, the wharf swirled with activity. It had originally been in my thoughts to seek Eamonn straightaway, but the scale of Tiberium overwhelmed me. The warehouses alone seemed enormous. Iskandria was the only city I had ever seen as large, and there I had been accompanied by Phèdre and Joscelin, who already knew it. Here I was alone, save for Gilot, who was little help. I was also tired and dirty, and it was growing late; the sun was hovering low over the seven hills. I looked around for a porter or a guide to hire, but it seemed all were engaged with bigger quarry than a pair of travel-worn D'Angelines. Gilot stood numb beside me, holding our horses.

In marked contrast to our sorry state, a trio of elegant young nobles disembarked from a pleasure-barge near us; young men, laughing and talking in animated Caerdicci. I plucked at my salt-stained doublet and looked enviously at them.

"Hey, D'Angeline!" one of them called. "What's the matter? Are you lost? Looking for the nearest brothel?"

His fellows laughed. I smiled ruefully. "A decent inn would do, my friend."

"Oh, friend, is it?" The one who had spoken eyed me. He had an unruly mass of dark auburn curls and young satyr's face, with sharp cheekbones and a wide, curling smile. "You're presuming a lot."

I shrugged. "A friend until proven otherwise."

He laughed. "I like that! Did you hear that, Aulus?" He thrust out a well-manicured hand. "Lucius Tadius da Lucca."

I clasped it. "Imriel nó Montrève."

A lively curiosity lit his gaze. "Montrève. You're adopted, yes? Do I understand D'Angeline nomenclature?"

"You do," I said. "And I am."

"The name strikes a chord," Lucius Tadius mused. "Ah well, no mind! What brings you to Tiberium, young Montrève? Another impoverished gentleman scholar come to try your luck at the University? I see your dumbstruck manservant standing by."

Gilot scowled.

I grinned, unable to help myself. Despite his insouciance, I sensed no malice in this Lucius. "Something like that," I said. "Can you point us toward an inn in the students' quarter?"

He raised his brows. "My dear, we can point you toward a dozen. We're all gentlemen scholars here. Aulus, Donato, come. Let us acquit ourselves of our civic duty and lead our hapless guests to lodging." Lucius gave me a sidelong glance. "And perhaps the baths," he added. "You're a lovely specimen, young Montrève, but a bit grimy."

True to his word, Lucius Tadius and his fellows escorted us into the heart of the city proper. I was grateful for his aid, realizing we would have gotten lost in short order. While the main road, the Via Appia, was wide and imposing, the students' quarter was a dense labyrinth, situated between the University and a major forum. It was a confusing jumble of inns, wineshops, and vendors, and the insulae, the apartments where most students dwelled, rose in staggering tiers. When we arrived, the sun was no longer visible and the narrow streets were filled with blue shadows.

"There," Lucius said crisply, pointing. "Or there, or there. If you want your mounts well-tended, I recommend Lollia's place. She keeps a clean stable if you can afford it." He watched as I dismounted. "That's a good-looking horse you ride, my friend."

I slapped the Bastard's speckled shoulder. "He's had a long journey."

"Haven't we all?" Lucius said cryptically. He pointed eastward. "The nearest public bath lies yonder, past the forum. I suggest you avail yourself of it."

"We will," I promised. "Thank you for your aid, truly."

Lucius shrugged. "Don't go noising it about. I've a reputation to uphold." He raised a hand in farewell. "Good luck to you, D'Angeline! Perhaps we'll see you in the lecture halls."

"Ass," Gilot muttered as Lucius and his companions departed.

I glanced at him. He was swaying in the saddle, glassy-eyed. "Come on," I said. "Let's see if this Lollia has a room to let."

She did, and we took it. I was glad to have a place to rest, glad to have our horses stabled and content. The Bastard eyed me with reproach, then sank his muzzle into a bucket of oats. We unloaded the pack-horses, staggering under the weight of our baggage, carrying it up several flights of stairs. By the time the transaction was fully concluded, the twilight that had settled over Tiberium was deepening to darkness.

"Baths," Gilot mumbled, his face sunk into his pallet.

I closed my eyes. "Tomorrow."

Behind my eyelids, darkness swirled; an abyss, dragging me downward. This time, I didn't fight it. In the city of Tiberium at last, I let sleep claim me.

THIRTY-ONE

I WOKE HUNGRY.

There wasn't much to be had at the inn, but we broke our fast with bread drizzled with honey and a handful of dried dates. The innkeeper Lollia assured us that the vendors would open ere long. Thus fortified, Gilot and I ventured out in search of the baths.

In the morning light, Tiberium was no less imposing, but one could see that it had fallen from its former glory. The buildings and monuments that marked the height of the empire were in poor repair. Still, if the tiles along the arching colonnades of the Great Forum were chipped and dirty, the space itself was still impossibly vast.

We found our way to the baths without difficulty. It was a huge structure, built to serve the needs of hundreds or mayhap even thousands of citizens. Early though it was, they were already doing a lively trade. The price was surprisingly reasonable.

"Oh yes," the attendant assured me with a pointed sniff. "It is in everyone's interest to make the baths affordable."

"I take your meaning," I said dryly.

After days at sea without a proper bath, it was pure bliss. Gilot and I indulged in the fullest, beginning in the steam

room. We sat on benches, sweat streaming, grinning at one
another through clouds of steam. Once we had sweated out
days' worth of grime, we moved to the caldarium, plunging
into scalding baths and sluicing away the sweat. There attendants poured olive oil over our skin and scraped it off
with curved metal strigils.

"It's an odd way to bathe," Gilot said. "But not
unpleasant."

Suitably scalded and scraped, we soaked in the warm waters of the tepidarium. It was a social place, with dozens of
men chatting amiably. Most were Caerdicci, though not all.
In the background, we could hear thudding and shouting coming from the palaestra, where others were taking
exercise.

We finished in the proper Tiberian style, plunging into
the cool waters of the frigidarium. I had to own, it was re-
freshing. It wasn't half as cold as Montrève's spring-fed
lake, but after the warmth that had preceded, it was a shock.
Gilot and I whooped, splashing one another like boys. An
older gentleman walking past shook his head at us.

"Ah, students," he said indulgently.

I tossed back my wet hair and grinned at him. "Not yet,
but I mean to be. Do you know, messire, how one goes about
seeking entrance to the University?"

He paused and drew up a stool. "Have you chosen a Master with whom to study?"

"No," I said. "I've only just arrived."

"Well, that's your first step, young D'Angeline. The next
is to convince him to accept you. Or her; there are a few
women licensed to teach." He smiled at me. "I suspect you
might do well in that area."

I flushed. "I have letters of reference, messire."

"Letters!" The gentleman chuckled. "They'll test you on

your own merits, lad. Luck to you." He heaved himself to his feet. "Tell them Deccus Fulvius said you were well-spoken," he said over his shoulder as he left. "It can't hurt your cause."

Gilot and I clambered out of the pool, and attendants toweled us off briskly.

"Thank you," I said. "Tell me, do you know that man?"

My attendant's eyes bulged. "Deccus Fulvius? How not?" Seeing my ignorance, he continued. "He is a senator, my lord, one of the most powerful; or the richest, at least." Glancing around, he lowered his voice. "He is one of the Restorationists."

"Restorationists?" I asked, bewildered.

"Those who wish to restore Tiberium to its glory as a *republic*," he whispered.

"Ah." I nodded. "Thank you."

By the time we returned to the antechamber and donned our clothes, there were food vendors strolling about and hawking their wares within the baths. It seemed strange to me, but the Tiberians regarded it as normal. We bought sausages and boiled eggs, venturing out of the baths and eating them as we went.

"So what's that about, Imri?" Gilot mused. "That Restorationist business?"

"I'm not sure," I admitted. "Tiberium was a republic, long ago. The Senate lost power when it became an empire. Even after it all fell apart, it's never regained its stature. I imagine there are some, like this Deccus Fulvius, who'd like to see it restored."

Gilot shrugged. "Precious little to quibble over."

"Not if you're a Tiberian senator," I observed.

Finishing our impromptu meal, we entered the Great Forum. To our amusement, we beheld the spectacle of a man in the velvet robes of a master scholar giving chase to a flock of pigeons. He yelled and shouted, thin arms protruding from his trailing sleeves, waving wildly. The pigeons took wing in unison, flapping and soaring. From time to time, he took a pinch of cornmeal from a pouch he carried, scattering it on the marble paving. When he did, the pigeons descended en masse; and then he plunged into their midst, shouting, while they swirled around him. Next he laid a trail of meal, while the pigeons followed, clucking and cooing, pooling around his feet . . . and then he startled them again, flapping his robes, revealing his bare shanks, skinny and hairy.

We couldn't help but laugh. It was Gilot who began it, but once he started, I was lost. We stood in the Great Forum, laughing like idiots, clutching one another, hard put to stand upright. The funniest part of all was that the scholar had students. A group of them stood by, watching and respectful. A few even made notes on wax tablets.

"Oh, Imri!" Gilot gasped. "You're sure about this University business?"

I wiped my streaming eyes. "Name of Elua! I said I was done with weeping, but I hadn't reckoned on this. Surely, the man must be mad."

"You'd better—" Gilot caught my arm. "Is that *Eamonn* among them?"

"No!" I looked in disbelief. There he stood among the students, half a head taller than the rest, his coppery hair glinting in the sun. I'd been laughing so hard I'd missed him altogether. "What in the world?" I raised my voice, heedless of all courtesy. "Eamonn! *Eamonn mac Grainne!*"

The bright head swung in our direction. Even at a distance, I could see the familiar grin spreading over his features. *"Imri!"*

His shout startled the pigeons anew. Laughing all over

again, I ran across the Forum. We met in the middle, embracing and pounding one another on the back, both of us grinning fit to split our faces.

"You made it!" he said happily. "You're here!"

I shook him by the shoulders. "Elua's Balls, but it's good to see you!"

"And you!" His grey-green eyes were alight. "Oh, Imri! There's so much to tell you. I've learned so much. Did you see Master Piero?"

I raised my brows. "The madman with the pigeons?"

"Oh, he's a brilliant man!" Eamonn said fervently. "I wrote to you about him, didn't I? Gilot, well met," he added as Gilot joined us. "Come, you both have to meet him!"

Gilot and I exchanged a look. I shrugged. "By all means."

We stood on the outskirts of the group. Master Piero had left off troubling the pigeons and was lecturing to his students. They listened, alert and attentive. I counted twelve of them including Eamonn. They were an odd lot. By their attire, a few of them looked to be less than wealthy; several were clearly not Caerdicci. There was a woman among them, tall and lithe, with tightly plaited blonde hair and a scowl of furious concentration. She was one of those carrying a wax tablet.

To my surprise, our saviors from the wharf, Lucius Tadius da Lucca and his companions, also numbered among Master Piero's pupils. I saw him glance at me out of the corner of his eye, wondering.

". . . thus we behold the workings of the group-mind," the Master was saying. "It is easily scattered by the unexpected; and yet, upon scattering, it moves swiftly to attain a consensus of direction, without leadership, without discussion." He broke off his words, smiling at us. He was a homely fellow with a wide brow and a thin beak of a nose that looked to

have been set askew, but there was an unexpected sweetness to his smile. "Welcome, friends. Will you join our
conversation?"

I bowed in greeting. "Forgive us, Master. We did not
mean to interrupt you."

"Surely there is no need to apologize," he said. "There
can be nothing but good in witnessing two friends reuniting,
can there?" There was a shrewd glint in his eye. "We agree
that friendship is a virtue. Does a display of virtue in others
not inspire it in ourselves?"

"Not necessarily, Master," Lucius Tadius observed. "It
may inspire envy."

"Ah!" Master Piero beamed at him. "Yes, indeed. What,
then, are the roots of envy? If a virtue inspires that which is
negative, is it itself lessened by it?"

"Master Piero!" The blonde girl spoke out in frustration.
I was startled to hear a thick Skaldic accent. "I am sorry,
please. But it is hard to follow when you wander."

"Are you in a hurry, Brigitta?" he asked gently.

"No, but . . ." She bit her lower lip, stubborn and vexed.
"You were talking about pigeons."

"And so we shall." Master Piero smiled at her. "Pigeons and
virtue and envy. We shall wander together, wherever the road
of thought takes us. It matters not how swift or straight our
path, merely that we travel it."

Having said so, he returned to the topic of pigeons and
the group-mind. Despite his demeanor and the fact that I had
laughed myself silly at him, I found myself listening, rapt,
as he expounded on his example.

". . . it is easily swayed by hunger and greed and flocks to
the promise of providence. It is easily led by a cunning hand.
It lives from moment to moment, forgetful of betrayal. Heedless of danger, it returns to the familiar . . ."

Upon concluding his lecture, Master Piero engaged in open discourse with his pupils. They speculated on the means by which the pigeons attained unspoken consensus in their flight, and how it mirrored the transmission of ideas and agreement among humans. They discussed how a swiftly propagated rumor turned into a held belief in a matter of days or even hours in a tightly knit community. I caught myself nodding at several points, thinking how members of the Court resembled a flock of pigeons in their behavior.

"You see?" Eamonn whispered to me when it ended.

I nodded, no longer inclined to laugh. "I do."

He hauled me over to meet the man. The other students made way for us with good-natured grumbles. "Master Piero di Bonci, may I present to you my very dear friend, Imriel nó Montrève de la—"

I coughed, covering my mouth with my fist, then executed a courtly bow. "Imriel nó Montrève, my lord. Thank you for permitting me to attend your discussion."

Eamonn, who was no fool, added nothing further.

Master Piero tilted his head, regarding me. I saw the same shrewd glint in his eye, and realized *I* was a fool, having thought I could hide my identity in a community of scholars. "Montrève," he said slowly. "Is that so?"

"Yes, my lord," I said humbly, willing him not to ask me about it.

He knew. I could see it in his expression. And I could see him read the unspoken plea in mine, measuring it with kindness and compassion. "Well," Master Piero said in a light tone. "You have listened. Is it your wish to study with us, Imriel nó Montrève?"

My heart soared with gratitude and relief. "I believe it is, Master Piero."

He patted my arm. "Come tomorrow," he said. "Eamonn can tell you where. We will see if we're suited to one another, eh?"

"I have letters of reference," I said.

"Letters!" Master Piero laughed. "I don't care for letters, lad." He poked me in the chest, then tapped my temple. "Only what's inside you, here and here."

Alarmed at the prospect of being judged and found wanting, I remembered the words the gentleman in the baths had spoken. "Deccus Fulvius said I might tell you he said I was well-spoken," I blurted.

"Deccus Fulvius!" Master Piero's brows shot upward. A few yards away, I saw Lucius Tadius raise his head like a hound on the scent. "Oh, lad, surely you've not been here long enough to dabble in politics." Master Piero shook his head. "Come tomorrow," he repeated. "And we will see, shall we?"

With that, he turned away to speak to Brigitta, the Skaldi girl, who had a host of concerns to address. Eamonn nudged me.

"Come on, Imri," he said. "Let's get a drink."

I wanted very much to speak with him alone. It was not to be, or at least not yet. A whole crowd of the Master's scholars accompanied us to the wineshop Eamonn chose, Lucius Tadius and his fellows among them. He found a seat at my elbow while Eamonn went to procure a jug of wine.

"So," he said, "you and Prince Barbarus know one another."

I frowned. "Prince Barbarus?"

"Yon Eamonn." He nodded toward the bar.

"Ah." The nickname made me laugh. "Yes, very well. Eamonn was fostered in our household for a year."

"Ah, I see. That explains the fond greeting." He regarded

me with interest. "The real question, my friend, is how you managed to acquaint yourself with Deccus Fulvius between sundown yesterday and midday today."

I shrugged. "Not through any intent of mine, I assure you. I encountered him at the baths this morning, and he was gracious to me. I'd no idea who he was until I asked an attendant. Why?" I added. "Do you know him?"

"You might say so." Lucius tapped his fingers idly on the tabletop. "He's married to my sister."

"I see," I said, though I didn't.

"What was the richest man in Tiberium doing in the public baths?" he mused. "Was he with anyone that you noticed?"

"No." I shook my head. "He was alone when I met him. But I hadn't noticed him before."

"Plotting conspiracy, no doubt. Ah, no mind." Lucius smiled absently at me. "Pay me no heed, Montrève. Master Piero is right, 'tis best to stay out of politics altogether and pursue the life of the mind."

"Is that why you're studying with him?" I asked, curious.

"Oh, in part." His focus returned, gaze sharpening. "I'm sincere in my studies, Montrève. There are those, many of them, who claim Master Piero is a lunatic. There are others, a dedicated few, who believe he is the purest natural philosopher since Sokrates. I happen to fall among the latter."

"I don't doubt you," I murmured.

Lucius Tadius' smile twisted on his satyr's face. "That's very kind of you," he said, glancing away. "And look, here comes Prince Barbarus with good red wine to free our thoughts and loosen our tongues. I'll move, shall I, and give you old friends leave to converse."

With that, he slid away to take a seat farther down the table. I frowned after him.

"Ass," Gilot muttered on the other side of me.

"I don't think so," I said slowly. "He seems . . . complicated."

"Well, that ought to suit you just fine," Gilot observed.

At that moment, Eamonn returned with a winejug in either hand, and I forgot all about Lucius Tadius da Lucca. We sat for long hours, drinking and talking. Eamonn told me in greater detail about the year he had spent in Tiberium. He had begun studying with a different Master, dull and conventional, who set him on an intensive course of Caerdicci grammar, reading and translating and performing endless recitations.

"I needed it," Eamonn acknowledged; and indeed, his Caerdicci had improved to the point where it was almost better than mine. "But Dagda Mor! It was *boring*!"

He had heard rumors about Master Piero, who was a controversial figure at the University. Unlike the other Masters, he refused to be confined to a lecture hall, venturing often into the city with his students. His methods were eclectic and his curriculum indeterminate.

Curious, Eamonn had sought him out.

"He's brilliant, Imri!" he said, glowing. "You saw him today, didn't you? The way he cuts through to the heart of the matter," he added, chopping his hand for emphasis. "Virtue! Envy! That's what I want to know!"

I smiled at him. "Well, I saw him try. The Skaldi girl wasn't having it."

"Brigitta." Eamonn looked pensive. "She struggles with the language. I've told her to study with Master Donato, my old Master. But she won't do it, she only has six months here. And Master Piero won't tell anyone what to do. He insists we must discover it for ourselves."

"There's sense in that, although I'm not sure it's a kindness in this instance." I refilled my winecup. "So why is a young Skaldi woman—"

"Where is the kindness in imposing our thoughts upon others?" Eamonn interrupted, lifting a finger. "Is common sense a virtue, Imri? We have agreed that it is. And yet it is one that cannot be taught, save by example. It must be discovered and admired on its own merits, even as one might see the foundations of a mighty building in a crude chunk of stone."

"—why is a young Skaldi woman studying in Tiberium?" I finished.

Gilot, bored witless, rolled his eyes.

"Sorry." Eamonn laughed. "I'm new to Master Piero's ways, and I get excited." He lowered his voice. "Truth is, I don't know. She's very serious, Brigitta. She keeps to herself. I tell you, Imri, make no mistake. She'll draw a dagger on you just for flirting. But Master Piero sees merit in her, so it must be there."

"No doubt," I said diplomatically. I nodded at Lucius Tadius. "What about him?"

"Lucius?" Eamonn dropped his voice another octave. "He's bright, very bright," he said. "But he is too lazy and does not always try." He looked troubled. "I'm not sure. There is some problem with his family. He is meant to be his father's heir, the Prince of Lucca, but there is some problem there. I think it involves buggery," he added in a whisper.

I choked on a sip of wine.

"They don't like it here, you know; or at least not exactly," Eamonn said in a serious tone. "They're very funny about such matters in Tiberium."

Gilot took an interest. "How so, my lord?"

"Oh!" Eamonn took a deep breath. "They're very strange. Anything a man might do with his shaft they reckon is right and fine. But to pleasure a woman with lips and tongue . . ." He shook his head. "That, they reckon debasing."

"Idiots," Gilot commented.

"Yes." Eamonn nodded. "And it is the same for a woman to take a man into her mouth, although I have never heard any man complain of it. And worse for a man who does it to another, and worst of all for a man who lets himself get buggered. They've no respect for it, or anyone who suffers it."

I glanced over at Lucius, seated farther down the table. He raised his winecup in mocking salute. "But that's just . . . silly," I said. Even to my own ears, I sounded as plaintive as Alais complaining at my nicknaming her.

Eamonn shrugged. "It's Tiberium, Imri, not Terre d'Ange."

"Nor Alba, either," I said sharply.

"No." He grinned. "That's why you'll find a good many Tiberian women interested in what you might offer them. I suggest you make the most of it."

Gilot lifted his winecup. "I'm for that!"

We drank to it, the three of us.

Day wore on into evening and Master Piero's disciples peeled away at last, making their farewells and leaving us alone. Once we were surrounded by nameless strangers, I felt myself relax, tense muscles easing.

"So," Eamonn said softly. "You do not wish anyone to know who you are, Imri?"

"It's not that, exactly." I met his gaze. "I'm not ashamed. I just want a chance to be myself, and not my history."

He understood, nodding. "I won't tell anyone," he promised, then paused. "How are my lady Phèdre and my lord Joscelin? I miss them."

"They're fine." I swallowed. "Worried. I miss them, too."

We blinked at one another, drunk and damp-eyed.

"No tears!" Gilot said adamantly. He wagged a finger at me. "You said, no more tears." Leaning forward, he proposed a toast. "To her ladyship," he murmured. "Let us three salute them. To Phèdre nó Delaunay, the Comtesse de Montrève, and her consort, Messire Joscelin Verreuil, heroes of the fair realm of Terre d'Ange." He raised his winecup. "May we aspire to be no less than them!"

We cheered while the other patrons watched, bemused and indifferent.

I set my lips to the rim of the winecup. The memory of my encounter with Phèdre the morning after Valerian House surfaced, abrupt and vivid. I felt again the startled leap of her pulse, the dark ache of yearning. The shock of desire, the bile rising.

I pushed the memory away. Here in Tiberium, everything would be different. I would seek to master my own desires. I would study what it meant to be good until I could live at ease in my own skin.

"May we aspire to no less," I whispered, and drank.

THIRTY-TWO

THE FOLLOWING DAY, I met with Master Piero and his students at the foot of the Capitoline Hill beneath the shadow of Tarquin Rock.

It was an inhospitable place, for the southern face of the hill was a sheer cliff. One could see nothing of the hill's summit, where the famous temple to the triad of Jupiter, Juno, and Minerva was perched; only barren ground broken into boulders and stony outcroppings. There was no shade, and in the late-morning sunlight it was already unbearably hot. Despite the blazing sun, there was a dark sense about the place that made me ill at ease.

We all disported ourselves and listened to Master Piero speak.

"There is blood on these rocks," he began. One of Lucius Tadius' companions sprang up with a curse, glancing at the boulder on which he'd been sitting, then sitting sheepishly when he found it clean and dry. "Ancient blood," the Master continued, then pointed toward the summit. "And there is blood above them."

He went on to tell the tale of how many centuries ago, one of Tiberium's Sacred Virgins, a priestess of Vesta, betrayed the city and opened its gates to the conquering

Sabinites. Sporting bracelets of gold, they promised to reward her with that which they bore on their arms; but instead of rewarding her with gold, they crushed her to death with the heavy shields they carried.

"She was buried atop the hill," Master Piero finished. "And when Tiberians regained the city and established their republic, they used this place to execute traitors, casting them from Tarquin Rock to their deaths."

I shuddered, imagining their broken bodies and wondering if there were old bones strewn among the rocks. No wonder it felt dark here. Lucius looked pale and grave.

Master Piero smiled genially at us. "So," he said. "Let us discuss the nature of betrayal. What is worse? To betray one's city? To betray one's gods? To betray one's family? To betray one's oath? To betray those virtues one holds to be true and good?"

Despite the heat, his questions loosened tongues and the discussion ranged freely. I sat and listened, sweat trickling beneath my hair. No two students made the same argument. Some of the arguments wandered into tangents. If it was worse to betray one's gods, was it due to the nature of the betrayal or because of divine retribution to follow? If it was worse to betray one's virtues, which virtues were those? Some argued for loyalty, while others countered with the possibility that loyalty might be betrayed in the service of a higher good.

"What do you say, Imriel nó Montrève?" Master Piero asked unexpectedly. "Surely you must know aught of betrayal, with all your country has suffered since your birth. Let us hear from a D'Angeline perspective. What is the worst thing one might betray?"

I gazed at him, his image wavering in the mounting heat,

and understood that he had chosen this topic to test me. Gritting my teeth, I answered. "Love, Master."

A few students chuckled, mocking and dismissive. One made a lewd gesture with his hands, low and covert. Master Piero merely nodded his head encouragingly at me. "A very D'Angeline answer," he said. "Tell us more."

I mopped the sweat from my brow and glanced around. "Blessed Elua left us with a single precept," I said. "*Love as thou wilt.* What do you love best? Your country? Your honor? The gods? A woman? A man? Truth? Whatever it be," I said. "*That* is the worst betrayal."

They fell silent, then, thinking; all save Eamonn, who beamed at me.

"But some people have impure loves." It was a young man I had not met who reasoned through the flaw in my argument; Umaiyyati, by the look of him, with fierce brows meeting over a hawk's nose. "What of gluttons who exist for gluttony's sake? What of those who seek power or wealth above all things?"

I shrugged. "Even they may serve a greater good without knowing it."

He blinked at me with a hawk's stare. "You *believe* this?"

I thought about Daršanga, and how I had ended there through my mother's treachery, though it was no fault of hers, for once. I thought about what might have befallen the world if the Mahrkagir's power had run unchecked, if Phèdre and Joscelin had not set out to rescue me. "I do," I said. "I have to."

He waved one hand. "Bah!"

"This greater good of which you speak." Brigitta, the Skaldi woman, spoke slowly, eyeing me with distrust. "What is it? Who determines it?"

I wished I had an answer for her, but I didn't; only bitter

experience I was reluctant to divulge. "I don't know, my lady," I said humbly. "That's what we're here to discuss, is it not? I know only what Elua bids me do as a D'Angeline." Glancing around, my gaze fell upon Lucius Tadius, who was seated on a nearby ledge, pale and sweating. "You've been silent," I said to him. "What do you say, Lucius?"

He lifted his head. Beneath his unruly curls, his eyes were wide and staring, hazel rims around stark pupils. "I say this place is full of ghosts," he said. "Don't you feel it?" He shuddered. *"Lemures,"* he said. "Angry ghosts."

Someone laughed, but it was a nervous titter.

Master Piero sprang to his feet, clapping his hands. "Enough!" he said with brisk good cheer. "We have gained many things to discuss this day. Let us gather in the lecture hall tomorrow and continue our conversation without distraction. It will please my fellow Masters for once." At that he smiled with impish glee, and his students chuckled, eased. As our gathering began to dissolve, he beckoned to me. "Imriel nó Montrève. Is it still your wish to study with us?"

"It is," I said.

"Good." He nodded several times, his gaze searching. "Come tomorrow, and we will speak further. We shall see."

I had hoped for more, but it would do. I inclined my head to him. "My thanks, Master."

He waved his hand. "It is what I do. If you wish to thank me, do a kindness for someone in need."

Thus we were dismissed for the day, straggling back toward the center of the city in groups of two and three. I listened with half an ear as Eamonn rambled on about Master Piero's talk. Mercifully, Gilot had agreed not to play nursemaid to me as long as I didn't wander the city alone, reckoning Eamonn and I combined were formidable enough.

Armed with advice from Eamonn, Gilot had taken on the task of finding us permanent lodgings in an insula today, and I wondered how he was doing. I didn't entirely trust him not to rent an entire townhouse.

From time to time, I glanced over at Lucius Tadius, whose companions were teasing him mercilessly. He had regained his color, but the set of his mouth was grim. Whatever the reason, he'd been genuinely frightened beneath the shadow of Tarquin Rock.

I thought about Master Piero's injunction.

"Lucius!" I called to him. Excusing himself to his friends, he came over. His eyes were wary. I knew the feeling. I hated for anyone to see me afraid. I clapped a hand on his shoulder. "We barely got to talk yesterday. Can I stand you a jug of wine? I owe you for your generosity."

Eamonn looked surprised by my overture—I wasn't known for being outgoing in matters of friendship—but said nothing.

Lucius' expression eased. "All right," he said, shrugging. "Why not?"

We went to the same wineshop, buying meat pies along the way. Either the garum in Tiberium was better than in Ostia, or I was getting used to the taste. At the door of the wineshop, Eamonn paused.

"Imri, maybe I should look for Gilot," he said. "He's new to the city, and like to get fleeced if he tries to bargain."

"A good thought." I nodded. "My thanks."

He grinned. "Ah, well, I know where to find you!"

Lucius watched him go, cool and speculative. "Prince Barbarus has more tact than I reckoned," he observed.

"Yes," I said. "He does."

Inside, it was dim and pleasant, sheltered from the sweltering heat outside. I bought a jug of watered wine and we sat at a wooden table. Lucius drank a cup straight off, then refilled it and met my gaze like a man girding himself for battle.

"I expect you're wondering why I looked wraith-ridden up there," he said.

"I thought you could use a drink," I said. "The rest is your choice."

"I'm afraid of ghosts." He smiled with bitter self-loathing. "I always have been. Terrified. *Lemures, larvae.* The angry dead. I swear, betimes I can feel their presence, even though there's naught to be seen. Stupid, isn't it?"

I shook my head and took a drink. "No."

Lucius' eyes narrowed. "I don't want your pity, D'Angeline."

"It's not pity," I said. "You're clever, Lucius. Even Eamonn says so, and he's a lot smarter than you credit him. If you're afraid, there's a reason."

He looked away. "My great-grandfather."

"Was he a cruel man?" I asked softly.

"By all repute." Lucius shrugged. "I never knew him. But he was a condottiere, one of the great ones."

"A mercenary warlord," I said.

He nodded, tracing a pattern in the condensation on the winejug with one fingertip. "We're an old Tiberian family. Hard times, you know. Gallus Tadius had a genius for warfare. He began as a sword-for-hire and ended up with his own company." Without looking at me, he smiled his twisted smile. "The Red Scourge, he called it, owing to the amount of blood they spilled. Half the city-states of Caerdicca Unitas hired him at one time or another."

I frowned. "I thought you were the heir to the Prince of Lucca."

Lucius' head jerked up. "Who told you *that*?"

"Eamonn," I said. "He said there was . . . some difficulty with your family."

"Let me guess," he said. "Buggery?" I didn't answer. "Ah, Prince Barbarus! The things that fascinate you." He ran a hand through his satyr's curls. "Yes and no, Montrève. There is difficulty, though it owes naught to buggery. And my great-grandfather, Gallus Tadius, did become the Prince of Lucca. But he was not well-loved."

I listened to the family history of Lucius Tadius da Lucca, whose great-grandfather's company, the Red Scourge, had seized the city of Lucca when its prince reneged on a contract. He married the prince's daughter and ruled with an iron fist until he died of an apoplectic fit. A generation later, his son was overthrown and the ruling Correggio family restored. The Tadeii remained, living in their shadow, vying for power with their considerable wealth.

"But"—Lucius raised one finger—"Gaetano Correggio has no heir, only a daughter."

"No heir?" I shook myself, remembering I was not in Terre d'Ange. "Ah. She's eligible to wed, then. And her husband becomes the heir to Lucca."

"You're quick, Montrève." Lucius pointed at me. "I'll grant you that." His voice softened. "She's a nice girl," he said. "Helena. That's her name. Helena, Helena Correggio da Lucca. She has a sweet nature."

I thought about Dorelei mab Breidaia. "And you're afraid to hurt her."

He looked quizzically at me. "Why would I do that?" he asked. "We've been friends since we were children. No, if I pressed for her hand, she'd accept, and there's a good chance her father would consent to it. The Tadeii have grown settled and respectable since old Gallus' day, and uniting our families would strengthen the city. But the truth of the matter is, she loves another, with all that deep, abiding passion you D'Angelines are so fond of."

"So it's gallantry, then," I said.

"Of a sort," he said wryly. "My father fails to appreciate it, and Helena herself is not exactly grateful."

I blinked in confusion. "Why?"

Lucius drained his cup. "Because the object of her desire is a charming, handsome scion of a very impoverished family, and there's not a chance under the sun that her father would ever consent to the union. And Helena's other foremost suitor is . . . distasteful to her." He set down his cup. "Why am I telling you this?"

"I'm interested," I said. "And you're haunted."

He shuddered. "Back to that, are we? Yes, Montrève, I am haunted. I am haunted by the ambitions of my father, who yearns to see a portion of his grandfather's legacy restored. One would think it would suffice that my sister wedded a Tiberian senator; and yet it does not. I am haunted by Helena's fears and my own cowardice. And I am haunted by my thrice-cursed great-grandfather."

"Gallus Tadius," I said.

"Yes." He eyed me. "His waxen death-mask sits in our *lararium*, scowling and fearsome. So it has since I was born. He feels cheated and angry. His spirit lingers. I know it. I have always known it. I feel his presence on my skin. As far as I have fled, it is not far enough. I am wraith-ridden and plagued by the dead." He spread his arms. "So, mock me!"

"Not I," I said. "I didn't care for the place much more than you did. But Lucius, if you care for the girl, why not marry her?"

"Would you?" he asked bluntly. I opened my mouth, then closed it. "Ah, hells! What could you know of it, Montrève?

You're D'Angeline. Your folk would let the girl wed a goat if that was her desire, wouldn't they?"

"It's not that simple," I said. "There's pressure in the Great Houses to make a good marriage, and it's not always a love-match." I grinned. "But we'd let her take the goat as a lover."

Lucius looked fascinated and appalled. "Truly?"

"No." I laughed at his expression. "Blessed Elua's precept has its limits."

"What if she truly *loved* the goat?" He smiled a little, then shook his head. "You're right, I know. I'm being stubborn. There's no reason for it, except it galls me. I can't abide the thought of being forced into doing my father's will. And too," he added, "I don't relish the idea of being made a cuckold. You D'Angelines may think nothing of it, but in Caerdicca Unitas it brings shame on a man. Any man."

"Do you think she would?" I asked.

He raised his brows. "*I* would! And women are weak when it comes to desire. They have no defense against it."

I refilled our cups. "You don't know a good deal about women, do you?"

"No," he said without apology. "But I know Helena, and I've seen the way she and Bartolomeo look at one another. She's a dear child, but she's too softhearted to be trusted. So what am I to do? Banish him?" He sipped his wine. "Old Gallus Tadius would have solved the problem by giving Helena a good beating and keeping her locked away. And betimes I hear his voice in my head, telling me I'm a craven coward for being unwilling to do the same. And that's nothing to his comments on the topic of buggery." Lucius gazed at nothing. "He roars," he said absently. "He's always roaring. Sometimes I think it will drive me mad." He shuddered. "I hate the dead."

"Have you spoken to a priest?" I asked.

"Oh, yes." His smile twisted. "My father performs the rites of exorcism every year during the Lemuralia, but I suspect Gallus Tadius' ghost is too stubborn to be driven away by a few black beans and banging cook-pots." He glanced at my puzzled face and shrugged. "It's an old ritual. The last time I spoke to a priest, he told me to obey my father and be done with it."

We sat in silence for a moment.

"Well!" Lucius said brightly. "Now I expect you must think I'm thoroughly mad."

"No," I said. "I don't. Haunted, but not mad."

"That's why I study with Master Piero," he said. "It helps. The more he prods me to *think*, the easier it is to keep the ghosts at bay. If I can keep my mind busy, I'm usually fine. Today was bad, though. You have no idea," he mused, "what it's like to live in fear."

"Oh, I might surprise you," I murmured. Lucius shot me a quick look, and I remembered that he was no fool. "Listen," I said, changing the topic. "How bad is this distasteful suitor of Helena's? Because that's the essence of the matter, isn't it? Which is worse? To wed her and take the risk of being made a cuckold? Or to condemn her to a life she abhors?"

"I hadn't thought of it thusly." He frowned. "He's a boor; a rather powerful boor. But their marriage would forge an alliance between Lucca and Valpetra. The problem is that it's more likely to benefit Valpetra." Lucius sighed. "Oh, enough! Would that I were an impoverished D'Angeline gentleman scholar, with nothing more to worry about than whether or not I could afford a second jug of wine." He lifted his cup to me. "You have no idea, Montrève, how fortunate you are."

"You're right about that," I agreed.

We talked of other matters, then. Before long, Eamonn and Gilot arrived, reporting on a successful mission. Gilot had ceded to my wishes, albeit reluctantly, and we would be lodged in a nearby insula like any other impoverished scholars. Eamonn had recommended a livery stable to board the horses, which would be cheaper than the stable at the inn.

Lucius Tadius excused himself shortly after their arrival.

"My thanks," he said to me. "I'll see you anon."

I nodded. "Tomorrow."

"So what was all that about ghosts?" Eamonn asked after Lucius had departed.

"It's a long story," I said. "I'll tell you later. Eamonn, I meant to ask the other day. Did you ever discover where Anafiel Delaunay learned the arts of covertcy?"

"Dagda Mor!" He smacked his forehead. "No, I forgot." He looked so remorseful I laughed. "And after all her ladyship did for me, too."

"Never mind," I said fondly. "She'll forgive you."

We shared a second jug of wine, one that I could easily afford, though I felt a measure of guilt at deceiving Lucius. Still, I was glad I'd talked with him. He'd been open and honest with me, and it was the first time since I was ten years old that I'd had a chance to extend a hand in friendship without being burdened by my complicated heritage. It felt good.

Afterward, with Eamonn's help, Gilot and I moved our baggage from the inn to the insula. The worst of the day's heat had passed and the streets were crowded with pedestrians. Eamonn led, forging a path, a heavy satchel on one shoulder. A good many people hailed him by name. I envied him his easy familiarity. He had been in the city long enough to make friends, to acquire a nickname that appeared more affectionate than not. Whereas I seemed to have managed to befriend the one soul in Tiberium perhaps more troubled than me.

Halfway down the block, I sniffed the air. "Are we near a temple?"

"Didn't I tell you?" Gilot, toting a pair of saddlebags, grinned at me. "The insula is behind an incense-maker's shop."

And so it was, filling the air with a wealth of aroma: frankincense and spikenard, cinnamon and sandalwood. I peered into the shop while Gilot fiddled with the gate on the passageway beside it. The incense-maker was there, grinding away with mortar and pestle. It reminded me of the first time I had seen Alais, grinding oak-galls for ink in the study of Thelesis de Mornay, and I felt a pang of longing for home.

We navigated the narrow passage, bumping against the walls of fired clay bricks. It opened onto a courtyard containing a well which everyone in the insula shared. The apartments rose in sturdy tiers above it, three stories high. A handful of women were waiting in line at the well, chatting amiably. A few of them waved, eyeing us with interest. Children ran about unheeded, and there was drying laundry strung on every balcony.

"Here we are." Gilot opened a wooden door without a lock.

The room behind the incense-maker's shop was just that; a room. It held a pair of straw pallets, a chamberpot, an empty brazier, a bathstand, and a rickety table with two chairs.

"Where do we . . . ?" I nodded at the chamberpot.

"There's a sluice in the courtyard. It's connected to the

sewers." Setting down the bags he carried, Gilot folded his arms. "My job, is it, your highness?"

"Don't call me that," I said automatically. "And no, I'll help."

"You can pay a woman to empty the chamberpot for you," Eamonn offered in a helpful tone. "And tidy and launder your clothes, too. That's what I do."

Gilot merely looked at me. "This *is* what you wanted, Imri."

I drew a deep breath, redolent of incense. It seemed to seep through the very walls. Blue twilight was settling over the courtyard beyond the open door. It came early here in the students' quarter with its tall buildings, blocking out the rays of the setting sun. I could hear women's voices, the high-pitched calls of children. Here in Tiberium, I was anonymous. No one wanted me dead. No one was gauging me for signs of treason. No one wanted me to wed a stranger and father a kingdom's heir. I could live like a pauper behind a door with no lock. I was just another impoverished gentleman scholar, one who could lend a sympathetic ear to a haunted friend.

It wouldn't last. Nothing good ever did without changing.

But while it did, I would revel in it.

"Yes." I smiled at Gilot. "It's perfect."

He sighed. "I was afraid you'd say that."

THIRTY-THREE

ON THE FOLLOWING DAY, I attended the University proper.

It is an ancient structure, situated alongside the Old Forum near the Curia, where the Senate still gathers. Once, I am told, it was used for judicial purposes; but the power of the magistrates and praetors who once legislated there has faded, their presence replaced by the trappings of academia.

Outside, students loitered before the colonnade, but inside, the marble halls bustled in a hushed fashion. The University Masters strode its halls, velvet robes flapping purposefully, respectful pupils trailing in their wake like so many ducklings. Unlike Master Piero's students, they all wore varying robes or hoods to indicate their status. Unsure where his lecture hall lay, I flagged down a passing student to inquire.

"Master Piero?" The Caerdicci student I had asked flapped one hand dismissively. "The madman's hall lies yonder, D'Angeline." He looked me over with scarce-veiled contempt. "So, has he decided to take on a fancy-boy, then?"

I stepped close to him, close enough to smell onions on his breath. My right hand hovered over the hilt of my sword.

"And what if he has?" I asked softly. "Do you wish to make an issue of it, my friend?"

He backed away, raising his hands. "Oh, please!" he said in disgust. "Spare me the posture. Go, and find your Master."

I went, troubled by the exchange.

The lecture hall was one of the smaller spaces, but it was large enough to contain us all in relative comfort. We sat perched on the funny little stools the Tiberians favor, while Master Piero paced the room and goaded us to conversation, pressing us to define the idea of the greater good in societal terms. For the first time in three days, I heard him cite many of the great Hellene and Tiberian philosophers, urging us to do the same.

I knew them; I knew them all, or almost. In her own scattered way, Phèdre had been an excellent tutor, and she had always hired the best available. And so I contributed, though I felt my words to be rote. When we had finished, Master Piero beckoned to me.

"Stay," he said simply. "Wait."

So I did, cooling my heels while he listened to the concerns of others, nodding and compassionate. It was in that time that Lucius Tadius approached me.

"Montrève!" he said, hailing me. "I come bearing an invitation."

His eyes were heavy-lidded. I peered at him. "Oh?"

"Oh, indeed," he retorted. "I extend it on behalf of my sister Claudia Fulvia and her husband, Deccus Fulvius, who invite you to join us at the theatre later today and for supper at their domus afterward."

Wary though I was of politics, I was curious. Already, I was hard put to imagine what Lucius' sister was like. And whatever dealings Deccus Fulvius was mixed up in, he had been courteous at the baths. It would be impolite to decline. "My thanks," I said. "I'd be honored."

Lucius merely nodded and told me where to find the theatre, near the Tiber in the vicinity of the butchers' market. I promised to meet them there.

By that time, Master Piero was awaiting me. I bid farewell to Lucius and followed the Master into his private study, a small antechamber at the far end of his lecture hall. He closed the door firmly behind us and invited me to sit.

It was a strange study, almost barren of books, but filled with all manner of oddments—plants growing in clay vessels; a variety of animal skulls and the fully articulated skeleton of a bird; geodes; glass lenses and prisms; an unnervingly large snakeskin; a number of intricate shells. I found myself cataloguing them in my mind the way Phèdre had taught me during our memory exercises, and swiftly succumbing to despair. There were too many items to count. I wondered what their purpose was.

Master Piero watched me. "You have a curious mind," he said. "Why do you suppose I keep these things?"

"I don't know, Master." I indicated the nearest object, a nautilus shell sitting on the corner of his desk. "May I?"

"Of course."

I picked it up and examined it. It sat lightly in my palm, a solid coil. Its outer surface was vividly striped. Inside, it gleamed with soft pearlescence. "Hellene mathematicians claimed it was a perfect spiral," I said. "A ratio of exact proportions building on one another to create a whole that is pleasing to the eye." I looked at him. "These are tools for thought, aren't they? Pondering the nautilus, one ponders the existence of perfection in nature."

He smiled. "You were taught well."

I set the shell down and chose not to tell him that I had

gleaned that particular piece of knowledge in the Hall of Games. The game of rhythmomachy is based upon such numerical sequences. "Does that mean you have decided to accept me as a student, Master Piero?"

He rose without answering and stood at the open window, gazing at the Old Forum below, his hands clasped behind his back. "The rostra is empty," he mused. "Once upon a time, it was seldom so. Every day, someone stood upon it to address the people of Tiberium." He turned around. "You have a quick mind, Imriel nó Montrève, and a solid grounding in knowledge. But I am troubled." His brow furrowed. "Does your family know you're here?"

"Yes, my lord," I said. "Of course!"

"Your *whole* family?" he pressed gently.

"Yes." I took a deep breath. "The Queen of Terre d'Ange is not pleased, but she knows. And as I am of age, the choice is mine to make. Master Piero, I'm not exactly the only student here fleeing family ties."

"No," he said. "You're not. But Lucca is a minor Caerdicci city-state, not a vast and powerful ally nation. And Lucius Tadius is not pretending to be someone he is not." The furrows on his brow deepened. "I do not like lies, Imriel."

"Where is the lie?" I protested. "Master Piero, I *am* Imriel nó Montrève. In my heart and soul, that's who I am. And I am here to find out who that is."

"But in the eyes of the world, you are someone else, too," he said quietly.

Bitterness and anger welled in me. "Do you know aught of my history?"

"I do." Sighing, Master Piero turned his troubled gaze back to the window. "Not all of it, but enough. We are not all hidebound here at the University, Imriel, heedless of that which lies beyond the borders of Tiberium, our noses stuck in the dusty tomes. We do pay attention, some of us, to that which passes in the greater world. Even I." Abandoning the window, he sat at his desk and regarded me. "Would that I knew naught, for it would make my choice easy. I would dismiss you despite your promise."

"Master Piero—" I began in alarm.

He held up one hand. "But I will not. I will tell you freely that I believe you would be better served by the truth than by evasion, which is the subtle kin to a lie. But I will give you the chance to make that decision on your own." From a cubbyhole beneath his desk, he drew forth a sheepskin parchment. "I will write your name on my matricula and number you among my students," he said, rummaging for an inkpot on the desk's cluttered surface. "You may see the bursar about paying your fee."

"Thank you, my lord, thank you!" I said with relief.

"It is what I do," he said. "You may go. Tomorrow, we meet at the Temple of All Gods."

I hesitated, watching him inscribe my name. "Master Piero?"

"Yes?" He looked up.

"How might a student at the University come to study the arts of covertcy?" I asked.

He blinked at me. "Covertcy? Is *that* what you wish to study?"

"No," I said. "Not exactly. I wish to learn how a student who was present"—I counted on my fingers—"some forty years past might have learned them."

Master Piero shook his head. His homely face was as innocent of knowledge as a blank sheet of parchment. "I've no idea, young Imriel. 'Tis before my time, but I've never heard of such a thing. Not here, not at the University."

"All right," I said. "Thank you, my lord."

"Go." He waved his hand. "You know how to thank me."

I went.

Outside, beneath the colonnade, I found Eamonn loitering and waiting for me. "Well?" he asked anxiously. "What did he say?"

I smiled. "I'm his student."

"Yes!" He gave me a bone-cracking hug worthy of his father, Quintilius Rousse. "I knew you would be!"

"Eamonn!" I wheezed.

"Sorry, Imri." He let me go. A pair of passing Caerdicci students shot snide looks in my direction. "I'm glad, that's all. Aren't you pleased?"

"Yes, of course." I watched the students. "Eamonn, am I imagining things, or is there a certain antipathy toward D'Angelines here at the University?"

"A bit, mayhap." Eamonn scratched his chin. "Truth be told, there aren't many here at the moment. Or any that I know of, other than you." He poked my arm. "Come on, let's go to the baths. We can talk there. Is Gilot about?"

"No." I laughed. "He's hovering in the courtyard at the insula, trying to find a woman to hire to empty the chamberpot."

We strolled together to the baths. It felt odd to me to walk everywhere in Tiberium, but everyone did it, patrician and commoner alike. There were strict rules regarding the use of carriages during daylight hours, and no one rode astride within the city proper unless they were coming or going. The main streets were wide enough and more, but it would be impossible to navigate the smaller ones. I found myself missing the Bastard, and thinking I must make time to take him for an outing. Surely he must be pining.

At the baths, we were sweated, scraped, and soaked.

Afterward, Eamonn talked me into availing ourselves of the services of the unctuarium for a scented-oil massage. I had to wait first while he saw the barber. Clad in a linen robe, I sat on one of the ubiquitous Tiberian stools while Eamonn stretched his length in a specially made chair, tilting his chin.

The barber on duty made a show of whipping the lather, spreading it over his face and throat with a boar-bristle brush. He dragged a keen razor over Eamonn's skin, scraping away lather and red-gold stubble. The sight of the blue-gleaming edge dragging against his throat made me shudder. Eamonn closed his eyes, heedless.

"You don't have to shave, do you, Imri?" he asked in the Alban tongue.

I shook my head, then remembered he couldn't see. "No," I said, replying in kind.

Eamonn smiled, eyes still closed. "Does it make you proud?"

"No," I said, feeling at my smooth cheeks. "Why should it? It's a matter of heritage, nothing more." I shrugged. "There are differences. Do they matter?"

"Aye." Eamonn opened his eyes. "They do to some."

In the unctuarium, we lay side by side on marble tables while attendants massaged scented oil into our skin.

"Make no mistake, Imri," Eamonn said. "There's envy at work. You . . ." He gestured at me with a languid arm. "You D'Angelines, you got lucky. You're a pretty folk, and you're a strong nation. Your gods gave you gifts you can number. And," he said candidly, "D'Angelines are nothing loath to boast of it."

I gazed at him through my lashes, eyes half-lidded. "I don't, do I?"

"True," he admitted. "You're different. But people here

don't know you yet. All they see is a D'Angeline face." He pillowed his head on his arms. "Give it time, Imri. They have long memories here in Tiberium. Their star has set, while Terre d'Ange's has risen; higher than ever, under the rule of Ysandre and Drustan. And now even D'Angeline scholars are disdaining the University for their own academies. It breeds resentment."

I sighed. "Can nothing ever be simple?"

"Ah, don't let it worry you." Eamonn grinned. "You worry too much."

"I have too many reasons to," I muttered.

Clean and fragrant, I returned to the insula to change my attire, reckoning the plain student's togs I was wearing weren't suitable for an evening with one of Tiberium's wealthiest citizens. Most of the clothing I had brought was simple and sturdy; well made, but nothing too fine. But I had brought one or two items I thought might suit, though they were doubtless worse for the wear after being crumpled in our packs.

A strange sight greeted me as I drew near the incense-maker's shop. A beggar had esconced himself near the gate that led to the courtyard of the insula. Somewhere he had obtained a vast pine-wood barrel, still intact, though its staves were cracked and sprung. An opening had been cut into it and the beggar sat cross-legged in its confines, cradling a wooden bowl, neat as a statue in an altar's niche.

He poked his head out as I approached. "Good day, young sir!" he called cheerfully. His Caerdicci was good, but he spoke it with an accent I couldn't place. He shook his wooden bowl, rattling the few brass sesterces it contained. "The wise man frees his soul from the burden of wealth," he said. "Will you not lighten your burden?"

I raised my brows. "And burden you in turn, my friend?"

"Ah!" A smile dawned on the beggar's face. Beneath the dirt and the lank hair, he was younger than I had thought at first glance, not yet thirty. Still seated, he gave a little bow. "I see you are kind. I thank you, young sir, for sparing me temptation. Perhaps, as my wisdom grows, I will learn to live upon air and sunlight." He inhaled deeply through his nose. "Or the sweet fragrance of incense, like the gods themselves. Yes! I shall become godlike in my wisdom."

Laughing, I dug into my purse. "Here," I said, depositing a silver denarius in his bowl. "Lest your mortal part fail you ere your ascendancy."

The beggar repeated his seated bow, eyes bright. "And thus in abjuring temptation, I am tempted thrice over. My thanks, young sir! I will seek to ascertain the meaning of this lesson."

"I wish you luck," I said, turning to the gate.

"Wait!" He beckoned to me. "I have a gift for you in turn." Ducking into his barrel, he scrabbled in the darkness, emerging with a rude clay medallion strung on a leather thong. "Here!"

I shook my head. "My thanks, but it is unnecessary."

"A kindness must be returned," he said stubbornly, thrusting out the medallion in one grimy hand. "Besides, everyone in Tiberium knows 'tis ill luck to refuse a beggar's gift."

I hesitated, then thought about Eamonn's words. I didn't want to further perpetuate the myth of D'Angeline arrogance, which was not entirely a myth. I accepted the beggar's gift with a bow. "My thanks," I said, placing it around my neck. "I, too, am seeking wisdom."

"I wish you the finding of it," the beggar said.

In the courtyard, I found Gilot sitting on the stoop of our apartment, conversing with a pleasant-faced young woman. She sprang up at my approach, blushing.

"Imri!" Gilot got to his feet. For the first time since our arrival, he looked glad, his handsome features alight. "This is the widow Anna Marzoni, who lives on the second floor of the insula. She has agreed to assist us with some small chores. We're going to the marketplace tomorrow," he added smugly. "To buy a few things so we don't have to live in squalor. Anna's promised to show me the best places."

"Oh, indeed?" I gave her a courtly bow. "Well met, Anna Marzoni."

She blushed more furiously and essayed an awkward curtsy. "Thank you, my lord!"

I smiled at her. "Imriel," I said. "Call me Imriel."

Whatever bargain Gilot had negotiated with Anna, it proved its worth within the hour. Upon seeing the state of the clothing we unpacked, she clucked her tongue in despair. I held up the sleeveless doublet of blue-and-silver brocade, eyeing its multitude of wrinkles and creases.

"It's not *that* bad," I said.

"Do you have a flatiron, my lord? And charcoal for the brazier?" Anna asked. When I shook my head, she snatched the doublet. "Give me the linen shirt, too," she said, holding out her hand. "Yes, and the breeches." I obeyed, and she nodded approval. "I'll be back in a trice." Arms laden, she paused in the doorway. "Polish his boots," she said to Gilot. "They're a disgrace."

Gilot rolled his eyes.

"I'll do it," I said hastily to him.

"Men!" Anna said in disgust, marching away.

By the time she returned, with my clothing neatly pressed, Gilot and I had concurred that whether or not it was a failing of our gender, we were woefully inadequate house-keepers. From a goatherd and a slave, I had vaulted into the

D'Angeline peerage. I had given little thought, in this venture, to how those in between the two lived.

I dressed inside while Anna Marzoni waited outside the apartment. On the stoop, she fussed with the collar of my shirt, straightening it until the lace points lay just so. Disdain for our inadequacy had given her the ease of familiarity.

"Very nice, my lord," she said, stepping back.

On impulse, I kissed her cheek. "Thank you, Anna."

She blushed. "Go on, then! You've a meeting to keep." Her gaze slid sideways toward Gilot, shy and hopeful. "Will you be back?" she asked.

"He will," I said firmly. "There is no need for him to dance attendance on me while I'm in the company of a prominent senator's family. And I do not believe the invitation was extended to the both of us."

Gilot and I exchanged glances and a test of wills. He sighed. "I'll be back."

"Good," said the widow Anna, still blushing. "I mean . . . well, good."

THIRTY-FOUR

OUTSIDE THE MARCELLAN THEATRE, I met up with Lucius Tadius, his sister, and her husband, the senator Deccus Fulvius.

The theatre was easy to find, being the largest structure alongside the Tiber River in the vicinity of the butchers' market. It was a vast marble circle, rising in tiers, glowing amber in the late-afternoon sunlight. Lucius' company was easy to spot, too. They were surrounded by servants carrying cushions and baskets of foodstuffs, keeping the crowds at bay. I wondered if they were slaves. Although the practice was not so prevalent as it had been during the height of Tiberium's empire, it persisted. I didn't like to think about it, having been one myself.

"Montrève!" Lucius lifted one arm, hailing me. "Join us."

"Go on," I murmured to Gilot. "I'll be fine, and Anna's waiting."

He scowled at me. "You don't make this easy, Imri."

I gave him a little shove. "Who asked you to come? Go, the widow awaits!"

He went, grumbling. I joined my new companions. Lucius looked better than he had earlier, his eyes clear. "I'm glad you came," he said. "Imriel nó Montrève, this is my sister's husband, Deccus Fulvius. I believe you've met."

Deccus Fulvius chuckled, thrusting out one hand. He was a solid figure of a man, silver-haired and affable. I recognized him from before, although he looked more substantial in formal attire. "In the baths, wasn't it? Well indeed, well met once more, young Montrève. I'm pleased you found yourself a Master to study with. We need more D'Angelines in Tiberium."

I clasped his hand. "My thanks, messire."

"And my sister," Lucius said. "Claudia Fulvia."

"Well met, Imriel nó Montrève," she said. Her voice was low and vibrant, the kind of voice made for uttering words of passion.

I took one look at her and felt the pit of desire open beneath my feet.

It was in the way she carried herself and the way she met my eyes, at once intimate and challenging. Claudia Fulvia had a look of her brother, but on her, his sharp satyr's features were softened to an earthy, feminine sensuality. Her dark auburn hair was arranged in an elaborate coif, curls descending to spill artfully over her shoulders. They had the same mouth, wide and mobile. Even in Terre d'Ange, she would have been reckoned striking, if not exactly beautiful.

I bowed, kissing her hand. "The honor is mine, my lady."

She laughed as I straightened. It made her breasts move beneath the bronze silk of her gown. She was tall for a woman and abundantly curved. I found myself trying hard not to gaze at the deep cleft of her cleavage. There was a faint sheen of sweat on her skin, and I wondered what it would taste like. I didn't want to, but I couldn't help it.

"Come, my friends," Deccus Fulvius said in a good-natured tone. "Let us take our seats and enjoy the pantomime."

Surrounded by a coterie of servants, we traipsed into the theatre. A box large enough to seat a dozen spectators was reserved for Deccus Fulvius and his family. The servants bustled efficiently, setting cushions on the stone seats and plumping them, bringing out tidbits of food and flasks of wine. All around us, the theatre filled with less fortunate folk, noisy and chattering.

Seated at her husband's right hand, Claudia Fulvia patted the marble bench beside her. "Sit next to me, won't you, Imriel?" She paused. "Do you mind if I call you Imriel?"

"Please do," I said, sitting. Our shoulders brushed.

"Call me Claudia." She smiled at me and lowered her voice, pitching it beneath the surrounding clamor. "Are you one of Lucius' playmates?"

"No, my lady." I held her gaze, shaking my head slowly. "I'm no one's playmate."

"Pity," she murmured.

Soon the pantomime began, though for the life of me, I couldn't recount it if asked. It was a comical farce based on an episode of ancient Tiberian history, about two quarreling generals and the Menekhetan Queen who outwitted them. The generals sported enormous leather phalluses laced to their breeches. They acted the part of buffoons while the Queen led them a merry chase. In the end, they battered one another with their phalluses, staggering about the stage until they collapsed. The hero of the piece appeared to be a wise old senator, who was aided by his prying servant.

Although the Tiberians laughed until they wept, doubling over in the stands at the antics of the dueling generals, I had the idea that there was somewhat subversive about the play. Betimes, when the sage senator spoke, Deccus Fulvius nodded his head in approval.

For the most part, I found it hard to pay attention.

It was not that the comedy was rude and absurd by D'Angeline standards, though it was. It was the pressure of Claudia's thigh against mine, and my own acute awareness of it. My resolve to be *good* began to seem distant and childish.

A short way into the play, the shifting sun put us in shadow. Claudia turned, beckoning to one of the servants. "A blanket, please." She spread it over her lap, solicitously extending a fold to me. "We wouldn't want you to take a chill."

Precious little chance of that, I thought.

It was not long before I felt her hand beneath the blanket. She was a woman grown—I guessed her age to be in her late twenties—and there was no uncertainty in her movements, no girlish groping or fumbling. Her palm slid over my tensed thigh, slow and firm, savoring the contact. Doing nothing to dissuade her, I glanced at her strong profile. Her gaze was fixed on the stage below, and she was laughing at the players. It looked for all the world as though she'd no other thought on her mind.

Meanwhile, her hand continued unerringly.

I twitched when she reached my phallus, hard and rigid beneath my breeches. On my other side, Lucius gave me an odd look.

"Are you all right, Montrève?" he asked.

"Fine," I said through gritted teeth.

Smiling at the stage, his sister stroked my phallus, filling her palm with it, her long fingers skillfully stroking its trapped length. For a terrifying moment, I thought I might climax beneath her hand, right there in the theatre. I took slow, deep breaths, thinking about maintaining Elua's vigil; the cold ground beneath my knees, the icy stars above.

It got me through the performance. Mercifully, Claudia released me ere the end. I muttered a prayer of thanks to

Blessed Elua, and set about regaining my composure. By the time the pantomime ended, I was able to rise without embarrassment.

Afterward, we went behind the stage to the players' rooms. Deccus Fulvius, it seemed, was the patron of this particular play. He greeted the players, congratulating them on a job well done, rewarding them with coin.

Lucius seemed to know them well. He mingled with them, laughing and jesting. I smiled to see him looking merry, although it left me standing with Claudia, which was a trifle unnerving.

"You're fond of my brother," she observed.

"We've only just met," I said. "But yes, I believe I am."

"I'm pleased to hear it." She sounded sincere. "He needs friends." Her voice shifted, low and amused. "And you seem to be a young man of singular will."

I looked her in the eyes. "I try, my lady."

I found myself regarding the pending meal with equal parts dread and eagerness. In Terre d'Ange, I might have enjoyed the game Claudia Fulvia played. But as Eamonn had reminded me, Tiberium was not Terre d'Ange. Noblewomen were not free to take lovers as they were at home. What the consequences might be, I wasn't sure, but I was fairly certain the wealthy and powerful Deccus Fulvius would not approve. And I didn't want to be in this position. After Valerian House and what had transpired afterward, I needed time to reflect.

I wanted her, though.

I wanted her badly.

After what had passed between us in the theatre, Claudia was the very model of a circumspect Tiberian wife. She excused herself as we entered their townhouse, or domus, as the Tiberians call it, going to check on proceedings in the kitchen. I gazed around the vast atrium, admiring the intricate mosaic on the floor. When a servant knelt to remove my boots, I started, and wondered again about slavery.

"A little taste of luxury, eh, Montrève?" Deccus Fulvius chuckled. "I thought a poor scholar might enjoy it."

I slid my bare feet into the soft sandals proffered and smiled at him, feeling guilt-ridden as I never would have at home. "You're very kind, my lord."

Deccus shrugged. "Not at all." He eyed Lucius, who was gazing into the open doorway of a small room to the right with a queasy look. "Come, Lucius, the *lares* of the Fulvii mean you no harm. Let's take some refreshment."

I glanced into the room as we strolled past it toward the peristyle. The light was dimming, but from what I would see, it held only a small altar laden with masks and bronze figurines.

"The dead?" I asked softly.

Lucius gave me a tight smile. "Always."

It was pleasant in the peristyle garden, with dusk falling over the city; though not so pleasant as Phèdre's courtyard at home. I sipped wine and found myself missing her, missing Joscelin, missing Terre d'Ange. Deccus Fulvius teased Lucius and me for our adherence to Master Piero, citing numerous examples of his erratic behavior.

"Oh, let the lads be, Deccus!" Claudia appeared in the doorway, her figure silhouetted in the lamplight behind her. "Come and dine."

We adjourned to the spacious dining room, which was set about with couches. There, Claudia joined us as a hostess in her own right.

I must own, after playing at being the impoverished scholar, it was a pleasure to indulge in luxury. Servants circulated with bowls of scented water. Reclining on couches, we dipped our hands and held them out to be wiped on soft linens. And then the food arrived; course after course, all of it washed down with good wine.

I hadn't realized the extent of my own hunger. Forgetting politics, forgetting Claudia's hand on my phallus, I ate until my belly was groaning: oil-cured olives, salty oysters, tender mussels, a capon so tender the meat fell from the bone, spicy fish stew. The taste of garum pervaded everything. I found myself growing fond of it.

"My!" Claudia smiled at me. "You do have a prodigious appetite, Imriel nó Montrève."

"What do you expect at his age, my dear?" Deccus Fulvius asked cheerfully.

I read the answer in the slight flicker of her eyelids and felt warm. I coughed to cover my embarrassment, loosening my collar and leaning forward to select a pear from the tray of desserts. The beggar's medallion still strung about my neck fell forward.

"What's that you have there?" Claudia asked, amused. "A luck-charm?"

"Oh, this?" I plucked at the pendant, removing it. I examined it for the first time, realizing it had the crude semblance of a lamp stamped on both sides. "Nothing, my lady. A beggar gave it to me. He said it was ill luck to refuse his gift."

She laughed. "Oh, he did, did he? It's a clever trick. He's bought your guilt, hasn't he? I'll wager you feel obliged to toss him a coin every time you see him."

Lucius frowned. "May I see?"

I passed him the medallion.

He looked at it and grinned. "He's a Cynic," he said, tapping the fired clay. "The lamp, that's their symbol." At her request, he passed the pendant to Claudia, who examined it with mild interest before returning it to me. "Your beggar's a philosopher, Montrève. Might as well keep it, it might be lucky."

"A Cynic, eh?" I shrugged and strung it back around my neck. "All right, then."

Deccus Fulvius clapped his hands. "Enough of philosophy!" he said. "Tell me, young Montrève, what you thought of the pantomime."

I opened my mouth to reply, but Claudia interrupted.

"Montrève," she said thoughtfully, tilting her head to regard me. She had light brown eyes like a fox, and the lamplight gave them an amber cast. "Something about that name's been plaguing me all night." I felt a stab of alarm in my belly. "Wasn't that the name of a D'Angeline poet you admired?" Claudia asked Lucius. "I seem to remember you were quite taken with his work some years ago."

Lucius snapped his fingers. "I *knew* I recognized it! Are you related?"

I heaved an inward sigh of relief. "After a fashion," I said. "I was adopted into his heir's household."

"What poet?" Deccus Fulvius asked his wife. He sounded disgruntled.

"No one you would know, my love." She smiled sweetly at him. "He wrote poems in the old Hellene style, lauding the noble virtues of manly love."

The senator gave a dismissive grunt.

Lucius leaned back on his couch, folding his arms beneath his head and gazing at the ceiling. "'O, dear my lord, let this breast on which you have leant, serve now as your shield,'" he quoted in a soft voice. He turned his head. "Did you know him? Is it true he was once a prince's lover?"

"Oh yes, it's true," I said. "But no, I'm afraid I never

knew him. He died before my birth. He studied here in Tiberium," I added. "They both did."

"Time was when all the best D'Angeline nobility sent their sons to the University," Deccus Fulvius said in an accusing tone. "In the last generation, it's changed." He pointed at me. "Your folk have forgotten where they come from. We *civilized* you."

Because I was his guest and there was a grain of truth to it, I didn't argue. "Yes, my lord," I said. "That's why I wanted to follow in Anafiel . . . de Montrève's footsteps." I caught myself stumbling over the name, though I don't think they noticed. It was a piece of irony, that. During his lifetime, Anafiel Delaunay was disowned by his father and took on his mother's surname. It was only after his death that he reclaimed the name that was his birthright, Anafiel de Montrève. His poetry, declared anathema in his lifetime, was released after his death under his given name. For a time, it had been quite the fashion.

But it was Phèdre who made the name he had borne in his lifetime famous.

And I had no intention of uttering it here. As Master Piero had said, they were not all hidebound. The name Delaunay might well ring a different chord than that of Montrève.

"There is a story," I said, shifting the topic, "that Anafiel de Montrève learned the arts of covertcy when he studied here in Tiberium, the better to serve his lordship, Prince Rolande. I asked Master Piero, but he'd never heard of such a thing."

All three of them looked blankly at me.

"Covertcy?" Lucius mused. "That would be useful."

"Bah!" Deccus scowled. "What's to teach a spy? Mind your loyalty doesn't stray, keep your ears open and your mouth closed." He shifted on the couch. "Now, back to important matters. Tell me, Imriel nó Montrève, what you thought of the pantomime."

I answered in diplomatic terms, which didn't entirely suit Deccus Fulvius. He pressed me for my deeper impressions.

"But what about the plot?" he insisted. "Did you grasp its relevance?"

I spread my hands, helpless. I couldn't very well tell the man I'd grasped only one word in three because his wife was fondling my groin. "Forgive me, my lord. I'm not well-versed in Tiberian politics."

"Deccus!" Claudia said with asperity. "The lad's only been here a few days. Let him get acquainted with the city before you try to drag him into your political snares."

"Forgive me, my dear," he apologized to her. "You're right, of course. But I wanted the impression of fresh eyes, untainted by bias."

She rose gracefully from her couch, bronze silks shimmering. "Well, why don't you settle for Lucius' tainted gaze and submit him to your inquisition. I'm sure he'd be happy to share his thoughts with you." She beckoned to me. "Come, let's give them their moment of intrigue. Have you seen our frescoes?"

"No, my lady," I said. "I haven't."

I could hear them behind us as Claudia led me away, talking pantomime and politics. My skin felt too tight, prickling with danger. I knew, without a doubt, that what I was doing was folly. And I knew I was going to pursue it anyway.

Lighting a taper at a lampstand, Claudia led me past the entrance to the peristyle. The servants who had attended us so solicitously stayed out of our way. We trod a corridor, entering a smaller room that lay off it. There she raised her taper, illuminating the darkness.

"You see?" she said. "Very fine, aren't they?"

There were two frescoes on the wall, both of them depicting a man and woman joined in the act of love. In one, she straddled him; in the other, he rode between her thighs. I had seen finer work in the Houses of the Night Court, but they were not poorly rendered.

I looked at them for a long moment, the blood beating hard in my veins. "What is this room, my lady?"

Claudia Fulvia smiled at me. "My husband's private salon."

"I see," I said.

"Good," she said, and blew out the taper.

In the darkness, it was she who found me; her hands lifting to cup my face. Her lips on mine, her tongue slipping between them to probe my mouth. I held her against me, sliding my hands down her waist, pulling her hips hard against mine to let her feel my stiffness. She groaned into my mouth. I could smell her musk.

The last remnants of my resolve crumbled. There was no good or bad, only unadorned carnal desire, banishing everything else. It sparked a deep craving in me, a yearning for escape. I wanted to take her then and there, hard and ungentle. I wanted to sink both hands into her elaborate coif and turn it into disarray. I wanted to tear away the bodice of her gown and bare her abundant breasts, shove up her skirts, and lose myself in her.

Claudia tore herself away. "Not here."

Her voice was breathless with urgency, but there was a thread of amusement there, too. The senator's wife liked to play dangerous games. I was eighteen, but I was D'Angeline, and descended from a long line of Kushiel's scions. I could be patient. I waited in the darkness for my blood to ebb and my pulse to slow.

"Where?" I said. "When?"

"I'll send word." Her fingers touched my cheek. "Where do you live?"

"In the students' quarter," I said. "Behind the incense-maker's shop."

"Beside the philosopher-beggar." I could hear her smile. Her fingertips trailed over my lips, down my throat, catching briefly on the thong of my medallion before they brushed lower, making me grit my teeth. "I'll find it."

In the corridor outside her husband's salon, Claudia drew a silk kerchief from her sleeve and reached up to wipe my lips. Her pupils were wide with darkness and desire. I wondered if she was haunted like her brother. If so, they were ghosts of a different nature.

"Carmine," she murmured.

I nodded. "My thanks."

We returned to the dining room. I felt horribly conspicuous and sure it must show; her mark, her scent upon me. But Deccus and Lucius were deep in conversation and neither noticed aught amiss. The remainder of the evening could not pass swiftly enough for me. I was grateful when Claudia excused herself. And after another polite cup of wine, I did the same, begging fatigue.

A generous host to the end, Deccus Fulvius sent a servant with me to light my way. He led me through the streets of Tiberium. It was late enough that the city had grown quiet, though a few taverns were still doing business. I thanked him outside the insula gate, giving him a coin for his trouble.

The incense-maker's shop was dark, but by the light of the servant's torch as he departed, I could make out the beggar's barrel, situated in the same place. The sound of snoring emanated from it and a pair of legs protruded into the street, grimy feet shod in worn, mended sandals.

I fingered the medallion around my neck and shook my head. Wisdom.

"You're better suited to the quest than I, my friend," I said softly.

In response, the barrel gave a hearty snore.

THIRTY-FIVE

DAYS PASSED without word from Claudia Fulvia.

On the first day, I was tense and fretful. Master Piero noticed it in the Temple of All Gods, though he said nothing. Although it was a misnomer, for it honored only the gods of Tiberium, it was an impressive structure, reminding me of the great Temple of Naamah in the City of Elua; perfectly round, with an oculus at the top. It was divided in quadrants in accordance with the four seasons. Listening to Master Piero speak about whether the pantheon of the gods represent a true multiplicity or a multitude of aspects, I found myself pacing its interior, thinking about the Cassiline spheres of defense and offense.

Without thinking, I traced the steps of the first hours, my empty hands moving as though I held the sword that hung untouched at my belt.

The Skaldic woman, Brigitta, wrinkled her nose at me. "Stop that," she said irritably. "I'm trying to listen."

I made myself halt. "My apologies, lady."

"Do you even *know* how to use that blade?" It was Aulus who drawled the question, one of Lucius' comrades. There had been a falling-out between them, and I sensed he held me to blame.

"Oh, he does!" Eamonn came behind me, resting his hands on my shoulders. "We fought a mighty duel once, didn't we, Imri?" He looked at Brigitta with interest. "Would you like to see us try it again?"

She sniffed with disdain and turned away.

Master Piero dismissed us early that day. I apologized to him, knowing I had behaved badly. He gave me a long, level look.

"Do not give me cause to regret my choice, Imriel nó Montrève," he said.

I tried not to. Sensing my mood, if not its cause, Eamonn suggested we go to a brothel as we used to do back in Night's Doorstep. Having already abandoned my resolution, I agreed, but the contrast was dispiriting. They were not Servants of Naamah, and there was nothing sacred in their calling. The girl I chose wept, turning over her hand-mirror in private, averting her face from me. She had never been with a D'Angeline before. I had chosen her for the way her face glowed when she looked at me, but once we were alone, she grew shy and timid.

"No," she whispered. "Don't look at me."

When I offered to choose another, she wept all the harder and begged me not to. So I stayed, though it was in my heart to go. I thought about what I had learned at Balm House, and I was gentle with her; unwontedly gentle. I aroused her as Emmeline had taught me, coaxing her with soft words and touches. She cried out at the end, hiding her face against my shoulder.

My own pleasure felt furtive and fleeting. It eased my body and troubled my soul. I reclined on my pallet, watching her perform her ablutions, feeling the black wings of melancholy descend upon me. I wished I hadn't come. In another room, I could hear Eamonn's laugh booming, echoed by feminine giggles. I still envied him.

I wished Claudia Fulvia would send word to me.

I hoped she wouldn't.

At the insula, Gilot had flung himself headlong into a romance with Anna Marzoni. She was a young widow with a two-year-old daughter, and she blossomed under Gilot's attention. They made a pretty picture, the three of them. Remembering his grief at the loss of Katherine and their stillborn child, I was happy for him. Envious, but happy.

Days passed, and no message came. Indeed, the nearest thing to a messenger to visit the vicinity was a pair of thieves bent on robbing the incense-maker's shop. I woke from a sound sleep to hear shouting and the slap of sandaled feet running over the cobbled street. Gilot and I both rolled from our pallets, alarmed.

"I'll go," he said briefly.

"We'll both go," I said.

We dragged on breeches, drew our swords in haste, and ran shirtless into the street. Our resident philosopher-beggar was there, wide-eyed with fear, hugging himself.

"Are you all right?" I asked him. "What happened?"

He pointed toward a dim figure lying slumped in a spreading pool of blood. By moonlight, it looked black. "T-two men," he said, his teeth chattering. "I heard them quarreling."

I turned the figure over. The man was dead, his throat slit. He was no one I recognized, but the sight reminded me of Daršanga, and I had to swallow against a wave of nausea. "Did you kill him?"

"No!" The beggar's eyes showed the whites all around. He shook his head violently. "I woke and shouted. The other man stabbed him and ran away."

Members of the city cohort arrived in short order, drawn by the shouting. We told our stories and the beggar told his. They examined pry-marks on the door of the shop, shrugged, and told us to go back to bed. Two of them carried away the corpse, slung between them like fresh-killed game, and one went to wake the incense-maker.

Gilot sighed. "We've got to get a bar for our door, Imri."

"All right," I said. "Ask Anna to recommend a carpenter." I eyed the shivering beggar. The night was cool after the day's heat, but I reckoned it was the shock of seeing a man murdered that made him tremble. "Fetch my spare cloak, will you, Gilot?" He did, grumbling, and I draped it over the beggar's shoulders. "Here."

He wrapped it tight around himself, burrowing gratefully into the fine-combed wool. Almost immediately, I could see his shivering ease. He peered over its folds, smiling at me. In the dim light, he looked younger and less filthy. "Surely kindness is a form of wisdom. Thank you, young sir."

I smiled in return. "'Tis the incense-maker owes you his thanks for saving his wares. What's your name, my friend?"

"I am called Canis," he said.

"Dog?" Gilot asked incredulously. "Your name is *Dog*?"

"He's a Cynic, Gilot," I said. "A philosopher. They believe . . ." I paused. "What exactly do you believe, Canis?"

"I believe I would like to lie down," he said, casting a longing glance at his barrel. "And forget that this unpleasantness happened."

"Some philosopher," Gilot muttered.

We let him go and returned to the insula. Gilot propped one of the rickety chairs against the door and examined the latchless shutters on the apartment's pair of windows, cursing under his breath. I thought about the elaborate precautions with security we took at Montrève and the townhouse, laughing softly at the irony.

"Stop smirking," Gilot said irritably. "You're mad, you know that?"

I shrugged. "They were thieves. They meant us no harm."

"Oh, and if they had?" He raised his brows.

"They didn't," I said in a peaceable tone.

He shook his head at me. "You *are* mad."

If nothing else, the incident served to put Claudia Fulvia out of my head. On the morrow, I resolved to dedicate myself to my studies. I was attentive during Master Piero's lecture and in the conversation afterward. He was pleased and called me over after dismissing us.

"I have been thinking about your question, Imriel," he said. "About the arts of covertcy. Master Strozzi has been teaching at the University for over fifty years. If there is anyone who would know if such a thing existed, it is he."

I bowed. "My thanks, Master Piero. I will ask him."

He gave me one of his hawkeyed looks. "You know how to thank me."

I went that afternoon to seek an audience with Master Strozzi, accompanied by Eamonn. He was curious, and still chagrined that he had forgotten his promise to Phèdre.

Unlike Master Piero's tiny study, Master Strozzi's quarters were quite fine. We were met in an antechamber by a soft-voiced servant. He laid a finger to his lips, hushing us. "My master is resting his thoughts," he murmured. "He is not to be disturbed."

Eamonn grinned. "He's sleeping?"

The servant permitted himself a slight smile. "Return in an hour, my lords."

We spent an hour idling. There was a stationer's shop

near the University, and I purchased supplies there: a pot of ink, a handful of quills, sealing wax, and a dozen sheets of pressed paper. I had been in Tiberium for over a week, and I had not yet written a letter home to assure Phèdre and Joscelin that Gilot and I had arrived safely. I felt guilty about it, for it might take weeks for a missive to arrive, and I knew they worried.

Afterward, Master Strozzi received us.

The soft-voiced servant ushered us into his presence. Master Strozzi was awake, sitting upright and erect on one of those infernal Tiberian stools. He was a formidable old man, well into his eighties, with a crisp white beard and the bald pate that seems strange to a D'Angeline eye. We may not be a hirsute folk in some ways, but what we grow, we keep in abundance.

"Imriel nó Montrève," he said, rolling the syllables of my name over his tongue with relish. "Prince Eamonn of the Dalriada. What seek you?"

It was not for nothing, I thought, that Master Strozzi had taught rhetoric for over fifty years. He had the portentous voice of a trained orator. I bowed. "Knowledge, Master."

"Aye," Eamonn echoed. "Knowledge."

"Knowledge!" Master Strozzi laid his wrinkled hands on his knees. "I could teach you to sway men's souls with the edge of your tongue, to move their hearts and minds, to leave them panting like dogs after your every word. But no." He shook his head. "You would sooner moon over that fool Piero, chasing pigeons in the Forum, gabbling over nonsense." His spine straightened further. "So be it. Speak."

We told him about Anafiel Delaunay—Anafiel de Montrève—and the arts of covertcy.

"Covertcy!" Master Strozzi's wrinkled eyelids creased. He drew his bearded chin against his breast, regarding us with distaste. "I assure you, young scholars, such a thing has *never* been taught at the University of Tiberium. It is the virtues we pursue in these hallowed halls, not the seditious craft of sneaking and spying."

"Yes, my lord," I said apologetically. "But he learned it somewhere, and I thought mayhap you would—"

"Not here!" Master Strozzi thundered. "Not in *my* University!"

Eamonn and I beat a hasty retreat.

"Dagda Mor!" he said outside the University. "He's a right old bastard, isn't he?"

"He is that," I said. "And he's lying, too."

"What?" Eamonn stared at me. "You think *he* taught Delaunay? Why?"

"I don't know." I shook my head. "A tell-tale around the eyes, and too much bluster. Mayhap he didn't teach Delaunay himself, but he knows more than he's saying."

Since our inquiry had come to naught, I spent the balance of the day composing a letter to Phèdre and Joscelin. I touched briefly on my futile search to uncover Delaunay's history, and wrote mostly about Master Piero and his students, and the sights and sounds and smells of Tiberium. I mentioned Lucius Tadius and his ghosts, omitting any mention of his sister.

I told them about Gilot and his budding romance. I wrote about our philosopher-beggar, too, living in his barrel in the street outside our insula, although I neglected to mention that a man had been stabbed to death there.

On the following day, I rose early and went to the wharf to hire a courier. I left Gilot sleeping and went alone, which would irritate him, but there was something pleasant about being awake while much of the city yet slept. A light mist hovered above the Tiber, its waters burnished and bronze in the dawn light. Through the mist, I could make out the small island that jutted from the waters and the Temple of Asclepius on it, dedicated to healing. I wondered if Drucilla, the Tiberian chirurgeon who had died in Daršanga, had made an offering there.

I watched the courier's barge draw away, bound for Ostia, and thought how it would cheer them at home to hear from me. I could picture Phèdre in her salon, cracking the wax seal, smiling as she scanned my words, while Joscelin read over her shoulder and others in the household—Ti-Philippe, Hugues, Eugènie—waited impatiently for news.

It made me at once glad and lonely.

I missed them. I missed them a great deal. I would have given a lot to spend a single hour in Phèdre's company, pouring out my worries and petty concerns, listening to her counsel. I would have gladly endured any awkwardness or discomfort it entailed. But this was the path I had chosen, and I would have to find my way on it alone.

Squaring my shoulders, I went to attend Master Piero's class.

We were planning to meet that day in the Old Forum outside the University, but for once, the rostra was occupied. Two men stood upon it, speaking in turns. A throng of students milled in the square, some listening and a good many others gossiping excitedly.

I caught sight of Eamonn's bright head above the rest and made my way to him. "What passes?"

It was Lucius who answered. "That's the pontifex maximus," he said, indicating the taller of the two men. "He's denouncing Deccus' pantomime on the grounds that it diminishes the *imperium* of our noble city. The aedile who sanctioned its performance is defending it."

"What *imperium*?" one of the other students muttered.

Lucius shrugged. "The princeps of Tiberium doesn't care for the play. He suspects it is a Restorationist ploy to feed the fires of disrespect."

"Is it?" I asked, remembering how Deccus Fulvius had queried me.

"Who knows?" Lucius gave me a tight smile. "But my sister's husband has departed for his country villa. I understand he plans to entertain a select handful of senators this evening. Oh," he added, "and that old stick-in-the-arse Strozzi has announced his retirement from the University." He nodded at a handful of merry students. "That's his lot. They plan to go out and get vilely drunk in celebration. Do you want to join them? I plan to."

A cold finger of suspicion made me shiver. "Next time, mayhap."

Since we could not meet in the Forum, Master Piero herded us into the lecture hall. We held a distracted conversation on tyranny versus democracy and the rights of hereditary rule. From time to time, the word *sedition* floated up from the rostra below. Almost everyone was nervous at the conversation, even Master Piero. Only Brigitta and Eamonn held forth with assurance, unperturbed by the shadow of Tiberian politics. Both of them argued in favor of leadership by strength of arms and surety of purpose.

"Oh, what would you know about it?" Aulus sneered. "Barbarians!"

Color flared in Brigitta's cheeks. "What would *you* know?" she retorted. "Your Tiberian princeps cowers in his castle and wrings his hands over a pantomime! What else have they done in living memory? At least Skaldia produced a leader that made the world tremble!"

The hall grew quiet in the wake of her words. A few peo-

ple glanced at me, wondering how I would react. I wasn't
sure myself. Mercifully, Eamonn saved me the trouble.

"Yes," he said in a thoughtful tone. "Waldemar Selig was
a powerful leader and sure in his purpose. But perhaps we
should consider the *nature* of a ruler's purpose, and whether
or not it is virtuous." He gazed at Brigitta. "I am named for
my uncle, who died on the battlefield facing Waldemar
Selig. He died bravely. I do not believe he trembled."

She looked away, biting her lip. "I did not mean to give
offense."

"Enough," Master Piero said mildly. He favored all of us
with a long, grave look. "We have all agreed to lay our personal quarrels and our national politics aside in the pursuit
of truth. It seems we find it difficult today. Let us adjourn,
and make a new attempt on the morrow. We will meet at the
Fountain of the Chariot, and hope its rushing waters lead to
cooler heads."

He dismissed us without lingering, retreating to his
study. I followed, hovering in the doorway until he looked
up.

"Yes, Imriel?"

"I heard that Master Strozzi announced his retirement
today," I said. "Is he . . . is he well?"

"He's fine." Master Piero looked puzzled. "I spoke to
him myself early this morning. It's not wholly a surprise;
the man is over eighty years old, and he's been talking
about it for some years. Why, did he seem ill when you saw
him yesterday?"

"No, no." I backed away. "I'm sorry to trouble you, my
lord."

In the lecture hall, Eamonn and Brigitta were immersed
in conversation. Her arms were folded and she wore a stubborn look, but she was listening to him. I waited a moment,

and Eamonn made a familiar gesture, one he used to give me during the summer we spent in Montrève when he was courting girls; a half-smile and a slight cock of the head, warning me to keep my brooding self at a distance. Brigitta noticed, following his gaze with a scowl.

I put up my hands and left him to it. I suspected Eamonn mac Grainne had met his match in that one, but I had underestimated his charms before.

The rostra was empty and the crowds in the Old Forum had dispersed, only a few knots of students standing around debating. By this time, the day's heat was at its zenith. I thought of the baths with longing, and decided to return to the insula to apologize to Gilot for vanishing this morning and see if he wished to accompany me.

Outside the insula, a powerful fragrance hung in the air, amplified by the midday heat. The incense-maker must be working hard at his trade. Canis the beggar poked his head out of his barrel as I drew near.

"Good day, young sir!" he called cheerfully. "Do you smell the myrrh?"

"I'd be hard put to miss it," I observed. "And my name is Imriel, by the way."

"Im-ri-el." He said my name slowly in his strangely accented Caerdicci, committing it to memory. "What does it mean, this name you bear?"

I shrugged. "Not much, I fear. 'Tis an old D'Angeline name." It was true, or almost. In Habiru, my name meant "eloquence of God," or so Phèdre had told me. Why my mother chose it, I have no idea. "Canis, where are you from?"

"From?" He looked surprised. "Why, I was squeezed out of my mother's loins, bloody and squalling. Where are you from?"

"Never mind." I shook my head at him, amused, and made for the gate.

"Wait!" He scrambled out of his barrel, his wooden begging bowl in one hand. I fumbled for my purse. "No, listen," Canis said. *"Smell."* He inhaled deeply. "There was a man once born of a tree," he said craftily. "Myrrha, the daughter of Kinryas, bore him. Her mother boasted of her beauty, and Aphrodite grew envious. She put a curse upon Myrrha and made her desire her own father, tricking him to her bed. When she got with child and he learned it was his, he tried to kill her."

My skin prickled. "That sounds like a Hellene myth," I said, striving to keep my tone light. "Are you from Hellas, Canis?"

He pointed at me. "The gods took pity on her," he intoned. "And they turned her into a myrrh tree. Ten months later, the bark was peeled away, and the boy-babe Adonis emerged." He gave me a gap-toothed smile. "And you know what happened to *him*!"

"Yes," I said. Memories descended on me: the banners of the Cruarch of Alba waving, the Black Boar of the Cullach Gorrym depicted on a red field. A scraping hoof, a looming shadow, the rank odor of pig and the rich scent of loam. Sidonie, trapped beneath me, laughing a full-throated laugh. I shuddered. "He was killed by a boar."

"Oh, the boar!" Canis waved a dismissive hand. "No, I meant the goddess of love, who made him her consort. Watch out for her, young Adonis. Betimes the gods take sides against one another, and we mortals are caught between them."

"Imriel," I said. "Who is this goddess of love, Canis?"

"Right." He nodded, ignoring my question. "Imriel." He held out his begging bowl, watching me place a few brass sesterces in it. "So tell me, pray. What was it like in the tree's womb, young Adonis? Did you find it a sticky place?"

"Canis!" I grasped his shoulders, exasperated. I was beginning to wonder if he wasn't a bit touched in the head after all. He stood steady beneath my grasp, blinking at me. His frame was unexpectedly sturdy. "My name is Imriel nó Montrève. And I was not born of a tree."

"Well, of course not!" He held himself with dignity. "That all happened a long time ago, didn't it? It's only the scent of myrrh that brings it back." He nodded toward the incense-maker's shop. "There was a messenger came for you, earlier today. He left a note with Master Ambrosius, I think."

I uttered a curse and let him go, banging on the incense-keeper's door.

He had closed his shop against the day's heat, but he opened it for me, peering through the gap with a dyspeptic look. "What do you want?"

"Master Ambrosius? My name is Imriel nó Montrève," I said humbly. "I live behind your shop. I think you hold a message for me."

I had to wait while he sought for it, sighing and scratching among his things. At length he returned, thrusting a scrap of sealed parchment through the gap. "Here!" he grumbled. "Take it and be done. I'm not your messenger boy, D'Angeline."

Standing on the cobbled streets, I cracked the note and read it.

The hand was unfamiliar, as was the device, though I spotted the Fulvii name in it. The impress of carmined lips that blotted the parchment, I recognized. I read the note, touching my own lips in memory.

Sundown. My domus.

There was no signature, merely initials. It didn't matter. None was needed.

My heart soared, and I felt the best and worst of me drawn aloft in its wake. Clutching the carmine-stained parchment, I luxuriated in the memory of Claudia's hand caressing my phallus, of her mouth taking mine.

Sundown couldn't come soon enough.

THIRTY-SIX

GILOT WAS FURIOUS.

    I didn't tell him about Claudia; he was angry enough that I had left him without warning this morning to wander the city alone. We quarreled about it, speaking in fierce, hushed tones.

"It was broad daylight!" I protested. "Gilot, I've spent the last eight years of my life being warded day and night. We agreed that you'd come as my companion, not my nurse-maid. All I'm asking for is a chance to live like a free man."

"Fine!" Gilot said. "You want to get killed, that's your business. Only you'd better get someone else to bear word to her ladyship, because *I* don't want to see the look on her face when she hears it."

"Fine!" I said, storming toward the door.

"Where are you going?" he asked.

"The baths," I retorted over my shoulder. "I have . . . an engagement this evening."

Gilot caught up to me as I wrestled with the new bar on the door. He held the door shut with one hand, leaning all his weight on it. "An engagement with whom, your highness?"

"'Tis no concern of yours!" I glared at him and jerked

hard on the door. "And don't call me that. This place is full of listening ears."

"Imri . . ." Gilot staggered off balance, then caught himself. "Wait a moment." He exhaled hard, and I could see him struggling for patience. "All right, then, don't tell me. But at least let me escort you wherever you're bound tonight."

I nearly refused, then paused. Claudia Fulvia might be a harmless libertine with no thought beyond her own desires, but her husband was a powerful man engaged in dangerous politics. I was taking a risk, and a foolish one at that. "All right," I said slowly. "If you'll swear to me in Blessed Elua's name that you'll keep my business in confidence."

Gilot gave me a hard look. "And whose business are you about?"

I grinned. "Naamah's."

His lips twitched. "Oh, aye? And who are you dallying with that you need swear me to secrecy? Not a widow, I'm guessing."

I shook my head. "No more questions. Do you swear?"

He put up his hand. "In Blessed Elua's name, I swear it."

Thus reconciled, we went to the baths. There was a buzz of gossip regarding the day's events. Although none of it seemed particularly urgent, the matter of the pantomime and the princeps' disapproval was discussed with avid interest. I had to force myself not to prick my ears every time Deccus Fulvius' name was mentioned. It was, I suppose, good practice.

I debated over my attire. Claudia Fulvia was a senator's wife; she would expect me to dress in my best finery. But she had already seen it, and mayhap it was better not to cater to her expectations. So I chose to dress simply instead, in lightweight woolen breeches and a white cambric shirt, open at the throat. It was fitting attire for an impoverished D'Angeline gentleman scholar, albeit one with access to a singularly skilled seamstress.

"So she's not a noblewoman, then," Gilot observed.

I smiled and did not answer. "If you mean to escort me, let's go."

We strolled through the city. It was much the same hour it had been the day we arrived, with the sun lowering over the seven hills of Tiberium, gilding the tops of buildings, casting the narrow streets in shadow. It seemed like a long time ago.

Outside the Fulvii domus, I paused. "Here we part ways, Gilot. Don't worry, she'll send a servant to escort me home."

He gazed at the townhouse, taking in the finely carved marble pediment above its door, the expensive potted trees. It was unmistakably the house of a wealthy man. "So she *is* a noblewoman." His brows knit. "Imriel, be careful. It's not like home, you know."

"I know," I said. "And I will be." I laughed. "Besides, what harm can I take? Her husband's away. The worst she's like to do is wear me out so that I can't keep my lids open during Master Piero's lecture."

"I don't know how you manage it as is." Gilot's smile didn't quite reach his eyes. "All right, I'll see you anon."

I watched him leave, then mounted the steps and knocked on the door.

It opened, and a servant with a downcast gaze ushered me inside.

Taking a deep breath, I entered.

Empty of Deccus Fulvius' presence, it seemed a different place: larger, yet charged throughout with uneasy energy. In the center of the atrium, the impluvium—the square pool Tiberians use to collect rainwater—reflected violet twilight from the opening in the ceiling overhead. All around the perimeter of the room, fat tapers were burning on gilt stands, wax stalactites dripping down their sides. The air smelled of beeswax and incense, although mayhap the latter was the scent of myrrh lingering in my nostrils.

I sat on a marble bench and let the servant remove my boots. He reached for a pair of the soft sandals they kept for guests.

"Leave them."

It was her voice. I looked up to see Claudia Fulvia in the far doorway, clad in a gown of yellow silk. Her auburn hair was dressed with a gold fillet, and one coiling tendril spilled over her shoulder, the color of dark fire.

"I heard D'Angelines approach their gods unshod," she said. "Is it not so?"

"Only Blessed Elua," I said. "Do you claim divine status, my lady?"

"Not at all." Her full lips curved. "But you have beautiful feet."

The tile mosaic floor was warm beneath my bare soles, retaining the day's warmth. I stood, opening my arms. "I place them at your disposal, my lady. Where would you have them carry me?"

She raised her brows. "Will you enter my presence armed, Imriel nó Montrève? I appreciate the manner in which your sword-belt clings to your hips, but it is not the sword at your belt I seek to employ."

I flushed, at once discomfited and aroused, and accorded her a bow. "Forgive me." I undid the buckle of my rhinoceros-hide belt, handing it to the waiting servant, then stooped to undo the dagger-sheath around my left calf. So I had done before when I had visited as Deccus' guest, but that had been mere courtesy.

It had not left me feeling as though I disrobed before him.

Claudia Fulvia watched me. "You do like to go well-armed, Imriel nó Montrève."

"Yes, my lady," I said. "I do."

She beckoned. "Come."

I went.

In the doorway, she took my arm, tucking hers beneath it. I felt her full breast brush against my forearm. She gave me a sidelong glance with her fox-brown eyes. "Are you hungry?" she asked. "Young men always are. I thought we might dine in the garden."

"As you will," I said in a thick voice.

So I dined in the peristyle garden of Deccus Fulvius with his wife. There, the flagstones were cooling and the scent of bruised herbs rose beneath my bare feet. The garden was set all about with hanging lamps, casting fretted shadows. Somewhere in the shadows, a flautist played, soft and piping. We reclined on a pair of couches, almost near enough to touch.

But not quite.

What we ate, I could not say, except that there were honey-drenched pastries at the end. I watched Claudia eat her portion, the sweet triangles disappearing between her carmined lips, the tip of her tongue flicking at errant flakes of pastry. Afterward, she licked her fingers, slow and lingering, sucking away the last traces of honey. I nearly groaned aloud at the sight.

"Ah, sweet boy!" Her eyes gleamed. "Do you hunger still?"

I clenched my fists and released them. "What do you think, my lady?"

She laughed, low and deep. "Oh, many things, Imriel nó Montrève! At the moment, I think you are a proud young

D'Angeline who fancies he knows somewhat of self-control." She shook her head. "You know nothing."

"Then teach me," I challenged her. "I came to Tiberium to learn."

Claudia's eyes narrowed. "Would you suffer yourself to submit to my will?"

I hesitated. "Mayhap."

"Are you afraid?" Another smile curled her lips. "I mean you no harm. I merely want to see what stuff this singular will of yours is made of."

"And if I agree?" I asked.

Her smile widened. "Oh, you will be rewarded."

I got to my feet. "Then let us find out, my lady."

Claudia led me to her bedroom. Whether it was one she shared with Deccus, I did not ask. Of a surety, it was large enough and sumptuously appointed. Everywhere, set in lampstands, on every surface, candles blazed, filling the room with golden light. It was like the inside of a temple, and the bed an altar in it. I stood in the center of the room while she prowled around me.

"So, my lady," I said. "What will you?"

"Nothing, yet." Her fingertips trailed over the fabric of my shirt. "I want you to stand there. I want to see you."

I stood. I could feel the heat of her as she moved behind me. Then she drew away and went to recline on the bed. Her eyes reflected the candlelight.

"Take off your clothes," she said.

I untucked my shirt and pulled it slowly over my head, baring my torso. On the bed, her breathing quickened. I unlaced my breeches and drawers and let them fall over my hips. At the sight of my erect phallus, the tip brushing my belly, she touched her lips with her tongue and swung herself off the bed.

"Why are you doing this, Claudia?" I asked, watching her approach. "Why me?"

"Ah, gods!" Her hands glided over my skin, and I heard her breath catch in her throat. "Deccus Fulvius is a good man," she murmured, circling me once more. "A good statesman and a good husband. But he is old, Imriel. He was old when I married him." Behind me, she slid both hands the length of my back. "I want this," she whispered in my ear. "I want to feel firm skin, and hard muscle sliding beneath it." Her skirts rustled as she moved around me, tracing the line of my collarbone with her tongue. "I want to taste clean, young sweat."

I gritted my teeth. The muscles in my legs were quivering.

"Do you want to know about self-control?" Her mouth moved lower, her tongue laving my nipples. "It is restraining oneself, day after day. It is weighing risks, parceling out pleasure in small, dangerous doses." She lifted her head, eyes bright. "It is seeing *you* and forcing myself to wait."

Her nails raked the flat planes of my chest, skimming my belly. I did groan then. My phallus twitched, a droplet forming on its crown. My testes ached.

"Poor boy!" Claudia gave a breathless laugh. "You begin to understand."

She kissed me as she had before, taking my face in both hands as though to drink me in through my mouth, plundering it shamelessly. No woman had ever kissed me like that before. I wasn't even sure I liked it, though it goaded my desire. This time, I forced my arms to remain at my sides, reciprocating only with lips and tongue.

"I want you." Claudia's fingers knotted in the hair at the nape of my neck. "I want to taste every inch of you," she whispered. "I want to suck you, bite you. I want to see the marks of my teeth and nails on your skin. And I don't want you to move."

"Do it," I grated.

She did.

It wasn't until the end that my control broke. When she knelt before me, doing what no proper Tiberian woman should, her mouth devouring my shaft, one hand milking it, the other squeezing the sac of my testes. I grabbed her head with both hands, holding it hard, shuddering the length of my spine as I spilled my seed in her mouth.

Spent, I stood panting.

Claudia laughed softly. "I'm not finished with you," she said, kissing me. I could taste myself on her lips. "Let me see how you return the favor." She nodded toward the bed. "Lie down."

I obeyed and watched her disrobe. Her bare shoulders emerged as she lowered her gown, and then her full breasts, tipped with wide, dark nipples. The swell of her hips, the shadowy juncture of her loins. I knew what she meant. I wanted to taste her everywhere. She removed the gold fillet from her disheveled hair, shaking it loose. It fell in a cascade, vivid against her pale skin.

Her breasts swayed as she crawled onto the bed, and I reached for her.

"No." She laid one hand on my chest, pressing downward. "My turn."

It was easier. I lay back as she straddled my shoulders, then cupped her buttocks, pulling her toward my mouth. I parted her with my thumbs. Her hidden lips were swollen, slick and gleaming with desire. Naamah's Pearl throbbed beneath my darting tongue, and she tasted of salt and honey.

I let myself get lost in her, the world reduced to this primeval darkness, flesh as fluid and surging as the sea.

Claudia's pleasure broke in waves, over and over, and I, thoughtless and blind, urged them to greater crests, higher and higher. I didn't stop until she pulled away to collapse on the bed beside me.

"Gods above," she whispered. "You are something."

I propped myself on one arm, gazing at her. Her dark red hair spilled in tangled coils over the pillows, and her eyes were heavy-lidded with satiety. My own desire, temporarily abated, had risen again. It was a deeper urgency, less acute, but as powerful as the tides.

"What will you *now*, lady?" I asked.

Claudia traced a line down the center of my bare chest, smiling as it caught once more on Canis' clay medallion. She cocked one knee, and candlelight gleamed on the soft skin of her inner thigh, damp with moisture. "You," she said. "All of you."

It began with languor; slower kisses, tongues entwining. I paid homage to her glorious breasts, filling my hands with them, suckling her dark nipples until she sighed with pleasure, hands sunk deep in my hair.

And it ended in hard, driving need, her voice urging at my ear, her ankles locked behind my buttocks, my body shuddering into hers.

"Blessed Elua!" I rolled onto my back and lay gasping. My heart was thudding, my blood roaring in my ears. The melancholy that befell me after love was nowhere to be found; held at bay, mayhap by the sheer force of our passion. I laughed. "Are you sure you'll not lay claim to divinity? I was warned today to beware the goddess of love."

"Quite sure." Beside me, Claudia sat up, curling her legs beneath her. "Would you be my consort if I was?"

I smiled at her. "Gladly."

"You look the part." She smiled back at me. "Or no, perhaps a young Bacchus." She ran her forefinger over my lower lip. "You've a mouth made for wine and love. I can see why he drove women mad. I could tear you apart and devour you."

"I nearly think you have," I said.

Claudia raised her brows. "Oh, are you finished, then?"

I eyed her. "What will you, my lady?"

"One more thing." She smiled again. "Sit up and close your eyes."

I heaved myself upright with a groan, kicking away a tangle of bedclothes to sit cross-legged. The candles had burned halfway down, and the room was filled with the scent of lovemaking. My body was as weary as though I'd spent a day laboring in the fields of Montrève.

"As you will," I said, closing my eyes.

I heard Claudia get up and move about the room, and then the bed dipped under her weight as she returned. She knelt behind me, her groin pressed against my lower back, the tips of her breasts brushing my shoulder blades. I felt the fingers of her left hand twining in the locks of my hair.

And at my throat, the keen edge of a dagger.

"What do you want with the Unseen Guild?" Claudia whispered in my ear.

My eyes flew open. A jolt of pure terror went through me, and I reacted unthinking, whipping my head backward with as much force as I could muster. There was a smothered cry as the back of my skull cracked hard against her face, and I felt a stinging pain at my throat. I caught her right arm, forcing it outward, and drove her backward with my own weight.

There was a scramble as I whirled to confront her. Claudia was strong, but I was stronger; and I had been taught to wrestle. I pinned her to the bed, grabbing her right wrist and digging my thumb into its underside until her hand opened involuntarily.

The dagger dropped, harmless.

"Damn it!" she swore irritably.

I lay naked atop her, panting, blood dripping from the graze at my throat, and stared at her in shock and disbelief. "What in hell is the Unseen Guild?"

"Let me up." Claudia struggled futilely, then scowled at me. Her lower lip was swelling where my head had struck it. "Oh, please! It's just a test. I wasn't going to harm you. I didn't expect you to be that fast."

I shook my head. Shifting, I braced one forearm over her throat. "Talk," I said. "And no shouting for help. I can crush your throat before the first servant arrives."

She rolled her eyes. "You won't."

"I will," I said grimly.

Claudia merely laughed, wriggling her fulsome body beneath me. Impossible as it seemed, I felt the stir of desire returning. A gleam of triumph lit her eyes. I cursed and sprang off her, scrambling for the fallen dagger.

"Feel better?" she asked wryly, sitting up and twisting her hair into a loose cable.

I felt like an idiot, actually, crouched naked and wielding a dagger in the private chamber of a woman I had just bedded. I could smell her juices on my skin. But the damp trickle working its way down my throat was blood, my blood. I stared at her. She sat, naked and unperturbed beneath my gaze. Slowly, my desire-besotted, terror-frozen mind began to work.

"This is about covertcy," I said. "Isn't it?"

Claudia Fulvia blew me a kiss. "Congratulations, Prince Imriel."

THIRTY-SEVEN

WE TALKED long into the night.

Once I let her off the bed, Claudia tended to my graze. With my wary permission, she rang for the servants, who brought clean water and supplies. Dipping a kerchief, she wiped away the blood and cleaned the wound, then dabbed it with alum to halt the bleeding.

It stung like fury. "Ouch!"

"Poor boy." She sounded amused. "Wasn't it worth it?"

I regarded her dubiously. "Was it?"

"Oh, gods, yes!" Her wicked smile left no doubt. She folded another moist kerchief into a cool compress, holding it to her swelling lower lip. "Though I'm not sure how I'll explain *this*."

"Deccus doesn't know," I said slowly. "Lady, who *are* you?"

"Claudia Tadia Fulvia," she said. Her gaze was frank. "Sister of Lucius Tadius, wife of Deccus Fulvius. And no, neither of them know. But I'm not pretending to be anyone I'm not, Prince Imriel de la Courcel."

Clad in a borrowed robe, I paced the bedroom while Claudia sat on the bed and watched me, volunteering nothing. At length, I fetched up before her, helpless and ignorant. "All right," I said. "So. What is this Unseen Guild?"

"A coterie of people with skills and interests in common," she said. "One that extends beyond the borders of any single nation or city-state."

"Spies," I said.

Claudia shrugged. "Some of them, yes. The Guild exists to discern and trade information, but it has influence, too. There are members with hands on a great many strings, and they can cause events to fall out in a certain way."

"And Anafiel Delaunay de Montrève was one such," I said.

"No." She shook her head. "He was approached, yes, while he was a student here at the University. And he was intrigued enough to consent to be taught, but I'm told he balked at swearing allegiance. 'Tis a pity," she added. "He would have been valuable. And things might have gone differently for Terre d'Ange. The Skaldic invasion might have been averted."

I shuddered. "How can you know such a thing?"

"I don't, not for certain," she said patiently. "I was only a child at the time. But surely the Guild knew in advance, and there were steps that might have been taken. Your Anafiel de Montrève would have been alerted. He would have had the right to ask the Guild's assistance. They could have diverted Waldemar Selig's interest. Offers of trade too sweet to ignore, perhaps a marital alliance. As I recall, Selig sought that route once. Even if it failed, they could have rallied the Caerdicci city-states to come to the defense of Terre d'Ange."

"I don't believe you," I said. "Any of it."

"What would you have me do?" Claudia asked.

"Prove it." I resumed pacing, thinking. There was no way

to prove the course of history might have been different, and Anafiel Delaunay was dead, unable to refute her claims. At this point, the only thing Claudia had done that remotely confirmed the existence of a vast web of covertcy was identify me, and that was no great trick. Master Piero had known me, too. Anyone with a passing interest in the doings of Terre d'Ange might have done the same. "Tell me something," I said. "Something I know to be true, and most of the world does not. Something you could not possibly have known if not for the Guild's existence."

Claudia made a face. "It's not that easy, Imriel. There are gaping holes in your history that not even the Guild can fathom."

"Oh, suddenly they're not all-knowing and all-powerful?" I asked sardonically.

"I never said they were." She sighed. "And I had a short time to memorize what *is* known about you. I'm only a journeyman, you know. Give me a moment."

I waited, watching her face. Thoughts flitted behind her eyes, sifted and discarded; her lips moved as though reading an invisible scroll. If she was dissembling, she did a good job of it.

"Tizrav," she said at length. "Tizrav, son of Tizmaht. That was the name of the Persian guide who led the Comtesse de Montrève and her consort into Drujan."

My knees gave way. I caught the bedpost with one hand and sat down hard on the bed beside her. "How do you know that?" I whispered.

"It's in the Guild's archive," Claudia said.

I sat, dazed, and listened while she told me more. What the Unseen Guild had known; what they had not known. Little of my vanishing, nothing of my whereabouts. No, their interest had been in the Drujani bone-priests, a mysterious, spreading presence that had even the Guild powerless and anxious. They had picked up Phèdre and Joscelin's trail in Menekhet, when they began asking questions about Drujan, and followed it as far as Khebbel-im-Akkad.

"After that . . ." Claudia spread her hands. "What did happen there, anyway? All the Guild knows is that a D'Angeline courtesan and a lone swordsman crossed a border the entire Akkadian army feared and emerged with a handful of freed slaves and the kingdom in utter chaos. How did they manage to stage a coup?"

"You don't want to know," I said, thinking about the Mahrkagir's festal hall drenched in blood. "Claudia, why are you telling me this?"

"The Guild is interested in you," she said simply.

"As a spy," I said with contempt.

"As a member willing to exchange knowledge, yes. As a prince of the royal house of Terre d'Ange, you would be uniquely valuable and well-situated. More so even than Anafiel de Montrève would have been." She rinsed her kerchief in the basin and dabbed her lip, then examined it for blood. "I wish you hadn't done that, Imriel."

"Well, I wish you hadn't drawn a knife on me!" I said. "Why on earth did you, anyway?"

Claudia shot me an irritable glance. "I was trying to impress the seriousness of the matter on you. This is no jest, you know. You've got to stop running around, asking questions. Someone could end up hurt."

"Master Strozzi?" I felt a stab of guilt and alarm. "He was lying, wasn't he?"

"Oh, that old blowhard!" Claudia rolled her eyes. "Yes, but he's fine. He was asked to step down as a precaution. It's just as well. It seems he can't seem to lie well enough to fool one half-trained D'Angeline dilettante. It was past his time, anyway. He hasn't been active in over a decade. No, I meant someone like you. Or," she added, "your friend Eamonn, or even Lucius. I won't stand for that."

"Why Lucius?" I asked. "You said he doesn't know."

"No, but he's clever," she said. "If you keep asking questions, he'll start wondering. The Guild protects its own, but it protects itself first."

"Elua's Balls!" I flopped down on my back and stared at the ceiling. "Why? Why the secrecy? This doesn't make any sense. If it's so damned important, why would the Guild train Anafiel Delaunay, then let him walk away? Why did he refuse to swear allegiance in the first place?"

Claudia leaned on one elbow and ran her fingers through my hair. "You have such beautiful hair," she observed. "There's a sheen to it, almost like a crow's feather. Why did you cut it so short? I thought D'Angeline men grew it long."

I glared at her. "Claudia!"

"What?" She wound a lock around her fingers and tugged it. "I'd like to feel it against my skin, wrapped around me. Will you let it grow?"

"Will you answer my questions?" I retorted.

She sighed. "The Guild operates in secrecy because if the web were exposed, it could easily be dismantled in a dozen places. Knowledge is only power if applied as judicious leverage. Collectively, we can do this in a myriad of subtle ways, but only if the web remains intact. Anafiel de Montrève refused the vow of allegiance because his mentor couldn't promise him that he'd never, ever be asked to do aught against his beloved Rolande's interests. And he was allowed to do so because his mentor held a knife to his throat and impressed upon him that he would die, and Rolande, too, if he ever sought to betray the Guild's existence. On pain of death, and the death of his loved ones, he swore he wouldn't."

I shivered under her stroking fingers. "Is that a warning?"

"Yes," she said softly.

I gazed up at her. Her fox-brown eyes were at once tender and canny. I had thought I'd learned every inch of her, but Claudia Fulvia had taken me in more ways than one. I knew nothing. And despite it all, I still wanted her. Her unapologetic ardor had struck a profound chord in me. I wanted to kiss her bruised mouth, bite her swollen lip. I wasn't sure yet to what extent I believed her. But one thing was certain; I wasn't about to jeopardize anyone I loved. Better to play the game and learn.

All knowledge is worth having.

"I won't swear allegiance," I warned her. "Not if it means betraying Terre d'Ange."

"Oh, you D'Angelines!" Claudia tweaked my hair. "So stubborn and single-minded. No, Imriel, you'd never be asked to betray your country. But you might be asked to support, oh, say, a trade measure that the Queen opposed. Nothing that would harm Terre d'Ange," she added indulgently. "Just something that benefited another. And in exchange . . ." Her shoulders moved in a shrug. The silk robe she wore slipped a few inches, revealing the shadowed valley of her cleavage. "You would gain knowledge. Knowledge that might *help* your country."

Her hand slipped beneath the folds of my borrowed robe, fondling me. I closed my eyes, allowing myself to succumb to the inevitable arousal. "What sort of knowledge?" I asked hoarsely.

"Oh, well . . ." Claudia leaned over me, planting soft kisses on my closed lids. Her fingers worked at the knot on my robe's sash, undoing it. "You might find out who wants you dead, Imriel de la Courcel."

"I've a good idea," I said. "There's a long list."

Claudia kissed my lips. "Are you sure?"

By the time she parted my robe and straddled me, grasping my rigid phallus and guiding it into her moist cleft, I was no longer sure which of us was play-acting. Inch by slow inch, Claudia impaled herself on my shaft, sighing with pleasure. I grasped her haunches, aiding her as she ground herself to climax.

"Sure enough," I gasped. "Are you my mentor, then?"

She gazed down at me, heavy-lidded and smiling. "How do you like your first lesson?"

I tried to answer, but only groaned.

I took my leave of her in the small hours before dawn, my head reeling and my body spent. I had made no promises and nothing was resolved between us, but when she kissed me good-bye at the door, I knew I would see her again. She'd dangled a mystery before me, and there was somewhat in me that couldn't stand not knowing.

And whatever else was true, the desire was real.

As before, a servant escorted me, carrying a lit torch. I glanced at his profile, quiet and disinterested, and wondered what he must think. They might know naught of the Unseen Guild, but there could be no doubt of what we'd been up to in her bedroom. I wondered, too, by what means Claudia assured herself of the discretion of her household staff.

I didn't dare ask.

At the insula gate, I thanked him. I stood there for a long time, my hand on the gate, watching his bobbing torch vanish and dwindle, my eyes adjusting to the starry darkness. It was late enough that all the taverns and wineshops had closed their doors here in the students' quarter. A faint odor of myrrh still hung in the air. All was quiet and still, save for Canis snoring in his barrel.

"You did warn me, didn't you?" I said to him. "Some goddess."

He smacked his lips in his sleep, uttering a long, gobbling sigh. I smiled a little, envying him his freedom. The thought of returning to our insula apartment made me feel stifled. Despite the lateness of the hour and my physical exhaustion, my mind was crowded with thoughts, too restless for sleep.

So I walked the city instead.

Foolish though it was, I couldn't help myself. I needed to be alone with my thoughts. I needed to feel the night air on my skin, erasing the scent of Claudia that clung to every inch of me. I had never been with a woman whose ardor more than equaled my own. This was a different game than the ones played in Valerian House, but it was a game of power nonetheless. It was intoxicating, as heady and dangerous as opium.

My thoughts went in circles, spinning uselessly. I tried to imagine what Joscelin would say, but I couldn't. I could only imagine him staring, blank and uncomprehending. He knew what it was to be driven mad by love, but not desire. The Cassiline discipline instilled in him ran too deep.

Phèdre . . . Phèdre would understand, all too well.

I wished, more than ever, that she was here. I wanted to tell her about the Unseen Guild, and ask her if she thought it was true. Whatever else lay unspoken between us, I would have given anything to hear her give her clear, unfettered laugh and dismiss it as a fanciful tale. Even the thought of it made me smile. It might well be nothing more; a wild falsehood invented by a bored senator's wife to toy with a besotted young lover. But as much as I wanted to believe it were so, I didn't.

There were those words.

Tizrav, son of Tizmaht. I remembered the Persian guide who led Phèdre and Joscelin into Drujan had met us two days away from the Akkadian border as we journeyed from Daršanga with the surviving remnants of the zenana in tow. He had only one eye, which is the sort of thing that one remembers as a child.

And there was no reason, no reason at all, for a bored senator's wife to know his name. Either the Unseen Guild was real, or someone was playing an incomprehensible game with me. Who or why, I couldn't begin to guess. Would it be wiser to walk away? Mayhap, I thought. But if I did, I would never know; and there might be more danger in ignorance. Claudia had hinted that mayhap I had an enemy I hadn't put a name to. At the very least, I could try to learn what she meant.

The sound of scuffling broke into my thoughts. With a start, I realized I had walked all the way to the wharf. In the fading starlight, I saw two figures struggling beside a darkened warehouse: a man and a woman.

"You—" She got out a muted squeak before he clamped a hand over her mouth.

"Hush!" He pushed her against the wall and fumbled with her skirts.

I drew my sword without thinking. "Let her go!"

The man spun in alarm, then leered at me. "Thought you were the city cohort, man! Go on, let be. We're just having a bit of fun."

I took two steps forward, angling the blade. Its well-honed edges glinted. "I'm not in the mood for fun," I said softly. "And it didn't sound like the lady was, either." I jerked my chin, pointing. "Get out of here."

He held his ground, fists clenched. For a moment, I

thought he might charge me, and I half wished he would. But the eastern skies were turning a somber grey, and the quarter was beginning to stir. I could hear voices carrying over the Tiber and footsteps in the street behind me, the dull thud and scrape of cargo being shifted. The man's gaze drifted past me.

"Go," I repeated.

With a curse, he fled. I sheathed my sword and approached the woman with a smile, thinking I hadn't done too poorly as a hero this time.

"Are you all right?" I asked her. "Did he harm you?"

She spat at my feet. "What business is it of yours? He owed me coin for his bit of fun, and now I'll never see it!"

I opened my mouth, then shut it. She stared at me, defiant. In the sullen grey light, I could see she was no longer young, and haggard with it. "My apologies," I said gently. Digging into my purse, I found a silver denarius. "Let me make good on it."

She accepted my coin without a word of thanks, turned her back on me, and scurried away. I shook my head. Savior of dogs, defender against deer, defrauder of whores. It seemed I wasn't cut out to be a hero. And, I thought, if I didn't make a swift return to the insula, I'd have Gilot's wrath to reckon with.

In my haste to retrace my steps, I nearly stumbled over a recumbent form in the street. Moments ago it hadn't been there. For the second time in less than a day, a jolt of terror washed through me. I ripped my sword clear of its sheath, spinning in a tight circle.

No one was there.

I forced myself to stand still, straining to hear over the sound of my ragged breath. All I could hear were the ordinary sounds of the wharf awakening—a few voices, the occasional splash, the creak of ropes. Swallowing hard, I knelt to examine the inert figure.

It was a man, his throat slit. I sprang back. His blood seeped between the cobblestones, filling the channeled cracks. Mine ran cold. I glanced around once more to find myself alone in the street, then turned the dead man over and studied him.

He was no one I'd ever seen before. He might have been Caerdicci or Hellene or Aragonian. Ordinary, rough-hewn features, half-hidden beneath thick black stubble. His mouth was slack and startled, echoing the gaping wound in his throat. His clothing was plain and unremarkable, the sort one saw worn by barge-hands on the docks. He had a sturdy cudgel still clutched in one fist, and his purse strings had been cut. I thought about the footsteps I'd heard, the dull thud and scraping sound, and my skin prickled.

While I was busy trying to be a hero, a man had been murdered. A man lurking somewhere behind me in darkened streets, a cudgel in his hand; murdered in a manner that was beginning to look uncomfortably familiar. I'd no idea what to make of the coincidence, no idea how it tied into Claudia's dire hints.

"Name of Elua," I muttered. "Why me?"

The dead man gave no answer.

I went back to the wharf and found the dock-master, yawning and bleary-eyed in the early dawn. I told him about the dead man, and he gave a weary nod.

"Not an uncommon occurrence, I'm afraid. I'll notify the city cohort." He eyed me dubiously. "You ought not be wandering these parts on your own at this hour, my lord. They're rife with footpads and cutpurses. That might well have been you."

"Yes," I said. "I know."

Mist was rising on the Tiber, shot through with gold where the sun's slanting rays touched it. It was as pretty a sight as it had been yesterday morning. A full day had passed since I'd risen from my bed and gone to post a letter to Terre d'Ange.

It felt like a lifetime.

THIRTY-EIGHT

W ATER."

Master Piero perched on the low ledge surrounding the Fountain of the Chariot and dipped one cupped
hand in the pool, raising it to let the water trickle through
his fingers. It sparkled in the sunlight, bright enough to
make me squint. My eyes felt raw and sand-scoured, and if
I looked too long at the brightness, spots danced before
them.

"It sustains and cleanses us, does it not?" he continued.
"And yet we may drown in it." He wiped his hands. "What
else is like water?"

"Fire," someone said. "For it, too, sustains us; and it, too,
can kill."

"Earth," another voice offered: Akil, the Umaiyyati. "All
things grow from it, but in my country, a man may be buried
alive in the sifting sands."

"In truth, all the elements, Master," Lucius observed.
"For without air, we die, but we starve on a steady diet of
it."

"So." Master Piero smiled at him. "When the elements
are in balance, there is life. Where there is imbalance, there
is death. Is this a true statement?"

I stifled a yawn and struggled to focus on the conversation. Like as not, I should have pleaded illness that day. But I'd barely made it back to the insula before Gilot awoke, and I didn't want to give him the satisfaction of chiding me. So I'd saved the tale of the murdered cudgel-wielder for later, poured a bucket of water over my head, put on a fresh shirt, and gone to Master Piero's lecture.

It felt strange.

I felt strange.

I felt like a man caught in someone else's dream. The sunlight, the fountain, the conversation of Master Piero and the students . . . all seemed unreal. Even the dead man in the empty street seemed unreal. There was a bottomless black well of profound exhaustion inside me, and at every instant my awareness threatened to succumb to it.

And there, beyond the brink, a bedroom lit with a hundred candles awaited, and Claudia, Claudia, Claudia. Kneeling, lips and hands devouring me. Naked, her breasts swaying as she crawled. Beneath me, astride me, taking her pleasure. Her yielding flesh, her avid mouth.

Uttering words, ripping my world asunder.

A room like a temple, a bed like an altar. But ah, Elua! No love. There was no love between us. Nothing sacred, not even pride. Only dark intrigue and desire like a conflagration, desire deep enough to drown. I wanted to put my hands around her throat and choke her until she gasped out the whole truth. I wanted to take her until she begged for mercy.

"Imriel."

I caught myself with a jerk, shaking my head to dispel the images in it. "Master?"

"We have spoken of the physical elements," he said patiently. "But in what other elements does imbalance bring about harm?"

"And don't say 'love,' D'Angeline," Aulus muttered.

I scrubbed my face with my hands. "Why not?" I asked. "After all, it does. A love that is not reciprocated in equal measure may hurt and breed bitterness."

He flushed and looked away.

"Wherein lies the fault if it breeds bitterness?" Brigitta challenged. "If you were to draw your dagger and prick me, it would be your fault, and I would be angry. But to love without being loved in turn . . ." She frowned, thinking through her logic. "It would be as though I thrust myself upon your dagger and blamed you for it."

Someone made a lewd comment. "Yes," I said, ignoring it. "But people do."

"Should we seek, then, the root of this impulse?" Master Piero asked with interest. "Should we seek to overcome it within ourselves? Or should we seek to redress the balance, that all people might love one another in equal measure?"

"Ah, now, here's a trick!" Lucius commented.

I closed my eyes, soaking in the sun's heat, listening to water splashing and the ebb and flow of discussion. Behind my closed lids, Claudia Fulvia awaited. There was so much we had not yet done. In my mind, I saw her cupping her breasts, holding them forth, nipples ripe as plums. Smiling over her shoulder, offering her haunches. Myself, lashing her buttocks with the flat of my belt. A gaping smile carved into a dead man's throat.

What do you want with the Unseen Guild?

Tizrav, son of Tizmaht.

"Imri?" A strong hand gripped my shoulder, shaking it.

Even dozing, I must have recognized Eamonn's voice, for I went for my daggers and not my sword. I found myself on my feet, glancing around wild-eyed, daggers crossed before me in the Cassiline style. Eamonn stood several prudent paces away, sucking at a scratch on his wrist. Lucius and Brigitta hovered behind him, as strange a trio as one was like to find in Tiberium. For the first time, the Skaldi woman regarded me with approval.

"All-Father Odhinn!" she breathed. "You're as fast as a snake."

I sighed and sheathed my daggers. If it had been an assassin, I would have been dead. Joscelin's words echoed in my ears. *Speed's not everything.* "Sorry," I said to Eamonn. "It was a long night."

"Oh, aye!" He gave his affable grin. "We noticed."

Taking stock, I realized that Master Piero and the others had departed. Only the three of them remained, and the charioteer in his fountain; legs braced, arms taut, the chiseled sinews springing forth in relief where his hands gripped the reins. His horses plunged, webbed hooves poised as if to churn the pool's waters, clear streams spewing from their lips. The charioteer's face was firm with resolve, his marble eyes filled with purpose.

Claudia, I thought, would enjoy him.

"So," Lucius drawled. He dragged a finger across his throat, echoing the line that grazed mine. The gesture made me shiver inwardly. "Looks like you landed yourself a proper hellion, Montrève. Who was she?"

I met his gaze without flinching and lied. "No one you know."

"More's the pity," he murmured. "Listen, do you want to get a jug? I've news since last we spoke. Prince Barbarus and yon shield-maiden are welcome, too."

All I wanted in the world was to stumble back to the insula and collapse on my pallet, letting the dark core suck me downward, past the corpses with slit throats, past the candlelit bedroom where Claudia and memory lurked, into utter oblivion. But I was young and proud, foolish and guilt-ridden, and however long I'd dozed at the Fountain of the Chariot, it was enough to sustain me for a while longer.

"Yes," I said. "Why not?"

And so we went, the three of us, to the wineshop; the same wineshop. This time, I noted the faded wooden sign that hung above its door. Though the wood was weathered to a silvery sheen and the paint untouched, one could make out the head of Bacchus, his curling black locks intertwined with vines.

I could tear you apart and devour you.

I nearly think you have.

It made me shudder, all of it. I found myself yearning toward Eamonn, longing to take comfort in his stalwart presence, his sunny disposition. But all his attention was bent toward Brigitta. There was a strange, wary courtship taking place between them, and it left no room for me. Instead, I was confronted with Lucius Tadius with his quicksilver intellect, and the dark red curls and wide, mobile mouth that reminded me of his sister.

"Listen," he said, leaning forward and pouring, filling our cups. "I've decided to take your advice."

"Oh?" I sipped my wine. "What advice was that?"

"I've made an offer for Helena's hand." Lucius frowned at me. "You were the one made me think, remember? The essence of the matter. Whether 'tis better to wed her and risk being made a cuckold, or condemn her to a life she abhors. I thought on it last night, stinking drunk. And I dispatched a missive this morning." He raised his winecup. "So. Here's to taking risks."

I clinked the rim of my cup against his. "To risks, then."

"What are we toasting?" Eamonn asked cheerfully.

"Lucius." I nodded at him. "He's made an offer for a wife."

"Oh, aye?" Eamonn drained his cup, then hoisted it. "To Lucius and his wife!" Brigitta made a guttural noise deep in her throat, and Eamonn glanced at her. "What is it?"

"You might at least ask her name," she said contemptuously.

Eamonn made to answer, then checked himself. The two of them exchanged a long glance. Whatever had passed between them since the sun rose and set and rose again over the Tiber River, there was substance to it.

I found myself envying them.

"True," Eamonn said slowly, turning his winecup in his big hands. "Has she a name, Lucius, this bride of yours?"

"Helena." Lucius permitted himself a tight smile. "Helena Correggio da Lucca. If her father consents, the wedding will take place later in the summer. You'll all be welcome as my guests, of course."

"Do you think he will?" I asked.

"Yes," he said. "I think so. Domenico Martelli, the Duke of Valpetra—the suitor I mentioned—has grown impatient. Overbearing, one might say. It's clear he's got designs on Lucca itself, and not just Helena. I suspect Gaetano Correggio will be glad of an excuse to tell him no."

"Well," I said. "Congratulations." I hesitated and lowered my voice. Eamonn and Brigitta had resumed their own conversation and were paying little interest. "Has it improved matters with the dead?"

"Oddly enough, it has." With a self-deprecating twist of his lips, Lucius tapped his temples. "I hate to admit it, but the old bastard's been quiet since I sent off the missive. Not a ghost in sight, not a rant to be heard." He raised his cup.

"Here's to peace and quiet in the confines of one's own skull."

"Indeed," I murmured.

"What's your family like, Montrève?" he asked curiously. "Any ghosts?"

"Only living ones," I said, thinking of my mother, then waved my hand in quick dismissal when Lucius gave me a sharp look. "Pay me no heed, I'm short of sleep. My family, they're . . ." I paused, words failing me.

"Oh, they're very beautiful!" Eamonn interceded helpfully.

"Naturally," Lucius said in a dry tone.

"No, it's true." He grinned. "Even in Terre d'Ange, because they're kind, too. Both her ladyship and her consort. She taught me to speak Caerdicci, you know. She spent hours teaching me, and she was so kind and patient. And even though they're welcome at Court, they don't put on insufferable airs like most D'Angelines. Sorry, Imri," he added, glancing at me.

I sighed. "I know."

"Her consort!" Lucius raised his brows. "She's not wed, then?"

"No," I said. "They never married."

"Why?" he asked.

I glanced at Eamonn, who shrugged. I was on my own with this query. "It's a long story," I said, temporizing. "Look, Lucius, we don't do things the way you do here in Caerdicca Unitas. Women are eligible to inherit as full-fledged heirs. They're free to take lovers outside the bounds of marriage. There are reasons," I added haughtily, "that we put on airs."

Lucius snorted into his winecup.

"It's not funny." Brigitta scowled at him. "In Skaldia,

too, women are treated with greater respect than you Caerdicci do."

"Alba, too, and Eire." Eamonn leaned back in his chair, stretching out his long legs. He was enjoying Lucius' discomfort. "My mother Grainne is the Lady of the Dalriada. With one word, she can send our people to war."

"Do not remind me," Brigitta muttered.

He smiled sidelong at her. "We did not start it, lady."

"All right!" Lucius raised his hands in surrender. "Yes, I'm willing to own that Caerdicci law is unfair to women. I'm certain Master Piero would agree. But I did not make the laws, and I am bound by them."

"You could change them," I suggested. "As Prince of Lucca, at any rate. Don't all the city-states maintain their own charters?"

Lucius shot me an annoyed look. "Yes. Yes, they do." He raked his hands through his unruly curls. The sight gave me an involuntary tremor, as though the shadow of his sister was present. Truly, I was haunted by the living. "And if I ever become Prince of Lucca," he said to Brigitta, "I will give the matter due consideration. Does that please you?"

She smiled at him. "Yes, thank you."

With the conversation steered onto less risky ground, I agreed to stay for another jug. Either the wine and my brief nap had restored me somewhat, or I'd travelled clear through my own exhaustion and come out the other side of it. Betimes, that can happen. When Phèdre and Joscelin and I rowed all through the night to Kapporeth, I had reckoned myself exhausted; but when Hanoch's men caught us and made to give battle, a ferocious energy had coursed through my veins. This was altogether different, but whatever the reason, I no longer felt as though I would fall into a well of oblivion.

So we sat and talked a while longer.

Lucius and I watched the interaction of Eamonn and Brigitta with bemusement.

"Are they lovers, do you think?" he whispered.

I studied them. They were careful of one another. He was solicitous, but he never touched her, and she held herself back; opening, but wary. "No, not yet."

"What a pair!" Lucius laughed.

"Well, from all I hear, his mother is an imposing woman in her own right," I said philosophically. "Mayhap he's predisposed." The thought touched too closely on my own situation. By all accounts, my mother Melisande had relished being steeped to the eyeballs in intrigue, not unlike Claudia Fulvia. I shuddered and changed the subject. "What of Aulus?" I asked. "He seems . . . out of sorts."

"Aulus!" Lucius drained his cup. "Oh, indeed. I suspect Master Piero may ask him to leave." He refilled his cup, contemplating its contents. "Aulus only asked to study with him to be with me."

"Was he your lover?" I asked him.

Lucius gave me a long, considering look. His eyes, Elua be thanked, were unlike his sister's: a dark hazel, and altogether a different shape. It made it easier to meet his gaze. "Have you ever felt you were born in the wrong time and place?"

"I'm not sure," I said. "Why?"

He cocked one leg, snagging his boot-heel on the rung of the chair, and laced his fingers around his knee. "'O, dear my lord' . . . it's beautiful stuff, Anafiel de Montrève's poetry. He modeled it on the ancient Hellenes. And there was nothing soft about *them*." A fierce light hardened his face. "Warriors, sworn lovers, each vowed to hold the other's honor more dear than their own. There was a city-state that fielded an army forged of such couples. The Sacred Band, they called it. Have you heard of it?"

I nodded.

"For a time, they were invincible," Lucius said softly. "I could have lived then. I could have been born in Terre d'Ange, where men still believe such things and write poems about them. They do, don't they?" There was a catch in his voice, vulnerable and hopeful.

"Yes," I said. "They do."

"Do you?" he asked.

His gaze was direct, and I returned it honestly. "No," I said. "I can understand it. Truth be told, there is no one outside Montrève that I have ever loved better than Eamonn mac Grainne. He is like a brother to me, and I would gladly spend my life to defend his honor. But . . ." I hesitated, then forged ahead. "Some bad things happened to me, Lucius, when I was a child, before I was adopted. Betimes I find it hard enough to be with women, although that has changed. Still, I find myself shying from the thought of being with a man. Mayhap that will change, too. But for now . . . no."

"I didn't think so." Lucius tilted his head and regarded the ceiling.

"Lucius." I laid one hand over his laced fingers. "I'm sorry."

"Not your fault." He bowed his head, contemplating our hands. "Though surely this must be the first conversation betwixt Caerdicci and D'Angeline that fell out thusly." His lips quirked and his fingers stirred, catching mine in a hard grip. "You named me friend when we first met, Imriel nó Montrève. Are you willing to stand by it?"

I returned his grip, hard. "I am."

"Good," Lucius said briefly. "I have need of friends."

After the second jug, we left the wineshop. Lucius bade

us farewell, and I accompanied Eamonn as he escorted Brigitta to the insula where she lodged. There was a landlady who rented her entire complex to female scholars only, and allowed no men past the gate. I loitered while they exchanged good-byes, trying not to eavesdrop.

We went to the Great Forum and bought skewers of grilled chicken from a vendor, sitting on the low steps that bordered the Forum to eat them. It was nearing dusk, and the street performers were getting in their last fleeting hour of work. We watched a fire-eater spew gouts of flame from his mouth, lurid against the gloaming sky, then lower the torch, extinguishing its flame with his mouth.

"I'd like to learn to do that," Eamonn said. "Do you think he'd teach me?"

"I have no idea," I said. My weariness was returning with a vengeance and my head ached with a dull, steady throb. The thought of lying on my pallet and letting myself slip into unconsciousness seemed like bliss.

Eamonn studied the fire-eater. "He must hold a sponge in his mouth, don't you think?" he mused. "But no, there has to be oil, too. I think he sips it from that flask and spits it into the flames." When I shrugged in mute reply, he turned his study on me. "What are you up to, Imri?"

"Me?" With an effort, I laughed. "What of you? Brigitta . . . you like her, don't you?"

"Yes," he said. "I do. And you are changing the subject, as you have been doing all day. I understand why you do it with Lucius, and I'm willing to help. He doesn't notice, because he's absorbed in his own concerns. But I know you. Why are you doing it to me?"

I gazed across the Forum. Beyond the fire-eater, I could make out a familiar figure, bare-legged, clad in a filthy tunic. He was talking to a group of students, gesturing animatedly with one hand, holding a wooden bowl out in the other. "Is that Canis?"

"Canis?" Eamonn frowned.

"My philosopher-beggar, the one in the barrel." I nodded. "Him."

"Yes, it looks like him," Eamonn said. "And you're doing it again."

"Sorry." I rubbed my eyes, trying to scour away the exhaustion. "I don't mean to. It's just all a bit odd, don't you think?"

"Well, he does live in a barrel," Eamonn observed. "Imri, we always swore we could tell one another anything, didn't we?"

Is that a warning?

Yes.

"I know." I rocked on the step, rubbing my palms over my knees. With a second corpse in close proximity to me, I was inclined to take the warning more seriously. "Eamonn, just . . . please. Don't ask, not now. I'll tell you when I can, I swear." I searched his face. "You do trust me, don't you?"

"With my life," he said simply. He sat for a moment longer, then sighed and rose. "Come on, let's get you back to the insula. You look half-dead." He eyed me. "Whoever she was, she rode you hard."

"You might say that," I murmured.

Halfway across the Forum, jostled by the milling crowds, I felt a hand catch my elbow from behind. I wrenched free, taking a step back and spinning, my sword hissing from its sheath. A half-step behind me, Eamonn followed suit.

"Sorry, sorry, sorry!" A small man in coarse homespun put up his hands, backing away. His voice squeaked with fear. "Sorry, young sir! It's only that my mistress would like you to call upon her, begging your interest. She may have work for you."

"Your mistress," I echoed. I stared at him, trying to determine if I recognized him from Claudia's domus. I didn't. "Who is she? What are you?" My voice hardened. "A procurer?"

Eamonn sniggered.

The small man drew himself up with dignity. "I'm an artist's apprentice, sir."

I blinked at him like an idiot. "Your mistress is an artist?"

"Erytheia of Thrasos?" he asked in a condescending tone. When I continued to blink, he sighed. "You're new to Tiberium, aren't you, young sir?"

"Rather," I said.

"I've heard of her." Eamonn sheathed his blade. "She's a painter, yes?"

"A painter." Her apprentice repeated the words with disdain. "Yes, young sirs, my mistress is a *painter*. A very famous painter." He measured me with his gaze. "She would like you to sit for her for a particular subject. The pay is good."

I shook my head, putting up my own blade. "Not interested."

He pattered after us when we turned our backs on him. "Wait!" He thrust a scrap of parchment into my hand. "Her patron was very specific," he said. "Think on it."

With his message delivered, he melted into the crowds, swift and darting. I gave a half a thought to pursuing him, then abandoned it. I was too damnably tired to give chase. Instead, I opened the note and read it.

Tomorrow afternoon. Erytheia's atelier.

There was no seal and no signature this time; not even a

set of initials. It didn't matter. I recognized Claudia Fulvia's hand. She wrote with the same bold assurance with which she made love, stark lines of ink etched on the blank parchment, staking claim to it. The mere sight of it roused memories that made me shudder.

I sighed and tucked the note into my purse.

"May I ask?" Eamonn inquired.

"No," I said. "Better you don't."

THIRTY-NINE

WHEN I RETURNED to the insula that evening, I told Gilot about the slain man. He listened without comment and gave me a long, sober look when I had finished. For the first time since we'd left Terre d'Ange, I felt the difference in our ages.

"Wandering the streets alone, at night," he said quietly. "I don't have to tell you how foolish that was, do I?"

I was abashed. "No. No, you don't. Gilot . . . do you suppose it's a coincidence?"

"Two dead men in a handful of days?" He frowned. "In a city the size of Tiberium, it may well be. Still, I don't like it. I'll see if I can have a word with the captain of the city cohort when you're otherwise occupied."

"My thanks," I said. "As it happens, I have an engagement on the morrow."

"And what might that be?" Gilot inquired.

I told him, and he laughed.

In the late afternoon of the following day, I presented myself at the atelier of Erytheia of Thrasos. It was easy to obtain directions; it seemed she was indeed well-known in the city of Tiberium. Since the note had not specified, out of some perverse impulse, I had chosen the worst time of day, when the heat was at its most stifling and most shops closed their doors. Only the baths were open at this hour. I knocked on the closed door of the atelier, then stood on the stoop, sweat trickling from my hairline.

"This is madness," Gilot muttered behind me.

"Like as not," I agreed.

Eventually the door opened. The artist's apprentice regarded me with round-eyed surprise. "You came!"

"I came," I said. "Am I welcome?"

"Oh, yes." The voice came from within the atelier, rich and resonant, speaking Caerdicci with the trace of a Hellene accent. Its owner came into view. A woman of late middle years, with strong features and streaks of grey in her black hair. "Iacchos!" she breathed, lifting paint-stained fingers to touch my face. "You are welcome." I flinched, and she took a step backward, gesturing. "Come," she said. "Enter."

"I'll wait," Gilot muttered.

"There is no need," the woman said. "I will send Silvio to accompany him."

Gilot cocked a brow at me.

"Go," I said softly. "You can take care of the matter we discussed."

"Fear not, loyal manservant." The Hellene woman—Erytheia of Thrasos, I presumed—smiled. "I have no desire to have the D'Angeline ambassador on my doorstep, asking questions. Your young lord will be restored to you in short order. I only ask leave to make use of his face in the pursuit of art."

Gilot rolled his eyes. I was not sure which he liked least: leaving me, or being called my loyal manservant. He went, though.

Erytheia's fingers lighted on my arm. "Come," she said. "And see."

I must own, I was startled by her work. There were three paintings in the atelier in varying stages of doneness, and all of them were good. Very good.

She watched my reaction with a wry eye. "You are surprised."

"Impressed, my lady." I stood before the largest, which depicted the abduction of Europa. The bull looked so life-like, I imagined I could feel the heat of his snorting breath. The churning waves were almost translucent, capped with frothing foam. The expression on Europa's face was fixed between ecstasy and terror.

"I studied in many places when I was young," Erytheia said. "Including Terre d'Ange, where I learned much about fixing pigments and the interplay of color." She lifted her hand to the panel, almost touching the bull's flank. It was coal-black, and yet it gleamed. "But," she said, "D'Ange-lines proved reluctant to commission a Hellene artist."

"We can be that way," I said, although I was growing weary of the accusation of D'Angeline snobbery. "Not all of us."

"So you are willing to model for me?" Erytheia asked.

"For this particular patron, yes." I paused. "Is she here?"

"No," she said shortly. "Take off your clothes."

Suddenly, sending Gilot away seemed like a bad idea. I doubted that one of the most famous artists in Tiberium intended me harm, but then again, I hadn't expected to find a knife at my throat the last time a woman said those words to me.

"Are you afraid?" Erytheia asked in amusement. She spread her paint-stained hands. "There is only Silvio and me here. You are quite safe."

Over at a long table, the apprentice Silvio was grinding pigment in a marble bowl, his head bowed in concentration.

I thought about the cudgel in the dead man's fist. The marble pestle in Silvio's hand could easily deal a crushing blow. The apprentice was a small man, but doubtless his labors lent considerable strength to his arms and hands.

"I would prefer to wait for the patron," I said.

"Oh, she is coming," Erytheia said. "Later." Her eyes held a worldly gleam. "It was my understanding that she wished to consult with you in private about this commission. She will be disappointed if there is no preliminary rendering to discuss."

So, I thought, I had the choice between disarming and stripping naked for strangers, or earning Claudia's ire. I wondered if it were a test. If it was, I resolved to play the game.

"Your man said you paid well," I said.

"Half a denarius for every hour you sit for me," Erytheia said promptly. "And a bonus at the end if the patron is pleased."

"All right," I said. "What do you want me to do?"

Once I had stripped, she had me stand in a shaft of sunlight and walked all around me, studying me, for all the world like Claudia in her bedroom. Except it wasn't. I could feel the difference in her gaze; an artist's gaze, absorbed and dispassionate. I might have been a marble statue as far as Erytheia of Thrasos was concerned.

At length, she handed me a swathe of deep purple cloth bordered with gold and bade me sit in an ornate upholstered chair. There she took her time arranging me to her liking until I was slouched in a pose of pure indolence, one leg slung over the arm of the chair, the purple cloth draped artfully over my groin.

"Hold this." Erytheia plucked a bunch of grapes from a nearby bowl and handed them to me. "No, as though you were about to eat them." She studied me and frowned. "Too coy. Hold them lower. Let your hand go slack, as though you're about to drop them."

The grapes brushed against my bare chest, cool and silken. "Let me guess," I said. "Bacchus?"

"Hush." She placed a wreath of dried vine tendrils on my head. "That will do for now. We'll get fresh later."

With that, Erytheia began to work, sketching on a white-washed panel with a piece of charcoal. She worked in silence and utter concentration, her gaze flickering between me and the panel. There was no sound in the atelier save the steady grinding of Silvio's pestle and the soft scratch of charcoal.

It was deadly boring.

The pose looked easy, but it wasn't, not really. After a while, I began to ache with immobility. The leg slung over the arm of the chair grew numb, and I yearned to lower the damned grapes. But every time I twitched a muscle, Erytheia made a disapproving sound deep in her throat.

So I held still and thought about Joscelin maintaining his vigil on the Longest Night. I thought about how I had offered my misery and vanity as penance to Blessed Elua, and the sense of mystery that had touched me.

Since then, I had been remiss.

Here in Tiberium, caught between scholarship and intrigue, I hadn't even prayed for guidance; not to Elua, not to any of his Companions. Nor had I offered honor to the gods of the place—the gods of Tiberium, stolen from ancient Hellas. And so, there in my chair, I offered up silent prayers.

"No, no, no!" Erytheia scolded me, breaking the long silence. "Not a *rapt* look, no!"

I grinned at her. "How is a god supposed to look?"

She clicked her tongue at me. "Iacchos! Drunk, drunk on wine and love and madness, but tender with it . . . not soft, but like a leopard with his prey. Think of something." She gestured with her charcoal. "Think of a woman you want."

Without warning, Phèdre's face surfaced in my mind. A thrill of horrified desire ran through me. I thrust the thought away with urgency, and tried to think of someone else, anyone else. Claudia Fulvia. No, there was madness there, but there was nothing tender about it. And surely there was no love. I wasn't even sure there was *liking*.

I thought about Sidonie.

After our parting, I had done my best to push her out of my thoughts, and what I had accomplished on my own, Claudia Fulvia had completed. But I thought about her now. The way she had stood, fearless, as I clutched her shoulders. Her dark Cruithne eyes set in a D'Angeline face. The spark of unfulfilled passion between us. On the surface, she was all cool composure, but there was somewhat wilder and deeper beneath it. Somewhat I longed to taste.

Do you forget that Kusheline blood flows in the veins of House L'Envers?

Oh, I had forgotten. But I remembered it then, and now.

"Better," Erytheia said. "Much better."

And so I lolled in my chair and thought about Sidonie and forgot the passage of time, until Silvio went to answer a knock at the door, and Claudia Fulvia entered. She glanced at me and her generous lips curved in a smile, and I stopped thinking about Sidonie altogether.

"Well!" Claudia said brightly. "Let's see what we have here."

My body creaked with protest as I stood, and my numb right leg nearly buckled under me. I put down the grapes, wrapped the purple cloth around my waist, and went to peer over Claudia's shoulder as she contemplated the rough sketch. Erytheia waited, her face filled with confident pride.

It is a strange thing, to see oneself captured in charcoal. The pose was everything Erytheia wanted, lounging and indolent. And yet there was tension in it, too. In a few bold lines, she had captured an expression at odds with the seeming ease of my body.

"Such a smolder!" Claudia murmured, stroking the whitewashed board and nearly smudging the charcoal. Erytheia bit back a protest. "Were you thinking of me, darling?"

I smiled at her. "Mayhap."

"Oh, *mayhap*." She arched one brow. "I'll have to make sure of it." She turned to Erytheia. "Yes, I'm pleased. Let's proceed. And the other matter . . . ?"

"Ah, yes." The artist raised her voice. "Silvio! Come, I want you to accompany me to the apothecary. He promised a shipment of lapis would arrive this day." She reached for an hourglass on a stand near her easel, which she used to track her models' time, and turned it upside down. "We will return anon."

Claudia inclined her head. "My thanks, Lady Erytheia."

I waited until they had gone to ask. "Is she one of you?"

"One of *us*?" Claudia put on a bemused tone. "What do you mean?"

"The Unseen Guild," I said.

"Mayhap," she teased. "Now why don't you go sit in your chair? I want to be certain I know exactly what you're thinking about when I look at this painting."

"Claudia." I caught her arms. "No. I'm tired of games."

"Will you threaten me?" She looked amused. "Dear boy, the game goes on whether you like it or not. And if you want to learn to play it, for now, you'll do it on my terms."

"And if I don't?" I asked.

Her nails raked my bare chest. I could feel heat coming

off her in waves, smell the scent of her arousal. Her fox-brown eyes were bright and sure. "Oh, but you do."

An answering ardor swelled in me, mindless and compelling. I took a sharp breath. "And what price do you offer, Claudia? Will you tell me about a dead man near the docks? Or another outside my insula?"

She pressed her body against mine, one hand reaching lower to cup and caress me. The blood pounded in my veins. "I might tell you all manner of things if you swear allegiance to the Guild, Imriel," she breathed. "But first, there's the matter of your training."

Fettered by desire and half hating her for it, I succumbed.

It was as raw and primal as it had been the first time. Claudia led me to the chair and bade me sit, and I watched as she undressed, the glory of her body emerging from folds of shimmering silk. The late, lazy sunlight filling the atelier made her flesh gleam. I stopped thinking as she knelt astride me, the tips of her breasts brushing my lips. I let myself get lost as she lowered herself onto me, rising and falling, the slow, steady churn toward rapture.

And then again, on a tumbled pallet where the artist napped; only this time, faster and more urgent, flesh sliding on sweat-slickened flesh. I wanted to punish her, I wanted to plow her like the earth, I wanted to fill her until she begged me to stop.

But there was no end to her, only more and more and more, and I kept going until I could go no further, the force of my climax pressing down on me like a vast hand. With a shudder, I spent myself in her.

"I told you so," she whispered in my ear.

I rolled onto my back and propped myself on one elbow, glancing around to make sure there were no weapons close at hand, then allowed myself to collapse on the pallet. "It's not the same thing."

"Oh, but it is." Claudia plucked idly at my hair, where the vine wreath was tangled. "Right now, the game and I are one, Imriel."

"And you call this *training*?" I asked.

She laughed and covered my eyes with one hand. "How many items are on Erytheia's worktable and what are they?"

"Six stone jars of pigment," I said. "A marble mortar-bowl and a pestle. A corked clay flask, probably oil. A pot of glue. A small hand-mill. A rolled leather bundle, probably brushes. Oh, and a bowl of eggs."

"You forgot Silvio's work-apron." Claudia removed her hand. "He took it off before he left and laid it on the table." She smiled at me. "Shall I have you walk through the atelier blindfolded?"

I held her gaze. "How did you know?"

"Oh." She shrugged. "We assumed." Glancing at the dwindling hourglass, she rose from the pallet and began to dress. After a moment, I followed suit, moving slowly. "I don't know your foster-mother, Imriel, but by all accounts, Anafiel Delaunay de Montrève trained her well. The things she accomplished, all on her own, are quite remarkable." She paused. "Actually, they would be quite remarkable *with* the Guild's aid."

"You don't know the half of it," I murmured.

"Yes, I know, and it's quite frustrating." Hunting up a hand-mirror, Claudia tended to her disheveled hair. "The point is, based on what we *do* know, Phèdre nó Delaunay de Montrève is a woman of fierce loyalties. Since she adopted you as her son, it was safe to assume that she would train you in every skill at her disposal." She thought for a moment. "Well, perhaps not *every* skill. Or did she?"

"No!" I yanked ineptly at my breeches.

"Well, she's not really your mother." Claudia glanced at me while I struggled with my tangled breeches and cursed. "What's that from?" she asked in a different tone, touching the Kereyit rune branded on my left flank. "I didn't notice it by candlelight."

I flinched away from her touch and got my breeches up. "Nothing. It's old."

"It looks like . . ." She frowned. "I'm sorry. Is it a slave-brand?"

"Something like it," I said briefly.

"I don't recognize the mark," she said.

"It's Tatar, Kereyit Tatar," I said. "The man who did it was named Jagun. He's dead." I smiled grimly. "What's the matter, doesn't the Unseen Guild have its tentacles amid the Tatar tribes?"

"No," Claudia said frankly. "We don't. There are a number of places where the Guild has no presence, Imriel. It's just that there are a great many others where it does. Especially here in Tiberium."

I dragged my shirt over my head. "So what is it you want from me, Claudia? What is it I'm supposed to be learning from you other than this?" I gestured at the pallet.

"Oh, you're already learning." Her smile returned. "How to deal with confusion and the shock of betrayal. How to keep your wits about you when you don't know who to trust. How to gauge risks, the merits of secrecy, the price of loyalty. Am I telling the truth? Does the Unseen Guild exist, or is it mad fancy? If it exists, who are its members? Erytheia? Silvio? Master Piero? Deccus? Lucius? After all, I might have lied to you. What of your friend Eamonn, your fellow students? Answering these questions *is* your training, Imriel."

I paused. "Canis."

"Canis?" Claudia laughed. "A *dog*?"

"The Cynic." I narrowed my eyes at her. If she was lying, she did it well; very well. "My resident philosopher-beggar."

"Canis." She shrugged. "All right, yes, perhaps. I might not even know myself. As I said before, I'm merely a journeyman. If you hadn't befriended Lucius, I would not have been selected for this assignment. The Guild operates in secrecy, and those of us in the lower echelons seldom grasp the whole of its intent."

"Who does?" I asked; but before she could reply, the door opened to admit Erytheia and her apprentice, along with Claudia's manservant, who had been loitering patiently on the stoop while his mistress took her pleasure. Although I was fully dressed save for my boots, I felt caught out and exposed.

By contrast, Claudia was the picture of composure. She thanked Erytheia and gave her a purse with the initial payment for the commission. "I added extra for the soiled linens," she added calmly, and I felt myself flush to the roots of my hair.

Erytheia merely nodded and turned to address me. "Come tomorrow," she said. "Not so early." Fishing in the purse Claudia had given her, she drew out a silver denarius and handed it to me. "Silvio will show you home."

The coin burned in my hand, and I wished I hadn't taken it. Blowing me a kiss, Claudia departed. Silvio watched with an ironic glint in his eye as I put on my boots and buckled on my sword-belt. I supposed I deserved it, having asked him with such contempt if he was a procurer. It didn't feel as though I was being paid for modeling.

It felt very much as though I'd sold my services to Claudia Fulvia.

"I don't need an escort," I said to Silvio. "'Tis nowhere near sundown."

"The lady's orders, young sir." He grinned, showing a set of rotting teeth. "She pays well for what she wants."

And so I suffered myself to be escorted, reminding myself that it was all part of the game that I was caught up in whether I liked it or not; and at any rate, Gilot would be pleased. Silvio trotted along at my side, taking three paces to every two of mine, his head bobbing at my shoulder. I asked him why he apprenticed with Erytheia, and he shot me a look of unutterable disdain.

"You saw her paintings, D'Angeline. Her colors . . ." His face softened and he kissed his fingertips. "Good enough to eat."

"What about Lady Claudia?" I asked.

His eyes went wide and mocking. "You're asking *me*! She's rich, sir. She does what she likes." He shrugged. "Right now, that's you. She pays for silence. I don't mind. My mistress doesn't mind."

"I'd think she might," I said. "She has pride in her work."

"Why?" His gaze turned curious. "You're a good subject. You sat well for her. A face like that . . ." He shook his head. "It's wasted on the likes of you."

"My thanks," I said wryly.

"No offense, young sir." Silvio sucked his teeth. "Beauty ought to lift people up, don't you think? Only it doesn't, all too often. At least not in the flesh. Captured in paint, rendered in marble . . . Ah, that's another matter, isn't it?"

"Is it?" I mused.

"Well, *I* think so!" Silvio stated.

Outside the insula gate, I tried to give him Claudia's coin, but he refused it, saying he was already compensated. If he was play-acting at being naught more than a proud painter's apprentice, I thought, he was a champion of dissembling. I lingered in the street and watched him trot away, sucking his rotting teeth, his head filled with color and beauty.

"Canis!" I rapped on the lid of his barrel.

There was a scrambling sound within, and then his head poked out. His matted brown hair was sticking every which way and his eyes were sleepy. "Yes, Imriel?"

I hunkered down in front of the barrel, holding out the coin. "For you."

He took it, blinking at me. "But I didn't even ask."

"I know." I hesitated. "Canis, why are you here?"

"Why am I here?" He knuckled his eyes. "Why are you here? Why are any of us here? I will tell you why, I think. Because the gods were lonely. Or perhaps only bored."

"No," I said patiently, tapping the cobblestones. *"Here."*

Canis inhaled a long breath through his nose. "Do you smell that? Master Ambrosius is grinding sandalwood today." He smiled sweetly at me. "I stink, do I not? So it should be, for I am a man, and I stink like a man. That is what we are, Imriel; men, dog-rank and stinking. And yet, here in this street, I can fill my nostrils like a god and never pay a brass sesterce for it. Do you not think it wise?"

I gave up.

It was true, Canis did stink; or at least his barrel did. It smelled like he had pissed in it, at least once, and mayhap more. If he was a member of the Unseen Guild, stalking me for their obscure purposes, he was going far beyond the call of duty to deceive me.

Why, I could not fathom.

"You might try the baths, my friend," I said, straightening. "They're very congenial."

"I'll consider it," Canis said obligingly, then tilted his head. "Would you mind moving? You're blocking the sunlight."

FORTY

THE WEEKS that followed were disorienting.

I took greater care with my safety and there were no further incidences of violence. The captain of the city cohort had shrugged off Gilot's concerns. The dead man near the docks had been a Tiberian barge-hand and sometime ruffian, the sort of fellow likely to turn up dead in a tavern brawl or a botched robbery. No one had claimed to recognize the corpse outside the insula, but there was no reason to suspect he was aught but the thief Canis had named him.

Gilot had been circumspect about my identity, saying only that he was in the employ of a D'Angeline gentleman. The captain opined that any D'Angeline lordling foolish enough to take up residence in the students' quarter and traipse around the docks at night got what he deserved.

Well, and so. At night, we barred the door to our apartment. In the city, I made a point of travelling with at least one companion. Tiberium began to seem reasonably safe once more.

But my life had been split into parts; parts that failed to add up to a whole. In the mornings, I attended Master Piero's classes, where I was a young scholar, earnestly pursuing the meaning of virtue. In the afternoons, I went to sit for Erytheia of Thrasos, where I was a paid model until Claudia arrived.

And then we were left alone, and I was . . . what? Her lover, at least at the beginning. Time after time, we coupled in Erytheia's atelier, sweating in the hot sunlight, the stink of linseed oil surrounding us. And then afterward, I became Claudia's reluctant acolyte, listening to her speak of the Unseen Guild.

It had rules and ranks like any other guild, she told me. Upon swearing allegiance, one became an apprentice. After seven years, an apprentice might be elevated to journeyman status; she herself had only recently been made a journeyman. In another seven years, she would be eligible to be named a master.

"Provided, of course"—she smiled sidelong at me—"that I make no reckless mistakes."

"Is that what I am?" I raised my brows. "A reckless mistake."

"No." She traced my jaw. "*You* are a dangerous assignment in which I am required to take dangerous risks. But you're tempting enough to make me reckless."

"What happens if Deccus finds out?" I asked. "Surely, all your servants must know."

"A good servant knows the value of discretion," Claudia said placidly. "And I'm a generous mistress with a husband much distracted by politics. My household is loyal, and my activities give them no cause to suspect the Guild's existence." Her expression turned serious for a moment. "I am fond of Deccus, you know. And I'm not usually this careless."

"No doubt," I said wryly. "So these masters control the guild?"

"No, not exactly." Claudia drew her finger down my

belly, leaving a line in the sweat that glistened on my skin. "The masters answer to the epopts."

I caught her hand. "Epopts."

She nodded. "It's an old word, a Hellene word. From the mysteries. You speak a lot of languages, don't you? Because that will be very useful."

"Yes," I said, keeping her hand trapped. "So the *epopts* control the guild."

Claudia blew out her breath in annoyance. "No, Imriel. The Unseen Guild is ruled by the Heptarchy. And don't ask me about them, because I don't know. Only that there are seven of them at all times. When one dies, another is chosen. Not even the epopts know the identity of all seven, only the Heptarchs themselves."

"So what makes you so certain they exist?" I asked.

There were other things she couldn't tell me—couldn't or wouldn't. On the matter of my alleged enemies, she refused to speak further, saying only that it was the price the Guild had set on my loyalty. But I continued to ask questions, hoping to reason my way out of the web in which I was entangled. And then Erytheia and Silvio would return and I would be paid my silver coin, and in their eyes I became somewhat else altogether, Claudia Fulvia's kept boy.

It shouldn't have bothered me, but it did.

I knew what it meant to serve Naamah. I had seen the profound reverence with which her adepts approached their work at Balm House, at once grave and joyful. I had seen kindness and compassion in those who answered Naamah's calling in Night's Doorstep. Even in Valerian House—especially in Valerian House—there was a singular pride, deep and untouchable.

It was different here.

And when I saw the way Silvio looked at me, I thought

about the young woman at the brothel, weeping and begging me not to leave. I thought about the whore on the streets, spitting at my feet.

I thought about Daršanga. And I wondered, betimes, about the damage done to me there. I told myself I only allowed myself to be caught in Claudia's thrall because of the intrigue, because I wanted to know the truth. But I knew, every time I went to her and she left me wrung out and gasping, that it was half a lie. I wanted her, too. I wanted to gain a sense of mastery over her, to drive her harder than she drove me.

And there was never enough time. I wanted *more*, more than Erytheia's hourglass permitted. Dangerous games with dangerous toys. Claudia made me promises, whispering in my ear, telling me things she longed to do. Ways she wanted me to take her; ways in which she wanted me to submit to her. She promised there would be another time soon when we could spend a night together.

I wanted it.

I dreaded it, too.

Worst of all were the evenings after I left the atelier and joined my friends in the wineshop. There I became yet another self, and it was the self I liked the least. I got into the habit of visiting the baths after I was with Claudia, but I could still feel her on my skin. I looked at Eamonn, who I claimed to love like a brother, and felt I was living a lie. I looked at Lucius Tadius, to whom I had promised friendship, and felt myself to be the worst kind of hypocrite. I looked at all of them, wondering who, if any, were part of the Unseen Guild, and I felt very alone and lonely in the midst of the camaraderie.

I'd come to Tiberium to find out who I was, and I had been divided against myself. I'd come to discover what it meant to be good, and I was floundering in lies, hypocrisy, and suspicion.

I was learning, though.

Claudia was right. I was being trained in the arts of covertcy. Not the skills of observation and stealth, but the deeper arts. The ability to navigate alone through a web of deceit and mistrust with a pleasant mask on my face. In time, I even got good enough to fool Eamonn, letting him believe a near-truth, that I was having an affair with a Tiberian noblewoman that I dare not risk exposing.

I'd told the same half-truth to Gilot, threatening him with dire consequences if he ever revealed the location of the domus he'd led me to on the night of that first liaison with Claudia. He believed it easily enough and kept his mouth shut. Gilot had no great fondness for Lucius, and as long as I didn't put myself at risk, wandering the streets alone, he didn't care what I did.

Lying to Eamonn was harder. It hurt. And I would never have done it if I wasn't afraid for him. If it wasn't for the nagging doubts. We were alone and far from home. If the Unseen Guild existed, I didn't dare risk telling him.

Is that a warning?

Yes.

Betimes I wasn't certain how much of it I believed. Of a surety, there was a conspiracy at work here, but there was no evidence of its scope, and Claudia was hard put to prove it to me. There was the Persian guide's name, yes; but that wasn't a secret, merely an arcane piece of information. I wanted a glimpse of the hidden mechanism at work.

"It's not that easy, Imriel!" she repeated in frustration. "There's a good deal I'm forbidden to tell you. And matters on that scale take months to play out, or years."

"Like what?" I challenged her.

"All right." Lying on her back, she gazed at the ceiling of Erytheia's atelier. "You know Deccus is a Restorationist." I nodded. "Well, it's not going to happen," she said. "The Senate won't get the popular support it needs to restore the republic."

"You're a senator's wife," I said wryly. "You're privy to information."

"Which is why I was approached in the first place." She rolled over. Damp tendrils of dark red hair clung to her temples. "But that's not why I know, Imriel. The Restorationists support diverting funds for the University to rebuild Tiberium's trade status. The Unseen Guild opposes this."

"Why on earth?" I asked, curious despite myself.

"Because the University of Tiberium attracts scholars from nations all over the world," she said. "It's an endless resource for the Guild's recruiting. We're careful and selective, but we do make use of it. And we don't want to see it reduced or eliminated."

"So you spy on Deccus and his comrades, and report to the Guild?" The thought gave me a chill. It seemed wrong, very wrong.

Claudia's eyes flashed. "I'm not a coldhearted monster, Imriel! I'd not do anything to endanger Deccus. Indeed, with the Guild's aid, I can protect him from the repercussions of his own politics. But yes, some things I report. And if I can sway his thinking on the matter of the University, it may be that the Restorationists will find the political balance tipping."

"I don't believe you," I said stubbornly. It wasn't true, but I thought that mayhap if I clung to my position, it would force Claudia to reveal more than she intended, one way or another. In that, I was mistaken.

"Believe what you like," Claudia said with a shrug.

Would that I could.

So I lived my divided life and reflected ruefully on the not very distant past, when it seemed that escaping to Tiberium and becoming a simple student, a scholar among many, would free me from the snares that entangled me.

As if to make matters worse, I returned to the insula one afternoon to find yet another unexpected missive awaiting me. It was sitting on the rude wooden table, creamy parchment stamped with the seal of an unfamiliar D'Angeline device, and my name written in a graceful, flowing hand: *Imriel de la Courcel*. The sight of it was like a dousing with cold water.

"Gilot!" I snapped. "Where did this come from?"

He glanced up from the sword he was whetting. "A messenger from Lady Fleurais, the D'Angeline ambassadress."

I tapped the letter against the table. "Did you *see* the name on it?"

"Aye." His gaze was steady. "So? What do you expect me to do, Imri? You are who you are. I'm not about to lie to the Queen's appointed envoy about it." Gilot frowned. "You're not exactly invisible, you know. If you wanted to vanish altogether, you should have run away and joined the Tsingani. Or at least registered at the University under a false name."

"The University doesn't require a residence of record," I pointed out. "And *you* were the one rented the apartment room, not me. We did that a-purpose, remember?"

Gilot shrugged. "You're not exactly inconspicuous."

I cracked the seal and read the letter. It was an invitation to dine with the ambassadress on the following day. Although it was couched in pleasant terms, it was clear that Lady Fleurais was doing the Queen's bidding and expected me to do the same. I tossed the letter on the table and flopped onto my pallet with a sigh.

"What is it?" Gilot asked.

"An invitation to dinner," I said. "It seems her majesty the Queen wishes a report on my well-being."

"Well, and why not?" he said pragmatically. "She has a right to be concerned. As I recall, she went to considerable lengths to secure it."

It was true, and I felt guilty. "I know. It's just . . . I don't like being so easily found."

"By the Queen's ambassadress?" Gilot raised his brows. "I worry about a lot of things when it comes to you, Imri. That's not one of them."

It was foolish and unreasonable, I know. If it hadn't been for the business with Claudia, it wouldn't have troubled me. I would have grumbled about Ysandre playing nursemaid, and not given it a second thought. I hadn't expected to disappear completely in Tiberium, only to live simply and quietly, as someone other than a D'Angeline Prince of the Blood. But as it was, it felt like yet another snare tightening around me.

I went, though.

There was no gracious way to decline, and I was half afraid that if I did, the ambassadress would only grow more persistent. And so the following morning, I sent Gilot with a reply of acceptance, and that evening I put on my shirt with the lace collar, the blue-and-silver brocade doublet, and went to call upon the Lady Fleurais.

I had seen the D'Angeline embassy from a distance, though I had avoided going near it. It was nestled on a ridge partway up the Esquiline Hill, which was one of the most verdant in the city, covered with dark green holly. The embassy itself was a modest palazzo. The walk was longer than it appeared, and I could feel the strain in my calves. Once again, I found myself missing the Bastard. I'd had precious few chances to ride in the past weeks.

It felt strange to hear Gilot give my name at the gates; yet another self, Prince Imriel de la Courcel. I had not been that self since I took leave of the City of Elua, and I didn't feel it now. But the guard admitted us with a low bow and straightened with a smile.

"Welcome, your highness," he said in D'Angeline. "Her ladyship is pleased that you've chosen to honor her."

Ah, Elua! The sound of his voice gave me an unexpected pang. It had been months since I'd heard anyone but Gilot speaking my mother tongue.

I hadn't realized, until that evening, how much I missed Terre d'Ange.

The guard escorted us into the palazzo, and Lady Fleurais emerged promptly to greet us. "Prince Imriel." She curtsied as protocol dictated, then gave me the kiss of greeting with seemingly genuine warmth. "Welcome."

The D'Angeline ambassadress was a woman of early middle years, with hair the color of new mahogany and shrewd eyes in a kind, lovely face—and all at once, I remembered why I knew her name. She had accompanied Lord Amaury Trente on his mission to Menekhet to retrieve me, and had taken over trade negotiations with Pharaoh when Amaury and the others had gone on to Khebbel-im-Akkad. It was where her career in diplomacy had begun.

Phèdre had spoken highly of her.

My eyes stung, and I blinked back unexpected tears. "Well met, my lady."

It was a pleasant evening; almost too pleasant. As the sun had not yet set, Lady Denise led me to see the garden temple at the rear of the palazzo. It was a gorgeous place, entirely hidden from view, lovingly tended. Roses of all hues grew in profusion and the scent of lavender hung in the air, another reminder of home.

We strolled around the perimeter. There were altars to all of the Companions; all save Cassiel, who served only Blessed Elua. I gazed at each in turn, the statues in their niches . . . gentle Eisheth with her harp, proud Azza holding a compass, clever Shemhazai with his tablet. Naamah held a dove cupped in her hands, while fierce Camael wielded his sword and a seedling sprouted from Anael's palm. And Kushiel; of course Kushiel, bearing his rod and flail.

Only Blessed Elua's hands were empty, open in blessing.

A priest in blue robes was pruning the rosebushes around his altar. I hung back, almost afraid to approach.

"Would you like to worship?" Lady Fleurais asked. "I often do at this hour."

"I'm . . . not sure," I murmured.

I did, though. I sat on the low bench provided and removed my boots. The grass was soft beneath my bare feet, damp with early dew. The priest smiled at me. Without a word, he cut a great handful of roses, laying them in my arms.

The amber light was fading, turning to soft twilight. Drawing a deep breath, I knelt before Elua's effigy and strewed the roses at his feet, their petals tender against the smooth marble. I could feel Elua's gaze upon me, filled with a love so pure it hurt. I felt unworthy beneath his gaze; profane and unworthy.

"Blessed Elua," I whispered. "Guide me."

There was no answer, but a tiny sensation of peace blossomed in me, tentative and delicate. I rested my brow against the pedestal. I could have stayed there all night just to keep the sense alive in my heart. I understood for the first time—truly understood—why Joscelin maintained Elua's vigil on the Longest Night. I would have liked to do the same.

But the ambassadress was waiting, and I was no Cassiline. No god's servant, no god's chosen. Only Imriel, alone and confused and far from home. With a sigh, I kissed Blessed Elua's feet and forced myself to rise.

"Thank you," I said to Denise Fleurais.

"Oh, you're quite welcome." Her kind, intelligent gaze searched my face. "It's difficult to be an exile, isn't it? Even if the exile is of one's own choosing."

"Yes," I said. "It is."

We dined in one of the palazzo's smaller salons, at a table set with white linens. After weeks of Caerdicci fare, it was a pleasure to dine on D'Angeline cuisine and drink good Namarrese wine. All the household staff was D'Angeline. They went about their business with quiet, efficient pride. It's a strange thing, how even the way a platter is placed on a table can remind one of home.

I'd missed it; missed it all.

Lady Denise Fleurais was an excellent companion. She inquired after my studies, listening with lively interest while I told her about Master Piero, laughing at the tale of his chasing pigeons in the Forum. In turn, I asked after news from home. Although it felt like I'd been gone for ages, in truth, it was little over two months and there was only one piece of news of any significance.

"The Queen has announced Princess Alais' betrothal to Prince Talorcan, the Cruarch's nephew," Denise told me.

I paused with my fork halfway to my mouth, then finished my bite, chewed and swallowed. Alais' tearstained face swam in my memory, her voice pleading, *Don't leave me, please!* "She's so young."

Denise nodded. "Fourteen," she said. "Of course, the

wedding won't take place for a couple of years. You're fond of her, your highness?"

"Very." I pushed away the memory of her tears. "What of Sidonie?"

"Oh, I daresay she has her share of suitors," she said, smiling. "But no, the Queen's letter said naught of her."

"And what did it say of me?" I asked.

Denise Fleurais beckoned to her wine steward, then dismissed him with a gracious word of thanks after he refilled our cups. She sipped her wine, considering me. "Her majesty is concerned," she said frankly. "It wasn't until after your departure that she learned you had left with a single attendant and were travelling in disguise as a commoner."

"Not exactly," I said. "And I'm travelling under my own name."

"Half of it, yes." She frowned. "Your highness, I will be honest. Yes, although her first concern is that I ascertain your well-being, her majesty asks me to urge you to return to Terre d'Ange. Failing that, she asks that I use the embassy's resources to ensure that you are esconced here in Tiberium with due honor and the privileges and protection according to your rank."

"Imriel," I said. "Call me Imriel."

She blinked at me. "I beg your pardon?"

I pushed my plate away. "No mind. My lady, I appreciate Ysandre's concern. Please tell her so, and that I am well. But I am doing what I believe is needful for my own sake. At the moment, that means living as Imriel nó Montrève and not a Prince of the Blood."

"May I ask why?" Lady Denise inquired gently.

It was the gentleness that nearly undid me. I looked away for a moment. It would have been easy, so easy, to tell her everything—Claudia, the Unseen Guild, all of it. She was an intelligent woman and a skilled diplomat; even Phèdre had said as much. It would be a blessed relief to lay the problem in her lap and shroud myself in the embassy's sanctuary.

But the seeds of doubt were there.

For all I knew, she was part of it. Of a surety, she had found me without difficulty. If the Guild existed and Denise Fleurais was complicit, this was a test I would fail. If she was innocent, then I placed her in jeopardy. She had a measure of status and power in Tiberium, but when all was said and done, Terre d'Ange was a long way away.

I couldn't be sure. This was a problem I needed to solve on my own, and giving up what freedom I'd acquired here for the mantle of the Queen's protection would change nothing.

And so I temporized. "My lady, you were in Menekhet, were you not? You know my history." I met her gaze squarely. "And you know my lineage, as does the whole of Terre d'Ange. Can you blame me for wanting a respite from it?"

"No," she said ruefully. "Not really."

The moment passed, and Lady Denise let it go with a diplomat's practiced grace. We spoke of other matters, touching on nothing of import, until the hour grew late and it was time for me to take my leave. I bowed and thanked her for her hospitality.

"You're a pleasant guest. I should have expected as much from Phèdre nó Delaunay's foster-son." She smiled at me, though her face was troubled. "Prince Imriel, I will respect your wishes and your privacy, unless her majesty orders otherwise. Only know that the embassy is here to serve you." She paused. "And I will leave a standing order with the guard. You are welcome here at any hour if you wish to avail yourself of the temple garden. Please consider it at your disposal."

"My thanks," I said. "That's kind of you."

Accompanied by Gilot, I departed the palazzo, and we made our way down the Esquiline Hill and through the city. He was in high spirits, having had a fine time dining, drinking, and dicing with the embassy guard while I met with the ambassadress.

"Elua's Balls!" he exulted. "It was like a taste of home. To be around people who look like you, think like you, talk like you . . . Ah, by all the gods, it felt good." Holding a torch aloft to light our way, he glanced sidelong at me. "It's not that I don't like Tiberium, mind, but . . . don't you miss it?"

"Yes," I murmured. "I do."

The fragile sense of peace I'd experienced in the garden was gone, long gone. I listened with half an ear while Gilot rattled on about the embassy, the guards, the possibility of taking a position there when I decided to return to Terre d'Ange. How Anna might feel about it, how her daughter would adjust to the change, how he might reconcile the two worlds.

My own thoughts were a jumble.

I wanted . . . what? A part of me wanted to go home. I wanted to see Alais, to hug her and promise to be the brother she wanted me to be. I wanted to find out who was courting Sidonie, especially if it was Maslin de Lombelon. I wanted Phèdre and Joscelin, so much so that it made me dizzy to think about it. I would have told them everything; everything. The Unseen Guild was no match for the two of them. That, I believed with all of my heart.

And another part wanted only to forget.

Forget the garden, forget the Lady Denise and her D'Angeline household. It only made me yearn; made me weak. I couldn't afford it. Unwitting or no, I'd walked into this maze of snares of my own accord. I didn't want to be rescued from it. I'd already played the role of victim in my lifetime, and it had left a trail of bloodshed and horror in my wake.

Once was enough.

I needed to make a choice. I could make an end to the affair with Claudia and refuse the Guild's overtures as Anafiel Delaunay had done, promising my silence in exchange for their tolerance. Or I could accept their offer, pledge my loyalty, and discover what deeper truths lay behind the tidbits of knowledge Claudia had dangled before me.

The first path meant accepting ignorance. That was the part that galled me. In Siovale, they say all knowledge is worth having, and I hated the thought of leaving the mystery unresolved, of always wondering what unseen forces were shaping the world around me. Still, Anafiel Delaunay had reckoned the Guild's price too high. He'd walked away from their offer, and so far as I knew, he'd kept their secrets and never looked back.

If he could do it, so could I.

At least I hoped so.

FORTY-ONE

"TO LUCIUS TADIUS DA LUCCA!"

Reclining on his couch, Deccus Fulvius raised his winecup, his broad face flushed. The rest of us followed suit.

"To Lucius!" we chorused.

"*And* Helena," Brigitta added pointedly before drinking.

Word had come from Lucca; Gaetano Correggio had accepted Lucius' suit on behalf of his daughter. The date of the wedding was fixed, some six weeks hence. And Deccus Fulvius had resolved to throw a fête to celebrate, deigning to invite his wife's brother's disreputable scholarly friends.

It was a full-blown Tiberian affair, complete with dancing girls and boys; players from the belated pantomime I had witnessed. The atmosphere was raucous and indulgent, and if it hadn't been for Claudia Fulvia, I daresay I would have enjoyed myself.

But there was Claudia.

I hadn't had a chance to speak to her since my visit to the embassy, and nothing was resolved. One thing was certain—if I had any lingering doubts about the efficacy of her training methods, I lost them that night. I had no choice but to engage in the practice of duplicity. It was hard, damnably hard, to be under the same roof with her and pretend there was nothing between us. Wherever she was, I could feel the heat of her. I couldn't look at her playing at being the proper senator's wife without seeing her in all her naked glory, spread out like a banquet.

And yet I managed to keep any of it from showing. Truly, I'd learned a measure of control.

The fête was too large to be contained within the dining hall. It spread throughout the domus. There were a great many people I didn't know present—Tiberian nobles and politicians as well as students. I shook hands and made polite conversation, all the while aware of Claudia moving smoothly throughout the throng while her husband and brother held court. Her decorum was a marvel to behold. Whether by dint of long practice or inborn skill, it seemed effortless.

I'd almost forgotten, since that first night I met her. Now I watched her through different eyes, wondering how much of her skill at dissembling was that of a woman cuckolding her husband, and how much owed to the arts of covertcy. Here in Tiberium, mayhap there wasn't much difference to choose between the two.

Whatever the case, Claudia's skill made it easier to fall into my own role—Lucius' friend, the D'Angeline scholar. I laughed with my companions, drank wine in moderation, spoke respectfully to my host, and began to relax.

Which, of course, was when Claudia struck.

It was in the atrium. I had been conversing with a trade merchant who was curious about the Master of the Straits. Outside of Terre d'Ange and Alba, his existence is regarded with a measure of skepticism. The merchant, who was interested in striking up a direct trade relationship with the Cruarch of Alba, asked me if the legends were true.

"Oh yes," I said. "They're true."

"I mean, *really*," he said, waving a dismissive hand. "I'm willing to allow that there are dangerous currents, mayhap a pernicious maelstrom . . . but surely, young sir, you don't expect me to believe there's a sorcerer controlling the seas surrounding Alba?"

I thought about Hyacinthe with his strange, sea-shifting eyes, stepping from the crest of a wave onto the deck of Admiral Rousse's ship. "Believe what you like," I said, hearing an echo of Claudia in my words. "But he is real."

The merchant turned to his wife. "What do *you* think?"

"Excuse me," Claudia murmured graciously, interposing herself. Her fingertips rested lightly on my arm. "Imriel, a moment?"

Not wanting to make a scene, I let her draw me away. With a deft motion, she slipped into the *lararium* where the household altar resided, taking me with her.

A single oil lamp burned on the table, low and guttering. It was barely enough to illuminate the waxen masks and bronze figurines with which the altar table was laden. The room seemed close and stifling, smelling of stale incense. There in the darkness, Claudia kissed me with familiar animal urgency, her tongue seeking to duel with mine.

"Claudia!" I wrenched my head away, hissing her name. Beyond the open door of the *lararium*, revelers laughed and chatted, only a few scant yards away.

"The world is filled with unexpected dangers, Imriel. Are you scared?" She pressed close, sliding one hand between us to fondle me. I swore softly as I grew hard under her touch. Her lips curved. "You don't *feel* scared."

I bit my lip and stared over her shoulder. On the altar, the waxen death-masks of the patriarchs of the Fulvii stared back at me. In the guttering lamplight, shadows moved over their features, altering their expressions. Their dead eyes were filled with disapproval. A current of cold air stirred in the close quarters. I thought about Lucius and shuddered.

The lares *of the Fulvii mean you no harm . . .*

So Deccus had said to him, and mayhap it was true, but of a surety, I did not think his ancestors welcomed my presence here in their sanctuary, with his wife's tongue in my mouth and her hand on my groin.

"Not here," I said firmly, removing her hand. "No."

For an awful moment, I thought Claudia meant to persist and I didn't know what I'd do. But no, she stepped away, her gaze light and amused. "Later, then."

I waited until she had gone, then turned to the altar with a low bow. Since I had no idea how to properly address Tiberian household gods, I merely said, "Forgive me, for I meant no disrespect."

Feeling the dead, waxy stare of the Fulvii *lares* betwixt my shoulder blades, I departed their chamber. All my hard-won composure was shattered. Mayhap it was what Claudia intended, and mayhap there was a purpose to it.

But if this was another difficult lesson, I meant to dodge it. And until I could put an end to this entire mess, I meant to avoid Claudia altogether.

"Lucius, my friend." Without asking permission, I joined him on his couch and addressed him with unwonted abruptness. "Let's celebrate your betrothal and get blind, stinking drunk."

He gave me a startled look. "All right. Let's."

We did so with great, rousing success.

I awoke the following day with an aching head, a mouth that felt stuffed with cotton, and hazy memories of ending the night by stumbling through the streets of Tiberium with Eamonn, singing an Eiran drinking song. It made me smile until I remembered the tired, stoic face of the Fulvii servant who had accompanied us to light our way. Then I felt the weight of my own hypocrisy descend, and sighed.

Although I'd slept through Master Piero's class, I managed to drag myself to Erytheia's atelier that afternoon, reckoning it a sort of grim punishment. At least in my sorry state, it would be easier to confront Claudia without fear of being seduced into prolonging the affair. Erytheia took one look at me and rolled her eyes.

"Iacchos! You look like you were scraped from the bottom of a wine barrel," she said, then paused. "Perhaps that's not altogether a bad thing. Strip, and sit for me."

I obeyed.

I'd gotten good at it by now. I took up my grapes and sprawled in the chair, slinging my leg carelessly over the arm, and stayed there without moving. Truth be told, I liked watching Erytheia work. There was somewhat beautiful in it, that pure and utter absorption; and somewhat fearful, too. I watched her face as she painted, at once blank and rapt, a kind of sight beyond sight. I had seen that expression on Phèdre's face.

I'd seen it in Daršanga.

And I'd seen it on Kapporeth, when she'd walked out of the temple with the Name of God quivering on her tongue, an unbearable brightness on her.

I'd seen a flicker of it, fleeting and elusive, the morning I'd ridden home from Valerian House and quarreled with her. Caught her wrist, hard, and felt her pulse leap beneath my touch. Seen the scarlet mote on her iris, a tantalizing challenge.

For months, I had struggled to keep that memory at bay.

And yet now, strangely, it no longer struck me like a fist to the gut.

We are what we are, Imriel.

It was true. She had drawn away from it, and so had I. Granted, I had heaved the contents of my belly onto the floor, but I had done it. And Phèdre had understood, and so had Joscelin. Although I could not help my own desires, I was not held helpless in their thrall. I was free to choose. I understood that now. And in a strange way, I had Claudia to thank for it.

Erytheia of Thrasos stepped backward and eyed her easel.

She nodded—once, twice, and thrice—and laid down her palette and brush. "It is finished," she said simply. "Will you see?"

I was lost in my own thoughts, and it took a moment for her words to make sense. Once they did, I rose, stiff-jointed, wrapping the purple cloth about my waist and coming to gaze at the panel on her easel.

"That's me?" I asked.

"Yes," she said.

It was strange—so strange!—to behold myself captured in paint. I cocked my head, gazing at the image. My own face stared out at me, indolent and predatory, all high cheekbones and languid eyes. A sensuous mouth, and firm brows. It was a compendium of contrasts. I felt at my face with my fingertips, trying to find the resemblance.

"Do you even *know* what you look like?" Erytheia asked curiously.

"No," I murmured. "I mean yes, of course, it's just . . ." I shook my head. "I don't look in the mirror very often. It's a long story."

The door rattled open to admit Claudia Fulvia.

"Lady Fulvia." Erytheia inclined her head in a formal greeting. "I am pleased to tell you that your commission is finished."

"Excellent." Claudia glanced at it. "Very nice. Magnificent. Will you keep it safe for me, Erytheia? I can't tarry." She caught my bare arm, and there was nothing playful or sensuous in the gesture. "Imriel, did you attend your lecture this morning?"

"No." I frowned. "Why? What is it?"

She sighed. "May we have a moment?"

The artist raised her brows, but made no comment, merely beckoning to her apprentice. The two of them stepped outside.

"Claudia, I need to talk—" I began.

"Listen." Claudia squeezed my arm. "I'm sorry, Imriel, but there's no time. I want you and your friends to stay off the streets tonight. It's not going to be safe in the students' quarter."

I stared at her. "Why?"

"Because," she said grimly, "one of Deccus' more hotheaded conspirators took it upon himself to call upon the Senate to enact a decree abolishing funding for the University this morning. And this afternoon, the consul of the citizen assembly stood up and agreed with him. The students are going to riot."

"They are?" I felt like an idiot. "We are?"

Claudia gave me an impatient look. "It's certainly going to look that way. Starting a riot's one of the easiest things in the world. Once there's bloodshed, the citizen assembly will back down. They don't have the stomach for it. Look, just heed my advice. Find your friends and convince them to keep their heads down and stay out of trouble." She gave my arm another ungentle squeeze. "And remember, I'm trusting you enough to warn you."

This was a different Claudia, one I'd never seen before, and she was deadly serious. I nodded and reached for my neatly piled clothing, with Canis' luck-charm sitting atop it. I strung it around my neck and began to dress. "I understand."

"Good boy." She gave me a swift kiss. "I'll send word to you later."

I managed to leave Erytheia's atelier without Silvio, which was a piece of irony. But I wanted to be able to move swiftly, and if trouble arose, I suspected he'd be more of a hindrance than a help. In the genteel neighborhood where Erytheia's atelier was located, all was fairly quiet, but by the time I reached the dense labyrinth of the students' quarter, I could sense the unrest.

All the wineshops and inns were full to overflowing. People stood around talking in knots, the way they had in the Old Forum when the pontifex and the aedile argued on the rostra. This was different, though. It had an ugly undertone, a low buzz of anger. I could feel it on my skin.

"Imriel!" Canis, perched cross-legged atop his barrel, called to me. "It is an interesting dilemma, is it not?" His brown eyes sparkled in his dirty face. "Myself, I have always found wisdom to be free, and thus there is no need for the state to sponsor its pursuit. And yet, where the purses of the few grow fat, the wisdom of the many is stunted. What think you?"

"I think mayhap you should roll your barrel into our courtyard tonight and sleep there, my friend," I said. "Canis, do you know if Gilot is here?"

"You worry on my behalf!" He beamed. "How kind. No, he departed for the market with his lady-friend and her daughter an hour ago. You're early," he added.

"I know," I said. "Do you know which market?"

He shrugged. "No."

With a curse, I plunged into the city in search of Gilot.

Along the way, I stopped in every wineshop I passed, looking for Eamonn or Lucius, or anyone else worth warning.

All I found was a steadily rising buzz of hostility. Students debated in heated tones, some of them still wearing their scholars' robes. Mostly they argued with one another, but in some places they quarreled with shopkeepers and other workers—members of the Tiberian citizen assembly that had supported the call for a decree. Some voices were louder than others, declaiming their outrage with an orator's skill. The citizens responding were beginning to sound nervous and unsure.

Master Strozzi, purported member of the Unseen Guild, had taught rhetoric. Claudia had called him an old blowhard, but mayhap his skills had their uses.

Starting a riot's one of the easiest things in the world.

There was no riot, not yet. But I could feel the tide of anger rising, and with it, my belief in the Unseen Guild's power. I wanted, with growing urgency, to find my friends and get them off the streets and into safety.

I made my way to the nearest market, which was in the colonnade of the Great Forum. Although it was an hour shy of sunset, the vendors there were concluding their last hasty transactions, packing away their wares. I pushed my way through an anxious throng; housewives, for the most part, clinging together in groups. In the Forum itself, students roamed in packs, chanting angry slogans. A phalanx of the city cohort stood, armed and watchful and vastly outnumbered.

"Gilot!" With a vast sense of relief, I spotted him and waved my arm. "Gilot!"

"Imri!" He waded through the crowd toward me, shepherding Anna and carrying her daughter Belinda on his shoulder. The child's eyes were wide and scared. For that matter, so were her mother's. "What are you doing here?"

"Looking for you," I said. "Come on, let's get off the streets. It's growing ugly."

Gilot must have felt anxious himself, for he didn't even bother to reprimand me for travelling the city alone. By now, the streets were well and truly clogged with irate students and nervous citizens. It took a long time to get back to the insula, and there were a few points where I had to push and shove. When at last we reached it, I was glad to see that if Canis had not moved his barrel, at least he had prudently removed himself from the vicinity.

"Name of Elua!" In the courtyard, Gilot set Belinda down and wiped his brow. "What in the seven hells is that all about?"

"Politics," I said briefly. "Have you seen Eamonn or Lucius?"

"No." He eyed me. The toddler Belinda clung to his leg, while Anna stood beside him, clutching an armful of green cloth to her breast. "Imriel, you are *not* going out there."

"They're my friends," I said.

We exchanged a long, hard glance which ended in Gilot rolling his eyes. I could be stubborn when I chose, and he knew me well enough to know when to cede ground. "Stay in your apartment," he said to Anna, "and bar the door. We'll be back ere you know it."

"You don't have to come," I said.

"Oh, I'm coming," Gilot retorted.

I waited while he kissed Anna farewell, then stooped and kissed Belinda. And then the two of us navigated the narrow gateway passage and plunged back into the streets.

It was beginning.

I thought about Master Piero's lecture as we hunted for

our friends; that first lecture I had witnessed. Here it was, the group-mind at work. And it could be directed and shaped, as surely as he had led the pigeons with scattered grain. The anger of the students was being shaped, directed against the Tiberian citizenry. Here and there, scuffles were beginning to break out. Young men with torches eyed closed shop-fronts, daring one another. Guards from the city cohort struggled inadequately to restore order, overwhelmed by sheer numbers.

"Blessed Elua!" Gilot said fervently. "This quarter would go up like a tinderbox."

"I know," I murmured.

In time, we found our friends. As I had guessed, it was in a wineshop; the same one we usually frequented, with the faded sign of Bacchus. I'd already checked it twice that evening. I would have been better served by waiting.

It was the shouting that drew us—two voices, raised in a shouting-match.

One of them, I knew.

"That's Lucius," I said, driving shoulder-first into the packed wineshop.

There I found Lucius in fine fettle, arguing against a slab-sided hulk in scholar's robes, his face alight with keen intellect. Eamonn was there, too, his back to the wall, watching the proceedings and looking cheerfully combative. And there at his side was Brigitta, merely looking combative, her hand hovering over the hilt of her dagger. The wineshop's patrons had withdrawn to give them space, clustering in a circle. The barkeep was nowhere to be seen.

"There is a *reason*," Lucius shouted, "for the rule of law!"

"Oh, aye!" his opponent growled. "To keep the likes of *me* in my place!"

"Will you *listen*, you idiot?" Lucius retorted. "You can't advance the pursuit of knowledge by violent means. It's antithetical!"

I began edging my way around the crowd, Gilot at my heels, intent on getting my friends out. I didn't think they fully reckoned how volatile the situation was.

"What does *he* care?" A new voice entered the fray, cool and disdainful. I glanced around to see another robe-clad scholar pointing at Lucius. He had sharp features and a contained, hooded gaze. "He's related by marriage to Deccus Fulvius. He's rich, and he'll only get richer. *He* doesn't care about the University."

The slab-sided scholar blinked, his color rising. "Is that true?"

"Oh, please!" Lucius said in disgust. "Deccus had nothing to do with this!"

"He's lying," the new scholar said smugly. "Everyone knows the Restorationists are behind this, and everyone knows Deccus Fulvius is behind them."

The comment drew murmurs. The tide of the group-mind was beginning to turn against Lucius. Claudia, I thought, your Guild takes an almighty risk when it decides to unleash the bottled lightning of a riot. Easy to start, hard to control. You should have protected your brother before me. Your nets are not so tightly woven as you'd have me believe.

"Imri!" Eamonn hailed me as I reached his side, rubbing his hands together with glee. "I'm glad you arrived. I think there's going to be a fight."

"Yes," I said. "And we're not taking part in it. Come on, let's get out of here."

"Why?" He looked at me with bewilderment.

Too late; already, too late. I'd missed the last exchange of barbed comments, but I heard the roar as the slab-sided scholar charged Lucius, barreling into him and hurling him against the wall. There was an audible thud and a grunt as the air left Lucius' chest.

I whirled without thinking, drawing my right-hand dagger and bringing the pommel down hard on the base of the big ox's skull. His eyes rolled back in his head and his knees buckled as he sagged slowly to the floor.

"My thanks!" Lucius said, half-breathless.

"Traitors!" It was the other one's voice, shrill and alarmed. I could tell without looking that he was pointing at us. "Traitors!"

"This isn't over," I muttered to Lucius. "We've got to get out of here fast."

He nodded, eyes wide and startled. "Whatever you say."

"Gilot, Eamonn!" I raised my voice. "Montrève, to me!"

I heard Gilot's voice answer, rising clear and ringing over the din. "Montrève!" And Eamonn's laughing bellow echoed his call, booming through the wineshop. "Montrève, and the Dalriada! Aye, and Skaldia, too!"

We forged a path toward the door with fists and elbows. There was no room to draw a sword, and I would have been reluctant to do so. I didn't want to draw blood unless it was absolutely necessary. Joscelin had told me not to take chances, but Joscelin had never been in a riot where innocent lives were indistinguishable from the guilty.

Without Eamonn, I daresay we would have been trapped. He waded into the fray, heedless of his own safety, tossing people aside like jackstraws. I felt a fierce grin stretch my lips as I followed in his wake. Brigitta stuck like a burr to his back, and I swatted away the hands that reached for her, Lucius hard behind me, and Gilot bringing up the rear. He *had* managed to draw his sword, and he walked backward with it, warding off pursuit as we spilled onto the street.

It worked for the space of a few heartbeats.

At first it wasn't even a fight; just a throng of bodies pressed against one another, pushing, shoving, and cursing. Too many people in the street, too many pouring from the wineshop. The throng surged in response to forces I couldn't see. I couldn't move, and my arms were trapped at my sides. I couldn't even raise my dagger. Bodies, pressed all around. Torchlight streaked the night, but it was hard to see. Nothing but swathes of cloth, bits and pieces of faces. Anyone who fell would be trampled, and it was hard to keep one's feet in the swaying, surging crush.

For the first time, I panicked and found myself struggling to breathe. Brigitta was no longer in front of me. I couldn't tell if Lucius was behind me, couldn't even turn my head. Someone's elbow was lodged in my ribs. Someone's heel stomped hard on my toes; hard and deliberate. I would have hopped with pain if I could have. As it was, it made me lurch. I felt another foot planted in the back of my left knee, and my leg buckled.

Somewhere Gilot was shouting my name: "Imri, Imri!"

I heard it, then I didn't. Someone had gotten to him, silenced him. And I was off balance, and the rioting throng was like a dark tide, threatening to pull me under. My left foot was trapped and I couldn't free it, couldn't straighten, couldn't move with the tide as I ought. A fist plowed into my bowed spine, driving me downward. Another blow, hard as a hammer. Helpless and furious, I pitched forward.

Somewhere above me, I heard a voice mutter, "Told to tell you, that's for Baudoin."

An intensified shock of panic ran through me. This was more than random violence; someone wished me harm. And if I fell, I'd never rise in one piece. Bodies, all around, thrashing and stomping and churning. No air, nothing to breathe. Only strange bodies, all too willing to crush the life from me. My attacker had hundreds of oblivious accomplices. I couldn't see faces, now; only backs and buttocks, legs and trampling feet. Before my eyes, the dim cobbled streets loomed close.

And somewhere, a faceless enemy.

Claudia had tried to warn me, but not hard enough.

Stupid, I thought as I fell, still holding the useless dagger, my arm pinned beneath me. Mayhap if I was lucky, I would fall upon its point and put an end to my foolish existence. I should have drawn them both, should have fought my way free. So what if I shed innocent blood? I could have claimed asylum at the D'Angeline embassy.

Stupid, stupid, stupid. What a stupid way to die.

Somewhere behind me, there was an anguished cry of pain; and then another. And then the throng shifted and the press abated and there was space, a little bit of space. I drew a ragged breath and yanked my left leg hard. With an excruciating twist of my ankle, it came free, and I nearly fell on my face once more. I thrashed, trying to get to my feet before my enemy struck again, but I was still unbalanced and flailing.

"Montrève!" Lucius was there, ducking under a reaching arm. He was wild-eyed, his hand clutching at my wrist, steadying me. "Give me your dagger!"

I let it go, drawing the second one from my boot-sheath as I forced myself upright. "Behind me!" I shouted. "Who is it?"

Lucius shook his head. "Never mind! Just get *out*!"

Of a single grim accord, Lucius and I planted ourselves shoulder to shoulder and fought our way free of the fracas, prodding with our daggers when a threat didn't suffice. I heard yelps of pain, and didn't care; it made people move.

Some had been less fortunate than me. Twice, I stumbled over fallen bodies and kept going, trying not to tread on anyone, desperate for air. By the time we reached the outskirts of the battle, I was gasping for it.

And then there was air, blessed air.

I bent over double, hands on my knees, sucking it into my lungs.

"What took you so long?" There was Eamonn, the battle-grin still plastered to his face. He'd drawn his Dalriadan longsword, and no one dared venture within its reach. Brigitta stood at his shoulder, dagger in hand, her face alight with fierce Skaldic pride. Prince Barbarus and his shield-maiden.

Still bent, I glared at him. "Someone tried to kill me."

"Oh, aye!" he agreed. "It's a right mess in there."

I didn't have time to explain. "Where's Gilot?"

Eamonn's expression shifted to dismay. "Dagda Mor!"

"Guard my back," I said to him.

And so we went back; back for Gilot. I gave my sword to Lucius in exchange for my second dagger and bade him defend Brigitta. He gave a terse nod; for a mercy, she didn't protest at it. Eamonn and I returned to the fray. I tried to identify my attacker, but I'd never even seen his face. By this time, reinforcements from the city cohort had arrived, dissolving the riots into knots. They meted out punishment with dispassionate equanimity, battering away at rioters and bystanders alike with the flats of their shortswords.

"Gilot!"

I knew him; even prone. His limp hand clutching the hilt of his sword, the fine D'Angeline profile against the cobblestones, bruised and swollen. He'd been beaten to the ground. One of his assailants drew back his foot, prepared to plant another kick to Gilot's ribs. I recognized him from the wineshop. He was the agitator, the sharp-featured scholar.

"Don't." In a flash, I was on him, crossed daggers at his throat. A cold, clean fury filled me. I leaned against him, breast to breast, close as a lover. "Was it you?" I asked softly. "Were you told to say, 'that's for Baudoin'?"

He trembled. "I don't know what you mean!"

"No?" I studied him. His voice was high-pitched with terror. Not the voice that had muttered the words I'd heard, not even close. "You provoked this," I said. "If Gilot dies of this beating, make no mistake, I will find you and kill you."

There was fear in his eyes. He kept his chin high to avoid the daggers, but there was fear, and the sight of it was sweet. With one swift, slicing motion, I withdrew both blades, marking his neck with a pair of shallow cuts. He cried out, clapping his hands to his throat.

"You'll live," I said with contempt. "Get out of here."

He went in a hurry, still clasping his throat, blood trickling between his fingers.

Although I would have liked to question them, Eamonn had dispelled the others. He stood over me while I knelt at Gilot's side, and even the city cohort gave him a wide berth. "Gilot." I peered at him, wincing in sympathy. Already, in the murky torchlight, I could see bruises blooming. His mouth was crusted with blood and the lids of both eyes were alarmingly swollen. I gave his shoulder a tentative shake, fearful of hurting him. "Gilot, can you hear me?"

He groaned, and one swollen lid opened a crack. "Imri?"

"It's me." My heart leapt with relief. "Where are you hurt? Can you walk?"

"I think so." With my assistance, Gilot sat upright, then coughed and spat out a mouthful of blood. "Ribs," he said with a grimace. "And my sword-hand. Some bastard stomped on it. I kept hold of it, though." He felt at his face with his left hand. "I can't see. Am I blind?"

"No." I slid my arm under his shoulders. "I don't think so, anyway. Come on, let's get you home."

With Eamonn's help, I got Gilot to his feet. We eased his sword from his broken grasp and got him over to the others. By now, the rioters were scattering, pelting every which way down the streets. Eamonn led the way, watchful and wary, no longer smiling. My wrenched ankle hurt like fury, and I struggled not to hobble under Gilot's weight.

Brigitta drew a sharp breath at the sight of his battered face. "Is he all right?"

"What do you think?" I asked grimly.

"Imri," Eamonn murmured.

"Sorry," I muttered. "It's just . . . this is my fault. He shouldn't be here."

"None of us should." Lucius, still holding my sword, shuddered. "You were right, Montrève. Let's get out of here."

Our insula was the closest shelter, so we made for it. It seemed to take forever. Every step sent a blaze of pain through my ankle. The worst of the riot had passed, but it was far from over. Students roamed the streets, taking to their heels at the sight of the cohort's legions. No one dared approach us, but here and there we saw skirmishes. It was impossible to tell who was fighting or why.

And there were still the torches.

Of all the possible dangers remaining, that was the worst. Gilot was right, the students' quarter was built of wood and clay brick, cheap and readily available. If one good blaze started, the whole thing would turn into a tinderbox.

We'd almost made our way home before the threat manifested.

I saw a pair of figures in front of the incense-maker's shop. One of them picked up Canis' abandoned barrel, hurling it at the shuttered windows; the other watched, torch in hand. With a loud crash, the shutters splintered, and an incongruous scent of sandalwood and myrrh wafted onto the street.

"Do it!" The one who had thrown the barrel laughed, drunk and reckless. "Aye, do it, Renzo! Why not? Let the merchant pay the price for his allegiance to the citizen assembly. Do you smell that? The gods never had such a tribute!"

The other cocked his arm, torch blazing. "You reckon?"

All at once, there was no time, and all the time in the world. I felt Gilot stir beneath my arm at their words, and I sensed his thoughts, clear as day. Anna. Belinda. The insula, a tinderbox. I saw Eamonn begin to move, sword naked in his hand, and knew he was too slow; too far away.

An arm; cocked. Flame and sparks, streaming into the night.

A snatch of a poet's tale, an impossible cast. There in the Temple of Asherat where my mother took sanctuary. It happened there.

Joscelin's voice, drilling me. *Again. Again. Again.*

"Take him!" I gasped, shoving Gilot's limp, heavy body in Lucius' direction. Already I was running, plucking the right-hand dagger from its sheath, ignoring the shattering pain with every step I took. "Eamonn!" I shouted. "Get out of the way!"

He ducked, bless him.

Whispering a prayer, I flipped the dagger in midair, catching it by its point. The steel felt slick and sweaty. I had done this before, done it a thousand times. Joscelin had taught me, had made me drill. At fifteen paces, my aim was good. This was farther. I was better at swordplay. But there was no time, no more.

The cocked arm began to describe an arc.

I threw.

It was a solid cast; a square cast. The dagger turned end over end, glinting dully in the torchlight. It pierced the back of the rioter's hand, pinning it to the wooden base of the torch. He shrieked and flailed, trying to shake himself free, flames dancing wildly around him.

"Thrice-cursed idiot!" I fell on him, wrestling him to the ground. We rolled on the cobbled streets. A searing pain lanced my shoulder, and his torch went out. A stink of scorched wool arose, and the odor of burned flesh. I could hear the pelting footsteps of his companion, beating a hasty retreat. "Do you know who I am?" I asked. *"Do you?"* He choked out an abject denial, weeping with fear. I wrenched the dagger out of his rigid hand, and he howled, blood welling in the deep, narrow wound. "Go," I said in disgust. "Go away."

He fled, sniveling.

I rolled onto my back and watched the others arrive. Gilot, blind and limping, leaning hard on Lucius. Brigitta, wary and sidling. Eamonn, extending a callused hand. I let him haul me to my feet.

"Right," I said, wavering. "Into the insula."

FORTY-TWO

GILOT WAS A MESS.

Eamonn volunteered to take first watch at the gate, and I dispatched Brigitta to fetch Anna Marzoni from her apartment. The whole of the insula was awake and nervous, many of them hovering around the courtyard well, buckets in hand. They knew the danger of fire.

Anna came in a hurry, bringing an elderly woman who had spent years as a chirurgeon's assistant. We laid Gilot on his pallet, lighting all the oil lamps in the room. In the flickering light, they undressed him with care. His torso was a solid mass of bruises, and his right hand was growing bloated and puffy.

"Ah, Jupiter!" Lucius looked sick. "What was he doing out there?"

"Trying to protect me," I murmured.

It was an awful feeling. Anna's daughter Belinda clung to her mother's skirts, wide-eyed and terrified, her thumb in her mouth. I watched, helpless, as the old woman—Nonna was her name—washed away the crusted blood with tender care, bathing his face. She bound Gilot's ribs with strips of clean linen and lashed his broken hand to a piece of board.

"'Tis beyond my ability to set, young lord," she said,

nodding at his hand. "And I can't be sure he hasn't pierced a lung. I don't like the sound of his breathing. When it's safe, take him to the Temple of Asclepius. You know it?"

"Yes." I remembered the island in the middle of the Tiber. "They can help him?"

She shrugged. "If anyone can. What of you?"

"I'm fine," I said.

Lucius lifted his head. "Don't be an ass, Montrève."

So I suffered Nonna to remove my shirt and probe at the burn on my shoulder, a raw, oozing patch. She swabbed it with salve and bound it with clean linen. I tried to drag the boot from my left foot, but my ankle had swollen and it wouldn't come. In the end, Lucius had to cut it off. He knelt on the floor of the apartment, cradling my foot gently, sawing at the leather with the edge of one of my daggers.

"Sorry," he murmured as I hissed with pain. One corner of his mouth quirked. "This isn't exactly how I imagined undressing you."

Despite everything, I laughed.

"There." Lucius eased the remnant of my boot away, and Nonna took his place, probing judiciously with her fingertips, turning my foot this way and that. It hurt like hell. I rolled my eyes skyward and concentrated on breathing slowly.

She grunted. "Bad, but not broken, I think."

"Imri?" On his pallet, Gilot turned his blind, swollen face in my direction. His voice was anxious. "You're all right? Tell me, please!"

"I'm *fine*." I heard the irritation in my tone, and softened it. Later, I'd tell him the truth. Not now. "It's nothing; just a wrenched ankle."

"Good." He sighed, the tense lines of his body relaxing. "Good."

Nonna bound my ankle, then left. Brigitta went to stand watch at Eamonn's side. Gilot drifted into a fitful sleep, with Anna curled alongside him on his pallet, drowsing and stroking his hair. Little Belinda slept soundly, nestled against her mother.

"A pretty picture," Lucius mused. "He's very loyal to you, isn't he?"

"Yes." Although it wasn't me, not really. Gilot served Montrève. Still, the burden of guilt remained. Here in Tiberium, I *was* Montrève, and keeping me alive appeared to be a tall order. I ran my fingers through my hair. It was growing longer; Claudia must have been pleased. I glanced sidelong at her brother. "And you, too. I owe you a debt, Lucius."

"Oh?" He arched his brows. "How so?"

"For keeping me afoot when I would have fallen," I said honestly. "Someone struck me from behind. You saved me, and you cleared a space when I needed it the most. I'd have gone down for sure if you hadn't." I paused. "How did you manage it?"

Lucius shook his head. "I didn't."

"What do you mean?" I was confused.

"'O, dear my lord' . . ." Head bowed, unruly locks falling over his brow, he toyed with an oil lamp, giving it a quick, secretive smile. "I wish I had. We were parted after the wineshop. All I saw was you starting to fall, and I tried to make my way there. But no. That was someone else broke up the throng and made a passage. I couldn't have gotten to you if they hadn't."

"Who?" I asked.

"I don't know," said Lucius. "But whoever it was, I think they killed to do it."

The night held no answers, only a prolonged period of

fear and uncertainty. After a time, I hobbled out to spell Eamonn at watch. He and Brigitta went to catch a few well-deserved hours of sleep while Lucius kept me company. The street outside our insula was quiet. We could still hear noise elsewhere in the quarter, but here, the worst of it had passed. For the most part we stood and spoke of inconsequential matters. I wasn't ready to confide in him. Not yet. There was too much to tell. First, I needed to tend to Gilot. After that, I wanted answers from Claudia Fulvia.

The rising sun caught us yawning.

"By the Triad!" Lucius rubbed at his bleary eyes. "I'm off, Montrève. I need to catch a few hours of sleep before Deccus Fulvius summons me to give him a student's viewpoint on the rioting. Say what you will, but I don't think he anticipated *this*."

"No," I said, thinking about Claudia's warning. "I daresay he didn't."

Lucius left, and I went out into the city on my own, barefoot and limping, to hire a litter to transport Gilot to the isle of Asclepius. My skin prickled with wariness and I kept my hand hovering over my sword-hilt. Gilot would have had a fit had he known, but he was in no state to protest. In any case, there was no sign of would-be assassins or rioters, only the wreckage left in their wake. The city cohort was on patrol, and wary shopkeepers were assessing the damage and looting done to their businesses. In the Great Forum, I begged an uneasy cobbler to sell me a pair of crudely made rope sandals. He agreed at length, eyeing me with distrust. A subdued pall hung over the city, like the aftermath of a fête that had turned poisonous. I had to go all the way to the wharf, but there I found bearers who agreed to my terms, and I returned to the insula to await them, ignoring the steady, piercing throb in my ankle.

There, everyone slept.

There were only the two pallets, meager and mean. I stood and looked. Gilot lay half on his side, his splinted hand outthrust. I could hear his labored breathing. Anna was curled against his back, Belinda's head tucked beneath her chin. And there on the other pallet was Eamonn, sprawled on his back in snoring splendor. Brigitta's head lay on one brawny shoulder, her limbs thrown carelessly over his.

I envied them. All of them.

"Gilot!" I raised my voice. "Your litter awaits."

By litter and barge, we made the journey.

The isle of Asclepius was a peaceful place; a place of healing. I felt calm descend upon me as we approached. The oarsmen dipped their oars with care, as though not to disturb their passenger. Everything was hushed, quiet. Even the barge docked in near-silence, somber attendants catching the ropes, mooring it noiselessly.

One of the priests of Asclepius glided from the temple on sandaled feet, clad in robes of fine-combed white wool. He had a short black beard and austere features; and dark eyes, as dark as those of the Cruithne, filled with wisdom and the knowledge of pain.

I stood at his approach, rocking the barge. "Please," I said humbly. "Help him."

His dark gaze rested on me. "What would you have me heal?"

I gestured to Gilot. "Him."

The priest bowed his head. "As you wish."

A strange question, I thought; Gilot's injuries were obvious. But then again, he was a priest. Mayhap he saw other wounds, deeper wounds. Of a surety, I had those. The attendants eased Gilot onto a narrow litter, and I followed as they bore him into the temple.

Inside, the priest examined Gilot, peering at his swollen face, gently probing his hand, laying his head on Gilot's chest and listening to his breathing. I stood by anxiously. At last, the priest turned to an acolyte; a grave, sweet-faced young woman. "Comfrey to bathe his eyes," he said to her. "And a tincture of opium and henbane for the pain. Once it takes effect, I will attempt to set his hand."

"Will I be able to use it?" Gilot asked through gritted teeth.

"Perhaps," said the priest. He beckoned to me. "Come."

I followed him through the temple. It was a light, airy space, unadorned save for a tile mosaic on the floor. The rear opened onto a grotto where a spring burbled, forming a natural fountain. I could see gold coins gleaming beneath the water. Behind the spring stood a statue of Asclepius, depicted as a hale, bearded figure. In one hand he bore a tall staff, with a serpent twining its length.

All around the grotto, hanging from every protrusion, were clay votive offerings: arms and legs, hands and feet, hearts, heads, eyes and ears—every portion of the human body. There was somewhat unnerving about the sight.

"Tell me," I said.

The priest faced me squarely. "I can make no promises. Many small bones are broken. He makes his living as a swordsman?"

"Yes." It seemed wrong to lie in this place. "He is sworn to the service of my foster-mother, Phèdre nó Delaunay, the Comtesse de Montrève."

Whether or not that meant somewhat to him, I could not say. "You would be well-advised to make an offering to Asclepius, D'Angeline," he said. "And pray to whomever you pray." The priest paused. "There are ribs broken, and something presses upon his lungs, yet he breathes. For that, there is nothing we can do, save wait. Do you understand?"

I nodded. "Pray."

The priest inclined his head. "Even so."

I sat with Gilot while the priest set his hand, though by that time Gilot was mostly unconscious. A good thing, too. It was a delicate business. By the priest's reckoning, three fingers were broken, and a myriad of the small bones in the back of his hand. Even if it healed without complication, he'd have a hard time gripping a sword. I watched distant flickers of pain cross Gilot's battered face and thought about what a good friend and protector he'd always been to me, despite my best efforts to thwart him. Like me, he was no hero; not like Joscelin, driven by the tireless discipline of his Cassiline vow, capable of impossible feats. He was just a good man, handy with a blade, loyal to a fault. And I . . . I wasn't even that.

I didn't deserve him.

He didn't deserve this.

Anger stirred in me, dark and full of loathing. I thought about my unseen assailant and the men who had done this to Gilot, and the one in particular; the one I'd marked with my daggers. I wished now that I'd done worse. I wanted to hurt him like he'd hurt Gilot.

Once it was done, the young acolyte gave him another draught of opium. With a sigh, Gilot settled into a deeper sleep.

"You'll watch over him?" I asked her.

"Yes, my lord." There was a trace of shyness in her voice.

"Good." I made myself smile. "What's your name?"

"Filomena," she whispered.

"Filomena." I touched her cheek. "My name is Imriel, and this is Gilot. If he wakes before I return, I pray you, tell him I'm fine and all is well, everyone is safe. He'll worry, otherwise. Will you help me in this?"

She swallowed. "Yes, of course."

I left the Temple of Asclepius, taking my anger with me. I didn't know what to do with it or where to go. Pray, the priest had said, but I couldn't. The anger was too big, like a boulder in my heart. I couldn't get around it. There was a dull ache radiating from the middle of my spine where my attacker had struck me. *Told to tell you, that's for Baudoin.*

Baudoin de Trevalion, long dead. He had aspired to the throne. My mother had been his lover, his co-conspirator. Ultimately, his betrayer. She had determined that he wouldn't serve her purposes well enough to suit her, and she'd brought him tumbling down.

I remembered the bitterness in Bertran's voice the night L'Envers had tried to frame me. *Baudoin de Trevalion was executed for treason, and the stench of the Trevalion name still reeked less than Somerville's after your mother was done with it.*

Elua, but I was sick of these coils of intrigue! And I was sick unto death at the thought that it was Gilot paying the price for all of it.

I walked swiftly through the city, heedless of my own safety. I'd gone beyond caring. I almost relished the stab of pain each stride provoked. Nonna had said the ankle wasn't broken; well and good, it would heal. It seemed a fitting punishment. For the first time, I understood why people visited Kushiel's temple to purge their hearts and souls.

Pain might not scourge away guilt, but it helped.

Outside the insula, Canis' barrel lay in the street, abandoned and half-staved. Master Ambrosius was supervising the repair of his shutters. He gave me a sour look as I drew near. "I hope you're pleased with this night's doings, young scholar," he muttered. "Ought to have you thrown out, you and your manservant."

My temper flared. "Oh, indeed?" I accorded him a cynical bow, laying my right hand on the hilt of my dagger. "Well, the next time some drunkard thinks to hurl a torch into your shop and send up a lifetime's worth of tribute to the gods, I'll not bother to stop him."

The incense-maker sucked his teeth. "You did that?"

"For all the good it's worth." I jerked my chin at the barrel. "Where's Canis?"

"The beggar?" He shrugged. "How should I know?"

"He kept your shop from being robbed, once," I said in disgust. "You might be bothered to give a damn."

Master Ambrosius repeated his shrug. "He stinks. It's bad for business. The other one was here, though," he added grudgingly. "The one who brought a message. Didn't leave one, just asked after you."

"My thanks," I said curtly.

I found Anna and told her what the priest had said. She bore the news bravely, but I could see her knuckles whiten as her hands clutched one another. She'd buried one husband young, and it had taken courage to risk caring for another man; her unlikely D'Angeline, nursing his own broken heart. It hurt to see the fear in her eyes.

"May I see him?" she asked in a low tone.

"Later, yes. He'll not wake for a time." I hesitated. "Is there someone who can care for Belinda?" She nodded. "All right, then. I'll come back for you, the city's not terribly safe yet. We can buy a votive-offering for Asclepius together and take it there. Does that suit?"

"Thank you, my lord!" The gratitude in her eyes was worse than the fear. Bobbing an awkward curtsy, she caught my hand and kissed it. I knew then that Gilot had told her who I was, and I repressed a sigh.

"Imriel," I said gently. "Just Imriel."

I left her then and went back into the city. I didn't trust myself to confront Claudia. Not yet. I went first to the Old Forum. It was teeming with a volatile mix of irate citizens and disgruntled students, held in check by a cohort of the princeps' own guard, recognizable by the purple stripe that bordered their white cloaks. I lost myself in the crowd and listened for a time while a group of senators stood upon the rostra and spoke in turn, denouncing both the night's violence and the plans of the Restorationists and the citizen assembly to diminish Tiberium's claim to academic glory.

Neither faction seemed pleased, but there was little to be said in anyone's defense. After the senators spoke, the lord chancellor of the University took the rostra and gave voice to his profound shame at the conduct of the students. He was a venerable figure, and I'd only ever seen him at a distance, but he spoke well, and a number of my fellow students looked abashed. I listened to the crowd, hoping to hear a familiar mutter.

There was no sign of my attacker, nor even the sharp-featured scholar whose neck I had marked. I guessed there wouldn't be; not him, nor a few others whose voices had been loudest in inciting the riots. Scholars' robes or no, I didn't think they were students.

When the lord chancellor had finished, Deccus Fulvius took the rostra and began to denounce his fellow Restorationists for acting in precipitous haste. I didn't stay to listen, slipping away instead to make my way to his domus, taking my coiled anger where it belonged.

Once there, I pushed my way past the servant who admitted me. The atrium was empty, save for the impluvium in the center and the shimmering reflection of sunlight dancing on the walls. When I raised my voice, it echoed.

"Claudia!" I shouted. "Claudia!"

She came.

Her face was anxious, brows knit into creases. They eased at the sight of me. "Imriel! I was worried. I sent Nestor to ask after you, but he could learn nothing."

I crossed the atrium in swift strides, grasping her face in my hands. A knot of fury twisted in my belly. "House Trevalion," I hissed. "That's it, isn't it?"

Claudia turned pale. "Are you hurt?"

"No," I said grimly. "But Gilot is."

Her lids flickered. "I begged you to stay off the street!"

"And you bade me to warn my friends." My thumbs itched, yearning to dig into her flesh. "Did you think I wouldn't listen? Did you *know* someone would try to kill me?"

She tried in vain to pull away. "No! I only knew it would be dangerous out there."

"Oh, it was," I agreed. "Lucius was caught in the middle of it."

"He wasn't supposed to be. Nestor was supposed to find him." There was a trace of fear in her voice. "Is he all right?"

I thrust her from me. "What do you care?"

"He's my *brother*!" Her eyes flashed. We stared at one another, breathing hard. I wanted to hate her, and did. But there was somewhat else there, too. Her face softened, the lines of worry returning. "Imriel, please. Just tell me, is Lucius hurt?"

"He's fine," I said shortly.

Claudia closed her eyes. "Thank you."

I sank onto the marble bench where guests sat to remove their boots, my fury giving way to a deep weariness. "So who is it, Claudia? Bertran? Ghislain? What member of House Trevalion wanted to avenge Baudoin's death badly enough to kill me? Do you care so little for me you were willing to let them do it?"

"I can't . . ." She swallowed. "I didn't think . . . All right. All right!" For a long moment, she stood silent and motionless. There was only the steady rise and fall of her breast. When she spoke, the words emerged flat, devoid of emotion. "It was his sister, Baudoin's sister. Bernadette de Trevalion."

"I see." I rubbed my face. "Does the Guild have proof of this?"

"Yes." Her tone remained even. "There's a man named Ruggero Caccini. He employs a number of unsavory types and accepts commissions for this sort of work. The Guild has found it . . . useful . . . to maintain contact with him. He provides affidavits detailing his commissions."

"For the purpose of blackmail?" I asked.

"For the purpose of information, for which he is remunerated and enjoys a measure of protection." Claudia took a deep breath. "Imriel, that's all I know. That's the coin I was given to entice you. To pay you for your loyalty, should you swear it. I don't even know who holds the proof, although it still could be yours if you prove willing. It's complicated. I swear to you, I didn't believe you were truly in mortal danger."

"Why?" I asked, my voice hard. "Why, Claudia?"

"I can't say," she said brokenly. "Please, please believe me."

"That's the problem." I stood. "I don't."

I meant to leave; I wanted to leave. My decision was made. I wanted to be done with the lot of it—Tiberium, Claudia, the Unseen Guild. But then Claudia drew near me, and I could feel the heat coming off her. In the wake of the riots, the revelation, my emotions were in an uproar. The unstoppable tide of desire rose, my resolve ebbing. Bowing her head, she touched the charred hole in the shoulder of my shirt, the clean bandage beneath. In my haste to get Gilot to the Temple of Asclepius, I'd forgotten what I must look like.

"You *are* hurt," she whispered. "Oh, Imriel! Come here, please."

Elua help me, I went.

Why, I could not say, save that I was angry and tired and hurt, and I wanted to punish us both. While Deccus Fulvius stood upon the rostra and proclaimed his innocence, I took his wife in their bedchamber. It was a fierce coupling, anger-driven. I left marks on Claudia's skin, the impress of my teeth in the full, white curve of her breast. She cried out, but she didn't protest. Not when I bit her. Not when I spread her thighs with an ungentle touch and pinned her hands above her head, driving into her. She didn't need to. In this battle, she had already won. I had already lost. I would take my leave of her without having gained mastery.

Still, there was a strange peace in it.

At least in bed we understood one another.

"Imriel de la Courcel." Claudia toyed with my hair. "What will you do?"

"I don't know." I glanced at her. "Take my concerns to the D'Angeline ambassadress, I reckon. It's about time, don't you think?"

Her brows rose. "Without proof? Imriel, you can't repeat what I've told you. Truly, you can't. Not without endangering us both for exposing the Guild. It's my fault. I shouldn't have trusted you."

I sighed and dragged myself out of her bed; Deccus' bed. "Fine. I've the proof of my own ears, lady. Last night, someone tried to kill me, or at the least, to do me grievous harm.

Baudoin's name was spoken. I don't need the Guild's evidence. I'm not even sure I *want* it."

She gazed at me, lips parted. "Why ever not? You could use it to bring down House Trevalion."

With a wince, I eased my sore and bound left foot into one leg of my breeches, and then the other. Claudia watched me with curious eyes as I stood to pull up my breeches, the way a child might watch a favorite toy being placed out of reach.

"You answer your own question," I said softly. "Because the Guild is ruthless, and it lacks compassion. And I am not certain I want any part of such a thing. I value my life, but I value my honor, too. I don't want to destroy House Trevalion. I just want to be left in peace. When all is said and done, I am D'Angeline, first and foremost. I honor Blessed Elua's precept, and there is little love here." I strung Canis' medallion around my neck and reached for my scorched shirt. "Claudia, I have to go."

She sat up, dragging her fingers through her disheveled hair. "Imriel, listen . . ."

There was a discreet tap on the door of the bedchamber. "My lady," said a muffled voice from the other side of the door. "His lordship returns."

Claudia's fox-brown eyes widened. "Go!"

I went.

Perforce, I exited from the rear of the domus. I ran through the peristyle garden, rope sandals clutched in one hand, leaving a scent of bruised herbs behind me. I gripped a handful of clinging vines and vaulted over the high garden wall.

The landing hurt, jarring my ankle, but mercifully, it was in an unattended property. Sandals in hand, I limped back toward the street. There, outside the Fulvii domus, I sat and donned my sandals, adjusting my sword-belt and the sheath strapped to my left calf.

Everything hurt, and I was tired; tired and confused and sore.

And yet, strangely, my anger had dwindled.

I was alone in Tiberium; alone and nameless. In that moment, I could have gone anywhere, done anything. I could have left the whole complicated mess behind me. House Trevalion, the Guild; all of it. No one knew where I was. Even Gilot had lost track of me. He was safe in the Temple of Asclepius, safer than he would be with me. There was only Claudia who knew my whereabouts, and not for long. If I had wanted to vanish, I could have chosen to do so, then and there.

I wouldn't, though.

"My choice," I said, standing and testing my unsteady ankle. "Mine."

No one heard and no one cared.

Being alone, I thought, was a lonely business.

FORTY-THREE

AFTER THE RIOTING, Tiberium was chastened and quiet. The city cohort and the princeps' guard patrolled the streets in significant numbers. The University closed its doors, presenting a blank face of disapproval to its students. No lectures were held, there or elsewhere.

It was peace, but a sullen one. A few of the shops opened, though one could see evidence of hasty repairs. The inns remained closed. Some students abandoned their scholars' robes, and others wore them defiantly. Still, they kept clear of the city cohort, and there was no violence. By and large, normality was restored, insofar as it was possible.

There was no sign of Canis, which troubled me every time I passed his abandoned barrel.

And, of course, there was Gilot.

In the morning, I escorted Anna to the Temple of Asclepius, where we spent a few hours sitting with Gilot. He had improved a bit with rest. Although his face was swollen and his eye-sockets were black and purple with bruising, he was able to open his eyes. He could see. His broken hand was splinted and immobile, and whether or not it would heal cleanly was anyone's guess.

I didn't say anything to him about the attack. Gilot would

only blame himself, and he needed to heal in peace. But afterward, I thought long and hard about what Claudia Fulvia had told me. Bernadette de Trevalion, mother of my erstwhile friend, Bertran. I barely knew her. I'd met her at Court a few times, but she spent most of her time at the duchy of Trevalion in Azzalle. It was hard to fathom her wanting me dead.

In the dispassionate light of day, it was also hard to imagine confiding in the D'Angeline ambassadress with scant evidence. One sentence muttered in the midst of a riot wasn't terribly convincing. I didn't doubt that she would take me at my word, but it was the uproar that would follow that made me wince. It would reach the shores of Terre d'Ange, acrimonious and bitter. I didn't relish the thought of following in my mother's footsteps and accusing Bernadette de Trevalion of conspiracy, even if it was true.

In the end, I held off telling Denise Fleurais. Instead, I confided in Eamonn.

"If I told you somewhat I couldn't prove and asked you to trust me, would you believe me?" I asked him in the privacy of my insula apartment, where we were sharing a skin of wine I'd bought from a street-vendor. "Because I've need of advice, and you're the only person here I trust unreservedly."

"Of course," he said readily, then hesitated. "Well, it's not about philosophy, is it? I'll not concede an argument unheard."

"No, no." I shook my head. "Do you remember what I said the night of the riot? Someone *did* try to kill me, Eamonn. I was pushed. And I think there may have been a couple other attempts, too. Either way, I know who's behind it."

He refilled my winecup. "Who?"

I took a gulp. "Bernadette de Trevalion. She hired a man here."

Eamonn looked blank. *"Who?"*

"Bertran's mother," I said. "You remember Bertran?"

"Yes, of course." He continued to look blank. "Why, though?"

I sighed. "Ah, gods! I don't know. There was a plot, ages ago. My mother betrayed it. And as a result, Baudoin de Trevalion and *his* mother Lyonette, who was my father's sister, were convicted of treason."

"Enough!" Eamonn held out one hand. "I don't know how you keep them all straight. So it's a blood feud, then?"

I nodded. "I suppose so. Baudoin and Lyonette were condemned to death. He fell on his sword, and she took poison. Bernadette and her father were merely exiled for complicity, although Ysandre gave them clemency later. The other business, that was under the old king's rule, Ganelon de la Courcel. My . . . uncle." It felt strange to say the words. I'd never felt myself to be a king's nephew. "But it was my mother's testimony that convicted them. And she did it a-purpose."

"So it's a blood feud," Eamonn repeated. "Vengeance."

"Yes," I agreed. "So it seems."

He gave me a shrewd look. "And have you told the D'Angeline ambassadress this?"

"Not yet." I met his gaze. "The problem is, I can't prove it, Eamonn. I know it's true. I even know the name of the man Bernadette de Trevalion hired. But I can't prove it, not beyond a shadow of doubt. And if I try, things are likely to get very ugly, here and at home."

Eamonn shrugged. "Would you rather risk another attack?"

"No." I drained my cup. "So if you were me, you'd go to the ambassadress?"

"Me?" Eamonn grinned. "Not likely! If *I* were you, I'd pay a visit on the fellow trying to have me killed, and tell him I'd slice off his ballocks and shove them down his throat if he tried it again. But that's the difference between the Dalriada and D'Angelines. You make everything complicated."

"You know," I said slowly, "you have a point. Not necessarily a good one, but a point."

"Aye, and I might make a better one if you'd tell me more," he observed.

I smiled wryly. "Call it misplaced gallantry, but I can't. I'm sorry. Eamonn, if I can devise a plan for dealing with this on my own terms, are you willing to help?"

He quaffed his wine. "Name the place, Imri. We swore to be like brothers to one another, didn't we? Well, I meant it, no matter how odd and mysterious you're being."

That night, I tossed and turned on my pallet. I thought about the proof that Claudia dangled before me and the Guild's methods. I thought about what Eamonn had suggested, and I thought about what Phèdre would have done and how she'd managed to gain evidence of L'Envers' plotting. Elua help me, I even thought about how my mother had used Baudoin's own private correspondence to condemn him.

By morning, I had conceived of a plan. Except for the foolhardy part, I thought Phèdre might have approved of it. And so, mayhap, would my mother. From what I understood, Melisande Shahrizai had been nothing averse to blackmail if it served her purpose.

I tried not to dwell on that thought.

First I went with Anna to visit Gilot. We had purchased two votive-offerings, a hand and a torso, and hung them in the grotto where the effigy of Asclepius stood. I went there to give her time alone with Gilot, spending my own time thinking and praying. To Asclepius, who ruled over healing in this place; to gentle Eisheth, who brought the healing arts to Terre d'Ange and taught them to her children, along with the gift of music.

I found myself praying to Kushiel, too. His mercy is cruel, but it is just. I offered up my anger and desire for vengeance along with my pain, vowing to lay them all at his feet in exchange for Gilot's life. In my mind's eye, I beheld Kushiel's face, calm and stern, promising nothing. One cannot bargain with the gods.

Still, it made me feel better to try.

Before we left, I met with the priest of Asclepius. I gave him a sealed letter I'd written. "My lord priest, may I trust you with this? It provides for Gilot and the woman Anna, should aught happen to me. It need only be presented to Lady Denise Fleurais at the D'Angeline embassy."

The priest gave me a long, unreadable look. "You may."

"My thanks," I said to him.

He inclined his head. "Perhaps I will ask a favor in return one day."

Afterward, I met up with Eamonn in the Forum as we'd agreed. His face brightened at the sight of me. "You've a plan, haven't you?"

"I do," I said. "Mostly, it calls for you to be silent and imposing."

Eamonn patted the hilt of his sword. "I can do that."

We went to the wharf, where I found the dock-master to whom I'd reported the dead barge-hand. Allaying his impatience with a bribe, I questioned him about the man.

"The city cohort identified him," I said. "A petty ruffian, they said. But since the riot, I've discovered there's reason to suspect he meant me harm. And I've reason to suspect an old enemy of mine may be behind it. Surely you see everything that passes on the wharf. I thought mayhap you might give me a name. Who in Tiberium might employ a man for such a task?"

He glanced sidelong at Eamonn. "Sorry, my lord. I've no idea."

"That's a pity." I sighed. "I was hoping there would be no need to trouble the D'Angeline ambassadress with a personal matter. You see, she's a dear friend of my foster-mother's. Once I tell her, she'll be obliged to see the matter investigated, even if it means closing the wharf to question every barge-hand and dock-laborer in the city."

The dock-master developed a twitch in one eye. "The princeps would never consent."

"Oh, he would, actually," I assured him. "And hold you to blame for it. Did I mention that my foster-mother is also a very dear friend of the Queen's?"

He held my gaze a moment longer, then broke. "Ah, Jupiter! It's nothing any cutpurse in the city couldn't tell you. Like as not it's Ruggero Caccini you're looking for. He's the one they answer to."

"My thanks." I doubled my bribe. "Where might I find him?"

The dock-master pocketed the coins and jerked his chin. "Inn of the Siren," he said sourly. "A few blocks that way."

We found the inn without difficulty. Unlike the inns in the students' quarter, there was no sign of damage sustained during the rioting here on the docks. It was a nicer place than I would have expected; sturdily built, with windows that looked out over the river. The sign above the door sporting a buxom, bare-breasted siren was freshly painted, the colors bright and crisp.

"Huh." Eamonn gazed at it. "Very fancy."

"Crime pays." I clapped his shoulder. "In fact, I'm counting on it."

Inside, the Inn of the Siren's pleasant appearance was belied by its patrons. Unsavory types, Claudia had called them; barge-hands and dock-workers for the most part. They eyed Eamonn and me with taciturn disinterest, more wary than hostile. I approached the bar while Eamonn lingered near the door, arms folded.

The barkeep raised his brows. "Are you lost, lad?"

"I'm looking for Ruggero Caccini," I told him.

He laughed. "Oh, indeed? What business might you have with him?"

"I'm quite curious myself," offered a smooth voice behind me. "Stand me a jug, D'Angeline, and I'm willing to listen."

I turned around. "Messire Caccini."

He went still, and I knew he'd recognized me. Like the inn, he wasn't what I'd expected. Ruggero Caccini was tall, dark, and lean, well-dressed and clean-shaven, with neatly barbered hair. I met his gaze steadily. He was some forty years of age, healthy and prosperous, but there was a shadow of old hunger in his eyes, a memory of gauntness in his face.

"Well, well," he said softly. "*You're* a brave little cockerel." He laid one hand on the hilt of a poniard he carried, and a dozen chairs shifted behind him, men preparing to come to his aid. "Come to beard the lion in his den, have you? Unwise. What makes you think you'd get out alive?" He nodded at Eamonn. "Yon strapping friend?"

"No." I smiled pleasantly. "A letter to be delivered to Lady Denise Fleurais detailing my whereabouts, should I fail to return. 'Tis a gambit I learned from my foster-mother long ago when someone else wanted me dead. But I'm pleased to hear you're inclined to be frank. You're a man of business, I understand. I come bearing an offer."

Ruggero stared at me, then uttered a sharp, barking laugh. "Stand me a jug, D'Angeline! I'm willing to listen."

The barkeep drew us a jug and Ruggero led me to a corner table. I motioned for Eamonn to stay where he was. He shrugged, watching attentively. Ruggero filled two cups, sliding one across the table.

"So," he said. "Offer."

I sipped my wine. "Here's the crux of the matter, Messire Caccini. It seems there have been two, perhaps three, ill-fated attempts on my life. The last occurred during the riot, in which my attacker divulged the name of an old enemy. It made me suspicious of the other occurrences. I've made inquiries among the city cohort and elsewhere, and I believe at least one can be traced to a man in your employ."

"Mayhap." He smiled sardonically.

"Mayhap." I nodded. "'Tis a gamble. I'm willing to take it if I must. But I would prefer to buy out House Trevalion's contract with you."

Ruggero said nothing, but there was a spark of interest in his gaze. He was greedy. From what little Claudia Fulvia had told me, I'd guessed as much. Now that I beheld him, I could see it was born of the old hunger, a childhood of poverty. Ruggero Caccini hungered for wealth, hungered for security. Nothing would ever be enough to allay those old fears.

He raised his winecup, wetting his lips. "Say that I know whereof you speak. And yet I'm a man of my word. I don't renege on a contract."

"Nor have you." I spread my hands. "Attempts have been made."

"For which you bear no grudge?" he asked with candid disbelief.

"If I bore a grudge, you would be dead." The words emerged so coolly that I nearly startled myself. "I could have chosen to come here with a squadron of D'Angeline guards. I did not. Messire Caccini, you are merely a weapon in a quarrel between two of the Great Houses of Terre d'Ange. I no more bear you a grudge than I would an enemy's blade."

"I don't believe you," Ruggero said, but there was doubt now.

I shrugged. "I, too, am a man of my word. Permit me to buy out Trevalion's contract, and I promise you no charges will be brought against you."

"And if I don't?" he asked.

I glanced over my shoulder at Eamonn. He grinned at me, a fierce battle-grin. "Well, messire," I said to Ruggero, "then the matter would become personal, and I would indeed bear a grudge. You and your comrades can take your chances with my friend and me, here and now. Eamonn is very good with his sword, and I'm quite fast. Fast enough, I believe, to take your head off before you could blink. We might not get out alive, but neither would you." I smiled at him. "Or, of course, you could let us go, and take your chances with the judiciary later."

Ruggero looked amused. "I might like those chances."

"You might," I agreed. "I wouldn't count on it. All in all, you might like a fat purse better. What do you care for the squabbling of D'Angeline nobles? This arrangement has failed to prove lucrative. I can cause that to change."

He narrowed his eyes. "Why the offer? What's in it for you? If you know who hired me, you know there's no way I can offer the same service in return. I'm a man of Tiberium, I've no resources beyond the city walls."

"Yes, of course." I took another sip of wine. "All I ask— in addition, of course, to the cessation of attempts on my life—is a signed letter acknowledging your contract with House Trevalion. I don't mean to use it against you, of course. I'll keep my word. But it's a surety against your changing your mind, and a means of keeping *them* in line."

Ruggero Caccini fixed me with another long stare, intent and wondering. I kept my face bland and blank. When all was said and done, I'd stolen a page from the Unseen Guild's book of intrigue, but there was no way he could be sure of it. He wasn't one of them, only one of their tools. And I'd been careful not to leave a trail. I was merely using the skills I'd learned.

Besides, it was a fair offer. It was a better offer than he deserved, but I'd made a promise to Kushiel. I wasn't seeking vengeance, only justice. Let Ruggero Caccini live, and let Gilot live in turn. As for Bernadette de Trevalion, I'd deal with her later.

"All right," he said at length. "Ten thousand denarii."

"For a letter and the privilege of keeping your head on your shoulders?" I laughed. "I'll give you a thousand."

"I've an embittered patron to consider," he said. "Nine thousand."

"Oh, please!" I waved a dismissive hand. "What are *they* going to do? Complain to the ambassadress? I think not. House Trevalion is far, far away and you're in no danger. I'll give you two thousand." I paused, curious. "How did they come to find you, anyway?"

Ruggero bared his teeth in a wolfish grin. "Seems the lady of the House made my old master's acquaintance many years ago, here in Tiberium. You D'Angelines ought to be more careful about who you send into exile bearing grudges. Eight thousand."

"Did the lady act alone?" I asked. "I'm minded to stand pat at two thousand, but it might be worth another five hundred to know."

We haggled back and forth, settling on a sum of four thousand five hundred denarii, which also bought me the information that, to the best of Ruggero's knowledge, the lady had acted alone. The sum was, fortunately, rather less than I had on account at the banking house where I'd presented a generous letter of credit from my factor. It was a good thing, after all, that I'd chosen to live as modestly as I had. We agreed to meet at the Fountain of the Chariot at sunset the following day to conclude our deal.

When it was settled, Ruggero and I both rose and shook hands solemnly. His grip was warm and solid. "You're an odd one, aren't you?" he said, bemused. "Tell me, why *didn't* you go to the ambassadress to accuse me? It would have been a good deal cheaper."

"Truly?" I frowned. "It's a personal matter. And I don't like to be indebted."

Ruggero smiled slightly. "Strangely enough, I believe I understand."

"Yes," I said. "I know."

I turned away from him. What alerted me, I could not say. A rustle of cloth, an indrawn breath. The sound of someone shifting in a chair, a belated realization dawning on Eamonn's face at the door. Heedless of my swollen ankle, I whirled, taking a step backward and drawing my sword.

Someone hissed through his teeth.

"Down, down!" Ruggero Caccini removed his hand from the hilt of his poniard and spread his arms, still smiling. The point of my blade was aimed at his throat. With a single step,

I could have run him through. "Down, lads," he repeated. "Forgive me," he added to me. "I was curious. You *are* fast."

"I wasn't boasting," I said shortly.

"No," he agreed. "But now I know."

I sighed. "Tomorrow, sunset."

"Of course," Ruggero promised. "I was merely . . . curious."

I shook my head. "I told you, messire. My word is good."

Eamonn opened the door to the inn. "Time to go, Imri," he said, ushering me out. He closed the door behind us, and no one followed. I breathed deeply, drawing in the scent of the Tiber River. The siren sign creaked in the light breeze.

"So!" Eamonn said brightly. "That seemed to go well."

I thought about it. "You know, it could have gone worse."

FORTY-FOUR

ON THE MORROW, Ruggero Caccini kept our appointment.

I hadn't been sure he would, not after the way we'd parted. He did, though. As the sun was setting over the seven hills of Tiberium, Ruggero appeared at the Fountain of the Chariot, accompanied by a pair of companions. I was glad we were meeting in the Great Forum with members of the city cohort in plain sight.

"Here," he said, thrusting a folded sheet of parchment at me.

I scanned it quickly in the fading light. It was written in a heavy scrawl, but it was legible. Everything was in order. He had not detailed the attempts made, but he'd rendered the commission clearly and identifed Bernadette de Trevalion by name. It would suffice. "Will you affix your thumbprint, messire?"

Ruggero scowled. "Where's my money?"

Eamonn stepped forward, jangling a heavy satchel. I raised my brows. "Your thumbprint, messire? 'Tis for surety's sake."

He grumbled, but he did it. I unstoppered a small bottle

of ink I'd brought, and Ruggero daubed his thumb and placed a clear impress at the bottom of the page.

"My thanks," I said, nodding to Eamonn.

Ruggero accepted the satchel and took a quick glance at its contents, then handed it to one of his men. "I'll count it later," he said. "If it's short, you'll hear from me."

I blew on his thumbprint to hasten its drying. "It's not."

"D'Angeline." His tone was flat. I glanced up. "If you fail to keep your word, if your ambassadress' guards come for me, you *will* die. That, I promise you. With nothing to lose, I will reach out from the gaol with every means at my disposal. Every brigand, every unscrupulous mercenary, every chambermaid and cook willing to be bribed, will become your enemy. I'll spend every last brass sesterce I've ever earned to ensure your death."

"Fair enough," I said.

Unexpectedly, Ruggero grinned. "On the other hand, if you *do* keep it . . ." He shrugged. "Consider me a friend. If you've enemies in Tiberium, I'd gladly do business with you again."

With that, he and his companions took their leave. Eamonn and I watched them until we were certain they were gone. I checked the thumbprint and found the ink had dried, folded the letter, and thrust it into my doublet.

"What *do* you mean to do with it, Imri?" Eamonn asked, curious.

"I don't know," I said. "I haven't decided."

"I'm sure it will be interesting." He eyed me. "Someday, I truly hope you'll be able to tell me what all this mystery is about."

"So do I," I said. "Believe me, so do I."

After the deal with Ruggero Caccini was struck, a pervasive sense of menace was lifted. I was glad to have settled the matter, for once on my own terms. Whether or not the Guild knew what I'd done, I couldn't say and didn't much care. I'd done nothing to expose them, given them no cause to object to my actions. All I had done was take matters into my own hands, using the very methods they'd instilled in me. No word came from Claudia, and I made no effort to contact her. I was content to let the matter lie.

I still felt ensnared, but the knot had loosened.

In the mornings, I went with Anna to visit Gilot. In some ways, his condition was improving. He hurt, though. It hurt him to draw breath. Not just his rib cage, but a sharp pain, somewhere deep inside. A bone splinter, the priest said. Left alone, it might heal, might fuse to the bones of his ribs. Or it might shift and kill him. There was nothing to do but pray.

So I prayed.

In the afternoons, I met with a handful of my fellow students at the wineshop, where we attempted to converse, bereft of Master Piero's guidance. There were only a few of us left—Eamonn, Brigitta and Lucius, Akil the Umaiyyati, and a quiet, thoughtful Tiberian named Vernus. The rioting had taken its toll and a number of students had left.

Brigitta was angry: angry at the rioters, angry at the Restorationists and the citizen assembly; angry at Master Piero.

"Why does he punish us?" she burst out one afternoon. "It is unfair!"

"Why do you assume it's a punishment?" Lucius asked mildly. "None of the masters are seeing their students." It had been Lucius who'd taken it upon himself to call upon Master Piero at his residence to ensure that he was well and wanted for nothing. I'd gained a new respect for him since the night of the riots, and not just because he had helped save my life. He seemed changed from the insouciant Caerdicci nobleman I'd first met.

Brigitta glared at him. "It's all right for *you*! I only have a short time here."

"Why is that?" I asked curiously. "Why can't you stay longer?"

"No reason you would understand," she muttered. "You're a man and free to do as you please."

I spread my hands. "Try me."

It was Eamonn who coaxed her to tell the tale; how, with her mother's aid, she had defied her father's wishes to come to Tiberium to study. She was a member of the Manni, a southern Skaldic tribe—they have a long history of dealing with the Caerdicci, and are reckoned among the most civilized of the Skaldi. Although of a surety, the Manni went to war alongside Waldemar Selig. I remember, Phèdre said it was one such who bore a letter from my mother to Selig. That was how she had uncovered the true depth of my mother's treachery.

Brigitta's father despised all things not of Skaldia, but her mother had a more pragmatic outlook. She was minded to see the future of their steading engaged in a broader discourse and trade with other nations. And so she had conspired to send her daughter to Tiberium, on the condition that she stay no longer than six months. Any longer and her brother Leidolf would be dispatched to fetch her back.

"Why did you want to come so badly?" I asked her.

"You ask a lot of questions." Brigitta fidgeted with her winecup, turning it in her hands. "Because I want to *understand*, D'Angeline." She looked up, a fierce light in her face. "Why things happen. Why we went to war. Why we lost. You don't know what it's like to grow up in the shadow of defeat. It's always there, always hanging over us. Why? Why are people the way they are?"

"Why, indeed?" Lucius murmured. "We are meant to be scholars, seekers after truth. And yet"—he gestured toward the door of the wineshop and the street beyond—"behold how swiftly we turned to violence."

"*You* didn't," Eamonn said helpfully. "You argued against it, Lucius."

"Oh, yes." He gave a wry smile. "Just before my opponent hurled me against the wall, Prince Barbarus. A most effective argument."

"There is honor in battle." Akil drained his cup, slamming it onto the table. His hawkish brows met in a scowl. "So my people believe, and I believe it, too. Even Master Piero acknowledges that honor is a virtue. Is it not so?"

"If the battle is honorable, of course," Eamonn offered. "But what if it is not?"

"And who decides?" Vernus added.

"Skaldia sought to better itself," Brigitta said hotly. "Waldemar Selig sought a better future for his people. Was that wrong? I say it was not. You may contest the means, but do you deny it was an honorable cause?"

Lucius waved a dismissive hand. "You can't separate the means from the cause, Brigitta. In theory, perhaps, but not in practice. We are dealing in realities here." His gaze lighted on me, keen and interested. "What do you say, Montrève?"

"I don't know," I said slowly. There was too much here, too much present at the table. And I knew too much. "I want to understand, too. Yes, the Skaldi were misguided. But . . ." I swallowed against the lump in my throat. "They were misled. Waldemar Selig was misled by those who preyed upon his desires, his ambition." My mother's face swam before my eyes, implacable and beautiful. I shuddered at the memory.

I'd only ever seen her twice. The first time, I had been a child. I had believed what Brother Selbert had told me, and I had loved her.

The second time . . . the second time, I had been a child in years only. That was after Daršanga, when Phèdre had taken me to see her. There had been tears in her eyes then. My mother's eyes, deep and blue as twilight. *Do you even know what you look like?* Erytheia had asked me. I did. It was why I wasn't overly fond of mirrors.

Melisande.

"That's true." Vernus frowned. "There was some plot within Terre d'Ange itself, wasn't there? It all took place before I was born. I never quite understood what happened or why."

Eamonn glanced at me and cleared his throat. "Perhaps we might speak of something else," he said. "It may have happened before we were born, but three of us at this table are children of that war, and it is a painful subject."

"I respect the lady's sorrow." Akil inclined his head toward Brigitta. "But why should it be a painful subject for you, Dalriadan? Or him?" He pointed at me. "You won."

"Have you ever been in battle?" Eamonn asked. "Any of you?"

Lucius and Vernus shook their heads, and Brigitta, reluctantly. I said nothing. Eamonn knew well enough what I'd witnessed, though I wasn't sure if the massacre at Daršanga could properly be called a battle.

"I stood three sword-challenges to earn the right to come to Tiberium." Akil pushed up his sleeve to reveal the pale welt of a scar on the brown skin of his forearm. He flashed a rare grin. "My father will have my head when he learns

I've been studying with mad Master Piero instead of learning to be a Caerdicci diplomat."

"Single challenges?" Eamonn asked. Akil nodded. "It's not the same." He poured wine all around, refilling our cups. "When I was sixteen, there was quarrel between a Dalriadan clan-lord and a clan-lord of the Tarbh Cró in the north." He shrugged. "A land dispute, but there is bad blood there, old blood. The Cruarch offered to send his army and mediate, but my mother refused. It is important for the Dalriada to maintain our independence. So we went to war."

I sat quietly while he told the story, having heard it before. Eamonn had killed two men and come through the battle unscathed, but he had watched comrades die, hard and ugly.

"There's glory in it," he acknowledged. "Dagda Mor! It's why I like to fight. When the battle-frenzy fills you, you feel like a god, I think." He paused, remembering. "But then you hear a friend's voice begging you to help, and you see your friend's guts falling out of a hole in his belly, and you can't stop to help, because someone is trying to kill you, so you have to keep going. You tread upon a corpse and realize it's a man who taught you how to hunt when you were ten years old. You see the woman who just got married run through by a spear, falling over her husband's body." The others were hushed, listening. Eamonn shook his head. "And when it's over," he said simply, "they're still dead. Victory doesn't matter to the dead, nor to the living who mourn them."

No one said anything.

"So!" Eamonn took a deep breath. "That is why war is a hurtful subject, even for the victors. And that is why I am here, trying to become wise."

Lucius raised his cup. "Hear, hear."

On the following day, word was released that the University was opening its doors, and Lucius went to see if Master Piero was in attendance. He wasn't, but there was a note pinned to the door of his study, bidding his students to meet him at the butchers' market early in the morning. Lucius passed the word to the rest of us, and I made arrangements with Anna to visit Gilot later in the day.

It was a strange choice of meeting places, and I daresay all of us wondered at it. The butchers' market was not an array of shops like those in the fora, where Tiberian housewives bought their goods, but a vast open-air market, adjacent to the slaughterhouses, where the country herders and farmsteaders brought their livestock for sale. It is not a place one visits for pleasure, and it was hard to imagine what lesson Master Piero wished us to take from it. Still, we went.

Even in the early hours, the stink and din was fearful. Pigs squealed, cattle bawled, goats uttered mournful bleats, and all manner of fowl raised a clamor. Everywhere, there was a smell of animals, dung, and feathers. Vendors and shopkeepers haggled with the owners, and a steady stream of animals was led to the slaughterhouses.

And there, in the midst of it, was Master Piero, his hands folded in the sleeves of his robe.

He looked thin and worn, but his eyes were clear and there was a calmness to his face. He waited until we were all assembled—the six who remained—before addressing us.

"Walk with me," he said. "And observe."

Without waiting for our responses, Master Piero plunged into the marketplace. Exchanging glances, we shrugged and followed him.

It was no pleasure-stroll. Since I didn't know what Master Piero wanted us to see, I treated the excursion as one of Phèdre's memory games. I numbered the different livestock, and listened to the cacophony of voices, marking accents and dialects. I marked faces, height and weight, attire. I marked the way their eyes cut toward us and sheered away, taking note of Master Piero's scholar's robe, the gaggle of students in his wake. We were not welcome here, but they endured our presence. How not? They were too busy to do otherwise.

Master Piero led us on a winding course through the market and into the slaughterhouses themselves, paying no heed to the mistrustful glances, but merely looking deeply at all he saw, his face grave and somber.

I'd never visited an abattoir before, and I never need do so again. Burly men bent to their tasks, splashed with blood to the shoulders. Cleavers flashed; animals bellowed and died. Carcasses were hung and drained, and rivers of blood ran in stone channels like it had done in Daršanga. I fought against a wave of sickness.

"Are you all right?" Eamonn asked in a low voice, steadying me with a hand beneath my elbow. I nodded, wordless.

"It's just livestock," Brigitta said irritably.

Lucius, too, looked a bit pale. "'Tis the scale that's daunting, lady."

I said nothing. When all is said and done, there is a great deal of difference between seeing a pig and a woman slaughtered before one's eyes. Still, the blood gushes the same from a slit throat, and I did not care to be reminded. How close had I come to doing it myself when I marked the agitator's neck during the riots? I didn't even want to think on it.

"It is the people I brought you to see," Master Piero said in his mild voice.

And so we looked. Men; it was almost all men. They performed their chores with brutal efficiency. Hoisting carcasses; skinning them, cleaving them into manageable portions. Striding through the slaughterhouse, hunks of meat on their shoulders. Shoveling masses of sawdust soaked with blood, piss, and dung.

Master Piero beckoned. "Come."

We followed.

He led us on a long journey that day; longer than any of us reckoned. From the butchers' market, we went to the wharf, and there we watched barge-men unloading other goods for sale, hopeful merchants and merchants' wives directing them anxiously. At least it smelled better. But the sun was growing high overhead, and my ankle throbbed with pain, an ache echoed by my burned shoulder.

We went to other places, too. We followed a Tiberian noblewoman in her litter, her bearers sweating beneath their burden, their faces stoic. We went to the baths, where we stood and watched the attendants at their labors, and they shot us wary glances. We went to a laundresses' establishment, where flush-faced women stirred massive pots of clothing with long-handled paddles.

I watched the people we saw, and I watched Master Piero, whose expression never changed. I watched my fellow students react with weariness, perplexity, and anger.

"No more!" It was Akil who balked, on the outskirts of the dyers' district. His nostrils flared, although whether at the stench or with outrage, I could not say. "Master, I demand to know. What is the meaning of this?"

Master Piero regarded him, then turned abruptly. "Come, and I will tell you."

For a mercy, he led us this time to a small park. There was a stele bearing an inscription informing us that it was a gift of his majesty Caius Maximius, the fifth princeps of the city-state of Tiberium. It was simple and unadorned, which made me think well of Caius Maximius. At Master Piero's invitation, we sprawled on the grass beneath a willow that bent its limbs over a small pond.

At least there was shade. I rubbed my aching ankle, suppressing a groan of relief.

"Dagda Mor!" Eamonn whispered. "I'm perishing of hunger."

"Shhh!" Brigitta favored us with a scowl.

Master Piero waited while we settled. "There is something I wanted you to see today," he said at last. "Do you know what it was?"

"Whatever it was, it stank," muttered Akil.

"Yes." Master Piero turned his gaze on him, luminous and tranquil. "It stank. It stank of humanity, of blood and sweat and labor." He stood before us, folding his arms in his sleeves. "I have been fasting," he mused. "Since the rioting. So many students, so angry! Why?"

"Master!" Vernus protested. "The University—"

"The University is a place of brick and stone," he said to Vernus. "Nothing more."

Lucius frowned. "Yes, but . . . it is, Master. Not the edifice, no, but that which it houses. Knowledge. Wisdom. The freedom to pursue them."

"And will wisdom die without a roof over its head?" Master Piero asked gently.

I thought about Canis; and I thought, too, of Jebe-Barkal and Saba. Of the Covenant of Wisdom that had been broken. "No, my lord," I said aloud. "But it will die if it is not passed on, mouth to ear, generation to generation. That is what the University stands for. It is the institution and not the edifice that matters. I think that is what Lucius was saying," I added, with an apologetic glance in his direction.

Lucius merely nodded.

"Indeed." Master Piero's gaze softened. "And yet, at what cost?" Seeing a belligerent look dawning on Brigitta's face, he raised one hand. "I cast no blame here. I trust you all conducted yourselves in accordance with the principles and virtues which we have agreed to hold dear. And yet there were many, many students angry with the citizen assembly for supporting the proposed decree."

"Shouldn't we be?" Vernus asked in genuine perplexity. "Are you not?"

"No." Master Piero shook his head. "I am disappointed in those in the Senate who call for Restoration at the cost of knowledge, for they should know better. But the citizen assembly is another matter." He gestured at us. "Vernus, your father is an aedile, is he not? And Lucius, all of Tiberium knows your sister is wed to a senator, and your family once ruled Lucca. Eamonn's mother rules his people, and Brigitta, your father is the lord of his steading. Akil, your father is a Sayyed, and holds a position of honor among the Umaiyyati. And Imriel . . ." He paused. "You were adopted into a noble D'Angeline household."

"What has that to do with anything?" Akil asked.

"And what were we supposed to *see*?" Brigitta muttered.

"Life." I remembered somewhat Canis had said. "Mankind, dog-rank and stinking. Why the fate of the University doesn't matter to the citizen assembly. And why we have no right to despise them for it; they, who perform the tasks we shun. Am I right, Master?"

Master Piero watched me with a steady gaze. "Do you take pleasure in being right, Imriel nó Montrève? Do you suppose this is merely an *exercise*?"

"No, Master!" It seemed unfair, this attack. After all, I was aiding him in making his point. I drew myself up, cross-

legged, and inclined my head, wrestling my temper into sub-
mission. "Forgive me, and give me your counsel."

He sighed, tucking his hands into his sleeves. "I did not
bring you here for counsel, merely to think about what you
have seen this day. The lives of the hardworking citizens
your fellow students treated with such disdain; and the lives,
even harder, of those who labor for them, slaves and freed-
men alike. It is true, they care little for the University. And
why should they, when they have no money to pay the bursar's fee and no time to spend in idle study? Why should
they, when they would benefit more from thriving trade than
a rabble of young gentry with tight purse strings?"

"Well." Lucius smiled. "Some of us spend freely."

"Oh, indeed." Master Piero didn't quite return his smile,
but there was a hint of one hovering about his lips. Clearly,
I thought with some annoyance, Lucius was his favorite student. "You do your part, Lucius Tadius."

"But . . ." Brigitta narrowed her blue eyes. "Master, are
you saying you favor closing the University?"

"No, child," he said gently. "You have not been listening.
I am saying I favor my students looking deeper into the
causes that move men's hearts. I am saying that you are children of wealth and influence." He did smile, then. "You may
not have it to wield here and now, but for most of you, it is
your birthright. When you do, I want you to do so wisely."

With that, he left us for the day.

We argued over his lesson all the way back to the students' quarter; all of us except Eamonn, who pronounced
himself too hungry to think. It hadn't sat well with Akil, and
Brigitta was perturbed, unable to see past the threat to the
University. Vernus said little, while Lucius argued both sides
of the matter. He did it well, though betimes I think he
merely did it to revel in his own cleverness.

For my part, I felt the burden of an obscure guilt.

Of course, there was little new in that. Whatever else I'd accomplished, I was still deceiving my friends, lying to Master Piero. Evasion was subtle kin to a lie, he'd said, and I was filled with evasion.

To my unexpected delight, when I returned to the insula, I found Canis struggling with his half-staved barrel. I was so relieved to see him, I nearly embraced him. "Canis! You're alive."

"Should I be otherwise?" he asked mildly.

"No, of course not." I helped him pound the broken slats, held in place by rusting strips of metal, into a semblance of their former shape, covertly studying him as I did. He looked marginally clean; cleaner than I'd ever seen him. There were fading traces of a bruise on his right cheekbone, and the knuckles of his left hand were scabbed. "Were you in a fight?"

"Weren't we all?" Canis smiled broadly at me, revealing a gap where a molar was missing. "You did try to warn me, Imriel. Thank you."

"Where have you been?" I asked.

He pointed in the direction of the Great Forum. "There is a barber who let me sleep in the baths until it was safe. I swept his floor and he pulled my tooth for free, although he made me bathe first." He looked thoughtful. "It hurt quite a bit."

"The tooth or the bath?" I inquired.

"Both," Canis said. "The attendant scrubbed very hard."

I laughed. "Canis . . . you can't go on living in a barrel. Why don't you let me ask about lodgings at the insula? I have coin, I'd be glad to pay."

"Oh, no!" His brown eyes widened. "Please, don't."

"Why ever not?" I asked him.

He looked away, his jaw working unconsciously as he probed at his missing tooth with his tongue. "Because it would take away my freedom," he said at length. "And I like it, Imriel. I like it very much. I live upon the kindness of others, and every day I see and learn so much. And yet I am beholden to no one, and no one is beholden to me. My life is my own, and I carry it with me." He looked back at me, guileless as a child. "Haven't you ever wanted to be free? To shed your name, to shed your very self?"

"Oh, once or twice," I said wryly.

Canis beamed at me. "Then you understand!"

"Yes." I sighed. "And no." I clapped a hand on his shoulder. "No mind. I'm glad you're well. I was worried."

"You're very kind," he said obligingly.

I thought about my recent expedition into the art of blackmail and extortion. I thought about Claudia and our violent lovemaking; and about the shadows that lay behind it. Valerian House, and Sephira in bonds, jerking as the whip kissed her skin. Saying farewell to Sidonie and gripping her arms hard enough to bruise. Phèdre; the look in her eyes when we recognized one another for what we were, in that single heartbeat before I thrust her away. Ah, Elua! Wanting, always wanting. And acting, heedless and impetuous. Gilot, his sword drawn to defend me on the outskirts of Night's Doorstep, where I'd nearly run down an angry nobleman's party. Gilot, seasick; Gilot, frightened and estranged on the dockside in Ostia, a foreigner far from home. Gilot, lying in the temple of Asclepius, battered and broken, a victim of my stubborn pride.

"No," I said. "But I try."

Canis tilted his head, considering me. An errant shaft of sunlight caught his face, turning it momentarily into a gilded mask. His thick black hair was curly with washing, no

FORTY-FIVE

LIFE IN TIBERIUM resumed its normal pace.

Or almost, at any rate. The number of Master Piero's students dwindled. I wasn't sure, not at first. He kept imperfect records, and attendance was betimes spotty. But within a few days, we learned. We had lost Akil and Vernus. They had transferred their allegiance, going to study with other Masters; ones who might prove more useful to their future careers. It surprised me, a little. Not Akil; I had known he was discomfited. But Vernus surprised me, for I thought he had valued Master Piero's lessons.

And it surprised me that despite everything, Lucius Tadius stayed.

One evening, in the wineshop, I told him so.

"Why?" he asked, swaying a little in his seat. He was drunk; we were all drunk. His hazel eyes glinted. "Why do you say so?"

I shrugged. "You're more serious than I reckoned on first meeting, that's all."

"I *am* serious." Lucius pointed at me. "Serious as death, Montrève. In less than a month's time, I'm off to be wed and assume my duties in Lucca. I mean to make the most of my time in Tiberium. What did I tell you? I told you Master

Piero was the purest natural philosopher since the Hellene Sokrates. I believed it then, and I believe it now. Don't you?"

"Near enough," I said, thinking of Canis.

"Oh, near enough, is it?" Lucius scoffed. "And *you* question *me*!"

"Peace, lads," Eamonn rumbled in his deep voice. "It's not a contest." He sat at his ease, one brawny arm slung over the back of Brigitta's chair. For better or for worse, it seemed they were a pair. She was still prickly, as prickly as ever. Only now, Eamonn seemed exempt from her distrust. Although it wasn't, it felt like a betrayal.

"No one said it was," I said pointedly. "We're just talking."

Lucius nodded. "Mind yourself, Prince Barbarus."

We chuckled, both of us, as Eamonn shot us a significant look and rose to see to the refilling of our empty winejug. I liked Lucius a great deal. The better I knew him, the more I liked him. Betimes I wished I could have grafted his nature onto Claudia's form, the way gardeners do with plants to create a new strain, combining the best of elements.

"What about you?" Lucius asked when Eamonn returned. "Brigitta's right, you do ask a lot of questions. But when all's said and done, Montrève, you're a bit on the reticent side when it comes to talking about yourself."

"Oh, there's not much to tell," I said.

Across the table, Eamonn snorted.

Lucius raised his brows. "Now that," he said, "I find hard to believe. I know how you came to find Master Piero, but what brought you to Tiberium in the first place? When so many D'Angelines have turned away from the University, what made you come?"

I traced the rim of my cup, thinking how best to reply.

"Lots of things. Eamonn. I wanted to study with him; we talked about it during his time in Terre d'Ange. And I wanted to follow in Anafiel de Montrève's footsteps and learn more about him."

"I remember," Lucius said. "The arts of covertcy, wasn't it? You said something about it at Deccus' dinner party. Did you ever find out?"

A hot flush suffused my face, and I found myself grateful for the poor lighting in the wineshop. With the memory of the dinner party came uncomfortable thoughts of Claudia. It seemed like a long time ago that I had spoken so rashly of matters concerning the Unseen Guild. "No," I said shortly. "Like as not, it was just a family fable."

"Pity," he mused. "It would have been interesting to know." Lucius regarded me. "So what *is* your family like, Montrève? The gods know, I've told you enough about mine, ghosts and all." He laughed. "What familial responsibilities are *you* shirking?"

Eamonn stirred. "Lucius—"

"No." I held up a hand to forestall him. "It's all right. It's just . . . Lucius, there are some things I'd rather not discuss."

The silence that followed was uncomfortable. "Fine," Lucius said at length, sounding puzzled and hurt. "I'll stop troubling you with unwelcome questions." He pushed his chair back and stood. "You know, Montrève, I'm glad of your friendship, but I'd appreciate it more if you'd let me reciprocate it."

With a courtly bow, he took his leave. I drained my cup and sighed. Once again, I'd managed to be hurtful and unfair to someone who meant me only good; a guilt compounded by the knowledge that I'd been carrying on a torrid affair with his sister, whose motives were suspect at best and mayhap downright dangerous.

"Sorry," Eamonn muttered.

I shook my head. "It's not your fault."

"Was it a lovers' quarrel?" Brigitta asked with interest. "Lucius likes men."

"I know," I said. "And no."

"Because Eamonn said in Terre d'Ange—" she persisted.

I raised my voice. "Will you please *shut up*!"

Rather to my surprise, she did. A few other patrons stared, then looked away. What had happened to all the polite D'Angeline niceties that Phèdre had taught me? Once upon a time, I'd had manners fit for an adept of the Night Court. Now it seemed all I could do was blunder about, causing damage to those I cared for. Master Piero wanted us to learn to be compassionate and wise, and I couldn't even help a beggar on the street.

Claudia's lessons and the Guild's scheming had had their effect. I'd been so proud of myself for using their tools to solve my own problem, so pleased with my success. And now it seemed I'd become better at plotting, lying, and dealing with thugs like Ruggero Caccini than engaging my friends. We spoke a great deal of *virtue* among ourselves, but there was precious little of it in my life.

"Imriel," Eamonn said gently, "go home and sleep. With all that's happened, and worrying about Gilot, and . . . whatever it is, you're worn ragged. Go."

He was right and he was worried. I could see it in his eyes. He was a friend; my one true friend. Phèdre said that about Hyacinthe, and I was coming to understand its value. I'd already confided in Eamonn once, and he'd trusted me enough to aid me without demanding answers. I wanted to stay, wanted to pour my heart out to Eamonn and tell him everything. But there was Brigitta beside him, her ire dampened to a low glower. And there was Claudia's threat hanging over me, backed by the menace of the Unseen Guild, capable of inciting riots. Mayhap its tentacles did not reach so far as Alba, but here in Tiberium, it was real. I'd learned that much.

I went.

On the morrow, I elected to miss Master Piero's lecture, and instead escorted Anna to the Temple of Asclepius.

Gilot's condition was improving, which was one shining spot of hope in my life. The swelling around his eyes had receded and the bruises were fading to unlikely streaks of greenish yellow, as though he sported a strange, sickly domino. He was able to hobble about on foot, though his chest hurt whenever he took a deep breath.

His hand . . . well. The priest said it would be weeks before the splints could be removed, and there was no telling what we would find. But he was better, or at least parts of him were.

"Name of Elua!" Gilot grimaced, trying to shove a twig beneath the bindings on his hand. "It itches."

Anna batted gently at the twig he held. "Leave it, Gilot."

"It *itches*!" he repeated plaintively.

"You're as bad as Joscelin." Perched on a stool beside his bed, I smiled at him. "When the chirurgeon examined him in Nineveh, after his arm was broken, he gave Phèdre a salve to use once the splint came off. She had to hide it, or he'd have torn off the splint and slathered himself night and day."

"Joscelin." Gilot smiled back at me. "Wish *he'd* been there, eh?"

"Ah, well." I thought about Daršanga, the Mahrkagir's festal hall, and the circle of bodies rising, rising ever higher, Joscelin at its center. "I don't know, Gilot. There were innocent people out there, caught up in the rioting. He might have wreaked an awful lot of Cassiline havoc."

"Still." Gilot drew a breath, then coughed and winced. "It worked, this salve?"

I nodded. "It helped, I think. But it was a Tiberian chirurgeon who set the arm in the first place." It wasn't, not really. Phèdre had done it, following the mortally wounded Drucilla's instructions; both of them weeping, Joscelin pale and sweating, cursing in terms no Cassiline Brother should know. *Remember this*, Phèdre had said to me. *Remember her courage. Remember them all.*

I did.

But I didn't think Gilot needed to know.

I told him another story, about how Phèdre had suffered broken ribs after falling from the cliffs of La Dolorosa into the ocean. A Tiberian physician had tended her, too; a Hellene, actually, a former slave. But he was trained in Tiberium, and it made Gilot feel better.

"So I have somewhat in common with them both," he mused.

"You do," I said, touching his good hand. I didn't tell him that Phèdre had never mentioned a persistent, stabbing pain when she sought to draw breath, or that it had been Joscelin's left arm that was broken and not his sword-hand. Anna's gaze dwelled upon my face, shadowed and somber. She knew, the way women do. "Have a care, Gilot. I'll be back."

I sat in the sunlight-drenched grotto, thinking. The effigy of Asclepius gazed across the isle, his shadow pooled at his feet in the burbling spring, pierced with golden glints from the coins that had been thrown there. I propped my own foot on the ledge of the fountain. The swelling in my ankle had gone down, and it was turning the hues of Gilot's face. Asclepius' serpent coiled the length of his staff, whispering counsel in his ear. Votive-offerings hung all around. For a while, I'd been able to pick out ours, but already it was hard.

New offerings eclipsed the old. The paint on the fired clay was fading, turning muted.

I unstrung Canis' medallion from around my neck, pondering it.

Wisdom. What was wisdom?

"What is it you have there?"

I looked up to meet the priest's gaze. "A luck-token, my lord," I said, handing it to him. "A gift of a philosopher-beggar, who may be more than he seems."

"A Cynic," the priest acknowledged, seeing the crude lamp stamped on the clay disk. He sat beside me, turning the medallion in his long, clever fingers. He paused, frowning. "Who gave this to you?"

"Canis." I felt silly, saying it. "He lives in a barrel."

"Canis, the dog." The priest bowed his head, his bearded lips moving in a smile. "Here," he said. "Feel."

I nearly pulled away; I still didn't like to be touched without my leave. But I relented and suffered the priest to grasp my hand and guide it. With my fingertips, I felt a series of notches etched into the rim of Canis' medallion.

"Once," said the priest, "there was one such as me, a healer, a priest sworn to the vows of Asclepius. But his eyesight failed as he grew older." He gave me a sidelong glance. "Still, he believed in his calling. And he continued to treat his patrons, experimenting with different treatments. He devised a system of notation that he might read with his fingers. His notes have all been transcribed, of course, but I saw one of his tablets once. My teacher showed it to me. On every tablet, he began with this inscription."

The hair on the back of my neck stood on end. "What does it say?"

The priest pressed the medallion into my palm, folding my fingers over it. "'Do no harm,'" he said simply. "It is the first thing we learn. It is our precept. And that is what it says here. 'Do no harm.'"

"Canis!" The word emerged in a hiss. The snare of intrigue tightened around me once more. Anger rising, I clenched my hand on the medallion. "So he *is* part of it. 'Do no harm'? What's that supposed to mean? I swear, in Elua's name, I am going to *beat* the truth out of him!" The clay disk cracked beneath the force of my grip, jagged edges biting into my palm. I glanced at it in disgust. "I'll crack *him* if I have to!"

"Perhaps his advice was not so poorly chosen," the priest said mildly.

His words brought me back to myself. "Forgive me," I muttered, shoving the broken medallion into the purse at my belt. "You're right, my lord priest. I did not mean to disturb your peace."

He gazed at me for a long moment, then sighed. "D'Angeline, I seldom offer counsel to those who do not ask it, for their ears are unwilling to hear. But this is a place of healing. Will you not seek it?"

"What do you mean?"

He reached out with one long finger, touching the center of my chest. "Not all wounds are of the flesh. You bear a wound deep inside you, and it festers. Will you hear my counsel? Stay. Pass this night in the temple, and let Asclepius guide you in your dreams. This is the favor I ask of you."

"Do you know who I am?" I asked him.

"Does it matter?" His eyes were as deep as wells, dark and fathomless.

"No." I thought about it. "I suppose not."

He nodded. "Then you will stay."

So it came to pass that I spent the night on the isle of As-

clepius and slept in the temple, after arranging with one of
the attendants to escort Anna home. In the wake of the rioting, they were understanding.

It was a strange experience. As darkness began to fall
over the isle, the priest led me to a chamber within the temple. Although it was roofed, it was open on three sides. A
warm summer breeze soughed through the painted columns.
In the center, there was a stone bier that served as a bed. Unbuckling my sword-belt, I lay down upon it. On the ceiling,
a faded fresco of Asclepius looked down upon me. The stone
was hard and unyielding, and I felt certain I would be unable
to sleep.

The priest closed my eyelids with a touch, light and sure.
"Sleep."

There he left me.

I opened my eyes, gazing at Asclepius on the ceiling until
darkness swallowed his image. I felt odd, like a corpse laid
out to await the funeral pyre. Asclepius, I remembered, was
born of death; Apollo's son, torn from his dead mother's
mortal womb. A strange way to beget a healer.

The bier was uncomfortable. I shifted, trying to find a position that didn't make my bones ache. Why on earth would
the priest think one could sleep in such a manner? Beyond
the columns, the night was full of noises. Small sounds; the
sounds of the isle. Birds and animals, whirring insects. A
chorus of cicadas. Night's predators and scavengers, stalking and scurrying. In Montrève, I wouldn't have noticed, but
I'd been living in the city for a long time.

After a while, I gave up, sitting and swinging my legs
over the edge of the bier. I walked to the edge of the chamber and leaned against one of the columns, peering out at the
benighted isle. The moon was dark, but there were stars. If I

craned my head, I could see them, high and distant behind scudding clouds.

"You are restless."

I startled at the sound of the priest's voice, reaching for the hilt of my sword. My fingers found only fabric, and I remembered I had disarmed. "Forgive me, my lord priest." I bowed. "I didn't hear you return. I tried to sleep. Is it forbidden to rise? I have not left the chamber."

He smiled into his beard. "Nothing is forbidden here."

"Good." I perched on the bier, squinting at him through the darkness. It was hard to make him out. "I don't wish to offend."

"Why are you restless?" he asked.

"You said I had a wound." I smiled wryly. "Lord priest, I have seen things, terrible things. I do not know how to unsee them. I am trying, very hard, to be *good*. And the harder I try, the more cruel I become." I shrugged. "Such is my birthright. Should I deny it? It seems it finds me no matter what I do."

The priest pointed at the fresco on the ceiling, lost in darkness. "From death comes life, and there is healing in it. Such is our mortal lot, those of us who strive. To wrest the good from the bad. Betimes, we succeed. Is it not enough?"

"No," I said. "Not always."

He nodded, leaning on his staff. In the faint starlight, the serpent's coils entwined around the staff stirred, gleaming. It was not the priest who addressed me. My hands rose unbidden, fingers sliding over my open mouth. All over my body, my skin prickled with a sudden mix of terror and awe.

"My lord Asclepius!" I whispered.

"I am here, Imriel nó Montrève." His voice was gentle, blending with the sounds of the benighted isle. "Kushiel's scion, you have seen terrible things, and you have witnessed glorious mysteries given unto few. This I know. It is hard to be a pawn of the gods. Even in loving us in all their numinous might, they are careless of our mortality. And I think you have been wounded by a darker god than any you or I serve. Is it not so?"

"It is." Tears came to my eyes unbidden.

Asclepius stood, pondering. His serpent lifted its wedge-shaped head, its forked tongue flickering as it tasted the air. At length Asclepius spoke. "It is not a wound I can heal," he said, and bitter despair flooded me.

"So this is useless?" I spat.

"I did not say that." He bowed his head, and the serpent's tongue flickered at his ear. He straightened. "Child, listen. That power lies within you alone. Nothing can be changed without undoing what was done. Yet even a stunted tree reaches toward the sunlight. Let the wound heal. Bear the scar with pride."

"How?" I asked.

The serpent's eyes glittered. Asclepius smiled. "You will find a way."

I opened my mouth to protest that his words were cold comfort, meaningless and worthless. Or at least, so I thought I meant to do. Instead, I found myself waking with a jolt, opening my eyes.

Opening them onto dawn's rosy light.

Morning was dawning, and I was lying on my back on the stone bier, stiff and aching, staring at the fresco on the ceiling. Sleep. I'd been asleep. When had I fallen asleep? I sat up in a panic, rolling over the side of the bier and dropping to a crouch, scrambling for my sword-belt. It was there where I'd dropped it. I snatched it and backed away from the bier, buckling the belt around my waist, checking my weapons.

Everything was there. I was alone in the temple's open-walled chamber of dreams. Beyond the columns, poppies bloomed in red-orange profusion. The summer breeze carried the sound of birdsong and the scent of the Tiber.

Behind me, on the one solid wall, the door opened. I spun about, hand on my sword-hilt.

It was the bearded priest. "Did you dream?"

"I did." I looked hard at him. There was no staff, no serpent. Although his eyes were dark and deep, he was a mortal man, no more, with dusty sandals and robe with a fraying hem.

"Tell me," he said gravely.

I let go the hilt of my sword and sat on the edge of the bier, feeling the strange sense that we had already done this. "Asclepius came to me in a dream. He said he could not heal my wound, but that the power lay within me." My lips curved in a mocking smile. "I am a stunted tree, my lord priest, reaching toward sunlight."

He frowned. "Indeed."

"Indeed." I meant to say the word with irony, but somehow it came out otherwise. I gazed at the priest, and it came to me in a thunderclap that all that Asclepius had said was true. I had seen terrible things and I had seen glorious mysteries. Against all odds, Elua and his Companions had triumphed over Angra Mainyu in Daršanga and turned back a tide of darkness that threatened to encompass the world. Ill thoughts, ill words, ill deeds. Against the might of a furious and dispossessed nation resorting to the darkest magics of hatred and despite, Blessed Elua had hurled a D'Angeline courtesan, a lone swordsman, and a ten-year-old boy.

And we had won.

Eamonn was right; war was a hurtful subject, even for the victors. I had been the lure that brought Phèdre and Joscelin to Daršanga. A victim; the perfect victim, until

Phèdre arrived. That had been many months; I would never be free of those wounds. The past could not be changed without altering the present. Cold comfort, yes; but it had awoken me from my torpor of self-pity. I could learn to bear the scars with pride—my own twisted pride. I slid from the bier, landing without a twinge from my injured ankle. I felt different; free from the bonds of fear and anger, lighter than I had felt for many weeks.

You will find a way.

I bowed to the priest. "May I see Gilot?"

He bowed in return. "Come with me, Prince Imriel."

Another time—a day ago—I would have startled at his address. Today I merely accepted it. He knew; so be it. I had been a fool to imagine I could flee my own self. I followed him through the door and into the temple proper, to the injured ward where Gilot was housed, the long line of cots in an airy space. He struggled to sit when he saw me, pushing himself upright with his one good hand, a grin breaking over his face.

"Imri!" he called, then coughed and winced. "How was it?"

I drew up a stool and sat at his bedside, taking his left hand in mine. "Fine," I said honestly. "It was fine. I learned somewhat of value." I paused. "Gilot, listen. I'm going to stay in Tiberium for a little while. Long enough to attend Lucius' wedding in Lucca. And after that, I think we should go home."

His hand tightened on mine. "You mean it?"

I nodded. "I do."

A flicker of distress crossed Gilot's features. He glanced at his splinted right hand. "Oh, Imri! What about Anna and Belinda? What if—"

"Listen." I squeezed his good hand. "Gilot, if you want to

stay here for their sake, no one will begrudge you, least of all me. I'll speak to Denise Fleurais. I've no doubt the ambassadress can find a use for a man of your talents. And if you wish to return to Terre d'Ange and bring Anna and her daughter with you . . ." I shook my head. "Name of Elua, Gilot! I've two holdings I've no use for. I'd as soon appoint you my liaison to deal with them. You've a knack for it, you learned enough at Montrève."

He looked steadily at me, his eyes as faithful as a hound's. "What of you?"

I made myself smile. "It doesn't matter."

"Why?" he asked. "What of *you*, Imri? What will you do?"

"I'll marry Dorelei." It felt odd to say the words aloud. I hadn't even known I'd decided until I spoke them. I freed my hand from his gently. "Gilot, I will take example from your loyalty. I'm doing no good here, not even for myself. After Lucius is wed, I'll take my leave of Tiberium. I'll do what the Queen wants, plight my troth to Dorelei mab Breidaia and go to Alba. I'll be a good D'Angeline Prince of the Blood and do my best to foster peace and harmony betwixt our nations." I laughed softly. "The stunted tree will seek sunlight."

Gilot sighed. "You promise? Because I'm mortally weary of worrying over you."

"I do," I said solemnly. "Only let me see Lucius wed first. It's only a few weeks hence, and you're not fit to travel. I have been a poor friend to him, and he deserves better."

"And then we go home?" he asked in a hopeful voice. "Because I think . . . I think if Anna is willing, I would like that. I would like it very much."

I nodded. "And then we go home. I promise."

FORTY-SIX

UPON RETURNING to the insula, I discovered Canis was gone.

Not absent; gone. The only trace of his presence that remained was a faint circle on the dusty street where his barrel had stood. I stared at it for a moment, then went to speak to Master Ambrosius.

The incense-maker was in good spirits. He had been more kindly disposed toward me since learning that I had kept his shop from being burned. "Smell this, young sir!" he greeted me, waving a bowl beneath my nose. "What think you?"

I sniffed. "Interesting."

"'Tis camphor and crushed cardamom seeds from Bhodistan." He beamed. "Do you reckon D'Angelines would find it pleasing?"

"I do, yes." I smelled it again. The mixture was pungent and spicy, but not displeasing. "It's a proud scent, I think. I would offer it to Azza. Master Ambrosius, have you seen Canis?"

"The beggar?" He shook his head. "No, he was gone when I opened the shop this morning, and his filthy barrel with him. And good riddance. Begging your pardon," he added. "You seemed fond of him."

"So I thought." I touched my purse, feeling the broken pieces of the clay medallion mingling with my coins. The incense-maker's eyes brightened. I thought for a moment. "Master Ambrosius, I'd like to make offerings to Blessed Elua and his Companions. Mayhap you might help me choose?"

He was more than eager. Together, we debated gravely over a dozen different incenses. He told me the components of each one and asked me which I thought suitable for each deity in turn, nodding at my comments. I made my selections, and he measured careful scoops into burlap pouches. Remembering Master Piero's lesson, I understood better why the incense-maker had shown little regard for the University's students in general, and me in particular. This was the first coin I'd spent in his shop.

In the end, I left with my arms laden. "Master Ambrosius, will you do me a kindness?" I asked him. "If Canis should return at any time, will you send word to me? Only don't let him know."

He nodded sagely. "Owes you money, does he?"

I hesitated. "Somewhat like, yes."

"I'll do it."

Obeying my whim, I departed the insula and headed for the D'Angeline embassy. The day's heat was rising and shops were beginning to close their doors, but I was able to purchase a cheap leather satchel in the Great Forum. It was poorly cured and stank a bit. I smiled, thinking about how we had cured gazelle hides to make waterskins by burying them in hot shale in Jebe-Barkal. It had worked better than whatever method had been used here. Still, the satchel served to contain my myriad pouches of incense, and I made my way to Lady Fleurais' palazzo trailing a most peculiar aroma behind me.

At the embassy gates, the guard on duty stared at me. "My lord?"

I stood before him in a miasma of ill-cured leather and incense. "Her ladyship said she would leave a standing order to admit me," I said. "But if she is available, I would speak with her." He continued to stare, his gaze travelling from my face to my feet. I realized, then, the figure I cut. I was wearing dusty student's togs, rumpled with sleep, and the crude rope sandals I'd bought after the rioting. Until today, my ankle had been too sore to consider replacing my boots. "I know," I said. "But it's important."

The guard gave himself a little shake, then opened the gate to admit me. "Name of Elua!" He grinned at me. "The Comtesse de Montrève would die of shame to see you thus, your highness."

I laughed. "Like as not."

He escorted me to the temple garden and went to send word to the ambassadress. In the height of the midday heat, the garden was empty. Not even the priest was about. I took off my sandals and knelt in the green grass, removing the pouches of incense and arranging them in order. And then, one by one, I made my offerings at each of the altars, filling the bowl before each effigy and kindling the incense with the fire-striking kit that had been our guide Bizan's farewell gift to me.

Another memory of Jebe-Barkal. It seemed fitting. As hard as the journey was, I had been happy there. It was there that Phèdre and Joscelin had found healing together. It was there that I had begun to know myself loved.

I said prayers as I lit each bowl; prayers for all those lost in the zenana, all who had not survived the uprising. *Re-*

member this. I said prayers for the survivors, and most of all for Kaneka, tall Kaneka, who had been a pillar of strength. I said prayers for everyone we had met in our travels who had done us a kindness, and a few who had not. I prayed for my kin . . . the family of my blood, Mavros and Roshana and Baptiste, Ysandre and Sidonie and Alais. And for the family of my heart.

Phèdre.

Joscelin.

And the others, too—all of Montrève's household, and most of all for Gilot. For him, I offered an incense of chamomile, hyssop, and cedar gum to Eisheth, praying she would send him healing. I prayed, surprising myself, for Maslin of Lombelon, a traitor's child who bore a dark shadow like my own on his soul. I remembered the joyous pride I had first seen in Maslin's face and offered Master Ambrosius' new mixture to Azza on his behalf, praying that he might regain it one day.

I prayed for Dorelei mab Breidaia, whom I barely knew.

And for Eamonn, whom I loved dearly, and Master Piero in his wisdom, and my haunted friend Lucius. For him I made an offering of attar of rose and amber to Naamah, hoping he might find love. I hesitated, then prayed for Claudia, too. I made her offering to Kushiel, spikenard and mastic, praying his justice would be merciful on the both of us.

It was a long process.

I saved the last offering for Blessed Elua: mistletoe and myrrh. And to Elua, I said no prayer, but merely knelt and bowed my head before his grace. I stayed there for a long time.

"Prince Imriel?"

I rose, stiff-jointed, and bowed. Midday had passed and the shadows were lengthening. In the center of the garden,

Denise Fleurais gave a soft, wondering laugh, gazing around her. From seven bowls on seven altars, dying trickles of fragrant smoke arose.

"'Tis a wondrous thing you've done, your highness," she said. "What does it mean?"

"My lady," I said softly. "I'm ready to go home."

We spoke long into the night, first over dinner and then over glasses of cordial. As it transpired, the ambassadress had canceled an engagement to put herself at my disposal. It felt peculiar. So often, this self seemed unreal: Imriel de la Courcel, Prince of the Blood, third in line for the throne of Terre d'Ange. I'd not grown up knowing it. I'd grown up a goatherd, not a prince and a traitor's get. It had been thrust upon me unwanted.

Inside, I was only me. Imriel; Imri to a few.

An orphan among orphans, a slave among slaves.

But it *was* real, and time enough I acknowledged it. And so I spoke of my thoughts and plans. I kept my word to Ruggero Caccini. I said nothing of the attempts against my life, and I said nothing of the letter I held implicating Bernadette de Trevalion in the matter. I would deal with her in my own time, and I hadn't yet decided the manner of it. But in everything else, I spoke candidly to Denise Fleurais. I saw the wash of relief that suffused her face. She was a diplomat. She knew what was at stake in Alba.

"May I tell her majesty?" she asked.

I shook my head. "I'd prefer to do it myself. You have couriers?"

"Yes." She rang a handbell. "I'll send for paper and ink."

I wrote two letters that evening. The first was to Ysandre, and it was formal and brief. I announced my plans to remain in Caerdicca Unitas for several more weeks to attend the wedding of a friend, and return to Terre d'Ange in autumn, before winter made the passage dangerous. I tendered my offer to wed Dorelei mab Breidaia in the spring, should all parties concerned still find it desirable.

The second letter was to Phèdre.

I lingered over it, but there was too much to put into words. In the end, I opted for brevity, with a promise to explain more upon my return. I smiled at the thought of the impatient happiness it would evoke in the household, and kissed the parchment before I sealed it.

"Will your courier see this is delivered first?" I asked, handing it to Denise Fleurais.

She raised her brows. "Before your missive to the Queen?"

"Yes," I said. "Please."

The ambassadress studied me. "Will you permit me to have my couturier attire you for this wedding you're determined to attend?"

I laughed. "I will."

Denise Fleurais inclined her head. "Then we have a bargain, your highness."

So the first step was taken, and I felt stronger for having made a decision and acted upon it. It was not the life I envisioned for myself, no. I wanted . . . what? I wanted what I had yearned after for a long time: to be a hero, like Joscelin. To love with the same desperate ferocity, to do impossible deeds. But such a destiny was vouchsafed to only a few, and it came at a terrible price. I knew; I'd seen him in Daršanga, and afterward.

It was not my lot, and I should be glad of it. I had a chance to do good in my own way. To pave the path of peace, to rise to the challenge of being tender and kind. To being a good husband to Dorelei, a Cruithne stranger with a lilting laugh. That would be my sacrifice, because I wasn't tender and kind, not really. I craved *more*.

But perhaps it would be enough to try.

Canis had said so.

So had Asclepius.

After I left the embassy, I sent a note to Claudia Fulvia. It was the second step, and harder than the first. Her reply came quickly, arranging for a rendezvous at the atelier of Erytheia on the morrow.

I kept the appointment. After so many, it felt strange not to strip and pose. Erytheia was working on another panel, but she eyed me with interest as I wandered her atelier, and Silvio watched, too, going quietly about the business of grinding pigments.

"We could use you," she said at length. "If you would be willing to sit . . . ?"

I shook my head. "Once was enough."

She nodded. "As you wish."

It wasn't long before Claudia arrived, and Erytheia and Silvio took their leave without comment. I watched the quiet nod the women exchanged, and knew with certainty that which I had wondered. Whatever other arrangement there was between them, the artist was complicit in Claudia's plans; the plans of the Unseen Guild.

"What is it?" Claudia made no move to touch me. The slanting sunlight turned her eyes to amber, and her gaze was curious and wary. "Are you well? You look . . . peculiar."

"I'm fine," I said. "Claudia, it's over."

A flicker of fear crossed her features, gone almost before it could register. "Over?" she asked lightly. "Oh, but Imriel! We've scarce begun. I was so proud to hear how you dealt with Caccini. You've a knack for this, you know." She smiled, coming toward me. Her hand rose to brush my lips, trailing down my throat. "And I have so much more to offer you."

My body stirred at her touch, but it was an automatic response, nothing more. For the first time, I didn't feel as though I were sliding helpless into the pit of desire. My thoughts remained clear. I stood outside myself and *saw* Claudia. I saw cleverness, cunning, and ambition. I saw her carnal nature, powerful and abundant, and the delight she took in it—wielding it as a weapon and a tool for her own pleasure. And I saw their shadow-sides, too. Fear; fear of failing the Guild. Fear of aging, of no longer being found desirable. Fear that the young D'Angeline lover she held in thrall would wake up one day and find himself repulsed by her.

I could have turned it against her, but I didn't.

"I'm sorry," I said gently. "Claudia . . . a day ago, I meant to beleaguer you with questions." I fished the broken pieces of Canis' medallion from my purse. "How do the members of the Unseen Guild acknowledge one another? Who is Canis and what is the meaning of the secret message inscribed here? And yet . . ." I tightened my fist, crushing the fragments, and let them trickle to the floor. "I find I don't care."

She inhaled sharply. "How can you *not*?"

I shrugged. "You know, it's easier than I would have reckoned. I don't want it, Claudia. You . . ." I paused. "You've given me a great gift, but the price is too high. The guilt, the secrecy . . . I don't like lying to my friends."

Her breast rose and fell rapidly. "Coward!" she spat.

"No." I thought about it. "Claudia, if we loved one another, no price would be too high." I accorded her a courtly bow. "You are all that is glorious in a woman, and I will always be grateful to you for showing me what it means to plumb the depths of desire. I have worshipped your body with every part of mine, and I have no regrets. But when all is said and done, we do not love one another, and you know it."

For a moment her face softened, and then it set in harsh lines. "And the Guild? Do you forget my warning?"

"No." I took a deep breath. "Anafiel Delaunay took his chances and walked away from the Unseen Guild. So will I."

"You're a fool!" Contempt laced her voice. "Delaunay could have prevented—"

"So you said." I cut her off. "But no one can know it for certain."

She trembled with anger. "You'll run back to *her*, won't you? Delaunay's little protegée, cocksure and ignorant! What gives an aging D'Angeline whore the right to think she can challenge—"

A wave of fury swamped my composure. *"Enough!"*

"You don't like that, do you?" Claudia laughed. "Oh, Imriel! Your precious Phèdre is overmatched here. You may cling to your foster-mother's skirts and have naughty dreams about sharing her bed, but don't think for a minute that she can protect you—"

"Enough." I repeated the word softly. "Don't provoke me."

Her chin raised in stubborn mutiny. "Do you dare threaten the Guild?"

"I do." I squared my shoulders. "And you, too, if you think to threaten me in turn. I'm sure Deccus would be quite interested to learn of our affair. Claudia, I will not expose the Guild. But understand, if anyone dear to me is harmed, I will break that promise. And if *I* am harmed . . ." I paused. "Yes, you will have Phèdre nó Delaunay on your doorstep; Kushiel's Chosen, filled with righteous fury, with the Queen's Champion guarding her back. She will ask questions, and she will find answers. It is what she does, and she does it well. And then you and the Unseen Guild will have the wrath of Queen Ysandre de la Courcel upon you, and the Cruarch of Alba, too."

"Politics," Claudia retorted. "The Guild doesn't fear *politics*. The Guild *is* politics!"

"No?" I asked. "How about the Master of the Straits?"

She was silent.

"He's real, you know," I said to her. "He can command the seas to rise, rain to fall, and the wind to blow. And he's not bound to the Straits, not anymore. Phèdre freed him, although she went through untold hell to do it, and Joscelin with her. I know; I was there." I smiled at Claudia. "His name is Hyacinthe, and he is her childhood friend, her one true friend. I imagine he could sink the port of Ostia beneath the waves if he took a fancy to do so."

Claudia had turned pale, very pale. "He wouldn't dare."

"Why not?" I asked. "What possible threat could the Guild use to deter the Master of the Straits?" I shook my head. "Claudia, let us both be wise and part as friends. I will stay for your brother's wedding, and then I will go. And nothing more will be said of this, ever."

"It's not that simple," she whispered. "Not for me."

"I say it is." I extended my hand. "Shall we part?"

"Friends." She pronounced the word bitterly. "You leave me little choice."

I shook her hand gravely. "There are worse things in the world, Claudia Fulvia."

To that, she made no reply.

Thus, the second step, that was in some ways the hardest. But once it was done, I felt good. I'd spent so much time and effort running away from my life and identity that it felt good to reclaim it.

I spoke to Eamonn that evening in private, just the two of us in a dark corner of the wineshop. We spoke in the Eiran dialect, which was one tongue I could be reasonably certain no casual bystander would know. I was rusty enough in its usage myself. If for some reason the Guild had set spies on me, well and so. If they were that determined and clever, there was little I could do about it.

I told him about Claudia.

Not about the Unseen Guild, of course; I wasn't fool enough to test their limits. But I told him about our affair. How it had begun, and how long it had continued. He let out a low whistle at the initial revelation, then sat quiet and listened while I told him the rest. I told him, then, of my night on the isle of Asclepius, and my decisions that had followed.

"I'll miss you," he said. "I understand why you're leaving, but I'll miss you. I'm glad you're staying for Lucius' wedding." He gave me one of his shrewd looks. "So it's over, then? You and Claudia Fulvia?"

"Definitely," I said.

Eamonn swirled his wine, then drank. "It's funny," he said pensively. "This would be nothing in Terre d'Ange. But here . . ." He glanced at me. "Do you think she'll talk?"

I shook my head. "She has her reputation to uphold."

He smiled a little. "Sounds like heavy lifting from what you say. Imri, are you going to tell Lucius?"

"Gods, no!" I shuddered. "No, I plan to tell him the truth about who I am. I reckon I owe him that much. But I don't think he needs to know I've been bedding his sister."

"I suppose not," he mused. "May I tell Brigitta?"

"About *Claudia*?"

"No." Eamonn grinned at me. "About you, your highness."

"You trust her?" I asked.

"Aye, I do," he said simply.

I thought about it. "Give me a couple days to talk to Lucius. And mind, while I've come to terms with the fact that I can't hide from who I am, I'd rather not have it noised about, either. At this point, it would just be compounding folly." I laughed. "You don't suppose she'll want to stab me through the heart for the honor of Skaldia once she knows, do you?"

Eamonn pursed his lips. "I don't *think* so."

It was another day before I had a chance to speak to Lucius. A message arrived from the Temple of Asclepius that Gilot was ready to come home. He had derived as much benefit as he could from their healing skills; from this point onward, only time and rest would help. I went to the market with Anna that morning, and we purchased an array of cushions and thick bolster pillows to make him more comfortable.

Her daughter Belinda accompanied us. She swung on her mother's skirts and chattered incessantly, no longer shy of me. I laughed when a mortified Anna tried to hush her.

"I don't mind," I said. "I used to know a little girl much like her."

"At the Palace?" she asked, then flushed to the roots of her hair. "Oh!"

"It's all right," I said gently. "Gilot told you, I know. Just don't speak of it in public. But no, it was at the sanctuary where I grew up. Her name was Honore," I said to Belinda. "I taught her how to climb trees when she was only five years old. Have you ever climbed a tree?" She gazed at me with wide eyes and shook her head. "Well, mayhap I'll

teach you, when you're older." I smiled at her. "Only a little one to start. And no honey trees, Belinda. That's where
the bees live."

"I like honey," she said solemnly.

"Oh, so do I. But you have to be *very* careful, or the bees
will get angry that you're stealing their honey." I made a
buzzing sound and snaked one hand through the air, landing to give her plump cheek a soft tweak that made her giggle. "And if you get stung, we'll have to slather you in
mud," I added, provoking a fresh fit of mirth. "All mud,
head to toe."

Anna regarded me with astonishment. "You're very good
with her."

I smiled wryly. "You needn't be so surprised."

She flushed anew. "No! It's just . . . I think you have a
kind heart, that's all. And I begin to see why . . . why Gilot
won't leave you, even though he grumbles."

I nearly made a self-deprecating comment, then caught
myself. "Thank you," I said sincerely. "It's good of you to
say so."

We fetched Gilot home that afternoon, and he did grum-
ble. He grumbled about the ungainly splint on his right
hand, his own slow-moving progress and general useless-
ness. He grumbled when I made him ride in a hired litter,
and when we propped him up on his pallet he grumbled
about the cushions being like a damned pasha's boudoir.
And then he fell asleep, exhausted. His face looked thin and
worn, still faintly discolored around the eyes.

"He's so beautiful," Anna whispered, stroking the hair
from his brow.

I perched on a chair, watching them. "Yes."

"Listen to me, saying that to *you*." Her soft laugh caught
in her throat. "But you're like something out of a picture or

a song, and he's . . . he's just Gilot. I can touch him, I can hold him. I never thought I'd feel that again, not like this." She bowed her head, but not before I saw the sheen of tears on her cheek. "Do you think he'll be all right?" she asked in a low tone.

"I don't know, Anna," I said honestly. "I hope so. But it will be difficult. He was a swordsman. It's all he's ever known, ever since he came of age and joined Phèdre's service. I promise, he'll want for naught. But he's going to need you, you and Belinda, to give him a reason to live."

She was still for a moment, then gathered herself, wiping her eyes. "Belinda. Forgive me, my lord. We're imposing. I'll take her home."

Belinda was sound asleep on my pallet, thumb in her mouth.

"Will she take a fright if she wakes here?" I asked. Anna shook her head. "Then stay." I rose. "I'll find lodging elsewhere."

"Oh please, my lord!" Anna got to her feet. "No, we mustn't."

Gilot stirred, murmuring restlessly in his sleep.

"I insist," I said, reaching for the door. "Stay."

She glanced at Gilot, then at me, her brows knit. "You would be welcome to my room, if it's not too humble."

"Is it worse than this?" I gestured around.

"No." Anna smiled through her tears. "You're a funny sort of prince, my lord."

"So I'm told," I said.

I left them there, lingering in the courtyard long enough to hear Anna bar the door against intruders. Through the irregular slats of the latched shutters, I could see her bend tenderly to kiss her daughter and Gilot, then blow out the last oil lamp. Oddly enough, my envy had dissipated. In its place, there was an aching tenderness, heavy and poignant.

"May Elua bless and keep you," I whispered.

And then I found my way to Anna's apartment, climbing the outer stair to the second story, and slept alone on the widow's pallet, with her daughter's empty cot beside me.

Even a stunted tree reaches for the sunlight.

FORTY-SEVEN

M ASTER PIERO LECTURED on the virtue of
honesty.

I swear, betimes the man chose his topics purely to provoke me. We met in his lecture hall at the University, and I
sat on my three-legged stool, chin in hand, listening to flies
drone while he railed against the myriad ways a lie can fes-
ter in one's soul, lies breeding lies, even as flies hatch maggots in an open wound.

"Ugh!" Brigitta commented.

Afterward, we argued the matter—lies of intent, lies of
omission, lies of kindness. Whether there was merit in any
of them. I argued that there was. That some secrets were
meant to be kept, too injurious to be made known.

"Truth, like fire, cauterizes," Master Piero said tranquilly.
"Can you think of a secret better kept than exposed, Imriel
nó Montrève?"

"I can think of a few, Master," I muttered.

He smiled at me. "Think harder."

I did, then. I thought about my mother's legacy of secrecy
and plotting; one for which it seemed I had a knack. I wondered, for the first time, what my life would be like if she
had simply succumbed, handing my infant self over to Ysan-

dre de la Courcel to be raised as a member of House Courcel. But as Asclepius had said, the past could not be altered without changing the present. If I had never been hidden by a priest's lie, there would have been no one to challenge Angra Mainyu in Daršanga. There were no easy answers.

It made my head ache to think on it.

I was glad when Master Piero dismissed us. "Lucius!" I caught his arm. "Are you free this afternoon? I'll stand you a jug of wine."

Things had been cool between us since I'd managed to insult his friendship, but he gave me a measuring look and nodded. "All right. Let's go to the baths first. It's perishing hot out there."

We spent a good portion of the afternoon idling in the pleasant waters of the tepidarium. The baths were crowded, so I held my tongue and listened instead while Lucius spoke of the wedding plans. The city of Lucca was preparing for a gala affair to celebrate the long-overdue union of two of its ruling families. Helena appeared content, and her beloved Bartolomeo had written Lucius a letter of thanks.

"Can you imagine?" he said wryly.

"It does seem a bit odd," I admitted.

"I don't think he could have borne seeing her wed to Domenico Martelli," he said. "From what I hear, he's nearly as bad as old Gallus Tadius. His first wife died. He put it about that she came to term early and died in childbirth, but I heard he beat her until she lost the babe. I suppose Bartolomeo has reason to be relieved."

"How is old Gallus Tadius?" I asked.

"Still quiet." Lucius grinned at me. "I hate to admit the priests were right, but he's been mercifully, blessedly quiet."

Clean and refreshed, we strolled through the city. Our usual wineshop was already doing a brisk trade, and I suggested we seek out less crowded quarters. Lucius looked puzzled, but agreed.

"You're being very mysterious, Montrève," he observed.

"I've reason for it," I said.

We found a place on the outskirts of the students' quarter. It catered to day-laborers for the most part; tradesmen and merchants who wanted a quiet drink during the midday hours. The wine wasn't very good, but it was mostly empty, which suited my purposes.

Lucius tasted his wine and made a face, then settled back in his chair. "All right. Out with it."

"Do you remember how you said you'd appreciate my friendship more if I let you reciprocate it?" I asked him.

"Quite well." He looked sharply at me. "This isn't about the time when I asked if there was any chance you might fancy me, is it? Because that's not what I meant. Don't flatter yourself, Montrève. I'm not pining."

"No, no." I shook my head. "I know what you meant. You've been honest and open in your friendship, and I've been . . . less than forthcoming."

"Mm." A corner of his mouth quirked. "You do cultivate an air of brooding mystery. It grows a bit tiresome."

I laughed. "It's not a-purpose."

"Good to know." He turned somber. "Why? Does it have to do with what happened when you were a child? Bad things, you said."

"It's part of it." I studied my hands encircling my winecup. "You asked about family."

"Is there a Gallus Tadius in yours?"

I glanced up at his sympathetic gaze. "Not exactly. There's a Melisande Shahrizai and a Benedicte de la Courcel. Lucius, I've not lied to you, but I've not been honest, either." I took a deep breath and braced myself for his reaction. "What I told you is true. I was adopted by Phèdre nó Delaunay, the Comtesse de Montrève. But I'm kin to Queen Ysandre, and in Terre d'Ange my name, my full name, is Imriel nó Montrève de la Courcel."

Lucius blinked at me, his mouth working soundlessly. He raised his winecup in an unthinking gesture. It slipped from his fingers and shattered on the wooden table. A puddle of wine spread between us and the barkeep hurried toward us with alacrity, a rag in his hand.

"Oh, sweet Apollo!" Lucius whispered. "You're the Bella Donna's son."

I stared at him. *"What?"*

It had to wait while the barkeep swabbed the table. Lucius muttered under his breath, pacing the wineshop and tapping his temples. I ignored him and thanked the barkeep for his troubles, giving him a few coins and procuring a new cup for Lucius, which I filled and thrust across the table.

"Sit," I said. "And tell me."

"Tell *you!*" He gave a harried laugh, but he sat and drained his cup, refilling it straightaway. "It's a legend, Montrève—or whatever I should call you. A Serenissiman tale, but it's cropped up in Lucca and elsewhere in the north of Caerdicca Unitas. Not here, not this far southwest. The Bella Donna, the handmaiden of Asherat." He gestured impatiently. "Asherat-of-the-Sea, the Bona Dea, Magna Mater. Whatever you wish to call her. As Master Piero says, the gods wear many faces."

"Lucius," I said.

He drank off another cup. "She's your *mother?*"

"No!" I raked a hand through my hair, still damp from the baths. "Lucius, my mother is very much a mortal woman. Her name is Melisande Shahrizai, and she took sanctuary in the Temple of Asherat to avoid being executed for treason."

He nodded and set his winecup down carefully. "The Bella Donna."

"She's a *traitor*!" I shouted.

Lucius winced. "Montrève, you asked. I'm telling you, that's all. That's the legend. She was a beautiful woman, wrongfully accused, her son stolen from her. She took the Veil of Asherat and the goddess granted her sanctuary. Year upon year, her grief and her beauty deepened. When her pain grew too much to bear, the goddess made the walls of the temple melt like mist and freed her to roam the earth in search of her lost son. There was a priestess who swore it was so." He picked up his cup, then set it down. "Women in desperate circumstances ask the Bella Donna to intercede with the goddess on their behalf. Little things, offerings at the crossroads. Blue beads. Helena did it once. That's how I know."

"Lucius." I spread my hands. "That's absurd."

He nodded. "I know."

"You don't," I said. We sat in silence for a moment. "Lucius, my mother was the architect of the greatest treachery in the history of Terre d'Ange, and my father . . . he was her dupe, her willing dupe, so far as I know, one in a long line of many. And me . . . I represent the least of her plots."

Lucius got up from the table and took our empty winejug to the barkeep. He returned, refilled our cups, and set the jug down between us. The shock had passed from his face and his hazel eyes were steady. "Tell me."

I told him.

Not all of it; not the full horror of Daršanga. On that, I touched lightly. I had told Phèdre all of it and Eamonn some of it, and I didn't think I'd ever speak of it to another living being. But I told Lucius my history, written in broad strokes.

Parts of it, he knew.

Lucius wasn't ignorant of the world's affairs; he'd simply failed to assemble the puzzle. Still, it was strange to speak openly to someone whose perspective was so vastly different from my own. The war that had left such deep and abiding scars on Terre d'Ange, Skaldia, and Alba was merely a historical point of interest to the Caerdicci.

"Are you sure?" he asked when I finished. "Sure of your mother's guilt?"

"Yes." I didn't elaborate.

"Where is she now?"

"Well, she's not roaming the earth in search of her missing son!" I said tartly. "Name of Elua! I was only missing in the first place because she had me hidden away, at least until the slavers took me. And I've been *found* for quite some years now."

"Fables have a way of outliving truths," Lucius murmured. "So you don't know?"

"I've no idea," I said shortly. "And so long as she keeps her promise, I don't care."

"Promise?" He raised his brows.

"To do naught to jeopardize the lives of the Queen and her daughters," I said.

Lucius looked blankly at me for a moment, then blew out his breath. "Which would put *you* on the throne, right? Jupiter Capitolinus, Montrève! What in the hell are you doing wandering around Tiberium pretending to be an impoverished gentleman scholar?"

I shrugged. "Hiding. Searching. I'm not sure."

"And they just let you go?"

"Not happily." I smiled at the memory of Ysandre's fury. "But I've come to realize I can't stay, Lucius. Truth be told, our situations aren't so different. After you're wed, I'll go back and face my responsibilities."

"I'm glad you're staying for it," he said. "And I'm glad you told me."

"So am I," I said.

In the weeks that followed, Lucius gave me no reason to regret my confidence in him. For all that he had an acerbic tongue, he was a loyal friend. As I had asked him to do, he kept the knowledge to himself and treated me no differently, although betimes I caught him giving me wondering glances out of the corner of his eye.

They were precious to me, those weeks; the last fleeting weeks of freedom before I would reclaim the mantle of Prince Imriel de la Courcel. Strange to say, I had more freedom now than I'd enjoyed since childhood or was like to ever again. With my decision made, I was free of the doubt and confusion that had plagued me ever since Claudia Fulvia seduced me and told me of the Unseen Guild. With Gilot confined to his sickbed, grumbling under Anna's care, I was free of any guard or caretaker. With Ruggero Caccini's letter in my possession, I was free of the threat of violence.

I treasured my time with Master Piero most of all.

I told him, of course. We met in his crowded study, and he listened as I told him why I would be leaving. When I had finished, he gave me that unexpectedly sweet smile, illuminating his homely face.

"I am pleased," he said simply.

"You are?" I blinked.

"Oh, yes." Master Piero nodded. "I will be sorry to lose you as a student, Imriel de la Courcel. Indeed, I find myself growing short of students!" Another Master would have been perturbed; Master Piero merely laughed. "Ah, but it is virtue we seek, is it not? And you will find more courage and strength of character in facing the things one dreads than in fleeing them, young prince."

"I hope so," I said.

The days passed quickly, summer's heat slowly diminishing with the advent of autumn. I spent my mornings with Master Piero and the other students. A few more joined; new ones, including a young pair of Tiberian tradesman's sons who had been wont to loiter around the outskirts of our conversations when we met in the public fora. They were rough-spoken, but eager to learn. I wondered at first how they had paid the bursar's fee; then I saw the look of quiet satisfaction on Lucius' face and guessed. He, too, had taken Master Piero's lessons to heart. I was envious I hadn't thought of it myself.

Still, it made me smile to see them gape at the way he framed ideas, asking pointed questions to make them think. They spoke with the same heady excitement that Eamonn had when I first arrived; the same I'd felt after Master Piero had first inspired me.

I felt older now.

To be sure, I had reason, but I think we all felt it, even Brigitta. She had grown easier in Eamonn's company, and no longer carried her wax tablet, scowling and writing furious notes. And too, the riot and its aftermath had changed things. We had seen our fellow students at their worst, and strived to be better. We were the ones who had stayed with Master Piero when he challenged our assumptions. We had survived the attrition.

We *were* older.

During the afternoons, I spent time with Gilot. He was improving. His bruises had faded and he could walk easily, so long as he did not walk too far or fast. Then his breathing grew labored and he clutched at his chest, where a sharp stitch of pain caught him. His hand was still bound in a cumbersome splint. Asclepius' priest had said it could be removed before we departed for Lucca. What we would find, he could not promise.

Gilot tried hard not to be bitter, although he was. He felt useless. We had a fight when he refused to accept his monthly stipend, claiming he had not earned it. So I gave the money in secret to Anna and found him work instead, sitting for Erytheia of Thrasos. She took one look at him and smiled.

"Endymion," she said.

"An *easy* pose," I cautioned her. "Nothing taxing."

"The easiest," she agreed.

So Gilot posed for her as Endymion, whom a goddess had loved, lying supine on a pallet, one arm outstretched and the other, with its splinted hand, hidden. It kept him quiescent and it restored a small measure of his pride. I visited the atelier from time to time and watched the painting take shape on Erytheia's panel. Sleeping Endymion, caressed by moonlight. I looked at Gilot's averted profile, the brown curls on his brow, the vulnerable curve of his torso, hearing Anna's broken whisper.

He's so beautiful.

I kept my promise to Denise Fleurais and paid a visit to her couturier. He was D'Angeline and far more pleasant than Favrielle nó Eglantine, of whom he spoke in terms of hushed awe. He took my measurements and began to work on a suitable wardrobe for Lucius' wedding.

It all went quickly, so quickly.

My favorite parts were the evenings. We gathered in the wineshop—our wineshop, with the faded sign of Bacchus above the door—and spun out the night in drink and conversation. Betimes the new students would join us, but often it was only the four of us, Master Piero's true acolytes. We had all grown easy with one another. Brigitta had abandoned her bristling defenses, and Lucius his careless posturing. I no longer hid from my identity with them. And Eamonn . . . well, Eamonn was Eamonn. He had never pretended to be aught else. But the difference was, the others saw his merit.

It was a good time.

Too often, such times pass unnoticed, unmarked; treasured only in hindsight. Knowing was a gift. I wish I had known, in Kaneka's village of Debeho, how happy I was. In Tiberium, I knew. And I treasured each moment, saying to myself, "Here, I have friends. Here, I am happy. *Remember this.*"

Soon, too soon, everything would change.

I had a hard decision to make in Terre d'Ange. Was it better to blackmail Bernadette de Trevalion or expose the truth? Once, I would have thought the choice easy. She'd tried to have me killed; she deserved no less. I'd wanted L'Envers to admit his guilt publicly and this was worse, far worse. And yet her punishment would be worse, too. Gaol or exile; mayhap even a sentence of execution. Although we were close kin, I didn't even know her well enough to hate her. Ruggero had thought she'd acted alone. What if it were true? Bertran had been a friend once; her husband Ghislain was the Royal Commander. Phèdre and Joscelin had ridden under his command in the Skaldic War. They considered him a boon companion.

If I exposed the truth, would it cauterize the wound as Master Piero said? Or would it merely breed another generation of blood feud? Somehow, I suspected the latter.

And beyond lay Alba. What I would find there, I could not guess. Alba was a different world; wilder and less civilized. I would be marrying a woman I scarce knew, and praying to Blessed Elua and his Companions that I could be kind and tender to her. That I could restrain my own dark desires and be a good husband. Dorelei had a laugh that made Alais smile.

Pray I did nothing to squelch that laughter.

Rejoice in the company of friends.

Love.

You will find it and lose it, again and again.

So Elua's priest had promised long ago. I drew my strength from cold comfort, and I loved without fear; my friends, Master Piero, Tiberium itself. I had grown to love the very city in all its decrepit grandeur. I had walked every inch of it by now. I knew it in the soles of my feet, in the sturdy muscles of my calves. Surely the finding mattered more than the losing.

It must be so.

Two days before we were due to depart for Lucca, we made our last excursion to the isle of Asclepius. The others had offered to come, and Anna had yearned to accompany us, but Gilot refused. He didn't want me to come, either, but I insisted. We made the trip alone. He sat in the barge, cradling his splinted hand in his lap.

"Are you afraid?" I asked him.

He shot me a dire glance. "What do you think?"

I kept my mouth shut then.

At the temple, the priest removed the splint, his mouth downturned and grave. He unwound what seemed like yards of linen bandages. Gilot watched fearfully as the wooden splints were removed and his naked hand was exposed. It looked strange; pallid and shrunken. The priest studied it.

"Make a fist," he ordered.

Gilot's hand twitched. "I can't."

"Try harder," the priest said ruthlessly.

He did; his thumb and forefinger described a circle. The

other fingers barely moved. "What good am I?" Gilot murmured. "I'll not even be able to grip a sword."

The priest shrugged. "Just as well," he said. "If you get into a swordfight, that bone-splinter in your chest is like to shift and kill you."

Cold comfort.

Gilot was quiet during our return trip. The priest had given him a salve—by the smell of it, it was much the same as the one Joscelin had used—and taught him a series of exercises to stretch and strengthen his hand. Still, it was clear that he'd never have the same use of it.

"I'm sorry," I said softly.

"I know." He stirred from his slough of despondency. "It's not your fault, Imri. You were trying to protect your friends, and I was trying to protect you. It's the only thing I've ever been good at. It's not your fault I wasn't good enough."

"That's not true!" I raised my voice. "Gilot, I could have *died* in that riot, but I didn't."

"Aye," he said. "No thanks to me. I got mobbed, Imri. Just like I did in that tavern where you picked a fight with the boatman. Do you remember?" He laughed, but there was a bitter edge to it. "Truly, when have I ever been of use? I've drawn my sword in your defense, but I've never been ruthless enough to use it. Joscelin wouldn't have hesitated. I did. Name of Elua, *Lucius* did more to save you that night than I did!"

I shook my head. "It wasn't just Lucius. There was someone else."

"I thought he was just a self-satisfied Caerdicci ass, with his clever tongue, and his 'your manservant this' and 'your manservant that,' but he kept a level head—" Gilot broke off his rant as my words penetrated. "What do you mean, there was someone else?"

In all this time, we hadn't spoken much of that night. I still hadn't told him about Bernadette de Trevalion; in fact, I'd sworn Eamonn to secrecy. Gilot carried enough guilt, a burden I knew all too well. This was different, though.

"Someone else," I said. "Someone broke up the throng, enough for Lucius to reach me."

Gilot frowned. "Who?"

"I don't know," I said honestly. "I wish I did. Lucius thought that whoever it was, they killed to do it. I remember hearing cries, and tripping over bodies, too. Gilot." I touched his pale, crabbed sword-hand. "You warded our backs. If you hadn't, we might not have gotten out of the wineshop in one piece. And if you'd begun laying about with your sword"—I shivered—"things would have gotten worse. You were right, the quarter was a tinderbox. There were a great many angry students with torches that night, remember?"

"Joscelin—" he began.

"Joscelin wasn't *there*!" I took a deep breath, calming myself. "Ah, Gilot! I do it, too. It's hard to measure one's actions against his. But the truth is, we can only do our best. You did, and I'm grateful for it. And I'm sorry you were hurt. But I still need you."

He lifted his broken hand. "For what?"

"I need your loyalty." I held his gaze. "Gilot, I know you. I *trust* you. Please."

After a moment, he nodded. "For whatever it's worth, I'll stay by your side, Imriel." His mouth twisted. "Not much, I fear. But I'll stay until you're ready to go home."

"My thanks," I said.

Gilot shrugged.

On the near side of the Tiber, our barge nosed the wharf.

I helped Gilot disembark. I would have hired a litter, but I gauged his mood and decided against it. We walked slowly through the streets of Tiberium to the insula.

"So," he said. "There was someone else that night. Who?"

I touched my breast, feeling for the clay medallion that no longer hung there. It was gone, crushed to shards and dust on the floor of Erytheia's atelier. Its secret message was gone. *Do no harm*, it had read. I thought about Canis, who had given it to me. Canis, who had vanished. Canis after the rioting, with a tooth missing and scabs on the knuckles of his left hand. "I don't know," I said. "But my wager's on Canis."

"Canis!" Gilot's head jerked. "Why?"

I shook my head. "I wish I knew."

FORTY-EIGHT

TWO DAYS LATER, we departed for Lucca.

It was a gay party, or at least to all appearances it was. We were all going—it made little sense for Lucius' friends to travel separately from his family—and so we travelled together.

All of us, including Claudia Fulvia.

Our party united outside the walls of Tiberium a little way along the Via Cassia, the wide road that led to the north. Truth be told, I was in good spirits. The day was bright and the air was crisp. I was attired in my new finery. And I'd had a joyous reunion with the Bastard earlier that morning at the lodging-stable. I'd checked on him from time to time during my studies to ensure that he was well cared for, but I'd had few chances to ride and I suspected the stable-lads hadn't exercised him properly. He was huffing and prancing, nearly bursting out of his spotted hide. I'd been hard put to get him out of the city without injuring anyone. No wonder everyone walked in Tiberium.

At the sight of the road stretching before us, Gilot, atop his rangy bay, actually grinned. "It feels good to ride astride," he called.

I grinned back. "That it does!"

Eamonn and Brigitta were awaiting us at the gate, and the four of us struck out together. We felt young and carefree, travelling lightly, with only two pack-horses between the four of us. The same was not true of Lucius' wedding party, which we overtook easily. It contained a very fine carriage drawn by a pair of matched white horses, several wagons loaded with goods, and a number of mounted outriders.

"Montrève!" Lucius caught sight of us and wheeled his mount. He rode back to meet us. In the brisk air, his satyr's face was aglow. "Prince Barbarus, Lady Brigitta, I'm glad you came. Gilot, how is your hand?"

"All right." Gilot eyed him grudgingly.

"Good." Lucius beckoned. "Come, join us." He led us to meet with his party. We jogged alongside the carriage. "You remember Deccus Fulvius, I trust," he said. "And my sister, Claudia Fulvia."

We all inclined our heads and murmured polite greetings.

It was the first time I'd seen Claudia since I'd ended our affair. She tilted her head, glancing out the carriage window and shading her eyes with one hand as she greeted us. Even in the shadowy depths of the carriage, I could see she was wearing a dress of bronze silk with ribbons laced beneath her breasts. I swallowed at the sight of the deep cleft of her cleavage.

"You remember my friends, Claudia?" Lucius asked.

"Oh, yes," she said.

Our eyes met. I felt a flush of heat that began in my groin and travelled upward. Beads of sweat sprang forth at my hairline, trickling down my temples. Sweat. I remembered the taste of hers all too well. And I hadn't been with a woman, any woman, for weeks. Not since the day after the riots. Not since Claudia.

"Imri." Eamonn touched my arm. "The Bastard looks restless. Shall we have a race to take the edge off?"

"*I* want to race!" Brigitta said promptly.

"Why not?" Lucius laughed. "Let's all race, shall we? All of Master Piero's loyal disciples." He pointed down the road. "To the tall cypress and back!"

Without waiting, he set heels to his mount; a sturdy black with a pronounced arch to its neck and a tidy gait. It surged forward and the rest of us gave chase, yelling and shouting.

It wasn't much of a race, not really; but then, Eamonn hadn't meant it to be. He'd proposed it only to distract me. His mount fell behind, and then Brigitta's, although she rode well. I held the Bastard back until I passed them. Ahead of us, Lucius reached the cypress and executed a neat turn, grinning as he passed me on the return leg. I had to fight with the Bastard, who wanted to keep going. At the cypress, I fought for control of the reins, guiding him hard with my knees. I was out of the habit, and he managed to spin around twice in a circle. Once I had him pointed in the right direction, I gave him his head and let him go.

He fairly exploded beneath me.

When it comes to breeding horses, the Tsingani know what they are about. The Bastard stretched out his neck and ran like a house afire. His nostrils flared, his striped hooves pounding the old Tiberian road as his forelegs reached and his hindquarters churned. I crouched low over his neck, laughing at Lucius' dismayed expression when we floated past him.

We overshot the party, and I had to wrestle the Bastard

into another turn. He acceded at last, prancing and preening all the way back.

"Nice horse, lad!" Deccus Fulvius poked his head out of the carriage. "Would you consider parting with him?"

I shook my head. "No, my lord."

He grunted. "Smart lad."

So our party was established, and we rode to Lucca. We were four days on the road, and the days I learned to endure. It wasn't hard. The days were easy, bright and clear. I was among friends, and I had Gilot at my side, trusted and faithful. Claudia was there, yes, but it was easy to pretend she wasn't, so long as she remained sequestered in the carriage.

It was harder at night.

We stayed at inns along the road to Lucca, and at night we were all there together in the common room, eating and drinking and enjoying Deccus Fulvius' largesse. He was no fool; he was investing goodwill in Lucius' future. The prospective Prince of Lucca was a formidable ally for Senator Deccus Fulvius. But ah, Elua! I had to see her then; be near her. And the truth came home to me: I still wanted her, badly.

It was a mercy that Deccus was there. His presence rendered Claudia's behavior circumspect. She bent most of her attention toward Brigitta, taking the young Skaldi woman beneath her wing, speaking to her of women's affairs. She was kind, which surprised me a little. It shouldn't have. Claudia Fulvia was trained in the arts of covertcy, and she used them.

Kindness could be a means to an end.

Deccus was pleased and magnanimous with it; Lucius was pleased, too. It made him happy to behold his sister's kindness. Eamonn, who knew the truth of my relationship with Claudia, was warier, though I daresay no one but I knew it. And who could say? Mayhap there was something genuine in it.

As for me . . .

I felt the heat between us.

Always, at night. It was dangerous to share such close quarters. The first three nights, I lay awake long into the night, tossing on my pallet while Gilot slumbered, aware that only a thin wall divided us. I gritted my teeth and thought about Deccus Fulvius, snoring beside his wife, his beard pointed toward heaven, and hoped it would cool my blood.

It didn't.

On the last night ere we reached Lucca, I gave in to my restlessness, rising from my pallet and letting myelf out of the room Gilot and I shared. I made my way down to the stable. All the world was sleeping; even the Bastard was dozing in his stall, his head hanging low, one rear leg cocked. I leaned on the stall door, watching his rib cage rise and fall, steady and comforting.

"Imriel."

I turned.

Claudia stood behind me, clad in a dress of russet velvet. She wore a shawl clutched round her shoulders and her hair spilled over it, dark red and abundant. She was shivering a little against the night's chill, and her face looked vulnerable.

"It wasn't just the Guild," she said. "It was never just the Guild."

"I don't believe you," I said.

"It's true." Her gaze was clear and candid. "And seeing you like this is driving me mad. I know, I was angry. I said hurtful things, but I didn't mean them, not really. It seems the Guild accepts your decision. Why does it mean everything has to end between us? There's so little time left."

"We can't do this." I shook my head. "Not under Deccus' nose."

"Why not?" Claudia asked.

I didn't answer and she drew near. Her heat and the scent of her skin surrounded me. I could feel my blood beating in my ears.

"I miss you," she whispered.

I kissed her then. A part of me cursed myself for a fool, but ah, Elua! It felt glorious. I slid my hands into the dense, silken mass of her hair. Her lips parted under mine, and I kissed her hard and deep. Her full breasts pressed against my chest. I wanted her. I wanted to take her there in the stable with straw in her hair. I wanted to build a seraglio and tie her to the bedposts with silken cords, to make love to her until she begged me to stop.

Instead, I let her go.

"No," I said simply.

She stood, breathing hard, her lips swollen and her eyes dark with desire. "You're sure."

I nodded. "It's not just Deccus. It's Lucius, too. I can't do this on the eve of his wedding." I closed my eyes. "Claudia, if you have any fondness for me, please go. Before I change my mind."

After a moment, the straw rustled. "You men and your silly codes of honor. What does honor have to do with desire?" Her lips brushed my cheek, and her fingertips brushed my aching groin. "I expected something different from a D'Angeline," she whispered. "But I'll go."

She went.

I waited until she was gone, then went outside. I gazed at the distant stars, willing my blood to cool and the ache of desire to subside. It took a long time, and I cursed myself for a fool all over again, then laughed softly and went back into the inn, where I lay sleepless on my pallet until dawn came.

On the morrow, I was glad of my decision. We got an early start. Lucca was a bit less than a half-day's ride away, and Lucius was hoping to reach the city in time for our midday meal. Whatever misgivings he'd had about this marriage seemed to have vanished; or mayhap it was merely gladness at the prospect of returning home.

I had to own, it was beautiful country, marked by green mountains and vast stretches of fertile plains, glowing golden in the autumn light. We had to ascend to a fair height on the last leg of our journey. At one spot, Lucius pointed toward the west, where a castle was nestled in the crags of another distant range. It looked nigh unreachable.

"You see that?" he asked. "Valpetra. The city's on the far side, you can't see it from here. But that's Martelli's stronghold."

"Looks imposing," I offered.

He contemplated it. "It is."

"Is Lucca in the mountains?"

"No." Lucius grinned. "But it's imposing, too, in its own way. Did I tell you the city walls are so vast they grow trees?" I shot him a skeptical look and he laughed. "Come on, you'll see."

I didn't believe him, not until we descended and rounded a curve in the gorge and the plain of Lucca stretched before us. There was the city, walled around with red brick and surrounded by a moat. Smaller villages clustered around its base, and a river glinted to the north with a canal feeding into the city's moat. At first I still refused to believe, certain that spreading oak-crowns visible above the city walls belonged to trees inside its perimeter. But as we drew near, I realized he spoke the truth. The trees were rooted atop the very walls themselves.

Brigitta frowned, pointing. "What is that?"

"Trees," I said. "Growing from the walls."

She shook her head. "Not the trees. *That*."

"That's the bell-tower." Lucius followed the line of her pointing finger. "They say that when Gallus Tadius and the Red Scourge descended—" He broke off his sentence.

"Smoke," Eamonn said briefly.

We all saw it, then; a trickle of smoke, rising to blend with the autumn haze, hanging over the city. I felt a feather of foreboding brush me.

Lucius turned pale. "Something's wrong." He rode alongside the carriage, pounding on the door. "Claudia! Deccus! Someone's set fire to the bell-tower."

"What?" Claudia's voice was incredulous.

"Stay here." Lucius was grim. "All of you. I'll go find out."

"I'm going with you," I said.

"So am I," said Eamonn. Brigitta merely narrowed her eyes.

"Montrève, you *can't*, you're—" Lucius paused and glanced toward the city. "I don't have time to argue."

"Then don't," I said.

We all went; all four of us, tearing hell-for-leather toward Lucca, and Gilot stayed behind only because I swore on Anna's head and in Blessed Elua's name that I'd dismiss him out of hand if he didn't. I meant it, too.

It was strange and unreal. Minutes ago, we had been laughing and jesting, anticipating our arrival. In a heartbeat, everything had changed. It might be nothing, of course. More often than not, fires happen by accident.

But the nearer we got, the deeper my sense of foreboding grew.

The gates of Lucca were sealed, the bridge drawn up and the portcullis closed. We drew rein on the far side of the moat. The tree-lined wall loomed over us.

Lucius shouted up at the guard towers flanking the gate. "*Guards!* What passes here?"

"Who asks?" a muffled voice called.

His voice was grim and precise. "Lucius Tadius da Lucca!"

The tip of a crossbow emerged from a high window atop the tower. "Show yourself."

Astride his black mount, Lucius opened his arms in a disgusted gesture. "What in the hell do you think I'm doing, you idiot? Look at me. Now open the gate and give us passage!"

Behind the crossbow, a guard peered out the window. "It's him," he called to someone inside, adding, "Sorry, my lord."

There was a grinding sound as the bridge was lowered and the portcullis raised. We followed Lucius across the bridge, the horses' hooves sounding hollow and echoing over the moat. The water stirred, sluggish and green. I knew that smell. It smelled like the fetid pool in the zenana. It stayed with me as we passed under the massive gatehouse.

Inside the walls, a contingent of the city guard awaited us. "My lord Lucius—" began one man, wearing a badge of rank.

"Captain." Lucius cut him off. "What the hell happened here?"

The captain gritted his teeth. "Valpetra."

Lucius swore violently and brought one hand down on

his mount's withers in a hard slap. The black startled under him and he wrenched at the reins with cruel force, jerking its head. Its eyes rolled wildly, and there were flecks of bloody foam at the corners of its mouth. Eamonn and Brigitta exchanged a glance.

"Tell me everything," Lucius said in a voice as cold as winter.

It didn't take long. We learned in short order that a few hours ago, Domenico Martelli, the Duke of Valpetra, had entered Lucca with an entourage of men-at-arms under the pretext of bringing the peace offering of a wedding gift to the Correggio family.

Instead, they had kidnapped the bride and strewn havoc in their wake, setting fire to the bell-tower and disrupting pursuit.

"And you just *let them*?" Lucius roared.

The captain winced. "My lord, they came under a sign of peace. They struck swiftly, and fled swifter. We did our best. I lost seven men, and there was a young nobleman killed, too."

"Who?" Lucius demanded.

The captain glanced around. "Bartolomeo Ponzi," one of his men offered.

"Bartolomeo." Lucius slumped in the saddle, and I remembered that was the name of the young nobleman his betrothed had loved. Lucius closed his eyes and shuddered, then straightened as though shouldering a burden. When he opened his eyes, he seemed to have himself under control. "Where's Helena?"

"Halfway to Valpetra, I imagine," the captain said apologetically. "An hour earlier, and you'd have seen them on the western road. I'm sorry, my lord. Come, we'll escort you to your father."

"Is the city safe?"

"It is now." The captain's face was dour. "The fire's contained and we sealed the gate."

"Good." Lucius pointed south. "My sister and her husband are awaiting word. Send a squadron to escort them. After that, no one comes or goes. Understood?"

"Prince Gaetano . . ." The captain paused. "Yes, my lord. Understood."

He escorted us through the streets of Lucca. It was a lovely city, or it should have been, charming streets lined with buildings of pale ochre with red-tiled rooftops, glowing in the afternoon sun. It was a merchant city and one could see it usually did a lively trade, but today the shops had closed their doors and the streets were mostly empty.

"Dagda Mor!" Eamonn muttered. "It's like Tiberium after the rioting."

"No," I said. "It's worse."

I couldn't have said why, not exactly. But the pall that hung over Lucca was different. It wasn't just the smoke, although as we drew near the center of the city we could smell it. There was somewhat else. The other smell, the fetid Daršanga smell, lingered in my nostrils. The air felt heavy and oppressive. Despite the sun's bright warmth, I was cold. Even the Bastard felt it, his hide twitching the way it did when flies plagued him.

In Lucca's central square, the bell-tower stood, fire-gutted and smoldering. Its stone outer walls were scorched and intact, but the wooden interior had largely collapsed and the roof was gone. A few lines of men stood passing buckets, tossing their contents inside the gaping opening. Others stood around muttering. Sullen tendrils of smoke wreathed the tower's crown, but it seemed for the most part, as the captain had said, the fire was contained.

So why did the sight of it fill me with dread?

Here and there, men made the old Tiberian gesture to avert evil, thrusting their thumbs out of clenched fists. Others spat on the ground. I listened to their muttering, and heard the same word over and over.

Lemures.

I looked over at Lucius. His face was stark and bloodless, and he was staring at the dark maw of the burned tower. His lips worked soundlessly.

"Lucius." I touched his arm. It felt rigid as a board. "What is it?"

He turned his stare on me. "The *mundus manes.*"

"The what?" I asked. "The world? What?"

"The *mundus manes!*" he shouted. "Sweet Apollo, are you an idiot? The pit! It was in the bell-tower!" He whipped his head around, pinning his stare on the captain. "What happened to it?"

The captain made the sign against evil. He was pale, too, though nothing like Lucius. "The cover cracked in the heat of the fire, my lord."

Lucius put his face in his hands. Another shudder racked him.

"I'm sorry," I said, bewildered. "I don't understand."

Eamonn cleared his throat. "It's the opening to the underworld. They uncover it once a year to appease the spirits of the dead and let them walk abroad." He shrugged at my expression. "I was in Tiberium last autumn for the festival. But I didn't notice anything."

"They're not *your* dead!" Lucius cried raggedly.

His shout rang in the square, and heads turned to stare.

"I'm sorry." Breathing hard, Lucius took up his reins. The color returned to his face so abruptly that he looked flushed. "Sorry. Come, my family is waiting."

No one said anything. We followed silently and Lucius sat bolt upright in the saddle as he rode, his back as straight as a spear, his hands steady on the reins. For some reason, even that made me uneasy.

The Tadeii villa was gracious and sprawling, occupying a generous tract of land. The gardens were green and lovely, laid out in stately lines. A pair of men-at-arms met us and the captain of the city guard ceded escort duty to them. Lucius rode up the pathway without looking to the right or left. Servants hurried from the stable to take our mounts.

"Careful," I murmured, handing over the Bastard's reins. "He bites."

Lucius was already striding toward the villa. Glancing helplessly at one another, Eamonn, Brigitta, and I followed.

It was an awkward moment, to say the least. We hung back discreetly, though it was difficult. The three of us weren't exactly a discreet trio. In the atrium, I sidled around, trying to get a look at the proceedings. I felt guilty doing it, but something was wrong, very wrong, and I was worried about Lucius.

"Oh, my boy!" It was his mother who greeted him first, her eyes red with weeping. She embraced him. "I'm sorry, I'm so sorry. That sweet girl!"

"Mother." Lucius returned her embrace. "I know."

"Son." His father's voice was hard and dry. He was a tall man with thinning hair and a mouth that had grown bitter with disappointment. One could see at a glance that Lucius and Claudia got their looks from their mother. "The honor of the Tadeii is at stake."

Lucius straightened, his face changing. "Yes, Father."

The air was heavy, too heavy. I struggled to draw breath.

There was darkness in the villa, darkness in the city. Darkness, crawling all around Lucius Tadius da Lucca. I backed away from him, bumping into the open doorway of the household *lararium*. Eamonn shot me a worried look; even Brigitta looked concerned. I shook my head at them.

"Yes, Father!" There was mockery, cruel mockery, in the older Tadius' voice. "Do you expect me to count on *you* to restore our honor?"

I leaned in the doorway of the *lararium* to brace myself. The altar was ablaze with newly lit candles and the offering bowls were full. The wax death-masks of the Tadeii patriarchs were sweating in the heat. One, prominently displayed, had cracked in twain. I reached for it without thinking, holding up the split halves and examining them. It was a strong face, set in cruel lines, scowling.

Only a mask, broken and empty.

I knew then.

"As opposed to *you*?" Lucius' voice was mild and insulting; at least until he raised it in a roar. "Ye gods, man! What's become of the Tadeii that you reckon *yourself* a man?"

I walked out of the *lararium* carrying the split halves of the death-mask in my hands; past Eamonn and Brigitta, to where Lucius stood. His father was dumbstruck; his mother looked terrified and confused.

Lucius scowled at me. "What's that you've got there, fancy-boy?"

I held up the halves of the mask, framing his scowl between them. I didn't need to see to know it mirrored his own. The resemblance was already etched in my memory, and the chill I'd felt earlier had settled into the marrow of my bones. "What does it look like?"

"Looks like me." He grinned, and it was an expression

FORTY-NINE

WHAT FOLLOWED WAS PANDEMONIUM.

Publius Tadius, Lucius' father, shouted at his son; Lucius shouted back. His mother, Beatrice, wept and begged them to cease. In the midst of it, Claudia and Deccus arrived. She looked at the scene in utter shock.

"What in the world?" she asked.

"Grief's driven your brother mad," Eamonn murmured. "He thinks he's his own ancestor."

I held up the broken halves of the death-mask. "Gallus Tadius."

"*Lemures!*" Deccus, solid Deccus Fulvius, blanched. But the hair on the back of my neck was crawling, and I was in no mood to mock Caerdicci superstition. Whatever possessed Lucius, I didn't think it was simple madness.

At that moment, the atrium echoed with a resounding smack as Lucius roared, "*Enough!*" and dealt his father a casual backhanded blow across the face. "Right," he said into the stunned silence that followed. "Let's all get acquainted." He pointed at Claudia. "You're a Tadius."

"Lucius," she whispered. "It's me, Claudia."

"Claudia." He nodded at Deccus. "Husband, right?"

"Deccus." The senator coughed. "Deccus Fulvius."

"A Fulvius!" Lucius clapped a hand on his shoulder. "Good man. The Fulvii know how to hang on to power, don't they? Not like my spawn." He strolled over to Eamonn and cocked his head. "And what do we have here? A fine barbarian warrior, by the look of you! Who do you serve, lad? You'd be welcome in the Red Scourge!"

"My thanks, my lord," Eamonn said with careful diplomacy. "I'm Eamonn mac Grainne of the Dalriada."

"*Prince* of the Dalriada," Brigitta announced, lifting her chin.

"Ooh!" Lucius laughed. "That's a fierce piece of chattel you've got there, *Prince* Barbarus!" He chucked her under the chin. "That's all right, sweetling. I like a bit of fight in a woman. Fierce women and fierce horses. All the better to break 'em." Brigitta's eyes blazed, one hand twitching toward her dagger, and Lucius laughed again. "Go on, sweetling! Make a move."

Eamonn clenched his fists and cast an imploring glance in my direction.

"Lucius!" I called.

He turned to me, abandoning Brigitta. "Lucius isn't here right now," he said in a conversational tone. "But you know that, don't you, fancy-boy?" I nodded. He came closer. "You're D'Angeline. What's a D'Angeline doing here?"

"I'm Lucius' friend," I said steadily.

"Friend!" He laughed. "That's a fancy word for a fancy-boy." He studied my features. "You're too pretty by half, you know that? I'm going to do you a favor."

Someone—Claudia, I think—let out a gasp as Lucius' fist plowed toward my face, but I was already moving. I swept his fist aside with my left forearm and slid inside his guard, planting my left foot behind his right leg. I splayed my right hand on his chest and shoved and he fell, hard, onto the atrium floor.

It wasn't pretty.

Apoplectic with rage, he got to his feet. "You buggering little—"

"Lucius." I slid out of range and caught Eamonn's eye. He nodded, circling behind Lucius, or Gallus, or whoever he was. "Lucius, think!" I said, desperate. "Where is the virtue in this? What would Master Piero say?"

He paused, a flicker of puzzlement crossing his face. "Master Piero?"

Eamonn took one step forward, raised his arms and clenched his fists together, and brought his right elbow down atop Lucius' skull. He was tall enough to do it, and he packed a wallop like a mule's kick. Lucius' eyes rolled back in his head and his knees buckled. Eamonn winced, rubbing his bruised elbow as our friend slumped to the floor.

"Imri?" Gilot entered the atrium. "They tried to pack me off to the servants' quarters, but I told them—" He halted, blinking. "What in the seven hells happened here?"

"Ghosts," I said wearily. "And Alais was right."

"What?" He stared at me.

I shook my head. "I'll explain later."

We had a long time to talk. After Eamonn had rendered Lucius unconscious, the Tadeii closed ranks and carted him away. The four of us were escorted to guests' quarters by polite, frightened servants. There we were made comfortable, while a steady stream of chirurgeons and priests entered and left the villa. Betimes we heard shouting, but no one told us anything. We ate the meal that was brought to us, availed ourselves of the villa's private baths and strolled in the gardens, and were no wiser by the time dusk fell.

The wing that housed the guests' quarters contained a

comfortable salon with a colonnade that looked onto the side garden, and it was there that we gathered. The servants brought wine and lit the lamps and left us in peace.

"Imriel," Gilot said. "Come morning, we leave."

"We'll see," I said gently.

He bowed his head, rubbing unconsciously at his crippled sword-hand. The fretted lamps cast a patterned shadow on his profile. "You'd stay because Alais had a *dream*?"

"No," I said. "Because Lucius is my friend."

"Loyalty." Unexpectedly, it was Brigitta who spoke. She and Eamonn were sharing a couch, and she lay in the curve of his arm. If there was any doubt that they were lovers, it was gone now. They looked like a pair of basking hunting cats, the two of them. Her blue eyes narrowed. "Loyalty is a virtue."

Gilot sighed. "And duty? What of duty?"

"Master Piero did not speak overmuch of duty," Eamonn said thoughtfully.

"Master Piero!" Gilot's voice rose. "I am nearly sick unto death of Master Piero!"

"Gilot." I reached over to touch his arm. "Go, then. I would sooner you did. This is my choice, and I have to live with it. I need to stay, at least for a little while. But Anna is waiting for you; and Belinda, too. They need you more than I do. On the morrow, go."

"I can't," he muttered.

"Why?" I asked.

He laughed, although there wasn't much humor in it. "Loyalty."

In the end we retired to our chambers and slept, and nothing was decided. I slept alone for the first time in many months. It almost seemed strange to sleep in a proper bed and not a straw pallet, without Gilot snoring in my vicinity.

I awoke to find Claudia Fulvia in my bedchamber.

I sat bolt upright, reaching without thinking for my sword, which I'd laid in easy reach beside my bedside ere I slept. She stood in the doorway and watched without blinking as I pointed it at her. She looked very tired, and the shadows beneath her fox-brown eyes tugged at my sympathies.

"He's awake," she said. "And he's asking for you."

I rose without comment, donned a shirt and breeches, and followed her, padding barefoot through the villa.

At the doorway of the invalid's chamber, Claudia paused. "He seems to be himself," she said. "I don't know how long it will last." Her throat moved as she swallowed. "Be kind to him, will you? He's my brother."

I nodded. "I understand."

She touched my cheek. "Thank you."

I went inside. It was dim and smoky, and there were herbs I didn't recognize smoldering on the brazier. I coughed, waving my hand before my face.

"Montrève?" The figure on the bed stirred. "Is that you?"

"I don't know," I said. "Is that *you*?"

"Near enough." Lucius' voice held a familiar wry note. He propped himself upright against the pillows. "Sorry about trying to break your nose."

I sat on the edge of his bed. "You remember?"

"Yes." He gazed at me with disarming candor. "I'm scared. He'll be back, you know. All of this"—he gestured at the smoking braziers—"it's just a stopgap. He's still here." He touched his breastbone. "Inside me."

"I know," I said.

"You saw it, didn't you?" Lucius asked, and I nodded. "I'm *not* mad?"

"No." I shook my head. "I don't think so. Lucius, my cousin Alais had a dream, years ago. The women in the Cruarch's family dream true things, sometimes. She dreamed I was helping a man with two faces fight villains." I smiled, remembering. "I teased her about it. And I asked why, if the man was my friend. She told me, 'One of him was.'" I took his hand. "I suspect that would be you."

He smiled back at me. "You know, in a strange way, it's almost a relief. The worst possible thing has finally happened. I don't have to worry about it anymore."

"It's not over, though," I said.

"No." Lucius' smile twisted. "No, he'll be back. I can feel him, like some awful bubble inside me, and he'll push until I burst. And the damned thing of it is, I'm afraid we're going to need him."

"What?" I looked blankly at him.

An odd expression flickered across Lucius' face and his hand tensed on mine. Then it vanished, and he was still himself. "Montrève, listen." He squeezed my hand, then let it go. "I'm grateful for your friendship, truly, but you can't stay here. That's why I sent for you."

"I'm not leaving you like this," I said.

"You don't have a choice!" His voice rose. He took a deep breath and lowered it. "Montrève, I don't give a damn what your little cousin dreamed. Listen to me. Get Eamonn and Brigitta and your man Gilot, and get the hell out of Lucca. *Now*."

"Why?" I asked stubbornly.

He swore at me. "Are you too stupid to take an order, D'Angeline? Go!"

Somewhere in the villa, there was more shouting, and then the sound of running footsteps. I heard Claudia's voice at the door and rose.

"Imriel?"

I opened the door. "What is it?"

Her face was composed, but there was fear in her eyes. "Lucca's under siege."

Behind me, Lucius laughed. I turned to see him sitting on the edge of the bed. He gave me a broad, cruel smile, and there was no trace of Lucius in it. "Too late, fancy-boy!" he said cheerfully. "I thought it might be. Valpetra doesn't give a damn about the girl, she's only a means to an end. He wants the city. And I'll be damned if I'll let him take it." Rising, he donned his clothing. "Right," he said to Claudia. "Let's go see about this, shall we?"

Without waiting, he strode out the door.

"Stay with him," I said. "I'll get the others."

By the time I'd roused them and we'd managed to get mounts saddled, Lucius was already on his way to the city walls. The city was in an uproar. The streets were thronged with terrified people, mounted and on foot. The air was thick with fearful rumors.

Oddly, the one calm point was Lucius.

We caught up with him before he reached the gate. He was in the midst of a group of Tadeii and their retainers, riding purposefully and straight-backed. He'd acquired a sword, and it looked as natural at his side as though he'd always carried it. His father was there, and Claudia and Deccus, but no one made a move to deter him. I suppose they didn't dare, and I didn't blame them.

At the gatehouse, the captain of the city guard saluted him warily. There was another man at his side; a nobleman by his dress. He was of middling to older years, with a high brow and a somber gaze, and by his air of authority, I guessed him to be Gaetano Correggio, Helena's father and the Prince of Lucca.

"Right." Lucius ignored him, addressing the captain. "Let's have a look."

"Lucius Tadius?" the other man asked, bewildered.

"Not likely." Lucius dismounted with careless ease, handing his reins to a retainer. He jerked his chin at the guard tower. "Come on, man! Let's go."

"Captain, don't—" Publius Tadius began, then fell silent as Lucius turned to fix him with a cold, hard stare. There was a faint mark on one cheek where Lucius had struck him yesterday. He cleared his throat. "Yes, all right, go have a look. Gaetano, a word?"

The four of us exchanged glances.

"I'll go," I said.

I left the Bastard in Gilot's keeping and followed Lucius and the captain into the guard tower on the right. No one moved to stop me, either. We climbed up the narrow winding stair and entered the chamber at the top. Lucius peered out the window, his shoulders blocking my view.

"Son of a bitch," he muttered, then withdrew. "I can't get a good look out this piss-hole. We're going out on the wall."

I caught the captain's arm as Lucius unbarred the heavy wooden door that led to the walls. "Captain, listen. He's not himself."

"So I see." He blinked. "Who is he?"

I hesitated. "Gallus Tadius."

"Oh." The captain thought about it. "Good."

Since there was nothing else for it, I followed Lucius, ducking my head and clambering through the door. I emerged into daylight, high atop the city wall. It was as broad as a Tiberian road. There were two walls, actually, an outer and an inner, both of them thick and sturdy, with dirt packed solid between them. Truly, the tall oaks that grew atop the wall were rooted in that very soil.

And beyond the wall was an army.

There must have been two thousand men. There was a

small cavalry contingent and a company of archers, but the rest were foot-soldiers. They were fully armed, short-swords and long spears, shields slung at their backs and their armor gleaming in the sun.

Lucius stood in plain sight, feet planted, hands on hips, contemplating them.

"Lucius!" I hissed, ducking back into the shadow of the guard tower.

He glanced over at me. "Oh, sweet tits of the Vestals, fancy-boy! They're not idiots, they're professionals. They're out of bowshot and so are we. Get out here."

I went.

My knees trembled as I did. There is somewhat unnatural about exposing oneself to an entire enemy army without cover. Lucius watched me with amusement.

"Well done," he said when I reached him, clapping my shoulder. "At least you're not a damned coward like the rest of 'em."

I heaved a sigh. "My thanks, my lord."

On the ground, a pair of figures rode forward; a man and a woman, the former leading the latter. Neither was armed. He wore elaborate robes glinting with cloth-of-gold trim. Her gown of red silk flowed over the crupper of her saddle. She kept her eyes downcast.

"Valpetra," Lucius muttered. "That must be the girl."

I glanced at him. "Do you . . . understand . . . what's happening here?"

He shrugged. "Enough."

"Lucca!" The man on the ground shouted. He grabbed the woman's unresisting hand and raised it. "How do you like my new bride? Come out and see her!"

There was a scramble at the door of the guard tower as Gaetano Correggio emerged, accompanied by the captain and a handful of guards. The Prince of Lucca stared at the scene before him and paled.

"That's my daughter," he whispered.

"His wife, now." Lucius shrugged. "That's him, right?"

"Domenico Martelli, Duke of Valpetra." Gaetano pronounced the words as though they were poison on his tongue. "Valpetra!" he shouted. "Let her go, damn you!"

The distant figure laughed. "Is that any way to greet your new son?" he called. "Lucca, I have a lawful claim by marriage as your heir. Open your gates and make me welcome!"

"And if I don't?" Gaetano asked grimly.

The Duke of Valpetra gestured. Behind him, a mounted figure barked an order. A squadron of soldiers unslung their shields and marched forward. The company of archers followed, taking up a kneeling position behind their line. "I'll open them for you!"

"*Guards!*" Lucius roared. "Take aim!"

They obeyed him without thinking, raising crossbows to their shoulders. Gaetano Correggio turned his stricken face toward Lucius. "What do I do?"

"Tell him to take your poxy whore of a daughter and go home," Lucius said promptly. He laughed as Gaetano gaped at him, too shocked for anger. "Oh, come on, man! This isn't about the girl. He wants Lucca." He nodded in the Duke's direction. "Unless matters have changed overmuch in a generation, Valpetra's a piss-poor holding compared to Lucca. That's a mercenary army he's hired, and I'll wager a mountain of gold against a steaming heap of dung that he's promised them spoils in lieu of wages." Lucius shrugged. "You want to see your temples stripped, your women raped, and your sons put to the sword? Go ahead, open the gates."

"How . . ." Gaetano Correggio licked lips gone dry with fear. "How can you be sure?"

Lucius smiled, or at least the thing that wore his face did. "It's what I'd do."

I tried to make myself as unobtrusive as possible. I didn't want any part of this conversation, let alone the tense stand-off between their archers and our guards. But there was nowhere to go atop the wall. Lucius stood there with a sublime lack of concern, the wind ruffling his dark red curls. Gaetano Correggio stared numbly at the figure of his daughter.

"But he'll kill her," he said.

"Her?" Lucius laughed. "Not likely. She's his only claim to legitimacy."

"No." The Prince of Lucca shook his head. "No. I won't risk her. There's got to be another way." His features strengthened with resolve. "Guards!" he snapped. "Stand down." There was a moment's hesitation before they obeyed, lowering their crossbows. "Valpetra!" he shouted. "I want a parley!"

"Idiot," Lucius muttered.

I nearly thought he might challenge Gaetano Correggio then and there, but he merely listened and scowled as they hashed out the terms of a parley meeting. In the end, Valpetra agreed to withdraw the bulk of his army and enter the city with an armed escort. Fifty men, no archers. Gaetano was reluctant to accede, but after much haggling, Valpetra offered to bring Helena into the city with him. At that, the Prince of Lucca relented.

"Correggio, listen." Lucius grabbed his arm as he headed for the tower. "It's a trick."

Gaetano Correggio shook him off. "Let be, man!" He took a deep breath. "Lucius Tadius, I'm sorry for whatever it is that's happened to you. But you've got to get a hold of yourself and stay out of the way until this is over." He glanced at me. "You're his friend?" I nodded. "Do what you can." He raised his voice. "Guards, to me!"

He strode away toward the tower. The captain and his guards fell in behind him. Two or three of them cast dubious looks behind them. I had the distinct sense that they would sooner take orders from Lucius; or at least from Gallus Tadius.

Lucius watched them go. "I'm not in command here, am I?"

"No," I said. "You're . . . dead, my lord."

"Right." He frowned. "It comes and goes. Knowledge, this knowledge, the knowledge of this flesh . . ." He thumped his chest. "My filthy buggering grandson. Great-grandson. It's slippery as an eel, knowledge."

"You should go lie down, my lord," I said.

"Are you out of your mind?" He fixed his wintry gaze on me. "By the Triad, D'Angeline! I thought I saw an ounce of sense in you. You had the balls to come out here, and the balls to knock me down. But hell, I've begun with less. Come on. We've got a lot to do."

"We do?" I asked.

He raised his brows. "Do you *want* to die?"

It almost sounded like Lucius, and for a moment I wondered. But it wasn't Lucius behind those cold eyes. Still, I stood atop the high wall of Lucca while Valpetra's army began to organize a slow withdrawal, and I knew that whoever he was, Lucius or Gallus, I believed him. Unwilling bride or no, Helena Correggio gave Valpetra's claim its sole basis of legitimacy. If he meant to negotiate in earnest, he'd never risk bringing her within Lucca's walls. Gaetano Correggio was blinded by a father's furious grief.

The parley was a trick.

"All right," I said. "What do we do?"

FIFTY

IT WAS A SLAPDASH PLAN, cobbled together in haste. And it all centered around Lucius'—Gallus'—conviction that he knew, with absolute certainty, what Domenico Martelli, the Duke of Valpetra, would do.

"He'll try to gain control of the gatehouse," he said. "It's what *I'd* do."

There wasn't time for anything else. Archers. Archers in the trees atop the walls, hidden from view, positioned to assail Valpetra's escort within Lucca itself. All the openings in the guard towers looked outward; any other position atop the wall was immediately visible and vulnerable to attack from the outside. The trees would serve. It was the best Lucius could do on short notice. The only thing that aided our cause was that Gaetano Correggio and every noble of influence in Lucca was closeted in hurried discussion prior to the parley, giving us leave to lay our plans.

"I can shoot," Brigitta said tersely.

"Brigitta . . ." Eamonn murmured. She glared at him, and I thought it was an argument he would lose. Lucius paid no heed to their exchange.

"Good lass." He nodded in approval. "Hunting bows . . . whatever we have. Gather them. There's a store at the Tadeii villa. I'd sooner have crossbows, but Correggio's ordered the guard to stand down." He slapped his thigh. "Can we recruit any of the guard?"

I thought about the way they'd gazed after him, and the captain's simple comment. *Good*. "A few, mayhap."

"Right," Lucius said. "Anyone they can spare, we'll post in the trees. But the gatehouse is the thing. That's a damn big army out there, and whoever controls the gatehouse controls our fate. They have *got* to be ready for an assault."

Gilot stirred. "I'll tell them." He gave me a crooked smile. "I understand soldiers. And I might as well be good for something, Imri."

I wanted to say no, and I knew it would break his pride if I did. "Go."

He went.

"We need *more*," Lucius said grimly. "Jupiter's Balls! It took me the better part of a year to put the Red Scourge together. I can't resurrect it in an hour."

"Bartolomeo," I said. "What of his friends?"

Lucius held my gaze. "Bartolomeo," he murmured. "Right."

While the elite of Lucca met and argued, preparing to treat with the Duke of Valpetra, we went to the impoverished Ponzi residence. They were holding a wake there. Incredible though it seemed, it was only a day since their son had been slain. Lucca might be under siege, but for the Ponzii, the worst had already happened.

The young nobleman lay on a bier. I didn't look at him, not right away. Instead, I watched Lucius circulate, speaking intently to those in attendance. There were quite a few; merchants and the lesser gentry of Lucca, left to grieve while the elite debated the city's fate. I followed, explaining to those who'd not heard the rumors that it was Gallus Tadius who spoke.

Most of them had.

Young men nodded at his words, pressing fists to their hearts and peeling away. I heard the sound of footsteps, running, and I knew they went to get arms—hunting bows, javelins, whatever they had. I was privy to Gallus' plan. I knew they would toss weighted ropes over the limbs of the oak trees atop the city walls, securing them and climbing to wait, hidden, in their foliage. The citizens of Lucca might witness their ascent, but from the outside it was invisible.

The Red Scourge was rising.

How much of it was pride and anger given purpose, and how much of it was the pall that hung over the city? I could not guess. The dead were afoot, but they were not *my* dead; nor Eamonn's, nor Brigitta's, nor Gilot's. Were we immune to the thrall of violence, the surety of command? I thought so, or I wanted to think so. We followed Lucius because he was our friend. Loyalty. And we followed him because I weighed the same circumstances Gallus Tadius did, and came to the same conclusions.

Phèdre had taught me well how to gauge men's souls.

I wondered, in that fleeting hour, what Claudia thought.

But there was no time; no time. Only time to pay my respects to the dead. I did, at last, pausing beside Bartolomeo Ponzi's bier. He lay stretched upon it, his skin the color of old ivory. It was a little sunken, nothing more. One could tell he had been a handsome young man, the dark brown hair swept back from his brow. His mother had wept for him; a small, round woman. I'd seen her escorted from the room. I did not wonder that Helena had loved him. He had been killed trying to prevent her abduction. Valpetra had cut him down where he stood. There was somewhat about his dead features, the proud, angled jut of his nose, that put me in mind of Joscelin. I didn't even like to think it.

"Bartolomeo." Beside me, Lucius shuddered. He touched the waxy flesh of Bartolomeo's cheek. "Forgive me."

"Lucius?" I thought it was him.

"Love as thou wilt." His mouth twisted. "Isn't that what you say? He never got the chance. Montrève, do me a favor."

"What is it?" I asked.

He looked at me and it *was* Lucius behind his eyes, scared and haunted. "Look out for Helena. Gallus . . ." He paused. "He reckons she's expendable."

I nodded. "I'll try."

"My thanks."

I watched Lucius' presence vanish as we left the Ponzi villa; his stride lengthening with brusque purpose, his spine growing rigid. By the time we reached the courtyard, he was gone. And Elua help me, as awful as I felt for Lucius, I was glad to see Gallus return.

Eamonn was waiting for us, holding the horses. Brigitta was already gone, hidden in the trees, armed with a hunting bow she'd chosen at the Tadeii villa. With luck, she'd never need use it. That was the only good thing about Gallus' plan. If he was wrong and Domenico Valpetra meant to negotiate in earnest, he'd never know we were there.

We mounted and rode toward the gatehouse square. The city was filled with a muted buzz. The streets were mostly empty, but people had clustered on the rooftops. Atop every building, the citizens of Lucca huddled and whispered.

The temples were crowded, too; mostly with the poor, hoping to claim sanctuary. We passed the Temples of Jupiter and Mars on the way to the gatehouse, and fearful faces peered from the open doorways. A squadron of the city guard was posted before both temples. Gallus Tadius—I had begun to think of him thusly—cursed at the sight. At the second temple, he dismounted and collared the reluctant squadron leader.

"Lieutenant!" he roared. "Who ordered you here?"

The lieutenant was a rosy-cheeked lad with a fuzz of blond down on his upper lip. He looked all of seventeen, and his voice quavered when he answered. "Captain Arturo, sir! Prince Gaetano's orders!"

"Greedy bastard," Gallus muttered. "I should never have told him Valpetra would sack the temples." He thought a moment, absentmindedly clutching the lad's tunic in one fist. "Right. Follow me."

"Sorry, sir!" the lieutenant squeaked. "We can't. Prince's orders!"

Gallus let him go and promptly knocked him down with a backhanded blow. "Idiots!" he said in a scathing tone. "Look at the lot of you. Green as they come, not a set of armor among the bunch. What do you think you're going to do if Valpetra brings his mercenaries in here?" He stood over the lad and shook his head. "A hundred bowmen could hold this city against an army. But no, Gaetano has to open the gates. Listen, boy. You hear fighting, you bring your men on the double."

The lieutenant rubbed his cheek. "Yes, sir!"

Gallus remounted and we continued. He muttered beneath his breath as we rode: numbers, arms, angles of trajectory—I don't know what. All the facts and figures that a good condottiere takes into account. Eamonn and I followed in his wake, glancing at one another.

"Imri." He touched my arm. "If this goes badly, don't hesitate to surrender and claim asylum."

"As what?" For a wild moment, I remembered how Lucius had reacted when I told him who I was. "My mother's son?"

"A political hostage." Eamonn's grey-green eyes were grave, as grave as I'd ever seen them. "You're a D'Angeline Prince of the Blood."

"What about you?" I asked. "What of the Dalriada?"

He shrugged. "We're a lot smaller and a lot farther away. Just remember, will you?"

"I'll try," I promised for the second time that day. "You do the same."

The square outside the gatehouse was packed. Gaetano Correggio, the Prince of Lucca, was there. Publius Tadius was beside him, and a few other noblemen I didn't recognize. There were no women. The bulk of the city guard flanked them, all on foot. I had to own, Gallus Tadius was right. They weren't an imposing sight. In accordance with the terms of parley, they were armed only with short-swords. None of them wore armor, only padded crimson gambesons.

"Stupid," Gallus seethed. "Stupid, stupid, stupid!"

There were mayhap a hundred members of the city guard all told. Forty of them had been dispatched to guard the temples. I cast my gaze over the ranks before us, and guessed that mayhap fifty were present; an equal number to match Valpetra's escort. That meant there were ten at best in the gatehouse itself. Less, if any were in the trees.

We drew rein behind them.

It was hard not to look. There were only two oak trees atop the walls that afforded sufficient cover to hide our archers and grew within striking range. Their dense foliage rustled, the leaves only just beginning to turn autumn's hues. I wondered how many archers were hidden within it, poised on thick tree limbs, prepared to shoot. I glanced at Eamonn and saw a muscle in his jaw jumping. I knew he was thinking of Brigitta. It was the first time, I think, I'd ever seen him afraid.

Gallus Tadius relaxed in the saddle, his hands loose on the pommel.

There was a small window in the chamber above the gate proper, overlooking the square. A guardsman's head poked out of it.

"Prince Gaetano!" he bawled. "Domenico Martelli da Valpetra and his bride Helena Correggio da Lucca request entrance! They bring an escort of fifty men, and their army has withdrawn!"

Gaetano Correggio nodded curtly. "Admit them."

Within the gatehouse, a winch was turned. Gears groaned as the portcullis rose and the wooden drawbridge lowered. I saw them, then, silhouetted in the opening. Two scouts, scurrying ahead to confirm the terms of the parley, ensuring that no ambush awaited them. Valpetra and Helena, riding. The hollow echo of hooves over water, the steady tramping feet of the men who followed them, clad in steel armor. They passed through the vast doorway of the gatehouse and entered the square, facing off against Gaetano Correggio. The mercenary soldiers fell into neat lines. The gears ground once more as the portcullis descended, the drawbridge closing like an angry mouth.

They wore armor.

They carried short-swords. They planted the butts of their thrusting spears on the dusty cobblestones and slung their shields over their forearms.

"Oh, we are in a sodding world of trouble!" Gallus muttered.

Domenico Martelli was a solid man with black hair and a fleshy face, deep lines inscribed on either side of his mouth. They deepened further as he smiled. "Prince of Lucca!" he rumbled, spreading his arms. Beneath his bridegroom's robes, a steel corselet glinted. "Father! Do you acknowledge your heir?"

Beside him, Helena kept her eyes downcast.

"I do not." Gaetano's voice was steady. "Valpetra, hear me. We are prepared to come to an accommodation. Do you cede your claim and leave in peace—"

That was as far as he got.

The Duke of Valpetra waved a casual hand. "Kill him," he said. "And take the gatehouse."

His escort didn't hesitate. A third, at the rear, peeled away to assail the gatehouse. Two-thirds of them simply settled their shields on their arms, lowered their spears, and charged.

"Archers!" Gallus roared. *"Now!"*

The air sang and hummed as flights of arrows passed overhead. I saw them find targets. I saw shields bristle with arrows. I saw armor pierced. I saw men wounded, and I saw some fall back and others press forward. Beneath me, the Bastard shifted restlessly, tossing his head. His nostrils flared. I felt sick with fear. Beside me, Eamonn drew his sword.

"Again!" Gallus called, and another flight of arrows sang. For a moment, it kept the assault in the square at bay, but in the gatehouse there was shouting and fighting and the sound of gears grinding. The portcullis was rising, the drawbridge lowering. Someone was blowing a horn over and over. Beyond the walls, Valpetra's withdrawn army was advancing in a hurry. Two thousand men, less fifty, ready to assail the city.

The portcullis rose to half-mast and stopped. With a rattling clank, the drawbridge halted in its descent, hovered at an angle over the moat. I prayed, silently, that Gilot was all right. He couldn't hold a sword. He shouldn't be there.

Domenico Martelli's face darkened.

"Lucca!" he shouted. "Are you willing to watch your daughter die?"

He reached for her, catching her wrist. In his other hand, he held a naked blade. All around them, men were beginning to fight and die. Luccan guardsmen, mostly, were doing the dying. The only mercy was that the Valpetran spears were hampered at close quarters; but by the same token, our archers could no longer shoot for fear of hitting their own men. Gaetano Correggio had fallen to his knees, his hands outstretched. I watched Helena's chin rise. Her eyes blazed with despair and pride.

Gallus Tadius laughed.

I swore.

It was too much; too much. I had seen that look on the faces of too many women in the zenana; the ones who went to their death and knew it, clinging to whatever small scrap of pride was left to them. Lucca's dead might not be mine, but I had my own to answer to.

A high-pitched ringing filled my head, obscuring the din of battle. All I could hear was the horn sounding the alarm, over and over, and a single voice uttering a fierce, wordless battle-cry. Heads turned slowly, knots of unmounted fighters disengaging. So, so slow! I felt the Bastard quiver beneath me, haunches gathering. Elua, but he was a good horse! When I touched my heels to his flanks, he shot forward like an arrow from the bow.

All the fear was gone.

There was only fury, a fury so vast my body couldn't contain it. It felt as though flames surged from the top of my skull. We plunged into the melee, guards and soldiers scattering. I guided the Bastard with my thighs and he wove between them, his striped hooves beating a fierce tattoo on the paving-stones of Lucca.

No one touched us.

I didn't even remember drawing my sword.

And then there they were, and we were bearing down on them. Domenico Martelli, the Duke of Valpetra, was slow to react. His fleshy face looked surprised, his mouth agape like a fish. His thick-fingered hand, clamped like a manacle on Helena's wrist.

Slow. Too slow.

I turned the Bastard sharply, coming broadside. I brought my sword down in a single swift stroke, severing the link that bound them, severing his hand at the wrist. Blood spurted from the stump. He stared at it in disbelief.

Helena gave a choked gasp.

Everything came back then. Time flowed in its usual channels, and the taste of fear filled my mouth. I smelled death; blood and feces and rot. Daršanga. Willing my churning gut to subside, I shoved my bloodied sword in its scabbard and grabbed the reins of Helena's mount.

"Lucius sent me," I said. "Hurry!"

She asked no questions, only followed. We fled on horseback, plunging past the fighting. It had grown fierce. Eamonn was in the thick of it, still mounted, laying about him on both sides with his sword. Other guardsmen had come at a run, swords drawn. Gallus Tadius rode along the fringes of the battle, calling out orders. A handful of guards were dragging Gaetano Correggio's limp form to safety. Here and there, a Valpetran soldier fell, picked off by a judicious arrow.

"Retreat!" the Duke shouted, clutching his stump. *"Retreat!"*

"Attack!" Gallus roared. "Archers, *forward*!"

Valpetra's men fell back; back to the gatehouse. On the far side of the moat, nearly two thousand reinforcements were hurrying to their assistance. But the drawbridge was stuck at its midpoint, and they wouldn't be able to cross easily. If they reached the moat before we could raise the bridge, it would buy us a few moments. Gallus Tadius' archers swarmed down from the trees, descending on ropes, fierce grins illuminating their faces. I breathed a sigh of relief at the sight of Brigitta, who looked remarkably happy. In the throng, Eamonn made his way toward her.

"Guards, *down*!" Gallus shouted. "Archers, *shoot*!"

Their untrained obedience was a marvel. The Luccan guards flung themselves flat and the ragtag band of archers knelt and took aim, shooting over their heads to drive back the invaders. Beneath the shadow of the gatehouse, Valpetra's soldiers began crawling beneath the half-raised portcullis and hurling themselves into the moat, leaping from the steeply angled drawbridge. Some stripped off their armor; others floundered and sank.

A dozen of them clustered around Domenico Martelli, the Duke of Valpetra, helping him toward the moat. Gallus Tadius issued furious orders to halt them, but the Luccan guards within the gatehouse were still struggling for control of the drawbridge mechanism, and a handful of Valpetra's men had made a stand, guarding his retreat from the onslaught of the guards in the square. Two of them died defending him, and four were wounded. Gallus was right; they were professionals.

The horn sounded an increasingly urgent alarm.

"The bridge!" Gallus roared. "Damn you, raise the bridge!"

I watched with my heart in my throat. Somewhere in the gatehouse, the mechanism was jammed. For long moments, the bridge stayed at half-mast. Valpetra and his men had made a successful retreat. On the other side of the moat, the entire bulk of his army was massing. It wouldn't be long before they mounted a second attack. If we couldn't seal the city, the lot of us were doomed. We were too few and too disorganized to hold off a sustained assault. And I didn't like my chances as a political hostage, not after I'd lopped off Domenico Martelli's hand.

"What is it?" a trembling voice asked. "What's wrong?"

I glanced at Helena Correggio, shivering beside me on horseback, her arms wrapped around herself. Her face was white, and her eyes were all pupil. "The bridge is stuck, my lady."

She swallowed. "Oh."

There was a clamor in the gatehouse; men shouting up and down the stairs. At length, a figure emerged from the right-hand tower and leapt onto one of the chains that held the counterweights. It didn't budge, not at first. But then a score of men followed suit on both sides of the gatehouse, several clambering up the chains to add their weight, others hauling on them with brute force.

Inch by inch, the drawbridge rose and the massive portcullis descended.

Until it was done, I hadn't realized I'd been holding my breath. I daresay all of Lucca breathed a sigh of relief as the drawbridge slammed into place and the portcullis shuddered to earth. The city was sealed. We were back to where we had been a mere hour ago. Under siege, and this time grateful it was no worse.

"Forgive me, my lady." I turned to Helena. "Are you . . . all right?"

She looked away and I knew she wasn't all right, not at all. She had been abducted and brutalized. She had watched the man she loved cut down before her eyes, and a man she despised violently maimed. One side of her scarlet wedding gown was splashed with darkening blood. But all she asked was, "Are we safe?"

"For the moment," I said truthfully.

She looked at me, then. Her pupils were no longer as stark, and I saw that her eyes were a clear blue. "Who are you?"

"Imriel," I said. "Imriel nó Montrève."

"You're D'Angeline." She put out one hand, then drew it back. "When you rode toward us, I thought you were . . . I thought . . ." She shook her head and did not finish the thought. "My father?"

"Let's go see," I said gently.

It was still mayhem in the square. Gallus had vanished into the gatehouse, for which I was grateful. Helena didn't need to know, not yet, what had befallen her betrothed. I counted the dead. Five of theirs, and eight of ours. There were another dozen, at least, badly wounded. The four injured Valpetrans were under guard, their faces stoic with pain and resolve. At least they were alive. Eamonn was right, war was ugly.

Gaetano Correggio was alive, too. He'd taken a blow to the temple. It wasn't serious, but his hair was matted with blood.

"Helena." His voice cracked and he raised his arms. She dismounted into them, hiding her face against his chest. He held her tight, his head bowed. I sat quietly atop the Bastard, thinking what a strange world it was where a man loved his only daughter enough to risk an entire city to save her, but not enough to permit her to wed a poor man. After a moment, the Prince of Lucca shuddered and lifted his head. "Thank you," he said. "My lord D'Angeline, you have my deepest gratitude and the eternal gratitude of my house." A touch of wonder lit his deepset eyes. "I don't even know your name."

I bowed in the saddle. "Imriel nó Montrève, your highness."

"Imriel nó Montrève." He repeated it. "Montrève."

"Yes, my lord." I saw Eamonn approaching across the square, Brigitta riding behind him, still clutching her hunting bow. Eamonn nodded toward the gatehouse. "My lord, forgive me, but I must see about a friend."

"Yes, of course," he said absently.

I paused, glancing down at the top of Helena's head. Her face was still hidden. Brown hair, straight and fine as baby-silk. "My lord, will you tell her about Lucius?"

"Lucius." The Prince of Lucca licked his lips. "Yes."

Eamonn and I entered the nearest guard tower without exchanging a word. We didn't need to. Even Brigitta had grown somber, agreeing to watch the horses without a quarrel. There were more dead in the tower; one Valpetran and two Luccan guards, blocking the narrow stair. We had to clamber over them.

The lower chambers were empty, which was absurd, but there were three guardsmen in the top chamber manning the arrow-slits with crossbows. In the far tower, we could hear Gallus Tadius shouting, but it was quiet here. One of the guards glanced around as we entered, the other two remaining intent on their duty.

"The D'Angeline?" he asked.

"Is he . . . ?" I couldn't ask.

"In there." He jerked his head toward the open door onto the inner chamber. "Tell him thanks for saving our arses."

With a surge of hope, I ducked through the door and entered the central chamber, Eamonn crouching as he followed. The windows were shuttered and bolted, and it took a moment for my eyes to adjust to the dimness. All I could see was the vast mechanism that took up a good portion of the chamber; a huge cog-wheel and pulley system with levers protruding at strange angles and the chains oddly disengaged.

"Gilot?" I called.

For a moment, nothing. And then a scrabbling sound and a faint cough. "Imri?"

"There." Eamonn pointed.

Gilot was lying propped against a wall. He raised one hand—his good hand—in greeting as we hurried to his side. I dropped to my knees.

"Are you all right?" I asked anxiously.

"No." He smiled at me. "Not really. But did you see what I did?" He pointed at the mechanism, and I realized one of the levers was a Valpetran spear, shoved deep within the gears of the cog-wheel. He coughed, and a bloody spume trickled from the corner of his mouth. "Damned engineers. You don't spend a year in Siovale without learning how things work. All knowledge is worth having, right?"

My eyes stung. "You did that? Stopped the drawbridge?"

He nodded. "Getting it unstuck was the hard part. I had to convince 'em to slip the chains and haul the weights by hand. Had to show 'em, too. They finally got it once the chains were loose." He laughed, then winced. "Sorry. Imri, I think mayhap that splinter . . . I think mayhap it's moved."

"Gilot . . ." I rubbed my eyes with the heels of my hands. "Eamonn," I said roughly. "He needs a chirurgeon."

Without a word, Eamonn stooped and gathered Gilot in his arms.

When the poets sing of glorious deeds, they leave out the awful parts. Phèdre always said so, and I knew it was true. I had heard the tales, and I had witnessed the reality. But this was the first time I'd done so as a man in my own right. I understood it anew that day. In a poet's tale, a valiant few might stand against the many, and a cunning hero prevails.

This was no poet's tale.

Eamonn had to sidle sideways down the winding stair, and even at that, Gilot's head and his trailing legs scraped the walls. And then there were the dead. One Valpetran, two Luccan. I had to move them all before Eamonn could pass with his burden.

Dead flesh, heavy and inert. Blind, staring eyes.

I took the Luccans first, hoisting one at a time over my shoulder and carrying them down the stairs. Dead limbs dangled and thumped against me and I could feel the slow seep of blood from their wounds soaking my shirt. It was hard work; harder than hauling stumps at Montrève and infinitely more horrible. I laid each down in the square with care. They were someone's son, someone's brother, someone's beloved. Already there was wailing in the city.

By the time I got to the Valpetran, I was exhausted. I had to strip his armor in order to move him. Beneath his helmet, he had an ordinary face. I hated him anyway. For a moment, I was tempted to grab his ankles and haul him down feetfirst. Let his skull crack as it bounced down the stair; what did it matter? He was dead.

Remember this.

I imagined Phèdre's expression, sighed, and hoisted the Valpetran's corpse.

Eamonn followed carrying Gilot. It was easier work than hauling the dead, but he had the physical strength to do it with a tender effortlessness I couldn't have mustered. Gilot hadn't uttered a word of protest. By that alone, I knew how badly he was hurt.

"Guard!" I caught at the nearest crimson gambeson. "I need a litter."

He jerked his head toward the northwest corner of the square, where a dozen wounded men lay groaning. "Wait your turn."

I swore at him.

"Imri." Gilot's breathing was shallow and thick, and blood bubbled over his lower lip. "Just put me on a damn horse, will you? I'll make it."

In the end, we did. Eamonn and I eased him atop the Bastard. We walked on either side and held him upright, while Brigitta took Eamonn's horse and raced ahead to the Tadeii villa to beg them to send for a chirurgeon.

Outside the walls of Lucca, Valpetra's army was settling in for a long siege. In the gatehouse, Gallus Tadius was rallying the city guard's defenses. So I assumed, at any rate. What had become of Gaetano Correggio and his daughter, I couldn't say. At the moment, I didn't care about any of them.

The Bastard was as good as gold. He picked his way with care, placing each hoof delicately. I swear, he knew.

"Remember that spotted horse, Imri?" Gilot coughed. "The one at the fair, the day we heard about your mother. What was his name?"

"The Salmon," I said softly. "I remember. You were going to save your wages."

"Never was any good at that." He bent his head, stroking the Bastard's neck. A few drops of blood fell from his chin, blending into the Bastard's speckled hide. "Take care of this one, will you?"

"Don't talk like that!" I said in alarm.

Gilot smiled, and winced. "Talk to you any way I please, today."

"Why not?" Eamonn said equably. "You always do."

It made us all laugh, and then Gilot coughed again and more blood came. We walked the rest of the way in silence, and Claudia Fulvia met us at the gate of the Tadeii villa with a handful of retainers, all of them armed and watchful. She looked tired and worried, but strong. Elua help me, I was glad to see her in a way I hadn't known existed. The courage of women is different from the courage of men; deeper and more enduring. A vast weariness crashed over me, and all I wanted was to sink to my knees and lose myself in her embrace.

"The chirurgeon is coming," she said. "Let's get him inside."

Eamonn carried Gilot into the villa. Without the presence of Gallus Tadius, the atmosphere was quiet and hushed. We made Gilot as comfortable as possible in one of the guest chambers, and settled in to await the chirurgeon.

There was nothing else to be done.

FIFTY-ONE

S O BEGAN THE SIEGE of Lucca.

It seemed like a fever-dream. From the moment we had spotted the smoke outside the walls, nothing had felt quite real. A single day had passed and the world had gone mad. It was, though. It was all horribly real.

The Luccan chirurgeon who examined Gilot shook his head. "Pray to Asclepius and Far-Sighted Apollo," he said simply. "There is nothing I can do."

I wanted to pray; I wanted to curse. I wanted to feel hope or fury. Anything to stem the awful tide of sorrow that threatened to swallow me. But there was nothing, only grief.

Gilot died in the small hours of the night.

I was with him. I never left his side, except once when Eamonn spelled me so I might change out of my blood-stiffened clothing and bathe. I did so hurriedly, leaving swirls of translucent red in the clear water of the baths. I didn't know how I'd gotten so much blood on me. Carrying the dead, I reckoned. I didn't even have a scratch. It seemed wrong.

Scrubbed clean, I knelt at Gilot's bedside. He slept, mostly. The chirurgeon had given him a tincture of opium. From time to time, I rose to tend the lamps. As long as I wiped the blood from his mouth, Gilot looked peaceful in repose. *He's so beautiful*, Anna had said. I thought of Anna and her young daughter, Belinda, awaiting his return from Lucius' wedding, and I wanted to weep.

He woke before the end and smiled to see me kneeling there. "Are you keeping Blessed Elua's vigil for me?" he asked thickly.

I took his stiff, broken hand. "I suppose I am."

Gilot laughed, or tried to. I let go his hand to dip a cloth in the basin beside me and dab his lips. "Elua! Do you remember when you took sick? Phèdre was so mad at Joscelin. I'd never seen her angry."

"No," I murmured. "It doesn't happen often."

"Will you tell her?" He groped for my hand. "Tell them both I tried."

"I'll tell them." I swallowed. "I'll tell them how you were a hero. How you saved the city, saved everyone. You were clever, so clever." I scrubbed my eyes with my free hand. "All knowledge is worth having. I'll tell them."

"Clever." Gilot smiled. "Who would have thought." He squeezed my hand. "Anna?"

I nodded. "I promise."

"Good." He sighed. "Good."

After that, he didn't speak. It was a long time before I realized that the silence I heard was the absence of his labored breathing. The peace that had settled over his features was a lasting one. His hand was growing cool in mine. I let it go for the last time and leaned my brow against the edge of his bed.

"Imriel?"

I lifted my head. Claudia was in the doorway, clad in a nightrobe.

"Is he . . . ?"

I nodded, wordless.

She opened her arms and I went to her. There was no guilt in it, not now; not even desire. Only a mortal, human need for contact. For a long moment, we stood in the doorway, holding one another. At length, Claudia shuddered and sighed. Her breath, warm and alive, stirred my hair.

"I'm sorry, Imriel."

I released her. "Thank you."

"I'll tell the chamberlain," she said quietly. "If it's acceptable to you, your friend will be given a place of rest in the Tadeii mausoleum, at least for now."

"Do we have a choice?" I asked.

Claudia shook her head. "At the moment, no."

A harsh laugh burst from me. "So much for the Unseen Guild!"

"Imriel." She touched my cheek. "The Guild can't control every vagary of human ambition. Right now, I'm trapped here as surely as you are. Be patient."

"Patient!" The anger came, then. "Name of Elua! It's a bit late for *patience*, isn't it? Surely it's too late for Gilot!" I drew a sharp breath. "I want out of here, Claudia. Out of Lucca. I want to take Gilot and go home. That's all he wanted, to go home to Terre d'Ange. I promised him we'd go home. Let him at least be buried there. It's all I ask."

"Well, mayhap you should have thought of it before you decided to play the hero!" Claudia said tartly. "Imriel . . ." She sighed and lowered her voice. "I'm sorry. I will do what I can. But understand, I don't control the Guild. They may move to aid us or they may not, depending on their interests. And when all is said and done, the Guild is not terribly interested in Lucca." Her wide mouth curled. "I'm only a journeyman. I'm expendable. It's another reason why I was allowed to approach you in the first place."

I shivered. "Cold folk."

"Yes," she said simply. "It might have been different if . . ."

"If I had sworn loyalty?" I asked.

"Mayhap." Claudia shrugged. "You were a prize they valued. Or if you hadn't severed the Duke of Valpetra's hand." She smiled ruefully. "It would have been a lot easier to negotiate safe passage for you and your friends if you hadn't."

I thought about the look in Helena's eyes. "He deserved it."

"I know." She took my sword-hand and stroked it, and a frisson of desire ran through me. In the presence of Gilot's cooling body, it felt at once wrong and right. There was a strangeness in it. Death breeds desire; and yet, should it not? I knew what happened if it didn't. Death breeding death, the three-fold path. *Ill thoughts, ill words, ill deeds.* One building on another. "I heard what you did."

"Gilot died a hero," I said hoarsely.

"Yes," she said. "He did."

I caught her fingers in mine. "Come with me."

In my guest chamber, we coupled. I daresay there is another word for it, a better word. Lovemaking; yes, there was love in it, or at least tenderness. But it was a form of grieving, too. And mercy, and redemption . . . I do not know how to speak of it. In the adjacent chamber, Gilot lay dead and cold. A life, two lives, would be darkened by that sorrow. And I made love to Claudia, because we were alive and warm. No games, no frills. I fell into her and lost myself. Her voice beckoned me onward, plummeting deeper into her core.

This, too, is sacred.

Afterward, I wept.

Tears, bitter tears. All the villa was asleep, Gilot was dead, and I wept onto Claudia Fulvia's shoulder, hot tears trickling over her skin. She held me and whispered words of comfort, and I was grateful for it.

"We have to be strong," she murmured at length. "All of us."

"I know." I rose and splashed my face in the washbasin, then dressed. "Tell the chamberlain to make arrangements. I'll speak to Eamonn and Brigitta." I looked at Claudia, tousled and weary, and lovely despite it. "Thank you."

She summoned a tired smile. "I told you it was never just the Guild."

Claudia left, and I went to tell Eamonn and Brigitta. He was in a deep, exhausted sleep, but Brigitta was awake, reading by lamplight, her brow furrowed in concentration. She glanced up as I entered the chamber, and saw by my expression what news I bore.

"He has died?" she asked in her Skaldic accent.

"Yes," I said.

Brigitta closed her book. "I am sorry. He died bravely." She paused. "Shall I wake Eamonn?"

I wanted to say yes, but Gilot was gone, and waking Eamonn wouldn't bring him back. There was no reason for it except that I didn't want to be alone with my grief. "No," I said. "Let him sleep and tell him when he wakes."

"Yes," she said. "I will."

I left her stroking Eamonn's hair as he slept. She understood her fortune; another woman's beloved had died while hers yet lived. I daresay Brigitta would have endured it better. My heart ached at the thought of having to tell Anna, who had already loved and lost one man.

Since I had nowhere else to go, I returned to Gilot's chamber.

For the rest of the night, I kept Elua's vigil for him, kneeling on the marble floor. We were alone here, the two of us.

We were strangers in Lucca. Eamonn and Brigitta had one another, Claudia had Deccus Fulvius, Lucius . . . well, Lucius had Gallus Tadius. Gilot was the only one who had come for me. And now he was gone.

I'd known him since I was thirteen years old. He'd been my present age when he joined Phèdre's service; eighteen and eager to make his name. He was the first to treat me as an equal—the only one. I smiled, remembering. At the time, I'd envied him the age of majority. Now Gilot at eighteen seemed younger, far younger, than I felt.

Elua, but I must have been a plague to him!

He'd endured it, though. My moody adolescence, my feckless young manhood. Endured it in good spirits, without complaint. Well, that wasn't exactly true. He'd grumbled incessantly for most of the time in Tiberium. It was fair, though. I'd given him cause, time and again.

I'd give anything to see him roll his eyes in disgust once more.

It was a piece of irony that Gilot had never known the truth about the danger I faced in Tiberium, the attempts on my life. And yet here in Lucca, where I thought I'd be safe, he'd done his duty to the utmost. He'd saved me, saved us all. And now he was dead.

I wished I hadn't let him go to the gatehouse.

I hadn't thought he'd stay. Or at least . . . No. I hadn't *thought*. That was the truth of it. Until Valpetra's men charged the gatehouse, I'd forgotten about Gilot. I'd been swept up in the fervor of the moment. I was responsible for him. I knew he was wounded. I should have seen to it that he was safely behind the lines. He wouldn't have liked it, but he would have gone if I'd ordered him on pain of dismissal. Mayhap.

And yet if he had, the drawbridge would never have been

raised. Valpetra's gambit might have succeeded, and many others might have died. I realized, that night, that I would never know. Gilot might have obeyed me; or not. He was loyal, but he was proud, too. He was Phèdre's man and sworn to protect me. Of a surety, he'd have been dead-set against my mad charge to free Helena. After five years, he knew me well enough to guess what I was about. I'd never opened my heart to him the way I had to Eamonn. But he'd been my companion, day in and day out, for a long time.

You've got a wild streak in you, my prince.

Gilot would have guessed.

And he might have thwarted me and lived, or he might have died trying. Valpetra might have killed Helena Correggio in front of her father's eyes. It might have turned the tide against us. Lucca might have fallen. All of these things or none of them might have happened.

I would never know.

In the early light of dawn, I heard Eamonn's tread. I got up, my knees stiff and aching. Eamonn put his arm over my shoulders and together we gazed at Gilot. Only yesterday, I'd stood beside Lucius at the bier of Bartolomeo Ponzi. It seemed like longer, much longer.

"*Slán agus*, Gilot," Eamonn said softly. "*Beannacht leat.*" The Eiran words brought a lump to my throat. We were all so far from home. He gazed at Gilot a moment longer, then gave me a light shake. "Come on. You need to eat something, Imri. Let's go find the kitchen."

I shrugged. "I'll wait."

"For what? The embalmers?" Eamonn read my expression and sighed.

"I will stay with him," Brigitta offered from the doorway. She shifted. "I know you think I do not like D'Angelines. I did not know him well. But he seemed like a good man. And I think you have not eaten anything since before yesterday."

I met her gaze and she returned it steadily. "All right," I said. "Thank you."

Brigitta inclined her head. "You are welcome."

We found our way to the kitchen, where the mood was tense. The servants of the Tadeii household spoke in urgent, hushed whispers. Nonetheless, a sweet-faced scullery maid came to our aid. Seated at the servants' table, we broke our fast on bread sopped in an egg posset and sprinkled with shaved curls of a hard, sharp-tasting cheese. Until Eamonn made me eat, I hadn't realized I was a trifle lightheaded with hunger. Brigitta was right, it had been a day and more since I'd eaten. I could have consumed a dozen possets.

"Is there more?" Eamonn asked hopefully.

The maidservant who had procured them for us glanced at the master cook. He hesitated, then scowled and shook his head at her.

"I'm sorry, my lords." She clasped her hands together and wrung them. "We're on short rations, all of us. Lord . . . Lord Lucius' orders."

"Lucius!" Eamonn exclaimed. "*Lucius* wouldn't—"

"Eamonn." I forestalled him. "Lucius wouldn't, but Gallus Tadius would, and rightly so. The city's under siege. Elua knows how long it will last. He's back, then?" I directed the last to the maidservant.

"Yes, my lord." Her head bobbed. "He came late yesterday evening. He works alone in his quarters. No one . . . no one wanted to disturb you, my lord."

"Imriel," I said. "My name's Imriel. What's yours?"

She flushed to her hairline. "Teresa."

"Teresa." I smiled to put her at ease. "Who came? Lucius or Gallus?"

"G-Gallus, my lord." The scullery maid swallowed. "So they say." She shivered. "Is it true, then? I think it is. I know it is. Everyone says so. I knew Lord Lucius before he left. He had a sharp tongue, but he was always kind beneath it. Now . . . it's all different."

"It's true." I stood up. "Eamonn, tighten your belt. Let's go."

By the time we left the kitchen, the Tadeii villa was awake. The embalmers arrived, and it was Claudia who directed them to Gilot's chamber and sent a runner to find me. I went and watched them prepare Gilot for removal. They were somber men and they treated his body with care, covering it with a linen shroud and easing it gently onto a litter.

"You wish the full treatment?" one asked Claudia. "It is costly. And in such times"—he shrugged—"more so."

She caught my eye and raised an inquiring brow.

"Yes," I said. "I mean to bring him home."

Deccus Fulvius laid his hands on his wife's shoulders. "I will stand the cost."

The embalmer bowed. "My lord senator."

I felt guilty at it, but not so guilty as I did at Gilot's death. If Deccus Fulvius wanted to stand the cost, well and good. When Gilot had jammed the cog-wheel that lowered the drawbridge, he had bought us all a respite. And when he had slipped its chains that it might be raised, he had paid the final price. We all owed him a great debt, Deccus included.

I watched the embalmers carry him away.

"My mother carried my uncle's head home from the battlefield of Troyes-le-Mont," Eamonn said thoughtfully. "Preserved in lime. You might consider it, Imri."

I shuddered. "I'll think on it."

Somewhere in that time, Lucius—Gallus Tadius— emerged. There was a good deal of confusion in the villa.

Publius Tadius had become a ghost in his own right, vanishing into the depths of his chambers. Beatrice had taken to her bed. What had happened had broken their spirits, at least for the moment. It was Claudia who had held the family together, backed by Deccus' authority and wealth.

A day had passed.

There were no more priests, no more incantations, no more herbs and braziers. In the scorched bell-tower, I understood, the *mundus manes* remained uncovered. And when Gallus Tadius sauntered through the villa, yawning and scratching himself, wearing Lucius' face, there was no doubt who was in charge.

If anything, there was relief.

He called us into the large dining room, where we perched uneasily on couches made for reclining. "Very good," he said. "I trust you all understand what's at stake here. I daresay the city guard understands, or at least they do now." He laughed. "So! I've called a conclave of whatever passes for authority in this forsaken city, that we might all agree. You need me. If we stand together, we've a good chance of beating this bastard. If we falter"—he shrugged— "you've seen what will happen. In the meantime, I want a thorough inventory of all the Tadeii holdings—arms, food stores, charcoal, firewood, money. All retainers or slaves of an age to bear arms. Anything of value. Claudia Fulvia, you may supervise it. The rest of you, lend her your aid."

"I want to attend the conclave," Claudia said coolly.

Gallus pinned her with a stare. "That won't be necessary."

"So do I," I said.

"And I," Eamonn added. Brigitta nodded.

"Ah, gods!" Gallus threw up his hands in disgust. "What do you fancy you lot are going to accomplish there?"

"We did well enough by you yesterday, my lord," I said.

"Well enough!" He snorted. "Oh, aye, fancy-boy. That was a deft piece of swordplay, but if you'd let Valpetra kill the wench, he'd have lost his claim to Lucca."

I shook my head. "Once he was inside the gates, it wouldn't have mattered. Not if he'd taken possession of the city. Anyway, that's not the point. Lucca may cede authority to you, but Terre d'Ange doesn't; nor Skaldia, nor the Dalriada, nor Tiberium. We deserve a voice."

"Tiberium has a voice." He pointed at Deccus Fulvius.

"I would speak for the Tadeii," Claudia announced.

Gallus laughed. "*I* speak for the Tadeii!"

"Not the living," she said.

A flicker of confusion crossed his features. Knowledge, slippery as an eel. "Our . . . your father may speak for the Tadeii."

"Our father is in his chambers, mumbling to himself, Lucius!" Claudia said tartly. "We need you, yes. But you need us, too. You'll get your inventory later. Don't be an ass."

They stared at one another, brother and sister; and yet not. It was a strange sight. In the end, rather to my surprise, it was Gallus who relented. He laughed aloud. "Sweet tits of the Vestals! I can see who inherited the balls in this family. Fine. Come, and welcome to it."

An hour later, the conclave was convened.

It met in the basilica, a stone's throw from the town square where the scorched husk of the bell-tower squatted. Lucius—Gallus—had been busy in the aftermath of yesterday's skirmish. Gaetano Correggio was there along with a cadre of other noblemen I took to be the elite of Lucca, but there were others, too. Lesser gentry, representatives of the merchant guilds, several priests, Captain Arturo of the city guard.

The central chamber of the basilica was vast and spacious, with a rostrum on the floor and tiers of benches rising on both sides. Eamonn, Brigitta, and I took seats on one of the lower tiers, behind Claudia and Deccus Fulvius.

Gallus Tadius stood on the rostrum and waited.

The benches filled slowly as people took their seats. Men; almost all men. Helena Correggio, huddled at her father's side, was one of the only other women present. I shook my head in wonderment. In Terre d'Ange, the numbers would have been equal. Brigitta's upper lip curled in disdain. I remember Phèdre said once that in Skaldia, women have the right to participate in their great councils.

It was cold and drafty in the basilica, a chilly autumn breeze stirring through the chamber. There were a number of charcoal braziers set about, but they were empty and unused. Gallus' orders, no doubt. And wise enough; it would only get colder.

Overhead, the vaulted ceiling was covered with plaster. It was divided into quadrants and painted with frescoes depicting the heavens—dawn, noon, dusk, and night. But the plaster was chipping badly, as though it had been laid in careless haste, and one could see bits and pieces of a tile mosaic that lay beneath it. A battle scene, I thought.

Gallus Tadius tilted his head to regard it and chuckled. "You covered over my triumph," he said to Gaetano Correggio.

The erstwhile Prince of Lucca accorded him a curt nod. "My father did."

Gallus shrugged. "No mind." He waited until all were assembled and settled, and then raised his voice. "My lords— and ladies!" He bowed mockingly. "I am Gallus Tadius da Lucca, and I claim authority over this city. Does anyone here contest me?"

No one did.

I watched their faces as Gallus spoke. Most were filled with a fierce hope. They wanted him to lead them. They hung on his words as he outlined the beginning of a plan. He spoke stirringly of sacrifice. He spoke of Lucca's defenses: its high walls, its deep wells. He spoke of hoarding stores and rationing food; of impending winter and the difficulty of feeding a mercenary army.

"All we have to do is outlast them," he said.

He spoke of our enemy, and there were things I learned. Domenico Martelli, the Duke of Valpetra, lived, one-handed and bitter. His hired army was under the command of a condottiere, Silvanus the Younger.

"I don't know him," Gallus allowed. "But condottieri are sensible men. It may be we can turn him for a bribe." At that, Claudia stirred. He raised a hand, forestalling any comment. "We'll need to find a discreet way of communicating with him. There are ways such things are done, and I know them. But first and foremost, we need to be prepared to deal with him from a position of strength."

I had to own, most of what he said made sense. Gallus Tadius had led a fair number of sieges in his day. He knew what was necessary to withstand one. He gave orders that every household was to conduct a thorough inventory and report the findings to him. Food stored in merchants' warehouses would be seized for future distribution. Armorers' stocks would be allocated at his discretion. And from this day forward, every man of fighting age was automatically inducted into the service of Lucca.

"You *are* the Red Scourge!" he roared, pointing at us.

Most of the men cheered. I felt it, the stir of martial pride. Yesterday I might have cheered, too. I'd been caught up in our defense of the city. But yesterday Gilot was alive. Today was different. I gazed at faces flushed with eager fury, and wondered.

The remainder of Gallus' orders were less stirring. He announced that Lucca was under a state of martial law. Any man refusing to serve would be executed as a traitor. Anyone, man or woman, who sought to leave the city by any means would be executed as a traitor. And then there was the harvest. In the fertile plain of Lucca, a good portion of the year's crops had yet to be harvested. The wheat was half gathered, while grapes yet ripened on the vine and entire groves of olive trees were unready to drop their bounty.

"It's a tricky matter," he admitted, scratching his chin. "We'll have to try to find a way to set fire to them."

At that, there were a few protests. I saw Claudia and Deccus exchange a glance.

"Gallus Tadius." Deccus Fulvius cleared his throat and stood. "Are you sure this is wise? Those olive groves have stood for hundreds of years. Surely there is a better way to save the city than by destroying its greatest resources."

Gallus shrugged. "It is a resource that will sustain our enemy. An army travels on its belly, Deccus Fulvius. We have no choice. Once Valpetra is defeated, we will replant and rebuild."

There were other arguments, but in the end, he swayed them. It was a remarkable thing to behold. He did it single-handedly, rousing their ardor and passion. There was a great deal of hatred toward the Duke of Valpetra in the basilica that day, and he used it to good effect. I sat and listened, remembering how well Lucius had always argued in Master Piero's classes, and wondered if some of his influence was present. Or mayhap the old condottiere had been a gifted orator himself, and passed his gift on to his great-grandson.

Or mayhap it was the presence of the dead among us. I could not say.

Indeed, for my part, I said nothing. None of us did. There was little, at this point, to be said. In truth, I'd not intended to speak out at the conclave. I wanted to know what Gallus Tadius was planning, and I suspected Claudia's motive was much the same. Any diplomatic gambit we might attempt would have to take his plans into account.

All knowledge was worth having.

"Right," Gallus said when he had finished. "You've leave to go, all save those I've asked to stay. I'll expect complete inventories and a list of the new militia on the morrow."

Almost everyone filed out of the basilica. We stayed, although Gallus hadn't asked us; but he didn't order us to go, either.

Gaetano Correggio stayed, and Helena with him. A handful of other noblemen stayed and a priest in a conical white hat, accompanied by several acolytes. I thought I had glimpsed them before in the temple of Jupiter.

"That's the flamen dialis." Claudia frowned. "What's Lucius up to?"

"Claudia Fulvia." Gallus beckoned to her. "Since you claim to speak for the Tadeii, you may serve as a witness to my wedding."

"What?" The word escaped my lips involuntarily.

Gallus Tadius grinned at me. "You put the thought in my head, fancy-boy. Why not? The lass was wed against the will of her paterfamilias. On Gaetano's word, the priest can decree a divorce and free her to wed me. It will undermine Valpetra's claim to Lucca and reinforce mine." He shrugged. "Might not have as much effect as we'd hope. He'll argue against it, and he's mad as hell since you lopped off his hand. I doubt he means to give any quarter. But it might help turn his troops against him, once they learn I'm bedding his bride. She's soiled goods, but I don't mind. Every weapon that comes to hand is fair game in war."

I glanced at Helena Correggio, and wished I hadn't.

She was terrified. The moment I looked at her, her gaze locked onto mine, mute and pleading. Begging for a hero to rescue her. All I could do was heave an inward sigh. This business of being a hero was a good deal more difficult than I'd reckoned. I'd saved the maiden from the villain and all it had done was infuriate the villain, complicate my own standing, and thrust the maiden into the arms of *another* villain—the one on our side. The man with two faces.

Was he a friend?

One of him was.

With a silent prayer to Blessed Elua, I steeled myself to make an enemy of Gallus Tadius. But before I could speak, Claudia intervened.

"My lord priest," she asked in concern. "Is this lawful?"

The flamen dialis looked profoundly uncomfortable. "Under certain circumstances, yes. If the paterfamilias seeks it. I trust the wedding was not *confarreatio*?"

"What does that mean?" I whispered to Deccus Fulvius.

"It's a binding form of marriage," he said, then hushed me.

Claudia turned to Helena. "Tell us," she said gently.

Betimes, men who know one another's minds have no need for speech. It is different with women. They need not know one another to communicate without words. I saw Claudia's subtle nod, and I saw Helena's eyes widen in understanding. Only slightly, so slightly. If it were not for Phèdre's training, I doubt I would have seen it.

"He took me to a village." Helena clenched her fists at her sides, then pointed. "Southwest. I don't know the name. The priest—his priest—was waiting there. The flamen dialis of

Valpetra." She bit her lip. "I didn't *want* to do it! But he said he would kill me."

The priest frowned. "How was it done, child?"

She told him.

A sheep was sacrificed, and there was a red veil and an oatcake; witnesses assembled, vows recited, and a contract written and signed. The details meant nothing to me, save that they seemed to fulfill the requirements for a *confarreatio* marriage—one that could not be dissolved.

Helena Correggio didn't lie well.

I daresay it was her sheer terror that sold her tale. Whatever else was true, she had been abducted and forcibly wed against her will, and the details she began to divulge of her nuptial evening held the ring of truth. The marriage had been consummated with violent glee on the part of Domenico Martelli. The flamen dialis cut her off and turned to Gallus Tadius.

"It is *confarreatio*," he said formally. "I do not have the authority to decree a divorce."

The news didn't sit well with Gallus. His face darkened with fury.

"Fine," he snapped, grabbing Helena by the wrist. "Then I will make a cuckold of him."

"My lord . . ." The priest's protest trailed off. Gaetano Correggio looked sick and did nothing; he had made his devil's bargain. Deccus Fulvius looked like he wanted to be elsewhere, like facing an angry mob in Tiberium. Claudia turned her palms up in a helpless gesture; she had done what she could. Eamonn caught my eye and moved to ward my back, and I heaved another inward sigh.

"Lucius." I interposed myself between him and the girl. "You don't want to do this."

There was no Lucius there. His face bared its teeth in a

battle-grin. In an eerie echo of Valpetra, he kept a tight hold on Helena's wrist, while she attempted to squeeze herself behind me, trapping me between the two of them. In a deceptively casual gesture, he raised his free hand and clamped it around my throat, hard enough to bruise. He had a strong grip. I'd noted it the first time we'd met, though I'd never expected to find it crushing my windpipe.

"What the hell do you know about what I want, D'Angeline?" he grated.

We were pressed close together, so close I could almost feel his heart thudding in his chest. His breath was hot on my face. I kept my hands at my sides, the fingers of my right hand brushing the hilt of the dagger at my belt. If worst came to worst, I was reasonably certain I could plant it in his belly before I blacked out. Behind me, Helena trembled, and I felt her rise on her toes, her soft breasts crushed against my back.

"Please don't kill him," she whispered in my ear. "He's Lucius, too."

I would have laughed, if Gallus Tadius hadn't been throttling me.

"'O, dear my lord,'" Claudia said unexpectedly, "'let this breast on which you have leant, serve now as your shield . . .'"

With a disgusted sound, Gallus thrust me from him, releasing Helena.

We both stumbled and fell. I landed on her and drew in a ragged gasp of air, then scrambled off Helena and onto my knees. Both of us were in Eamonn's way. Too fast for him to prevent it, Gallus Tadius drew his sword and wedged its point beneath my chin.

"You know," he said in a conversational tone, "I almost

like you, D'Angeline, but you're a far sight more trouble than you're worth. Give me one reason not to kill you."

I tried to speak and burst into a fit of half-choked coughing.

Gallus laughed.

"I'll give you one." Eamonn moved into view in the corner of my eye. His face was calm. He'd drawn his blade and held it angled for a sweeping blow. "Do it, and your head rolls on the floor before you can draw breath."

"Will someone call for the guard?" Deccus Fulvius muttered to no one in particular. "This is absurd."

I felt the tip of Gallus' sword pierce the skin as he applied pressure, and a trickle of blood ran down my throat. Like sister, like brother. It *was* absurd.

"Lucius!" Claudia faced him. "I'll give you a better reason. If you kill Imriel, you'll bring the wrath of Terre d'Ange upon you, upon me, upon all of Lucca. He's third in line for the throne."

"He *is*?" It was Deccus, dumbstruck.

Helena made a small sound.

The sword's point withdrew to hover beneath my nose. I breathed slowly, struggling against the anguished protest of my abused windpipe. Gallus Tadius glanced between me and Claudia, looking confused. "How do you know that?"

"You told me," she said steadily.

He blinked, the lines of his face softening. "I did?"

"Yes." Unlike Helena, Claudia lied well. "His name, his full name, is Imriel nó Montrève de la Courcel, and he's a Prince of the Blood. You told me he wanted it kept a secret, Lucius, and so I have."

"I don't remember that," he said, but he lowered his sword. Eamonn moved swiftly, hauling me to my feet and thrusting me behind him. The priest, his acolytes, Gaetano

Correggio, and Deccus Fulvius all stared at us with varying degrees of astonishment. Gallus Tadius shook his head, and the tip of his sword began to rise. "No," he said. "I don't believe it. Any of it."

"Lucius," I croaked. "The Bella Donna's son. Remember?"

There was a soft thud behind me as Helena Correggio slumped to the floor in a dead faint.

FIFTY-TWO

For a mercy, Gallus Tadius gave up on the lot of us. In the face of united opposition, he abandoned his plan and stomped out of the basilica to attend to more pressing matters elsewhere in the city. The rest of us attended to Helena.

Brigitta, who had been closest, cradled her head in her lap. Gaetano knelt at her side, chafing his daughter's hands. But when her lids fluttered open, it was at me that she gazed, her blue eyes soft with wonder.

"I knew it," she whispered. "I knew it!"

I sighed. "It's not what you think."

"What *is* it, then?" Deccus Fulvius demanded.

So I told him, apologizing for my deception and explaining the bizarre legend that had spun out of my mother's twelve-year exile in the sanctuary of Asherat's Temple and subsequent disappearance.

"Women!" Deccus snorted. "The tales they'll conjure."

"Indeed," Claudia murmured.

He glanced sidelong at her. "You never believed such nonsense, I hope."

She smiled at him. "Of course not."

"My lord," I said to Gaetano Correggio. "I fear your

daughter is unnerved by her travail. It would be best if you took her home to rest. And it would be best, I think, if she were kept out of sight of Gallus Tadius."

"Yes." The Prince of Lucca—or former prince—seemed stunned. "Yes, of course. I shouldn't have . . . I'm not . . ." He touched the ugly gash on his temple, a souvenir of yesterday's battle. "Forgive me, child," he said to Helena. "I'm not thinking clearly."

He led her away, walking like an old man, stiff and defeated. She glanced backward over her shoulder at me as they went, her face suffused with a glow of hope and faith. Whatever I'd said, it hadn't sufficed to dispel her belief. My throat hurt, and I was weary to the bone with guilt and grief. "My mother," I said to no one in particular, "is a traitor. A monstrous, monstrous traitor. And this is truly, deeply wrong."

Eamonn shrugged. "It gave the lass joy, poor thing. Don't begrudge it."

Once they had gone, we returned to the Tadeii villa, where Claudia set about supervising the inventory. I wanted only to take to my chambers to snatch an hour or two of sleep, but it was not to be. Instead, Deccus Fulvius sat me down in the salon and gave me a thorough grilling about my connections and influence, his politician's mind at work. He knew Queen Ysandre by name, of course, but he had met the D'Angeline ambassadress Denise Fleurais and thought highly of her.

"Good woman," he said, nodding. "*Smart* woman. She knows you're here?"

"Yes," I said wearily. "I don't recall if I told her the exact dates."

"Pity. But she'll figure it out once the news reaches Tiberium. It's bound to sooner or later." Deccus rubbed his chin. "Like as not she'll send a delegation to negotiate for your freedom when she does. Trouble is, you made it a lot harder when you lopped off Valpetra's hand. What in the hell were you thinking, lad?"

I didn't answer directly. "Deccus, does this all seem a bit strange?"

"Ah, lad! War's an ugly business," he said in a kind tone. "Never fear, you'll get used to it. And Gallus Tadius may be a hard man, but he knows what he's about."

"That's just it," I said slowly. "Deccus, Gallus Tadius is *dead*. Two days ago, we were trying to drive his ghost out of Lucius. Now we're happily taking orders from him."

"Two days ago, Lucca wasn't under siege!" Deccus sighed. "Lad, listen. You saw what a mess Correggio made of it. If you're asking if this whole business makes my skin crawl, well, it does. But let's be honest, man to man. We're stuck here. And frankly, as long as there are two legitimate claims to Lucca, no one in Caerdicca Unitas is going to raise a finger to intervene. Warring city-states are altogether too common. They'll wait it out to see who wins and reestablish ties. Since we're stuck, I'd as soon wager on winning, even if it means letting a walking dead man rule the damned city. Understand?"

I nodded.

"Good lad." He clapped me on the shoulder. "Go on, get some rest. You look as hollow as a scraped gourd." He paused, his hand heavy on my shoulder, and gave it a sympathetic squeeze. "Sorry about your friend."

My throat tightened. "Thank you."

I didn't deserve his kindness; but Gilot did. So I accepted it and stumbled off to my guest chamber. There I fell onto my bed, the sheets still rumpled from my lovemaking with Deccus Fulvius' wife. A trace of Claudia's scent hung in the air. Tired beyond guilt, I sank into the depths of a sleep at once deep and restless, plagued by fragments of fitful dreams.

A few minutes later, Eamonn shook me awake.

At least it seemed that way.

"Imriel!" He shook me again. I opened my eyes to see his face hovering above me. A low amber light slanted through the shuttered windows of my bedchamber, indicating that I'd slept for hours. "We're to report for duty."

I sat up, confused. "Duty?"

Eamonn nodded and perched on the side of my bed. "Mounted night patrol," he said in a cynical voice. "Gallus' orders."

I rubbed my face, half-blind with sleep. "Why us?"

"Not just us." Eamonn shook his head. "Every man of age with a sword and a horse, Luccan or no. And if you don't move and hop to it, he's like to confiscate the Bastard and assign him to someone who will."

"Like to see him try," I muttered, but I moved with alacrity.

We reported for duty in the central square of Lucca, along with a score of others. We assembled in two lines, while Gallus Tadius rode slowly back and forth, surveying us. Since earlier today, he had obtained armor; a full corselet, vambraces, and greaves. It was very fine and a little outdated, and I wondered if it had been his own. The gilded steel glinted in the fading light.

Everyone else bore a mishmash of armaments: swords, spears, hunting bows. Some carried bucklers slung over their backs. There were padded gambesons and chainmail shirts, and one lad with a helmet the size of a bucket, riding low on his brow. But all of them were armed, one way or another, and all were mounted. Several of their mounts bore unmistakable harness marks on their hides, and at least one, I was sure, was a plowhorse, placid and gentle, with feathered fetlocks and hooves the size of dinner plates.

That was the one the boy with the bucket-helm rode.

Elua, but he looked young.

"Greetings, warriors," Gallus Tadius called. "Welcome to the Red Scourge!" He paused to acknowledge the resulting cheer. "Captain Arturo, give them their badges."

The captain of the Luccan city guard nodded to a lieutenant. It was the rosy-cheeked lad from before, the one Gallus had struck outside the temple. He looked different, proud and somber, despite the down on his upper lip and the yellowing bruise on his cheek. He paced along the lines, handing out scraps of crimson cloth as though bestowing a grave honor.

Eamonn and I watched others lash them about their upper arms and followed suit.

"Right!" Gallus said crisply. "You're to divide into pairs and ride along the inner walls. I want a constant circuit, no more than a few minutes between each pair. We're mounting guards atop the wall at every tree. Not my choice of crenellation, but we might as well use 'em. You will check in with each and every guard. Is that understood?"

We agreed that it was.

"Good." He leaned over and spat on the ground. "Aught's amiss, you ride like hellfire. One to the gatehouse to alert Captain Arturo, and one to find me. Understood?"

We agreed, again, that it was.

"Good." He eyed the sky. Sunset's last afterglow was vanishing and a pale half-moon hung on the rise. Whatever warmth the day had held was vanishing, and autumn's chill was setting in with the night. "Daresay you'll make do without torches tonight. Get used to it. We'll make do without wherever we can."

On his order, we paired off. Gallus Tadius gave us the night's password and countersign we were to use with the guards and began ordering us to leave, one pair at a time. He sat astride his horse, motionless, and each rider saluted as they passed him. When Eamonn and I took our turn, he gave us both a long, hard stare.

"Behave yourselves, my princelings," he said. "Whoever you may be outside these walls, so long as you're inside them, you're under my command. As far as I'm concerned, we're all Luccan here. Understood?"

"Aye, sir!" We both saluted.

He jerked his chin. "Go on."

Through the deepening twilight, Eamonn and I rode toward the outskirts of the city. It was disconcerting. I was barely familiar with Lucca, and the streets looked less familiar than ever in the purple dusk. No one was about. We passed the closed doors and shuttered windows of shops and inns. Here and there, in townhouses, we could see a spark of lamplight, but already people were hoarding their stores as Gallus had ordered.

We reached the city wall, and beneath its looming shadow began to ride in a slow circuit around the inside perimeter of Lucca.

Gallus Tadius had been busy. At every substantial oak tree, there was a sentry posted. I craned my head at the first one, but I could see nothing save the vague silhouette of branches and leaves against the dusk.

"Mundus," I called.

"Manes," came the soft reply. "All quiet."

We rode onward.

"Gallus Tadius has an odd sense of humor for a dead

man," Eamonn remarked. My stomach rumbled in answer. "Have you eaten since this morning?" he asked. When I shook my head, he rummaged in his saddlebag and handed me a meat pastry pie in greasy cloth. "Here. Filched from the kitchen."

"My thanks," I said gratefully.

Eamonn shrugged. "Thank Brigitta. It was her idea."

I ate one-handed, juices dripping down my chin. "She's . . ." I swallowed. "You're very fond of her, aren't you?"

"Aye." Eamonn glanced at me. "Does it bother you?"

"Because she's Skaldi?" I asked.

He shrugged. "All of it."

I thought about it as I finished my pie and Eamonn exchanged password and countersign with the next sentry. All was still quiet atop the walls of Lucca. "A little," I said honestly. "Not because she's Skaldi. In the zenana, there was a young man, Erich . . . did I tell you about him?"

Eamonn nodded. "At the Midwinter Masque. Remember?"

It seemed like a thousand years ago that we had attended the Queen's fête, dressed as Skaldic deities, reveling amid all the glittering panoply. I remembered Eamonn attired as Donar the thunder-god, dancing so carefully with Alais. And I . . . I had danced with Sidonie, and we had quarreled. That was the night I'd sworn fealty to her on a perverse whim.

"I remember," I said.

"It seems like a long time ago," Eamonn said softly. "And another world."

"It was." I tucked the grease-stained cloth in my belt. "Eamonn, I'm happy for you, truly. And yes, a little bit envious, and a bit jealous, too. It had naught to do with Brigitta. I miss you, that's all."

"I'm right here," he said.

"I know," I said, "but . . ."

"I know." He sighed. "It's different, it's all different. Why can't things be simple?"

I opened my mouth to reply. Up ahead, in the darkness, we heard shouting and splashing. Eamonn and I glanced at one another and set heels to our horses, racing toward the sound.

It was coming from the point along the wall where the aqueduct that fed the moat entered into the city, passing through a pair of sluice gates beneath the wall itself. The two riders ahead of us had dismounted and plunged into the canal. There was a good deal of splashing and grunting, but it was too dark to make out why.

"Hey!" a voice shouted from above. "Mundus!"

"Manes!" I squinted at the sentry-tree. "What's happening?"

There was scraping sound of a flint striker and a flurry of sparks atop the wall. A pitch-soaked torch kindled and I saw the sentry who held it, pointing. "Intruder. I saw him slip into the moat."

By the light of his torch, I could make out the dim sight of three figures struggling in the water. Whoever the intruder was, he was putting up a hell of a fight. Uttering a curse, I dismounted, unfastened my cloak, and jumped in to aid my fellow guards.

The water was only chest-deep, but it was cold and dank. In a heartbeat, I was soaked and chilled to the bone. The intruder wasn't a big man, but he was slippery as a fish and deceptively strong. One of the other guards gave up the moment I entered and flung himself over the edge of the canal, panting for breath.

"Get behind him!" the other guard gasped.

I waded with difficulty through the deep water. The guard made a move to grapple with the intruder, and I saw the intruder's arm rise, dripping, above the surface of the water. Distant torchlight struck a faint gleam from the dagger in his hand.

There was no time to think, so I didn't. Taking a deep breath, I grabbed his shoulders and hauled him backward. He wasn't expecting it. Off balance, he fell atop me and both of us plunged beneath the cold, dark waters. Before he could struggle, I wrapped my arms and legs around him in a death-lock. Entwined, we sank to the bottom of the canal.

He did struggle then; he thrashed like a gaffed fish. But I'd learned to wrestle in Siovale, and I had a good grip on him.

And I was stubborn.

I held him until the air began to burn in my lungs, and he went limp. Guessing it for a trick, I relaxed my grip a cautious degree. When he began thrashing anew, I tightened it and squeezed him hard, shifting my arms so that my doubled fists dug into his belly and jerking upward. This time, a stream of bubbles issued from his lips. I'd nearly drowned once. I knew how it felt.

I squeezed him until no more bubbles came.

The second time he went limp, I gauged it was real and shoved him toward the surface. My limbs were cold and leaden, my lungs ached, and I barely had the strength to lever myself upright. I did, though, sputtering and coughing. That first gulp of air, drawn through a throat still bruised by Gallus Tadius' ire, was as sweet as anything I'd ever tasted.

Our intruder floated like a sodden log.

Comfortable and dry, Eamonn leaned over the canal and caught a fold of the man's tunic. "Nice work, Imri," he said cheerfully, tugging him over to the edge and hoisting him out of the canal with annoying ease. "Let's see what you've caught."

At that point, the only thing I cared about was getting out of the water. I dragged myself onto the cobblestones and sat in a puddle of spreading wetness, breathing hard, with my arms propped on my knees.

Eamonn gave our captive a helpful shake. The man groaned, rolled onto his side, and spewed out a considerable volume of canal water. His hair was plastered to his face. His dagger was long gone, and he wore only a tunic of rough homespun; not even sandals on his bare feet. Already he was beginning to shiver in the cold air. Whoever he was, he looked miserable.

"Poor bastard," I murmured.

Over at the wall, our fellow guards shouted back and forth with the sentry. I watched him lower a rope ladder and climb down awkwardly, the flaming torch held in one hand. Once he descended, all three approached, the torch bobbing. It threw everything into high relief, casting stark shadows.

"So who is he?" the sentry asked.

Squatting behind the intruder, Eamonn hauled him upright and yanked on his lank, dripping hair, angling his face so that the torchlight fell upon it.

Canis.

All I can say is that it was a mercy that I was half-drowned, since no one thought anything of my choked gasp and subsequent coughing fit. Canis' gaze flickered toward me; briefly, so briefly. He gave his head an infinitesimal shake.

"Who are you?" one of the guards demanded. "Are you with Valpetra? Are you a spy? What do you want?"

What followed was a pantomime. Canis shook his head in vigorous denial, water spraying. He opened his mouth and pointed to it, shook his head again. He placed both hands over his ears and shook his head.

"A deaf-mute," the guard said in disgust.

Oh, he was good.

By this time, a small audience had gathered. Two other sets of riders had arrived. All of them watched, bemused, as Canis, half-clad and shivering, went through an elaborate set of gesticulations, miming his actions. He pointed to where his village lay outside the wall, he depicted Valpetra's soldiers arriving, sweeping through the village with sword and spear, laying claim to all it held. He mimed himself quaking with fear, his eyes stretched wide. He pointed to the sluice gates and showed, with his hands, how he had dismantled them underwater.

When he had finished, *I* was half-convinced.

"Ah, the poor dumb bastard!" The sentry took control of the situation. As the only person present who'd been a member of Lucca's city guard prior to nightfall, I supposed he was entitled. "Take him to the gatehouse," he said, nodding to the first pair of guards. "Let Captain Arturo decide what to do with him. The rest of you, resume patrol."

I stood up, my boots squelching. "All of us?"

He gave me a wary look. "Did Gallus Tadius order otherwise?"

I glanced at my fellow conscripts. The boy in the bucket-sized helmet was there atop his plowhorse, looking scared despite the scrap of red cloth tied boldly about his upper arm. If the *lemures* of the Red Scourge were afoot—and I believed they were—they were not finding so consistent or congenial a host as their commander. I sighed, catching the Bastard's reins and setting one foot in the stirrup. "Right." It was a half-conscious echo of Gallus Tadius. I swung myself astride, plopping wetly into the saddle. "Patrol."

Eamonn handed me my cloak without comment. At least it was dry. I settled it over my shoulders and huddled inside it as we resumed our circuit of the city walls. Within a few minutes, an acrid funk of wet wool surrounded me.

We rode for hours. I noted the landmarks and reckoned that it took almost an hour to make a complete circuit of the city. I had learned, in Saba, how to gauge the passage of the stars across the night sky. Although I'm no horologist, I've always had a good sense of time ever since then.

We made nine circuits that night.

By the fifth, I was sore. It was much like keeping Elua's vigil on the Longest Night. The air was cold and I was soaked. My muscles tensed and fought one another as I shivered until I ached as with an ague. I thought about the boy in the bucket-helmet, and I thought about Joscelin, his profile silhouetted against the winter stars. I kept riding, and the Bastard paced along the walls, tireless and steady. From time to time, I blew on my fingers and warmed my hands on his spotted hide.

"Damn, that's a fine horse," Eamonn muttered.

I summoned a weary smile. "You want a rematch?"

He eyed me. "You know, I don't fancy it. You're a little mad, you."

By the eighth circuit, I was beyond sore. Everywhere my sodden clothing rubbed me, my skin felt raw. Circuit after circuit, sentry after sentry. Mundus manes, mundus manes. All was quiet, and if I never heard the words again, it would be too soon.

The ninth circuit ushered in the dismal grey light of early dawn and Gallus Tadius, grinning. "Go home, princelings!" he called to us. "Your replacements are here, and your warm beds are beckoning you."

I sneezed. "Thank you, my lord."

Gallus studied me for a moment and I found myself straightening in the saddle, squaring my shoulders. Damned if there wasn't a part of me that wanted his approval. He gave a slow nod. "I heard what you did. That was a nice piece of work at the aqueduct, D'Angeline. The deaf-mute may be harmless, but one of the guards swore he drew a dagger on him."

"I didn't see a dagger," I lied. "Where is he now?"

"Oh, Captain Arturo tossed him in gaol with the Valpetran prisoners." He shrugged. "We'll see if he changes his story," he added, then laughed. "Not that he could *tell* us, mind!"

"Indeed," I murmured.

Eamonn and I wasted no time in heading for the Tadeii villa. His mount was plodding and exhausted, which was how I felt. Eamonn was quiet, watching Gallus Tadius ride away on another indefatigable errand.

"Does he ever sleep?" he asked when Gallus was out of earshot. I shook my head, too tired to venture a guess. "I don't think he does." Eamonn glanced at me out of the corner of one eye. "That intruder looked a lot like your beggar, didn't he?"

"Canis?" I asked.

"Mm-hmm."

"Yes," I said. "I suppose he did."

FIFTY-THREE

AT THE VILLA, I turned the Bastard over to the stablehands and went straight to my chamber, where I stripped off my cold, wet clothing and burrowed under a pile of blankets. I slept through the morning and woke, ravenous, in time for the midday meal.

The braziers were unlit and the hypocaust that heated the private Tadeii baths was no longer stoked at any hour, another victim of Gallus' orders. I couldn't bear to submerge myself in the chilly waters, so I settled for scrubbing myself at the washbasin in my room, naked and shivering, dunking my head for good measure. A faint odor of canal water clung to my hair, but it would do. Thrusting aside the memory of Daršanga it evoked, I went to join the others.

It was almost a homey scene. Lunch was being served at a long table in one of the less formal dining rooms. Beatrice, Lucius and Claudia's mother, had emerged from seclusion. She seemed determined to impart a sense of normalcy to the household through sheer force of will. When I arrived, she rose from her chair at the head of the table and greeted me with a deep curtsy.

"Welcome, your highness," she said. "Forgive us our neglect."

I bowed in return. "My lady Beatrice, forgive *me* this imposition on your hospitality, for which I am most grateful." I smiled at her as I straightened. "And please, call me Imriel."

"Imriel." A dimple appeared and vanished as she smiled back at me. "Please join us."

The meal was simple: mutton in a thin sauce, black bread, and wild greens. As hungry as I was, it seemed a veritable feast. Beatrice apologized for it several times over. "It's not what you're accustomed to, I know," she said anxiously. "But there are . . . orders."

She didn't mention Gallus Tadius by name. It was hard for me to see what had befallen Lucius, who I reckoned a friend. I couldn't imagine how difficult it was for her. I'd known him for only a few months. She was his mother.

"My lady, it is delicious," I said truthfully. "And I am grateful for your generosity."

Her dimple returned. "You're too kind . . . Imriel."

On the other side of the table, seated beside her staid husband, Claudia Fulvia caught my eye and smiled with quiet amusement. She got her looks from her mother, at least in part. Both of them did, brother and sister. They had inherited Beatrice's dark red hair, thick and unruly, and a certain sense of luxuriance, of being comfortable in their flesh. But there was a rondeur to Beatrice; a soft, bustling plumpness that made one feel at once protective and at ease. Unlike her children, she had no hard edges.

That, I guessed, came from the Tadeii blood.

Beatrice worked gallantly to make us all feel welcome. She fussed over Eamonn until I half thought she was ready to adopt him as a son, and Brigitta . . . well. In her own mind, I nearly think she *had* adopted her.

"Oh, child!" She clapped her hands together and flushed

with pleasure. "You should wed, the two of you! After all . . . after all, here we were, ready for a wedding."

Eamonn and Brigitta exchanged a considering glance.

"Why not?" Eamonn's sunniest, most infectious grin creased his face. "Aye, why not? What say you? Will you have me, lass?"

"Eamonn!" Brigitta tugged her blonde braids with both fists. "Where would we go? How would we live? What about . . . ?" She hesitated. "I have a family, I have duties. I shouldn't have come here; I wouldn't have, if I'd known. My six months are nearly gone. You know my brother Leidolf will come looking for me. Soon."

"Aye." He nodded. "In Tiberium, where he'll not find you."

"But . . ." She cast an imploring glance around the table, settling on Claudia. "You gave me wise counsel on our journey. What do you say, Lady Claudia?"

"In this matter?" Claudia raised her brows. "Oh, I believe the world defers to Terre d'Ange in matters of love, my dear. Isn't that so?" She addressed the last question to Deccus Fulvius, who rumbled good-natured agreement. With a hint of a smile, Claudia nodded at me. "What do *you* say, Prince Imriel?"

I stood up, and I looked at them, all of them. Deccus Fulvius with his open expression, doing me the courtesy of treating me as an equal, knowing so little. Claudia Fulvia with her smile, knowing too much, knowing how I wanted her. Beatrice Tadia, who knew nothing, nothing, her face alight with the hopeful pleasure of wresting somewhat *good* out of the wreckage of her family and the deadly siege of Lucca.

Eamonn.

Brigitta.

Elua help me, whether I liked it or no, they loved one another. It shone forth between them, as steady as a well-made lamp, as sure as a pair of joined hands. I lifted my cup, filled with cool well-water. "Need you ask?" I said lightly. "I am D'Angeline. When all is said and done, there is but one tenet to which we adhere." I hoisted my cup to them. "Love as thou wilt."

So it was decided.

Having seized upon the notion, Beatrice set about implementing it in all haste, deciding that the celebration should take place on the morrow. In truth, there was little point in delaying. None of us knew what the morrow would bring. Lucca was holding strong under Gallus Tadius' leadership and looked likely to do so for weeks on end, but even so, war was an uncertain business.

I left them to their plans and went to seek out the gaol.

It was a squat, solid building near the basilica with lodging for the guards on the main floor and a single great dungeon-chamber below. A lone guard stood duty; the rest were posted elsewhere. When I remarked on it, he shrugged.

"There's no one down there but the Valpetrans and the deaf-mute. Gallus Tadius freed the rest."

"He did?" I asked. "Why?"

"Well, he gave 'em a choice, anyway. A red armband or a hemp necklace." He chuckled. "None of 'em chose the noose over the Red Scourge. Anyway, you want to get a few licks in on the deaf-mute, go ahead. From what I heard, I reckon you owe him." He plucked a ring of keys from a stand and unlocked the door to admit me, then kindled a lantern. "Here, you'll need this. Bang on the door when you're done, and I'll let you out."

It was unnerving to hear the heavy wooden door slam shut behind me, the key turning in the lock. The stairs led down into darkness and a fetid odor. The dank smell of my hair. I stood for a moment, willing my heartbeat to slow, then descended the stairs.

"Canis?" I lifted the lantern.

It illuminated a vast open space. There were chains along the wall, enough to hold several dozen prisoners. There were only four, though. Three of them lifted their heads, wary eyes glittering in the lantern's glow. The fourth was sitting cross-legged, watching me, a calm expression on his battered face.

"Canis!" I crouched beside him. "What in the seven hells are you *doing* here?"

He didn't answer.

"Dog." One of the Valpetrans gave a wheezing chuckle. "Good one, D'Angeline. But Dog don't talk. Didn't even make a sound when they beat him."

Sitting back on my heels, I regarded Canis with frustration. He returned my gaze with implacable calm. I wanted to shake him, to squeeze answers out of him as surely as I'd squeezed the breath from his lungs. But as long as Gallus Tadius believed him a simple deaf-mute seeking the safety of the city walls, there was a good chance he'd be offered the same bargain in time—the Red Scourge or the noose. I'd already been careless, calling him by name. If it had been any other name, we might both be in trouble.

I sighed. "In Elua's name, I swear . . . one day, Canis, we'll have this out."

He bowed his head, scrabbling in the loose, filthy straw of the gaol floor with one hand. The chain shackled to his wrist clanked. At least the chains were long enough to allow the prisoners a measure of ease. In the pleasure-dungeons of Valerian House, they were a good deal shorter. I smiled wryly at the thought. Canis tapped the stone floor with one grimy fingernail, rhythmic and insistent. Glancing down, I

saw that he'd arranged stalks of straw into letters, spelling
out two words.

Hit me.

"No," I said involuntarily.

He tapped the floor again, raising his chin. *Hit me.*

The other prisoners were watching with interest.

And why not? They had nothing else to do. Valpetrans,
we called them out of convenience; but they weren't. They
were mercenaries hired by Valpetra. If they were loyal to
anyone, it was their condottiere. And like as not, any one of
them would sell Canis short for an extra ration of food. Why
I was trying to protect him, I couldn't even say. He'd done
nothing but haunt my shadow and feed me smiling lies. And
he *had* drawn a dagger on the guardsman; I'd seen it.

But whatever game Canis was playing, he meant me no
harm. I was sure of it. In Tiberium, he'd had ample chance.
Name of Elua! He knew where I lived, where I slept . . .
Gilot and I hadn't even possessed a bar for our door or
latches for our shutters until the night Canis claimed to have
seen two thieves attempting to rob Master Ambrosius' shop.
I eyed him, wondering what had really happened that night.
"Why are you doing this, Canis?"

His brown eyes never blinked. *Hit me.*

So I did. I brushed away the straw, making the words he
had written vanish, clearing a space on the stone floor. I set
the lantern down. And because I was angry, I feinted with
my right hand and made him flinch, then punched him hard
with the left.

I hit him high, a little off the center of his forehead, where
it wouldn't break any bones. Still, his head snapped back,
and I felt my knuckles bruised to the marrow. Canis' breath
hissed through his teeth. I followed up with an open-palmed

slap with my right hand, hard enough to wrench his head sideways.

It made a loud sound in the confines of the dungeon.

And it felt good.

Too good. I didn't want to do this. I didn't want to be here. I got to my feet, fists clenched. Canis righted himself. Shielded from the view of the Valpetrans, he grinned at me, his eyes bright with approval. There was a knot rising on his forehead and blood on his teeth. He must have bitten his cheek when I struck him.

"That's for last night," I said to him. "I reckon we're even."

Grabbing the lantern, I marched toward the stairs, shadows swinging around me.

"Hey!" The Valpetran who'd spoken before called to me. "D'Angeline, listen! I don't know what your stake is in this, but Commander Silvanus is open to barter. And he's a man does right by those who swear allegiance to him." He moved his arms, rustling his chains. "Our freedom for yours?" he asked cunningly. "You're a foreigner here. Think on it."

I nodded at him. "I'll think on it."

"Think swiftly," he shouted after me. "We've already lost one."

At the top of the stair, I pounded on the door. It seemed an eternity before I heard the sound of the key turning in the lock and the guard opened it with a grin. Even as I emerged into the open air, he snatched the lantern from my hand and blew it out. "Mustn't waste!" he remarked. "Gallus Tadius' orders." He eyed me. "Did you have fun?"

"Fun." I shook out my bruised hands. "Oh, aye."

"Good," the guard said cheerfully. "Good."

I'd elected to walk, having grown accustomed to it in Tiberium; and I reckoned the Bastard needed his rest. By the time I returned to the villa, the shadows were growing long. It seemed I'd barely risen and already it was nearing time for another night of mounted patrol. I was wondering if I might catch a few more minutes of sleep before reporting for duty, but Claudia Fulvia met me in the atrium, a sealed letter in her hand.

"A letter came for you," she said.

It was fine parchment, sealed and stamped with red wax, and for a foolish moment my heart leapt. I would have given anything to see the impress of a familiar seal—the Courcel swan, the moon and crag of Montrève, the lily and stars of Blessed Elua. Gods, even the intertwined keys of House Shahrizai! It wasn't, of course. There was no way a missive could have arrived so swiftly, even from Denise Fleurais in Tiberium; and no way it would have been delivered if it had. I didn't recognize the seal, which bore a crude lion.

"It's from the Correggii," Claudia added.

I cracked the seal and opened the letter. A scattering of rose petals drifted to the floor of the atrium; plucked from the season's last blooms, already dry and brittle. Claudia leaned against the wall and watched me read, her arms folded beneath her breasts. I schooled my face to impassivity, folding the letter and tucking it into my belt when I'd finished.

"Helena," I said. "She wished to thank me."

"Oh, indeed." Claudia gave me a wry smile that didn't quite reach her eyes. There was a complex mixture of worry and affection in her expression. "Have a care with her, Imriel. After what the poor girl's been through, she's not quite in her right mind."

"I know." I gazed at her, thinking that a man might look at her face for a long, long time without ever growing weary of it. I hoped Deccus Fulvius felt the same way. "Don't worry, I know how she feels. Better than I'd like to."

"I remember." Claudia touched my left hip, close to where the Kereyit Tatar mark was seared onto my buttock. She wasn't smiling anymore, and her eyes were grave. "Something like a slave-brand, wasn't it?"

Ah, Elua! I wished we could have known one another like this before. It could all have been so different between us without the games, without the invisible force of the Unseen Guild in play. There would still have been Deccus, but, well . . . it would have been different. There might have been love alongside the passion. Love, wild and dangerous, the sort that believed every risk worth taking, destroying reputations and shattering lives. Mayhap we had been capable of that, Claudia and I. And mayhap it was better that we hadn't tried . . . but I would never know.

You will find it and lose it, again and again.

"Yes," I said belatedly, easing her hand from my hip. "Something like it."

All too soon, dusk was falling and it was time for Eamonn and me to report to the town square. Gallus Tadius made a brief, distracted appearance before dispatching us on our rounds. It was the first time I'd seen him since dawn. If he'd slept in the past day, it wasn't at the Tadeii villa. I wondered if Eamonn was right.

"He's up to something," Eamonn said. "They're building something atop the gatehouse."

"A ballista?" I asked.

He shrugged. "It's meant to lob things at Valpetra's men."

"Huh." I thought about it. "What's Valpetra doing?"

"Nothing that I've heard." Eamonn grinned at me. "Nothing to interfere with my wedding, I hope! Do you know, Deccus Fulvius has offered to take my place tomorrow night and ride patrol with you so that Gallus Tadius doesn't put up a fuss."

A twinge of guilt caught me. "That's a kind offer."

"Aye." Eamonn gave me one of his sidelong looks. "You're not . . . ?"

I thought about Claudia touching my hip earlier today; Claudia stroking my hand beside Gilot's deathbed; Claudia in the theatre, caressing my swelling groin beneath the blanket; Claudia in her husband's salon, her tongue probing my mouth; Claudia by lamplight in the bedchamber, and the taste of her on my lips; Claudia in the painter's atelier, her white limbs spread and languid, all her naked abundance glowing in the sunlight.

"No," I said. "We're not."

"Good," Eamonn said simply.

It was an uneventful night, which was fine with me. The only surprise in the whole affair was that Gallus Tadius had ordered the sluice gates that Canis had dismantled left unrepaired. On the heels of a dry summer, the river was running low, so it made no difference. Still, it was odd. An extra sentry was posted atop the wall there, and a quartet of footsoldiers lounged in the shadows. We all exchanged what gossip we'd overheard, but none of it came to aught.

"So how *is* Canis?" Eamonn asked when we were out of earshot.

"Silent," I said. "And mysterious."

He laughed. "Well, that ought to suit you."

We talked of a great many other things as we rode together that night. Mostly, I asked questions, which Eamonn answered freely. I hadn't realized, until that night, how remiss I'd been in *his* interests. I'd been too wrapped up in my own concerns. It came as a surprise to me to learn that he planned to travel to Skaldia with Brigitta to meet her family, assuming they both survived this siege. He hoped to coax them into blessing their union, and giving Brigitta leave to travel to Alba with him and make a home there.

"Why not?" he asked pragmatically. "I know there's a history of enmity. But we're all barbarians alike, aren't we?"

"You?" I said. "Never."

"I am, though, Imri. We both are." He rode without comment for a while. "Please don't take this amiss," he said eventually. "Because I know you don't think like most D'Angelines. But Brigitta and I understand one another. History is a lottery of sorts. We come from people who hunger for what they were denied, through whatever accident of birth or geography. They've known it longer in Skaldia. In Alba and Eire, the Dalriada are only beginning to realize it. The Master of the Straits kept us in isolation for a long, long time."

I shook my head. "Not a-purpose. The curse—"

"I know." Eamonn leaned over to touch my arm. "Dagda Mor! I don't mean to blame you. You, of all people; you and Phèdre and Joscelin . . ." His voice trailed off. "And yet," he mused, "when all is said and done, we are still subject to the Master of the Straits."

I summoned a memory of Hyacinthe; Hyacinthe, whom Phèdre had named her one true friend. *Didikani*; a Tsingano half-breed, with a worn, beautiful face, black curls, and color-shifting eyes filled with lost knowledge won through the long, lonely years of his forced apprenticeship. I remembered how he had walked on the waves, clutching his folio of pages. The lost Book of Raziel. Speaking the charm that held him aloft on their surface.

Held Phèdre aloft.

And she had summoned Rahab and banished him, speaking the Name of God.

"A different Master," I said softly. "A *better* Master. The Straits are open, Eamonn, and he protects both our shores,

Alba and Terre d'Ange alike; aye, even from the ambition of
the Skaldi, who would raid your shores if they could. Should
he put aside his knowledge? Banish it from human understanding? Do you say it is ill done?"

"No!" Eamonn hesitated, then repeated it. "No."

"Good," I said. "Because Elua knows, it was hard-won."

"I know." He put out his hand, and I clasped it. "I know
it was, Imri. I just want you to understand, that's all."

I nodded. "And I am trying."

Come dawn, we were relieved of duty and made our way
back to the villa. Once more, I stumbled to my chamber and
threw myself down on my bed, where I slept the sleep of
pure exhaustion.

I dreamed, though.

In my dreams, I held the two halves of Gallus Tadius'
broken death-mask and sought to join them together. It
seemed to me that all would be right if only I could make it
whole. The siege would be lifted and Lucius restored to himself. Everyone would be happy and free. I couldn't do it,
though. The wax was old and brittle, crumbling beneath my
hands. The harder I tried, the faster it crumbled. And I knew,
somehow, that there was a charm that would make it stop,
that would make time run backward in its course until the
mask was whole and Gilot was alive again and everything
was right in the world, only I didn't know the words, the
right words. It was somewhat I'd known a long time ago, a
very long time ago, but I had lost it. Because I was too careless, because I was bad.

I woke myself mumbling.

"Imriel!" Eamonn's voice boomed in the bedchamber. I
opened my eyes and squinted at him. He was standing before the window, sunlight making a fiery halo of his red-gold
hair. "Wake up! I'm getting married today."

FIFTY-FOUR

FOR A CEREMONY thrown together in haste, it was a touching affair.

Nothing was quite as it ought to be, of course; there simply wasn't time. It didn't matter, though. The bride was Skaldi, the groom was Dalriadan. Neither had family to stand for them, and neither cared aught for proper Caerdicci customs. It was the exchange of vows, spoken and witnessed, that mattered.

It took place in the atrium. By all rights, there should have been a procession from the bride's household to the groom. Since that wasn't feasible, the groom's "household" was established in the far end of the atrium. A young priest from the temple of Jupiter was in attendance—not the flamen dialis himself, but a priest nonetheless—and an altar had been set up there.

Flames danced in the gilded offering bowl that sat atop the altar, fueled by bundles of juniper twigs tied with red wool and laid carefully across a charcoal base. Beyond the atrium, a banquet table awaited in the dining room, laden with food and brimming jugs of wine. The Lady Beatrice had elected to ignore Gallus Tadius' proscriptions for the occasion.

"Do we know where Gallus is?" I whispered to Eamonn, who looked resplendent in a toga of fine-combed white wool with a crimson border, his gold torc around his neck. I was standing at his side, along with Deccus Fulvius and a bewildered-looking Publius Tadius. Something inside him had cracked the day his son struck him across the face, and what will remained, the siege had broken. I was surprised he was there.

Eamonn shook his head. "Up to his plans, I imagine."

"Does he know about this?" I asked.

"No," he said.

"Excuse me." Publius leaned forward and peered at Eamonn. "Who are you again?"

I bowed to him. "My lord Publius, this is Prince Eamonn mac Grainne of the Dalriada, who has fought bravely for Lucca. He is grateful beyond words that you have extended the hospitality of the Tadeii to him on his wedding day."

"Oh, indeed!" Eamonn agreed.

Publius blinked at me. "Who are you?"

"Imriel," I said.

Deccus Fulvius clapped a hand on Publius' shoulder. "Let's have a quick cup of wine, old friend," he murmured, steering him toward the banquet table. "I'll explain it all again."

At the other end of the atrium, the doors opened to admit Brigitta, escorted by Claudia and the Lady Beatrice. Deccus and Publius hurried back, wiping their mouths. Brigitta was clad in white, too: a long white gown, with a gold cingulum tied around the waist in an elaborate knot. It made me think, briefly, of the sacred girdles the Magi had worn in Daršanga; the ones the bone-priests had used to strangle their loved ones.

I pushed the thought away, determined not to taint Eamonn's wedding day with my own dark memories.

Brigitta looked lovely. Her golden hair was arranged in an elaborate coif, adorned by a wreath of myrtle. Her cheeks glowed pink, and her blue eyes shone. Eamonn straightened at the sight of her, his tunic straining across his broad shoulders.

There was awkwardness with the ceremony itself; and how not? But in the end, none of it mattered. All together, we managed to get them before the altar. And there, each in turn, Brigitta and Eamonn spilled incense into the offering bowl and held their hands above the flame and declared their willing consent to this union. There was some business with a bronze scale and a distaff that went wholly amiss; I had to repress a laugh at the dubious gaze Brigitta cast toward the latter.

The young priest was perspiring. *"Iuppiter, Iuno atque, dii me omnes testes vos testor mihi,"* he said in formal tones, wiping his brow with his sleeve. "I call the gods to witness. In their presence, in good faith, make now your vows."

Eamonn took Brigitta's hand. "Upon my life and by my honor," he said solemnly, "I pledge myself to you, for as long as I live."

Her blush deepened and her Caerdicci dwindled. "So do I."

Once it was evident that nothing more was forthcoming, the priest beckoned for a winejug and a chalice. He filled the chalice, and indicated that they should both pour an offering to the gods and then drink from the nuptial cup. When it was done, he heaved a sigh.

"By the gods immortal," he pronounced, "you are joined together in matrimony."

We all cheered, and Eamonn swept Brigitta into his arms

and carried her over the threshold of the atrium toward the banquet. She flung her arms around his neck and kissed him in a rare moment of unreserved joy. My eyes stung with an odd mixture of affection, envy, and grief. And strangely, the person I missed most in that moment was Lucius. He would have understood.

After the ceremony, it was all revelry.

There was a hectic gaiety in feasting during a time of siege, in defying orders. I ate and drank deep of all that was placed before me, making a concerted effort to thrust aside any feelings of ill will, to take joy in the happiness of my friends. And in others, too. Claudia and Deccus shared a couch, the apparent picture of wedded contentment. The Lady Beatrice was happy, and I could not begrudge her that. Even Publius Tadius seemed pleased in a befuddled manner, if only because his winecup was steadily refilled, the poor man.

I kept my dire thoughts at bay and raised my cup in a toast. "To Eamonn and Brigitta!" I called, and then slipped into D'Angeline. "May Blessed Elua hold and keep you in his hand, and may his Companions grant you mercy and kindness."

Amid the general acclaim, a shadow darkened the doorway.

"What in the name of Hades is *this*?" a voice grated.

I got unsteadily to my feet. "Lucius . . ."

"Lucius be damned!" he roared. His gaze scoured the dining room, the picked-over banquet table. "Did I not give orders? What *is* this? This excess, this folly! Do you not understand that we are under siege? This is treason!"

The Lady Beatrice emitted a faint sound and fanned herself anxiously. Her husband stared blankly at his empty lap. No one else moved, although Claudia watched me.

"Lucius." I approached him. The sockets of his eyes were bruised hollows, his eyes burning like embers. They were mistrustful, and yet there was something within them I knew. Without thinking, I took his face in my hands. It felt stiff and hard. The skin was taut over the bones of his face, the scowling lines on it were engraved cruel and deep. And yet, unlike my dream, it didn't crumble under my touch. "It's a wedding. Eamonn and Brigitta's wedding."

For the space of a few heartbeats, Lucius surfaced.

I saw it; I saw his satyr's mouth twist in a familiar, wry smile. "Prince Barbarus and his shield-maiden?" he whispered.

"Yes," I said. "Will you celebrate it with us?"

Lucius was there; and then he was gone. He yanked his head back and swatted my hands away. "Jupiter! Get off me, you damned D'Angeline, before I have your balls for juggler's toys." I stepped back, raising my hands in a placating gesture. "Right," he said, breathing hard. "We've a special mission planned for tonight. I'll need you to report early, both of you."

"Gallus Tadius." Deccus Fulvius swung himself off the couch. "I will be taking Prince Eamonn's place tonight that he might spend it with his bride."

"Oh, you are, are you?" Gallus gave him a hard look, but Deccus stood firm. At length, Gallus shrugged. "As long as you follow orders," he said, then jerked his chin at the banquet table. "Clean this up. And don't let me see anything like it again."

With that, he strode away.

"Well," I said. "That could have been worse."

The Lady Beatrice had tears in her eyes. "My poor boy! This is devouring him from the inside out. Is this worth it? Is *Lucca* worth his suffering?"

"Lucca," her husband murmured vaguely. "Oh, yes."

"I don't know, my lady," I said to her. "I wish I did."

Deccus Fulvius cleared his throat. "Come on, lad. We'd best be off."

"No, my lord." Eamonn rose. "I can't let you take my place. It's not right. Whatever Gallus Tadius is planning, it may be dangerous."

"Bah!" Deccus chuckled. "Do you take me for a milksop, lad? I was holding a sword before you were born. There's fight in the old republican yet. Isn't there, my love?" he added to Claudia. She smiled at him with genuine fondness. Deccus nodded at Eamonn and Brigitta. "Take your happiness where you find it, children, and don't ask too many questions. Life is too short and uncertain to do otherwise."

Eamonn protested; Deccus prevailed. And so it was that he and I reported for patrol duty together that evening.

The square was already crowded by the time we arrived. The usual riders were there, as well as a squadron of the city guard and a handful of the newer conscripts on foot. The latter wore dark clothing and no armor, though they had the scarlet band of the Red Scourge tied around their upper arms.

Gallus Tadius waited until we were all assembled, the riders in a neat double line, the foot-soldiers clustered in front of us. Behind him, the burned hulk of the bell-tower loomed in ominous warning.

"All right, lads!" he shouted. "Tonight we set fire to the fields!"

Almost to a man, they cheered. Deccus and I exchanged a glance. "Surely he jests," he murmured.

I shook my head. "I think not."

He didn't. In a few broad strokes, Gallus Tadius outlined his plan. Over the last two days, he had prevailed on Lucca's carpenters to build a crude trebuchet atop the gatehouse, hidden behind the parapet. Others had scoured the city's parks and gardens for rocks and boulders large enough to make suitable missiles. Once darkness fell, he meant to launch an attack on Valpetra's forces.

It was unlikely to do much damage, but in the darkness it would sow confusion. And while Valpetra's men were distracted, a detail of handpicked conscripts would exit the city by way of the dismantled sluice gate. Once they were out, guards atop the wall would lower bundles of weaponry—hunting bows, pitch-tipped arrows, torches, and oil-filled bladders.

"It's a dangerous detail," he said grimly, then raised his voice to a roar. "But there's gold and glory for any man who makes it back alive! What do you say, lads? Are you game?"

They roared back at him. *"Gallus! Gallus! Gallus!"*

He flashed a feral grin. "Then come forward and be anointed!"

Twenty men crowded forward, touching his stirrup, his saddlecloth, his booted foot. Eager faces strained upward. Dipping into a pouch at his belt, Gallus Tadius leaned down and smeared a dark substance on each face; a streak on both cheeks and one down the center of their brows. Ashes, I thought. Ashes from the burned bell-tower. Fire for fire.

"This is madness," Deccus said quietly. "Is it always like this?"

"No," I said. "This is new."

"Right!" Gallus straightened and pointed. "Off you go to await my signal!" He watched them pelt through the streets of Lucca, then turned to the rest of us. "Riders, heed. This mission's to be run from the walls. You'll patrol as usual, but your primary job is to carry orders; mine from atop the gatehouse, and Captain Arturo's from the sentry-point near the canal. The watchword is 'firestorm.' You hear it, you do whatever you're told and ride like hell. Understood?"

"Aye, sir!" we called.

He dispatched us in short order and headed off toward the gatehouse. Deccus was quiet as we set out on patrol together. It was a cold, cloudy evening. He wore a heavy wool cloak fastened with a gold brooch. I wondered if Claudia Fulvia had fastened it for him. It was the sort of Tiberian wifely gesture she did so well.

There were no orders at the first sentry-points we passed. At the canal, we found a throng of men clustered under the shadow of the wall, their soot-streaked faces eerie in the twilight. "Any word?" one called eagerly.

"Not yet," I said.

"Firestorm!" a voice hissed from above. "One campfire in range, a dozen of the enemy posted. No movement. Continue and report to Gallus Tadius."

I gave a wave of acknowledgment and we rode onward.

Presently, Deccus spoke. "They're dead men, you know."

My skin prickled. "You sense it?"

"What?" He glanced at me. "Oh, the *lemures*, aye. It's been turning my stomach long enough I'm nearly used to it. I meant those poor lads." He frowned. "Glory and gold! They don't stand a chance. They might get out safely, and they might even succeed. But there's no way they're getting back alive."

I didn't think so, either.

"And if Gallus Tadius is half as ruthless as I think he is," Deccus added in a low voice, "he knows it, too. He's sending those lads to their deaths."

We reached the gatehouse without event, although I could barely make it out. Full darkness had fallen. The moon was hidden behind clouds, and only a few stars were visible.

I called out my report to the unseen faces atop the gate-house. It felt as though I were talking to myself.

"Firestorm!" A voice floated down from above. "Report to Captain Arturo, now!"

Deccus grunted. "We can't damn well *see*!"

"Now!"

I leaned over in the darkness. "Follow me, my lord."

Without waiting to see if Deccus followed, I nudged the Bastard's flanks. His hooves rang on the cobblestones as he shifted into a smart trot. I could barely see, either; but I could hear. The nearer we were to the wall, the more muted the echo of his hoofbeats. Closing my eyes, I could hear the difference.

Behind me, Deccus huffed. "What are you, lad, a *bat*?"

I smiled. "Can you see?"

"I can see your damned spotted horse," he retorted. "And that's all."

"That's enough," I said.

Behind us both, we heard a deep thumping sound as the trebuchet released its first missile. Atop the gatehouse there were cheers; and beyond the walls, a distant thud and shouts of alarm. Again and again, the sounds were repeated. We could hear them all the way to the aqueduct.

"Firestorm!" Captain Arturo's voice rang out, exultant. "The enemy is moving away! Report to Gallus Tadius, *now*!"

"I'll go," I said briefly.

Deccus nodded. "Take care."

I gave the Bastard his head. He stretched into a canter, veering only once to avoid a pair of startled riders picking their way cautiously along the wall. I daresay his night vision was better than mine. I grinned as we whipped past them. Deccus was right; this was madness. Still, there was somewhat infectious about it.

"Enemy at the sluice gates moving away!" I shouted up at the gatehouse.

The trebuchet thumped, its counterweight slamming into the roof. Another load of rocks was launched toward Valpetra's army.

"Firestorm!" roared the voice of Gallus Tadius. "Tell Arturo, *now*!"

I saluted. "Aye, sir!"

I rode the Bastard at a hand-gallop, trusting to my ears and his eyes. We tore a path along the wall, his striding legs eating up the cobbled streets. At the aqueduct, there were torches lit and men waiting, conscripts and guardsmen alike. In the sudden blaze of light, I reined the Bastard hard.

"Captain Arturo!" I cried. "Gallus Tadius says, *now*!"

"Firestorm!" came the reply. "Red Scourge, *go*!"

Gallus' handpicked troops swarmed into the canal. One by one, they dove beneath the dark waters, shadowy figures disappearing beneath the wall. I shivered at the thought, knowing damn well how cold it was. Atop the wall, there was an anxious, waiting silence. After what seemed a dangerous length of time, we heard faint splashing sounds on the far side of the wall.

A pair of rope ladders slithered down from the sentry-tree. "Weapons up!" Captain Arturo ordered. "Riders, lend a hand."

The bows and torches were bundled into sacks, each one tied with a generous length of rope, and stacked along the inner wall. Already, the guardsmen were beginning to ferry them up the ladders. Dismounting, I grabbed one and slung the sack over my shoulder. It was awkward work, climbing the slack, twisting ladder with one hand, an ungainly array of weapons banging at my back, the dangling rope entangling my legs as I climbed.

On the other ladder, Deccus Fulvius puffed and grumbled. "Surely there's a better way to do this."

I reached the top and set my sack down. "Toss me the end of your rope."

It felt strange to be atop the wall in open air. The work went quicker once the other guards saw what we were doing and followed suit, letting those of us already on the wall hoist the weapons. I suppose they hadn't dared earlier, with the enemy sentries watching. We worked as quietly as we could. Below, Gallus' troops hauled themselves dripping from the moat and fanned out along its outer edge. Except for the whites of their eyes, they were nearly invisible in the darkness.

"Lower weapons!" Captain Arturo ordered in a strident whisper. "And mind you clear the moat."

One of the guards slung his sack of weapons toward the far side of the moat, letting it fly. It landed with a loud splash, not even halfway across. I winced at the sound.

"Damn it!" Arturo hissed.

"Sorry, sir!" The guard cringed. "It's farther than it looks!"

I studied the sentry-tree. "Help me a moment," I said to Deccus. He followed with both weapon bags as I scrambled up the tree-ladder. It was a sturdy old oak, good for climbing, with low, broad limbs. I shinnied out onto one, wrapping my legs around it, then leaned down and extended one hand. "The rope."

It took a couple tosses, but once I had it, I started swinging the heavy sack of weapons, getting a good momentum going and trying to gauge the distance. The captain watched without comment. When I thought I had it, I let it fly at the height of its arc. Until I heard the rattling thud of impact, I wasn't sure that it had cleared the water.

"Good work," the captain said laconically. "Next!"

Another guard took a post on a different limb, and between the two of us, we managed to get all twenty sacks of assorted bows, arrows, torches, and pitch across the moat. Vague figures scrambled to retrieve each one as it landed, melting away into the night. I lay along the tree limb for a moment, gazing out at the darkness.

Over at the gatehouse, the trebuchet was still thumping sporadically, but Valpetra's troops had retreated out of range. From this height, I had a clear view of their abandoned campfires and the milling mass of soldiers beyond. Here and there, riders peeled away, torches streaming with sparks as they began to scour the perimeter of Lucca. Either Valpetra or his condottiere was growing suspicious. I thought about our twenty soaked, shivering conscripts lugging heavy bags of weapons, and I liked their chances even less.

Somewhere behind me, I heard slow, plodding hoofbeats and a scraping sound. Something heavy was being dragged along the streets of Lucca on ill-made skids.

"All right, lads." Captain Arturo's voice was low and grave. "Get it in place."

I didn't want to look. The rough bark was oddly comforting beneath my cheek. It made me think of happier times, like Queen Ysandre's Festival of the Harvest. And then I remembered that I'd promised Anna Marzoni's daughter Belinda that I'd teach her to climb a tree and the feeling vanished, so I climbed back down to the wall.

Below, the boy with the bucket-helm was stroking his lathered plowhorse's neck and praising him. Captain Arturo's guardsmen were rolling a massive millstone into position at the edge of the canal. One careful shove, and it effectively would seal off the sluice gates.

I looked wordlessly at the captain.

"Gallus Tadius' orders." His face was stoic. "We'll wait as long as we dare."

Deccus Fulvius was watching the fields. "There!" he said suddenly, pointing. "Fire!"

It was quite a distance away; farther than I would have thought anyone could have gotten on foot carrying such a burden. I wondered if Gallus Tadius had chosen his twenty recruits for fearlessness, loyalty, or merely foot-speed. A low orange-red blossom of fire, blooming and spreading. It hadn't rained since we'd arrived. I reckoned the wheat fields were good and dry.

"There!" someone else cried as another bloom appeared.

Two . . . five . . . a dozen. There, a blazing arrow arched across the night like a shooting star, and fire bloomed where it landed. There, an unseen figure raced along a furrow, lit torches in both hands, leaving a trail of fire in his wake. The red blossoms took root and spread.

And Valpetra's cavalry responded, trying to outrace the flames, trying to ride down the perpetrators. The infantry was in retreat, horns blowing, organizing a swift march toward the river. The cavalry was in pursuit.

Dark figures on dark horses, silhouetted against a rising sea of fire. They cut down anyone on foot. They cut down Gallus Tadius' conscripts; they cut down folk from the outlying villages, fleeing for the river.

I felt sick.

Luccan riders within the walls came with reports from the north and east; the vineyards were burning. Atop the walls, we watched as the olive grove to the west was set alight. For a time, it seemed as though the ancient olive trees would withstand their efforts, but Gallus Tadius had armed his men well. They flung oil-filled bladders which burst against the bark, and the fire clung and spread until the gnarled trees were engulfed in flame.

"Firestorm," Deccus Fulvius murmured.

I glanced at him, remembering how he had spoken against this. He looked old; old and weary. He met my gaze and forced a smile, laying a hand on my shoulder. "Is it worth destroying a thing to save it?" he asked.

"I don't know," I said humbly.

Deccus squeezed my shoulder. "Nor do I."

Beyond the walls of Lucca, everything was ablaze. The burning fields flung a roaring blaze of heat and light upward, as though night had become day and earth had become sky. The air was filled with smoke. I prayed silently that the moat and wall would prove an adequate firebreak. Captain Arturo shielded his eyes, gazing out toward the roaring maelstrom.

"That's it, then," he muttered, then raised his voice. "Guards! Lower the millstone!"

There was a grinding sound as they hove to. The millstone rolled over the edge of the canal and entered the water with a deep, resounding splash. It sank beneath the surface and settled into place.

"*Captain!*" My voice emerged high and taut as I pointed.

A figure, a lone figure, running like a coursed hare, burst into view. His soot-blackened face was set in a rictus of terror and exhilaration, teeth bared. He hit the edge of the moat and dove without a pause.

"Oh, sodding hell," Captain Arturo said quietly.

There were three Valpetran cavalrymen on his heels, singed and furious. By the time he breached the surface of the moat, they were fifty paces away. He trod water, calling to us. "Something's wrong! I can't get through!"

Captain Arturo cursed. "Run! Run, you idiot, *run*!"

There was light; too much light. A sea of flame by which to see Valpetra's men close the distance and draw rein as Gallus' exhausted conscript sought to drag himself out of the moat. A lone figure, damp and bedraggled, a sodden length of red cloth tied around his upper arm.

"Guards!" Captain Arturo shouted. "Crossbows!"

There was a quick flurry of exchange as weapons were discharged, and I saw none of it, borne down by the weight of Deccus Fulvius, who flattened me atop the wall. I heard the whizzing sound of a flung javelin passing overhead, and the squeal of a horse struck by the bolt of a crossbow. When Deccus' weight rolled off me and I lifted my head, there was only the vast, roaring silence of fire beyond the walls, speaking in inhuman tongues of flame.

Valpetra's cavalrymen were gone, riding for the river.

A lone figure floated in the moat, two javelins protruding from his back.

Captain Arturo heaved a sigh. "Go," he said to Deccus and me. "Back to your patrol."

We climbed down the rope ladders and reclaimed our mounts. The Bastard was nervous, rolling his eyes and stamping. I didn't blame him. Once I got him quieted, we resumed our patrol. There were no stars visible, not anymore. Only a low ceiling of clouds and dense smoke, lit from beneath with a hellish glare. Beneath it, we passed from sentry-point to sentry-point, carrying reports. Every one was the same. All was burning; the enemy had retreated.

Once again, Deccus was quiet.

I gazed at his profile as we rode together, set in somber lines. And I did not think about Claudia, but only about how he had been kind to me the first time we met: in the baths, where Gilot and I, newly arrived in Tiberium, were acting like fools together, splashing about.

It hurt to remember.

Deccus Fulvius had always been kind to me.

We were relieved of duty beneath a sullen, smoky dawn. Everything that could burn had burned. It was left only to smolder. I dismounted wearily and handed over the Bastard's reins. Outside the Tadeii villa, I made a deep bow to Deccus Fulvius. Although he didn't know it, in the D'Angeline court it was a bow accorded a superior.

"My lord Deccus," I said softly. "I was careless atop the wall. I owe you my life."

He dismounted with a grunt, rubbing the small of his back. "War's war, lad. It's an ugly business. 'Tis a petty mind keeps score." He summoned a tired smile. "Let us hope your Dalriadan friend enjoyed his wedding night, eh? The cost was a trifle higher than I reckoned."

"Than any of us did," I agreed.

Deccus grunted again. "Except Gallus Tadius."

FIFTY-FIVE

O N THE NEXT DAY, the D'Angeline delegation
arrrived.

To his credit, Gallus Tadius sent for me as soon as their
banners were spotted; or mayhap it was due to Lucius'
prompting somewhere deep inside him. I couldn't say and
didn't care. All I knew was that I was glad beyond telling to
see them.

For all of that, the view from the gatehouse was devastating. The delegation rode slowly along the road to Lucca. On
either side of them, the once-fertile plains were scorched
and smoking. Overhead, the sky was low and angry, the
color of tarnished silver. It seemed as though all the brightness in the world was concentrated in the approaching company of D'Angelines.

They were a squadron of embassy guards, I guessed.
They rode fully armed, some thirty strong, with surcoats and
cloaks of Courcel blue. There on their banners were two of
the seals I'd longed to see—the golden lily and stars on a
green field that represented Elua and his Companions, flying
above the silver swan of House Courcel.

And, too, they carried the pure white banners that requested a peaceful parley.

Valpetra's cavalry interecepted them before they reached the gate, galloping across the blackened fields. I watched with my heart in my throat, praying they wouldn't be turned back. After an interminable length of time, one of the cavalrymen headed back toward their new encampment on the far side of the river. The rest waited out of range while the D'Angeline contingent moved forward.

Gallus Tadius pulled me back from the window. "Hold, D'Angeline. Don't be hasty."

I glared at him. "They're my people!"

"And it's my city." He shrugged. "Let's just see, shall we?"

Outside the gate, the delegation drew rein. Gallus nodded to his guards, who took careful aim at them, crossbows cocked. "State your business!" one of them called.

"Quentin LeClerc, servant of her majesty Queen Ysandre de la Courcel of Terre d'Ange, commander of the Tiberian garrison of her ladyship the ambassadress Denise Fleurais," came the reply in D'Angeline-accented Caerdicci. "We come seeking the ransom of his highness, Prince Imriel nó Montrève de la Courcel of Terre d'Ange!"

Gallus glanced at me with a hint of amusement. "I take it that's you, fancy-boy?" I nodded. "Well, I'll have a word with them."

Without further ado, he ducked through the outer door and sauntered out onto the wall. From the tower chamber, I watched him fold his arms and address them.

"Right," he said easily. "I'm Gallus Tadius, Prince of Lucca, and as far as I'm concerned, you're welcome to the whelp. But unless your whoring Queen's sending a few thousand more like you to guarantee the bargain, I'd think twice about it." He jerked his chin toward the north. "You want safe passage for him, barter with Valpetra."

"My thanks, your highness, on behalf of her majesty and Terre d'Ange, for your generosity. We will negotiate with the Duke of Valpetra." The unseen commander's tone was circumspect. "Might it be possible to speak to Prince Imriel? I would confirm his well-being."

"Why not?" Gallus beckoned. "Come on out. You've leave to talk as long as you like," he added, passing me and heading back for the tower. "It's your lookout if you get shot by the enemy. And mind, the guards have orders to shoot you themselves at the first hint of treason."

Ah, Elua! All the homesickness I'd been holding at bay overwhelmed me at the sight of my countrymen. D'Angeline faces, clear-cut and handsome. I found myself beaming involuntarily at Quentin LeClerc. He was a tall man with dark brown hair braided in a tidy cable, a bemused look on his face as he peered upward. He accorded me an uncertain bow from his saddle.

"Your highness?" he asked in D'Angeline. "Prince Imriel?"

In my haste to see them, I'd thrown on last night's worn, dirty attire. I hadn't had a proper bath since before Eamonn's wedding, either, just another cursory wash at the basin. I dragged my sleeve over my face, smearing lingering soot-stains. "Forgive me, messire. Last night's patrol was . . . eventful."

"So I see," he said.

One of the guards laughed. "That's him, my lord. He turned up at the embassy dressed like a beggar and smelling somewhat fierce one day."

I flushed, remembering. "Not me. It was the satchel."

"Oh, aye!" He winked and bowed. "The satchel it was."

"No mind." I sat on the edge of the wall, dangling my legs over the moat. The water was higher than it had been since Gallus Tadius ordered the sluice gates blocked. "Messire LeClerc, how did her ladyship get word so quickly? We expected it might take weeks."

Quentin LeClerc shook his head. "I couldn't say, your highness. All I know is that she received an urgent dispatch and sent us posthaste." He paused. "We? There are others with you?"

"Friends," I said. "Eamonn mac Grainne of the Dalriada and his wife, and Senator Deccus Fulvius of Tiberium and his wife. I'd like safe passage for all five of us. And there is the matter of my man-at-arms, Gilot, who was slain during the fighting. I promised to bring him home."

"Of course." He nodded. "May we be confident that the Prince of Lucca will honor his word? I thought . . ." He hesitated again. "Forgive me, highness, but I understood Gaetano Correggio was the Prince of Lucca, or so Lady Denise told me. And it seems to me . . . as a student of military history, it seems to me that Gallus Tadius is . . . was . . ."

"Dead?" I lowered my voice. "'Tis a long story, messire. Get me out of here, and I'll tell you. But yes, I think he'll honor his word. And anyway, he's right. It's Valpetra we need to worry about." I gazed at the cavalrymen watching us from the smoldering wreck of Lucca's fields, and my last trace of gladness ebbed away. "I don't suppose he'll be in a good mood."

"No." Quentin LeClerc followed my gaze. "I don't imagine so." He squared his shoulders. "Still, he's no cause to blame you, has he?"

"Ah, well." I smiled ruefully. "He might."

I told him about cutting off the Duke's hand, and watched his face turn grave. When I finished, he gave me a resolute bow. "Sensible men understand the vicissitudes of war. I

will beg an audience with him and pray I find him reasonable. I will return, your highness."

They rode back across the barren landscape, vivid banners bobbing in the grey air, carrying all my hope with them.
I watched them join Valpetra's cavalrymen and head toward
the river. I offered a silent prayer to Blessed Elua for their
success, then descended back through the gate tower and
went to report on the latest doings.

At the Tadeii villa, I found Claudia. Deccus Fulvius
hadn't risen yet, nor had Eamonn and Brigitta, though I
daresay for different reasons. Claudia listened intently, re-
questing that I repeat our conversation in its entirety.

"There was no other news?" she asked when I was done.
"No promise of aid from other quarters?"

"No." I frowned. "Should there have been?"

She sighed. "Not necessarily."

"The Unseen Guild?"

Although the two of us were alone, her nod was almost
imperceptible. "If word has reached the D'Angeline ambassadress' ears, then surely the Guild knows, too. Such news
spreads swiftly. There would have been word if they meant
to act. They don't."

"I'm sorry." I took her hand. "But what could they have
done?"

"Oh, plenty of things." She smiled, but her eyes were red-
rimmed and weary. "They could have prevailed on the Duke
of Firezia to intervene. He's a vested interest in Lucca's
trade and a considerable standing army. Or they could have
dispatched an assassin to take out Valpetra, though I suppose
it wouldn't be easy under the circumstances." She shrugged.
"Perhaps they have. We can hope, I suppose."

"The Guild employs assassins?"

"The Heptarchs do, or at least so it's rumored. Possibly

the epopts." Claudia rubbed her eyes. "I told you, Imriel, I'm only a journeyman." She gave me another wry smile. "And a failed one at that."

I held her hand tighter. "I won't leave without you. I swear it."

"Don't be stupid." Her gaze sharpened. "If you have a chance, take it. This is no time for foolish heroics. Speaking of which . . ." She withdrew a letter from her bodice. "This arrived."

It was another letter from Helena Correggio. I walked away to read it. Although there was nothing in it Claudia couldn't have guessed, the words were naked and vulnerable on the page, and it didn't seem right to expose them to other eyes. Despite my denials, she believed I was the belated answer to her prayers: the Bella Donna's son, sent to rescue her in a time of need. As she had before, she begged me in fulsome terms to call upon her.

If I'd thought it would do any good, I would have; but I feared the opposite was true. Betimes, women in the zenana had clung to desperate delusions. Indulging them only made it worse when their delusions were shattered. And they were; they always were. It was another part of why I'd hated Phèdre for so long. She'd held out an impossible ray of hope, and hope killed quicker than despair in that place.

The other part . . .

Death's Whore.

I shuddered at my memories. But Lucca wasn't Daršanga, and I wasn't sent by Blessed Elua to save anyone. It was just a city under siege, and I was a mortal man struggling to set aside his childish notions of heroism to save his own skin. Still, I thought, it would be cruel to reply with naught but silence. And with luck, on the morrow I would be gone. In time, Helena would find the healing she needed.

"I'd like to send a letter," I said. "Have you the means?"

Claudia inclined her head. "Lucius hasn't begun rationing stationery yet. I'll have paper and an inkpot delivered to your chambers."

I submerged myself in the chilly waters of the unheated bath, scouring away the stench of smoke that clung to my hair and skin. The water wasn't stagnant yet, but it would be before long. Lucca's drinking water came from its deep wells, but the aqueduct fed the baths and fountains, public and private. They'd all be stagnant soon.

Afterward, I scrubbed myself dry and dressed hastily, trying to beat the chill, then sat down and penned a letter to Helena Correggio. It was innocuous and impersonal. Using formal language, I thanked her for the invitation to call on her and tendered my regrets. I offered condolences for her losses and extended my best wishes for happier days to come.

I signed it with my full name.

It felt strange and I felt guilty. I wanted, very much, to get *out* of Lucca. It wasn't my city and it wasn't my battle. Gilot had already died for it; surely that was enough? There was Lucius and loyalty . . . but Master Piero had never told us how to answer questions of loyalty when one's boon comrade was possessed by the spirits of the dead. And there was the mystery of Canis, languishing in Lucca's gaol . . . but I hadn't asked for that, either. If he couldn't be bothered to be honest with me, why should I care?

Anyway, I could do more good outside Lucca's walls than within them. I thought about what Claudia had said. If the Unseen Guild could exert such influence, well and good. If they wanted my allegiance that badly, let them bargain for it on *my* terms. And if they didn't . . . when all was said and done, I was a D'Angeline Prince of the Blood and not without influence. For the first time in my life, I might as well use it.

Feeling better, I sealed the letter and gave it a Tadeii servant to deliver.

By the time I had finished, it was late afternoon and Eamonn and Brigitta were awake. The past night's events had cast a pall on their nuptials, but even so, it was clear they had taken Deccus Fulvius' advice. They'd taken happiness where they found it, and I couldn't begrudge them. In the salon of the guest wing, I told them what had transpired earlier today with the D'Angeline delegation.

Brigitta's face lit up when I told them, almost as bright as it had yesterday at her marriage. "You mean we might be free to leave?"

"Might," I said cautiously. Hope kills. "Might."

"Oh, Eamonn!" She kissed him. "You could come to Skaldia!"

"And you to Alba, my heart." He returned her kiss, then settled her head on his shoulder. "What do you reckon the odds, Imri?"

I shook my head. "I've no idea."

He stroked Brigitta's golden hair, and his grey-green eyes were thoughtful. "So who sent an urgent message to the D'Angeline ambassadress in Tiberium?"

Our eyes met over Brigitta's head.

"Does it matter?" I asked. "If it works, does it matter?"

Eamonn shrugged. "Not if it works." Planting a last kiss on Brigitta's temple, he swung himself upright. "Time for patrol!" he said cheerfully. "Mustn't disappoint Gallus Tadius."

After the hectic events of last night, tonight's patrol was mercifully uneventful. We assembled in the central square, and Gallus Tadius addressed us briefly. His mood was somber. He bowed his head and offered a prayer for the dead, speaking stirringly of their sacrifice. In the lowering twilight, his face looked horribly like a mask. I closed my eyes and listened to his words, trying to shut out the vision of the lone conscript treading water in the moat, his face terrified and bewildered. His body, floating, a pair of javelins protruding from his back.

Not my fault. Not my responsibility.

We were given lanterns that night, as it was well and truly too dark to see without them. Eamonn and I traded ours back and forth, taking turns carrying it. Nothing was happening; everything was quiet. We chatted with the sentries atop the wall, who reported that the fields were still smoldering. One could see it at night, they said; the sullen glow of embers. The enemy remained where they were, encamped on the far side of the river. Gone, but within striking distance. The D'Angelines were there, yes, but no word.

So it went, around and around.

At dawn, I went to bed and dreamed of home.

It was another full day before the D'Angeline delegation returned. Every hour that passed seemed to drag into eternity. I was impatient; impatient at waiting, impatient at not knowing, impatient at being trapped in Lucca. The day wore on endlessly. I'd risen after a few hours of sleep and spent my time pacing the city, pestering the sentries for word. There was some activity at the river no one could make out, but the D'Angeline company showed no sign of movement.

Indeed, the only thing of note to occur that day was that I discovered Canis had been released. He was part of a group of conscripts laboring at the entrance of the aqueduct, hauling dirt and stones to reinforce its blockage, Gallus Tadius having determined it was a point of vulnerability. Rising water in the moat was trickling past the broken sluice gates and the millstone. Lucca's walls were too sturdy and well-defended to be easily breached by sappers, but if Valpetra was minded to try, that was the place he'd pick.

Canis sported a few fresh bruises and a red armband, already grimy from his labor. He gave me a covert grin when no one was looking. I had a nearly overpowering urge to grab him by the scruff of the neck and shake the truth out of him. Since it was highly unlikely to work, I merely shook my head at him and kept walking.

At least he was free of the gaol. Whatever else he was about, it was his own doing. I reckoned my conscience was clear on that score.

Another night.

Another endless round of patrolling.

This time, the distant sound of horns awoke me. Either Valpetra was launching a new attack or the D'Angelines were returning. I rolled out of bed and dragged on my boots and sword-belt without bothering to wait for word.

It was the D'Angeline delegation.

Gallus Tadius was already atop the wall engaged in a negotiation with Quentin LeClerc. I couldn't make out what they were saying and the guards wouldn't let me into the gatehouse until it was settled, which drove me half-mad. At length, one took pity on me.

"Your D'Angeline captain wants to enter the city," he said. "Seems he wants to talk to you in person."

Not for anything would Gallus Tadius open the gates of Lucca. It took the better part of an hour, with riders dashing back and forth to various sentry-points, before an accommodation was reached. The sentries confirmed that the bulk of Valpetra's army remained stationed across the river. The cavalry had taken up a position blocking the road almost a quarter of a league away. There they remained motionless.

Gallus grudgingly agreed to lower a rope ladder and permit Quentin LeClerc and two men into Lucca, provided they came unarmed.

It was a considerable operation since the ladder had to stretch all the way across the moat, and by the time it was pegged into the ground, it was at a difficult angle. All I could hear were shouts and grunting, and a splash when someone fell off. I waited, breathing slowly and forcing myself to a state of composure.

At last, I caught a glimpse of Courcel blue. A pair of guardsmen helped LeClerc and his men atop the wall, while another pair stood by with swords drawn, ready to sever the ropes at the first indication that Valpetra's men were moving or the remainder of LeClerc's men attempted to scale the ladder. After the assault on the gatehouse, they weren't taking any chances.

But neither thing happened. The ladders was retrieved safely and LeClerc and his men were escorted through the tower and into the gatehouse square where I waited. All three of them bowed deeply. One was the embassy guard from before, the one who had remembered my stinking satchel of incense. None of them looked happy.

My heart sank. "He refused?"

"Not exactly." Quentin LeClerc glanced over at Gallus Tadius, who was lounging against the wall, arms folded over his chest. He was flanked by a pair of city guards. Their crossbows were cocked, and while they weren't aimed at the D'Angelines, the warning was clear. "Must we do this in public?"

I shrugged. "It's his city."

"So be it." LeClerc drew a deep breath. "Domenico Martelli, the Duke of Valpetra, maintains that his claim to

Lucca is valid by right of marriage. He is willing to grant your highness mercy and allow you to leave . . . for a price."

"That's all?" I laughed, buoyant with relief. "Name of Elua, man! Why didn't you say so? Whatever it is, whatever markers Lady Denise has to call in to pay it, I'm sure the Queen will see her compensated. What does he want, the moon and stars?"

"No." He pointed. "Your left hand."

FIFTY-SIX

I N T H E E N D, Gallus Tadius decided that LeClerc was in
earnest and three unarmed D'Angelines represented no
threat to Lucca, and allowed us to retreat to the villa for further discussion. We met in the grand salon, where the others
might hear and give their counsel, for there were other issues
at stake.

But in the matter of me, it was simple; Valpetra was
adamant.

My hand, or nothing.

That was why the cavalry was waiting on the road. Once
they'd severed my left hand, they'd allow me to pass. And
once it was done, they'd return to Valpetra with their grisly
token.

"I'm sorry, your highness." Quentin LeClerc's voice was
strained. "I argued through two nights and a day with him,
but he wouldn't hear reason. Not on this point." He took a
sip of water. "He's a little mad, I think."

Claudia Fulvia leaned forward. "And the condottiere, Silvanus? He owes no allegiance to Valpetra beyond whatever
spoils he and his men have been promised. Can he not be
bribed?"

He shook his head. "My lady, believe me, I tried. He

means to stand by the Duke until Lucca falls. They're all mad for war, and I don't quite know why." He glanced uneasily at the cup he held. "Something in the water, mayhap?"

None of us laughed. "What of the others?" I asked.

"Ah." LeClerc's expression eased. He cleared his throat and lifted his cup to his lips, then set it down untouched. "Yes. A touch of sanity, here. Valpetra's willing to barter, or at least Silvanus is and the Duke allowed it. They're willing to grant you"—he nodded at Deccus, Claudia, Brigitta, and Eamonn—"safe passage in exchange for the release of four of Silvanus' men."

"Excellent," Deccus said wryly. "All we have to do is convince Gallus Tadius."

"*Lucius* would do it," Claudia observed.

"Aye, but Lucius . . ." Eamonn sighed. LeClerc and his men looked at us with utter bewilderment. I explained to them about the *mundus manes*, the *lemures*, and the death-mask. It sounded mad when I said it, and they looked scarce less bewildered when I was done. Mayhap it *was* something in the water.

"Well, it's worth a try," Claudia murmured. "We'll speak to him. He seems to respect Deccus, and I was his sister once. Or perhaps Mother can reach him." Her face was troubled. "I don't like to leave her."

"They'll only grant safe passage for a direct exchange," Quentin LeClerc said apologetically. "Four for four, and no Luccan citizens. I'm sorry, my lady." He gave her a halfhearted smile. "You're lucky to be Tiberian by marriage. I wouldn't mention your family ties if I were you."

Four for four . . .

I swore, remembering. "One's dead," I said grimly. "One of Silvanus' men. There are only three."

The others exchanged glances.

"I'll stay." Deccus Fulvius spoke without hesitation, taking Claudia's hand. "Let the young people go. It's not their battle. You know who to see in Tiberium, who to speak to?"

She nodded, still troubled.

"What about Imriel?" Eamonn asked.

Quentin LeClerc cleared his throat again. "Terre d'Ange will act, of course! Make no mistake. Only I fear it will take time. Our presence in Caerdicca Unitas is thin, and Lady Fleurais will have to rely on diplomacy to raise a sufficient force of allies."

"Hire a condottiere," I suggested.

"Yes." His eyes were a trifle glazed. "One such as Gallus Tadius would be ideal." He gave himself a shake. "We will act," he said firmly. "But any course we take will take some time. The choice is yours, your highness."

I stood and paced restlessly around the salon, rubbing my left hand. Did I risk the uncertainty of waiting or take certain freedom and the loss of my hand? Not my sword hand, at least, I thought, remembering Gilot. I wished he was here. He always had sensible advice, even if I usually ignored it. I wondered what he would say.

"I'm staying."

"Eamonn," Brigitta breathed. "No!"

"What?" He shrugged. "Imriel's not about to let Valpetra lop his damned hand off. Lucca's got high, strong walls, plenty of water, food enough for weeks, and a mad genius in command of its defense, even if he is a dead man." He grinned at her. "You can help rescue us when the D'Angelines come. We'll be here."

It was the beginning of a lengthy argument. I led Quentin LeClerc and his men quietly out of the villa and escorted them back to the gatehouse. He agreed to report back to

Valpetra and return on the morrow. Whatever was decided in the argument, there was still the matter of getting Gallus Tadius to agree to the exchange.

"Your mind's settled?" LeClerc asked me atop the wall.

"Yes." I rubbed my hand. "I'm staying."

Under the watchful eyes of Gallus' guards, the ladder was lowered and they made their precarious, swaying descent. The last to go was the one who had remembered me from the embassy. He laid a hand on my shoulder.

"Have a care, your highness," he said. "Valpetra's up to somewhat over at the river."

I frowned. "What?"

"He's got his men digging a trench." He pointed. "Over on the far side. I don't reckon you can get a good look at it from the wall. But I grew up in Siovale, and unless I miss my guess, he means to try and dam the river."

"Ah, well." I relaxed. "Mayhap no one told him Lucca's got deep wells."

He nodded. "All the same, have a care."

"My thanks." I bade him farewell, then watched as they departed. The D'Angeline banners still fluttered brightly in the breeze, but they no longer carried any hope with them. The distant Valpetran cavalry began to move and the lieutenant in charge of the wall that afternoon ordered me down.

I went to find Gallus Tadius.

He was in the empty common room of the city guard's barracks, poring over inventory lists and muttering to himself. I gazed at the top of his head, the familiar burst of dark auburn curls. It evoked fond memories of Tiberium. In a strange way, I was glad I wasn't leaving.

"Lucius Tadius da Lucca," I said without thinking. "What's Master Piero got you studying now?"

His head came up with a jerk. "Montrève?"

My heart skipped a beat. "Lucius?"

He blinked. "I don't . . ." He pressed his fingers to his temples and grimaced. "Sweet Apollo! My head hurts."

"Lucius." I yanked out the chair opposite him and sat. "Listen to me, quickly. You've got to give an order to free the Valpetran prisoners."

His face shifted. "Why?"

Leaning across the table, I grasped his arms, willing him to stay. "Valpetra's agreed to an exchange. Three for three. Claudia, Deccus, and Brigitta." I didn't expect Eamonn to lose that argument. "Safe passage to Tiberium."

"Tiberium," he murmured. "Montrève . . ." His brow furrowed. Elua, it looked like the lines were cut into his flesh by a chisel. "People have died because of me, haven't they?"

"Lucius, please." I tightened my grip. "Just do this."

He stared at me, his eyes lost and haunted in their bruised, sleepless hollows. "What must I say?"

I gave him words to say and dragged him bodily from the room, hauling him by one arm, terrified that he'd turn on me without notice. Outside, he shook me off, but said nothing. I watched his stride lengthen and his shoulders straighten as he flagged down a pair of mounted riders on day patrol.

"Soldier!" he snapped. "Carry a message to Captain Arturo for me. Tell him I've authorized the exchange of the Valpetran prisoners on the morrow."

They saluted. "Aye, sir!"

Once they'd ridden onward, he turned to me. His face was unreadable, neither quite Lucius or Gallus. "You know, I might change my mind about this."

"Please, don't." I couldn't think of anything else to say.

"Is that all you wanted?"

"Yes," I said. "I mean, no. I came to tell you . . ." I wasn't quite sure who I was talking to. "That is . . ."

"Spit it out, man!" he said impatiently.

Gallus.

"One of the D'Angelines told me he thinks Valpetra's trying to dam the river," I said. "I thought you'd want to know."

"Huh. He is, is he? Interesting." Behind the mask of his face, one could see the thoughts working. Clearly, the news meant more to Gallus Tadius than it had to me. He gave me a brisk nod of dismissal. "My thanks, lad."

"Aye, sir." I turned to go.

"D'Angeline!"

"My lord?"

He gave the back of his left hand a meaningful tap. His face wore the peculiar in-between look again. "Staying or going?"

"I'm staying," I said.

"Good." Gallus nodded, or Lucius did. "I'm glad."

With that, he strode back to the barracks. I watched him go, feeling more than a little bewildered myself, then made my way back to the villa.

Despite my news, the atmosphere there was grave. I was right, Eamonn had refused to be dissuaded. Brigitta was furious and grief-stricken. I stayed well out of their way and spent my time composing a letter to Phèdre and Joscelin. If all went well, if Denise Fleurais succeeded in raising an army of allies or hiring a condottiere's mercenary company, if Lucca held strong, I'd be free and on my way home to Terre d'Ange before winter.

If it didn't . . . well.

What does one say in such a letter? I didn't know. So I wrote about what had happened, and about Gilot's death. I told them that Eamonn was here with me. There was so much I wanted to say—about Claudia, the Unseen Guild, Bernadette de Trevalion, the mystery of Canis. But it would all take too long. Once I started, I knew I'd write myself dry; and I was wary of committing anything that might endanger them to paper. I thought about enclosing the letter that Ruggero Caccini had given me implicating Bernadette. I'd brought it with me for safekeeping. And yet, if it came to it, I didn't want my last act to be one of retribution. Let the blood feud die with me and pray that Kushiel's justice prevailed in the end. It was the farewells that mattered.

I told them how much I loved them, or tried to.

For that, there weren't enough words.

I nearly tore up the letter and started again, but there wasn't time. So I left my inadequate words on the page. I asked them to thank Mavros for the kinship of the Shahrizai, to give my love to Alais and my apologies to Queen Ysandre. After some hesitation, I asked them to tell Sidonie I wished her happiness. I fought down a wave of homesickness that brought tears to my eyes, and signed my name. I folded the letter, then reopened it and scrawled a postscript.

Thank you for the gift of my life, I wrote.

I sealed it without blotting it, before I could change my mind. And then, with dusk falling, I went to report for night patrol.

It was a quiet night. Quiet beyond the walls, quiet in the city, quiet between Eamonn and me. We spoke a little bit about his decision.

"I knew what you'd choose," he said simply. "And I couldn't let you stay here alone."

"Yes, you could."

"And let Deccus Fulvius take my place?" He glanced at me. "He's too old for this, Imri. I'm not, and I'm good at fighting if it comes to it."

"True," I said. "But as Deccus said, it's not your war. And you just got married."

"Oh, I know!" Eamonn grinned. "Brigitta is very angry. But Imri, listen. All that talk with Master Piero about virtue . . . honor, loyalty . . . what's it worth if we don't put it into practice? It's when the choices are hard that it matters."

At dawn we returned to the villa, yawning. I was thinking about how the nights were growing longer as the siege wore further into autumn and wondering if Gallus Tadius would be amenable to splitting the night patrol into two shifts. It felt like weeks since I'd had a proper night's sleep. Come to think on it, it likely was. Even on the road from Tiberium, I'd slept poorly, distracted by Claudia's proximity. And these days, no one got to sleep much.

"Imriel."

I blinked at Claudia, standing in the chilly atrium with a thick robe wrapped around her gown. For a few heartbeats, it seemed as though my thoughts had conjured her.

"I'm sorry," she said quietly. "I know you're tired. But I wanted to see you."

Eamonn touched my shoulder. "I'll be in my chamber."

He took his leave, and Claudia and I went to the salon in the guest quarters. It was cold there, too. We sat side by side on one of the couches, she huddled in her robe and I wrapped in my cloak. Since I didn't know what to say to her, I waited for her to speak.

After a moment, she gave a short laugh. "I had a speech in mind. I lay awake half the night thinking of the right words. Now it's gone."

"Too little sleep," I said. "None of us are in our right wits."

"Imriel nó Montrève." Sliding one cold hand out of her sleeve, Claudia touched my hair, which hung long enough to touch my shoulders. "You let it grow," she murmured. "Do you remember I asked you to?"

I smiled. "All too well, my lady."

"Oh, indeed." A faint glimmer of her old carnal mischief surfaced in her answering smile. "I owe you my thanks."

"For my hair?" I asked stupidly.

"For my freedom." Claudia's expression turned grave. "For Deccus' and Brigitta's. And I promise you, whatever I can do to bring this siege to an end, I will. I will use any influence at my disposal to ensure that the D'Angeline ambassadress' negotiations fall upon willing ears and help comes swiftly."

I eyed her. "At what price?"

Claudia winced. "I deserve that, I suppose. There is no price, Imriel. I'll not use this to try to bind you to a promise, if that's what you're thinking."

It was. I gazed at her face, touched by the dawn light slanting through the window. There were fine lines at the corners of her eyes that had not been there before. The siege had aged her. She had watched her brother descend into madness, her father's spirit broken, her mother reduced by grief. "The Guild abandoned you," I said slowly. "And yet you're still loyal to them?"

"Yes." She offered no justification.

So be it. "Thank you," I said. "I appreciate your aid."

Claudia nodded. "I will do my best. Imriel . . . this is no price, but only a favor I ask. Will you do what you can to look out for my family?"

It was on the tip of my tongue to say yes, of course. I hesitated. "Will you answer a question for me? Honestly and truthfully?"

"I'll try," she said.

"Who is Canis?" I asked. "Who sent him?"

"The beggar?" Her brown eyes were steady and clear, touched to amber by the dawn's rays. "I don't know."

"He's here, you know." I watched her pupils dilate. She hadn't known. "I think he may have been the one to send a message to Lady Denise. And I think he's done other things, too. Is he Guild?"

"I don't know." Nothing in her face betrayed her, but Claudia held my gaze too long. Only that, the most subtle of tell-tales. She lied very, very well. "I'm sorry, Imriel."

"So am I." I smiled at her, rueful and tired. "Yes, my lady. I will do all that is in my power to look out for your family, including your wraith-ridden brother. However," I added, turning my hands palm upward, "I fear that while the siege continues, my power is limited to whatever lies within these."

"No." To my surprise, Claudia took my hands in hers. Raising them to her lips, she kissed both my palms. "You have a kind heart."

"Not really." I swallowed. "Deccus . . ."

She laid her fingers over my lips, silencing me. "Deccus Fulvius is a good man with an unfaithful wife. It changes nothing. The truth of what I said stands." Taking her hand away, she kissed me, then rose. "And I have no regrets."

Elua, but she was a strong woman! I laughed softly. When all was said and done, I didn't want to trade my memories, either. "All right, my lady. No regrets. Except mayhap for a few deeds left undone."

Blowing me a final kiss, Claudia Fulvia left.

Too tired to seek my bed, I rolled myself in my cloak and fell asleep on the couch.

When I dreamed, I dreamed of Claudia.

FIFTY-SEVEN

THE TRANSFER WENT SMOOTHLY.

We were all there to see it effected. I was in an agony of fear that Gallus Tadius would change his mind and rescind his order, but he was nowhere in evidence. The three Valpetran prisoners were released. They were dirty and disoriented, blinking at the sudden emergence into daylight, but their wounds had been tended and all three were alive.

It took some time to get them down the ladder, and longer for Quentin LeClerc's men to escort them into their condottiere's custody, where their identity was confirmed. The wall was bristling with armed guards, but Valpetra's men agreed to the continued truce and maintained their distance.

Once it was done, it was time for our three to go.

We said our farewells. Claudia was warmly cordial. Deccus Fulvius shook my hand firmly. He would have shaken Eamonn's, too, but he and Brigitta were locked in a tight embrace.

"Don't worry, lad," Deccus murmured. "I'll do my damnedest to see to it that Lady Fleurais gets all the aid Tiberium can muster."

No regrets.

"Thank you, my lord," I said.

Eamonn and Brigitta stood motionless, folded together in his cloak. His head was bowed, his coppery hair mixed with her gold. They looked almost like one figure. Not until Deccus and Claudia were safe on the ground and one of the guards gave a conspicuous, apologetic cough did Eamonn tear himself away.

"I will find you," he said to her.

"I will be waiting," she whispered.

She went down the ladder with her face averted. Eamonn watched her all the way.

When all was in readiness for their departure, I beckoned to Quentin LeClerc. He brought his horse to the edge of the moat. I withdrew my letter, wrapped in an oilskin packet. "Messire LeClerc," I called. "Will you ask the ambassadress to see this is delivered to the Comtesse de Montrève?"

He bowed. "Of course, your highness."

I tossed the packet. It was light and sailed easily across the moat. The waters seemed to have sunk a bit.

He caught it handily. "Have you any message, Prince Eamonn?"

"Yes." Eamonn was still watching Brigitta. "Tell my mother . . . ask the Comtesse de Montrève to let the Lady of the Dalriada know that her son married well. And to tell my father I'm glad I met him."

Quentin LeClerc bowed again. "It will be done."

There was nothing left to say. Everyone was mounted, with six of the guards riding double to free up horses for the hostages. LeClerc saluted and gave the signal. They struck out across the burned fields at a steady jog. I laid my hand on Eamonn's shoulder and we watched them go. For once, none of the guards disturbed us.

Valpetra's cavalry had withdrawn to their post on the road. They halted the D'Angeline contingent, inspecting the released hostages and LeClerc's men to make sure none of them was me, trying to sneak out of Lucca with both my hands attached at the wrist.

It didn't take long.

Domenico Martelli must have gotten a good look at me, I thought. Then again, I suppose one doesn't forget such things. I will see the Mahrkagir's face in my nightmares until I die.

Still, I breathed a sigh of relief when the cavalry let them pass. Valpetra's soldiers wheeled and beat a path toward the river, vanishing beyond the wall's curve. The D'Angeline contingent labored onward, dwindling into specks as they neared the foothills of the mountains and began to ascend. Eamonn and I watched them until the last banner was out of sight.

Eamonn sighed. "So."

"So," I echoed.

"A few weeks, do you think?" he asked.

Time. Time for the delegation to return, time for Lady Denise Fleurais to set the wheels of diplomacy in action, time for Claudia Fulvia to prevail on the Unseen Guild to grease those wheels, time for Deccus Fulvius to convince the Senate to put Tiberium's collective shoulder to the wheel. Time for mercenaries to be hired, time to report and muster. Time for messages to fly to Terre d'Ange and back. Time for the wrath of a nation's Queen to gather.

"A few weeks," I said. "Mayhap."

He grinned at me. "Ah, well! If that's all, we can hold."

"Can and will," I agreed. "Can and will."

The Tadeii villa felt deserted upon our return. The Lady Beatrice, who had bade her daughter farewell at the door, haunted it like a ghost, wringing her hands. I'd gotten over the awkwardness of imposing on her hospitality—after all, I was engaged in the defense of *her* city—but it came back to me that day. She got around it by plying Eamonn and me with food. There was an abundance of it, since no one had alerted the kitchen staff that three members of the household were departing. Food was rationed yet, but there were enough rations for five.

If it was a deliberate oversight, it was much appreciated. I suspected Claudia. She'd been the one to hold everything together.

"So they're well?" Lady Beatrice asked anxiously. "They're well away, my Claudia and Senator Deccus, and oh! Your lovely bride?"

Eamonn nodded, shoveling food into his mouth.

I swallowed a mouthful of lentil porridge. It was tasteless, but filling. "They are, my lady. Away and safe under the aegis of Terre d'Ange."

She was glad, and we were sated.

Afterward, we slept; or at least I did. I wouldn't have thought it possible, but the body's exhaustion takes its own toll. One of the Tadeii retainers came to wake me near sundown, and Eamonn and I reported for night patrol.

There, Gallus Tadius greeted us with another pleasant surprise. As though he'd read my mind, he was dividing the night patrol into two shifts. Half the riders were dismissed, and the rest of us remained. I blew on my cold fingers, already luxuriating in the thought of returning to my warm bed hours earlier than anticipated.

"I expect a quiet night," Gallus said. "But stay alert."

"He doesn't look happy," Eamonn whispered.

"Does he ever?" I whispered back.

He was right, though. Gallus Tadius flagged us down as we rode past and saluted. His face was engraved in unwontedly somber lines. "The exchange was made?"

"Yes, my lord," I said.

"Good." He leaned over and spat. "It's worth the price of Valpetra's wounded baggage to see the Tadeii bloodline carried on safely. Lads, I'm calling a conclave tomorrow. I expect to see you there."

"Aye, sir." I hesitated, trying to see if there was anything of Lucius in his sunken gaze. It was hard to tell in the dusk. "My lord, if you don't mind my saying, you should get some sleep."

"Sleep!" He gave a hollow laugh, his eyes glinting briefly in their bruised sockets. "Plenty of time for that when you're dead."

"Some jest," Eamonn muttered after we'd ridden onward.

"Not really," I said.

As Gallus Tadius had predicted, it was an uneventful night. We rode our endless circuits, exchanging password and countersign, but nothing was stirring beyond the wall. Valpetra's forces remained withdrawn. There was no stealthy advance, no attempt to drag siege engines within range under cover of darkness, no effort to bridge the moat or begin the long process of tunneling beneath it to sap the walls.

So what, I wondered, were they doing?

Whatever it was, it had Gallus Tadius worried.

We found out on the morrow.

As before, the conclave met in the basilica. It was a smaller gathering and there were no women present, only men. Captain Arturo was there and two of his lieutenants. Gaetano Correggio and a handful of other nobles, though fewer than before. No sign of Publius Tadius. Several of the more competent conscripts in the Red Scourge were present, sporting their scarlet armbands. For that matter, I supposed

Eamonn and I numbered among them. Others looked to be tradesmen, work-hardened and sturdy.

We all crowded in the lower tiers, while Gallus stood on the rostrum and waited for us to settle. He had a table of sorts set up there; a low, shallow tray filled with loose dirt. We sat and shivered, chafing our hands in the cold air, peering at the tray and wondering.

"Right," Gallus said without preamble. "Here's the thing. We're in trouble."

He used the tray to demonstrate. While we were exchanging prisoners for hostages, Gallus Tadius had spent the better part of the day atop the northwestern section of the wall, staring toward the river and trying to determine what Valpetra was doing. He watched the distant figures of the condottiere's men bustling and digging, and while he couldn't make out much of their activity, by the day's end, he reckoned he had a good idea.

"I had the same idea myself, see," he said dryly. "Back in the day. Turned out I didn't need to use it."

Hands in the dirt, Gallus Tadius shaped a mounded curve to represent Lucca's outer wall. With a stick, he traced the river's broad, winding course, with a smaller line representing the canal that fed the moat.

"So," he said, sketching in the dirt. "Valpetra diverts the river to the west, *here*, and builds two dams, one above the canal and one below it. He fills in the trench and returns the river to its proper course. The water backs up here, in Lake Emarus. Once it threatens to flood, he breaches the upper dam, and the water goes *here*."

His pointed stick traced a swift course along the canal, bursting through the mounded dirt that represented Lucca's wall.

"Trouble," he said.

Gaetano Correggio descended to examine the model. He shook his head. "It will not happen. The walls are strong, and the moats will disperse the water's impact. The river has overflowed its banks and flooded the plains before. It happened when I was a child. Lucca stood then, and it will stand now."

"Oh, you think so, do you?" Gallus eyed him.

The former Prince of Lucca paled. "I know my city."

"*Your* city." Gallus snorted. "Let me tell you something about your city, Correggio. It's got trees growing atop the walls. Very pretty. Oak trees have deep roots." He tapped the mounded dirt. "All this dirt between the walls ought to be packed hard as rock. And it's not. You know why? Your damned pretty oak trees. We're not talking about a river flooding its banks, Correggio. We're talking about a river in full flood changing its *course*. And when the gods alone know how many tons of rushing water hit that spot, with the sluice underneath it and roots eating through the dirt above it, it's going to burst like a rotten melon."

"Odds are he's right, my lord." A burly man in tradesman's attire rose.

Gaetano frowned at him. "Who are you to say?"

"He's the head of your Masons' Guild," Gallus Tadius commented. "Didn't you bother to learn anything about *your* city? Master Varrius spent several hours examining the wall at my behest yesterday. He concurs."

Beside me, Eamonn groaned.

"My lord," I said. "How long do we have?"

Gallus shrugged. "Who can say, D'Angeline? It's a huge task, but Valpetra's got two thousand men at his disposal. By the look of it, they're trained in the old Tiberian manner." He looked approving. "They know how to set their hands to hard labor. They know what they're about, and they needn't do a bang-up job of it, either. It's only got to hold for a little while. And they'll work fast, because we've burned their food supplies out from under them, and because now they're worried about Terre d'Ange making a fuss." He slashed idly at the model of Lucca with his stick. "A few weeks, perhaps?"

A nobleman I didn't recognize glanced at his fellows, then cleared his throat. "So what do we do, Prince Gallus?"

He told us.

In short, we prepared for the worst. Master Varrius and his masons would do all they could to shore up the wall, but we were to assume Valpetra's plan would succeed. We were to prepare for flood and invasion. Every household with an upper floor was to move their living quarters. Every household without one was to seek an alternate shelter. The conscript army of the Red Scourge was to begin drilling in preparation to fight.

"We've got nearly a thousand men," Gallus Tadius said cheerfully. "So the odds against us are a mere two to one." He rubbed his chin. "I'd like to say we'll hold the breach, but the truth is, we've got an inexperienced army with a piss-poor assortment of arms and precious little armor to speak of. We'd be overrun in an hour's time. So we'll fall back in stages. Trick 'em, trap 'em, lead 'em into ambush. And I want your wives and sisters and daughters to hit them from the rooftops and upper stories—stone them, scald them, whatever they can muster. No safe havens." Gallus chuckled. "It's our city, lads. We can do this."

There were nods and murmurs of agreement all around.

I caught Eamonn's eye, wondering if I'd gone mad. It seemed to me there was an enormous flaw in Gallus' plan. Eamonn looked equally perplexed, so I asked. "My lord . . .

how are we to do this if the city's flooded? What about the water?"

"The water?" Gallus jabbed his stick into the center of the tray. He grinned at me, baring healthy white teeth in his death-mask face. "Why, we're going to send it straight to hell, D'Angeline."

No one seemed to find this strange.

I opened my mouth to protest. A dozen blank stares fixed me. The pointed stick stood upright in the tray, quivering. I hadn't gone mad. Whatever haunted Lucca, they weren't my dead, weren't Eamonn's dead. But everyone here had gone a little bit mad, except for Gallus Tadius, who was either a lot mad or right. I thought about the blackened husk of the bell-tower and the *mundus manes* beneath it. The pointed stick quivered. I thought about the cold, barren firepit in the Mahrkagir's festal hall. Joscelin had flung his torch into it like a warrior planting a spear, and the Sacred Fires had ignited across the whole of Drujan.

What did I know?

"Right," I said. "Straight to hell it is."

Once the conclave ended, Gallus Tadius dismissed the masons to their labors and dispatched the noblemen to see to it that his orders were spread. He called his conscripts together and informed us that we would be performing drills in the public park from this day forward.

"Tell the others," he said. "You'll get orders when to report. I'll make my decisions after I've gauged your skills. You lot seemed among the best, but we'll see."

"Does that mean no more night patrol?" Eamonn asked hopefully.

Gallus stared at him. "Hell no, Prince Barbarus! After all, I might be wrong."

No orders came that day. Eamonn and I spent most of it

conferring with the Lady Beatrice and her household staff on preparing for the eventuality of a flood. Most of the villa's stores were in cellars. We studied the inventory together and made up lists of what should be hauled to the second floor of the villa, and what could safely be abandoned. She flung herself into the task, seeming grateful to have a purpose. Neither of us mentioned the part about the floodwaters being sent to hell, not until that night's patrol.

It was a clear night. The clouds had retreated and the lingering pall of smoke had finally cleared. The moon was three-quarters full, drenching the city with silvery light. It seemed almost peaceful. I wondered if Quentin LeClerc and his contingent was riding beneath the same stars. I hoped so. Their mission seemed a good deal more urgent than it had yesterday.

"What do you think?" Eamonn asked in a low voice.

"I don't know." I shivered, drawing my cloak tighter around me. "It's possible, I suppose. A lot of things are possible."

He gazed at the stars. "You would know, wouldn't you?"

"I ought to." I rubbed my eyes. "Ah, Eamonn! I wish you'd gone with them."

"I wish I'd sent a letter," he said quietly.

That was all we spoke of it. In the small hours of the morning, the sentries passed word that our shift was ended and we headed back for the villa. The Bastard was lazy that night, his head nodding. He'd preferred the wild rides the night of the fire. I didn't blame him. Amid the horrors of war, the poets seldom saw fit to mention the deadly tedium. I was thinking about the possibility of a flood and the stables, and trying to determine where the highest ground of the Tadeii property lay. As we drew upon a crossroad, the hooded figure blocking our path took me by surprise.

"Prince Imriel."

For a wild instant, I was flung back into the past. A cold, crisp night outside the Cockerel, and a figure speaking my name. Bertran's fury and Gilot's faithful response. A chase, a cap. My reputation in tatters. I yanked my sword from its scabbard, the Bastard startled into skittering life beneath me.

"Who asks?" I demanded.

Somewhere in the darkness behind us, there was a faint scuffling sound. With a curse, Eamonn rounded his horse and drew his blade, riding to investigate.

The figure lifted its head.

It was a woman's face within the hood; young, scared, and adamant, leached of color by the moonlight. I put up my blade. I knew her.

Helena.

"Please," she breathed. "I only want to speak to you."

Eamonn returned at a lope, indicating his failure with a shrug. When he saw Helena, he let out a sigh and sheathed his sword. "My lady," he said, bowing in the saddle. "You should not be here. Let us escort you home."

Her gaze never left my face. "Please?"

Having wrestled the Bastard under control, I spread my arms. "What is it you *want* of me, my lady? I'm cold and tired, and very, very mortal. Whatever it is you think I am, I assure you, I'm not."

"I know." She bowed her head and opened one clenched hand. Three small objects fell rattling onto the cobblestones. Beads, glass beads. In the daylight, I guessed, they would have been blue. Little things, Lucius had said; offerings at the crossroads. Helena nudged them into a crevice with one slippered toe, then lifted her head. "I've been foolish, but I'm not stupid." She was trembling with cold, but the set of her delicate jaw was no less adamant.

Her wide eyes searched my face for meaning, for a sign, for somewhat that wasn't there. "I know what you're not," she whispered. "I don't know what you *are*."

"Just Imriel," I said tiredly. "A stunted tree reaching for sunlight."

She blinked at me and shivered.

Eamonn raised his brows at me.

What could I do? I was D'Angeline and taught by Phèdre nó Delaunay. Swallowing my own cruelty, I dismounted and bowed to Helena, holding it for an extra heartbeat. "Forgive me," I said to her. "I am weary and sharp-tongued. And Eamonn is right, this is no place for you. We will escort you home."

I cupped my hands to cradle her slippered foot, hoisting her astride the Bastard. Ah, Elua! She weighed little more than Alais. I took the reins and began trudging in the direction of the Correggio palazzo, trying not to think about what she had endured.

"Will you not ride with me?" Her teeth chattered. "Can he not carry two?"

The Bastard snorted.

So I mounted, settling myself behind her while she perched on the pommel, and took up the reins. Eamonn and I exchanged a long, silent look that spoke volumes.

"Fine," I said shortly. "I'll see you at the villa."

He saluted me and cantered away. I took Helena home. She held herself taut, and I did nothing to discourage it. Still, I could feel her growing warmer between my arms and in time her shivering stopped.

The Correggio palazzo was untended in the moonlight, the gate unguarded. Small wonder that she had been able to slip away unnoticed. I supposed their retainers had been impressed into Gallus Tadius' army, too. The Bastard paced into the courtyard as though he owned it. I dismounted and lifted her down from the saddle, my hands around her waist.

"Will you be all right?" I asked her.

"Will I?" She looked up at me with that soft, aching gaze. "I don't know. You . . . you were taken, too, weren't you? Father explained it to me. I understand about your mother, a little bit. But that part of the story is true, isn't it? You were lost and taken."

"Yes," I said.

"When does it stop hurting?" she asked.

I was silent for a moment, and it came to me that it wasn't Helena I'd tried to protect by avoiding her, not entirely. It was me. It wasn't just the women of the zenana I saw reflected in her broken gaze. It was my ten-year-old self.

And my ten-year-old self owed her an honest answer.

"Never," I said. "But it gets better."

Helena nodded. "Will you come and talk with me? Please? I only want to understand. And I think . . . I think you matter. What you did . . . it matters to me. I just want to make sense of it. Please?"

"All right," I said. "I'll come when I can."

FIFTY-EIGHT

ON THE MORROW, there were orders awaiting.

Eamonn and I reported to the park. In the summer, doubtless it was a green and pleasant place, but dry autumn had taken its toll. What remained of the sere grass was already flattened by treading feet. There were a few late-blooming flowers, but most were already dead, straggling and unpruned. All the ornamental trees were losing their leaves, which lay scattered on the trodden ground. Like everyone else, Lucca's gardeners were conscripts. Only the tall cypresses retained their dark green majesty.

We were to begin drilling in groups of forty. Gallus Tadius reckoned that was the maximum size that could maneuver swiftly within the city streets. And we were to train on foot. There would be no cavalry for the Red Scourge.

Several other squadrons had gone before us. There was an array of armor laid out in piles; all the oddments and remnants that Gallus Tadius had managed to confiscate based on the inventories. He pointed to one of the piles and gave us a few minutes to scavenge whatever fit to augment our gear, or lack of it.

We all scrambled.

I didn't hesitate, going straight after a pair of rusted vambraces. Manners be damned; if there was anyone else there who could make as much use of them, I'd eat my boots. When the flurry was over, I had my vambraces, as well as a leather jerkin stitched with small metal disks, which I reckoned would turn a glancing blow if not a straight thrust, and an open-faced helmet with a shallow brim and a missing chin-strap.

Eamonn had a cuirass that actually fit him and a tall, kite-shaped shield. Since he was the only one who could lift it with ease, no one had challenged him for it. Everyone had something, though almost no one had a full set. There were bare heads, unprotected limbs, vulnerable throats and sides. All in all, it was a motley assortment.

Lucca was a trade town. It had always hired merchant armies for its defense. After Gallus Tadius had seized it and established himself as Prince of Lucca, the Red Scourge had disbanded. Within two generations, the descendants of those who had settled there had long since sold their arms and been absorbed into society.

Gallus shook his head, watching us don our armor.

"Right," he said when we were more or less assembled. "Here's the thing, lads. It's not going to get much better. We're ransacking the city and I've got carpenters and smiths working day and night to pound out bucklers and spears. They won't be much to look at, but they'll serve. Until then . . ." He shrugged. "We'll work with what we've got. Now let's see what *you've* got."

Arrayed in a loose circle, we watched as he called us out one by one to test our mettle with a quick bout.

Gallus Tadius was good.

Not great, but good.

He was a deceptively straightforward fighter, although I couldn't really tell until his bout with Eamonn. Most of the conscripts had little or no training. He dispatched them quickly, pointing out the death-blows he could have dealt and leaving them a few bruises and scratches as a reminder to take the matter seriously.

And he never got tired.

I wondered how many bouts he'd already fought that day. Forty? Eighty? I didn't know how many groups had trained before us. And I wondered what toll this tireless energy was taking on Lucius' body. When I watched him fight Eamonn, it gave me an idea.

It was a good bout. Eamonn had learned a measure of patience since that day so long ago when we'd dueled with wooden blades, betting the Bastard against his golden torc. His tall shield covered him from chin to knees, and he used it to full advantage. They sidled around one another, trading blows.

Gallus was cunning and efficient. Every move was economical. He kept his feet planted and his guard high, moving only for an occasional feint. Eamonn watched him warily, circling with slow deliberation. For a moment I thought the bout would turn earnest, but then Gallus Tadius put up his sword and grinned.

"Ah, Prince Barbarus!" He clapped a hand on Eamonn's shoulder. "You'll do. Next!"

When my turn came, I stepped forward and bowed, then drew my sword and settled into a two-handed Cassiline fighting stance, angling the blade across my body.

Gallus eyed me with dour amusement. "What in the hell do you think you're doing, fancy-boy?"

"Preparing to be tested, my lord," I said politely. "Would you care to make a wager?"

"A *wager*!" He roared with laughter. "Oh, aye, lad, I'll wager aught you care to wager!"

"All right." I hesitated. "I'll wager I can disarm you. If I lose, I'll . . ." I swallowed. I couldn't bear to wager the Bastard, the only living reminder of home I possessed. I reversed my sword, offering the hilt. I pushed aside the memory of Joscelin and me conferring with the master smith. It was only metal, wrought in a pleasing shape. "I'll give you my sword."

There was a good deal of whispering among the conscripts, and not a little snickering. "I don't want your sword, lad," Gallus said absently, examining it. "I want you to use it in my service. Nice piece, though." He nodded and returned it. "All right. Mine for yours if you lose. And if by some poxy D'Angeline miracle you don't?"

"You sleep, my lord," I said steadily. "A full night's sleep."

His sharp brows, Lucius' satyr's brows, shot toward the rim of his helmet. "Oh, sweet tits of the Vestals! Now you're a damned nursemaid!" He turned toward the conscripts, laughing. "What do you say, lads? Does Gallus Tadius da Lucca need *sleep*?"

"No, sir!" they shouted.

Gallus might not, but Lucius did. "Do we have a bargain, my lord?" I asked doggedly.

He shrugged. "Why not?"

It went fast. I'd watched him fight. Nothing in his experience had prepared him for the fluid Cassiline style, but if I gave him a chance to adjust, he would. So I didn't. I brought my sword around from right to left in a high, sweeping circle, raising his guard, then continued the circle with a low feint at his legs. I ducked low under his counterthrust and rolled toward the right, coming up outside his guard.

His head was turned the wrong way. I could see a few

inches of exposed skin between his helmet and his gorget where his pulse beat.

I didn't strike. Instead, I spun behind him, turning my back to him, keeping my blade high and tight against my body. Circles within circles, as Joscelin had taught me. Gallus was caught inside my circle, his sword-arm over-extended. He was turning toward his left. I was on his right, where he didn't expect me. With my two-handed grip, I brought the pommel of my sword down hard on the back of his gauntleted hand.

It opened in an involuntary spasm.

He dropped his sword.

There was a collective gasp from the watching conscripts, with Eamonn's low chuckle resonating beneath it. I sheathed my sword, stepped back, and bowed.

"Well," Gallus Tadius said mildly. He slung his shield aside and shook out his hand, which must have stung somewhat fierce. "Well, well." He picked up his sword and sheathed it. "You're full of surprises, D'Angeline."

"Yes, sir," I said.

He stepped closer to me. I couldn't read his expression; I only knew there was nothing of Lucius in it. But there was no malice, either. "Do you know," he mused, "I had a D'Angeline in the Red Scourge once. Doucet, or something like. Got in some trouble back home, took to the mercenary life. Don't suppose you know of him?"

I shook my head. "'Tis a large nation, my lord."

"Aye." Gallus nodded. "And he's been dead a while, I imagine. Hailed from Camlach, as I recall. He got a little crazy when he fought, too. Different style. A sodding pretty bastard, though not as pretty as you, not by half. Used to pray to one of your poxy D'Angeline gods before a battle."

"Camael," I said, relaxing. "Most likely."

"Camael. Aye, that was it." He nodded again, then punched me in the face.

It hurt like fury. He'd caught me high on the left cheekbone with his gauntleted fist, knocking me clean off my feet. I felt the ground break my fall and rolled backward, grabbing instinctively for my daggers. There was no room to draw a sword, but room enough for those. I came up hissing, half-blinded, my left eye watering, daggers in both hands.

Gallus Tadius regarded me, hands on his hips. "See, here's the thing, lad. If we're going to beat these pox-ridden Valpetran sons of whores, we're going to have to stand shoulder to shoulder, shield to shield. Every man knows his duty. Every man counts on the fellow beside him to know his. That's what keeps you alive on the battlefield. That's what it means to be an army. I don't know who the hell taught you, but this is war, not a gladiator's arena. You go twirling around like a high-priced whore on an acrobat's stage, you're like to get your fellows killed. Understand?"

I didn't want to, but I did.

"Yes," I grated.

"Good." He jerked his chin at the waiting conscripts. "Next!"

One by one, Gallus Tadius tested the remainder of our company. And when he had done, he arranged us into pairs according to our levels of skill and set us to sparring. He appointed Eamonn to lead our squadron.

"Teach 'em the basics, Prince Barbarus," he said. "That's all I ask. You'll drill here every day until you receive further orders. You've got an hour till the next batch comes. Make good use of it."

He mounted his horse and made to leave.

"My lord!" I called after him. Gallus looked over his shoulder. "It's bad luck to dishonor a wager."

He stared at me for a long moment. One corner of his mouth curved with the hint of a smile, and he shook his head. Unexpectedly, I found myself grinning. Without a word, Gallus Tadius rode away, still shaking his head.

My sparring partner was a young man named Orfeo. He seemed familiar, with a narrow face with wide eyes that gave him a curious, birdlike look. I'd watched his bout and seen enough to guess that someone had taught him the rudiments of swordplay, but whatever he'd learned, he'd forgotten for lack of practice.

"My brother, Giancarlo," he confirmed. "He taught me some before he left."

"Left?" I asked.

He nodded. "To seek his fortune with a mercenary company."

I remembered where I'd seen him. "You were a friend of Bartolomeo's."

"Yes." Orfeo's narrow face darkened. "They cut him down like a dog in the street! I hope they *do* invade," he said savagely. "I mean to get revenge for him." He paused. "Can you teach me to fight like you do?"

I explored the tender knot rising on my left cheekbone. "Not likely."

We spent the hour sparring. It was difficult. Ti-Philippe had taught me to fight in the conventional manner with sword and shield, but I'd spent so many long hours training with Joscelin. Out of practice though I was, the body remembers. And too, I was fighting without a shield. I tried to keep to a straightforward approach, but without intending it, I'd find my feet moving in familiar patterns, circles within circles, marking and blocking the quadrants with my blade. And Orfeo tried to emulate me, spinning awkwardly, leaving himself horribly open. He had a round buckler, but only a leather jerkin like mine, and I was fearful of injuring him by accident.

Eamonn took his charge seriously. After demonstrating the proper usage of our weapons, he strolled around, watching us all, offering corrections and advice. After a few passes, he returned with a second buckler, having come to some arrangement with one of the other conscripts.

"Here." He handed it to me, his face serious. "Gallus Tadius is right, Imri. At least in this matter."

I shoved my left arm through the arm strap and flexed my hand around the smooth grip. "I know, I know." I tested the shield's heft. It felt cumbersome, but I supposed I'd get used to it. "You're good at this."

Eamonn grinned. "I am, aren't I?"

For the remainder of the time, Orfeo and I hacked and battered at one another. I felt awkward and unbalanced, which made us a better match. By the time the next batch of conscripts arrived, my left arm felt like a lead weight, and I was glad to stop.

So began the new pattern of our days in Lucca.

It was a miserable time. I hated a great deal of it. I hated the broken nights of riding patrol and the broken days of drilling. I hated the buckler, and being constrained to a style that made no use of my hard-won skills. Everything I'd been taught was to preserve *my* life. Everything Gallus Tadius taught us emphasized the need to stand together, to defend one's brother in arms. As much as I understood it—and I did, even Joscelin would be the first to admit that Cassiline Brothers aren't trained to the battlefield—I still chafed at it.

Gallus did honor his wager, though.

I found out that night, when Eamonn and I returned from patrol. Despite the lateness of the hour, the Lady Beatrice met us in the atrium. It gave me a start, reminding me of her daughter. Her dark red hair was loose around her shoulders, her round, pleasant face alight with gladness as she hushed us.

"He's *sleeping*!" she whispered.

Eamonn glanced at me. "I'll be damned."

I liked to think it helped, at least a little. When I saw him next, Gallus Tadius wore Lucius' face a little easier. It didn't last, though. He was up day and night; tracking the progress of Valpetra's labor, tracking the progress of the Red Scourge, tracking the progress of the masons' efforts to shore up the wall. He rode through the city, scouring every inch for defensible positions and vantage points.

He spent long hours conferring with priests.

Since he didn't seem overly concerned with the Tadeii villa, which wasn't situated in a strategic location, I kept my promise to Claudia Fulvia and concerned myself. With Lady Beatrice's blessing, I confronted Publius Tadius.

I came straight from the training-field and strode into his study uninvited. He had issued a standing order to be left undisturbed, but his wife countermanded it. I found him seated by a window, immersed in reading, for all the world as though Lucca weren't under siege. He looked up when I entered, his gaze vacant.

"Yes?"

I stood in front of him, dripping on his carpet. It was raining. The long dry spell had broken with a vengeance, and it had been a miserable day of drilling. We were staging mock skirmishes now, squadron against squadron, and I'd spent the better part of two hours ankle-deep in cold mire, locking shields, thrusting and grunting.

"My lord," I said. "Do you know who I am?"

His expression changed slowly, a measure of clarity surfacing. It was cold and disapproving. He marked his place in his book and set it down. "If you're speaking of your relationship with my son, I don't particularly care to hear it."

"Your son." My hair was dripping into my eyes. I swiped it out of the way with one vambraced forearm. "My lord, your *son* is a good man, and I pray to Blessed Elua you have a chance to learn that one day."

His mouth pursed. "You have no right to pass judgment on me."

I gazed at him, through the bitterness and disappointment and self-righteousness, and beheld the shadows on his soul. Fear and longing and deep-seated self-loathing. "You were afraid of him, weren't you? Your grandfather?"

He looked away. "Please leave."

"My lord." I opened my arms. "I fear, too. But I'm here and I'm fighting for Lucca at the behest of your wraith-ridden son and your mad, dead, awful genius of a grandfather. And if a prince of Terre d'Ange can do this much for a foreign city, surely the grandson of Gallus Tadius can bestir himself in the defense of his own household."

Publius' jaw trembled. "You don't understand."

"Yes," I said. "I do. You've not gone mad, my lord, you've only taken refuge there. It's time to return. Lucca needs you. Your family needs you."

He looked at me, his glance flinching away, then steeled himself. "What must I do?"

I led him through the villa, explaining about the dam and the prospect of flooding, and how the city wall might be breached. I showed him what we'd done to shift foodstuffs and certain delicate valuables to the upper story.

"You think it will happen?" he asked.

"I think it might," I said. "And my lord, if it does, I won't be here to protect the villa from looting. I won't be here to defend the Lady Beatrice's honor. I'll be in the streets, fighting. You've got to help."

"I can do that." His eyes were clear and young, younger than they'd been. "Yes."

I smiled. "Good."

As it transpired, he had a certain knack for it. In the days that followed, the upper level of the Tadeii villa was transformed into a bastion. Stairways would be sealed, doors barred and blockaded. A hail of arrows and scalding water would rain down from the balconies. If Lucca held, the villa would hold.

At least for a time.

Everywhere across the city, others were doing the same thing. For a trade city, there was precious little trade afoot. No one could enter or leave, and Gallus Tadius had put a halt to trade among those merchants who were trapped here. I had to own, he was evenhanded in his approach. All goods that were confiscated were shared alike. Anyone caught hoarding was put to death. It only happened twice. Both times, the offenders were strung up on a gallows in the central square.

It was an effective deterrent.

"Hear me!" Gallus roared, riding back and forth before the second swaying corpse. He pointed his finger at the gathered crowd. "Lucca stands. And while it stands, *no one*, not the least among us, man, woman, or child, will starve while there is a handful of grain to share." He gave his death's-head grin. "And share you will, on pain of death."

There was no word from Terre d'Ange, no word from Tiberium, no word from the Unseen Guild. On occasion, I caught sight of Canis when our squadrons passed. We began training with thrusting spears. Once we skirmished together, although he was some distance down the opposing line from me. I could barely see him for the rain. He seemed to acquit himself well. Afterward, I saw a couple of his fellows slap his back in approval. A few of ours complained that the deaf-mute had a heavy hand. And then Gallus Tadius changed our orders, and we began training in the city streets, each squadron assigned a specific section.

It kept raining.

The water in the moat kept falling.

I went to see Helena Correggio.

FIFTY-NINE

I WAS RECEIVED GRACIOUSLY in the Correggio household. Gaetano was elsewhere when I called upon the palazzo, but Helena's mother, Dacia, greeted me with a deep curtsy. "Your highness," she said. "We owe you thanks beyond words."

She was a tall, elegant woman with kind eyes, and I liked her immediately. Indeed, whatever madness had befallen Lucca, the women bore it with infinitely more grace than the men. Then again, their dead had not been tyrants and mercenary soldiers.

After brushing off my polite demurral, she escorted me into a salon and went to summon her daughter. A servant arrived with a carafe of watered wine and a plate of dates; the height of hospitality during the siege. I ate a date and sipped sparingly at the wine, mindful that it was a portion of someone's daily ration. More days than not, I felt hollow with hunger.

Within a few moments, Helena arrived.

It surprised me, knowing what I did of Caerdicci culture, that we were allowed to meet unchaperoned. And then I remembered that Helena was a married woman, and no longer a maiden. Whatever virtue the Caerdicci place in virginity, hers was no longer at issue.

It was awkward at first. Although we shared a common bond, we were strangers to one another. We spoke of desultory matters; the siege and its effects, mostly. It was Helena who cut through the awkwardness and went straight to the heart of things.

"Will you tell me your story?" she asked. "The true story?"

I hesitated. "My lady, why do you want to know?"

Her hands were clasped hard, fingers working unconsciously. "I know the tale my nursemaid told me; the tale of the Bella Donna and her missing child. My father told me that it wasn't true, that it was only women's foolish superstition making something false out of politics and intrigue. It's not, though, is it? Not only that. I want to know the *true* story."

"I don't speak lightly of it," I said.

She knotted her fingers. "I don't ask lightly."

And so I told her.

At another time, in another place, I might not have done it. I cannot say. She seemed so young to bear the burden of my dark tale, with her shining, baby-fine hair and her clear blue eyes. But she bore her own burden of betrayal and lost innocence behind those eyes, and once I began to speak, the words kept coming. I told her of being raised in the Sanctuary of Elua where my mother had hidden me from the world, all unwitting of my own parentage. I told her of my own abduction by slave-traders, of being sold to the merchant Fadil Chouma. Of travelling to Menekhet, where Chouma sold me to the Âka-Magus, the Drujani bone-priest.

Daršanga.

I told her only that it was a foul place with a mad ruler

who did terrible things. It was enough. I told her that some died and others lived and all of us kept despair at bay one minute, one hour, one day at a time. And I told her how Phèdre came into the midst of it, bearing an impossible gift of hope. How Phèdre and Joscelin rescued us, and the zenana rose up and overthrew the garrison. How I had learned who I was.

Helena listened to it all without comment, drinking in my words as the parched earth drinks in water. When I had finished, we sat for a moment in silence together.

"So it is true," she murmured at length. "In a way. True and not true."

"Most stories are, my lady," I said.

A quick smile flickered over her face, so fleeting it was barely there. "I prayed to her," she said. "When Lucius told me he wouldn't marry me, that he was going away to Tiberium instead. I snuck out beneath a new moon. I went to the crossroad before our home, where we make offerings to the *lar compitale*, and I buried three blue beads beneath a cobblestone like my nurse told me." She drew up her knees, hugging them. "I prayed to the Bella Donna to find a way to save me from Domenico Martelli da Valpetra and let Bartolomeo and me be together."

"You should have been more specific," I said wryly.

Her eyes widened and a startled laugh escaped her. "Oh, Bona Dea!" She stifled her laugh with her hands. "It's not funny. But when I saw you, I was so sure . . ."

"I'm just—"

"I know," Helena said, growing somber. "I do. But it's true, too, isn't it? True and not true. Do you think . . . do you think the gods always answer our prayers like this? Sideways?"

"Mayhap." I smiled. "That's a good way of putting it."

She smiled back at me; a real smile. It faded, though. "I'd take it back if I could." She rubbed her knees. "If it meant bringing Bartolomeo back."

"It's not your fault," I said gently. "Valpetra's a cruel, greedy man. He wanted Lucca and he was bound to act on it, Helena. Your prayers had naught to do with it."

"Didn't they?" She rubbed harder. "Bartolomeo died because he loved me. I wanted to die that night. I did. But I was afraid, and Valpetra promised . . . he promised he would spare my parents if I did what he said. So I did." Tears filled her eyes. "Oh gods! I should have let him kill me. If I had any courage, I'd take my own life and join Bartolomeo."

"Helena, no." I knelt on the floor beside her couch and eased her hands into mine. "It would only break your mother's heart. None of this is your fault."

"It feels as though it is," she whispered.

"I know." I nodded. "You'll carry guilt like a stone in your belly because a bad thing happened to you. I don't know why. I don't know why we do that. Mayhap because it's easier than acknowledging that the world can be cruel and unfair, and the gods only answer our prayers sideways at best."

Helena sniffled, but her eyes were intent through her tears. "How do you live with it?"

I sat back on my heels. "You just do. Day by day. It gets easier to bear. You accept the gift of your life with grace and try to be worthy of it." I squeezed her hands. "Does that make sense?"

"Some, yes." Freeing one hand, she touched my bruised cheek, a touch as delicate as the brush of a moth's wing. "You wouldn't be here if you hadn't saved me, would you? I heard about what Valpetra told the D'Angelines who came for you."

I shrugged. "It doesn't matter."

"It does to me." Her face was grave. "I'll try to be worthy of it."

We gazed at one another a moment too long.

Long enough for me to realize I wanted to take her in my arms and kiss away her tears, to soothe the ache in her heart with gentle words. To let her know that love is a trust, a sacred thing, that no debasement can besmirch it, that no betrayal can destroy it. To give her a haven, to offer her protection. Ah, Elua! I yearned for tenderness.

"I should go," I murmured, pulling away.

Her voice broke. "Please, don't!"

"I have to." I stood up, and she followed. "Helena . . ."

"I know. It's just . . ." She scrubbed away the marks of her tears with fierce determination, though a fresh onslaught stood brimming in her eyes. "What was it you said about a stunted tree?"

I touched her hair. It felt as silken-fine as it looked.

"Asclepius came to me in a dream," I said to her. "At his temple. We spoke of wounds. He told me to bear the scars with pride. He told me, 'Even a stunted tree reaches toward the sunlight.' You shine very brightly behind your tears, my lady. But I fear this is the only gift we are meant to give one another."

She closed her eyes, new tears falling. "It's enough."

I nodded. "It is."

I felt lighter when I left the Correggio household; all at once melancholy, yet lighter and strange within my own skin. Peace. I was at peace with myself. I hadn't felt that way since I'd left Balm House, healed of the aching wounds of my adolescent desires. The rain-washed streets of Lucca seemed uncommonly beautiful to me. All throughout the city, people were going about their daily chores, striving for normality. They were cold and hungry and frightened, but they were surviving as best they might, quarreling and living and loving. I wished I could protect them all, fold them all within my arms.

A vast tenderness filled me.

I have been blessed in my life, I thought. For as much darkness as I'd endured, there had been brightness, too; brightness beyond telling. If I died here in Lucca, my life would not have been lived in vain.

In the central square, I dismounted. Heedless of the curious glances, I stooped and touched the cobblestones. I bowed my head, my damp hair hiding my face. "Blessed Elua," I whispered, "I am in your hand. If you have sent me here for a reason, let me serve you well. Mighty Kushiel, accept your reluctant scion's prayer. If I may serve as the instrument of your justice, wield me as you will."

There was no answer, only a waiting stillness. Rising, I gazed at the scorched bell-tower. In all the days I'd been here, I'd never dared enter it.

Today, I did.

There wasn't much to see. The interior was gutted by fire, with only the remnants of a stair winding its way up the inner walls. The outer walls rose around a hollow shell. There were a few blackened timbers at the roofless top where the bell had once hung. A handful of roosting pigeons took flight as I entered, the clap of their wings echoing in the empty tower.

In the center of the floor, half-hidden by rubble, was the *mundus manes*.

The circular slab of marble that covered it had cracked in half. No one had disturbed it since the fire. The gap between the two halves was slight, no more than a few inches at its widest. I stood before the *mundus manes*, gazing at the dark, jagged crevice, trying to imagine what lay beneath it.

An earthen pit or a portal to hell?

If I'd had a torch, I might have dragged aside one half of the broken slab and cast light into that darkness. And I knew, as surely as I knew my own name, what I would see. An earthen pit, dug by human hands. Crawling segmented bugs, scuttling away from the light on a multitude of legs. That, and nothing more.

And yet the hair at the back of my neck prickled.

True and not true.

A thing may be both, I thought. Helena was right. And so I bowed my head once more and offered prayers; prayers to the gods of this place, the Caerdicci *lares* of family and city and field. Prayers to the honored dead, and prayers to the dishonorable dead. Prayers to Dis Pater, lord of the underworld, and his bride Proserpina. There was no blasphemy in it. When all is said and done, D'Angelines are Earth's youngest children, and we seek to tread lightly on her bosom, honoring the gods of all places.

Mounting the Bastard, I departed.

My sense of strangeness stayed with me. It had settled over my shoulders like a cloak, and I was enfolded in it. Eamonn noted it when we rode on patrol together that night. I was unwontedly quiet, wrapped in my own sensibilities.

"You're in a fey mood," he said.

"Thinking about life," I said. "And death."

Eamonn nodded. "Good to do."

The nights were quiet. Inside Lucca's wall, we rode in uneventful circuits. Outside the wall, Valpetra's small company of cavalry did the same. They rode in shifts, day and night; circling the city to ensure that no one attempted an escape, riding the length of the canal to ensure that we didn't endeavor to sabotage it. Our sentries kept watch to ensure Valpetra didn't launch a surprise offensive and a lookout for any lapse in his men's vigilance. Gallus Tadius had a company of saboteurs at the ready, armed with pickaxes and prying bars. We were poised to carry word at the first opportunity. If the saboteurs could demolish a section of the canal, the river would be diverted to flood the fields outside the city.

But there was no lapse, and at the river, the dam took shape.

I went to see it the day after I visited Helena.

There was a massive pile of rubble where once the aqueduct had flowed beneath the wall. The masons had done their best to construct a solid bulwark, but they were hampered by a lack of building materials. They'd salvaged bricks from buildings in ill repair, cobbling together a graceless structure held together by mortar that refused to set properly in the rain. On top of that, they'd simply heaped as much dirt and debris as they could haul. Whether or not it would hold, and for how long, was anyone's guess.

The sentry on duty, a good-natured fellow named Pollio, let me come atop the wall. Gallus Tadius didn't discourage us from getting a good hard look at our enemy's labors. He reckoned we were better off knowing what we were up against. Some of the men preferred not to know. I wasn't one of them.

It was a dismal view. A steady fall of rain soaked the fire-blackened fields. Beyond lay the river. It no longer cut a path like a silvery ribbon across the plain. Valpetra's men had done exactly what Gallus Tadius had predicted. They'd built a pair of dams flanking the canal and filled in the trench, returning the river to its proper course. The dams were as ugly as our bulwark; uglier, I daresay, built of packed earth and felled trees. Neither one was likely to hold for long.

But they were holding now.

Above the upper dam, the river was rising. It was rain-swollen and angry, forcing paths around the edges of the dam. I could see Valpetra's men scurrying atop the dam's surface, building it higher, reinforcing the sides. Others worked furiously on the lower dam. It didn't need to hold long, not long at all. Only long enough to shunt that first, furious surge of water into Lucca's waiting canal.

"It's coming," Pollio said. "Any day now."

Beyond the river was a forest of tents, sagging in the rain. I thought about Valpetra's men, Silvanus' men. They must be soaked and weary, chilled to the bone. And hungry, too. As miserable as the endless days of drilling and nights of patrol were, at least I was able to retire to the villa where I had a ration of food, a proper roof over my head, and a bed laden with warm, dry blankets. It seemed bizarre to me that unless fate intervened, we'd all be doing our best to kill one another in a fairly short amount of time. After all, we were strangers to each other. I asked Pollio if he found it odd.

He eyed me as though I'd spoken in a foreign tongue. "That's war, isn't it?" he said. "Anyway, you're no stranger to Valpetra. He'll remember *you*."

"I know," I said.

Every free hour was filled with drilling, now. We rehearsed Gallus Tadius' plan of engaging and falling back. By now, there was no squadron but had developed some degree of proficiency. I had to own, as much as I disliked it, that I took a measure of pride in our progress. We invented friendly rivalries, staging mock invasions of one another's territories. The squadrons acquired nicknames—ours was Barbarus, of course—but we were all part of the Red

Scourge. We drilled in the streets, we memorized alleys and byways, and the horn signals that would carry Gallus Tadius' orders. We stashed caches of food and waterskins in the emptied lower stories of buildings, worked out plans for ambushes and pitfalls.

There was a fierce camaraderie in it like nothing I'd ever known. All the men in Barbarus came to know one another in a way wholly outside my experience, at once superficial and intimate. For the most part, I didn't know their histories, their hopes and dreams . . . indeed, we seldom knew one another's surnames. But I knew that Orfeo wanted revenge for Bartolomeo Ponzi's death and was apt to be hotheaded. I knew that quiet Constantin never flinched at a feint and was a good man to have at your side. I knew that Matius struggled to hold his position when he locked shields with an opponent, and Baldessare could always be counted on for a jest. I knew somewhat about all of them.

All men; ordinary men.

What they thought of me, I couldn't say. At first, there was a mixture of awe and disdain, which seemed to be the common attitude toward D'Angelines among the Caerdicci. And too, word had gotten about that I was a Prince of the Blood, that I had cut off the Duke of Valpetra's hand and he wanted vengeance for it. But after the bout with Gallus Tadius, I did nothing to draw attention to myself and worked without complaint. I found a leather-worker to repair the chin-strap on my helmet. In the rain and muck, one muddy, helmeted conscript looks much like any other, D'Angeline or no. In time, they forgot.

Eamonn, they adored.

Truly, he had a knack for leadership. He was clever, good-hearted, and fearless, and he had a gift for making men like him. No one seemed to care that he was a prince in his own right and half-D'Angeline to boot; he was Eamonn. He won their respect with Gallus Tadius' praise and his own actions, and their affections with a grin. He worked as hard as or harder than any man in Barbarus during the drills, bareheaded in the rain, his red-gold hair plastered to his skull and his loud, cheerful voice calling out orders.

I didn't begrudge him, not a bit. It was a heavy burden. And there wasn't a man among us, myself included, who didn't know beyond a shadow of doubt that Eamonn would be the first to advance and the last to retreat. Betimes, I wished for his sake that he showed a little less valor.

Gallus Tadius did us one kindness, though. There were twenty-four squadrons all told, and Barbarus would be stationed near the rearguard. If the wall was breached and Valpetra's men were engaged, we would be among the last to peel away before the rearguard made its final stand in an effort to halt the enemy. The section of the city Barbarus was to defend lay in the farthest outskirts, backing up against the gatehouse itself.

It was the most safety he could offer us . . . save, of course, forbearing to execute us for treason if we refused to fight for Lucca.

I thanked him for it anyway.

He gave me one of those long, gimlet stares. He'd gone back to his old ways, going without sleep, and his face had resumed its hollow-eyed, fearsome aspect. There was no trace of Lucius behind the mask. "You're welcome," he said.

That was all.

SIXTY

WE WERE BREAKING our fast at the villa when the horns blew.

There were a dozen signals Gallus Tadius had devised, but the one that signaled the advent of a flood was simple and unmistakable: a single sustained blast, repeated over and over. Once the first sentry on the wall gave it, twenty others picked it up and echoed it.

For the space of a heartbeat, we all stared at one another.

The Lady Beatrice went white.

"Get your gear," Eamonn said to me, taking charge. And to Publius Tadius, "My lord, you know what to do. Will you see the horses are led to high ground?"

"I will." His jaw was set. "Go!"

We donned our gear in haste and raced for the basilica. My heart was beating like a Jebean war-drum. This was the part of Gallus Tadius' plan that remained vague, the part he had devised with his priests. He'd given no counsel to the Red Scourge. We only knew that we were to assemble atop the basilica.

Eamonn and I pelted down the rain-slick streets of Lucca. Everywhere, from every doorway, other conscripts poured

into the streets. We exchanged fierce grins, recognizing one
another by our motley arms and tattered red armbands.

Behind them, families scrambled to seek refuge in the
upper stories of townhouses and insulae. Shopkeepers and
innkeepers barred their doors and abandoned their places of
business. All the warehouses were already sealed, perishable
goods raised out of the flood-path. All across the city, horns
blared atop the roofs, issuing the same warning.

Flood, flood, flood!

There were four stairways leading to the roof of the basilica, and two hundred and fifty men trying to crowd their way
up each one, all of them carrying shields and spears. I got
caught up in the crush and felt the breath pressed out of me.
It was as bad as the riots in Tiberium, except that the stair-
way was deadly narrow and everything smelled of damp
stone and unwashed flesh. I shoved hard with my buckler
against someone's back, cursing.

"Slow and orderly, lads!" Eamonn bawled behind me,
nearly deafening me. "Slow and orderly!"

It worked.

We spilled out atop the roof of the basilica. All the
squadron leaders were shouting for their men to assemble.
Eamonn spotted the city guard sentry poised at the northwest edge of the roof, his horn at his lips and his crossbow
slung over his back, his padded crimson gambeson dark
with rain. He nudged me. "Over there."

The roof of the basilica was made of red tile. It had a
shallow peak, merely enough to shed the rain. We ran easily
across it and reached the sentry.

"Is it coming?" I asked, panting. "The flood?"

He barely spared me a glance, pointing. "They're breaching the dam."

"Barbarus!" Eamonn shouted, hoisting his tall shield. "Barbarus, to me!"

By twos and threes, they came; all of them. All of us. The Red Scourge assembled atop the roof of the basilica, and by virtue of Eamonn's quick wits, Barbarus squadron had the best vantage point. We clustered along the edge, spouting water pouring beneath our feet, and peered toward the river. Valpetra's men were tiny and distant, swarming over the upper dam with prying bars.

"Where's Gallus Tadius?" someone asked.

The sentry pointed again. "There."

I craned my neck. Gallus Tadius was in the gutted bell-tower, along with a handful of priests. I recognized the fla-men dialis by his pointed hat. I didn't know the others. They were arrayed along the winding stair. One of them held a black lamb, struggling and half-grown.

"Dagda Mor!" Eamonn frowned. "What do they think—"

"The *mundus manes*," I said. "He means to—"

And I got no further, for in the distance, the upper dam gave way.

The river was unleashed.

It wasn't a mighty river. I'd seen those; I'd nearly drowned in one and I'd sailed on others. The Nahar's majesty is unprecedented. Even the Aviline River, which threads the City of Elua, is larger. But this was an angry river, rain-swollen and held in abeyance. It burst through the upper dam in half a dozen spots, and I daresay it took half a dozen of Valpetra's men with it. It dashed itself against the barrier of the lower dam, throwing up mighty grey waves. I found myself chanting under my breath, hoping the dam would burst.

It leaked, but it held.

As the waves crashed back upon themselves, the pent-up

force of the river seized upon the outlet that it was afforded. Sinuous as a snake, it sought egress. It sped down the long, shallow channel of the canal, obliterating it from view and heading straight for Lucca. And it was such an awesome sight, all of us watched it in gape-mouthed silence.

It hit hard.

From our vantage point, we saw it all. We saw the wall shudder, we heard a deep cracking sound from somewhere within it. For the space of a few heartbeats, it held. A few men cheered. But the water kept coming and coming, an unbearable pressure mounting.

"Name of Elua!" I whispered.

There was a sound like a groan. The wall sagged, and then it simply burst. It burst, collapsing onto itself. The sentry-oak fell, taking its sentry with it. The painstakingly constructed bulwark burst in a furious hail of bricks and debris. A torrent of grey water surged into the city.

There was so *much* of it!

It was like a living thing, an invading army. It kept coming and coming. It ate away at the breach in the wall, tearing down its edges. It took possession of the city, spreading and dividing, flowing down every street, every alley, every nook. It battered down doors and splintered shutters. If the populace hadn't been warned, scores of them would have been washed away and drowned. It happened that fast. We stood atop the basilica and stared, aghast.

And the water continued to rise.

"They think to flush us out like rats," Eamonn murmured. "And it looks like they're doing a fair job of it."

We traded glances.

"Straight to hell," I said. "Now's the time to believe."

He nodded and raised one hand. "Barbarus, *hold*!"

Although we had little choice—after all, where would we

go?—his firm command heartened the men, and I heard other squadron leaders echo his lead. Far across the fields, Valpetra's camp was in disarray, his men scattered by the flood's backwash. I daresay the force of it had overwhelmed them, too. The lower dam gave way almost languidly, packed earth dissolving into a swirl of muddy water. The surging river forked, half of it returning to its proper course, the rest continuing to flow into Lucca, although its force had lessened. It would take some time before Valpetra was able to get his army sorted out and ford the river, let alone take advantage of the breached wall, through which half a river still flowed. I said as much to Eamonn.

"He never meant to." Eamonn nodded toward the south. "Valpetra expected us to fling open the gate and wash out into the arms of the cavalry in a great, half-drowned tide of surrender. He reckoned he'd keep his infantry safe and dry on the far side of the river." He grinned. "Buys us some time, anyway!"

I peered over the edge of the roof. "We're going to need it."

It looked so strange to see the city half-submerged, all its buildings rising out of the water. I hoped the Bastard was all right. We'd determined the highest point on the Tadeii grounds, but it was a fairly shallow rise.

Something was happening in the bell-tower, though it was hard to make out what. I sat down and straddled a rain-spout, dangling my legs over the edge. It felt good to lay my buckler aside. I studied the tower.

Water lapped at the step on which the flamen dialis stood. He held his hands extended over the rising water, his white sleeves trailing. The faint sound of chanting reached us, too faint to make out any words. From time to time, one of the other priests would hand him an object: a smoking incensor, a pitcher of wine, a dish of grain. The flamen dialis poured libations and offerings into the water above the *mundus manes* and the chanting continued, punctuated by the occasional clash of a bronze cymbal. Gallus Tadius stood beside him, still as a statue.

It went on for a very long time.

The water continued to rise. Trapped within the city walls, it had nowhere to go.

The men began to mutter. I kept silent, but I didn't blame them. Despite my bold words, I was filled with doubt. It had been a lot easier to believe before the flood hit. Why had we taken Gallus Tadius at his word? Why hadn't we questioned him? When all was said and done, it was a piece of madness. We'd put our faith in a dead man; or a madman. It had all happened so quickly. What if there was no Gallus Tadius? What if Lucius *was* mad? I'd believed he wasn't . . . why? Because of Alais' dream, the man with two faces. Because of what I'd witnessed in my life, terrible darkness and glorious mystery alike.

And, in truth, because of the sheer force of Gallus Tadius, real or no. He'd swept over us like a river, brooking no argument. He'd offered us hope and purpose, and we'd taken it. We'd asked no questions, or at least far too few. Now Lucca's fields were razed by fire, its streets drowned in water. I thought about what Deccus Fulvius had said atop the walls the night of the firestorm, his hand heavy on my shoulder.

Is it worth destroying a thing to save it?

I hadn't had an answer then, and I still didn't. I only knew that as the morning wore onward, this was looking a lot more like destruction than salvation. At least Deccus and Claudia and Brigitta were safe. Counting back in memory, I reckoned it had been two weeks and a day since they left. It seemed like longer. I cast a hopeless glance behind me, just in case there might be a bright army of D'Angeline allies emerging from the twisting mountain road.

There wasn't.

In the tower, the priest holding the lamb descended. He held it while the flamen dialis cut its throat. I shuddered as they held it above the water, letting its blood drain. In Terre d'Ange, we don't offer living sacrifices. Then again, we don't believe in hell, either; not in the same way. Oh, we invoke it in casual curses, but it's not for us. When Blessed Elua refused to return to the One God's heaven, he barred the way to hell, too. Only the Cassiline Brothers—the truly rigid ones, not apostates like Joscelin—believe otherwise. Our fate lies elsewhere.

When I was a child, Brother Selbert taught us that in time, all of Elua's children will pass through the bright gate into the true Terre d'Ange-that-lies-beyond, though it may take us many lifetimes. I used to daydream about it in Daršanga, where I thought I'd die and sometimes wished I would. In those days, I reckoned it must be a lot like the Sanctuary of Elua where I grew up, only the honeybees never stung and no one ever got hurt, ever.

I couldn't imagine it, now.

I could imagine hell, though. It was a lot like Daršanga.

Sitting atop the roof of drowned Lucca, I wished Master Piero was there. We'd never talked about the afterlife. I wondered what he would have said about this. Was hell merely human cruelty? Was it a place? Was heaven? Were there truly different places for different peoples? In Caerdicci belief, it lay beneath our very feet and heaven and hell lay side by side, the Elysian Fields and Tartarus.

Mayhap it was true; but all I could see was water.

The Caerdicci believe there is water in the underworld.

Five rivers—the River of Woe, the River of Lamentation, the River of Fire, the River of Unbreakable Oaths, and the River of Forgetfulness. Mayhap, I thought, they should add a sixth: the River of Demented Folly. Despite everything, the thought made me smile.

"Eamonn—" I began.

He poked me. "Hush. Look."

In the tower, Gallus Tadius moved. After all the endless ritual and sacrifice, his action was the essence of simplicity. He worshipped the way he fought, without a wasted motion. He stepped forward and held up an object; two objects. Two halves of a whole.

His death-mask.

He dropped it into the rising water.

My skin prickled even before the water began to stir in a circular motion. As though my hearing had grown achingly acute, I heard the bronze cymbals clash. It sounded like wings, bronze wings beating. It sounded like it was inside my skull. On the tower stair, Gallus Tadius lifted his head, gazing through the broken wall. Impossible as it was, it seemed as though he looked right at me. I could see his lips moving.

Forgiveness.

On my feet, I clutched at my ears, trying to suppress the bronze din. Loud, so loud! Within the tower, the waters were swirling faster. A maelstrom. I'd seen one before, but as terrible as Rahab's wrath had been, it had been bright, bright beyond telling. This wasn't. And it was on dry land, or land that should have been dry. Wrong, all wrong.

Men were shouting in terror, a sucking wind rendering their cries wordless. At the edge of the rooftop, I staggered, the rain-spout careening in my vision. Strong hands hauled me back and Eamonn's voice bellowed in my ear, anchoring me.

In the tower, Gallus Tadius crumpled.

Oddly, my head cleared.

Faster and faster, the waters spun. In the pit of the maelstrom, darkness blinked open like an eye. A fetid taste filled my mouth. Water, foul and stagnant. My hell, my memory. But this wasn't mine.

The pit yawned wide; no pit, but the *mundus manes* itself. It had grown as wide as the tower, as deep as . . . I don't know what. There was no measuring it. It opened onto darkness, utter and complete blackness. A sigh of wind breathed forth from it, and it was at once fair and foul as anything I'd ever smelled; as sweet as a dew-laden rose, as horrid as a rotting corpse. A thousand emotions flickered through me, quicker than thought, bitter and joyous. All around me, men were laughing and crying.

Water cascaded into the *mundus manes*, falling and falling. It no longer spun in a maelstrom. Whatever drew it, drew it straight down, and where it fell it was black, as though the abyss cast darkness the way the sun casts brightness. Cataracts of gleaming blackness, spilling over the edge. There was a roar like a waterfall, as deafening as the Great Falls of Jebe-Barkal. There seemed to be no end to it, no bottom to the abyss. On and on it went, rippling curtains of smooth obsidian descending in a sheer, endless plunge.

A strange exhilaration filled me. I yearned to follow the black water, to descend into those lightless realms. What an adventure it would be! To walk the underworld like a hero out of legend, to speak with the storied dead . . .

No.

The word brushed my thoughts, as soft as a bronze-edged feather. I shuddered and drew back from the edge of the roof. My place was among the living. I clung to the thought and kept a firm grip on my place in the world.

In the city, the level of water began to drop.

How long it lasted, I couldn't say. It felt like hours, and I daresay it may have been. And yet it all took place like a dream. It may have taken minutes. The abyss gaped, the cataracts roared, the water fell and fell and fell . . .

And then it was gone.

All of it.

Atop the roof of the basilica, we blinked at one another like men waking from a shared dream, dazed. The streets of Lucca were wet and shining, filled with shallow puddles and strewn with debris, but the flood was gone.

"Straight to hell," Eamonn said.

In the tower, the abyss was gone. There was only an earthen pit some five paces in diameter, damp and muddy. No offerings, no dead lamb, no wax death-mask. The cracked halves of the marble slab that covered it lay on either side. Even as we looked, priests hurried down the winding stair and began dragging the slabs back into place, their robes trailing in the mud.

Others attended to Gallus Tadius, obscuring him from sight. A sentry appeared, descending from a high post. He leaned in close, nodding, then trotted back up the winding stair, vanishing behind an intact portion of the wall.

A few seconds later, we heard his horn sounding. Three short blasts, high and piercing: Stand and await orders. Our sentry replied with a single, brief note: Acknowledged.

He turned to us. "You're to assemble downstairs. Captain Arturo will be here presently. Check the upper tiers, there should be dry supplies."

"What of Gallus Tadius?" one of the other squadron commanders asked. Others echoed the query with rising anxiety. "Where is he?"

"He'll need time to recover," the sentry said wearily. "So we were told. Until then, Captain Arturo's in command."

There was some grumbling, but most of the men were too shocked to protest or wonder. The squadron leaders began shouting commands and the Red Scourge began trooping down the four narrow stairs.

I lingered atop the roof as long as I could, gazing toward the breach in the wall. Water was still flowing into the city, but it was merely a stream, scarce overflowing the aqueduct. For the most part, the river had returned to its proper course, where it was still swollen and flowing swiftly, trapping the bulk of Valpetra's army on the far side.

Not the cavalry, though.

More than a score of sentries were posted to defend the breach, vulnerable and exposed, their crossbows cocked and aimed. Valpetra's cavalry lingered out of range, their horses mired to the fetlocks, watching and assessing.

I pointed them out to Eamonn. "Think they'll charge?"

He rubbed his chin, his grey-green eyes troubled. "They might. They don't know what we've got here, and we can't afford to get caught wrong-footed." I watched him wrestle with a decision and come to it. "I don't think we'd better wait for Arturo."

Downstairs, the basilica was teeming with soldiers. It held all of us, but barely. The men of the Red Scourge spoke in hushed whispers of what had happened, and muttered in anxious tones about what would happen next. The sense of awe that had pervaded us atop the roof gave way to the exigencies of mundane reality. We squeezed rainwater from sodden cloaks and broke into the cache of stores in the upper tiers, passing around dry blankets and rags, rubbing down ourselves and our weapons. The entire place reeked of floodwater, wet wool, and rank humanity.

As the last to descend, Barbarus squadron was stuck with a post on the damp lower tiers and last pick of the dry goods. I got a scrap of muslin. It didn't do me much good, but I wiped down my sword assiduously and watched Eamonn shove his way through the throng. It was always easy to spot him, half a head taller than anyone else. I wished he'd found a helmet.

He spoke to several of the other squadron leaders, and there were nods all around. Eamonn hopped up onto the rostrum.

"Right!" he called cheerfully. "Here's the thing, lads."

I laughed; everyone did. He sounded for all the world like Gallus Tadius. Eamonn grinned and waited for us to stop laughing.

"Here's the thing," he continued. "There are a hundred and fifty Valpetran horse-soldiers trying to decide whether or not to charge twenty sentries. We're going to give them a reason not to. Until Captain Arturo or Gallus himself tell us otherwise, we'll hold the gap and squadrons will rotate out every two hours. We'll go in order. Understood?"

There were cheers and shouts of agreement. The commanders of the 1st and 2nd squadrons—Cutpurse and Horsethief squadrons—hustled their men out the door. As motley a group as they were, they moved with brisk efficiency, settling their bucklers, striding with their spears held upright.

Canis was among them.

They were first in order, and if Gallus Tadius' plan held, they would be first in line when the full-forced attack came, bearing the brunt of it. Among the eighty men in Cutpurse and Horsethief, most were former prisoners who had chosen the red armband over the noose. A few were just unlucky.

My erstwhile philosopher-beggar gave me a long look as he left, filled with meaning I couldn't decipher. All I could do was shrug. After what we'd witnessed, I didn't much care. If there was somewhat Canis wanted me to know, he should leave off pretending to be a deaf-mute.

But all he did was shrug in reply and leave.

Eamonn ordered us to get what rest we might, since no one knew what the next hours would bring. Someone found a stash of charcoal untouched by the flood in a storeroom, and lit the braziers. The basilica grew marginally warmer and a good deal smokier. We lounged on the tiered benches, checking our gear. There were oatcakes and salt cod in the caches, so we shared those around, along with skins of water to wash it all down. Through the windows, I could see the cloudy sky lowering. However much time had passed, it must be nearing sunset. I wrapped myself in my damp cloak and tried to doze.

In time, Captain Arturo arrived, accompanied by a lieutenant.

He looked exhausted, and I daresay he was. The city guard had carried a heavy burden these last weeks, with worse yet to come. He listened as Eamonn and the other squadron commanders reported and nodded with relief.

"Good men," he murmured. "Good plan. Stick to it."

"Where's Gallus Tadius?" someone called. Others took up the call, turning it into a chant. *"Gal-lus, Gal-lus, Gal-lus!"*

Captain Arturo winced. "Resting, damn you!" he shouted. "The man opened a portal to hell! Can you not give him a moment's peace?" With an effort, he gathered himself.

"He'll be with you by daybreak," he said curtly. "We're keeping a watch. Valpetra's men won't attack before then."

Some cheered; some groaned. I understood both parties. The waiting was hard.

Captain Arturo raised his hands and spoke, trying to placate them.

The captain's lieutenant snaked through the crowd, clambering over the tiered benches. It was the young one, the one with the rosy cheeks and the peach-fuzz. The one Gallus Tadius had struck. Wrapped in my cloak, I watched him come. I didn't realize he was coming for me until he leaned down, whispering in my ear like an inept lover.

"He wants to see you!" he hissed.

I knew.

I'd known since I saw Gallus Tadius cast his death-mask into the waters. But I couldn't show it, not here. I sat up, raking a hand through my damp hair. "I'll come," I said quietly, settling my helmet on my head and grabbing my gear.

I told Eamonn what I was about, and he gave me a puzzled nod. I did my best to slip away unobtrusively, following Captain Arturo and his lieutenant through the streets of Lucca. There were a few people about, cleaning up flood-borne debris, but for the most part the citizens of Lucca huddled in the upper stories of their homes. The flood may have been banished, but Valpetra's army had not.

They led me to the Temple of Jupiter. It hadn't been spared by the flood, but the god's mighty effigy was none the worse for wear. He sat on his marble throne, staring out toward the entrance with a fierce gaze. Captain and lieutenant alike offered a salute in passing, touching their fingers to their brows, and I followed suit. At the doorway that led out of the main chamber, the flamen dialis met us. He looked weary, too.

"Prince Imriel." He inclined his head. "This way."

There was a small sanctuary beyond the central chamber where the water hadn't penetrated. They'd laid a pallet in there, piled high with pillows. Half a dozen candles were blazing atop the small altar and in niches built into the walls. I entered, gazing at the figure reclining on the pallet.

Lucius.

He looked awful. Beyond weary, beyond exhausted. Even by candlelight, his satyr's face was haggard and grey. Still, he shoved himself upright as I entered, and a trace of his old smile flickered. "Montrève."

"Lucius." I set down my buckler and spear, removed my helmet, and sat on the edge of his pallet. "He's gone, isn't he?"

"I'm afraid so."

SIXTY-ONE

W E DIDN'T SPEAK of it at once. The lieutenant had stayed behind, but Captain Arturo entered the sanctuary after me. Lucius listened to his report, then nodded. "Thank you," he said. "Tell me . . . tell me if anything changes."

"Aye, sir." There was fear in his eyes, and a question writ large. What will *you* do if it does? He knew. But all he said was, "The men are counting on you, my lord. Your men."

"I know," Lucius said. "I'll be there."

The captain hesitated, then departed with a salute. Once he had gone, Lucius gave a shuddering sigh and buried his face in his hands. A deep tremor shook him.

"Sweet Apollo," he said in a muffled voice. "I can't do this."

"I think you may have to," I said quietly.

"I know," he said. "Believe me, I do."

"How much do you remember?" I asked him.

"Enough." Lucius raised his head and gave the ghost of a smile. "Knowledge is a slippery thing, Montrève. But I know what he had planned. I still do." He studied me, his hazel eyes steady in their sunken hollows. "You weren't surprised."

"No," I said. "I knew it when he dropped the mask."

"He knew." Lucius shivered. "Sweet Apollo, he *knew*."

I propped my elbows on my knees. "He was making atonement, Lucius."

"Yes." His gaze dwelled on me. "I saw you. *He* saw you, there at the end. And you knew. You see things other people don't, don't you, Montrève?"

"Sometimes," I said.

"Why is that?" Lucius asked.

I reached out and took his hand. It had grown gaunt and callused under Gallus Tadius' usage, but the strong grip was purely Lucius. I smiled wryly, remembering the buffeting sound of bronze wings within my skull. *If I may serve as the instrument of your justice, wield me as you will.* Kushiel's reluctant scion, called to bear witness. I could hardly explain it to him when I barely understood it myself. "Does it matter?"

"No." Lucius leaned his head back against the pillows, closing his eyes. "I suppose not. What do you see in *me*, Imriel nó Montrève?"

I told him.

All of it, good and bad. A quick wit and a generous spirit; a thorny sense of pride. A love of justice that wrestled with inborn prejudices; an abhorrence of hypocrisy. Stubbornness and kindness commingled. Courage, and a surprising capacity for endurance.

In short, a good deal of myself.

When I finished, Lucius was watching me with open eyes. "I'm not afraid to fight," he said. "And I'm not afraid to die. I'm not even afraid of the dead, not anymore." His mouth twisted. "But I am not my great-grandfather. And I am terrified to the core of my being at the prospect of ordering men to die in *his* name. Because they will, you know. A good many of them."

"Yes," I said. "I know." I wished I had words of comfort to offer him, but I didn't. There weren't any. "Lucius, you need food and sleep, as much of both as you can manage. Have you eaten?"

He shook his head. I found a priest loitering outside the door and sent him to fetch food. They must have anticipated the need, for he returned with alacrity bearing a steaming bowl of stew, hearty with beans and rich chunks of mutton, and a sizable chunk of black bread. After weeks of short rations, it looked delicious.

I shoved it at Lucius. "Eat."

He ate slowly at first, but after a few mouthfuls I could see his appetite return. I refused his offer to share and watched with satisfaction as he devoured the entire bowl, wiping it clean with the last of the bread.

"More?" I asked.

"I'd burst." Lucius set the bowl aside. "Thank you, that was good."

I nodded. "You need to sleep now."

He grimaced. "I think I've forgotten how. My mind keeps working and working, and I don't even know whose thoughts I'm thinking. I've gone so far beyond tired, I've come out the other side. Anyway, I need to get a look at Valpetra's forces and—"

"No." I pointed at him. "Look at you, you're about to fall over. You're no good to anyone in this state. Sleep."

A faint spark of humor lit his eyes. "What do you mean to do? Sing me a lullaby?"

"Mayhap." I stood and removed my sword-belt, then began stripping off my leather jerkin. Lucius watched me with bemusement. "Move over."

"Montrève, I hardly think—"

"Don't be an ass." Clad in a woolen shirt and breeches, I crawled onto the pallet beside him. "You've got pillows enough for an orgy here. Move over."

In the end, Lucius was too exhausted to protest. I propped myself against the pillows and pulled him toward me, trying to settle his head on my shoulder.

"Come here," I said. "I'll tell you a story."

"I'm not a child," he murmured. "And I do *not* need your damned D'Angeline pity."

"Shut up." I tugged a lock of his hair. "This is a true story. You've heard of the Master of the Straits?" He nodded. "Well, there was a curse that bound him to his island. And it bound him to immortality, too; but an immortality of endless aging. It was the angel Rahab who uttered the curse, and the only thing that would break it was the Name of God . . ."

As the candles sank low throughout the night, wax dripping, I told him the story of our quest to Saba. I told him about stowing away on the boat to Menekhet, praying Phèdre and Joscelin wouldn't send me away. I told him of our voyage down the Nahar, and sang the children's counting songs in Jeb'ez that our felucca-captain Wali taught me. I felt Lucius' cheek move in a smile. I told him about crossing the desert on camelback, and the stark, awful majesty of the desert. He called me a liar in a sleepy voice.

Stroking his hair, I told him about the splendors of Meroë, where Queen Zanadakhete ruled and soldiers rode oliphaunts in the streets. I told him about our journey southward, about the rhinoceros and the immense fish that Joscelin and I caught. I told him about the Great Falls. I told him about Saba and the lost Tribe of Dân with their ancient bronze weapons.

As I was telling him about following the stars across the Lake of Tears, rowing and rowing, Lucius fell asleep.

Sleep eased the stark lines from his face. He looked ten years younger; almost like himself, albeit a worn, thin version. I held him close and kept talking, keeping my voice low. It seemed to soothe him, and I thought he'd like to know the story had a happy ending, even if he wasn't awake to hear it. But between the warmth and the peaceful sleeping weight of Lucius, I fell asleep before the end.

It seemed like only a few minutes.

"Montrève!"

I snatched the dagger from my boot-sheath, eyes snapping open. Lucius was standing a safe distance away, regarding me with a bemused look.

"I've seen the way you wake when startled," he said dryly. "O, dear my prince, you are an odd one, aren't you?"

I grinned at him, sheathing my dagger. "So I've been told. How do you feel?"

He stretched his arms, flexing his hands. The lines had returned to his face, but they were carved less deeply, and his color was better; much better. "I'll serve. I don't feel like a strong wind might blow me to pieces anymore. That's an improvement." He met my eyes. "Thank you. Someday I'll have to hear how the story ends."

I nodded. "Get us through this, and I'll tell you."

"I'll do my best."

Daybreak was nigh. A scuttling priest came with a breakfast of dates, black bread, and hard cheese. We both ate as much as we could, washing it down with water, then assisted one another in donning our armor with unself-conscious ease. There was a strange sense of intimacy between us, born of the night's shared sleep and the morning's imminence of death.

"You know I have to send you back to your squadron," Lucius said quietly.

"I know." I yanked the mended chin-strap of my helmet, testing its strength. "I'm ready. We're ready. And Eamonn's a good leader. You—Gallus—did a good job of training us."

"He wasn't all bad, was he?" Lucius mused. "Not wholly."

"No," I said. "And when all is said and done, he believed in you. He'd never have left if he didn't. Gallus Tadius believed you could do this. Remember that."

"I will." Leaning over, Lucius plucked something from the tangle of blankets and pillows on the pallet—a length of crimson cloth, loosened during the night. "Here." He knotted it firmly around my upper arm. "The badge of the Red Scourge."

I gave him a half-bow. "My thanks, my lord."

"Imriel . . ." Shaking his head at me, Lucius took my face in his hands. "Don't be an ass," he said, and kissed me.

It was sweet.

It was sweet and strong and firm. There was amusement in his handsome satyr's face as he drew back from me; what my own expression was, I cannot guess. I was struggling with an unexpected swell of desire.

"For luck," he said lightly.

"Luck," I echoed. The flamen dialis was standing in the doorway, his brows raised and his lips pursed in disapproval. In that instant, I despised him. I wished I could give him the sort of devastating look that Phèdre had given me the day I'd quarreled with Mavros, that deep, penetrating, self-aware gaze before which all accusations quailed and all shame rebounded upon the accuser.

Lucius did it for me.

The priest dropped his gaze. "Captain Arturo is awaiting orders."

"Right." Lucius donned his gilded helmet, which bore a tall plume of horsehair dyed red. It had belonged to Gallus Tadius once. He fastened his chin-strap and checked his sword-belt, then settled his buckler on his arm. He drew a deep breath, as though to better fill out the armor. Beneath the helmet's gilded peak, a look of grim resolve suffused his features. "Let's go."

He strode out of the sanctuary, back upright, shoulders squared.

I trailed behind him, a lowly foot-soldier once more, clad in motley attire.

Beneath the shadow of Jupiter's mighty effigy, Captain Arturo saluted, his weary face surprised and hopeful. "My lord?"

Lucius gave him a curt nod. "Report."

"They're coming."

SIXTY-TWO

IT WAS RAINING AGAIN.

A light rain, little more than a steady drizzle. We held our position, periodically twitching our cloaks to shed the rain. Barbarus was the 22nd squadron. We were posted on the right side of the aqueduct. On the left side was the 21st, and behind us were the 23rd and 24th, which were called Stone and Anchor. All of the best or most foolhardy soldiers were in the latter two. Either trait would serve.

Before us was the 20th, called Senecus owing to the age of their commander, a grizzled oldster with fierce eyes and narrow jaws like a pike eel. A good fighter, his men said.

I hoped so.

We were in a narrow formation, each squadron split into two lines of twenty men. Eamonn stood directly in front of me, blotting out most of my view; in front of him, there was a sea of cloaks belonging to the other squadrons of the Red Scourge. We were backed up all the way to the residential district.

Gallus Tadius rode back and forth along our ranks.

Not Gallus; Lucius.

Even I, who knew, had to remind myself. He did a beautiful job of it. The set of his shoulders, the straight line of his back, the defiant angle of his chin—it was pure Gallus. I suppose he'd had time to learn it. Bone-weary though I knew he was, it didn't show. When he called out mocking assessments of the enemy's fears and ordered us to hold firm, even I drew heart from it.

"Is he . . . ?" Eamonn had asked when I slipped back into the basilica.

"He'll do," was all I said.

We couldn't see what was happening beyond the breach, but word filtered down from the sentries atop the wall and passed through the ranks. Valpetra's men were massed and waiting. During the night, they'd managed to ford the river. In the grey light of dawn, they'd slogged across the burned, half-flooded fields. The cavalry, a mere hundred and fifty men, had fallen back to take a position at the rear. Almost two thousand infantry stood just out of bowshot, awaiting orders.

And we awaited them, a thousand strong.

I tried to clear my mind.

I tried to imagine I was Joscelin. What must he have felt in such moments? A clarity of purpose, the essence of his oath and long training, purified and distilled. But I wasn't him. There was no charge to protect, no oath to obey, no act of solitary heroism pending. I was only a soldier, a single cog on a mighty wheel, a single brick in a vast wall.

Imriel.

A soldier.

Beyond the wall, Valpetran horns sounded a charge. Atop the wall, Lucca's horns echoed a warning, caught up and repeated throughout the city, atop a dozen rooftops. We all braced ourselves, bucklers on arms, the butts of our spears planted. I was on the inner edge beside the aqueduct on my left, the water flowing high but contained. I spared a glance to my right, where Matius gave me a nervous grin. Not a good man to have beside me.

"Here they come!" Lucius shouted. "*Hold*, lads!"

They came.

They came hard and fast, charging the gap. They came in waves, the first wave ducking low and running, bent double beneath their raised shields. Our sentries' crossbows twanged, bolts flying, thudding into wood and flesh. The second wave of Valpetra's infantry followed hard on the heels of the first, hurling javelins. Atop the wall, men staggered and fell, pierced through.

"Cutpurse, Horsethief, *hold*!" Lucius roared. "Everyone, *hold*!"

The sound of that first clash was like nothing on earth. A screech of metal on metal, the crash of shields, battle-cries and howls of pain. We felt it, all of us. All the way through the ranks, we felt the impact as Valpetra's first wave struck our vanguard. It rocked us on our heels, setting us to scrambling, until we got our feet beneath us and leaned forward, shields pressing.

"Bar-bar-us!" Eamonn chanted. "Bar-bar-us!"

I found myself grinning.

Ahead of us, someone took up the chant anew. "Sen-e-cus! Sen-e-cus!"

We held, all of us, squadron by squadron. Cutpurse and Horsethief were borne backward, taking casualties, bearing the brunt of the first wave's attack. It seemed forever until the Luccan horns blew, echoing the command of Lucius' bellowing voice. As the 3rd and 4th squadrons stepped up to take their places, they peeled away at a dead run, dropping back into the city. I looked for Canis among the retreating figures and saw only a blur of men, faces undistinguishable.

Again.

Again.

Again.

It went on and on. With each squadron's retreat, Valpetra's men seized the chance to push farther into the city. Despite our best efforts, they had taken control of the gap. Rank by rank, squadron by squadron, the Red Scourge opposed them, pitting fresh soldiers against weary ones, trying to reduce the odds against us, trying to hold them long enough for the retreating squadrons to take up defensive positions in the city.

And with each squadron's retreat, I took a step closer to combat.

"Senecus!" Lucius roared.

Ah, Elua! I saw them die, then. I saw it at close range, helpless behind them. The Valpetrans were wading through their own dead and wounded, and so were we, by now. We were packed too tightly to move them. There was a body at my feet, stirring. I could hear him moan. I didn't dare look down and put a face to him. I was afraid to know.

More and more Valpetrans were streaming through the gap. The newcomers began edging around in an effort to flank us.

"Double up the ranks!" Lucius shouted. "Now!"

Our commanders echoed his order and we obeyed. In front of me, Eamonn's line spread out, stretching and thinning. Just as we'd practiced a hundred times on the drilling ground, those of us in the second line stepped forward and the two short lines of our squadron meshed into one long one, staving off the attack on our flanks. Now I had Eamonn on my left, and a taciturn cooper named Calvino on my right instead of Matius. I barely had time for a guilty twinge of gratitude before the horns blew another retreat and Senecus' line began to peel away.

My mouth went dry and my limbs tingled all over with fear. Despite the chill, my palms were sweating so hard I was afraid the wooden shaft of my spear would slide through my grasp. I flexed my fingers around the grip of my buckler, willing myself not to drop it.

"Barbarus!" Lucius roared.

Leveling our spears, we stepped forward.

They were on us instantly, flinging themselves forward. The Valpetran opposite me evaded my jabbing spear-thrust. He was left-handed, and if he'd had a spear of his own, he'd long since lost it. They were tired and half-starved, and they'd been fighting in the vanguard long enough to grow reckless and desperate. His shield crashed hard against mine and he pressed forward, his short-sword stabbing. I twisted sideways, avoiding his blade, and felt him overbalance. Shoving hard with my buckler, I hooked my left foot behind his forward leg.

If not for the surging ranks of men behind him, he would have fallen; as it was, he staggered backward, clad in heavy armor. I settled my spear, holding it tight between my elbow and my body, wishing I had his armor. For the space of a heartbeat, we stared at one another. Men; ordinary men. Then he gritted his teeth and charged me again. At the last instant, I shifted, raising the tip of my spear.

It caught him under the chin, nearly lifting him off his toes. His mouth gaped and I could see the wooden shaft between his reddened teeth, dark and bloody. It nearly made me vomit. I yanked it loose, and blood spilled out of the round hole it had made.

He fell.

Another Valpetran took his place, and I killed him, too. He got tangled in the first man's dead limbs and sprawled at my feet. I shortened my grip on the spear and punched downward, driving into a gap at the base of his back-plate. This time, my spear stuck. I braced my foot on his armored back and tugged. Out of the corner of my right eye, I saw a blade flash toward me and Calvino's buckler rise to intercept it.

"My thanks!" I gasped as the spear came free.

He grunted.

On my left, Eamonn was singing. An Eiran song, fierce and bloody, filled with grim joy. He'd gone to his sword and was laying about him left and right, half-hidden behind his tall shield. Where he struck, men cried out in pain. The sheer force of his blows was devastating. Already, they were trying to give him a wide berth.

Blessed Elua, I thought, I am not made for this.

On my right, Calvino's buckler cracked and split, pierced by a Valpetran spear. It had saved my life, but it cost him his. He grimaced at it, and the Valpetran ran him through. Spitted, he sagged. I had a glimpse of his hands rising to touch the shaft of the spear that had killed him, and then the Valpetran line pushed forward and he was gone, trampled underfoot.

"Barbarus, *hold*!"

I didn't want to hold. I wanted the retreat to sound, wanted to run. I had Matius to the right of me once more. He'd dropped his spear and was shoving futilely with his shield. I saw the Valpetran opposite him grin and race forward, his sword raised. I hated him without knowing him. Taking a step forward, I dropped to one knee and planted the butt of my spear, wedging it in a crevice, letting him hurl himself on it. The shaft snapped under the impact.

It didn't pierce the Valpetran's armor, but it drove the breath from his lungs. He gaped, fish-mouthed, clutching at the dent in his breastplate. His helmeted head bowed, baring brown curls at the nape of his neck.

I drew my sword and struck him there. Half-severed, his head lolled, exposing the bone-white knuckles of his vertebrae. I had killed my third man.

No time to vomit.

After that, I lost count. There were others I struck, but I don't know if any of them died. Mostly, I tried to stay alive. My shield-arm felt jarred to the bone with the blows I turned aside. I shouted at Matius to draw his sword, to fight. Somewhere, he found courage and did. It was exhausting and brutal and awful, and it seemed like forever before the horns blew, sounding our retreat.

"Anchor and Rock," Lucius roared. "Anchor and Rock!"

"Barbarus, *go*!" cried Eamonn.

Our outside line peeled away. Those of us caught inside struggled to disengage. And then the men of Anchor squadron stepped forward past us, fresh and ready, driving back the Valpetran line with leveled spears and forging an opportunity.

We fled.

Through the damp city, past the empty square, panting in our makeshift armor. All across Lucca, the squadrons that had gone before us lurked in streets and alleyways, calling out encouragement, offering us pumped fists in salute. Women and children called to us from the rooftops and the upper stories of buildings.

"Is it well?" they asked.

"Well enough!" Eamonn called, answering for us. "Be ready!"

We didn't stop until we reached our designated territory. Our first stand—and hopefully our last—was outside the deserted public baths. Eamonn called a halt. There was a clatter of shields and weapons dropping as we all doubled over, gasping for air.

"Who's gone?" someone asked.

"Calvino," I gasped.

"Adolpho."

"Orfeo."

The names kept coming; seven, all told, dead or wounded too badly to flee. It hurt with a numb and distant fury, in a way I couldn't have imagined. I hadn't known them well, but I had known them. They were my brothers in arms. Orfeo had been my sparring partner. I hoped he'd gotten a taste of his revenge before he fell. Calvino had saved my life, and I hadn't been able to save his. It had all happened so fast.

"Grieve later, lads," Eamonn said soberly. "We've work to do."

Across the city, Luccan horns were sounding the final retreat, picked up and echoed by sentries on the rooftops. Anchor and Stone would be turning tail and fleeing for all they were worth, scattering down a myriad of streets. With luck, Valpetra's army would pursue them in disarray. Splinter and divide, and fight them on *our* ground. That was Gallus Tadius' plan.

Lucius' plan, now.

I prayed he was safe.

On Eamonn's orders, we regrouped, checking our weapons and binding our wounds. There was a cache of bandages and waterskins in the baths. I'd taken a graze to my left thigh that was beginning to sting, and a slight cut on my upper right arm that I'd not even felt. There was a dark blotch of blood spreading on my red armband. Since it didn't hurt, I left that one alone. The knot on the armband held; Lucius had tied it securely.

For luck.

Mostly, I was thirsty. When Matius passed me a water-skin, I drank deep, as much as I could hold. Lowering it, I remembered the first man I'd killed, the glimpse of the wooden shaft between his gaping jaws. I turned away and vomited up the water I'd drunk, splashing my boots.

"Steady, Imri." Eamonn clapped a hand on my back.

"Sorry." I wiped my mouth with my sleeve.

"I puked, too, my first time." He nodded at the waterskin. "Drink more, you'll need it. It'll stay down this time." I obeyed, and Eamonn raised his voice. "Listen, lads! You did a good job, a *damn* good job."

"*You* did, Captain Barbarus!" Baldessare called. "You were so deep into their line, I thought we'd have to send a scouting party to retrieve you!"

Eamonn grinned. "Ah, we all did! Imriel here killed . . . how many?"

My stomach lurched and a mixture of bile and water surged into the back of my throat. I swallowed and kept it down. "Only three, I think."

Someone gave a low whistle.

"Three!" Eamonn said cheerfully. "How do you like that, eh, lads? Now we've got ourselves a little game of hare and hounds coming, and I've a mind to make it a merry chase."

Was three a lot? I didn't know and I didn't have time to wonder. The sentries' horns were calling out a warning: Valpetra's men were advancing throughout the city. They hadn't reached us yet, but they were drawing near. On Eamonn's orders, we laid our traps and took up our new positions. The majority of the surviving members of Barbarus lurked in the baths themselves, and a handful took posts behind the columns in the portico.

I was a hare.

There were five of us: Eamonn and me, Matius and two others. We walked slowly to the corner of the street that marked the farthest end of our territory, conserving our energy. There was a jeweler's shop on one side of us, boarded tight against flooding and looting. On the other side was a wineshop and inn. The innkeeper was a conscript, but his family was there. They were assembled atop the roof, along with one of the sentries, recognizable by his crimson gambeson. Eamonn sketched a salute and the sentry nodded in brief acknowledgment.

Although the flood-swept street in the block before us appeared empty, we could hear fighting and shouting elsewhere in the city, accompanied by periodic crashes. Lucca's citizens were hurling objects—furniture, kettles, whatever they had—from the rooftops, raining down missiles upon the invaders. I squinted at the roof of the inn, nudging Eamonn and pointing. There were two empty wine-barrels perched at the edge, grim-faced women poised to roll them over.

"Have to lead 'em close to the eaves," he said. "I don't imagine they'll get much distance with those. Can you do it, Imri? You're probably the fastest."

"I'll try." The barrels made me think of Canis. I wondered if he was still alive.

Eamonn nodded. "Good."

He carried his kite-shaped shield lightly, seemingly untired. He was still bareheaded, rain sparkling on his coppery hair. I wished I'd thought to grab him a helmet from one of the dead, but there hadn't been time. It seemed there was never time in battle, except when there was too much time and nothing to be done.

Like now.

"I hate this." Matius shivered, shifting from foot to foot. "I hate the waiting."

"Be glad you're alive to do it." Eamonn's gaze was fixed on the far end of the street. I was glad he was our commander. I opened my mouth to tell him so, when a sentry's horn blew somewhere in the next block. Our sentry atop the inn echoed the call, loud and piercing. "Here they come, lads!"

Valpetra's men.

There must have been over a hundred of them, driving in a hard wedge. Too many, too many to have come this far with their numbers intact and unchallenged. Three men of the Red Scourge pelted before them; not playing hare and hounds, but running for their lives.

And behind them was the cavalry.

"Dagda Mor!" Eamonn whispered. "Why are they *here*?"

There was no time. No time to wonder, no time to form a new plan. Elsewhere in the city, the sentries' horns were calling anew. I almost fancied I could hear a familiar voice roaring orders. No time to decipher it, no time to guess. There was only now.

Eamonn gathered himself and stepped forward. "Now, hares!"

He beat his shield with the flat of his blade, jeering and shouting insults to the Valpetran army. We all did. They held formation and advanced steadily. Not what we wanted, not what we'd planned for. And then one of them pointed, calling out to his fellows. Halfway down the street, a few in the forefront broke into a jog.

From the doorfronts and alleys, hidden soldiers of Senecus squadron stepped forth to challenge them, sowing chaos in their ranks. But they were too few, outnumbered. They'd laid their traps to catch stragglers, not an entire company. I watched them fight and die, their grizzled commander holding off several attackers, and my feet began to carry me forward unthinking until Eamonn's shield blocked my path.

"Hold," he said grimly.

Senecus' commander was borne down in a mass of men. Valpetra's men resumed their advance. One of the fleeing Luccan conscripts stumbled and was cut down from behind. We beat our shields and shouted. The other two conscripts reached us. One flashed past us without pausing. The other halted and grabbed my sword-arm.

"He wants *you*," he said in a rusty, accented voice. "Run!"

I stared blankly into Canis' face, blood-streaked beneath his helmet. "Who *are* you?"

And then Valpetra's men were on us.

"Hares, *go*!" Eamonn shouted.

I shook off Canis' hand and ran, darting beneath the eaves of the inn. There were footsteps behind me, and then the cobblestones trembled beneath my feet as two heavy barrels crashed down from above. I heard groaning and cursing. Overhead, the sentry's horn gave a new, frantic call, no signal we'd agreed upon, high and clarion.

I ran.

Never in my life had I felt more vulnerable. Not even in Daršanga, stripped naked and shivering, awaiting the Mahrkagir's lash or Jagun's brand. The space between my shoulder blades itched, protected only by a metal-studded leather jerkin. One arrow, a single well-thrown javelin, and I was dead.

It didn't come.

The charge through the city had taken its toll; Valpetra's men were down to hand weapons. I drew abreast of Matius and the other two, passing them as we raced up the marble steps of the baths and through the arched doorway.

An army followed at our heels. I didn't look back; I didn't dare. With the grunt and clash of swordplay ringing in my ears, echoing in the vast space, I ran past the openings onto the caldarium, the tepidarium, ducking into the room that held the frigidarium. The pool was brimming with floodwater and there was a single narrow plank laid across it. Discarding my shield for the sake of balance, I ran across the plank. It dipped and bent beneath my weight, but it held me. I turned around to find that a full score of Valpetra's men had followed me.

"Come on, then!" I shouted, settling into a two-handed stance.

Valpetra's men hesitated, arraying themselves around the edge of the pool. One ventured onto the plank. I jerked my chin, beckoning him onward. He edged toward me, wavering.

"Bar-bar-us! Bar-bar-us!"

A half dozen of my comrades emerged from hiding to charge them from behind. No skill, no finesse, simply a hard, shoving charge, shields to the fore. Valpetran soldiers staggered, tumbling into the flooded pool, flailing, borne down by the weight of their armor. It was chest-deep; too shallow to drown them, but deep enough to render them ineffectual.

I pointed my blade at the exposed face of the nearest. "Surrender your swords."

He grimaced at me. "Die, D'Angeline."

'Tis a terrifying thing to feel how easily sharp steel shears through human flesh. I cut him; I cut him a-purpose, the tip of my blade etching a thin line across his cheekbones and the bridge of his nose. It wouldn't kill him, but it would scar.

Blood ran down in a sheet, making a scarlet mask of the lower half of his face, stirring crimson tendrils in the water.

"Surrender your swords," I said softly.

This time, they did.

"Imriel!" Canis pushed his way through the members of Barbarus squadron as they collected Valpetran arms. He ran lightly across the plank, balancing his shield with ease. "They're coming. You've got to get out of here."

"They're sodding well *here*, Canis," I said. "Where do you expect me to go?"

He shook his head impatiently. "Not just Valpetra. Help from Tiberium. Didn't you hear the horns?"

"What?" I gaped at him.

Inside the baths, Barbarus was whooping with unexpected triumph. Our ambush had been a success. Dead Valpetran soldiers blocked the doors and temporarily barred further pursuit; live ones splashed and floundered in the pools. The tiled floors were awash with blood and water, and it stank of death and mildew. It was a scene out of some macabre farce. Outside, the sound of battle continued to rage, too fierce to be limited to a handful of resistance.

"Go!" Canis began shoving me back along the plank. "This will be over in an hour, but if you don't damn well get out of here and hide, you're like to be dead before they get here."

"You want me to *desert*?"

He bared his teeth at me. "I want you to *live*!"

Others were beginning to stare. I glanced around desperately for Eamonn; as my friend, as my commander. We needed him. I didn't know whether to believe Canis, whether to heed him. No one knew whether we should attempt to hold the baths or retreat out the rear entrance to the fabric warehouse that was our next stronghold. Remembering my earlier reget, I snatched a helmet discarded by one of the Valpetrans who had surrendered.

"Eamonn!" I shouted. "Where's Eamonn?"

There was a surge at the door. Two Valpetrans burst through. Constantin and another Barbarus member killed one; the other retreated. Outside, it was getting louder. I craned around, looking for a glimpse of copper-bright hair, half a head taller than anyone else.

"Imriel." Matius touched my arm. "Eamonn never made it to the baths. He—"

His lips continued to move, forming words I couldn't hear. There was only a high-pitched ringing sound, the sound of fury. It coursed through me in waves, filling my veins with dark fire. I could taste it on my tongue, acrid as steel.

Enough.

I don't know if I thought the word or spoke it. I tore away from Matius' grip, from Canis' urging, and made for the arched doorway at a dead run. Members of Barbarus squadron turned their heads slowly. I plowed past Constantin and hurdled a Valpetran corpse. There was another Valpetran in the doorway, a live one. He stared at me open-mouthed. I ducked under his raised sword and slid past his shield, dropping to one knee and executing a one-handed backward thrust. As though from a great distance, I heard him bellow as my sword pierced the back of his thigh. Without pausing, I yanked my sword free and continued onto the portico.

"Eamonn!" I shouted.

It was madness outside the baths. The streets were clogged with almost two hundred Valpetran infantry and mounted men, and hundreds of Luccan soldiers. Hundreds. They must have rallied from every quarter of the city. As

though a door had been flung open wide, my hearing returned, and the sound of it slammed into me: clashing, grating, deafening. Over the top of it all rode the sound of the
horns calling out an alarum. Somewhere through it ran the
thread of a familiar roar. There was a mounted figure amidst
the advancing Red Scourge, clad in gilded armor, a crest of
crimson horsehair bobbing.

Lucius, alive. Not Eamonn.

"Eamonn!"

I couldn't hear my own voice in the din. I shook my head
in frustration. Another Valpetran charged across the portico
toward me. Realizing I still held the useless helmet, I flung
it in his face. When he staggered backward, I plunged the
point of my blade in a gap beneath his armpit.

A lot more of them attacked me then.

I don't know how many. I didn't count. Out of the corner
of my eye, I'd caught a flash of red-gold hair some distance
from the portico, backed up against the ledge surrounding
the baths. I fought my way toward him. No shield; no shield
line. No comrades in arms to worry about. I fought in the
Cassiline style. They weren't men anymore, just obstacles to
surmount. Shields to dodge, blades to parry, bits of moving
armor to pierce. I didn't care about killing them, I only
wanted to get past them. Somewhere behind me, I could
hear a voice cursing steadily in a language that sounded like
Hellene, but wasn't.

I saw Eamonn go down, and I cursed, too.

It was the helmet, the damned lack of a helmet. A big
Valpetran with a thrusting spear gave him a glancing blow
to the head and his knees began to sag. A helmet would
have turned it. I'd taken several. Small wonder my ears were
ringing.

"Eamonn!" I shouted, and he turned his head. Blood was

spilling down one side of his neck. Our eyes met and he pitched forward. The Valpetran grinned and raised his spear for the finishing thrust.

Whispering a prayer to Blessed Elua, I ran for the edge of the portico and leapt. His arms began to descend. There was no time to strike a blow. I simply lowered my head and ran into him. He dropped his spear as the impact sent us both sprawling. I landed atop him, losing my sword in the process.

There were more horns blowing, a confusion of horns. There were hoofbeats on the cobblestones. Someone was shouting an order to surrender. It didn't sound like Lucius or Gallus Tadius. The Valpetran soldier beneath me glared and heaved, nearly throwing me off him. I fumbled for the dagger in my boot-sheath and planted it between his eyes, sinking it to the hilt. His glare faded, eyes fixed and open.

A heavy weight fell across my back

"Surrender arms!" the voice shouted.

For the first time, I panicked, flailing out from beneath the weight. A body. Finding my sword, I scrambled to my feet, gripping the hilt in both hands and breathing hard, terrified of what I might see.

D'Angeline banners and Tiberian soldiers massing on the outskirts of the battle.

Silvanus the Younger calling on his men to surrender.

Lucius making his way through the throng, accompanied by three guardsmen.

Canis at my feet, clutching the haft of a javelin, his lips drawn back with pain.

And Domenico Martelli, the Duke of Valpetra, seated astride a black horse. His men, Silvanus' men, had drawn back to give him a wide berth. Lucius was yet to reach us. We might have been alone on the street. Although we were strangers to one another, a strange sense of intimacy settled between us. He gazed down at me, his fleshy, rain-streaked face impassive. One hand ended in a bandaged stump. In the other, he held a javelin, cocked and ready to throw.

"I've been looking for you, D'Angeline," he said conversationally. "I blame you for all of this. I'm not sure why, but I do."

I nodded. "I carry a lot of guilt, my lord."

"Valpetra!" Lucius' voice; Gallus' voice, raised in an ear-splitting roar, carrying over the mass of soldiers. "It's over! Your condottiere has surrendered! *Drop your weapon*!"

"Ready to die?" Domenico Martelli asked me, ignoring him.

"Not really," I said honestly.

Lucius shouted an order, and a trio of crossbows sang out over the crowd. Martelli jerked hard as one bolt struck home, jutting from his left shoulder. The other two missed. Lucius shouted again. The guardsmen struggled to reload, but it was a slow process. At my feet, I could hear Canis moving feebly. Martelli gathered himself, cocking his right arm and setting his javelin, aiming its point at my heart. Now, at last, I wished I had my shield.

"Well," said the Duke of Valpetra. "Ready or not."

I bowed to him in the Cassiline manner. I wished there was sunlight to cast a shadow, I wished I'd thought to remove my helmet so I could hear better, I wished my ears would stop ringing. I closed my eyes and listened, shutting out the din and clamor. Hard, harder than I'd ever listened during one of Phèdre's games. All the world narrowed to this moment. With my eyes closed, I stepped outside myself and concentrated on this Duke, this stranger, closer to me in this moment than any lover had ever been.

And I heard an indrawn breath, softer than a lover's gasp.

I didn't wait for the exhale. By the time he threw, it would be too late. I straightened, sweeping my vambraced forearms before me, my eyelids flying open. All around me was knife-edged brightness. The jolt of the javelin's impact against the outer vambrace struck me to the bone, my arms aching at it. Everything ached. For the space of a heartbeat, I wasn't sure if I was alive or dead. Then I heard the javelin clatter harmlessly to the cobblestones and the crossbows sang once more.

This time they were closer. No one missed.

Bristling like a pincushion, Domenico Martelli, the Duke of Valpetra, slumped sideways and fell off his horse. He landed with a dull thud and lay without moving.

"You alive, Montrève?" Lucius called.

"Yes," I called back. "I think so."

"Good."

They were surrendering, all of them; laying down their arms and surrendering. I supposed I was glad. If Eamonn was alive, I would be. I made my way to his side. He was slouched against the ledge, one hand clamped to his head. Blood trickled down his neck and leaked between his fingers.

"Are you—?" I asked anxiously.

"I'll live." He gestured with his chin, then winced. "Look to him."

Canis.

He was still alive when I returned, though barely. The javelin had pierced him clean through, the bloody point exiting from his chest. Like me, he wore only a leather jerkin. He was curled on his side, his hands clasped loosely around the head of the shaft. I knelt beside him, understanding what he'd done. Valpetra had cast two javelins, and the first when my back was turned. Canis had taken the death-blow meant for me.

"Why did you do it?" I asked softly.

There was a froth of blood on his lips, but his brown eyes were clear, filled with a mixture of pain and rue. Canis the Cynic; the cheerful philosopher-beggar; Canis the deaf-mute; Canis the Unseen Guildsman; Canis the soldier. All along, he had been there. I had a thousand questions and he held a thousand answers, but time to speak only one. I had to bend low to hear his faint voice.

"Your mother sends her love," he whispered.

There was no more. With a quiet, bloodstained smile, Canis died.

The siege was over.

SIXTY-THREE

IN THE DAYS that followed, I pieced together all the varying accounts to make sense of what had transpired. Gallus Tadius' plan had worked to a point. Bent on looting and slaughter, most of Valpetra's men *had* scattered throughout the city, falling prey to traps and ambush. A good many had surrendered of their own will. I daresay the madness that had befallen everyone when the *mundus manes* was uncovered had begun to disperse after Gallus Tadius sent the floodwaters to hell.

Not Valpetra's.

He'd held a core of his men together and gone hunting me, consumed with the notion of revenge. When Lucius realized it, he'd rallied the Red Scourge in pursuit, turning the hunted into hunters. The sentries atop the walls had spotted the approaching army of D'Angeline and Tiberian forces, and their appearance in the city had tipped the balance; Silvanus the Younger had cut his losses and surrendered.

And Canis . . .

No one knew for sure. Cutpurse squadron had sustained heavy losses, and none of his fellows remembered seeing him after their initial retreat. They'd assumed him dead. I could only guess that he'd deserted. Like Valpetra, he'd gone looking for me.

Your mother sends her love.

I knelt beside his body for a long time, there on the cobbled streets of Lucca, rain dripping from my helmet. I was too tired to know what I felt, other than pain. All around me, there were men—cheering and groaning, sullen, wounded, dying. I would like, I thought, to spend a good deal more time in the company of women.

More hoofbeats; an uncertain voice. "Your highness?"

I pried myself to my feet, aching in every part, and gazed upward. "Messire LeClerc."

Once again, I was filthy and bedraggled in the presence of the D'Angeline ambassadress' guardsmen; clad in motley armor, splashed with mud and gore. This time, there was no hint of amusement in their regard. Quentin LeClerc dismounted and his men followed suit. There in the filthy street, they all dropped to one knee.

"Your highness," he repeated, bowing his head. "We came in all haste."

"Thank you." There were lines of Tiberian faces behind the kneeling D'Angelines, alert and attentive. And clean. They all looked so clean. I took off my helmet and rubbed my face with a fold of my sodden cloak. "Mayhap . . . mayhap you could help with the wounded."

Quentin LeClerc stood. "Of course, your highness."

"Call me Imriel," I said wearily.

He began to give orders, calm and efficient, and they spread through the streets, helping sort the dead from the wounded, giving what comfort they might to the latter. Atop the roofs and the walls, the sentries were sounding the all-clear, and Luccan citizens were beginning to emerge, wailing or rejoicing at the fate of their loved ones. Lucius was busy organizing the surrender of Silvanus' men, who were being gathered from all quarters of the city and herded into the empty fabric warehouse where Barbarus squadron would have made its second stand. There was a great stack of weapons piling up on the portico.

I stooped and gathered Canis' body in my arms, carrying him over to the ledge where Eamonn was waiting. He was on his feet, weaving a little, the rain making pink rivulets through the blood seeping along his neck. I laid Canis down gently, then eased the bloody length of the javelin from his chest and set it aside. We both gazed at him. He looked peaceful in death.

"So," Eamonn said. "Who was he?"

"I don't know," I said. "My mother sent him."

"Phèdre?"

"No." I shook my head. "My mother." I touched his arm. "Come on, Captain Barbarus. Let's get you patched."

Eamonn nodded at a dead Valpetran. "Your dagger."

The hilt jutted forth between the man's eyes. A part of me was tempted to leave it. I didn't want to remember killing him with it. But Joscelin had given them to me when I'd turned fifteen. It was after the winter when I'd first kept Elua's vigil on the Longest Night with him. I remembered the carriage ride home, shivering and delirious, when I'd told him I wanted to be like him.

Ah, love, he'd said. *Don't wish for that.*

I had, though.

I put one foot on the Valpetran's breastplate, grabbed the hilt, and yanked. It came out hard; I'd planted it with a good deal of force. There was a cracking sound and it came free. The corpse's helmeted skull bounced on the cobblestones. I thought about that vast pit opening beneath the city, the obsidian curtains of water spilling downward, downward, and wondered if the Valpetran's spirit was wandering a flooded Caerdicci hell, all its five rivers swollen and raging.

I wondered how many others I'd sent there.

I didn't know.

"Imri," Eamonn said.

I laughed, or at least I made a sound that resembled a laugh. "Is three a lot, Eamonn? I wanted to ask you before. Because I didn't think it was, but you made it sound like it was. And now I don't know how many. Four, anyway."

"I owe you my life," he said simply.

It was enough; it had to be enough, because if it wasn't, there was nothing else. Standing in the cold, drizzling rain, I met his steady grey-green gaze and forced myself to smile. "Do you suppose Brigitta will think better of D'Angelines because of it?"

Eamonn managed a grin. "No."

In the baths, where most of Barbarus still loitered, we were greeted as heroes; or at least Eamonn was. Me they regarded with a renewed wariness—whether it was because of Canis, or Valpetra, or LeClerc and his men kneeling in the street to me, I couldn't say—but they fell over themselves to pound Eamonn's shoulders, his back. He bore it with stoic good humor, looking a little green and sick. Matius, who was neat-handed, bound his bleeding head with a length of clean bandage.

Outside, we heard a chant begin.

"Gal-lus! Gal-lus!"

Eamonn caught my eye. "We should be there."

I nodded. "Tell them."

He rose. "Listen, lads!" he called, and they fell silent. "Barbarus squadron will pay homage to the man who led us to victory. When the time comes, follow my lead, eh?"

They agreed, chanting Gallus Tadius' name with cheerful

oblivion. We spilled onto the portico. The streets were still thronged, though mostly with the living and victorious now. Lucius was in the thick of it, soldiers surging around him, the red horsehair crest bobbing.

"Gal-lus! Gal-lus!"

I leaned against a column. Somehow, amidst the turmoil, Lucius glanced toward me. Beneath the shadow of his gilded helmet, I saw his wide mouth quirk in a smile. I thought about his kiss and smiled in reply.

"Lucca!" he called, his voice clear and carrying; his voice, *Lucius'* voice, Master Piero's prize student, capable of arguing black into white and night into day. "Know this! In your hour of need, Gallus Tadius served you well. He taught you, he trained you, and he laid his plans. He loved Lucca so well, he returned from the underworld to serve it; he loved Lucca so well, he returned to the underworld to save it! It is only thusly that the flood was dispelled, and Gallus Tadius banished. And I have done my best to lead you in accordance with his wishes."

There were cheers, but there was a note of bewilderment amidst them.

Lucius raised his hand. "And for that, I, Lucius Tadius da Lucca, honor the spirit of my great-grandfather, and give thanks for your courage!"

A confused silence settled.

Eamonn drew a deep breath, his broad chest swelling, and loosed his booming voice. "Lu-cius! Lu-cius! Lu-cius!"

To their credit, Barbarus squadron scarce hesitated. For the space of a heartbeat, my voice was the only one echoing Eamonn's; and then the others arose. As though we had set spark to tinder, it spread, until his name resonated through-out the city.

"Lu-cius! Lu-cius!"

There were tears on Lucius' face, which was etched with lines I suspected would never be gone; not wholly. He had worn the mask of Gallus Tadius too long. I shouted for him, rejoiced for him, grieved for him; for myself, for Helena, for Gilot, for Lucca's dead and all those things that might have been had intrigue and warfare and humanity's incalculable cruelty not intervened.

He belonged to Lucca now.

As I belonged to Terre d'Ange.

After the cheering ran its course, Lucius met with Quentin LeClerc and Marcus Cornelius, the commander of the Tiberian legion. It was a smaller force than I'd reckoned; only seven hundred strong, plus a delegation of thirty mounted D'Angelines. Tiberium no longer fields a mighty army as it did in the days of empire. I wondered what they would have done if they hadn't found the city in chaos, Valpetra's men already dispersed. Lucius must have wondered, too, for he asked them.

Marcus Cornelius shrugged. He was a stolid veteran in his late forties, with plain, pragmatic features. "The Senate reckoned Valpetra would back down."

I didn't think he would have, but I supposed it didn't matter now. The Duke of Valpetra was dead. His body lay where it had fallen, untouched. By all accounts, Silvanus and his men were eager to quit the city and put the debacle of the siege behind them. Arms, armor, horses; all their goods would be forfeited.

"You mean to simply let them go?" I asked.

"What would you have us do?" Lucius asked reasonably. "Feed and shelter them? No, they'll go, and they'll take their dead with them."

The Tiberian commander agreed to lend his company to the task of overseeing the exodus, giving the exhausted men of the Red Scourge a chance to rest, and Lucius dismissed us with a gracious word of thanks. Many left; others stayed, Eamonn and I among them, watching as the long file of soldiers began winding their way out of the city, the living carrying the dead, heads bowed beneath the cold drizzling rain, defeated and dispirited.

"Such a waste," I murmured.

"Aye." Eamonn shivered. The white bandage Matius had tied around his head was soaked through with bright crimson blood. "I think I'd like to lie down now."

Quentin LeClerc insisted on escorting us to the Tadeii villa. At my request, he'd already dispatched several of his men to assist Publius Tadius and the Lady Beatrice in restoring order to the estate. One of his men dismounted with a bow and proffered the reins of his mount. I watched the other surviving members of Barbarus squadron limping through the streets and shook my head.

"I'll walk."

Instead, Eamonn rode. It seemed fitting to me. He was our leader; Captain Barbarus. I walked beside his horse's head. A few of the men raised their hands in salute to him as we passed, weary and proud. All throughout the city, we saw the extent of the damage the flood had caused; debris and rubble, animal carcasses beginning to bloat.

Although dusk was only beginning to fall, the Tadeii villa was ablaze with lights, a welcome beacon. I felt the full extent of my exhaustion as I plodded toward it. My legs were leaden, the muscles of my arms aching with exertion. The courtyard had already been cleared, but the grounds were floodswept, the grass flattened, bushes uprooted. I peered toward the rise of high ground and found it empty.

"Is the Bastard safe?" I asked the D'Angeline guardsman who met us.

He blinked at me. "Your highness?"

"My horse," I said wearily. "The spotted one."

"Oh, the hellion!" He grinned. "Aye, your highness. In the stables. The straw's sodden, but the grain is dry."

"Good." I rubbed my eyes. "Good."

Quentin LeClerc spoke to me about plans to safeguard the villa and the city, the disposition of his men and the Tiberian company, plans for our swift return. I nodded, listening with half an ear, until he took pity on me.

"Rest, your highness," he said. "We'll speak on the morrow."

Inside the villa, the Lady Beatrice laughed and wept, covering her mouth with her hands, her eyes shining in the lamplight. She would have fallen upon us had I not begged off with an apology. She wore a gown of finespun wool, dyed a rich saffron hue, and I was acutely aware that Eamonn and I were besmirched from head to toe with things best left unmentioned.

"What . . ." she whispered. "What of my son? They said he lived."

"Your son." I drew myself up and bowed, formal and deliberate. I bowed once to her and once to Publius Tadius, silent in the background. "My lady, your son, Lucius Tadius da Lucca, is a hero today. I imagine he will be here presently."

"And Gallus Tadius?" Publius' voice was rough.

"Gone," I said.

True and not true.

His shadow would always be there, lurking behind Lucius' eyes, carved into his features. It would hang over the city he had conquered as a living man and defended as a dead one. It dwelled beneath the marble slab that covered the *mundus manes*, and in the scorched, stubbled fields outside the walls. It would live in the memories of ordinary men who had been transformed into the Red Scourge. I didn't think any of us would forget him.

I wouldn't.

Still, it was only a shadow.

The private baths were filled with murky floodwater, but the kitchen had been scoured and fires lit in the stoves. Lady Beatrice had ordered vats of water heated and a tin washtub dragged into the guest quarters. I let Eamonn have the first turn at it, while Beatrice found salve and hunted up clean linens to use for bandages. They had sent for a chirurgeon, but all of them were busy tending to more urgent needs. Afterward, the servants refilled the bath and I tied a fresh bandage around Eamonn's head. He ate a bit of black bread and hard cheese, drank a good deal of water, and went straightaway to bed.

Lady Beatrice had offered her attendants, but I'd declined them. Alone at last, I stripped with care. The woolen shirt and breeches I'd worn were stiff with dried blood, some of it mine. I was half afraid to see what lay beneath my clothing.

The washtub steamed invitingly, smelling faintly of roses. Someone had scattered a handful of dried petals in the water. It made me think of Lady Denise Fleurais' garden sanctuary, and I whispered a prayer of thanksgiving to Blessed Elua at finding myself alive. By the warm glow of a trio of oil lamps, I assessed the damage.

It could have been worse, much worse. The shallow slice on my left thigh was crusting over, and the triangular gouge on my upper right arm was narrow enough that it needn't be stitched. I'd taken a myriad of nicks and cuts during the fighting on the portico, but none that wouldn't heal on their own. Mostly, I was bruised.

There were massive constellations of bruises already blossoming beneath my skin, their hues indistinct in the lamplight. Except for the one on my right forearm where Valpetra's javelin had dented my vambrace, I couldn't even remember what had done it, whether they were inept blows I'd taken or impacts resulting from my own attacks.

It didn't matter. I was alive.

I eased my body into the washtub. Every wound, no matter how small, stung in protest. The gash on my thigh cracked open and bled, and the tub was so small that I had to sit with my knees drawn up tight. I didn't care. For a long moment, I rested the back of my head against the rim of the tub and simply sat there, luxuriating in the heat.

I sat there for a long time, until the water began to cool. Then I took up the ball of soap and scrubbed myself, thoroughly and methodically. My hands were stiff and aching from clutching weapons all day long, the knuckles swollen and split, battered against the shields and armor of my opponents. Although I'd washed them before tending to Eamonn, there was blood ingrained all around the beds of my nails. They looked like someone else's hands.

Someone good at killing.

When I had finished, I climbed dripping from the tub and dried myself on a clean towel, leaving blotches of fresh blood on the linen. I smeared salve on my wounds, bandaging the worst two, using my teeth to tie a knot around my right arm.

Somewhere in the villa, I heard the sound of Lucius' returning and his mother's glad cries, his father's voice filled with a new note of respect. I should go greet him, I thought, but I was too tired. No, let them have their moment. I was a guest in their household and I had fought for Lucca, but I had no place here, not really.

I wanted to go home.

I wanted it so fiercely, I ached with it. I wanted to walk into Phèdre's study and sit at her feet, leaning my head against her knee. I wanted to pour out my heart to her, while she stroked my hair and told me there was nothing inside me that I needed to fear, only shadows.

I wanted to be a child again.

Her child.

But I wasn't and I couldn't. And so I took myself to my lonely bed and lay awake for a long time, staring open-eyed into the darkness, thinking about Canis and Domenico Martelli, the Duke of Valpetra, my fellow soldiers who had died and the men I had killed, until sleep took me unaware, and I slept and dreamed of war.

SIXTY-FOUR

THREE DAYS LATER, we departed Lucca.

It took that long to get the city restored to some semblance of order. Marcus Cornelius' men loaned their aid unstintingly, helping clear away wreckage the flood had left, digging graves for the dead, posting a guard at the massive gap in the wall. There wasn't much to be done about the breach, not until the Masons' Guild could procure the vast quantity of materials needed to repair it. Between the breach and the short harvest, Lucca faced a hard winter.

Lucius spent long hours in council with the Tiberian commander, Gaetano Correggio and various Luccan aristocrats, the flamen dialis and his priests. They came to a settlement regarding aid from Tiberium in exchange for certain trade rights to be granted in the future.

They came to a settlement regarding Helena, too. The priest declared a mourning period of six months in order, after which she would undergo a ceremony to effect the dissolution of her unwanted marriage. In the spring, she would be free to wed Lucius.

I took no part in the discussions. At first, I spent my time worrying about Eamonn, who slept for almost a solid day, waking only briefly to eat. The chirurgeon who came at last to examine him peered at his eyes, slapped a poultice on his wound, and shrugged. Eamonn promptly went back to sleep, slept through the night, and woke in good spirits the following morning, declaring himself ravenous.

The embalmers came with Gilot's body in a casket, having completed the long process of preservation. They had kept him safe during the floods, for which I was grateful. He was given a place of honor in the Tadeii mausoleum while Quentin LeClerc made arrangements to procure a wagon to transport the casket. I meant to keep my word and bring Gilot home.

Canis was buried in the Luccan graveyard. I commissioned a stele from a stonecarver's shop to mark the site, although it would be a long time before it was finished. The carver had been a member of Stone squadron. He'd reckoned the name would prove lucky for him, and I suppose it had, since he had survived. I didn't tell him why I wanted the stele and he didn't ask. He promised on the honor of the Red Scourge to see it installed properly. We clasped hands on the deal.

I visited Canis' gravesite.

There wasn't much to see; only a mound of raw earth, one of over a hundred, each marked with a crude identifier. For Canis, it was the javelin that had killed him, thrust into the damp soil. I stood there for a long time, not knowing what to say. A priest had performed the rites for all of the dead, but I didn't even know what gods Canis had prayed to.

Your mother sends her love.

My mother, my beautiful, treacherous mother. Canis had been her dog, her faithful hound. And he'd been good at his job. I'd even been fond of him for a time. I smiled a little, remembering the bright-eyed beggar in his stinking barrel.

"Peace, my friend," I said, pouring out wine from a flask I'd brought. "May your journey bring you wisdom."

Since I didn't know his country or his gods, I prayed to mine. I prayed as I had in the embassy garden, and although I had only wine to offer, I conjured the scent of incense in my mind and offered prayers—for wisdom and for healing, for strength and pride, justice and mercy, and love.

Always, love.

On our final night, the Tadeii held a dinner in our honor. I'd tried to demur, but like Eamonn's wedding, the notion brought Lady Beatrice too much pleasure to deny her. It was good to see her happy. Alone among the wives and mothers and sisters of Lucca, she had regained a son during the siege, and war had brought peace to the Tadeii household.

It was a small gathering. The Correggii were the only other guests. But it would be the first time that Lucius and Helena had met since everything had happened, and he was nervous. We spoke of it beforehand in the salon of the guest quarters.

"I tried to . . ." He swallowed. "I tried to force her into my bed, didn't I?"

"Gallus did."

Lucius shot me a look. "Wearing my face. Do you think she'll forget it?"

"No," I said honestly. "But you were there, too, Lucius. You were there all along. When you knew Gallus would have let her die, you bade me look out for her. Helena knew it. When Gallus tried to throttle me, she begged me not to hurt *you*."

"Gallus Tadius," he mused. "There was good in him along with the bad. But when all's said and done, he wasn't all that different from Valpetra, was he?"

"Not really." I thought about it. "But he was ours. And he gave himself for Lucca."

"He did do that." Lucius sighed. "Ah, Montrève! There's a part of me wants to hide away in your entourage and flee back to Tiberium, back to Master Piero. Let him help me make sense of this all. Or even continue on to Terre d'Ange with you." He grinned at me, raising his satyr's brows. "I might do well there, don't you think?"

I laughed. "Oh, yes."

"Mayhap I'll visit." His smile turned wistful, fading. "So what do I do about Helena?"

"Treat her gently," I said, remembering the day I had called upon her and what I had felt. "Treat her with kindness and respect. Earn her trust. She deserves it, Lucius. You were friends once, and you've got six months to learn to be friends again. It's a good place to start."

He leaned forward, knotting his hands between his knees. The furrows that would never leave deepened on his brow. "What if she's with child?"

I gazed at him, at the shadow of Gallus Tadius. "Love the child."

"As simply as that?" he asked bitterly.

Kushiel's bronze wings stirred in my memory. "Yes."

Lucius held my gaze for a moment, then looked away. "You're a strange one, Imriel nó Montrève," he murmured. "Strange and beautiful and, I think, a little bit dangerous to know in your own peculiar way. I wish . . ." He shook his head.

"What?" I asked.

He looked back at me. "Oh, perhaps that my sister hadn't gotten to you first."

Fiercely and unexpectedly, I flushed a hot red to the roots of my hair.

Lucius gave a wry laugh. "One thing about Gallus Tadius, he was no fool. He saw things I didn't." He regarded me with rueful affection, then rose and extended his hand. "Come on. I imagine our guests are waiting."

By the time we arrived, they were all assembled in the dining room, reclining on couches. All of us exchanged formal greetings. Lucius bowed low over Helena's hand. Her fingers trembled in his grasp, but he whispered somewhat to her as he straightened, and I saw her expression soften. They would be all right, I thought. Both had been used cruelly by hard men in different ways, but both had survived. In time, they would be all right.

So we drank and dined and strove to make pleasant conversation, although it was hard to talk about anything but the siege. It was still too fresh in all our minds. If the evening could be counted a success, I reckon it was due to Eamonn. He overrode every awkward pause and silence with cheerful anecdotes, his sunny good nature on full display. He told stories of his childhood in Alba, and stories of his courtship of Brigitta that made everyone laugh. He even told stories of the siege that made it bearable. He charmed them all, men and women alike. I knew he was doing it a-purpose, and I loved him for it. As always, Prince Barbarus had more tact and shrewdness than anyone credited him.

I was glad, so glad, he was alive and well.

And I was glad when it was over.

We said our farewells in the atrium. Helena took both my hands in hers, and her fingers were warm and didn't tremble at all. She gazed at me without fear, her blue eyes wide and candid.

"Thank you," she said softly. "For what you did, and for what you said to me. I will always remember it."

I bowed. "Be well, my lady."

Her fingers tightened on mine. In Terre d'Ange, I would have given her the kiss of parting without hesitation. But this was Lucca, and she was Domenico Martelli's widow and Lucius' betrothed. I returned the pressure of her fingers, then let her go.

After the Correggii had departed, I found Lucius eyeing me oddly. "You didn't . . ."

I shook my head. "No."

He blew out his breath in a sigh. "Good."

On the morrow, there were more farewells to be said. Quentin LeClerc and a score of his men gathered in the villa's courtyard to escort us. They had procured a mule-drawn supply wagon, and Gilot's casket was loaded ceremoniously into it.

There wasn't much else. Eamonn and I had travelled light, expecting to spend no more than a few days in Lucca. After enduring weeks of the siege, most of our clothing wasn't fit to salvage. I was clad in what would have been my wedding finery, a velvet jacket and breeches in Courcel blue, trimmed with silver; Eamonn had been reduced to rough-spun woolens.

We bade farewell to Publius Tadius and Lady Beatrice in the villa. He shook our hands solemnly and thanked us for our service to Lucca and the Tadeïi. She enfolded us both in a warm, heartfelt embrace.

"You be good to that wild girl of yours," she said to Eamonn, rising on tiptoe to take his face in her plump hands. "Remember your vows."

"I will, my lady," he promised.

Lucius walked into the courtyard with us. LeClerc and his men were waiting, holding our mounts. The Bastard was restive and stamping, his hooves ringing on the paving-stones, snorting plumes of frost. It was a bright, crisp day, with only a few wispy clouds in the blue sky. Lucius stood beside the wagon and laid his hand on Gilot's casket.

"Lucca owes him a debt," he murmured. "I won't forget."

I nodded. "Thank you."

He turned to Eamonn, smiling slightly. "Prince Barbarus."

Eamonn grinned. "Lucius Tadius."

They clasped one another's hands, strong grips vying to make the other wince. Neither did. They parted with a laugh, and Lucius turned to me. In the clear daylight, his face was as open as a book.

"Good-bye, Montrève."

I hugged him, hard and fierce, feeling him stiffen, then relax and return my embrace. I held him tight enough that I could feel his heart beating in his breast, strong and steady. Turning my head, I kissed his cheek. "Good-bye, Lucius."

Thus we took our leave.

The Bastard took all my attention, sidling and chomping at the bit. It wasn't until we reached the gate onto the Tadeii grounds that I had him under control. I turned back in the saddle. Lucius was still standing in the courtyard. I raised my hand, and he did the same. And then we entered the street, and I lost sight of him.

We passed swiftly through Lucca. Despite the damage, it was bustling and lively. It seemed strange to see it thus. I'd known it only as a city under siege. Now, only the ruined bell-tower stood as a stark reminder, a hollow shell pointing toward the heavens, its scorched walls hinting at what lay beneath it.

An earthen pit.

A portal to hell.

At the gatehouse, we found the portcullis raised, the

drawbridge lowered. The sentries on duty saluted as we swept through. "Captain Barbarus!" one of them called, and Eamonn waved in acknowledgment. He'd ventured into the city early yesterday to bid farewell to all the surviving members of Barbarus squadron he could locate. I felt a twinge of guilt at having failed to do the same, but only a twinge. We had been brothers in arms, and strangers out of them. The moment had already passed.

Our mounts' hooves clattered over the drawbridge, the wheels of the wagon creaking. There was a whiff of stagnant water from the moat, and then we were past and through, and the walls of Lucca were behind us.

I drew a deep breath, tasting freedom.

The rest of LeClerc's men were waiting on the outskirts of the Tiberian encampment, and fell in alongside us as we passed. Marcus Cornelius and his company would remain in the city for a few weeks until Lucca could be adequately secured. Although the speed of Tiberian foot-soldiers was still legendary, we could travel quicker without them.

We rode alongside the fire-razed, flood-sodden fields, the twisted stumps of the ancient olive grove visible in the distance. One of the guards lifted his voice in song; a L'Agnacite hymn to Anael, who taught us husbandry and to be good stewards of the land. Several other clear D'Angeline voices joined in, and I felt tears sting my eyes at the beauty of it.

"Pretty," Eamonn commented.

"Yes." It made me yearn for home. I gazed at Gilot's casket, jolting along in the wagon, thinking how he'd never really wanted to leave Terre d'Ange. "It is."

Beyond the fields, the road began to wind into the mountains. I called out to Quentin LeClerc before we entered the gorge. Our company halted, and I turned for a last look at Lucca.

It looked peaceful and pleasant, save for the stark fields surrounding it. None of the damage was visible, not even the crumbling gap on the far side of the city. The red-tiled buildings were warm and beckoning, the mighty oaks rose up from the vast wall, spreading their crowns, a few russet leaves clinging to the branches. No unwitting traveller could guess what had transpired there.

I sat in the saddle and remembered it all. The smoke rising from the bell-tower, the *mundus manes*. The cracked death-mask, and Gallus Tadius. Arrows singing from the trees, blood spouting from the stump of Valpetra's wrist. Gilot. Nights of patrol, the firestorm, and Deccus Fulvius atop the wall.

Rain, and endless drilling.

Helena.

The breaking dams, the flood. The cracked mask and the maelstrom, the bottomless pit sheeting with obsidian water.

The battle, and Valpetra.

Canis.

The defeated living carrying their dead; the victorious living burying theirs. A hundred graves covered with raw earth.

Remember this.

No one spoke. After a time, Eamonn leaned over and touched my shoulder. I looked into his grey-green eyes, knowing he shared the same memories. There were others there, too. A wedding celebrated in joy, a bittersweet farewell.

"Are you ready?" he asked. "I've got a wife to find."

"I'm ready."

I turned the Bastard, who snorted and surged forward. Quentin LeClerc gave the order and our company continued, passing beyond the first curve of the gorge. Gilot's wagon

SIXTY-FIVE

I T WAS A SWIFT and uneventful journey.

We rode hard, pushing the horses and the tireless mules, pausing only long enough to catch a few hours of sleep at night in makeshift camps. Quentin LeClerc apologized for the hardship. Eamonn and I laughed. Although we'd been sleeping softer in Lucca, we'd been living harder. We were used to going short of sleep.

At night, we talked about the battle. I found out he'd lagged behind when Valpetra's men charged us, trying to safeguard his "hares'" flight.

"I got caught," he said ruefully. "Too slow." He'd seen me trying to reach him, there at the end. He laughed at the memory of it in a way that only Eamonn could. "Twirling around like a high-priced whore on an acrobat's stage," he said, grinning. "Gallus Tadius would have whalloped you a good one."

I rubbed my fading bruises. "I know."

We talked about Canis and my mother, though not much. Eamonn wanted to speculate; I didn't. The nearer we drew to Tiberium, the more I felt the shadow of the Unseen Guild hanging over me. I didn't want it to touch him. Being Eamonn, he didn't press.

We spoke of Lucius and the tremendous reserve of courage he'd found within himself to carry through with his charade of Gallus' plan, adapting it as circumstance dictated.

"He was good," Eamonn marveled. "So good! I tell you, if I ever have to fight again, I hope it's under someone half as good. If he hadn't sent for you that night, I'd never known aught was amiss." He eyed me curiously. "What did you say to him, anyway?"

"Not much." I smiled. "But I got him to sleep."

Eamonn snorted. Being D'Angeline, I let him wonder.

We spoke of friendship and loyalty. I'd come to understand a good deal more about friendship during my time in Tiberium; and Lucca, too. It required a standard of honesty and openness I'd shunned in my dealings with everyone but Eamonn. I was resolved to do better to meet it henceforth; and to demand it in turn, too.

We spoke of the Duke of Valpetra, and the mortal demons of avarice, ambition, and vengeance that may possess men, as destructive as any supernatural force. We spoke, in hushed Eiran, of Bernadette de Trevalion and the devastating madness that lay seeking to wreak retribution for past sins in innocent blood, passing down hatred from generation to generation. And when we had done speaking of the past, we spoke of the future.

"Have you decided what you'll do about it?" Eamonn asked. "Will you accuse her?"

"No," I said slowly. "No, I think not."

"It's a hard thing, choosing to be the one to put an end to a blood feud." He picked up his whetstone. "Worth doing, though. So you'll wed Dorelei mab Breidaia, then?"

"In the late spring." I sat with my arms wrapped around my knees, gazing at the campfire and trying to remember what she looked like. Dark eyes, Cruithne eyes. Sidonie's face surfaced in my memory. I pushed it away. "Will you come?"

"Mayhap." Eamonn ran the whetstone over his sword, head bowed and intent. His coppery hair spilled over the bandage that still bound his wound, glinting in the firelight. "It depends."

"On Brigitta?" I asked.

He nodded. "She may be awaiting me in Tiberium, or she may already be on her way to Skaldia. I don't know. But I *will* find her. And if I can come, I will."

I lay back on my bedroll, folding my arms beneath my head. "How did you come to conceive this great love?"

In truth, there wasn't much to tell; or at least little I didn't know. He'd known her for months before I arrived in Tiberium and hadn't bothered to court her. It had begun as a whim, spun out of idle intrigue after the day when they'd argued over Waldemar Selig in one of Master Piero's classes. But once it had begun, he found himself well and truly hooked. He began each day yearning to see her, ended each day hating to part from her. While I had been immersed in my affair with Claudia, keeping my secrets, they had spent endless hours together.

"We're a lot alike," he said.

I thought about Brigitta's scowl and ill-temper. "You're nothing alike, Eamonn."

He shot me an unreadable glance. "You don't know her, Imri. Not really."

"So tell me," I said.

The litany of Brigitta's praises was a lengthy one. He loved her fearlessness, her fierce pride, her determined independence. He saw through all the prickly defenses in which she cloaked her true nature, which shone forth to his eyes like a bright flame. She made him want to be a better man. Together, the two of them formed a greater whole.

I listened to his endless litany, to the rapt tone of his voice. And I listened to the hidden meaning, too. There were sides to Eamonn I didn't know; the secret self that lay beneath his cheerful exterior. Although we were as close as brothers and I had risked my life to save his, Brigitta had touched him in a way I never could. It lay beyond friendship.

I wondered what it was like.

Watching the stars, I tried to imagine it. What would it be like to love a woman so? I knew what it was to *want*. I'd wanted Claudia so badly it was like a fever under my skin. And there were other desires, too; deeper and darker than sheer carnal yearning. I had not forgotten Valerian House. I had known tenderness, too; the healing gift of Emmeline of Balm House. I had even yearned to share it with Helena Correggio. And I knew the compulsive allure of infatuation, ill-conceived and dangerous, complete with attendant jealousy, in the form of my cool and haughty royal cousin, Sidonie.

But love . . .

There was Alais, of course. The thought of her made me smile. She was the one person in my life I loved with a pure and uncomplicated simplicity. Even during her irritable adolescence, her spirit brought me joy. But that was different. There was no desire there, no hidden undercurrent.

I couldn't imagine all of those things combined into one woman.

And if they could be, it wasn't Dorelei mab Breidaia.

Well and so, I thought. I have made my choice, and I should be content that I'm alive to see it through. And so I listened to Eamonn dream aloud about his love, pushing away my envy and knowing that I would never feel as he did. Perhaps it was just as well. There were women in my life who cast long shadows.

My mother, wrapped in a tissue of myth and lies.

Phèdre.

Better to love a man, mayhap. Half-drowsing, I thought about Lucius' kiss and the unexpected desire it had evoked. I was glad he'd done it. It pitted a spark of brightness against the black tide of horror that was Daršanga. And I had come to love him.

You will find it and lose it, again and again.

Then I thought of Claudia Fulvia in her bedchamber ablaze with candlelight, kneeling on the bed and gazing at me over her shoulder, her heavy breasts swaying. And I knew it wasn't the same. I wanted *that*. I wanted carnal desire so intense it cleaved my tongue to the roof of my mouth, opened a pit beneath my feet. But I wanted aching tenderness and purity, too.

I wanted it all.

The dark mirror and the bright.

Laughing softly at myself, I drifted into sleep with Eamonn's voice still droning musically above me. I slept, and for the first time since the siege, dreamed of somewhat other than blood and war.

On the morrow, we reached Tiberium

I had first entered the city as Imriel nó Montrève, impoverished gentleman scholar. This time, I entered it as Imriel de la Courcel, Prince of Terre d'Ange. There was no point in trying to hide it. All of Tiberium knew that a company had been dispatched to Lucca at the behest of the D'Angeline ambassadress. I'd learned from Quentin LeClerc that the decision had been made with unprecedented speed. The princeps had made his will explicit; the Senate had voted unanimously to endorse it. The consul of the citizen assembly had lodged a protest, and withdrawn it within a day.

So we entered with fanfare, and the people of Tiberium gawked at our company. A few of the bolder ones shouted out for news. One of LeClerc's men—Romuald, who'd warned me about the dam—called back the news of victory in Lucca.

There were cheers then. And the Tiberian citizens stared at Eamonn and me, nudging one another. They gazed with open curiosity at Gilot's casket, carried in the open cart. It was very fine, made of polished walnut and draped with a banner bearing the lily-and-stars insignia of Blessed Elua and his Companions.

"Who died?" someone called.

"A hero!" I raised my voice. "A hero of Terre d'Ange."

Beside me, Eamonn nodded.

We made our way tò the embassy. A crowd followed us, many of them reaching out to touch the hem of Gilot's banner as the cart passed them. Tiberians are very fond of dead heroes, even D'Angeline ones. I clung to the memory of Gilot staring gape-mouthed around him on the quai in Ostia, and blinked back tears. The Bastard pranced and stomped, glaring around him with white-ringed eyes, forcing the onlookers to keep a wary distance.

At the embassy gates, the guards turned them back and we passed into relative quietness. Lady Denise Fleurais was awaiting us in the courtyard. Since it was a formal occasion, she bowed low in greeting.

"Your highness," she murmured. "Prince Eamonn. Be welcome."

We were made welcome, extravagantly welcome. Although the Lady Denise, with her shrewd diplomat's instinct, took care not to overwhelm us, the sudden immersion in luxury made for a stark contrast with the lives we'd been leading. Every amenity of the embassy was laid at our disposal. Our mounts were whisked away to the stables; Gilot's casket was carried with careful honor into a stateroom where it would reside until returning home.

The palazzo's private baths were cleared for our usage. Barbers and masseurs were sent to attend us in the unctuarium. While we soaked and luxuriated, Lady Denise's couturier measured our discarded clothing and made hurried alterations to near-finished garments intended for other clients. A leather-worker undertook to replace the cracked heels and worn soles of our boots. By the evening, we had been scoured and scrubbed, oiled and rubbed and combed, and in Eamonn's case, shaved. We were clad in clean, unworn attire, the fabric soft against our skin. Our newly resoled boots shone with polishing.

It felt good.

And it felt strange.

I sat down at Denise Fleurais' table in the small salon where we had dined before. The table was draped in white linen so pure it was dazzling in the candlelight. All the accoutrements on the table gleamed with polishing. I rested my fingertips on the edge of the table, feeling the fine weave of the cloth, and gazed quizzically at the backs of my hands. They were clean and familiar again. My hands, well-shaped and sinewy. The knuckles were no longer swollen, and only a few deep nicks remained. The squarish nails had been trimmed and buffed. I'd once heard Phèdre remark in an unguarded moment that I had my mother's hands.

I turned them over. They were still callused, a ridge of thick skin along the base of my fingers. I stared at the whorls inscribed there.

"Are you all right?" Denise Fleurais asked gently.

"Yes." I hid my hands beneath the table. "I'm fine."

"Good," Eamonn remarked. "I'm famished."

There was an abundance of food. I hadn't reckoned myself as famished as Eamonn, but as soon as the soup course arrived, I found my appetite. For what seemed like the better part of an hour, we ate our way steadily through course after course—sorrel soup, fish in a galantine sauce, goose stuffed with dates and almonds, all washed down with glass upon glass of good Namarrese wine. By the time we finished with custard tarts in a flaky pastry, my belly was groaning.

Lady Denise watched us with amused indulgence. Although she had no children of her own, she was familiar with the appetites of young men. Picking at her own plate, she drew the story of the siege from us. Eamonn told most of it, in between chewing vigorously and swallowing enormous bites of food.

When it came to the *mundus manes* and Gallus Tadius, her expression turned somber. She didn't question it, though; not even the portal opening. I supposed she had seen things in Menekhet that had inured her to doubt. A Drujani bone-priest, for instance.

"I'm sorry," she said when Eamonn had done. "If I had known . . ."

I wiped my mouth with an immaculately clean linen napkin. "How did you know, my lady? Quentin LeClerc said there was a message."

"Yes." She drew a much-folded scrap of vellum from a purse at her girdle and handed it to me. "This."

I unfolded it. The parchment had been used before and scraped clean. It was thin and a little greasy. It bore only a few words written in Caerdicci, the ink blurred and difficult to read by candlelight. *Lucca is under attack.* I fingered the ragged edges. "Who brought it?"

She shook her head. "He didn't give a name. The guard at the gate said he looked like a peasant. He took the message and turned him away."

I raised my brows. "And yet you believed."

"I didn't dare do otherwise. Better to believe in error and be made a fool than risk the alternative." Denise Fleurais smiled briefly. "The Queen would have my head if I'd let harm come to you when I could have averted it, and I daresay I'd rather answer to her than Phèdre." Her expression turned somber again. "I thought a small delegation would suffice, since Lucca's attackers would have no reason to quarrel with Terre d'Ange. I was wrong."

"You couldn't have known. Obviously, whoever sent this had no idea the Duke of Valpetra wanted vengeance on me. I didn't know it myself." I ran the ball of my thumb over the parchment, wondering if it contained a hidden message. I gave her what I hoped was a disarming smile. "May I keep this?"

"Yes, of course."

There was no hesitation, no trace of guile. I tucked the scrap away. "Thank you, my lady. For this and for securing Tiberium's aid. You must have been most persuasive."

"Ah, well." With a self-deprecating gesture, Lady Denise spread her hands. "Queen Ysandre may be displeased with me after all once she learns what I had to promise the princeps. It will cost dearly. But the matter seemed urgent, and Deccus Fulvius was most helpful in securing the Senate's support."

"He's a good man," Eamonn offered.

She nodded. "Yes, he is. He has a message for you, too, Prince Eamonn; or at least his wife does." A hint of amusement returned to her voice. "From a young Skaldi woman?

It seems she wished it held in safekeeping and out of D'Angeline hands."

"Brigitta!" His face kindled, then fell. "She's gone, then."

"Is there word from Terre d'Ange?" I asked.

"Not current, no." She turned to me, sympathy in her gaze. "There are two letters that arrived while you were gone, but they would have been sent some weeks ago. I'll have the chamberlain bring them to you in your chamber. There hasn't been time since the news from Lucca arrived."

I remembered the letter I'd written there. "Was my missive sent?"

"Yes." She was quiet for a moment. "Prince Imriel, I dared not send word until I knew you were well. I will send it on the morrow, if you wish, but I suspect you will be your own best message. There is a ship standing by at Ostia, ready to transport you."

Ah, Elua! I'd nearly forgotten. They must be going mad there, wondering if I was dead or alive. I should leave; tonight, tomorrow at the latest. Already, it was growing late in the season to make the passage. But there were a few things I needed to do ere I left Tiberium. I rubbed my face with the heels of my hands and sighed.

"Give me a day," I said.

Lady Denise inclined her head. "Of course."

SIXTY-SIX

A S MATTERS TRANSPIRED, I couldn't have departed on the morrow. By dawn, there was a summons awaiting us. The princeps of Tiberium had received word of our return, and we were bidden to an audience with him.

"I should have anticipated this," Lady Denise apologized. "You may refuse, of course, but . . . it would be better if you don't."

"We'll go," I said. Eamonn, not bothering to hide his impatience, grumbled reluctant agreement.

A squadron of the princeps' personal guard arrived to escort us. As a sign of honor, we were allowed to ride. They fell into formation around us, clad in shining breastplates, their white cloaks with the purple border swinging briskly about their bare legs as they marched. I wondered if they felt the chill. I had no idea what to expect of the princeps, Titus Maximius. In my time as a scholar in the city, I knew him only as a distant figure of derision among the University students, who had little respect for the office he held, diminished as it was from its long-ago glory. I'd never expected to meet him in person.

Like the Temple of Asclepius, the royal palace was located on an island in the Tiber River, though it was closer to shore and joined by an elegant bridge. Our escort marched us across it. We dismounted in the courtyard and were conducted inside.

Here, the vestiges of Tiberium's splendor remained on display. We were led into the throne room, which sported a polished floor of pink marble, high ceilings, and a border of gilded friezes. There was a throne, too: an ornate affair of gilded wood crusted with jewels, a purple cushion on the seat. It was empty.

"Dreadful, isn't it?" A man emerged from behind the throne. He was some thirty years of age, with bad skin and a prominent bulge to his skinny throat. In one hand, he held a scroll; the other was extended in greeting. "Well met, Prince Imriel de la Courcel."

I clasped it unthinking. "Well met, messire." Even as I said the words, I realized he wore a simple diadem, a purple ribbon tied around thinning brown hair. I released his hand and bowed deeply, mindful of Court protocol. "Forgive me, your highness."

"Oh, call me Titus," he said. "Please."

I straightened and found him smiling. "Imriel."

"Imriel." The princeps of Tiberium turned to Eamonn. His gaze rested on the gold torc around his neck, oddly wistful. "And you must be Prince Eamonn mac Grainne of the Dalriada, from the far reaches of Alba. I've just been reading about it."

"I am." Eamonn bowed.

Titus Maximius sighed. "Come and take a cup of wine with me, won't you?"

We spent an hour with him, drinking and talking. He wanted to hear of our adventures, here in the city and in Lucca. To my surprise, I found I both liked and pitied him.

The princeps had led a sheltered, protected life. He yearned for more, more than his role would ever allot him.

"I wanted to go, you know," he said sadly. "To Lucca. I wanted to lead the army myself. But the Senate refused to allow it."

Eamonn coughed. I daresay he thought it was the right decision.

"Terre d'Ange is grateful beyond telling for Tiberium's aid in this matter," I said diplomatically. "To risk yourself in such a manner would have been far too much to ask."

"That's what *they* said." Titus Maximius snorted. "You needn't be grateful. I would have done it for the sport. For the glory. And unless your ambassadress is a liar, and I am assured she is not, your queen will pay dearly for our assistance. After all, it was a prince's ransom of sorts."

"Lady Denise's word is Queen Ysandre's bond," I assured him.

"That's good." He drummed his fingers restlessly on the arm of a chair. I noticed his nails were bitten to the quick. "It was my wife's idea, you know. She's very clever."

I met his gaze. Although his pale blue eyes were a trifle watery, it was frank and ingenuous. I wondered if his wife was a member of the Unseen Guild. If she was, I wondered if he knew. "Will we be meeting your lady wife?"

Titus blinked his watery eyes. He looked from me to Eamonn, then back at me. He was an unlovely man with unrealized dreams of heroism and glory, and I didn't need to step outside myself to see the shadow of envy that lay on his soul. But he knew it, and he bore it with a kind of forlorn dignity.

"No," he said, slow and sorrowful. "No, I don't think that's a good idea."

We parted with mutual assurances of goodwill. I left in a

pensive mood. There are all sorts of prisons in this world, and Titus Maximius was trapped in one of them. I'd often felt the same way myself before I'd reached my majority. While Tiberium had been my escape, its princeps would never taste freedom. I could not help but pity him.

At least he was shrewder than Deccus Fulvius where his wife was concerned.

"Dagda Mor!" Eamonn shook himself. "I'm glad *that's* over." He punched my arm and grinned. "Come on, let's go find out what message the lovely Claudia holds for me. If I wait any longer, I'm like to burst."

We arrived at the Fulvii domus unannounced, but not unexpected. A heavy knot of guilt settled into my belly as I entered the atrium, rendered all the worse by Deccus Fulvius' hearty greeting.

He embraced us both, pounding our backs. "Good lads, good lads! By the gods, I'm glad to see that dead madman didn't get you killed!"

I smiled at him. "Thanks in large part to you, my lord."

"Eh." Deccus shrugged, a twinkle in his eye. "I promised you I'd do my best. I'm an old lion, but not yet toothless."

Claudia emerged, a letter in her hand.

She was every inch the Tiberian matron, clad in a demure gown of amber velvet with a high throat, her extravagant hair braided in a coronet. It didn't fool me, not for a heartbeat. I could see the way her breasts moved beneath the velvet, the sway of her hips. I swallowed hard as we exchanged greetings. Eamonn, quivering with impatience, didn't notice. His gaze was fixed on the letter she held.

"Prince Eamonn." She handed it to him. "This is yours."

He tore it open, scanning the page, his lips moving soundlessly.

"Well?" I asked.

Eamonn showed it to me. I thought he'd been reading a lengthy missive, but I was wrong. He must have been uttering a silent prayer, or whispering place-names to himself. There was a crude map of Skaldia drawn on the parchment, with one spot circled over and over again. At the top, it simply read, *Come.*

"What happened?" There was a note I'd never heard before in his voice. "And when?"

"Ten days ago?" Claudia glanced at her husband for confirmation. "Her brother came for her," she said gently. "I'm afraid that's all we know. One of Master Piero's students brought this, along with the tale that Brigitta was returning to her family in Skaldia. You might question him."

He nodded. "I will."

Out of the dictates of politeness, we stayed for a while longer, sipping wine and telling them all that had transpired since they had left Lucca. This time, the telling fell to me. Eamonn was distracted and restless. I recited the tale of the battle, all the while racking my wits to find a way to have a private word with Claudia Fulvia. When one of Deccus' colleagues called upon him in a business matter, he excused himself and Eamonn sprang to his feet.

"We should go," he said.

Claudia rose. "I'll show you out."

I let Eamonn hurry ahead and caught her by the arm. "I need to see you."

She turned her head. I could feel her quivering under my grip, but no trace of distress showed in her calm profile. "Afternoon. Erytheia's atelier."

I exhaled hard. "My thanks."

It left me with time to spare. Since I had naught better to do with it, I accompanied Eamonn; and in truth, I wanted to see Master Piero. Like fools, we searched in the least likely places first, remembering all the tricks he'd played upon us to get us to think and to see. The sun was standing high overhead by the time we thought to look in the Great Forum. People scattered before us, some cursing in irritation, some shouting in recognition. A flock of pigeons rose, wings clattering.

By all rights, we shouldn't be riding roughshod through the city, but Eamonn reckoned the honor Titus Maximius had accorded us was good for the span of a day, and I was in no mind to argue with him.

"Master Piero!" Eamonn shouted.

He was seated on the ledge of the Fountain of the Chariot, clad in his scholar's black robes. There were a handful of students with him, most of them strangers. At Eamonn's call, he lifted his head and smiled.

"Dismount!" I hissed at Eamonn. "Show a measure of respect."

"Sorry," he muttered.

We both dismounted and led our horses across the Forum's plaza. The Bastard behaved himself admirably, although once we reached the fountain, he shoved his muzzle unceremoniously into it and drank in noisy gulps. The new students gaped at us in what was either awe or appalled shock.

Master Piero laughed and stood.

"Master." Eamonn dropped to his knees, still holding his reins, and gazed humbly at him. "What can you tell me of Brigitta?"

"Ah." He laid his hand on Eamonn's shoulder. "We were speaking of the virtues and pitfalls of love, were we not?" he asked his students. "And here we behold them both, wrapped up in one mortal package." He looked at Eamonn with fond sympathy. "I fear your Brigitta's brother Leidolf came to fetch her home, accompanied by several strapping companions. He threatened violence if she did not consent immediately."

Eamonn gritted his teeth. "He threatened her?"

"No," Master Piero said mildly. "Me."

"Oh." Eamonn was quiet. "I'm sorry."

Master Piero shook his head. "Why should you be? You are not responsible for his actions, Eamonn, only yours. And as Brigitta is responsible for hers, she chose to avert his anger by acceding to his demand. So, all is well." He took one look at Eamonn's expression and laughed again. "Ah, lad! You'll find her. I trust you received her map?" Eamonn nodded, and Master Piero patted his shoulder. "Try the University archives," he said kindly. "I daresay you'll find more detailed maps in their keeping. Brigitta sketched in haste."

Eamonn bounded upright and embraced him. "Thank you, Master!"

Since Eamonn was in a fever of impatience, I bade him go on to the University without me, promising to meet him later at the embassy. He swung himself into the saddle and raced away in a clatter of hooves, scattering pigeons and pedestrians.

With Master Piero's permission, I stayed and listened to the end of his lecture. Having drunk his fill, the Bastard was in a placid mood, dozing in the autumn sunlight with one rear leg cocked. Despite the day's chill, the sun was warm. I listened with half an ear, mostly thinking how young all the students looked, their faces keen and attentive. I thought about the harsh lines engraved on Lucius' face. I couldn't imagine any of us had looked that young.

When he had finished, Master Piero dismissed them. They wandered off in groups of three and four, talking animatedly. Heading for their favorite wineshops, no doubt. I smiled, remembering the excitement, the profound engagement in a heady world of ideas.

"Thank you for allowing me to stay, Master," I said to him. "It's good to see you have new students."

"There are always students." Master Piero sat beside me on the ledge and patted my hand. "And you will always be welcome among them, Imriel nó Montrève. Tell me, how is Lucius Tadius?"

"He's well," I said. "And grateful for your teaching."

"And you?" he asked.

I glanced at the charioteer in his fountain, his face filled with stern resolve. Sunlight reflected on the glittering water, dappling the Bastard's spotted hide with bright, moving patterns. I listened to the music of the falling water, the cluck and coo of pigeons, the ordinary sounds of the marketplace. All sounds of life, with all its myriad pitfalls and virtues. There was so much I yearned to discuss with Master Piero, but it would take a lifetime. I didn't even have a day.

"I'm well," I said. "And grateful for your teaching."

"Then I am pleased," he said.

I stood, and Master Piero rose with me, clasping the hand I proffered. He smiled at me one last time, that smile of unexpected sweetness that transformed his plain features. He was a good man and a wise one. I was lucky to have met him.

I bowed, according him the respect due to a sovereign. "Good-bye, Master."

Taking my leave of Master Piero and the scholar's life, I led the Bastard across the crowded Forum and into the narrow streets. The stable-lad at Lollia's inn, where Gilot and I had stayed on our first night, agreed to sell me a half-day's lodging.

I still had things to do.

I went to the banking house where I'd drawn on the letter of credit Jacques Brenin, Phèdre's factor, had given me. It had been a considerable sum and I'd been living frugally. Even with the payment I'd made to Ruggero Caccini, the balance would suffice for my purposes. At the banking house, they issued me the monies I requested and a new letter of credit for the remainder under the name I specified.

Lady Denise had been generous and thoughtful. She'd had our things collected from the insula weeks ago, after the first news from Lucca, and settled our debt.

But I had other debts.

By the time I was done, it was nearly time. The sun moved more swiftly across the sky than it had during the summer weeks. I hurried to Erytheia's atelier. Her door was closed, but she opened it to my knock, inclining her head in greeting.

"Prince Imriel," she said. "You are expected."

"Yes, my lady," I said wryly. It was the first time she'd acknowledged knowing who I was. "I know." I jangled the purse at my belt, newly bulging with coin. "I come as a patron, too. Have you sold it?"

Her brows arched. "The Bacchus? You know that was—"

I shook my head. "The Endymion."

"Oh." Erytheia of Thrasos touched her lips with paint-stained fingers, studying my face. "The model . . . ?"

"Dead, my lady," I said.

"I am sorry," she said simply.

"So am I," I said. "Is it available?"

"Well, there is a—" A flicker of calculation crossed her strong Hellene features, then vanished. "Yes. For you, yes."

The artist named a price and I agreed to it without bartering. It would have felt unseemly. As it was, it was strange to be in the atelier once more, filled with slanting afternoon sunlight and the strong scent of linseed oil. Wishing to retain my composure, I didn't dare glance at the painting. I paid her in hard coins. Her assistant Silvio was wrapping it in burlap when Claudia Fulvia arrived, enfolded in a thick woolen cloak.

Entering the atelier, Claudia drew back her hood. By accident or design, a shaft of light turned her glorious hair to a blazing crown. She didn't speak, merely tilted her head toward the door. The sunlight caught her eyes, turning them amber. Erytheia nodded, beckoning to Silvio. They departed with alacrity. I supposed we were past the point of dissembling.

"So." Claudia smiled. "You wished to see me?"

All the old yearning returned. Ah, Elua! It would have been good, so good, to lose myself in her. To purge myself of all the horror of battle, the shrouds and remnants still clinging to me, in the glory of her naked body. We were well matched, Claudia and I, at least in the bedchamber.

"Yes." I took a deep breath. "Tell me about my mother."

"Your *mother*?"

It caught her by surprise. I watched her carefully. Her voice was untuned, and a brief flare of outrage surfaced in her fox-brown eyes. Claudia was older than me. She thought it was some cruel game I played.

"My mother sent Canis," I said.

The outrage vanished and comprehension dawned. "Canis," Claudia murmured. "Your philosopher-beggar."

"Yes." I drew up Erytheia's paint-encrusted stool and sat, still watching her. "You lied to me in Lucca, Claudia. You may not have known who he was, but you knew he was Guild. You knew from the beginning."

She gazed at me unflinching. "And you knew there were

things I was forbidden to tell you. I'd already erred once. I couldn't afford the risk. I'm sorry."

"'Do no harm,'" I quoted. "It was the medallion, wasn't it?"

The color drained from Claudia's face. "How did you know?"

"Canis told me before he died." I'd rather risk lying to Claudia than putting Asclepius' priest in danger. "'Do no harm.' And he told me my mother sent her love, and then he died with a javelin stuck through him that was meant for me. So I'm asking you, Claudia. It means my mother's in the Guild, doesn't it?"

Claudia sighed. "Imriel, I don't know. I'm just—"

"A journeyman," I finished. "I know. Is my mother, Melisande Shahrizai, a member of the Unseen Guild?"

She looked away. "If she sent Canis, yes. Or she's learned our secrets and is using them to get us to do her bidding. From what I know of her, either could be true." Claudia looked back at me. "I truly *don't* know, Imriel."

"What did the message mean? 'Do no harm'?" I watched Claudia begin to pace back and forth in the atelier, passing easels with rude charcoal sketches, half-finished paintings. "Name of Elua, Claudia! Canis *died* before he could explain it to me. A man died for my sake, and I'm owed answers. Do you want me to raise a fuss and start asking questions? Because I will."

"No, don't. Please." Claudia flung herself into the chair in which I'd posed as Bacchus, sighing. "Imriel . . . the message on the medallion simply meant that a powerful Guild member had placed you under the seal of his or her protection. That you weren't to be harmed by other members. I heeded it and passed it on. Does that satisfy you?" She regarded me. "When you told me about Canis, I assumed someone had appointed him to guard you."

"Someone did," I said. "My mother. He did a good job of it, too, although I don't think he reckoned on having to deal with a riot." I stared at her, thinking. "That's why you didn't think I was in mortal danger from Caccini's thugs? Because of Canis?" Claudia nodded. "How did you know the medallion held a message?"

She made an impatient gesture. "It's one of the signs they use. The Cynics' lamp, only reversed. It pointed left. Most people never notice. *You* didn't."

"So all this business about the Unseen Guild's threats . . ." I shook my head. "It was a lie, all a lie. I was never in any danger from the Guild."

"Ah, well." Claudia smiled wryly. "It depends on how powerful the Guild member who placed the seal on you is."

I thought about that, and I thought about Canis. "Powerful enough to send a man willing to die to protect me."

Claudia shrugged. "I'm told men have died for Melisande Shahrizai's sake before."

"Not wittingly," I said. "And not smiling." The more I thought about it, the angrier I became. In the midst of all the Guild's intrigues, there was my mother, cursed and inevitable, squatting like a spider in a web. No wonder they had wanted so badly to recruit me. There was a cold fury singing in my blood. I rose from the stool and paced over to her, putting my hands on the arms of the chair and leaning forward until our faces were mere inches apart. Claudia shrank back in the chair, trapped. I could see her pulse beating under her jaw and smell fear in her sweat. "Where is she?"

"I don't know!" Her voice broke. "Imriel, please."

"Where?" I shouted.

"I don't know." Closing her eyes, Claudia swallowed. "I swear to you by the Triad, on the lives of my family, I don't know. Only what I've told you."

"But you know who does," I said grimly. "Erytheia, perhaps? Artists travel. Or perhaps the princeps' wife. Or Lady Denise, Terre d'Ange's own ambassadress?" Drawing back, I fished the scrap of parchment out of my purse and thrust it below her nose. "Tell me, is there a hidden message on *this*?"

Opening her eyes, Claudia took it from me. "No." Her voice was taut as she felt at the edges. "If there was, it's been torn away. I don't . . . I don't believe Lady Fleurais is involved. I don't know. Not for sure."

I believed her. Abruptly, my anger drained away, leaving me tired. I took the scrap back from Claudia and sat down heavily on the stool, putting my face in my hands.

"Imriel." A softer tone. I lifted my head. "Go home," Claudia said gently. "Go home and wed your Alban princess, and forget about this. You can't win this game. Above all else, the Guild protects itself. You'll lose if you try, and whatever power your mother wields, it won't be enough to save you. Or me. Or the people you love."

"Are you so sure?" I asked bitterly. "Elua! What if she's . . . what is it? A Heptarch?"

"She's not." Her gaze was steady. "Trust me, if she had *that* kind of power, her dog Canis would have had a vast Caerdicci army marching on Lucca at a day's notice. As it was, it took all the influence Deccus, Lady Fleurais, and I could muster to get seven hundred Tiberian soldiers under way in less than a week's time." A hint of smile curved her generous mouth. "And you're welcome, by the way."

A reluctant smile tugged at my lips in response. "Thank you."

Claudia inclined her head. "You're welcome." She paused. "Why are you so angry?" she asked curiously. "Your mother did no harm. She sought only to protect you."

I opened my mouth and found I had no answer; or at least none that wouldn't sound childish. My mother was a villainous traitor. She had borne me out of sheer ambition and bequeathed me a heritage of treason and mistrust. And when I had gone missing, she had swallowed her pride and sent the one person in the world capable of finding me to do so.

I would be dead if she hadn't.

And I would be dead, spitted through by Domenico Martelli's first javelin, if she hadn't sent Canis to protect me. For once, she'd given me no cause to hate her.

"I don't know," I said honestly.

SIXTY-SEVEN

SINCE THERE WAS NOTHING left to say, Claudia Fulvia and I said our farewells in Erytheia's atelier. It was fitting. I'd bid her good-bye once before in this place.

There were no recriminations this time, no cruel words. When all was said and done, we had been through too much together. I had seen much to admire in her and much to despise. A great deal to desire. I had learned from her, as surely as I'd learned from Master Piero.

The bright mirror and the dark.

I bowed over her hand and kissed it, remembering our first meeting. Her hand, bold and sure, reaching for me beneath the blanket. Her husband's salon in the darkness, her mouth on mine and her urgent, probing tongue.

"Good-bye, my lady," I said. "Elua's blessing on you."

Her mouth, smiling. "So it has been."

And so I left her to carry out my last errand, carrying a painting wrapped in burlap. I navigated the narrow streets of the students' quarter. The sun was sinking beneath the hills of Tiberium, filling the streets with blue shadows. It was growing cold, cold enough to turn my breath to frost.

I went to the insula.

A fit of cowardice overcame me and I nearly turned back.

It would have been easy to have the painting and the cruel news delivered. I'd already spoken to Lady Denise about my intentions, and she had agreed freely to lend her aid. No doubt she would see it done with every courtesy and kindness.

But she hadn't known Gilot.

The courtyard was empty. No one was drawing water from the well, emptying chamberpots into the sluice. Drawing a deep breath, I tucked the painting beneath my arm, mounted the rickety stairs, and knocked on the door of the widow Anna's apartment.

"Yes?" It opened a wary crack. "Your highness! Forgive me."

She opened the door.

"Anna . . ." I said raggedly.

She knew. I saw the knowledge break over her like a wave, and she turned her face away. A pleasant face, ordinary and pretty. She closed her eyes as she turned, not quickly enough to hide the tears. Her shoulders shook.

"I'm sorry," I said. "I'm so sorry."

"Mama?" Her daughter's voice, high and frightened. "Mama?"

Anna Marzoni dashed away her tears and faced me. "Come in. Please."

I entered quietly. It was a quiet place, neat and tidy. A table, two chairs. A single oil lamp, an unlit brazier. A dish of olives. A pallet with clean linens, the child Belinda huddled in it, her eyes wide and scared. She had known me, once. All that mattered now was that I had made her mother weep. I set down the painting, leaning it against the wall.

"What is this?" Anna asked me. A quiet voice.

I swallowed. "For remembrance."

She unwrapped it with steady hands, then knelt before it, her palms resting on her knees.

"Gilot!" Belinda crowed.

Gilot as Endymion, sleeping. His face half-averted, lashes curling on his cheek. Brown hair curling over his brow. One arm outflung, moonlight silvering his flesh like a lover's caress. The other hand, the splinted hand, hidden from view.

He's so beautiful, Anna had said.

"Yes, darling," she said now; softly, so softly. "That's Gilot."

"He died . . ." I paused, hearing the rawness of my voice. "He died a hero—"

"Stop." A quiet fierceness. Anna covered her eyes with her hands, then lowered them. "I don't want to hear it," she said to me. "Not here. Not now. I don't care."

I nodded and withdrew the banking house's letter of credit from inside my doublet, setting it on the table. "A beginning," I said quietly. "For you and Belinda. It was his wish. There will be more soon. If you have need of aught, you need only ask. There is a standing order at the embassy."

"Need!" Anna drew a long, shuddering breath, then loosed it, her shoulders slumping briefly. "Thank you, Prince Imriel," she said formally, rising to her feet. "It was good of you to come."

"Anna . . ."

"Please go." There were tears in her voice. "Please go now."

I went.

I heard a single sharp, choked sob as the door closed behind me, and then the low murmur of Anna's voice attempting to explain to her daughter that Gilot was gone, that Gilot, like her father, was never coming back. I leaned my brow against the door and wept.

So it was done, my last errand and the hardest one. I gathered myself and walked away from the insula. Away from a young widow's grief and a child's incomprehension. Away from the self that had lived in this place. Only a lingering scent of myrrh from Master Ambrosius' shop followed me, and within a block, that, too, was gone.

At the stable, I reclaimed the Bastard, tipping the stable-lad a silver denarius. He gaped so widely he nearly forgot to thank me. I didn't care. Anna was right, money meant nothing. Tomorrow, after the worst of grief's blow had been absorbed, it might. Tonight it didn't.

I rode slowly through the streets of Tiberium, alone with my thoughts. Gilot would have scolded me for it. If he hadn't been so damnably worried about my safety, he'd never have gotten hurt in the rioting, never had sustained the injury that killed him. He was always trying to protect me.

I carry a lot of guilt, I'd said to Valpetra.

And when all was said and done, the worst danger I'd faced had come from a man I barely knew. A stranger, bound to me by ties as narrow as the edge of my sword. A woman's terror, a missing hand. I'd created an enemy for myself far more determined than those I'd inherited from my mother's legacy.

And Canis had saved me from them all.

At the base of the Esquiline Hill, I drew rein and gazed back at the city. There had been the riot, of course; and the footpad in the alley the night I'd wandered the streets of Tiberium alone. The dead man outside the insula, his throat slit. Canis, trembling with fear, telling a tale of quarreling thieves. I'd taken pity on him, given him my cloak.

"I'm an idiot," I said aloud.

The Bastard snorted in agreement, pricking his ears toward the embassy.

The Guild had known about Bernadette de Trevalion. Surely, my mother must have known, too. But she had withheld her hand from seeking vengeance, content merely to protect me. Or was it the only thing it lay in her power to do?

I didn't know.

I might never know.

And yet if I had other enemies I couldn't put a name to, enemies known to her, I didn't doubt she would seek to protect me. It was a strange thought. I stared out at the darkened city, sprawling across Tiberium's hills. Light spilled from the wealthier homes; the poor quarters were dim. I wondered if my mother was out there somewhere, or if she was elsewhere, far, far away. I never had succeeded in identifying Canis' accent.

I raised one hand. "Kushiel's mercy on you, Mother."

A shudder ran through me, a memory of bronze wings. There was a taste of blood in my mouth. The Bastard shifted restlessly beneath me, pebbles rattling under his hooves. I turned his head back toward the embassy and we began to climb.

It was quiet when we arrived.

Since it suited my mood, I was glad. After the visit to Anna's, I craved it. Lady Denise was entertaining Eamonn and a noted Master of Skaldic studies in the dining hall. I begged off on the invitation to join them and retired to my chambers.

All my things were there; mine and Gilot's. It didn't amount to much. We'd travelled light, he and I. I went through his things. Two shirts, one neatly mended. A pair of breeches. Nothing anyone would want to keep for remembrance. There was only his sword, and that lay in his casket with him.

I thought briefly of retrieving the blade for Anna; and then I thought better of it.

My own possessions were scarcely more notable. I stowed a few of the less disgraceful items of clothing in my bags, preparing for the morrow's departure. There wasn't much else. My sword, my daggers. A whetting stone, and the flint striking kit given me long ago in Jebe-Barkal. A pair of waterskins. The letter written by Ruggero Caccini.

Letters.

As Lady Denise had said, two had arrived while I was gone. One was thin and bore the crest of House Courcel. That one I'd cracked open and read last night. It was from Ysandre, a gracefully worded acknowledgment of thanks on behalf of Queen and Cruarch alike for my decision to return to Terre d'Ange and wed Dorelei mab Breidaia.

The other letter was thick and the seal of House Montrève was stamped on it. I hadn't opened it. It would have been written before they heard the news from Lucca; only word that I was coming home. I could envision Phèdre in her study, dipping her pen in the inkwell, her brows drawing together in a faint frown as her hand flew over the page. Joscelin leaning over her shoulder, offering a wry comment as she shared some bit of gossip he deemed too trivial to interest me.

I was afraid I'd devour it too fast. Better to save it.

"Imri?" Eamonn poked his head in the door, startling me.

"Come in," I said.

There was a fireplace in my chambers, with a pair of chairs set before it. One of Lady Denise's servants had laid a crackling fire in the fireplace, though I'd let it burn low.

They'd brought a light meal and a decanter of brandy, too. I poked at the fire and poured brandy for us.

"Here," I said, handing it to him.

"Ah!" He drank deep, then sank into one of the chairs. "That's good." He held up his glass. "Joie."

I smiled and echoed his toast. "Joie."

We sat for a time in companionable silence. Eamonn gazed at the fire, his head nodding a little. I wondered how much wine he'd drunk at dinner. Then he caught himself and gave a prodigious yawn, jaws cracking. "Dagda Mor! I still feel short of sleep."

"Night patrol," I agreed. "Too many nights."

"Aye." He chuckled. "'*Here's the thing, lads . . .*'" We both laughed, remembering Gallus Tadius. Eamonn rubbed his chin. "Here's to the madman, eh?" he said, hoisting his glass again, and we both drank. "So." Eamonn set down his glass. "You mean to go home."

I nodded. "On the morrow. And you to Skaldia?"

"Aye." He regarded me steadily, no longer sleepy. "Come with me?"

Because it was Eamonn asking, and because I loved him, I thought about it. I thought about the tales Joscelin had told me of Skaldia in winter, of cold so intense it froze the sap in the trees until they made loud cracking sounds, of a world blanketed in whiteness beneath the blue dome of the sky. Of wolves and ravens and battles fought on a stretched hide. Of a people who were harsh in some ways and kind in others. And I thought about Eamonn and me wandering into the midst of it, huddling over campfires, depending on the kindness of our former enemies as we sought Brigitta's steading.

It would be an adventure.

It stirred my blood a little. But then my gaze fell on Phèdre's letter, filled with what was surely gladness and hope at the news of my return. Like the poor princeps of Tiberium, I had my own dutiful prison to return to. Unlike his, mine was built on a foundation of love. I shook my head. "I can't."

"Ah, well." Eamonn refilled his glass. "I had to ask."

"Are you scared?"

"Some." Another man might have lied; Eamonn didn't bother. He gave me his steady look. "The Skaldi have no reason to love the Dalriada. I don't know what I'll find. She's worth it, though."

I raised my glass. "To Brigitta."

"To Brigitta." Eamonn drank. "Shall we toast your betrothed-to-be?" He read my expression and understood. "Ah, it's too soon, isn't it? You barely even know the lass. How about Claudia Fulvia?" I sputtered mid-sip and Eamonn grinned at me. "To Claudia, then."

"To Claudia," I agreed. "May the gods protect her from herself."

Eamonn laughed. "To the long-suffering Deccus Fulvius!"

"Oh, yes." I drank. "May he never know what is better left to ignorance."

Other toasts followed as we refilled our glasses and tried to outdo one another. We drank to Lucius for his courage and to the valor of the Red Scourge. We drank to our fallen companions and toasted the living. I toasted Eamonn for his leadership of Barbarus squadron, and he toasted me for saving his life. We drank to Master Piero for his wise teaching, and then we drank to wisdom itself and to all the virtues we could think of, making a muddled job of it.

By that time, the decanter was nearly empty and we were both more than a bit drunk. After the short rations in Lucca, neither of us had a head for drink anymore. I poured the last of the brandy into our glasses.

"To Gilot," I murmured.

"Gilot," Eamonn echoed.

Silence settled over the room, broken only by the soft crackle of the fire. A charred log settled, sending up a burst of sparks, and Eamonn heaved himself to his feet.

"To bed," he said, swaying. "You're off in the morning?"

"Early, yes."

"All right." He knuckled his eyes. "I'll see you then."

I almost wished he would stay, that we were sharing a bedchamber as we had in Phèdre's townhouse. For once, I wouldn't have minded his snoring. But we weren't overgrown boys anymore, exchanging confidences in the dark. We were grown men who had fought in and survived the siege of Lucca. We were royal guests of the D'Angeline embassy, entitled to the privilege of privacy. I closed the door behind him and climbed into bed.

I'd thought to lay awake for hours that night, staring at the darkness and remembering the stricken look on Anna Marzoni's face, but the brandy had done its work. I fell asleep almost the instant my head touched the pillow, and slept soundly until a servant came to wake me at daybreak.

It was time to go home.

SIXTY-EIGHT

ALL WAS IN READINESS.

An honor guard of four men would escort me to the City of Elua. I'd argued against it, but Lady Denise was adamant. When I learned they were drawing lots for the privilege—which was less about my royal personage than it was the chance to return home—I'd ceded the point.

We assembled an hour after dawn and rode in procession to the wharf. Gilot's casket had been fitted with brass rings. Sturdy poles were thrust through the rings, and four embassy guardsmen carried it on their shoulders. Eamonn and I rode on either side of the casket, exchanging glances, bleary-eyed and rueful.

I hated the thought of saying good-bye to him.

There was a barge awaiting us at the wharf. It was reserved for our usage, flying the banner of Elua and his Companions. I lingered on the docks while Lady Denise's guardsmen oversaw the loading of the horses, our goods, Gilot's casket.

Then it was done, and there was no excuse for further delay. I bowed to Denise Fleurais. "Thank you, my lady, for all you have done. May Elua bless and keep you."

Lady Denise bowed in reply, then gave me the kiss of parting. "Be well and be safe, Imriel de la Courcel," she said. "I need no other thanks."

Eamonn.

He had dismounted and given one of the guards his reins. We gazed awkwardly at one another. "Here." He thrust a packet of letters toward me. "For my mother, mostly. There's one for my father, too, if he ever comes to port." He gave a lopsided grin. "Didn't want to forget this time."

I took them and tucked them inside my doublet. "I'll make sure they're received."

"Good." Eamonn cleared his throat. "So."

"You've got everything you need?" I asked him.

He nodded. "Nearly. I'll leave within a day or two. Mayhap I can beat the snow."

"Good." I drew a breath. "I'll miss you."

"Ah, Imri!" Eamonn grabbed me in a bone-cracking hug, then held me by the shoulders. "Try to stay out of trouble until I get back," he said gruffly. "Don't let anyone kill you. And try not to brood so damnably much, will you?"

"I'll try." I blinked back tears and laughed. "Come home safe?"

"I'll try," he promised.

All we could do was try. I boarded the barge and the barge-captain gave the order to shove off. We swung away from the wharf and the oarsmen began to stroke. In a few short minutes, we were on our way, travelling down the wide expanse of the Tiber. The figures on the shore began to dwindle. I stood at the aft end of the barge, watching until I could no longer see the glint of the autumn sun on Eamonn's bright hair.

"You all right, your highness?" one of the guards asked—Romuald, who'd ridden twice to Lucca and warned me about the dam. He was the one who'd laughed at me at the embassy gates the day I'd arrived with a stinking satchel full of incense. I was glad he'd drawn one of the lots.

"Yes," I said. "I will be."

Our journey to Ostia was swift and uneventful. We were travelling with the current and there was little traffic on the river this late in the season. As the seven hills of Tiberium fell away behind us, I stood beside Gilot's casket, remembering. There was the bridge we'd passed under before, the worn figure of Janus maintaining his vigil, his two faces gazing in opposite directions. Last time, a finger of foreboding had touched me as we glided beneath the bridge's shadow. This time, I saluted him, thinking of the split halves of a wax mask falling into the floodwaters. The man with two faces. Alais had been right, I'd met him after all.

Was he a friend?

One of him was.

As Lady Denise had promised, there was a ship awaiting us in Ostia. It was a Tiberian ship, and its captain had been paid handsomely to make the late crossing. He was a short, rotund man named Oppius da Lippi, good-natured and merry.

"You're the D'Angeline prince's party?" he shouted from the deck as we made our way across the quai. When one of the guards answered in the affirmative, he nodded so enthusiastically that his chins quivered. "Come aboard, come aboard!"

All his men were in good spirits. I watched in bemusement as they loaded our gear and horses quickly aboard the ship, laughing and dodging as the Bastard balked on the ramp, snapping at his would-be handlers.

"Here." I took the reins. The Bastard eyed me with profound mistrust, but he suffered me to lead him aboard. Once he was safely ensconced in a narrow stall in the dark hold, he settled down, and I returned abovedecks.

"A right bastard, eh, sir?" asked a cheerful sailor.

I smiled. "You might say so." They were loading Gilot's casket and I was worried that they'd handle it carelessly, but they treated it with the respect due a dead hero, at least until the casket was safely stowed away below.

"Your highness!" Captain Oppius approached me with a florid bow. "Welcome aboard the *Aeolia*! 'Tis the first time she's carried royalty, but I promise you, she's up to the task. Cradle you on the bosom of Ocean, she will, as safe as a babe at the teat."

"My thanks, lord captain." I extended my hand. "Call me Imriel."

"Imriel!" He pumped my hand, beaming with delight. "Not one to stand on ceremony, eh? Wise, very wise! Makes for a more pleasant journey, and a good thing, too, since we're like to run into a few rough patches. Call me Oppius. Do you dice?"

"Betimes." I glanced around. "Captain Oppius, forgive me, but why the merriment?"

"Marsilikos, lad!" A wide grin spread across his plump face. "We'll be forced to winter there, and every man of us with a fat purse thanks to your lady ambassadress' generosity." He rolled his eyes and kissed his fingers. "Have you *seen* the women there?"

"Ah." I smiled. "Yes."

"They look like . . ." The captain's voice trailed off and he stared at me for a moment, his lips pursed. "Don't really need to tell *you*, do I?"

"No," I said. "Not really. But do me a kindness and bid your men treat Naamah's Servants with the courtesy and respect they would accord their own mothers and sisters and daughters. In Terre d'Ange, they are."

"Oh, aye." Shrewdness surfaced in his gaze. "You needn't

tell an old sailor, lad. We're a superstitious lot. I see to it that my boys give your Naamah her due. Patron-gifts and all. I know what's proper." He clapped a hand on my shoulder. "No fear, young prince! Your lady ambassadress knew what she was about when she chose the *Aeolia* and her captain."

I felt better hearing it, and better still observing Captain Oppius as he took command of the ship and ordered the anchor hoisted and the oarsmen to their posts. For all that he cut a comical figure, striding over the deck in a rolling waddle, it was clear he was an able commander, admired and respected by his men.

They obeyed his orders with alacrity. Men sang out in a steady rhythm as they bent their backs to the oars and the *Aeolia*'s prow nosed toward open water. Although the sun was shining overhead, the water in the harbor of Ostia was grey and choppy.

Beyond the harbor, it looked worse.

And indeed, it was.

For the entire journey, the winds were blustery and capricious. The *Aeolia* was buffeted mercilessly. On a good day, we'd find the ship running before a strong tailwind, sails taut and straining, only to have the wind shift without warning. The sails would empty, slack and flapping, and the ship would wallow while Captain Oppius shouted orders at the wheel and his men raced around the deck and clambered in the rigging. And then we would catch the wind once more, making headway until the wind changed again.

On a bad day . . .

On a bad day, the skies were dark with storm clouds that spat angry rain down on us, and the winds would lash the sea into churning waves. Far from cradling us tenderly on Ocean's bosom, the *Aeolia* rode the waves like an unbroken horse, bucking the crests, plunging into the troughs. On those days, there was no laughing, no singing. Only grim determination, rain-whipped sailors, and dogged Captain Oppius at the wheel. Whether or not we made progress, I couldn't have said. We stayed afloat, which was all that mattered on a bad day.

It was a long journey.

It was Phèdre's letter that kept me sane. I cracked it open and read it as soon as Ostia was out of sight. The whole first page was filled with accounts of the joyful reception the news of my homecoming had met. Despite the fact that it was weeks in the offing, Eugènie had begun turning the household upside down, plundering the markets in order to make my favorite dishes. Hugues had written some very bad poetry in celebration—she included a sample that made me laugh aloud—and Ti-Philippe had gotten roaring drunk in the Hall of Games and had to be carried home. Joscelin, she reported, had actually kissed everyone in sight and gone about grinning from ear to ear for an entire day, which had caused a number of people to ask if he had a touch of the fever.

And she reported on the reception at the Palace, assuring me that Ysandre and Drustan's gratitude was deep and genuine, and that they appreciated the difficulty of the decision. Alais, it seemed, had burst into tears of joy when she learned of it. I wondered what Sidonie had done, but Phèdre didn't say.

There was other news, most of it inconsequential. Court gossip, for the most part. My former friends among the young gentry had not been idle in the Game of Courtship. It might interest me to learn, Phèdre wrote, that Maslin de Lombelon was in disgrace after beating Raul L'Envers y Aragon very badly in a duel, which was believed to be over a slight Maslin had offered Colette Trente. The Captain of the Guard had reprimanded him and sent him away to winter in Camlach with the Unforgiven.

I must own, I smiled at that.

For all its length, it was a light letter, written with a glad heart. If there was bad news, it was nothing so serious that Phèdre didn't deem it could wait. I kept it close to me throughout the journey, a talisman of hope, reading it over and over, until I could almost hear Phèdre's voice reciting it in my head, humorous and wry and filled with affection.

At the end, she sent her greetings to Gilot and Eamonn, and then wrote simply, *Come home safely, love. I will count the hours until you do.*

Alone in my cabin, I traced those words with one fingertip. It made my heart ache to imagine how Phèdre must have felt when she received the letter I'd written in Lucca; how they all must have felt. The awkward postscript scrawled at the bottom. *Thank you for the gift of my life.* I almost wished I hadn't written it. And then I remembered Valpetra's javelin, cocked and aimed at my heart, and I was glad I had.

It had been a near thing.

On our last day at sea, it stormed. It grew calm, first, late in the afternoon. The *Aeolia* bobbed like a cork, going nowhere. Captain Oppius cast a grim eye toward the bruised, luminous sky and muttered to himself. His sailors went about lashing things down, striking the mainsails and hoisting the storm-sails.

"This is going to be ugly, your highness," he said soberly to me. "Once it hits, stay in your cabin and tell your men to keep to their berths."

I nodded. If he hadn't meant it, he'd have used my name. Oppius da Lippi hadn't been jesting about dice; we'd passed a fair number of hours together and my dwindling purse was lighter for it. "How ugly?"

He pursed his lips. "Ugly."

It was.

A right bitch of a storm, Eamonn would have called it. It came for us an hour before sunset. We watched it approach from the deck, Lady Denise's guards and I. A smudge of darkness on the southern horizon moving closer, lightning dancing on the waves. Storm clouds piling above us in layers, dispelling the strange, livid light. Sea-swells rising, the *Aeolia* bobbing ever higher. I glanced at Romuald, who stood beside me, his gaze fixed on the moving darkness. I remembered his kindness toward me on the barge.

"Are you all right?" I asked him, echoing him.

"Aye." His throat moved as he swallowed. "Don't much like the sea."

And then it hit, faster and harder than I could have reckoned, fierce and primal, all roaring darkness and water, splintered by lightning.

"Get down!" someone shouted. *"Down!"*

It was terrible and glorious, and I wanted to stay. I wanted to see, wanted to see it all. I'd heard tell of such storms, other storms. Storms the Master of the Straits had sent; the old one, before Hyacinthe took his place. The storm that drove Phèdre to Kriti on the ship of the blood-cursed pirate, Kazan Atrabiades. I wanted to *see*, to know.

And men might die if I did.

"Down!" I shouted, shoving Romuald before me. "Down!"

The ship lurched and wallowed, half-swamped. A wave washed the deck, water spilling into the open hatch. No time to find my cabin. Romuald and the other guards scrambled before me, and I scrambled after them. Above us, the hatch slammed closed. A single lantern swayed wildly, hanging from a hook, illuminating scared faces.

"Blessed Elua!" someone gulped. "We're all going to die."

"The hell we are!" I grabbed the tin lantern, steadying it in both hands. Bilgewater sloshed around my ankles. "Right," I said to them, thinking of Gallus Tadius who had made us believe in the impossible. "You think this is bad? Listen, lads . . ."

I told them the end of the story, the story I had begun telling Lucius Tadius on the eve of battle and fallen asleep before completing. Rahab and his maelstrom, the bright mirror of the dark. The form that had risen at last in terrible, anguished brightness, the watery chains. How we had wept, had all wept at its beauty. Hyacinthe and his ragged voice, chanting charms in a forgotten tongue, pages of the lost Book of Raziel clutched in his arms.

Phèdre, dripping.

Phèdre, dripping and half-drowned, finding her feet.

Speaking the Name of God.

They knew the story. They were D'Angeline. But they'd never heard it from one who was there. I remembered the syllables of the Sacred Name, each one tolling in my head like a bell as it fell from Phèdre's tongue. I didn't remember what they were. I couldn't speak them, any more than I could give voice to the sun or the moon or the earth. But I had been there. I had heard them. I knew the shape of the word they formed, and the word was *love*.

I'd never doubted her in that moment.

Never.

"That's a good story, Prince Imriel," Romuald whispered when I finished.

"It's a true story," I said hoarsely. "And I swear, by Blessed Elua, I am *not* dying by water after it. Not here, not now, not like this. And neither are you."

For a mercy, I was right.

The storm passed and the *Aeolia* endured. We were bruised

and battered, and one of the horses had suffered a badly wrenched foreleg after panicking, but we were alive. After checking on the Bastard, who eyed me with a look that suggested all of his misgivings had been more than justified, I went abovedecks to greet the dawn.

All the sailors looked weary, but glad. No one had been lost. After a night of raging turmoil, the sea was almost tranquil. Captain Oppius was just handing over control of the ship's wheel when I emerged, and I greeted him with a deep bow.

"You are a master sailor, my lord," I said to him.

He gave me a tired grin. "That I am. Come here, lad. Have a look." Oppius led me to the prow of the ship. Cocking his head at the rising sun, he pointed directly in front of us. "Ought to catch sight of it in a bit."

I peered across the water. For a long moment, I saw nothing. Only the breeze ruffling the water into wavelets, tinged pink with the dawn, and a few raucous gulls soaring. Then the sun inched higher and I saw a distant spark of gold on the horizon, like a lit candle in a faraway window. The sailors erupted in cheers.

"Is that—?"

"Marsilikos," Oppius said. "The Dome of the Lady." He clapped me on the shoulder. "We'll be an hour or two yet. I'm off to catch a wink."

Our progress was slow, but I couldn't tear myself away. I stood in the prow and watched as the shoreline appeared, and the sprawling harbor city of Marsilikos. The gold glint resolved itself into the gilded Dome of the Lady, set high on the sloping hills.

Terre d'Ange.

Home.

I wished Gilot was here beside me to see it.

By the time we reached the mouth of the harbor, Oppius had reemerged, refreshed and cheerful. His men went to oars, singing once again. The harbor was mostly empty, only a handful of fishing vessels afloat. Oppius took the wheel and guided the *Aeolia* smoothly to the quai, and sailors leapt to the dock to secure her.

"Hey, *Aeolia*!" A figure in sea-blue livery approached, cupping his hands and shouting to the ship. By the gold braid and the crest on his doublet—Eisheth's gilded fish, the insignia of the Lady of Marsilikos—I guessed he was the harbor-master. A pair of men trailed behind him. "A little late in the season, aren't you? What's the urgent cargo?"

Oppius came up beside me and leaned over the railing. "Just this!" he shouted back in passable D'Angeline, pointing at me. "Says his name's Imriel."

The harbor-master drew nearer and shaded his eyes, peering up at me with a puzzled look. "Not . . ." His eyes widened. "Elua's Balls! Your highness?"

"Just Imriel," Oppius said affably. "He doesn't like to make a fuss."

"Oppius, you fat, prattling—" the harbor-master began in irritation.

I laughed. "Leave him be, messire. After last night's storm, I suspect we owe our lives to this fat, prattling, and most able ship's captain. I'm Imriel nó Montrève de la Courcel."

"On behalf of her grace Roxanne de Mereliot, the Lady of Marsilikos, well met and welcome home, your highness." He bowed, then straightened and elbowed one of his men, adding in a hiss. "Go tell her ladyship! *Now!*"

The man started, then took off at a run.

Despite the difficulty of the crossing, I was glad it was late in the season and the harbor was quiet. Rumor flies swifter than an arrow in Terre d'Ange, and I didn't want an audience gathering to bear witness to my arrival.

As it was, I had my hands full with the Bastard. One look at dry land, and he charged down the ramp, as headstrong and determined as a Jebean rhinoceros. I clung to his lead-line and swore at him, dancing in an effort to avoid his stomping hooves.

"Nice horse," a good-natured voice offered.

Wrestling the Bastard into a semblance of control, I glanced up to see an escort had arrived. It was led by a man I guessed to be in his mid-thirties, with coal-black hair. He grinned and bowed, then extended his hand.

"Gerard de Mereliot," he said. "The Lady's son and Captain of her Guard."

I clasped his hand, keeping a wary eye on the Bastard. "Imriel."

"Don't I know it!" Gerard laughed. "Mother's nearly bursting. You know she counts Phèdre nó Delaunay among her most valued friends? We've been on the lookout for news, any news, for weeks now. I daresay the courier's already on his way. She . . ." He looked past me. "Ah. I'm sorry. A friend?"

I turned to see Romuald and the other guards hoisting the carrying-poles of Gilot's casket. "Yes," I said honestly. "Would that I'd been a better one to him." My eyes stung, and I rubbed them with the heel of my free hand. *I'm done with weeping,* I'd said to Gilot as we left the City of Elua. *No more, do you hear me?* "My apologies," I said now to Gerard de Mereliot. "It's been a . . . difficult . . . journey."

He nodded. "I understand."

After that, Gerard was all tactful efficiency; ordering his men to assist with Gilot's casket, presenting Captain Oppius with a purse of coin to be distributed among his men as a token of the Lady's thanks.

I was grateful for it. As glad as I was to be safe on D'Angeline soil, it was a bittersweet gladness. It was impossible to retrace the steps of my journey without feeling Gilot's absence; impossible to rejoice at the prospect of being reunited with the people I loved best in the world without feeling a shadow of sorrow and guilt hanging over me.

Try not to brood so damnably much . . .

He knew me too well, Eamonn did. I wished he was here and not headed to an unknown fate in Skaldia, giving me one more damn thing to brood over. The thought made me smile a little. I gave the Bastard into Romuald's uneasy care and went to bid farewell to Oppius, who was also a difficult man around whom to remain brooding.

"Oppius, my friend," I said to him. "My thanks to you."

I'd caught him squirting the contents of a wineskin into his wide-open mouth. He lowered it with a grin, wiping his lips. "The pleasure was mine, friend Imriel. If you ever have need of a ship, send for the *Aeolia*."

"That I will," I said.

"Ready?" Gerard called.

He was waiting; they were all waiting. I reclaimed the Bastard from Romuald and mounted. In the distance, the Dome of the Lady glittered. Beyond the borders of Marsilikos lay the road home. Taking a deep breath, I turned my back on the harbor, on Captain Oppius and the *Aeolia*, on the last vestiges of my Tiberian adventure.

"I'm ready," I said. "Let's go."

SIXTY-NINE

ROXANNE DE MERELIOT, the Lady of Marsilikos, was a gracious hostess.

I'd met her before and liked her. When Ysandre had been a young Queen thrust into an unsteady perch on the throne, faced with treason and invasion, the Duchese de Mereliot was one of the few nobles she had dared trust. Phèdre held her in high regard and with a great deal of fondness.

I'd behaved badly the last time I saw her, though. Until we arrived at the Dome of the Lady, I'd forgotten. It had been at a fête in her honor that I'd danced with Sidonie and we'd quarreled. I'd left rudely and without word, trailing loyal, worried Gilot in my wake. That was the night I'd gone to Mavros, and Valerian House.

It felt strange to remember.

If Roxanne de Mereliot remembered it—and I daresay she didn't—she'd long since forgiven me the slight.

"Ah, child!" she said simply. "I'm so glad you're here."

There were tears in her eyes as she embraced me. She was rising seventy, and the coal-black hair her son had inherited was mostly grey, but she had fine dark eyes, filled with compassion and warmth. I returned her embrace, thinking to myself, *No more tears.*

"Thank you, my lady," I said to her. "So am I."

We passed the night there. I'd had it in mind to set out immediately for the City of Elua, accompanied by Lady Denise's guards, but the truth was, we were all weary after the long, storm-tossed night. Even the Bastard was off his feed, which was a rarity. A night's respite would do us all good. Like as not, we'd travel more swiftly for it.

And Gerard had guessed rightly, or nearly so—his mother sent a courier to the City within moments of our arrival at the Dome of the Lady. I felt better knowing that Phèdre and Joscelin wouldn't be kept in suspense a heart-beat longer than necessary.

I dined that night with Roxanne, Gerard, and Jeanne, the Lady's daughter. She was younger than her brother, with the same black hair and smoky grey eyes. As her mother's heir, she would one day bear the title Lady of Marsilikos. Eisheth's city was ruled by a woman, always. We flirted gently with one another. I liked her, too. I liked them all.

"We studied in Tiberium, too," Jeanne said to me. "Gerard and I."

"What did you study?" I asked.

"Wineshops." Gerard laughed. His sister smiled.

"Medicine," she said. "I wanted to see how it differed from what we're taught in Eisande. I'm a chirurgeon."

"Truly?" I asked, surprised.

"It's in our blood." Jeanne stretched out her hands, regarding them. "Eisheth's line."

"Medicine or music," Gerard added. "Or storytelling. What did you study?"

I told them about Master Piero, chasing the pigeons in the Forum, about how he taught us natural philosophy. They laughed, but they listened, too. We talked about what it had been like in Tiberium then, and what it was like now. In some ways, nothing had changed; in others, it was different. There had been more D'Angelines studying there in their day, far more.

"Times change," Gerard remarked. "Right, Mother?"

"They do." Roxanne de Mereliot smiled at her grown son. "And I have lived to see it. The Queen has wed her Cruarch, the Straits are opened, and Terre d'Ange occupies a new place in the world. New ties are forged, old ones are neglected."

I turned my winecup in my hands, thinking about the Unseen Guild. They'd lost a greater prize than they reckoned when Anafiel Delaunay walked away from their offer. How it must have terrified them years later when Terre d'Ange and Alba united to triumph over the Skaldi, when Ysandre wed Drustan! Alba was a vast unknown, rich in resources, isolated for centuries. The Guild had no foothold there, and they'd lost the best one they might have gained in Terre d'Ange.

Small wonder they'd wanted *me*. For all I knew, my mother was the least of it.

"Imriel?" Jeanne was looking at me. Caught up in my own thoughts, I'd lost the thread of conversation. "If you're willing to speak of Lucca, we'd like to hear it. There was a siege?"

"Yes." A siege, a dead madman, a terrified bride. A broken mask. Trees growing from the walls. An abyss of black water, the dark mirror of the bright. I was tired, too tired. "There was a siege," I said slowly. "And I survived it."

"Enough." The Lady of Marsilikos rose from her chair. She came around behind me, laying her hands on my shoulders. She had a gentle touch. "I think we should let Prince Imriel sleep," she said. "And not plague him for stories."

Prince Imriel.

I remembered lying on a lumpy pallet beneath a thread-bare blanket in a cheap travellers' inn in Marsilikos, within sight of the Dome of the Lady, and explaining to an irritated Gilot that we weren't calling upon her grace Roxanne de Mereliot because I'd been raised a goatherding peasant in the Sanctuary of Elua.

I wondered if *Prince Imriel* would ever sound right to my ear.

Now I was led to a guest-chamber beneath that very dome, splendid and spacious. Gilot would have reveled in it. The windows, shuttered against the autumn chill, looked out toward the harbor. There was no fireplace, but a char-coal brazier glowed merrily. The bed was piled high with eiderdown quilts.

I lay on it and stared at the ceiling.

A thousand thoughts crowded my brain. I thought about my mother and the Guild and the Skaldi invasion. She had known. She had been complicit in it. Had *they*? Elua, it would have been a coup! A horrible, marvelous coup! How long had my mother been a part of the Guild? And *how*?

She had known Anafiel Delaunay for a long time.

They'd been lovers, once.

I shied away from the thought, and thought instead about what Jeanne had said at dinner about Eisheth's line. What a marvelous thing that must be, to have music and story and healing in one's blood! A far nicer legacy than mine. Kushiel's stern mercy had its place—I would never forget the way Gallus Tadius had glanced up at me as he stood in the bell-tower, the broken mask in his hands, and prepared to die a second death—but it wasn't a pleasant one.

Except when it was.

Dark pleasures, violent pleasures. Remembering Valer-ian House, I felt a flush of heat rising to my skin, the awful tug of desire. It hadn't gone away. I supposed it never would. After all, I was my mother's son.

True and not true.

All at once, it seemed too hot in the room. I threw off the heavy quilts and lay naked atop the bed. When a soft knock came at the door, I went to answer it unthinking, pausing only to grab my sword-belt.

It was Jeanne, the Lady's daughter. Amusement lightened her dark grey eyes. "Did I disturb you? I thought you might be awake."

"No, and I was." I laughed. "How did you know?"

"Because I'm a healer who ought to know better than to ask pressing questions of a battle-weary soul." She touched my bare chest with her chirurgeon's fingers. "And so I came to offer . . ."

"Healing?" I asked.

"Respite." Jeanne smiled at me. "Ease. Eisheth's mercy, if you want it."

"Yes." Taking her hand, I drew her into the room. "Oh, yes."

This, too, is sacred.

It was, all of it. And there was healing in it, and ease and mercy. She opened all of the shuttered windows to let the night breeze blow through the chamber, tasting of salt from the ocean. I could feel the chill on my skin, and yet I was hot, too. The embers in the brazier blazed in answer, bright shadows moving in their burning hearts.

No brooding.

No thinking.

Only a woman, warm and kind. She touched me with her healer's hands, stroking my skin. It felt as though my scars melted under her touch; brand and lash, sword and spear. She took me into her, and we lay for a long time, barely moving. Propped on my arms, I gazed at her black hair spread on the pillow like sea-grass, the flickers of pleasure shifting in her grey eyes. At last, I closed my eyes and rocked slowly, a ship come home to safe harbor, until I felt her sigh into my ear and shudder beneath me and around me, long, slow ripples as inexorable as the tide. And then I sighed, too, and spent myself.

It was quiet and good.

Afterward, I was peaceful and sleepy. Jeanne laughed softly at me, sitting on the edge of the bed and twining her hair into a loose braid. When I made to get up and escort her to the door, she shook her head at me.

"Sleep." She bent down and kissed me, then regarded me for a long minute, a smile still hovering on her lips. "Eisheth had a fondness for beautiful sailor-boys, too."

I laughed.

Jeanne kissed me again, then rose and closed the shutters. The room felt pleasant now, neither too cold nor too warm. I fell asleep listening to the rhythmic swish of her skirts. I never even heard the door close softly behind her as she left.

It was a gift that stayed with me. I rose in the morning, later than I'd meant. There was no guilt and no shame, only a lingering sense of tenderness. This was Terre d'Ange, and I was D'Angeline. I was home.

At the breakfast table, Jeanne and I caught one another's eye, and I couldn't help but smile. Gerard noticed it and grinned, raising his brows at his sister.

"Oh, so that's how it is, is it?" he teased her. "You didn't light a candle to Eisheth, did you? It's high time you thought about an heir of your own, you know."

"Of course not!" She rapped his knuckles with a serving

spoon. "I've time. And I'd never do such a thing without asking."

"Women do," he observed.

"*I* don't." Her gaze rested briefly on me, filled with bright amusement and somewhat more. "Though you'd be a good choice if I did, Imriel."

I stared at Jeanne. *"Me?"*

"Well, of course," she said. "Why not?"

I opened my mouth to reply, then closed it. She didn't mean it, not really. Already their conversation had moved onward to other matters, brother and sister bantering in a long-familiar pattern of exchange. But she hadn't *not* meant it, either. I glanced at Roxanne de Mereliot, sure she must be appalled. But no, she was listening to her adult children's sibling banter with a mother's fond patience. She had no objection to the notion that her daughter found me worthy of fathering an heir. It didn't disturb her.

It was a strange thought.

I'd be expected to when I wed Dorelei. Although I'd not let myself think on it, I knew it was true. It was the whole purpose behind the betrothal, securing the succession of Alba in a manner that was acceptable to Terre d'Ange. But that was different. It was politics, nothing but politics. And Dorelei mab Breidaia, poor girl, couldn't be expected to know.

House Mereliot was different.

They knew who I was, *what* I was. A traitor's get on both sides. And they didn't care. Or if they did, they cared more that I was Phèdre nó Delaunay's foster-son. Or mayhap just myself. Me. Imriel. Not the what, but the *who*.

It surprised me, pleasantly so.

Let the wound heal, Asclepius had told me. *Bear the scar with pride.*

I shook my head in wonderment. I was glad, more than glad, that I'd chosen to tarry a night in Marsilikos. A respite, and more. Whether she knew it or not, Jeanne had spoken truly. Eisheth's mercy brushed me; a feather-touch of grace, kinder by far than Kushiel's.

"Forgive my quibbling offspring," Roxanne de Mereliot said to me. "You must be impatient to be off."

I thought for a moment that she'd misread my gesture, then I saw in her fine dark eyes that she had not. They were filled with understanding and wisdom gained through long years as a ruler, as a mother. As a woman of Eisheth's line, who carried healing in her blood. I smiled at her, and knew it was true. "Yes, my lady. I am."

"Well, then." The Lady of Marsilikos clapped her hands. "Let's be about it!"

Another day, another journey.

She had insisted on providing an escort of twenty men under Gerard's command, and for once I had the sense not to argue. I left Eamonn's letter for his father in her keeping. She and Quintilius Rousse were friends of long standing, and whenever he put to port, she would be the first person he called upon. She promised to see it delivered, and I had no doubt it would be.

Since I no longer had need of Lady Denise's guards, I dispensed the last contents of my purse among them, thanking them for their service. Three of them accepted it gladly, eager to depart for their own destinations and make the most of their time in Terre d'Ange before returning to Tiberium in the spring. Romuald scratched his head and regarded me dubiously.

"Think I'll stay in your service, if you don't mind," he said. "Until we reach the City."

"Of course not."

"Like to tell her ladyship I saw the job through." He watched Gerard's men loading Gilot's casket carefully into a cart. "And then there's him. It's a funny thing, your highness. I never knew him, but I came to think of him as a friend of sorts, on the road together so long." He gave an embarrassed chuckle. "You must think me a little mad."

"No." I laid a hand on his shoulder. "You would have liked him."

Another parting, another farewell.

Jeanne embraced me. I closed my eyes, remembering her black hair spread on the pillow, the sea-surge of love. "Come visit us," she said. "Anytime. You could come in the spring for the Moon-Tide Festival. Have you ever seen the taurières at sport or a Mendacant perform?"

"No," I said. "Not a real one."

"Think on it."

I promised I would, and then Roxanne de Mereliot gave me a kiss of parting; a mother's kiss, gentle on my brow. "A safe journey," she said, patting my cheek. "And my love to Phèdre and her lovely Cassiline." Her dark eyes crinkled. "He makes a terrible Mendacant."

I laughed. "I know."

And then we were off. Another journey, a last journey. At least for a while. Despite the chill, the sun was bright and Marsilikos was doing a bustling trade. The harbor might be quiet for the season, but the city wasn't. All manner of folk would winter here. We passed shops and taverns and markets, temples and brothels. Native Marsilikans recognized Gerard and called out cheerful greetings as we passed, then fell silent when they saw the casket. I saw a few offer prayers to Blessed Elua, and I was glad.

The city behind us, the road before. One of Gerard's men

brought out a wooden flute and began to play as he rode, and another beat the time on a tambor. After a moment, Gerard began to sing. He had a fine voice, deep and rolling.

"What was all that about Mendacants?" Romuald asked curiously. "I saw one, once. Came to town when I was a boy. No offense to your highness, but Elua, could he spin a tale!"

I cocked my head at him. "A *true* tale?"

"Ah, well." He grinned. "Who's to say?"

So I told him, as we rode, about how Joscelin had taken on a Mendacant's guise to cross the country with Phèdre and Hyacinthe; a wandering Eisandine storyteller in a multicolored cloak, travelling in the company of the Tsingani. He knew the story, of course; he was D'Angeline. But he knew only the poets' version, which didn't mention igno-minious disguises. I knew the version Phèdre told, laughing at the memory of Joscelin Verreuil practicing the dramatic swirl of his Mendacant's cloak, glaring with stiff, irritable Cassiline dignity at Hyacinthe's persistent coaching. There were some stories they'd never told me; ones I'd learned elsewhere, like how Waldemar Selig sought to skin her alive. From Gilot, mostly.

But this one, Phèdre had told.

And Joscelin . . . Joscelin listening with wry patience. When I was younger, I'd begged him to demonstrate. He'd done it, too, telling some wild, half-remembered tale they'd concocted between them. He'd actually made a good job of it, which made it all the funnier. Phèdre and I had laughed until we wept. I'd rolled on the floor, helpless with it.

Ah, Elua!

"Are you all right, your highness?" Romuald asked in

concern; the same kind, decent concern he'd shown on the barge.

"Yes." I willed my voice to steadiness. It was the nearness of it that had caught me. The nearness to the journey's end, the nearness to those I loved. My heart swelled within me, aching, but I made myself give him an answer, the same answer I'd given before. "I will be."

Romuald nodded gravely. "That's good, then."

SEVENTY

NEVER IN MY LIFE had I been so glad to see the white walls of the City of Elua. From the first glimpse, I found myself standing in the stirrups and craning for a better look. The Bastard caught my mood and began straining at the bit, arching his neck and sidling. He wanted to run, and I wanted to let him.

Gerard laughed at me. "Eager, are we?"

"You've no idea," I said fervently.

It seemed to take forever to reach the gates, and then we had to wait while the guards examined the contents of a merchant's caravan. At last they waved him through and it was our turn.

"Marsilikos, my lord?" a guard asked Gerard, noting the banners and his crest.

"Gerard de Mereliot," he said cheerfully. "And friends."

The guard looked us over. His gaze passed over me at first and lingered on Gilot's casket. He frowned. "Who died?"

"He was the Comtesse de Montrève's man," I said.

"Why—" He gave me a startled glance. "Oh. Oh! Your highness?"

"Imriel, yes."

A pair of Tsingano lads idling over a game of knuckle-bones in a patch of sun leapt to their feet. One of them stuck his fingers in his mouth and gave a sharp whistle. "Hey! Is that *him*?" he called.

The guard grinned. "Aye, it's him!"

With dueling whoops and shouts, they dashed away, pelting through the City.

"What in the world?" Gerard asked, bemused.

"Tsingani." The guard shrugged. "They've been hanging about for a few days. I don't mind, as long as they don't steal."

Another time, I might have stayed to defend the reputation of the Tsingani, but not today. I could well guess that the lads were there at Phèdre's behest; or mayhap Emile's out of the affection he bore her. Even now, they were racing to carry the news. Filled with impatience, I pushed past the guard to follow in their wake.

"Welcome home, your highness!" he called after me.

The City of Elua.

It seemed bigger than I remembered it. I'd thought it would seem smaller, but it didn't. We crossed the arched bridge over the Aviline, the river sparkling in the wintry sun. Pedestrians made way for us, casting respectful glances at the casket. No one recognized me in the midst of Gerard's men, surrounded by Marsilikan banners and livery.

My heart was thudding in my chest.

We got almost as far as Elua's Square when the sound of pounding hoofbeats shattered the air. I recognized Ti-Philippe by his seat, riding hell-for-leather, with Hugues on his heels. A grin split my face, and I gave the Bastard his head.

"*Imri!*"

It's a wonder no one was killed. We collided in Elua's

Square in a churning tangle of horseflesh, limbs, and leather. Hugues embraced me so hard, I thought he meant to lift me clean out of the saddle, and then the Bastard reared and nearly unseated me, spooking Ti-Philippe's mount in turn. Somehow, laughing and talking all at once, we managed to get ourselves untangled and righted.

"Where—" I began.

"Imri, love."

Phèdre's voice.

I'd not even heard them arrive in the confusion. They had already dismounted. Standing in the square, Joscelin a half-step behind her. I stared at them. My mouth had gone dry and the blood was pounding in my ears until I felt dizzy with it. Phèdre's eyes shone. She was wearing a dark green gown. It hurt to look at her. At them.

No one spoke.

I dismounted in silence, dropping the Bastard's reins. My legs were trembling. I made myself move them. I walked into her arms, and his arms came around the both of us.

Home.

How long we stayed that way, I couldn't have said. A long time, I suppose. It didn't feel like it. But at length, I became aware of the murmur of voices, other voices, low and somber. Taking a deep breath, I pulled away.

Joscelin looked at the cart. "Gilot?"

I nodded. I didn't trust myself to speak, not yet.

"Ah, love!" There was sorrow in Phèdre's voice; an ocean of sorrow. Tears gleamed on her beautiful face. "I'm so sorry."

"I know," I whispered. "So am I."

Thus was my homecoming, filled with shared gladness and grief. We didn't go home straightaway, but took Gilot's casket to the cemetery. All was in readiness. Phèdre had written to his family when she received the news of his death. It would have been his wish, his mother had written in reply, to be buried as a member of Montrève's household. His service to House Montrève was his greatest pride.

Gerard and his men accompanied us; and Romuald, too. An elderly priest of Elua met us at the cemetery gate, emerging from the humble gatehouse there. It was a duty many of them took upon themselves in the last years of their lives.

"Comtesse." The priest inclined his head. His hair was white, as white as snow. Even his lashes were snowy, barely visible against his wrinkled eyelids. "Come with me."

The men of Montrève bore the casket; Joscelin and I in the front, Ti-Philippe and Hugues at the rear, the poles resting on our shoulders.

It was heavy.

We followed Phèdre and the priest through the city of the dead, along aisles of grass turned brown and sere. The priest's bare feet were gnarled beneath the hem of his blue robe. Only the members of the Great Houses of Terre d'Ange were buried here. Some of the mausoleums we passed were ornate, adorned with elaborate statuary, surrounded by dozens of grave markers. Others were simple.

Montrève's was simple. There is a graveyard on the estate where most of the members of House Montrève lie. Only two lay within the mausoleum in the City: Anafiel Delaunay de Montrève and Alcuin nó Delaunay. It was built on Ysandre's orders, following their murders.

And there, beside it, a new grave had been dug. The freshly turned soil lay in a neat pile on the far side, a pair of shovels crossed atop it. It had been made ready as soon as the courier from Marsilikos had arrived. We lowered the casket on the near side of the grave and slid the poles from the brass rings.

"Has he been blessed and anointed?" the priest asked Phèdre.

She glanced at me, and I shook my head. "No," I said.

I undid the latches myself while the priest offered a prayer, and then the four of us lifted the lid from the casket. A powerful odor of myrrh filled the air. I was half afraid of what we might find—I daresay all of us were—but the embalmers had done their job well.

Gilot.

True and not true.

It looked like him, like a Gilot carved of marble, bloodless and pale. His closed eyelids were smooth and serene, his mouth closed and somber. The priest drew a vial of oil from his vestments and smeared some on his brow, uttering the formal words of blessing. He kissed his fingertips and touched them lightly to Gilot's breast.

"Go forth in love," he said. "May you pass through the bright gate to the true Terre d'Ange-that-lies-beyond."

We replaced the heavy lid and I reclosed the latches. And then we picked up the casket and lowered it into the earth. Phèdre stooped and grasped a handful of soil. "Blessed Elua hold you in his hand, Gilot," she whispered, letting it trickle through her fingers.

I followed suit, and others after me. And then I took up a shovel and began filling in the grave. Others helped, and I let them, but I didn't relinquish my turn. It was something I needed to do. I had promised to bring him home.

I keep my promises, my mother had written.

So did I.

And then it was done. I set down my shovel and straightened, running my sleeve over my brow. I felt tired and sad, but lighter, too. A burden had passed from my keeping.

"You all right, your highness?" Romuald asked me a last time.

"Yes," I said. "I am."

We parted ways after the cemetery. Gerard was bound for the Palace to carry his mother's greetings to the Queen, and his men would accompany him. I thanked him for his kindness.

"Oh, anytime!" he said cheerfully. "Mind what Jeanne said and come visit, will you?" He laughed. "Watch out for candles, though!"

I flushed. "I will."

Romuald left us, too. Phèdre had offered him hospitality, but he had declined, stammering somewhat about an inn and friends in the City. He was ill at ease in her presence, awestruck and overwhelmed. I didn't blame him. Gilot had been like that at first. He used to stare at Phèdre when he thought no one was looking, blushing and tripping over himself to apologize when he was caught out at it. He'd gotten over it, though.

"You're welcome, highness," Romuald said when I thanked him for his service. "I couldn't risk having you turn up on her ladyship's doorstep looking every inch a ragged beggar, could I?"

I laughed. "I wouldn't have dared!"

"Oh, no?" He grinned at me, then dared a sidelong glance at Phèdre, who looked bemused. "Ah, well . . . I'm glad to have seen you home safely." He nodded in the direction of the cemetery. "And him."

I clasped his hand. "Do me a kindness. He left a woman behind in Tiberium, Anna Marzoni. She's a young widow, with a daughter. I've seen to it that they'll be provided for, but if you think on it, will you call on them when you return and make certain they want for naught?"

Romuald nodded. "Of course."

He rode away whistling. I watched him go, thinking he was a good man, a kind man. Gilot, who'd always rolled his eyes at Lucius, would have liked him. I wondered if Anna would find him beautiful. She would, I thought. She might even let herself care for him. Who could say? It was worth hoping, at any rate.

"Ah, love!" Phèdre's voice broke my reverie. "How you've grown!"

I smiled at her. "I'm just me."

She shook her head, but said nothing. There was time. Time to talk, time to tell her everything. Time to speak of Tiberium, of Master Piero, of Claudia Fulvia and the Unseen Guild. Of Bernadette de Trevalion and Ruggero Caccini. Of Lucca and Gallus Tadius, Canis and my mother, Eamonn and Brigitta. Time to speak to Joscelin, to tell him about the siege—the parts I didn't want Phèdre to know. To ask him how long it took before one stopped seeing one's dead in dreams.

"Are we ready to go *home*?" Ti-Philippe asked plaintively. In his haste, he'd ridden out without a cloak, and he was shivering in the cold air. "I'm perishing out here!"

Joscelin glanced at me. "Imri?"

"Elua, yes!" I said. "Home."

At the townhouse, it was mayhem all over again. There was a lieutenant of the Queen's Guard waiting on us. Eugènie hadn't known that we would go to the cemetery before returning to the townhouse—it had all happened so quickly—and she was beside herself with anxiety. I'd scarce gotten through the door when she seized me.

"Oh, you bad child!" she said, hugging and scolding me while the lieutenant looked on with horrified amazement. Tears ran down her plump cheeks. "What *took* you so long?"

"Gilot," I said.

"Ah." Eugènie went quiet for a moment. "The poor lad. I'd forgotten."

The lieutenant cleared his throat. "Your highness? I'm Zacharel Clarence of her majesty's personal guard. I'm bidden to summon you to the Palace. Her majesty is most eager to see you."

"I'm sure she is." I gave Eugènie a kiss on the cheek and moved away. I gave Lieutenant Zacharel a friendly smile. "Tell her majesty that I will present myself on the morrow."

He blinked at me. "Pardon?"

"Tell her majesty that I will present myself at Court on the morrow," I repeated. I waited until he opened his mouth to protest. "Lieutenant, I've come a very long way, and I've just buried a man who died because he was loyal to me. I'm tired. I wish to spend the remainder of the day with my *family*." I gave the word a deliberate emphasis. "You've seen with your own eyes that I'm alive and well. Pray tell her majesty as much, and that I look forward to seeing her anon."

He stared at me for a moment, then glanced around. Phèdre met his gaze with a mild look. Ti-Philippe opened the door for him, bowing as if to usher him through it. Joscelin leaned against a wall, vambraced forearms folded over his chest.

"I'll . . . I'll tell her," the lieutenant said.

I inclined my head. "Thank you."

He left. For a moment, I nearly thought Phèdre would follow to offer some words to soften the message—she watched him go, her expression thoughtful—but she didn't.

Joscelin straightened and grinned at me. "And how did *that* feel?"

I smiled back at him, and knew he knew exactly how I

felt. Good and proud, and a little bit foolish, too. Ysandre would pay dearly for Tiberium's aid in Lucca and I was grateful for it, but she was getting her money's worth. I'd agreed to her plans for Alba. It didn't mean I was placing myself at her beck and call. "It feels . . . ah, Elua!" I took a deep breath. "Good, mostly. And very, very good to be home."

It was a late night.

The story came out in bits and pieces. Everyone wanted to hear it, from Eugènie and Clory to Benoit the stable-lad, and certainly all of Gilot's comrades. With her usual grace, Phèdre acquiesced, inviting the entire household to dine with us. There was enough food prepared for a small army, a fact which I appreciated. One of the retainers—Marcel, who had known me for years—teased me at the dinner table.

"Are you sure you've got enough on your plate, your highness?" he asked. "I can still see the top of your head."

Eugènie glared at him. "Hush, you!"

I swallowed a succulent mouthful of roast beef. "You'd have an appetite, too, if you'd spent weeks on Gallus Tadius' rations."

"Gallus Tadius?" Ti-Philippe frowned. "I was the Admiral's man, but wasn't there a Caerdicci warlord—?" He shook his head. "No, no mind. Old sailors swapping tales, that's all. He's long dead."

"Well, he was," I said.

Throughout the course of the dinner, and afterward in the salon, I told them about Lucca. About Helena's abduction, my haunted friend Lucius, the *mundus manes* and the broken mask in the *lararium*. Gallus Tadius. The battle for the gatehouse, Valpetra's hand.

Gilot's death.

I didn't try spinning a tale out of it, I just told them. Told them that what Gilot had done in the gatehouse had saved countless lives, mine included. How he was a hero after all.

Phèdre was quiet throughout my telling, sharing a couch with Joscelin. Truth be told, I would rather have been alone with them. I could have sat for hours without talking, just content to know I was here and they were here, all of us together.

But there was time.

And I owed a debt to Gilot, and to everyone in the household of Montrève who had known him, who had cared for me and protected me, and worried in anguish alongside Phèdre and Joscelin when they received my last letter, wondering if I lived or died.

So I told the rest of it. The D'Angeline embassy, the dams. Training with the Red Scourge, and Barbarus squadron. Eamonn's leadership, which sparked smiles and nods all around. There was no one in the household who didn't remember him fondly. I told them about Brigitta and his wedding, and how he had gone to Skaldia in search of her.

"What about the siege?" Benoit asked.

"And the dam?" Ti-Philippe added. "Was there a flood?"

"Yes." I glanced at Phèdre. I'd heard Eamonn tell it before; I'd told it myself to the princeps. This was different.

The flood—the flood was easy. I could still see it in my mind's eye: the vast, awesome force of it bursting the wall, churning through the streets. The bell-tower, Gallus Tadius and his death-mask. I faltered a little there. I caught myself gazing at Phèdre, wondering if she would understand what I had felt atop the basilica. Kushiel's presence, beating in my skull.

Probably better than I did. His blood ran in my veins, but I was only his scion, and a reluctant one at that. My blood was purer than most—House Shahrizai saw to that—but there were thousands of us. He had parted the veils of the worlds to touch her in the womb, pricking her eye with his crimson sign. She was his Chosen.

And then the maelstrom and the pit, the waters receding, falling in an ebony cascade into the unknown depths of hell. I could hear the awe in my own voice. They listened and believed. House Montrève had known stranger things.

Lucius, and his courage.

The battle.

If I had been telling it to someone else—Charles Friote, mayhap—I might have told it differently. I don't know. In the warm, loving confines of home, the terror and the stench and the screaming seemed farther away. And yet they weren't, not at all. Every time I glanced at Phèdre, I remembered. She had taught me to do so.

Remember this.

So I told it quickly, without belaboring my role. Without telling about holding the line with Barbarus squadron or my mad charge to rescue Eamonn, about Canis, about the Duke of Valpetra and his javelins. I would, later. It could wait. I told them only that Lucius rallied the Red Scourge, and the D'Angeline and Tiberian troops arrived on their heels. That Valpetra was killed, the condottiere Silvanus surrendered, and it was done.

"The rest," I said, my voice hoarse with talking, "you know."

It was Joscelin who dismissed everyone, dispatching them to their respective beds. Only the three of us were left. Phèdre sat curled in the corner of the couch, watching the fire. I couldn't read her face, not at all. It was inward-looking, lost in contemplation.

"There's somewhat else I have to tell you," I said to them.

"Well, a number of things, including news of my mother, but this one's pressing." I took a deep breath. "I've thought about this, long and hard. And I'd like to handle it myself, quietly. You should know, though."

Phèdre stirred. "What is it?"

"Bernadette de Trevalion hired a man to kill me in Tiberium," I said simply.

For a moment, both of them merely stared at me. A flush of anger rose to Joscelin's cheeks; Phèdre closed her eyes. "Are you certain?" she whispered.

I nodded. "I've proof."

"No." Joscelin shook his head. "Oh, no! Not this time. Not after L'Envers. This time, it will be done in the open. Let the world know—"

"Joscelin." I spread my hands. "No. Ysandre brought me into the fold of House Courcel to break the chain of vengeance and retribution. This is a chance to do that very thing." I smiled wryly. "Through the gentler coercion of blackmail, at any rate."

"You can't—" he began.

"He can, Joscelin." Phèdre cut him off. "It's his choice." Her deep gaze rested on me, familiar and unnerving. I met it without flinching. The tension between us was there, it would always be there. But I could bear it. And there was so much more besides. "You're sure?"

"Yes," I said. "I am."

For the second time that day, there were tears in Phèdre's eyes. "Elua! It's such a short time for you to have grown so much, Imriel."

Joscelin touched her hair. "Love?"

She shuddered and slid into his arms, burying her face against his shoulder. He held her for a moment, then let her go. She gathered herself and rose.

I stood up. "I'll go. I should sleep."

"Not on my account." Phèdre lifted one hand to my face, her touch lingering. Not quite a mother's touch; not a lover's either. Hers, and hers alone. "We'll talk later. About this, and about the other things, too." She smiled at me, the crimson mote of Kushiel's Dart floating on her dark iris. "There's time. Right now, I'm just happy you're home and safe."

I bent and kissed her cheek. "So am I."

Once Phèdre had gone, Joscelin got up and stirred the fire until it crackled merrily. He sat back down, drawing up one knee, his fingers laced around it, and fixed me with a steady regard.

"All right," he said presently. "I'm willing to cede you Bernadette de Trevalion. Not the rest. How bad was it?"

I thought about the Valpetran soldier with his jaws agape, the bloody length of spear visible between them. "Bad enough."

Joscelin nodded. "It always is."

"What . . ." I hesitated. "What was it like for you the first time?"

"Hard." He leaned his head against the back of the couch. "It was in Skaldia. One of Gunter's thanes. Evrard, Evrard the Sharp-tongued, they called him. He challenged me to the holmgang. I didn't want to kill him. I barely knew him."

"You knew his name," I said softly.

"Yes," he said.

"Do you ever dream of him?" I asked.

"I dream about them all." Joscelin lifted his head and looked steadily at me. I remembered him in the festal hall in Daršanga, a ring of corpses rising around him. He might have known the name of the first man he'd killed, but I doubted he could even number those who followed. A leopard among wolves, they had called him there. "And so will you."

"Does it . . ." I swallowed. "Does it get easier to bear?"

"It shouldn't." His mouth twisted. "But it does. The Cassiline Brothers have a prayer for the slain. It helps. Do you know it?"

I shook my head. "Will you teach me?"

"Of course."

We knelt together, Joscelin and I, before the dying fire; heads bowed, hands clasped. He spoke the words of the prayer in a low, firm voice. To my surprise, he spoke in Habiru.

"Mercy, mercy, mercy, o lord of lords! Grant this soul swift passage, and forgive me my need that dispatched it to your keeping."

"A Yeshuite prayer?" I asked.

"A Cassiline prayer," Joscelin corrected me.

"But . . ." I said helplessly.

"Imri." Joscelin touched my face, much as Phèdre had done. "Anathema or no, I *am* Cassiline. If you're asking whether I believe everything they taught me, the answer is no. But some things are ingrained too deeply to be removed."

"Like Daršanga," I murmured.

"Yes." He knelt quietly, sitting on his heels. The low firelight flickered over his austere, beautiful features. "You'll find your own way, Imri. Your own words, your own prayers. You've already begun."

I shrugged. "Even a stunted tree reaches toward the sunlight."

"You're not *that* stunted," Joscelin said in an unexpectedly acerbic tone. "Name of Elua! When it comes to melodrama, you're as bad as Phèdre."

"I am not!" I laughed. "I brood, that's all. That's what Eamonn says." I shifted to sit cross-legged, hugging my knees. "Did I tell you I saved his life?"

Joscelin raised his brows. "Oh *did* you?"

I told him about it in hushed tones; about the battle-fury, the ringing in my ears. About flinging myself into the fray, heedless and unthinking. About my enemies being reduced to mere obstacles. Joscelin knew; Joscelin understood. He listened to me with a complicated expression on his face, all at once rueful and horrified and proud.

"Ah, love!" he said when I was done. "I didn't teach you to fight to—"

"Be like you?" I asked.

"No." Head bowed, he regarded his hands, resting loosely on his thighs. "Not for that."

"You think I am, then?" I asked. "Like you?"

"No." Joscelin raised his head and gave me his wry half-smile. He uncoiled to rise with an easy grace I would envy until I died, extending his strong right hand. I took it and got to my feet. "I think you're like *you*, Imriel. Quick to admire kindness and courage and loyalty in others; slow to see it in yourself. At your age, I promise you, I was quite the opposite. And I think you've room in your heart for more than I ever did."

"Phèdre—" I began.

"Takes up a lot of space," Joscelin agreed. "And the rest is yours."

My eyes stung. "Joscelin . . ."

"Oh, hush." He embraced me, then loosed me, tousling my hair as he used to do when I was younger. "Go to bed, will you? I'll see to the fire. I don't want to be blamed if you're exhausted on the morrow."

"I'm going, I'm going." I reached for the railing and began mounting the stairs. "See?"

"Imri?"

"Yes?"

Joscelin looked up at me. His summer-blue eyes were wide and clear. Whatever shadows lay behind them—and I knew, now, that they were there—he'd learned to live with them. "When you tell Phèdre whatever else there is to tell . . ." He shook his head. "Don't tell her about rescuing Eamonn. It was a foolhardy thing you did."

"All right," I promised. "I won't."

"Oh, she'll know." He smiled at me. "Or she'll guess. But you don't need to *tell* her. Not the details of it. She worries enough as it is."

"And you don't?" I asked.

"Always," he said simply. "But I'm used to it."

SEVENTY-ONE

IN THE MORNING, I presented myself at the Palace.
I'd learned, rather to my relief, that the news from
Lucca had been kept fairly quiet. It had leaked out, of
course, but it was only rumors. Ysandre didn't want the fact
that her wayward young kinsman was trapped in a besieged
Caerdicci city to become common knowledge.

"Who knows?" I asked at the breakfast table.

"Officially?" Phèdre counted on her fingers. "The
Queen's Guard, and Sidonie and Alais. And House
Shahrizai."

"She told them?" It surprised me.

"You sent a message for Mavros," she reminded me.

"Elua!" I set down the piece of jam-smeared bread I'd
been holding. "That letter . . . I'm so sorry."

"Don't be." Phèdre reached across the table and took my
hand. "Imri, if you hadn't come back . . ." She shook her
head, unable to finish the thought. "Don't be sorry."

I squeezed her hand. "You told Mavros, then?"

"Mmm." She nodded. "And Roxanne de Mereliot."

"The Tsingani?"

She smiled. "Only Emile. After all, they've found you before. You saw the boys at the gate?" I nodded, and Phèdre

laughed. "He promised them I'd give a gold ducat to the first to bring word you'd been sighted. Only he didn't bother to tell *me*."

"Did you?" I asked.

Her smile deepened. "Of course."

"So what might I expect today?" I smiled back at her. "Will Ysandre be angry with me, do you think?"

"Over yesterday?" Phèdre let go of my hand, propping her chin on her fist. "No, I don't think so, Imri. I know you have your quarrels with her, but Ysandre's not petty."

"She was with *you*," I said.

"Ah, well." She raised her brows. "That wasn't pettiness. I gave her cause."

It was true, so I didn't argue. "What about Barquiel L'Envers?" I asked, pronouncing his name with distaste. "Will he be there?"

"No, I doubt it." Phèdre looked thoughtful. "He's not been much in evidence this autumn. What that means, I can't say, but he's not likely to be there."

"Well, he got what he wanted, didn't he? By this time next year, I'll be out of his way in Alba, exactly where he wanted me." I picked up my bread and put it back down. "Has my . . . betrothal . . . been announced?" The word sounded strange to my ears.

"Not officially, no. She was awaiting your return." Her voice was quiet. We hadn't spoken of it yet.

"Unofficially?" I asked.

"Well, you know Alais was delighted." She hesitated. "She took the other news, the news of the siege, hard."

"There was a scene," Joscelin added wryly.

"Poor little thing." I pushed my plate away, no longer hungry. The gossip of the Court could be cruel. "No wonder there are rumors. What . . ." I cleared my throat and schooled my voice to casualness. "What about Sidonie? I nearly expect she'd be glad to be rid of me."

"Imri!" Phèdre sounded shocked. "That's unkind."

"What?" I shrugged. "You know there's never been any love lost between us."

"You do her an injustice," she said softly. "She didn't take it lightly. No one did."

I met her gaze, feeling at once guilty and glad. "I know. It's just . . . no mind. What of House Trevalion? Bertran was courting Sidonie, wasn't he?"

"He was and is," Phèdre said. "Not with much success, I believe." She met my eyes. "He's wintering at Court, though. And so is his mother."

"She's not in Azzalle?" I asked, surprised.

She shook her head. "Not since Ghislain was named Royal Commander."

I thought about it. "Well, good. That will make this simpler."

"Come on." Joscelin pushed his chair back and rose. "Enough idle speculation. The Queen is waiting. Let's get you to Court."

It struck me harder than I'd reckoned.

I'd never had any great love for the Palace, or at least I hadn't thought so. But when we disembarked from the carriage in the courtyard, a lump rose to my throat. It was a beautiful building, massive and proud, overlooking the Aviline River. Its white marble walls glistened, maintained with loving pride. I tilted my head and gazed at its high towers, silhouetted against the cold, grey sky. If I had died in Lucca, I would never have seen it again.

D'Angelines had built this.

I thought about Lucca, and how Gallus Tadius had been willing to die a second time in defense of the city he'd made his own. I wouldn't gladly lay down my life for the City of Elua, for this building. But I would do it for Phèdre or Joscelin; I would do it in a heartbeat.

And I would do it for Terre d'Ange itself.

A pretty folk, Eamonn called us, teasing. We were. And a vain folk, too. Proud—proud of our beauty, proud of our heritage, proud of our knowledge and skills. The world chided us for it, and rightly so. Some of it was folly, some of it was conceit.

Not all. Never all.

"Prince Imriel!" One of the Queen's Guard greeted me with a deep bow, snapping his fingers at a comrade. "Welcome home, your highness. Comtesse de Montrève, Messire Verreuil, welcome. Her majesty awaits you."

We were ushered into the Palace. It was busy; it was always busy. The marble halls rang with the sounds of merriment from other rooms. I turned my head as we passed the Hall of Games, remembering Gilot dicing there, swearing cheerfully as he lost his wages. D'Angeline gentry strolled the halls, heads turning as we passed, speculation rising in our wake.

Like the first time, only different.

Elua, how they had stared! And I'd cared then. I'd cared so much, hating them. It all seemed a long time ago. I'd struggled to ignore them, keeping my chin up and my eyes fixed forward, rehearsing in my mind the words I meant to say. I'd snuck covert glances at Phèdre, drawing strength from her intent fixity of purpose. At Joscelin, taking heart from his careless glower.

It was easier now. There's not much to be said for the experience of standing one's ground before the onslaught of a charging army, but it put matters into perspective.

I'd thought we were bound for the throne room, but no.

The reception took place in the Queen's private chambers. The room had tall windows that looked out onto a garden, sere and frostbitten. Ysandre paced before them, her hands clasped behind her back, pensive and anxious. Even as the guard announced us, she turned.

"Imriel!" she said with pleasure.

Phèdre was right, there was no pettiness in Ysandre de la Courcel. Her face was alight with gladness, and I was ashamed. I bowed deeply, muttering words of gratitude and apologies for yesterday's rudeness. Ysandre laughed and clasped my shoulders, raising me to give me the kiss of greeting, sweetly and nicely.

"Ah, no," she said, overriding my protestations. "I'm glad you're well, cousin. After your travail, there's naught I begrudge you. I should have known to wait. After all, I've had long dealings with House Montrève." The Queen of Terre d'Ange cast an affectionate glance in Phèdre's direction, then turned her head toward the far door. Her profile was still as clean and lovely as an image on a coin. "Alais!" she called. "He's here!"

There was a choked sob in the other room, and a flurry.

Alais barreled into me, hard and fast. Her head butted into my chest, and her thin arms wrapped around my waist. I wouldn't have fallen if it wasn't for the wolfhound Celeste bounding after her, tangling my legs. We went down in an undignified tumble.

"You promised, you promised, you promised!" she chanted.

I could barely make out her words, uttered through sobs and muffled against my doublet. "I know, I know! And Alais, I did. I came back." I hugged her and stroked her black curls, which was all I could see of her, sprawled on my back as I was. "See, here I am."

She lifted her tearstained face, laughing and sniffling. "I knew you would!"

"Oh?" I teased gently. "That's not what I heard."

"I was scared." Becoming self-conscious, she extricated herself and knelt on the floor beside me, folding her hands in her lap. For all that her face was blotched with crying and her nose was running, Alais had grown older. I'd been gone for half a year, and the awkward girl I'd left behind was turning into a young woman, although I daresay she'd forgotten it for a moment. Not for long, though. "I'm very glad you're home, Imriel," she said in a formal tone.

"So am I, my lady Alais." Sitting up, I took her hand and kissed it in a courtly gesture. "And you were right, you did dream a true dream. Do you remember the man with two faces? I met him."

Her eyes widened. "You did?"

The wolfhound sat beside me, and I scratched her ears. "I did."

Alais smiled and wiped at her tears. "And my other dream, too . . . it's true, isn't it? You're to be my brother after all."

"I am," I said solemnly.

"Cousin Imriel." Sidonie's voice, light and composed. It sent a tingle through me. "Have you not saved a greeting for me?"

I got to my feet and bowed. "Hello, Sidonie."

"Welcome home." She gave me the kiss of greeting, her lips cool and soft; so soft! It might almost have been impersonal, except it wasn't. Our fingers touched briefly. I could see her pulse beating in the hollow of her throat. She, too, had grown while I'd been gone. There was knowledge stirring behind those dark Cruithne eyes that hadn't been there before; knowledge and power, a woman's power. "We've missed you."

Oh, but I'd had practice, too. I knew all about the banked heat of an illicit love affair. I could be patient and predatory. I could lie and dissemble in the service of desire. I had Claudia Fulvia in all her amorous glory to thank for it.

How do you like your first lesson?

"My thanks." I smiled at Sidonie. "And I you, cousin."

Her lips twitched in a slight answering smile.

"Well!" the Queen said brightly. "I think this calls for a fête."

We spent the better part of the day at the Palace. I told parts of the story of Lucca—Alais wouldn't have forgiven me if I hadn't told her about the man with two faces—but I begged off on the rest and promised to tell it later. Ysandre began planning immediately for the fête at which my return to Terre d'Ange would be celebrated and my betrothal to Dorelei mab Breidaia would be announced.

It brought her pleasure, simple and pure.

I watched her confer with Phèdre, their heads bowed in merry conspiracy, laughter spiraling upward as they plotted together. To this day, there are those who believe Phèdre is the Queen's lover, due to the intimacy between them. It wasn't true, though; or at least to my knowledge. I don't think it ever was. It is true, there is Kusheline blood in the veins of House L'Envers, but I suspect Ysandre was wary of it.

I watched Joscelin's gaze linger on them, quiet and content.

All was well in Terre d'Ange; or at least it would be.

In Lucca, it was Lady Beatrice who'd clung to simple pleasures, drawing strength from the ability to spread joy to those around her. She'd taken such care planning Eamonn and Brigitta's wedding. But it was Gallus Tadius—and Lucius—who had borne the heavier burdens. The ones that called for sacrifice, right or wrong. I had not forgotten the night of the firestorm, atop the walls with Deccus Fulvius, gazing in horror at the soot-smeared face of the conscript racing across the burning fields with Valpetra's cavalry on his heels. Whether or not it had been needful, I could not say. It was a ruler's burden to make such choices.

Ysandre carried them all.

She was a strong ruler, and a good one. After Lucca, I had a better idea what that meant. I might not agree with her choices—despite my own decision regarding Bernadette de Trevalion, it still galled me that Barquiel L'Envers had gotten away without any acknowledgment of his attempt to smear me with treason's brush—but I understood why she made them.

As I had made mine.

There among my family, the family of my heart and the family of my blood, I felt myself settle into a kind of peace with it. When all was said and done, it was good to be home . . . and that meant the Palace, too.

Later in the day, we strolled through the halls together in a deliberate show of unity, attended by the Queen's Guard and seen by the Court. We visited the Salon of Eisheth's Harp, where Gerard de Mereliot was playing a lap-harp and singing ballads for an appreciative audience. He caught my eye and winked without losing a note.

"Imriel!" A familiar figure leapt to his feet. Mavros wove through the crowd with lithe elegance. He sketched a quick, courtly bow to the Queen, then grabbed me in an exuberant hug. "Name of Elua! It's good to see you."

"And you." I grinned at him. Mavros . . . Mavros looked the same. His braids were caught back in a silver clasp, leav-

ing his face bare. He, too, was family. The dark mirror of
House Shahrizai, dangerous and beautiful. "And you."

His twilight-blue eyes narrowed. "What *have* you been
up to, cousin?" he mused, holding my shoulders and studying me. His fingers flexed, digging lightly into my muscles.
"Quite a bit, by the look of you."

"Enough," I said. "I'll tell you later."

"Oh, indeed," he agreed. "I'm all ears until you do."

There were others there; other members of the Shahrizai,
and other friends I had known, or people I'd called friends,
once.

One of them was Bertran de Trevalion. He greeted me
with wary courtesy, uncertain of his reception; and well he
should be, I thought. I clasped his arm in ostensible friendship, pleasant and amicable.

"Tell me," I said. "Is your mother here?"

"My mother?" He looked confused. "Somewhere, yes.
Well, I think she's visiting a friend in the City today. Why?"

He had an open, earnest face. He always had. Even in the
passionate throes of mistrust, Bertran had been honest about
it. Now that I saw him once more, I couldn't imagine him
dissembling well. If I were recruiting for the Unseen Guild,
I'd never choose him. And if I were his mother, I'd hide my
intrigues from him. Mayhap that was one of the reasons
she'd waited until I was well away from D'Angeline soil to
make a bid for vengeance. Or mayhap she simply thought no
one would find out, so far from home.

In that, she was sorely mistaken.

"Oh, I've a lengthy message for her from an old friend in
Tiberium," I said lightly. "It's a private matter. I'll call on her
later to deliver it in person. Ruggero Caccini is his name." I
clapped his shoulder. "Be sure to tell her that, will you?
Ruggero Caccini."

"Ruggero Caccini." Bertran nodded solemnly. "I'll tell her."

I smiled at him. "My thanks, Bertran."

As for the rest of those I'd once called friends, although they greeted me warmly, I hadn't forgotten the cold shoulders they had turned in my direction when I was suspected of conspiring to treason. And I'd learned a great deal about what it meant to be a friend.

But I could forgive, or try to.

It seemed petty not to try.

And it was good, truly. Somewhere along my journey, I'd managed to lay down bits and pieces of the hurt and anger and fear I carried. Even, mayhap, a little of the guilt. Not all of it, no. I doubted I ever would. But I could carry it with better grace.

We left late in the day, with promises to return on the morrow. Eugènie had supper waiting for us. She served me herself, hovering at my elbow and heaping my plate until I laughed and bade her stop. Still, I managed to do justice to it.

Afterward, Phèdre excused herself to her study. I sat for a while talking with Joscelin in the salon, casting glances toward the hall where her study lay. At length he jerked his chin toward the door. "Go. Talk to her."

I hesitated. "Do you want to—"

"Does it have aught to do with your mother?" Joscelin asked.

"Yes."

He gave his familiar half-smile, wry and loving. "Tell it to Phèdre. She may actually understand it."

The door to her study was closed. I knocked lightly on it.

"Come in, love," she called.

I entered and closed the door behind me. The room was

cozy, warmed by a brazier and lit by a pair of oil lamps. It held at least a hundred texts written in a dozen tongues. Some of them had been Delaunay's, and some Phèdre had purchased in her long quest to find the key to freeing Hyacinthe. Many had been salvaged from the bottom of the sea and found languishing in the Master of the Straits' library. There were others at Montrève, too.

All knowledge is worth having.

Phèdre sat at her desk, but her chair was pushed away from it. A finished letter sat atop the desk, the ink drying. I glanced at it and saw it was to the Lady of Marsilikos.

"I'm sorry," I said. "Were you—"

"Waiting for you?" Phèdre smiled. "Yes."

I sighed and folded my legs, sitting at her feet. I leaned my head against the arm of her chair and closed my eyes. After a moment, she began to stroke my hair. We sat like that for a long time. After a long, long while, I began to talk.

I told her about Claudia Fulvia.

I told her about the Unseen Guild.

I told her how I had learned about Bernadette de Trevalion, and what I'd done about it.

And I told her about Canis, and my mother.

She listened to it without comment. Once I'd begun, the words spilled out of me, tumbling one after another. Ah, Elua! Too many secrets, secrets I'd never wanted. I'd been keeping them too long.

When I had finished, I shuddered. I was spent, wrung out. I rubbed my hands over my face, then got up and sat in the guest chair. I'd let myself be a child for a moment, but it couldn't last.

"What do you think?" I asked. "Are the Guild's claims true?"

"It would explain a great deal," Phèdre said quietly. "I always wondered how Melisande came to conspire with Waldemar Selig. Through the Duc d'Aiglemort, everyone assumed, but . . ." She shook her head. "She knew things he didn't. And she was able to contact Selig without his knowledge. She always *knew* too much. It would make sense."

"What do we do, then?" I asked.

"Wait," she said simply. "Watch and listen, as always. The Guild has played their hand; they're not like to take any further chances soon. We'll learn what we may." She glanced at the shelves and cubbyholes filled with tomes and scrolls. "Asclepius' priest said the system of notation on Canis' medallion was devised by a blind healer? A fellow priest?"

"Yes. Long ago, I think." I smiled, knowing she wouldn't see it. Phèdre's face had taken on the absentminded expression she wore when lost in thought. I'd first seen it in the zenana. Not at the beginning, but later, when she was busy hatching the impossible scheme that freed us. "Do you think you might find a reference to it?"

"Mm-hmm."

I liked it when she wore her absent face, because it was safe. I could look at her and wonder what she was thinking, or just look at her. There were no disconcerting undercurrents, no terrible, wonderful hints of transcendence clinging to her. Only Phèdre, thinking. I watched her for a while before speaking again. "It's dangerous," I reminded her. "If the Guild is half as powerful as Claudia claimed, their threat is real."

"Oh, I know." She returned from wherever it was her thoughts had led her. "Don't worry, love. I don't mean to take any risks. You've not told anyone else, have you?"

I shook my head. "Not even Eamonn. Will you?"

"Other than Joscelin?" Phèdre frowned. "I'd like to speak to Hyacinthe about it. Elua knows, if there's anyone in the world safe from reprisal, it's him. I'd trust him with it without fearing I'd put him in jeopardy."

"Not Ysandre?" I asked.

"No," Phèdre said slowly. "No, I don't think so."

Our eyes met. "Delaunay," I said.

"I know."

"Do you think . . ." I swallowed. "Do you think he told anyone?"

"Like your mother?" she asked gently. I nodded. "I don't know, love. He might have. They played a strange game with one another. Anafiel Delaunay was a complicated man, and Rolande's death had a profound impact on him. There are things about him I daresay I'll never understand."

"Like my mother," I murmured.

"Yes." Phèdre gave a wry smile. "Ah, well. Yes and no."

"Why did she save my life?" I asked. "Does she still think to *use* me?"

The words emerged, abrupt and bitter. I hadn't meant to ask it; and yet I had. Although I'd not given voice to it, it had been burning in the back of my thoughts ever since Canis died. Phèdre looked at me for a long moment. "Do you remember the promise I extracted from her in La Serenissima?" she asked. I nodded. As if I could forget. *I keep my promises.* "I bargained with her. I told her I'd adopt you only in exchange for her promise not to raise her hand against Ysandre or her daughters, nor to leave her sanctuary. She bargained me down to one promise, and made me choose. And after she agreed and swore an oath, she laughed and told me I was a dreadful liar." Her mouth quirked. "I didn't think I'd done that badly."

"Why did she do it, then?" I asked.

"'One day—not soon, but one day—tell my son that this bargain I have made with you today is my gift to him, the only one he would accept from me,'" Phèdre recited from memory. "Those were her words. There wasn't a great deal Melisande did out of kindness," she said softly. "Although mayhap she sees it differently. But that, yes. It was a gift, pure and simple."

"Do you think . . ." I paused. "Mayhap she isn't *all* bad?"

"No one is, Imri." Her voice was gentle. "Nor all good, either."

There was a great deal more she could have said, although she didn't. When all was said and done, I think no one in the world knew my mother better than Phèdre. Not her own Shahrizai kin, not Anafiel Delaunay, not anyone. They were two sides of a coin; Kushiel's deadliest scion and Kushiel's Chosen. The dark mirror and the bright, and which was which depended on one's vantage point. They had reflected the best and worst of one another.

And I was both of their sons.

True and not true.

I took a deep breath and prepared to shoulder a burden I'd long avoided. "I'd like to read her letters, please."

Phèdre nodded as though she had been expecting me to ask. Like as not, she had. Without comment, she folded and sealed her letter to Roxanne de Mereliot and set it to one side. I remembered with a guilty start that I'd forgotten to ask Ysandre to send a courier to the Lady of the Dalriada with Eamonn's letter.

I would do it on the morrow.

There was time.

She got up and fetched the coffer from a shelf. It was made of polished wood inlaid with mother-of-pearl. Phèdre set it on her desk and unlocked it with a gold key that I hadn't seen since I was fourteen years old. She laid the key beside the coffer and stepped back.

"There you are, love."

I got up. Phèdre watched me. Her eyes were dark and luminous, filled with tenderness. The knowledge of the Name of God lay behind them, and the word it spelled was love. Every letter of the alphabet in which it was written, every stroke of every letter, was love. I sat down at her desk.

"Thank you," I whispered.

She didn't answer, only kissed my brow and left.

I sat for a long time, gazing at the coffer. At last I lifted the lid. A faint, spicy scent of sandalwood emerged. The letters lay there, seals cracked, neatly refolded. No one had touched them for four years. Not since Melisande Shahrizai had vanished from her sanctuary in the Temple of Asherat-of-the-Sea.

Melisande.

My mother.

I thought about Helena Correggio opening her hand in the streets of Lucca, and beads of blue glass falling onto the cobblestones. The Bella Donna's son. I'd forgotten to tell Phèdre that part. It didn't matter. There was time. I thought about the tears in my mother's eyes the last time I had seen her, and her voice breathing my name.

Imriel.

I took out the first letter, my hands trembling. I unfolded it and laid it flat on the desk, smoothing its creases. It was the one I'd hurled unopened into a brazier, and there were marks of charring along one edge where it had scorched before Phèdre had rescued it. It was old enough that the parchment was growing brittle. It was legible, though. There was a date on it, penned in a firm, elegant hand. It had been written the day after we left La Serenissima. There were others following it, dozens of others.

I read the first line.

To my son, Imriel . . .

Bowing my head, I whispered a prayer to Blessed Elua for courage to bear the understanding that might come, for compassion to use it wisely. I had no idea what these pages might hold. I was afraid to know. Afraid to know my mother had loved me, truly loved me. Afraid to see her as a mortal woman, capable of grief and regret. Afraid to discover that her actions had merit viewed through her eyes. Afraid to find an echo of myself in her.

But I would do it anyway.

The flickering lamps cast a warm glow over the parchment. Beyond the door, I could hear the ordinary sounds of an evening in House Montrève's household, muffled and indistinct. Joscelin's voice asking a question; Phèdre's low reply. A scuffle of boot-heels, a winecup rattling against a table. Eugènie scolding. Hugues laughing, Ti-Philippe protesting.

A host of people who cared for me, gathered under one roof. Everyday happiness, common and precious. I let out a breath I hadn't realized I'd been holding.

My mother's letters waited.

I lifted my head and began to read.

ABOUT THE AUTHOR

JACQUELINE CAREY's previous publications include various short stories, essays, the nonfiction book *Angels: Celestial Spirits in Legend and Art,* the novels *Godslayer, Banewreaker,* and the nationally bestselling series Kushiel's Legacy. She lives in Michigan.

Enjoy a sneak peek
at the sexy new novel by

JACQUELINE
CAREY

Please turn this page
for a preview of

**KUSHIEL'S
JUSTICE**

Available in hardcover.

A GAIN!"

In the gloaming, Joscelin's teeth flashed as he took a stance opposite me, his wooden sword angled before him. I grinned in reply and launched a fresh attack.

Our blades flicked and clattered as we circled one another in the courtyard, testing each other's defenses. There was hoarfrost beginning to form on the slate tiles and I placed my feet with care as we revolved around one another. Out of the corner of my eye, I watched Joscelin's feet move. Hugues' bad poetry not withstanding, he *did* seem to glide. His footwork was intricate and impeccable.

He was good; better than I was. I daresay he always will be. At ten years of age—the age at which I was learning to beg for mercy in the Mahrkagir's zenana—Joscelin entered the Cassiline Brotherhood and began to train as a warrior-priest. Day after day he had trained without cease.

It wasn't just the training, though. There were other Cassiline Brothers. But none of them had ever made his choice. None had ever been tested as he was.

I pressed him on his bad side; his left side, where he was slower. His left arm had been shattered in Darŝanga. He relinquished ground in acknowledgment, step by gliding step, and I pressed him. And then, somehow, he leaned away from my thrust with a subtle twist of his torso and I found myself overextended. The sharp point of his elbow came down hard on the back of my reaching hand.

"Oh, hell!" My sword fell and my hand stung. I shook it out.

Joscelin chuckled.

"Show me?" I asked.

"Here." Setting down his blade, he placed one hand on my belly and the other on my lower back, applying pressure. "Weight on the rear foot, knee flexed. See?"

I leaned as he'd done. "I feel off-balance."

"Widen your stance." Joscelin nudged my forward foot. "Better." He patted my belly. "It all flows from here, Imri. You can't be stiff. Have you kept up your practice?"

"No," I admitted. "Gallus Tadius didn't approve. He had us training with—"

He wasn't listening. He was smiling across the courtyard. Nothing had changed, but his face was alight. Since there was only one person in the world who made Joscelin Verreuil's face brighten so, I knew without looking that Phèdre was there.

I looked anyway. She stood before the doors that opened onto the courtyard, hugging herself against the cold as she watched us spar. There was so much love and gladness in her eyes, I had to look away. What I wanted wasn't meant for me.

"Show me?" she asked, teasing.

Joscelin laughed, low and soft. He crossed over to her and placed his hands on her, as he'd done to me, only not. Not at all the same. She twined her arms around his neck, the velvet sleeves of her gown falling back to lay them bare, white and slender. He bent his head to kiss her, his wheat-blond hair falling forward. For the span of a few heartbeats, nothing else in the world existed for them.

I stooped, picking up our fallen swords. It shouldn't hurt. When I was younger, when I was a child, it wouldn't have. I loved them; I loved them both so much. They had rescued me out of hell and they paid a terrible price for it. Together, we found healing. We reknit our broken selves as a family, and their love lies at the core of it. I will never, so long as I live, begrudge either of them the least crumb of happiness. They have earned it a thousand times over.

It did hurt, though. I never thought it would, but it did.

Ah, Elua! Jealousy is a hard master. I'd known love and I'd known desire, but never the two at once; not this kind, the kind that shut out the world. And there was a darker strain, too. Like it or no, I was my mother's son; Kushiel's Scion, albeit a reluctant one. It was there, it would always be there. Phèdre was Kushiel's Chosen, born to yield; Naamah's Servant and a courtesan without equal. It was there between us, it would always be there.

My mother had written of it:

> When, I wonder, will you read this? Not soon, I think. You are too angry, now. I think you will be older. I think you will be a man grown.
>
> I should speak of Phèdre nó Delaunay.
>
> You will wonder, did I love her? No . . . and yes. I will tell you this, my son: I *knew* her. Better than anyone; better than anyone else.

I let out my breath in a sigh, wondering what Phèdre had made of those words. When all was said and done, I do not think she disagreed. Still, whatever lay between them, it was Joscelin she loved. And he knew her, too. I watched her withdraw from him, smiling. In the lamplight spilling from the open doors, I could make out a faint flush on her cheeks.

"Are you coming, love?" she called to me. "It's perishing cold out here."

"I'm coming," I said.

How is it that two people so unlikely, so unsuited, find one another? I thought about it that night, watching them at the dinner table. And I thought about the fact that I was unlikely to do the same. I had met my bride-to-be, Dorelei mab Breidaia, the Cruarch's niece. She was a sweet young woman with a lilting laugh, and I couldn't possibly imagine sharing the kind of all-consuming passion that I craved with her.

I heaved another sigh.

"Why so somber?" Hugues asked me. "Did Messire Cassiline give you a drubbing?"

"No," I said, then amended it at Joscelin's amused glance. "Well, yes." I flexed my bruised hand. "It's not that, though. I think . . . I think I would like to go to Kushiel's temple on the morrow."

"*What?*" Joscelin stared at me in disbelief. "Are you mad?"

I hadn't known what I was going to say until the words emerged from my mouth. I mulled over them. "No," I said slowly. "I think I need to make expiation."

"For *what?*" He continued to stare.

I thought about my recent excursion into extortion and blackmail. I thought about the soldiers I had killed in Lucca, about Canis with the javelin protruding from his chest and Gilot after the riot, battered and broken. I thought about cuckolded Deccus Fulvius and mad, dead Gallus Tadius standing above the maelstrom, meeting my distant gaze as he dropped his death-mask. I thought about the night

Mavros took me to Valerian House and the morning after, when I grabbed Phèdre's wrist and felt the pulse of desire leap.

"Things," I said.

Joscelin shook his head. Phèdre rested her chin on one hand and fixed me with a deep look that gave away nothing. I returned it steadily. "You're sure?" she asked. "It's like to stir memories. Bad ones."

"You go," I said. "What do you find in it?"

She smiled slightly. "Oh, things."

I nodded. "I'm sure."

I wasn't, not really; at least not on the morrow. I couldn't even say of a surety what had prompted the urge. After Darŝanga, I would have said I would never voluntarily submit myself to any man's lash, nor any woman's. And yet, the idea had fixed itself in my thoughts.

By morning, Joscelin was resigned. "You know, betimes I think you *are* a little mad, Imriel nó Montrève," he said to me in the courtyard outside the stable, holding the Bastard's reins.

"You never said that to Phèdre," I reminded him.

"Ah, well." He grinned despite himself. "In her case, there's no question." His expression turned sober. "Imri, truly, I know the dead weigh on you. I know it better than anyone. And I may be Cassiel's servant, but I don't deny Kushiel's mystery. It's just that it may be different for you."

I swung astride. "Because of what happened to me?"

"Yes." His eyes were grave.

"I know," I said. "But Joscelin, I'm tired of having a terrified ten-year-old boy lurking inside me. And I need to deal with my own blood-guilt and . . . other things. You told me I'd find a way, my own way. So. I'm trying."

"I know." He let go the reins. "You'll see him home

safe?" he said to Hugues. Ti-Philippe had offered to go, too, but I'd rather have it be Hugues. If the ordeal took a greater toll on me than I reckoned, I trusted him to be gentle.

"Of course."

It was another cold, bright day in the City of Elua, the sky arching overhead like a blue vault. All the world seemed to be in high spirits. Hugues brought out his wooden flute as we rode and toyed with it, then thought better of it, tucking it away.

"It's all right," I said to him. "Play, if you like."

He shrugged his broad shoulders. "It doesn't seem right."

"Have you ever been?" I asked.

"No." His face was open and guileless. "I've never known the need."

It had been a foolish question; I couldn't imagine why he would. I had known Hugues since I was a boy, and I'd never known him to say an unkind word. I wondered what it would be like to be him, unfailingly patient and kind, always seeing the best in everyone. I tried to look for the good, but I saw the bad, too. The flaws, the fault lines. I was of Kushiel's lineage and it was our gift. My mother's gift that she had used to exploit others.

But I was Elua's Scion, too.

I wondered, did Elua choose his Companions? Nothing in the scriptures says so. They chose him as he wandered the earth; chose to abandon the One God in his heaven to wander at Blessed Elua's side until they made a home here in Terre d'Ange, and then a truer home in the Terre d'Ange-that-lies-beyond.

He loved them, though. He must have. And if Blessed Elua found something to love in mighty Kushiel, who was once appointed to punish the damned, then mayhap I would, too.

Elua's temples are open places; open to sky and grounded by earth. In the Sanctuary of Elua where I grew up—until I was stolen by slavers—the temple was in a poppy field. I used to love it there.

I'd never been to one of Kushiel's temples. It was a closed place. Though it was located in the heart of the City, it sat alone in a walled square. There were no businesses surrounding it; no shops, no taverns, no markets. The building was clad in travertine marble, a muted honey-colored hue.

"Funny," Hugues mused. "I'd expected it to be darker."

"So did I," I murmured.

The gate was unlocked and there was no keeper. We passed beyond it into the courtyard, hoofbeats echoing against the walls. I thought about the wide walls of Lucca, so vast oak trees grew atop them. A young man in black robes emerged from the stables.

"Be welcome," he said, bowing.

We gave our mounts over into his keeping. I watched the Bastard accept his lead without protest, pacing docilely into the stable, and thought once more about the Sanctuary of Elua and an acolyte I had known there.

Hugues nudged me. "This way."

The stairs leading to the entrance were steep and narrow. The tall doors were clad in bronze and worked with a relief of intertwining keys. It was said Kushiel once held the keys to the gates of hell. House Shahrizai takes its emblem from the same motif. The door-knocker was a simple bronze ring, unadorned. I grasped it and knocked for entrance.

The door was opened by another black-robed figure; a priest, his face covered by a bronze mask that rendered his features stern and anonymous. Or hers; it was almost impossible to tell. The sight made me shiver a little. He—or she—beckoned without speaking, and we stepped into the foyer. He waited, gazing at us through the eyeholes of his mask.

"I am here to offer penance," I said. Save for a pair of marble benches, the foyer was empty of all adornment and my voice echoed in the space.

The priest inclined his head and indicated the benches to Hugues, who took a seat, then beckoned once more to me. I followed, glancing back once at Hugues. He looked worried and forlorn, his wide shoulders hunched.

I followed the black-clad figure, studying the movement of the body beneath the flowing robes, the sway of the hips. A woman, I thought. I wasn't sure if it made me more or less uneasy. She led me through another set of doors, down a set of hallways to the baths of purification.

Although I'd never gone, I knew the rituals. I'd asked Phèdre about it once. It used to bother me that she went, betimes. I was fearful of the violent catharsis she found in it. The dark mirror, Mavros would say.

And now I sought it.

The baths were stark and plain. Light poured in from high, narrow windows. There was a pool of white marble, heated by a hypocaust. The water shimmered, curls of steam rising in the sunlight. The priestess pointed at the pool.

"Do you know who I am?" I asked her.

She tilted her head. Sunlight glanced from the mask's bronze cheek. In the shadows of its eyeholes, I could make out human eyes. The bronze lips were parted to allow breath. I thought she would speak, but she didn't answer, merely pointed once more.

I unbuckled my sword-belt, pulled off my boots and stripped out of my clothing, piling it on a stool, then stepped into the pool. It was hot, almost hot enough to scald, and yet I found myself shivering.

"Kneel."

A woman's voice, soft and sibilant, emerging from between the bronze lips. I knelt, sinking shoulder-deep in the hot water. It smelled vaguely of sulfur. She took up a simple wooden bucket, dipping it into the pool. I closed my eyes as she poured it over my head in a near-scalding cascade; once, twice, thrice. When no more water came, I loosed the breath I'd been holding and opened my eyes.

The priestess beckoned.

I clambered out of the pool, naked and dripping. Water puddled on the marble floor. She handed me a linen bath sheet. I dried myself and looked about for a robe, but she pointed at my piled clothing.

"Seems a bit foolish," I muttered. She said nothing, so I put on my clothes and followed as she led me out of the baths, feeling damp and anxious.

We entered a broad hallway with a high ceiling and another pair of massive, bronze-clad doors at the end of it. The temple proper. The doors clanged like bells as they opened. My mouth was dry.

Kushiel's inner sanctum.

All I could see at first was the effigy. It towered in the room, filling the space. I wondered how they'd gotten it through the doors, then realized the entire temple must have been built around it. His arms were crossed on his breast, his hands gripping his rod and flail. His distant face was stern and calm and beautiful, the same visage echoed in the mask of the priestess who led me, and those of the priests who awaited us.

One held a flogger.

I couldn't help it, my throat tightened. At the base of the effigy was the altar-fire. A few tendrils of smoke arose. The stone walls of the temple were blackened with old soot.

The flagstones were scrubbed clean, though. Especially those before Kushiel's effigy, where the wooden whippingpost stood.

"Damn it!" I whispered, feeling the sting of tears. I thought about Gilot. No more tears, I'd promised him when we set out for Tiberium. Impatient at myself, I strode forward. I made an offering of gold and took up a handful of incense, casting it on the brazier.

Fragrant smoke billowed. I'd offered incense to Kushiel in the ambassadress' garden in Tiberium; spikenard and mastic. This was different. This was *his* place.

A bronze mask swam before me. A priest, a tall man. He bent his head toward me. "Is it your will to offer penance?"

"Yes, lord priest." I blinked my stinging eyes, rubbing at them with the heel of one hand. "Do you know who I am?"

"Yes."

A single word; a single syllable. And yet, there was knowledge and compassion in it. Behind the eyeholes of his mask, his gaze was unwavering. The decision was mine.

I spread my arms. "So."

Hands undressed me; unfastening my cloak, unbuckling my swordbelt. Anonymous hands belonging to faceless figures. Piece by piece, they stripped away my clothing, until I was naked and shivering in their black-robed midst. A heavy hand on my shoulder, forcing me to my knees. I knelt on the scrubbed flagstones.

Hands grasped my wrists, stretching my arms above my head. I willed myself not to struggle as they lashed rawhide around my wrists, binding them tight to the ring atop the whippingpost. The incense was so thick I could taste it on my tongue, mingled with the memory of stagnant water, rot, and decay.

The chastiser stepped forward, his bronze-masked face

calm and implacable. He held forth the flogger in both hands, offering it like a sacrament. It was no toy intended for violent pleasure, no teasing implement of soft deerskin. The braided leather glinted and metal gleamed at its tips. It was meant to hurt.

My teeth were chattering. All I could do was nod.

He nodded in acknowledgment and stepped behind me.

I braced myself.

Ah, Elua! The first blow was hard and fast, dealt by an expert hand. White-hot pain burst across the expanse of my naked back. I jerked hard against my restraints, feeling my sinews strain near unto cracking. Again and again and again it fell, and I found myself wild with panic, struggling to escape. I flung myself against the coarse wood of the whippingpost, worrying at it with my fingernails. And still the flogger fell, over and over.

I saw Daršanga.

Dead women, dead boys. The Mahrkagir's mad eyes, wide with glee.

Phèdre, filled with the Name of God.

Brightness.

Darkness.

All of the dead, my dead. Daršanga, Lucca. Everyone's dead.

Kushiel's face, wreathed in smoke.

"Enough." The tall priest raised his hand. I had ceased to struggle, going limp in my bonds. On my knees, aching in every part, I squinted up at him. "Make now your confession."

I craned my neck. "I'm sorry," I whispered, "and I will try to be good."

There was a pause; a small silence. I let my head loll. From the corner of my eye, I saw the tall priest gesture.

There was the soft sound of a dipper sinking into water, and then another voice spoke. "Be free of it."

A draught of saltwater was poured over my wounds. I rested my bowed head in the crook of my elbows, sighing at the pain of it.

It was done, then. My penance was made. The anonymous hands untied my wrists and helped me to stand. Patted dry my lacerated back, helped me to dress. Though I stood on wavering feet, strangely, I felt calm and purged.

"So." The tall priest regarded me. "Is it well done, Kushiel's Scion?"

If I had wished it, I thought, he would have spoken to me as a man, mortal to mortal, both of us grasping with imperfect hands at the will of the gods. I didn't, though. I bowed to him instead, feeling the fabric of my shirt rasp over my wounded flesh. It was a familiar feeling. I'd known it well, once. This was different. I had chosen it.

"It is well done, my lord priest," I said.

He nodded a final time. "Go, then."

Hugues leapt to his feet when I entered the foyer. "Are you . . . how are you?"

I ran my tongue over my teeth, thinking. I could taste blood where I'd bitten the inside of my cheek, and the lingering taste of incense. Nothing else. I hurt, but no worse than I'd hurt after a rough training session with Barbarus squadron. The weals would fade. And I wasn't scared inside. "I'm fine," I said, surprised to discover it was true. I smiled at Hugues. "Come on, let's go."